Whatever it Takes to Win

Also By Eric Rice

America at the Brink series
What Can One Man Do?
Our Choice: Freedom or Obedience
The Cost of Standing Up

Whatever it Takes to Win

America at the Brink (Nick Turner, Book Four)

Eric Rice

Disclaimer: This novel is a work of fiction. It contemplates a 'what if' scenario in an imaginary United States, along with imaginary interactions with the rest of the countries of the world. The novel's characters and story are fictitious. Any reference to historical events, real people, or actual places are all used fictitiously. Any resemblance to those living or dead, actual events, and to any actions is entirely coincidental. I reference long-standing institutions, such as American Government entities, agencies and other public offices, both in the US and abroad. The actions of these agencies, their policies or the characters involved with or working in said agencies portrayed or implied in our tale are entirely fictitious and wholly imagined as of the point of time of publication.

Dedication

Writing a book is bound to be influenced by your life experiences. You can research history, clever facts, and quotes. Ultimately, you have a story to tell. It is a journey with a start and a finish. The difference between a novel and life is you get to start at the end and work backwards from your desired ending in a novel.

Life is exactly the opposite. You have no idea where the next step takes you. Only a direction. Your life is the sum of your choices. The actions you take, the people you meet, and the places you go.

I have been fortunate to travel extensively in my life. This, combined with a love of history, gives me insight and knowledge of many places and events. All valuable when weaving tales from imagination.

Best of all, I was blessed to interact with a host of different people all over the world. This is almost entirely because of my luck in being married to a wonderful woman who could start a conversation with any stranger and make an acquaintance for life.

This opened us to broad exposure to cultural differences, experiences and the wonderful interaction between people from varied backgrounds and locales, influencing our outlook on the world.

I started this saga with a dedication to my wife, my inspiration and soulmate. She was a huge believer in fate and faith. I can only assume there was a greater need in heaven. I must soldier on alone, telling the story of Nick Turner. Helping you, the reader, understand what and why you must wake up, stand up, and think for yourself.

This and all our happy memories will have to be enough to sustain me going forward. It is what she would have wanted. Mary Sue, I'll love you forever.

Where are we so far?

The first three books of the saga, America at the Brink, describe a time in America's history where our country was divided along ideological lines. Into this arrived Nick Turner. These episodes are specifically about his role in this history. The decisions, their actions and consequences, and how they shaped where we are today.

This book is being written in the middle of the 21st century after we have experienced tumultuous decades of upheaval and change both here and around the world.

My intent is to detail these decisions so future readers can see what to do to prevent similar events from repeating themselves. This is the entire purpose of documenting history. To learn and not continue to repeat the mistakes of the past in our future. The books in 'America at the Brink' take us back several decades to where this all started.

Military veteran Nick Turner was perfectly happy as an obscure college history professor. He'd foiled a terrorist attempt to blow up a crowded subway station in New York City years previously. Forgoing the money and fame this deed offered him, he opted to return to teaching until fate intervened once again. The first episode of this series, *What Can One Man Do?*, detailed Nick's introduction to Washington politics.

Appointed to fill out the term of a Colorado Senator who died. Nick is quickly disillusioned after arriving in DC. He discovers most of Congress is more concerned with re-election and growing their financial opportunities after Congress, instead of looking out for their constituents as their voters expect.

I have changed the predominant political parties to the more generic Party and Opposition. You can no doubt figure out which represents which. Nick is a member of the Party, who also has control of both branches of congress and the presidency. The Party was finally on the verge of removing the last of the Constitutional rules designed to prevent a tyranny of the majority, the legislative filibuster.

Without it, a simple majority of 51 to 50 would enable the ruling party in the Senate to pass sweeping changes to any laws. The founders designed the Constitution to make wholesale change hard and force compromise. They understood the danger of the unchecked majority. The Party leaders viewed this archaic rule, and the Constitution, as an impediment to the changes required to solve society's problems.

In a show of political bravery not seen since Lincoln, Nick cast a deciding vote against the bill, and the will of his Party. Sacrificing any chance at a political career, while earning the undying hatred of his Party colleagues and their media allies. It turns out to be for naught, as the Party leaders orchestrate a miracle and pass the bill.

The legislative filibuster, the last of the checks and balances of the Constitution, is now gone. Nick sees the problems the country will face if Vice President Lexi Smythe-Thomas, the overwhelming favorite to win the presidency in a year, is elected. With unchecked power and control of all branches of government, the progressive platform she favors will remake America. This first episode ends with Nick announcing he is leaving the Party. He also astounds everyone by announcing a run for President as an Independent, not seeking the nomination of either party.

In the second episode, *Our Choice: Freedom or Obedience*, Nick discovers just what his impulsive decision means. With no money, no staff, no organizations, either nationally or in the states, he is woefully unprepared. Without a campaign manager and a million other things, he is starting a year later than everyone else and with nothing for his presidential campaign.

When asked why he was doing this, he said his goal was to educate and wake up the silent majority. Those cowering in fear who disagree with the direction and policies of the elites in power. People too afraid to stand up in disagreement for fear of being canceled.

Nick hits the road, meeting with everyone who will stand still long enough to listen. His message: use common sense. Defying every conventional method of successful campaigns, he promises *nothing*, refuses to court big money donors, and limits his donations to small dollars from individuals.

At first, Lexi and her team and media pundits laugh at the announcement. As it becomes clear he will not go away, she uses the agencies of the administration to start monitoring his activities. As the elderly President continues his slip into mental oblivion, Lexi takes over stage managing the country from the Vice President position. As a popular Vice President, with a clear path to becoming president, the media doesn't question this charade, ensuring her path to power.

Nick builds his following. Limiting his media exposure to a lone semi-friendly cable news network. Working closely with a technology mogul, his message slowly spreads. These unconventional methods, along with old-fashioned word of mouth, lead to a gathering of momentum.

Working his way through the country, at each stop Nick leaves behind converted *and* motivated followers, the Turner Rabble. Committed to his ideal of staying under the radar, his public polling stays low as his followers lie to pollsters about their support for Nick. His message resonates with the increasingly ignored common man and woman. Those toiling to make ends meet each day. Through his journeys, Nick goes places and talks to folks the other campaigns shun. Most of all, he listens to what the people have to say and what they think of his stances.

His growing popularity and moderate stances lead both campaigns to offer him a spot as their Vice President. He turns down both offers. EXN invites Nick to provide commentary in their cable news booth for each of the political party's conventions. Lexi's nomination and subsequent speech clearly shows she and the Party have big plans. Intending to fix American democracy through increasingly radical progressive policies and government oversight.

The Opposition can't even agree on a candidate as they enter a brokered convention without a clear winner. After several nominating votes, failing to gain a majority for one candidate, a coalition tries to nominate Nick in a surprise move as a compromise candidate. As the nomination hangs in the balance, he turns down the opportunity and the Opposition chooses their candidate.

The third book, *The Cost of Standing Up*, is the sprint to November. We are now three months from the election. This episode follows Nick as he tries to fend off the endless litany of attacks being thrown at him by PACs, SuperPACs, both candidates, and his own self-inflicted mistakes.

The people and money working in the background, ensuring the outcomes for the major parties, reveal the true stakes of presidential politics. Having jumped to legitimate status, Nick is forced to be much more front and center. Both to layout his platform and stances, and to defend them in more places, and to larger audiences.

He faces a pivotal moment when he speaks to both the Pro-Life and Pro-Choice conferences laying out a middle ground abortion strategy. His attempt at a pragmatic solution cannot be allowed and galvanizes the extremes of both sides against him and his followers.

Their machines of destruction spring into action, trying to destroy Nick's reputation and render him irrelevant. A seemingly catastrophic unforced error sees him squandering his momentum by supporting a Marine accused of murdering half a dozen sheriff's deputies. His popularity suffers as the relentless press hammer him and his support for a 'cop killer'. The fundraising dries up and some of his grass-roots organizations seek to dissolve, having become disillusioned.

Nick delivers a speech at a Nebraska state fair and explains not that the Marine is guilty or innocent, but that he deserves a fair trial and not a public lynching. How this is part of the problem with society, with everyone so easily whipped into a frenzy by the media mob. Without stopping to consider or find out the truth before jumping to a conclusion.

This message gets traction among his followers, forcing them to think for themselves rather than consume only what the media is peddling. Nick's pet term for the media, American *Pravda*, is now trending as folks wake up. Just as he is making headway, he is shot while speaking on stage at the Minnesota state fair.

While wounded, the shot missed any vital organs. The convenient timing of this helps shift public opinion and sympathy to Nick and away from his support for the Marine. The VP and her team and their many allies in the America *Pravda* media speculate he had himself shot to raise his popularity. In a dramatic live conversation on EXN, Nick easily debunks this theory.

He continues to campaign and fight back against the growing barrage of fake scandals and roadblocks continuously thrown in his way. Finally, the trial of the Marine occurs. The parents of the slain deputies have all been appearing on shows for months leading up to the trial, continuously vilifying Nick for his support of the Marine. However, they are nowhere to be seen as the trial begins.

Instead, they have gathered together in New York to appear on an evening news show. When asked why they're appearing together in New York, rather than attending the trial in Denver, they explain it is because Nick took the time to meet with each of them and explain why he did what he did.

Not to claim the Marine was innocent, but to have them understand mistakes made. Putting their children into the line of fire where they should not have been and to highlight the Marine was not even the target of the raid. Nick asked them to review the facts of the case, never reported on American *Pravda*. And finally, to highlight the most important of Constitutional safeguards available to all Americans. Innocent until proven guilty.

The media are outraged at Nick for what they see as preying upon the feelings of these poor grieving parents and loved ones for his own political gain. The parents stand up to the media and behind Nick and his desire for a fair trial for the Marine. The Marine is found not guilty.

Ignoring this outcome and the fact the parents of the slain deputies agree with the verdict and the truth presented, the American *Pravda* media continues the public lynching. Shouting the Marine is guilty despite the evidence or the verdict. Realizing there is no hope of leading a normal life, the Marine commits suicide.

Nick is furious at this turn of events. His speeches getting angrier and more passionate, driving his audiences into a frenzy. As his opponents turn up the pressure and attacks, Nick is physically attacked several times trying to rebut false accusations. While not hurt and always the one being attacked, the media takes the footage and makes it appear Nick and his followers are inciting riots and violence.

They highlight how he has attracted white supremacist militia lunatics who are delighting in attacking peaceful gay and minority protestors at his rallies. Nick disavows them and makes sure his teams film every rally, providing footage refuting all the rhetoric.

The footage clearly shows Nick and his followers being attacked, while always advocating for tolerance and centrist, common sense stances. This information is never acknowledged, nor is the footage shown on any but EXN and his few remaining social media accounts. All the violence is being funded by groups affiliated with PACs supporting both political parties to ensure negative coverage of Nick's rallies and to manipulate public opinion against him.

These tactics limit Nick's ability to get to national audiences. Lexi and her minions increasingly pressure Nick's campaign and his few allies. Opening official FBI, Homeland and DOJ investigations regarding their actions, his rhetoric and the violence he is inciting.

As we approach October, a month before the election, the attacks are coming more often, requiring more of Nick's time, keeping him off the campaign trail. Even a motion to Censure him in the Senate is granted. This will take Nick back to Washington at a crucial time, with only weeks before the election.

One network drops a bombshell on the Opposition candidate. His inept handling of the news and the true nature of the story are so damaging he is rendered almost unelectable.

The VPs team speed up their efforts to discredit Nick to keep the Opposition voters from going to his banner. They launch relentless attacks against Nick and his staff, including both a catastrophic debanking decision, hamstringing his ability to continue to spend campaign funds, and accusations of sexual misconduct among his staff.

While entirely fabricated, Nick cannot prevent the staffer accused from deciding it is in the best interests of Nick's campaign to remove himself as the problem. Nick tries unsuccessfully to convince him to not commit suicide. The book ends with Nick resolving to make people pay for the needless pain and loss of life his opponents are perpetuating solely for the sake of winning an election.

Nick has come far, survived physical attacks and near-death experiences, to mount a credible campaign as an independent. But he faces opponents committed to doing whatever it takes to win.

Eric Rice
Undisclosed location
Near the middle of the 21st Century A.D.

Prologue

Maksim Pavlovich sat in his massive library in his equally massive Swiss estate. Projected in the air in a half circle in front of him were eleven holographic symbols representing the Chinese zodiac. Ten were orange, showing they were connected to this highly encrypted call. The Chinese Dragon symbol was still white. They had yet to join. Maksim knew why and waited patiently.

These twelve symbols represented the Council of the Konigschloss Group. The leaders of the movement, dedicated toward global management of the world's people, countries, resources and preservation of the planet through forced cooperation and common goals.

His own symbol, of the Chinese Rat, would be in the center of each of the other participants' calls, as the leader of the Council. Having helped form it, he alone knew the identities of all the other symbols.

Pavlovich glanced up at his council. Since he had ascended to the top of the hierarchy, he'd replaced various members as others had died or gotten cold feet and been eliminated. They all mingled at the annual KSG event, but none was entirely sure who the other council members were or even who Rat was.

Maksim had chuckled at the American movie, where their motto had been the first rule of the club was there was no club. This had been the mantra shared by all in the council for over half a century. Long before the movie adopted *their* motto. The first rule was there was no council. Everyone understood it was an irrevocable membership. A blood pact. To betray the council would bring death and retribution against the betrayer's family as well.

As he waited for Dragon, Pavlovich remembered when he 'took' the top role. Though over fifty years ago, it was still as clear as yesterday in his steel trap mind. He could see the pale face of the former

Rat, a billionaire when their total number was only in the teens around the globe.

He and Pavlovich formed the Konigschloss Group during the height of the Cold War. When nuclear arms proliferation, terrorism, and anarchy were at their high point. It was becoming increasingly clear, both elected political leaders and dictators were equally likely to make irrational decisions leading to the destruction of civilization if not the planet as well. There was a need for a surer hand on the tiller.

The charter of KSG was to manipulate and control all aspects of the global community to prevent this impending Armageddon. Unlike Pavlovich, the first Rat lacked the killer instinct necessary to see their charter become reality.

Balking at some recommended actions under his leadership, the council did not act when necessary to avert potential disasters. The original Rat envisioned an exclusive club of rich playboys pontificating ala Bilderberg. Strategy and advice, not overt kingmaking. Maksim knew this would be insufficient. They needed actions, not words. Or public accolades.

Maksim had watched as Rat drank his 'hemlock', passing from heart failure. Giving his life to the cause and preserving his fortune for his family. He chose to save his family from ruin, humiliation, and bankruptcy after Maksim's threat to expose how much of his wealth was accumulated from Nazi collaboration.

Pavlovich looked down at the plain green jade rat figurine in his hand. He'd picked it up from the hand of his deceased predecessor. Rebuilding the council, he recruited those he knew he could count on to complete their objectives. Of course, he'd still sent the prior Rat's family into ruin and disgrace, adding much of their fortune to his own. Without remorse. Such was the pact. His predecessor should have expected nothing less. Further proof of his weakness.

The new council also created what he would call the 'second circle'. Much like the Council on Foreign Relations, which also served his purpose tangentially, the members of the KSG second circle comprised influential members in business, media and government, all sworn to secrecy. The second circle was unaware of the existence of the KSG council. Believing they were part of an exclusive and small clandestine group focused on global good. Useful idiots, one and all.

Pavlovich chuckled at the ease with which he manipulated magnates and heads of state to do his wishes. It all came down to one thing. Money. Jesus had been right to throw the money changers out of the temple.

KSG controlled the money supply of the entire planet. Either directly through its members, or indirectly through its ability to put pressure on commerce and sovereign countries through those in the second circle. This gave the council, and specifically Pavlovich, the power to control many aspects of life.

He laughed at the annual rankings of the richest individuals. His own access to wealth dwarfed that of the individuals listed. He needed no silly acknowledgement of the power he wielded.

Yet again, KSG was on the cusp of tipping the last domino to ensure their plans could finally come to fruition. For all its uses, money was not *everything*. Movement in the air caught his attention.

"Dragon, I see you have arrived," he commented, seeing the dragon symbol turn orange. "My friends, we have a dilemma."

Each of their voices was masked and delivered in mechanical sounding voices. There were men and women on the council, but the voices all sounded the same to preserve anonymity.

Maksim continued speaking. "What was once assured appears to be in doubt, namely the landslide victory of the Vice President in the US election."

"I disagree," said the hologram represented by the Dragon. As the members spoke, their hologram would flash from orange to green, showing who was speaking. "The election is still clearly favoring the Vice President. The abysmal showing by the Opposition candidate is allowing the independent Turner to get some traction, but it is all at the expense of the Opposition. The Vice President will win. Of this, I am still confident."

The Chinese Pig turned green as its owner spoke.

"While I appreciate your confidence, we have heard this before. Too many times. We must move now. Too many plans have come to fruition in too many places around the globe. Sovereign nationhood has never had less command of their citizenry. Many are on the verge of anarchy and chaos. Shortly, the citizens of many of these countries will be ready to accept radical changes to replace anarchy with order. If America is not removed as a stabilizing force, they may still step in and assist with mitigating the controlled chaos we have worked so hard to cause. As they did in Ukraine and Israel."

"I warned all of the unintended consequences, when I counseled against releasing the COVID plague. Both times," responded Dragon. The voice washing software could not convey emotions or tone, but Dragon's concern was clear in his choice of words.

The Goat symbol turned green before Pig could retort. "I remind you it would not have been necessary if *you* had not failed during her election. You told us it was assured as well. If not for the release of the plague, we may have lost yet again."

"Perhaps, but it also disrupted so many other of our plans and altered the entire structure of global supply chains, accelerating nationalistic tendencies. Something *we* had worked decades to eliminate. This makes some of our expected change uncertain. Look at recent elections in the EU. They are trending more towards 1914 national identities than our post-war socialist cooperatives."

Rat spoke again. "Dragon, we have been extremely patient. Destabilization through the United States electoral processes has been our goal for decades. You have provided guidance to this council during this time, saying this is the only way for this to work. Yet we never seem to quite achieve the goals of leaders who can be manipulated and successfully implement the required changes in America."

Dragon's symbol turned green, as he sighed.

"I understand your frustration. America is difficult. I can only assume most of you are *not* here. I am. America is unlike any other country and culture on the planet. Entirely unpredictable. They rally around the strangest things. Threats and bullying will not work. They are too diverse. You must be patient and stay the course. If the Vice President is not elected, then you can assess alternatives."

Goat spoke again. "This is the exact speech you have given several times after *our* candidate *did* win. Now four times. They were still unable to accomplish the tasks and implement the policies we all agree are needed to start this process. Each time you council patience. This time, we were assured it would not be the case. We have accelerated the timetable in so many other ways. Activities we cannot stop or reverse. They will proceed and some of our efforts will be squandered if your part of the plan is not concluded successfully."

Before Dragon could respond, Rat broke in.

"Goat, you are correct. Regardless of the outcome, we proceed with our plans. Dragon, we will begin after your election. Either the VP will be the leader pushing the United States fully into the global community or we will take matters into our own hands and force the change without the help of American leadership."

Dragon sat in his office, watching the twirling zodiac symbols in the air above his desk. He fully understood their impatience.

"Understood. I will leave you again with my warning. America is unpredictable. They will not react as you think. Whether we can account for this remains to be seen. Expect the unexpected and plan accordingly," finished Dragon, knowing the admonition would go unheeded. Their patience was gone.

"We will reconvene after the US election," finished Rat, ending the call.

Pavlovich sat contemplating. The sole roadblock to implementing his vision continued to be one country. The United States and its ideals of personal freedom and individuality. The ability to spread this ideal to the weak-minded citizens in the world constantly undermined his goals of creating dependent societies and people.

America. Freedom. Individual choices. These were the sea walls they could not exterminate. Breach, yes. Undermine, in some areas, culturally yes. Ultimately, still unable to bring about complete collapse. Politically, they had chipped away at the protections the Constitution provided. Slowly they were reaching their culmination. It teetered on the edge of success.

Lexi Smythe-Thomas was handpicked by Pavlovich. Nurtured and supported for decades in the background. Given enough free rein to think her accomplishments were her own, while being controlled in subtle ways. Recruited to the second circle at the right time. She was his angel of death. Delivering death to America. Whether or not she knew it.

Part One

Bruised but not Defeated

"Experience is a brutal teacher. But you learn. My god, you learn."

C.S. Lewis

Chapter 1

Senator Nick Turner sat in his presidential election campaign office in a downtown high-rise in Denver, Colorado. On the desk was a single black loafer. He stared at the shoe, looking up at the knock on his open door. His campaign manager, Denise Rojas, entered taking a seat opposite. The shoe now between them. She glanced at it, then back at Nick.

"Please, let me at least put it on the bookshelf. It is not healthy sitting here staring at it all day."

"We almost had him. I should have told Earl to move sooner. I should have charged him faster," fumed Nick, looking away from the shoe.

"Right. Then I could be having this conversation with Neill. Asking him who he wants as *his* VP after you went over the side of the building with Greg."

Nick nodded as Denise took the shoe and put it on a bookshelf. Handling it like a holy artifact.

"Did you get the video to Tommy?" he asked.

"He'll air it tonight. I assume you want to be on?"

"Yes."

"The news is covering Greg's suicide carefully. They are trying not to make him sympathetic, but they're also trying not to pile on him either. They know it could make him a martyr to many and help you," noted Denise.

"The recording will put a lot of this to rest," remarked Nick.

"What's on it?" Denise stared at him intently.

"You'll have to wait like everyone else. It's what Greg wanted," replied Nick, holding up a hand at Denise's scowl.

"You know?"

He nodded. "Where are we on everything else?"

"You mean from the most epic day from Hell a campaign has ever had?" groaned Denise.

Nick smiled briefly. "Let me have it. Good news first, please, if there is any."

Denise returned his smile, just happy to have something else to focus her boss on.

"The good news is we seem to be turning the corner on the Blue Morpho accusations. The interviews with the homeless who are in the program are resonating. Our requests for the names of the whistleblowers who claim to have worked for our campaign are being ignored. We, of course, are broadcasting this from the rooftops. For any who will listen, anyway."

"Make it clear they are afraid to come forward because they know they won't hold up to any questioning. This is all manufactured by the VP and her lackeys."

Denise nodded at Nick as she continued.

"Coach Sampson was great on the morning shows, as was Laura Wood, our Orange County campaign office supervisor. Once she got done telling her story, there wasn't a dry eye in the place. The interview on NWN with the Blue Morpho founders, Summers, Spalding, Patterson, and Williamson went well."

"Good."

"They opened their books. Providing access to their taxes and the deductions they are *not* taking on what they donated. Tens of millions, by the way. In return, they asked for the list of assets and how these were obtained. Including copies of the warrants the DA used to seize them," said Denise with a small smile.

"Nice, calling their bluff."

"Everett Spalding was loaded for bear. Right after the appearance, his lawyers filed defamation lawsuits against LN1. Naming the news reporters, and the network president Kaufmann, citing their 'inflammatory and reckless rhetoric with no facts to back up the accusations'. That should get some sphincters tightening."

Nick grinned at Denise's statement. Once again thanking his stars for his rich, honest, *and* brave allies.

"That means they either have to produce the illegally seized asset lists or the warrant we know they don't have," explained Denise. "They are screwed. Spalding has both the money and the desire to stick it to them. They picked a fight with the wrong guy. Martha, Carson, and Howard are also thinking of joining the lawsuit as well."

"I'm glad we finally have someone who can't be canceled. Someone able to stand up to the bully tactics and make them pay. I assume they will keep this front and center in the media and not let them wiggle out of it?" asked Nick.

Denise smiled a big smile for the first time in the last few days. "Oh yeah. This one is going to be everywhere. Martha spends a ton advertising on all the networks for her stores. No way any of them want to lose her advertising spend by not covering this."

Nick leaned back in this chair, thinking as Denise continued.

"They got their digs into the administration and the failure of the California Governor to even come close to what Blue Morpho has done for the homeless in less than six months. It is not a good look when Party donors, who have provided billions to the coffers for decades, are suddenly solving problems their candidates and the Party chose not to."

"Not to mention supporting me," added Nick.

Denise flipped through her notes.

"Luckily, their interview finished before they started playing the drug deal footage from Bergamo on ANC. You are going to get around to telling me how we fight that, right?" asked Denise, exasperated. "You know how you and Earl are on camera at a drug deal with you holding a bag of heroin? With an ANC reporter filming from a car as a rival gang shows up shooting at all of you?"

"Eventually. Earl headed to Chicago?"

"First flight out this morning," she answered.

"Good, he'll handle our Chicago response. I need to buy thirty minutes of prime time on any station that will have me."

"That'll cost a pretty penny. EXN will be fine. The other networks will take the money." grunted Denise.

"Fine, we have the money, lets buy some attention to what we have to say. Don't offer it to ANC and FLCN. I'm not giving them a dime of my donor's money."

"Got it. When?"

"Monday night?" asked Nick.

"Let me see what I can do on this short notice."

"They'll find me time. They all need eyeballs. This is guaranteed to get a bunch. They think they've got me. Anything they can do to help Lexi. They'd even delay the football game if she asked. Trust me. She has them all on speed dial. Monday night should give Earl enough time to get what we need," responded Nick with confidence.

"And that is?" fished Denise.

"Nice try. Trust me, you are better off not knowing. Anything else on my truckload of write in ballots you ordered in Michigan?"

"That's not funny," accused Denise tersely.

"Hey, that's what the driver said. I'm just repeating what he told the FBI," Nick said with the hint of a genuine smile. His first since Greg's suicide.

"This is serious. We need to figure out how to fight this and prove these are fraudulent or at least not printed by us or any allies. Right now, everyone thinks you are stuffing ballot boxes."

"We're working it. Earl has already contacted folks who are looking into this. We'll get enough info to debunk it. This one is bad optics, but the people who are going to vote for me aren't going to fall for this. We aren't even on the ballot in Michigan, so why would we waste our time and effort trying to get three million write-in votes? In Michigan, solid Lexi territory? That is ridiculous and on the surface it would be looked at that way by a non-biased FBI."

"Except we know the FBI is not unbiased. Just so you know, I would not do well in prison."

"I won't let you go to prison."

"Gee, that's heartening. 'I'm sorry, Mr. FBI agent, but my boss says I can't go with you. Please come back another time'. Exactly how would you stop them?" retorted Denise.

"What proof do they have? The driver has a rap sheet a mile long. He is not exactly an upstanding citizen. We'll have to reverse engineer this entire process back to the source. They only have his word you were involved. No proof," explained Nick.

"I'm sure they will let me use my laptop and Wi-Fi from my cell for the next few weeks," offered Denise sarcastically.

Nick ignored her tone. "Earl has some local law enforcement contacts in the Detroit area. Someone knows something. Then we have to figure out who is paying for them. My guess is if they are printing ballots with my name, they are probably also printing ballots for Lexi."

"No doubt about it. She is obsessed and she'll stop at nothing to ensure she doesn't end up like the last female candidate."

"Lexi is way worse than her," commented Nick.

"What do you want to do about Little Rock?"

"Right, the Arkansas state fair. That's tomorrow night? They still want me after all the stuff yesterday. Knowing I'm not dropping out or resigning?"

"Yep, they're still game if you are. The music acts are cool with it as well. They don't believe any of it," assured Denise.

"Ok, I'll fly down. Can the jet fly me to Chicago after the speech in Little Rock?

"Sure. You going to help Earl?"

"I just had an idea and I need to be there to make it happen. Is it possible to get a studio setup in Chicago so I can do the broadcast live from there?"

"You want to do it live? Are you nuts? We should record it to make sure it's what we want. Too many things can go wrong doing it live."

"It *has* to be live. We need credibility. Doing it live shows I am not afraid," said Nick with conviction. "Plus, what I'm thinking has to be done live to be effective. Make sure the networks don't cut me off like they did on *The Sunday Hour*. It's my money this time and I am paying to be seen."

"Ok, I guess at this point we have little to lose. I'll make the point it is our money. Our terms or no eyeballs for them."

"We have everything to lose. That's why it has to be done this way," shared Nick.

Denise shrugged, intrigued, worried, and a little pissed. She had no idea how her boss was going to handle five bombshell October surprises dropped in the last twenty-four hours. One thing was for certain. Lexi was out for blood.

Chapter 2

Nick sat in the green room at EXN's studio in Washington. He was by himself, sipping a Pellegrino and contemplating the events of the last 48 hours. He had arrived an hour earlier, having flown in from Denver to do this segment in the studio. Tommy's producer stuck his head in.

"Senator, we're ready for you."

Nick shook Tommy's hand as he arrived on the studio soundstage. "Nick, we have the last thirty minutes of the show for you. What they are doing to you is a travesty," said Tommy Charles, host of *Tommy Charles Tonight*, the top rated EXN opinion show.

"Tommy, they are doing it to all of us, not just me. Greg is the latest in a long line of people they have chewed up and spit out," answered Nick in a calm, but dangerous sounding tone. Tommy picked up on this, a bead of sweat appearing through the makeup on his forehead, below his crewcut.

"Nick, I'm taking an enormous risk here. Letting you run this footage sight unseen on live television. You aren't doing anything that'll cost me my job?" he laughed nervously.

"Hardly Tommy. The nation, or at least the part watching your show, needs to see and hear firsthand from the innocent victim."

"Trust me, we'll have plenty of folks tuned in. We have been hyping your appearance non-stop since you asked for it. On *their* stations, too."

"Five seconds," said Tommy's producer Warren.

"Welcome back to this special Saturday night edition of our show. As promised, we are joined by Senator Nick Turner, independent candidate for President. Senator, before we start, I would like to offer my condolences for the loss of Greg Simmons," stated Tommy.

"Thank you. It is truly a sad and unnecessary tragedy, as you will soon see and hear," challenged Nick, setting the tone.

Tommy nodded, continuing. "I want you to know, and I think I speak for most of my viewers as well, these attacks on you, your campaign, and your staffers are a bit too coincidental to be believed?"

"Tommy, there can be no doubt our campaign has been the target of a concerted effort to smear and damage our reputation prior to the election. Just like what happened to the Governor. Politics is a dirty business. No one knows this better than the Vice President who has left a trail of broken and ruined challengers in her wake for decades now. Reputations destroyed personally by the VP or her many minions and willing allies in American *Pravda*," accused Nick.

"This time, they have crossed the line. A good and innocent young man in the prime of his life is dead. A direct result of spurious and sensational claims made using Kevin Moss as their latest weapon. A 22-year-old junior staffer from my team."

Nick was trying to remain calm, but his anger was clearly visible. Tommy looked on, prepared to interrupt if Nick went too far.

"No doubt he will suffer the same fate as all the others this Party campaign has used and sacrificed. Lest we forget, it was only days ago, we finally came to know the two young women who accused me of sexual harassment were thoroughly discredited, having admitted to being paid to accuse me."

"They are paying the price for being used. Now canceled, sentenced to live a life of shame and regret. Manipulated and discarded, their usefulness over. I am hopeful this will not be Kevin's fate as well. Tommy, this is an evil machine. Hopefully whomever paid them will be unmasked. Clearly, those supporting the Vice President will do or fund whatever it takes to win," concluded Nick.

"Those are pretty substantial accusations, Senator. Do you have anything to back them up?"

"I don't. But Greg Simmons does."

"Beg your pardon, Senator," responded Tommy, confused.

"Tommy, I provided you with a phone earlier today. It is Greg's phone. He made a video on it before he committed suicide. I would like you to play it for your audience."

"When did he do that, Senator?"

"Just before I was trying to talk him out of jumping off a 20-story building last night," replied Nick.

"Jesus," blurted Tommy incredulously. "You were there when he jumped?"

"I was. What makes it worse, Tommy, is Greg was jumping out of guilt. Not guilt for the alleged deed the Vice President's team has blackmailed this poor young man into perpetrating. No, it was guilt over the damage he was causing to *my* campaign. Can you believe that, Tommy? Greg killed himself because he was more concerned about damaging my f-ing campaign than his own life and reputation. That is so wrong." Nick paused for a second to shake his head.

"Greg did not want to be the story. But Lexi and her minions have made him the story," said Nick emotionally. "Tommy, he killed himself to save a stupid political campaign. This is a burden I'll have to bear," Nick turned from looking at Tommy to looking into the camera.

"Know this. These dirty tricks, innuendos, frame jobs, and hit pieces are all contrived by someone. Blood has been spilled. I won't give up. Now or ever. I'll fight for every Greg and Dusty out there and I will find who did this and make sure justice is served. This I promise," said Nick to the camera.

"Senator, let's play the video Greg left," interjected Tommy, sensing Nick's restraint was weakening. He interrupted to keep Nick from directly threatening the VP.

"Good idea Tommy. Just so everyone knows, I am the only one who has seen this footage. I gave it to Tommy on the condition he would not preview it," explained Nick.

"Play it please production room," ordered Tommy.

Up on the screen, a video started playing, showing Greg's face.

"For those of you who do not know, I am Greg Simmons. I am the assistant chief of staff for Senator Turner's campaign. Recently, accusations were made of an inappropriate relation with another male staffer. These are false. The accuser in question, Kevin Moss, is a 22-year-old staffer in our office. Kevin is a great kid, but he is just a kid. I am a gay man. As any gay man in politics can tell you, it is not an easy task. I have been working first with Senator Richards and now Nick since he took over. The one thing I have learned in DC is when you are a staffer, you should *never* be the story," said Greg on the video with emphasis.

"Because of this and the sensationalism of gay relationships as pushed by our overzealous media, I chose to never put any of my bosses at risk. I have had no relationships since arriving in Washington. You can research to your heart's content, but you will find no credible evidence of one," Greg stopped and took a deep breath.

"Kevin knows this, because yes, I spent time with him. It was not an affair. I was counseling Kevin on what it means to be gay and work for a senator and then on a high profile presidential campaign. I told Kevin those same words. Whatever he did, to remember the staffer coda. Never embarrass the boss. Never be the story. Ever," continued Greg.

"It is precisely because of this, I am going to do what I can to fix the issue. I refuse to be used to bring down Nick Turner. He is the last hope for our country. I believe only he can convince a majority of the people to wake up. To see the damage the Party and its allies in the media have done with its full-on shift to fascism disguised as Progressivism. I cannot be a party to them taking him down and I will not allow it."

Greg's face on the recording had a slight smile as he continued.

"This is a cause worth dying for. So maybe I am the Crispus Attucks of this revolution. Maybe the first sacrifice is a gay white man instead of a free black man. Regardless, I am willing, and I believe in the cause enough to make the sacrifice." Greg's voice became more confident and assured as he delivered his challenge.

"Finally, Kevin, I know you didn't want to do this. I know you needed the money to pay for your mother's rehab in California. You had mentioned you did not know how you could afford to keep her there. You were worried because this time it seemed to be working. I checked and found $100,000 had been wired to the rehab facility to pay your mother's bills for the remainder of her time there."

"I know you did not have this money or know anyone who did. Now I know why you did this. *They* offered you the money to make up these lies. I know you were desperate. I get it. Family first and all that. But you should have come to us and the Senator. We would have helped. You know that. You know the kindness, faith, and hope he gives to all those around him. You were caught in the spider's web of politics. And the Black Widow got you." Greg shook his head on camera at the tactics of their enemies.

"I am sure the money won't be traceable back to the VP's campaign, but her tentacles are long and wide and no doubt some organization who gives large amounts to the Party and her coffers funded your mother's rehab. Kevin, I forgive you. I do. I hope you can find it in your heart to forgive yourself. You know Nick forgives you." finished Greg as the video went to black.

Tommy was visibly upset. "Nick, what can you do about this? There has to be a crime here somewhere," said Tommy, forgetting to call him Senator.

"What do I do? Go after a kid because he lied to save his mother? He already has to deal with the guilt of Greg's death. That is burden enough. One he should not have to bear at twenty-two. Or at any age."

"The crime is perpetrated by the people who cannot win a free and fair election. Who are sacrificing good people and extorting others into deeds they will regret. The real crime is the unwillingness of the progressives, the Party, and the American *Pravda* media to let the will of the people stand in our democratic republic." Nick sat up straight and tall, staring into the camera while towering over the diminutive Tommy, even on his elevated dais.

"Every totalitarian regime is born when the people fail to stand up and stop it in its infancy. They fail to unify in their strength. Instead, allowing inattention and an unscrupulous minority to gain power and use the tools of the state against them. By then it is too late. Inevitably, much suffering must happen before they are overthrown, as they always are. Must we always repeat the mistakes of history? Over and over. We either fight and defeat Progressivism now, or we do it later, after much loss and deprivation. It is *our* choice. This was our Boston Massacre, and like the Sons of Liberty, we will take up the cause of freedom and defend it against all who would take it away." Nick finished his speech as Tommy nodded vigorously in agreement.

"Well said Senator. It is what we say every night on this program. It is what every thinking person in this country knows in their gut. It is what we see in our cultural rot promoted by Hollywood. What we hear and see daily from the *Pravda* press and cable and the hatred spewed on social media. We are already at war. It is Progressivism vs Constitutionality. We see the results of each. I choose constitutionality over progressive totalitarianism every day," ended Tommy.

"As do I Tommy. As Ben Franklin challenged, we need to prove once more, we deserve our Republic with its democratic freedoms. Freedoms, our forefathers rose in rebellion to win for us. We should not lightly squander the opportunity we have. To take back our destiny via the ballot box."

"Agreed. Senator, we have a few more minutes. Do you care to comment on the other accusations against your campaign? There were so many. My head is spinning. I can only imagine the chaos it is causing you and your team."

"Sure Tommy. I think we have already debunked the idea that Blue Morpho is in any way fraudulent. Clearly, Party operatives delivered a package to LN1 on Blue Morpho, similar to what they did against Governor Blackbird for NWN. It appears LN1 failed to do their due diligence. The mistake they appear to have made is to accuse some of our most civic-minded philanthropists. It probably doesn't help that they were also once upon a time some of the Party's biggest donors. That is testimony to the current direction of the VP and her policies."

"To throw out unsubstantiated accusations and innuendo when one only has to take a trip to Venice Beach today, versus April, when we started this effort. What you will see is success. Success at helping the homeless get back on their feet and get their lives in order. The billions of tax dollars, yours and mine, thrown at these problems by state and federal governments. Through various NGOs and other organizations could not accomplish in decades what we did in less than six months," Nick laughed.

"I do not need to defend the backers of Blue Morpho. They can do this themselves and will. They cannot be canceled. They will not stop until they clear their names. We should celebrate their efforts and the results. Not try to malign people who donate billions without asking for anything in return. That sounds like someone I would want to emulate, not smear."

"Thank you, Senator. And the accusations of your campaign taking advantage of these homeless?"

"Tommy, we are transparent. There is not a single member of the Blue Morpho organization working for us who is not being paid well above minimum wage. Our books are open. Our Orange County campaign chairperson, Laura Wood, appeared this morning on several shows. She is herself a graduate of the Blue Morpho program. There can be no more credible witness to the success of the program than her."

"We welcome the scrutiny. Blue Morpho's founders and Coach Sampson will seek to have their day in court, where we can confront these anonymous accusers and their mouthpieces in the American *Pravda* media. It is our hope we can set a precedent to ensure these types of spurious attacks by the press with no due diligence or actual vetting of facts are penalized heavily."

"Who knows, perhaps we can finally hold the press accountable and repeal the *Sullivan* Supreme Court decision they have been hiding behind for decades now. Enabling them to make shit up about their enemies claiming everyone in the limelight is fair game for innuendo and accusation without fact. Our ministry of truth should look closer to home, at our American *Pravda* media. There they will find the most dangerous mis- and dis- information."

"If we don't fight back against cancel culture and the threat of it, we are allowing them to take away our rights and freedoms. Then we have no one to blame but ourselves." Nick again sat up and delivered his speech to the camera and not Tommy. This was his last chance to reach a broad audience, refuting the megaphone of accusations being broadcast non-stop.

"Senator, we are almost out of time. I have to ask about the footage Lauren Bergamo showed in Chicago. It's fake, right?" laughed Tommy, hopefully. "This one is comical. How far has ANC fallen?"

"Far indeed. However, I won't address that one tonight. We have purchased time Monday night on every network who will take our money. I will discuss these allegations then. Trust me, it will be must see TV, to borrow a phrase," laughed Nick.

"My producers are yelling at me and we have not taken a commercial break, but I have to ask about the ballots and the debanking?" asked Tommy

"Tommy, I'm not on the ballot in Michigan, Pennsylvania and Wisconsin. Activist state Supreme Court judges, appointed and elected by the Party in each state, kept me off the ballot. Sometimes even overruling their own legislatures, as in Pennsylvania. Their excuses were weak considering there are at last count close to 17 other candidates who will receive mere hundreds to maybe a thousand votes and yet I am kept off?" Nick could see Tommy's producer rolling his hand to speed it up off camera.

"The winner in Michigan is probably going to have at least 3 million votes. Any idea what it would take to fake three million write-in votes to stand up to any scrutiny?"

Tommy laughed in reply.

"There are 83 counties in Michigan. In the last two elections, less than 10,000 ballots in three states decided the outcome. You can't just print up three million ballots in Wayne county for Detroit. I'd need a majority in most of the counties. And you would have to do it in such a way to withstand challenges. It is an enormous task to consider. Frankly, it is much easier to win the battle of ideas and count on our citizens to vote for the candidate with the best policies. I am perfectly happy to take my chances with the voters. This is why I tell them to vote on election day. We'll expose this accusation as another attempt to divert our attention and try to sway impressionable voters with rhetoric and dirty tricks."

"Wow Senator, it appears you have put some thought into it," laughed Tommy, nervously.

"Tommy, I gave a speech at the CST conference in February and I explained why everyday folks doubt our elections are honest any longer. I explained just how systematic cheating could occur on so many levels, especially with mail in balloting and ballot harvesting. What I just explained to you is just one of many ways this can occur because we lack the simple check of forcing folks to show a picture ID when they vote."

"This simple step makes fake ballots an impossibility. It makes people voting for others an impossibility. It makes ballot box stuffing an impossibility. You simply count the number of IDs and names checked off and count the votes and if there is a discrepancy, then you know how many ballots were faked. It is easy to restore confidence. All of this shows how this charge I am printing ballots is ridiculous. Anyone who has listened to a single speech knows I only want to win one way, honestly. I am all in on voter IDs. One legal vote from each *legal* citizen."

"The real question should be directed at whoever did gin up these fake votes and then have them *conveniently* found implicating me and my campaign manager, at the same time as these other accusations? Somebody obviously *can* print and fake these ballots. What else might they be doing? Now that is what we should be investigating."

"Senator, we have beat that to death on this program," responded Tommy, nodding vigorously.

"Nobody who wants to vote legally would complain about having to show an ID to cast a vote. Use my other technique, the Mirror. Reflect on them what they are saying about you. They claim you are the fraud or the racist for wanting IDs. Actually, they are the ones committing the fraud, advocating for the fraud by fighting this obvious remedy to cheating. Voter IDs. If you aren't cheating, why else would you fight it? It is common sense," finished Nick.

"Senator, thirty seconds left. Debanking? How are you going to pay your staff and your bills?"

"Tommy, we're working on it. Obviously, this is another coordinated attack. It is too convenient for it not to have been orchestrated. The three largest banks all decide to stop me from banking *on the same day* and with no notice? Have no fear, we have plenty of money. We are exploring other options to pay folks."

"Senator, thank you for your time. Again, our condolences on the loss of Greg Simmons. That had to be heartbreaking. Hopefully tonight's airing of the video will allow for some closure and help the American public realize the lengths to which your opponents are going in order to win an election," closed Tommy.

"Thanks Tommy, see you Monday night."

As they went to break, Tommy looked at Nick, "I truly am sorry, Nick. I had no idea you saw him jump."

"Earl was there too. We had him for a second, but his weight was too much," said Nick, shaking his head.

"Just so you know, my producer was yelling in my ear. Corporate wanted to cut away once the video started, but I told him to ignore it. There may be hell to pay. I, and a few others on my team, may need a job in the morning," laughed Tommy.

"No worries, I'm sure we need folks to make calls and fill envelopes," responded Nick with a smile.

"See you Monday night, I hope," said Tommy, half seriously.

Chapter 3

Like many others, Vice President of the United States, and Party candidate for president, Lexi Smythe-Thomas, sat watching Nick's appearance on *Tommy*. Along with her chief of staff Mel Arenson, her campaign manager Harriet Jordan, head of security Roland Gill, and Merri Wilcox, her pollster. They were sitting on various chairs and couches in her expansive DC campaign office.

Lexi was in a festive mood as she watched. Mel muted the TV waiting for Turner's segment.

"Well Merri, what are the latest snap poll results? Surely Blackbird and Turner are finished," she gloated.

Mel glanced at Merri, who appeared unsure how to answer.

"Lexi, it is still early to see results from all the activity. Not everyone watches the networks. Cable pundits and our social media influencers are ramping up their commentaries to reinforce all the disclosures yesterday," remarked Mel.

"You're telling me it's not affecting polls yet?" responded Lexi in a dangerous tone, well aware of Mel's attempted deflection.

"Having Turner's man commit suicide turned the sympathy from the staffer to his guy. Yesterday, they were outraged against him and Turner. This morning not as much. They feel sorry for them," answered Mel for Merri, still trying to shield her from Lexi's wrath.

"It's also too early to show any response to the revelations from ANC and Bergamo about the drug deal. Our man on the street is mixed. Some think he should resign and drop out. Others think it is an outright hoax perpetrated by ANC to help their sagging ratings," shrugged Merri.

"If it's true? Pretty hard to deny *that* footage. Where did you ask the questions, outside EXN's building?" asked Lexi, her sarcastic tone signaling danger the analytical Merri was oblivious too.

"Actually, no, we did it in Rockefeller Plaza, outside the NWN studio during their weekend morning show," responded Merri, missing Mel's subtle hand motion.

"Really?" glared Lexi, her voice rising. "Mel, why isn't this working? We called in a lot of favors and greased a lot of palms."

"It may have been a mistake to dump all five of them simultaneously. They stepped all over each other and I think the public is a lot more skeptical of anonymous sources, especially after Blackbird's scandal," explained Harriet Jordan, Lexi's campaign manager, jumping in to help Mel.

Lexi turned to look at the middle-aged large black woman, with her steel gray hair pulled back in a bun. Harriet had been managing Lexi's campaigns for decades now.

"Count on Turner to have someone willing to jump off a building for him," admired Lexi. "Let's see what else he has to say on that jarhead prick's show. Why can't we get him off the air?" Lexi stood and headed to the bar for a refill of her scotch. Everyone else tried to avoid any eye contact with the candidate.

Mel caught the eye of Roland Gill, Lexi's head of personal security and their resident 'fixer'. He returned Mel's gaze with a steely one of his own.

"We try. Every time we have a sponsor boycott his show, they get killed in the market and sales of their products just wither and die. It ends up hurting the sponsor to the point they are no longer willing to take our direction. We have tried putting pressure on the show producers, but they just laugh. You know the EXN president, maybe you can put more pressure on Sheila," remarked Mel with a shrug. "She is the *only* female media president."

"I have tried. She says their ratings are the best in the business, and Tommy routinely beats the networks now. Anything she does would be seen as completely political and even though she supports me, she has to be mindful she *is* running a business."

"She's right. He is their cash cow," agreed Mel in a resigned tone.

"So how bad is the polling?" Lexi came back to her chair with a fresh drink.

"Oh, it's not bad at all for you. You still have a 30 plus point lead. It's just Turner has not fallen as far and as hard as we had expected or hoped. You are at 56, Turner is now at 15 and Blackbird is around 23. Blackbird is down about 15 from his highs and not likely to recover. He has not handled his scandal well. Turner picked up a few points from Blackbird and so have you," explained Merri, trying to sound encouraging.

"Crap, I was hoping Turner would fall too far to join the debate," worried Lexi. "Any chance we can change the criteria again? Like 20% or being on the ballot in all 50 states?"

"We tried the ballot thing, they turned us down. They had already turned us down on raising the poll percentage. There is still hope the Chicago or ballot thing has legs and he sinks before the last qualifying poll in a few days. My bet is on Chicago to do it," hoped Mel.

"Turner is on," said Harriet, nodding at the muted TV.

They listened in silence, with an occasional snort. When Nick admitted he was on the roof when Greg jumped, Harriet and Mel both said "Shit" at the same time and looked at each other.

"What?" asked Merri, confused.

Roland answered. "He just blew our entire story out of the water. Once again, he is bullet proof. Now he is the Hero attempting to save the victim once again. You continue to keep underestimating him." He glanced from Lexi to Mel as he finished his statement.

"Merri, we need to talk," ordered Mel in a tone she was not used to hearing. Merri glanced at Lexi, who met hers with an icy stare as she sat confused before processing the request.

"Oh, right. I'll let you know when we get the latest poll results." She picked up her laptop and left Lexi's office. Mel got up and flipped the light curtain and SCIF mode, securing the office from any surveillance. As Mel returned to his seat, the video was just starting to play.

"The payment can't be tied back to us?" asked Lexi.

"No, but it can be tied back to our donors and maybe even the Party National Committee," replied Harriet. Roland made a noise, earning a look from Lexi.

They continued to watch as Greg's face came on the screen. "Shit, shit, shit," cursed Lexi, dialing the phone, now pacing.

"You shut it down. You shut it down now or we'll pull your fucking FCC license tomorrow. You hear me? Now!" screamed Lexi into the phone, furious, as she watched Greg continue to describe how he found the payment and the motive for the accusations.

"What do you mean, he is not listening to your direction? Aren't you the president of the fucking network? Then have someone cut the goddamn power to the building. I don't care," said Lexi, yelling at Sheila Caruthers, the president of EXN on the other end of the line.

They watched as the video ended. Lexi hung up on Sheila and dialed another number. "I want that kid back on the air in an hour. I want him rebutting everything Turner's guy said. I don't care how you do it, but get it done. This is your mess. Clean it up," said Lexi, once again turning off her phone.

They watched as Nick continued to defend against the various attacks and made his accusations, laying all of this at the feet of Lexi.

"How much?" asked Lexi, looking from Mel to Harriet.

"5 points, maybe more if they track it back to a Party donor," answered Harriet.

"Crap," vented Lexi. "We should have cut his legs out at the beginning," Lexi looked at Mel, who simply opened his hands.

"It was a judgement call, giving him attention versus not. This is a very different campaign and a very different electorate. We control almost all the news sources, yet he is still thriving. Our tactics should have worked and did with Blackbird. The Opposition is even more feckless than usual. We just never counted on an independent having this staying power and an ability to get to the people directly," commented Mel.

"What about all the accusations? He is saying the attacks against him lack evidence. Blaming me for all of this. Where is *his* proof? Can we sue *him* for libel?" challenged Lexi.

"It would give him what he wants. Airing the accusations in the press and on TV. He probably thinks he has enough examples to at least cast doubt on us for causing this. Plus, it gives him the free press we have been denying him all campaign. He wins if we make a big deal defending against this. I suggest we just accuse him of hypocrisy, claiming we are behind this with no proof. Turn his Flip and Mirror against him," finished Mel.

Roland shook his head. "Do not underestimate him. *He* would not make the accusations if he was not sure he could defend them. Has he not already bought airtime on Monday? And there is the Censure debate in the Senate as well. When you provoke the viper, you must be prepared for the strike in response."

Mel and Lexi were both about to retort when Lexi's phone buzzed before she could respond.

"Yes? It had better be good," she said, ending the call. "The kid's going on FLCN in an hour to rebut the video."

"Do you think that is a good idea?" counseled Harriet. Her tone expressing her concern.

"It is his word against a dead guy. So what if he got paid? It doesn't change the story if we stick to our storyline. There is no one to say this kid wasn't violated by Turner's guy. He did commit suicide. If he was innocent, why off himself? They can say it was to save Turner. We have many more mouths and outlets to say it was because he was guilty. If we stick to the plan, it can still work, especially if the kid can sell it. Then we don't have to worry about the money. He had a legitimate story to sell, and he did it for the money. People do it all the time," reasoned Lexi.

"It could work, but you are putting a lot of faith in an emotional 22-year-old giving the performance of a lifetime," worried Mel.

"Do we have a choice? Time for him to earn that money," said Lexi unemotionally.

\#

"Nick, FLCN is putting Kevin on again. Supposedly, to rebut what Greg said," warned Chuck Robinson, his chief of staff, on the laptop ZOOM call. Nick was in his hotel room with a room service dinner.

"Really? I feel sorry for Kevin. They must have put the screws to him. Dealing with all this at his age. I wish he would have just come to us," sighed Nick.

"It's a dirty business, Nick. Nothing dirtier than vying for the most powerful job in the world," remarked Chuck.

"Then why do I feel so helpless?" asked Nick.

"Hey, Denise and Jer just walked in. They were still in the office as well," said Chuck as they came into view around the office conference table where Chuck and Margie, the campaign's communications director, were already seated.

"Does anyone have Kevin's number? Maybe I can call him before he goes on."

"Let me get it," said Denise, looking through a file on her laptop. She gave Nick the number.

"I'm putting you on mute to see if I can get him on my cell." Nick walked away from the laptop webcam, dialing. It went to voice mail.

"Kevin, it's Nick. Look, I know how tough this is for you and we can help. All of us. You are part of our family. Don't let them destroy you like they did Greg. Come in and we'll work through all of this together. I forgive you for what you did. I know you needed to help your mother. Don't let them use you. They don't care about you at all. We do. We can fix this. Please for Greg, let us help you through this," finished Nick, walking back into view of the laptop sitting on the small table in the hotel room.

"No luck, voicemail. I told him he did not have to do this and to come in and we would help him get through it. We'll see if it works."

"You would do that, after everything he did to Greg?" This question from Jerry Kingston, a skinny young white guy with black-rimmed glasses. All he lacked was the nerd's pocket protector to complete the stereotype. Despite the appearance, there was no one better at analytics and polling.

"Jer, of course I would. Kevin was used, plain and simple. Even Greg forgave him. We have too little faith in each other and no trust. We have to rebuild it as an entire community. That means making mistakes, admitting them, and being granted forgiveness. Kevin didn't make Greg jump. He chose to. I didn't agree, but it was his and his choice alone to make."

Margie blew her nose loudly. Then shook her head while wiping at some tears streaking down her light brown face. Jer handed her a tissue, putting a hand on her shoulder tenderly. "Nick, I don't know how you do it. I hated Kevin and in three sentences you cut to the heart of the issue. This country needs your wisdom more than ever. And your healing words."

Denise and Chuck were also nodding their heads in amazement at Nick's willingness to forgive Kevin.

"We are all responsible for our own actions, period."

As they were speaking, Kevin came on remotely on FLCN. He was flanked by Tate Vick, one of the opinion show hosts in the studio. A very nervous Kevin appeared on the other side of the split screen.

"Kevin, thank you for joining us once again on such short notice. As you no doubt know, Senator Turner showed a video allegedly from the person who assaulted you. Of course, he claimed you made all of this up and then conveniently committed suicide rather than face you in court." Tate delivered this opening salvo in a snide tone, as if nothing less was expected of a political operative like Greg.

"It is our belief he merely did this because he was guilty and did not want to face the consequences of his actions. We brought you on once more to reiterate your statement and accusations. We realize how difficult this is for you. Especially given the heinous nature of the crime. We feel it is important for America to know you won't be silenced by the bullying tactics of the Turner campaign."

"Thank you, Tate," answered Kevin nervously. "As you can imagine, it has been a tough couple of days for me. It took lots of soul searching to make the accusations. My mother is indeed sick, and I needed the money to pay for her continued rehab. So yes, I got paid to tell my story." Kevin paused.

"It's OK Kevin, take your time. Getting paid to tell a story is nothing to be ashamed of. The truth must be exposed. You have suffered. There is no reason you shouldn't get paid to make up for the pain you've endured at the hands of Turner's hate filled campaign. It is no surprise you are a victim considering what Turner claims he will do if elected," explained Tate, laying on the moral outrage, his face twisted in disgust.

Kevin stiffened at the characterization of the Turner campaign as hate filled. "You know, I was part of a family. A job I liked, people I liked, a cause I believed in," Tate could be seen nodding in his window. "But I was in a tough spot, and I took the easy way out. Instead of trusting my gut. I believed this was the only way to solve my problem. I didn't believe I could count on those around me to support me in my time of need. I didn't confide in enough people," paused Kevin.

\#

"Uh oh," said Mel in Lexi's office, sensing danger.
Lexi sat impassively watching the unfolding drama.

\#

Nick buzzed out of the call in his hotel room and dialed Kevin's number as he too understood where this was going.

\#

"But," continued Kevin. "I was wrong, horribly wrong, and now good people have been hurt needlessly. I made it all up. Greg was always the gentleman, trying to help me. He never made a pass at all. I killed him." A phone was ringing in the background behind Kevin, who turned slightly. Kevin now had a wild look in his eyes as his voice quavered.

"I got Greg killed. I hurt my candidate, Nick Turner. The most wonderful person I have ever met. An honest and great man. I became the story Greg," said Kevin, looking into the camera, tears rolling down his cheeks. "I am sorry, but I cannot forgive or live with myself and what I have done for *money*." Kevin finished, drawing a large kitchen knife across his throat, spraying the webcam with blood and falling over out of his chair. The camera cut to a full screen of Tate Vick, an astonished look on his round face for five seconds, unable to speak at what he had just seen. They finally cut to a commercial.

Nick buzzed back into the conference call.

"Someone call 911," yelled Nick into the laptop microphone

"Already done," said Denise crying "we gave them his home address."

"Goddamn you, Lexi," shouted Nick out loud, as those on the phone heard a loud crack.

"What the hell was that?" asked Chuck in a worried tone.

Nick looked down at his hands. He held up a two-inch-wide piece of wood. He'd snapped it off the end of the table in his anger at Lexi. Everyone looked at Nick, startled, as he looked up, his eyes ablaze with anger.

"Margie, please get a statement out, offering our condolences to the family and again highlighting the dirty nature of politics and how no one's life is worth throwing away to win votes. The Party obviously feels otherwise," said Nick in an unnaturally calm voice.

"Got it, we'll have it out on the wire ASAP," said Margie, who was also dabbing her eyes from crying and being held by a visibly shaken Jer. Greg *and* Kevin had been popular members of their campaign family.

"Chuck, make sure we handle and pay for the expenses of both funerals. I want to speak at both," said Nick in a commanding tone.

"Are you sure he's dead?" asked Denise, almost sobbing.

"Yes, once the carotid artery is cut, it only takes a few seconds," replied Nick. "He wouldn't have suffered long, nothing like the last couple of days. Poor kid. I should have seen this coming."

"I'll take care of everything, Nick," said Chuck quietly as Nick closed his laptop, ending the call.

Nick stood and walked to his hotel door, startling his bodyguard standing outside the door as he opened it suddenly.

"Jason, I need to take out some frustration. Can you find me a gym or a dojo with someone willing to take a potential pounding?"

Jason nodded in understanding. Earl had already texted him about what had just happened.

"Sure boss."

"Krav Maga, Ju Jitsu, Taekwondo, whatever, and make sure they have at least a black belt. I don't want to hurt them," explained Nick.

"Senator, I have a fifth degree black belt in Ju Jitsu and level five in Krav Maga," answered Jason without batting an eye.

"Great, then find us a gym. And some ice."

Jason looked skeptical for a moment. He was shorter and leaner than Nick and at least a decade younger. He'd fought side by side with Nick at the scuffle in Austin, but those attackers were hardly skilled.

Nick sensed his hesitation. "Don't worry. I hold you blameless. I'll be ready in ten. Better let Mike know as well," finished Nick, referring to the second of his now ever-present ex-Green Beret bodyguards, who was probably downstairs or at the stairwell.

As Nick closed the door. Jason called Earl first, then let his partner Mike know the plan. Earl just laughed and told Jason to be careful. He *also* suggested they have ice ready.

#

"Jesus Lexi," faltered Mel. Even he was appalled at watching the kid slit his throat on live TV.

Lexi just sat, staring into space pensively. "Harriet, get a statement out saying this was brought on by the hateful rhetoric of the Turner campaign. His willingness to keep black, brown, LGBTQ and others from getting equity from the white dominated society. Nick's aide and Kevin are just examples of how Turner's warped view of reality cause others to blindly follow his lead in a last-ditch effort to maintain white privilege at the expense of others," said Lexi in an icy voice.

She looked at Roland, who sat silently in the room, his face betraying no emotion. She turned her gaze on Mel and Harriett. She made a slight motion with her eyes and head. They both stood and left the conference room.

#

Mel and Harriett entered the conference room next door where Merri was busy on her laptop, FLCN still in commercial on the big screen in the room.

"10 points?" asked Mel.

Merri nodded. "8 at least. It'll be bad. She needs a good debate to make sure still wins with a good margin. That was horrible. No way Turner doesn't get a sympathy bump after that."

"Mel, this is a disaster. This is going to be all they talk about now," groaned Harriet, running her hand through her hair in concern.

"We need to double down on Chicago. Make sure our pundits focus on that. We have no other choice."

Roland stuck his head in the conference room, looking at Mel.

"She wants to see you." Roland continued on to his office.

Mel knocked and walked into Lexi's campaign office.

"Sit," she commanded.

Mel promptly sat in the chair.

"Do you want to win?" asked Lexi, toying with a letter opener on her desk.

"What kind of question is that?" asked Mel, worriedly.

"From the beginning, you have counseled going easy on Turner and focusing on Blackbird. Are you a closet Turner sympathizer?" asked Lexi, rising from behind her desk.

"Or perhaps you are more than a sympathizer. Perhaps you are working for Turner," said Lexi, the letter opener clenched in her hand as she stood in front of him.

Mel barely outweighed the Vice President and knew she could stab him and there would be nothing he could do about it from his sitting position. From the look in her eyes, he could tell she was both capable of and thinking about doing it.

"Good grief Lexi. How long have we known each other? You need to think before acting. Roland's advice to kill everyone who crosses you is not good counsel. How many campaigns have we been through? And how successful have our tactics been in the past? Everything I did was based on conventional wisdom. You can ask any campaign manager. Hell, call up Denise, even she would agree," prompted Mel nervously as Lexi backed off and began pacing.

"Picking on Turner in the beginning would have just given him even more exposure and validated you thought he was legit. It was and still is the right play. He has benefitted more by luck and unintended consequences of events than us making bad moves. These tactics are tried and true and they *always* work on the Opposition," assured Mel, getting up, wanting mobility. Just in case.

"Of course, except for that lone exception," said Lexi tellingly, looking at Mel putting distance between them.

Mel nodded. "But Turner is no egomaniac. He has a conscience. He isn't self-centered, concerned with self-preservation and future earning power like most here who capitulate at even the hint of scandal. Every other Opposition target retires or resigns and slinks home to earn their money in family businesses or lobbying. That is the reason it never works on Party politicians."

"Why is that? Because we in the Party are all heartless and cruel?" said Lexi with a smirk.

"No, realistically look at your congress. The bulk of the Party congresspeople aren't any good at anything *but* politics. Most have never had a decent job and certainly have not run a business. Bartenders, failed businessmen, shitty teachers, and career public servants in local and state government. That is why they stay and weather any storm. This is *their* meal ticket. They can't do anything else."

Lexi smiled at his description of the bottom feeding Party congress members.

"Only Party members survive these scandals. Opposition always caves in to public opinion. Public opinion we control. We were treating Turner like Opposition. Our only mistake was not understanding two things: honor and backbone. He has both in spades. No money, family, or job to lose, and no political record. He sure as shit couldn't care less about his earning potential from serving in Congress. He showed that with the filibuster vote. If someone wanted to handpick a candidate best qualified to beat you, they would have picked Nick Turner," informed Mel.

"How do we know someone didn't do just that?" asked Lexi, walking back to her desk to lean on the edge.

"Who? We do the picking. We pick judges, we pick AGs, we pick prosecutors, we pick Supreme Court justices, we pick Party candidates. We *pick* the winners. Who the hell else is there to pick, groom, or support a candidate like Turner? And if they exist, why now? After letting us get away with all our other shenanigans in the last 60 years?" asked Mel.

Lexi smiled. "Just a silly thought on my part. You have my complete confidence. So how do we recover from this shit show? Our October surprises are hurting us, not him."

"The debate. Get him on stage and use his own words against him. Show all the things he is going to take away from the poor, the LGBTQ, the minorities, and the rich Party members. How his way is hard and requires them to have a lower standard of living. To give up things. To have less. To enjoy less. Show how he is going to tear down their cozy little world, like Robespierre and his guillotine. You need to scare them into getting off their asses and," Mel did not finish his sentence, instead looking at Lexi.

"And what?" she asked.

"You need to cheat like hell."

"I assume you and Harriet have that under control,"

"We do," agreed Mel.

"No pussyfooting around this time. Hit them hard and don't hold back on election night. When we win, we can cover it up."

"Let's see how the debate goes. Not having a chance in Wisconsin, Michigan, and Pennsylvania is a tremendous advantage. We don't have to push hard there," said Mel.

"Push anyway, like I said, no squeaker."

"Why risk it?" asked Mel.

"Because of the last few elections, that is why. We are not winning because we are popular. Turner got that part right. We are winning because we have ensured disinterested people are voting to keep their free stuff. We win because we are keeping the Opposition depressed and at home with shitty candidates. We are winning because we know what it takes to win and we are not afraid to do it," explained Lexi in the firm tone.

"It helps that we own all the judges, DAs, Secretaries of State, the FBI, NSA, CIA, Congress and media," said Mel sarcastically.

"Everyone hates a winner. Just ask Brady," said Lexi, finally smiling.

"We need to get started on debate prep. You can give Blackbird the 'coup de grâce' and tag Turner with a few good ones, and this thing is over," said Mel.

"Any film on Turner debating."

"Not a lick. It'll be a hell of a place to do your first debate,"

"Let's hope so," countered Lexi.

Chapter 4

It was a beautiful October Sunday evening at the fairgrounds in Little Rock, Arkansas. Nick stood off stage, having flown in from DC earlier in the day. He was surrounded by his now beefed-up security, as the band finished in front of him. He grimaced when he glanced over at his bodyguard, Jason.

At least his eye was now opening up more, but the black surrounding it showed various shades of purple. Jason noticed Nick looking and gave him a rueful smile. He wouldn't underestimate Nick the next time they sparred.

Rather than wait to leave, the front man for the opening band introduced Nick. "Before we leave, we want to invite the Senator on stage with us."

Nick, surprised at the early intro, walked onto the stage at the urging of the band. He approached the singer, shaking hands as the crowd cheered its support. "Senator. Sorry Nick," he laughed at Nick's look.

"First, thank you for all you have done for this country and for what you are trying to do. I want you to know the state of Arkansas is behind you one hundred percent." the crowds cheered accordingly.

"We know you have been through some tough times and our hearts and prayers go out to the families of your lost staffers. What has happened in the last week is a reminder of why we need you in office. Anyone who would organize such a stunt using people's lives like playing cards deserves far more than just losing. Anyway, this is not our song, but Lee won't mind. I think we can do a reasonable cover. Everyone in the audience, please sing along. Nick, we dedicate this one to you and hope to God you prevail in this election."

With that, the singer turned to his bandmates as they broke into a rousing rendition of Lee Greenwood's *God Bless the U.S.A.*

The crowd and Nick sang along to this modern anthem of American patriotism and love for the country. When the song was over, the crowd was jumping up and down and cheering, screaming the name of the band and Turner. The band came together around Nick and a photographer came out to shoot some pictures, followed closely by two of Nick's very big and imposing bodyguards, who remained standing nearby.

Nick turned to the crowd as the band left and they calmed down.

"Folks, I wish I could maintain the high they just gave us with that rendition. Thank you, Lee, for writing the song. I'm afraid reality is intruding. We live in strange times. Others throughout history have faced these same situations. Most made the bad choices that cost them their livelihoods, their society, even their civilization. The one constant in these is their bad choices often cost them their lives." The crowd quieted as Nick continued in a somber tone.

"You see, this election is not simply whether we are ruled over by a Party president or *governed* by an independent candidate who will swear an oath to uphold the laws of the Constitution. No, this election is about a clear choice. A choice, I believe, can only go one way."

"The current administration has failed in their oath of office. I could sit here and give you chapter and verse on all the ways they have failed to live up to their oath to protect and defend the Constitution. We do not have until December," said Nick as the crowd laughed a bit, not quite knowing if they should or not.

"I also have to leave for Chicago so I can go on TV tomorrow and show everyone the truth about the footage ANC showed. I can assure you I am not a drug dealer and there is actually a reason I was there. Stay tuned tomorrow night, putting that footage into the correct context. It is worth your time. Trust me." This statement met with loud cheers.

"Thomas Jefferson intentionally chose the words in the Declaration of Independence. They were risking everything to throw off the shackles of servitude to an all-powerful government. To enable a society founded on the idea of making one's own choices for Life, with Liberty and the freedom to choose how to *pursue* Happiness. Not to be entitled to it." The crowd roared again.

"All the founders were guaranteeing was the *opportunity* to achieve the American Dream. Our Constitution codified these principles, and we fought a Civil War to ensure there would be equality for all."

Nick shook his head as the crowd continued to yell their support.

"Today, in this administration, this is no longer the case. Those same rules so many followed to become American, to reap the benefits of citizenship, have been ignored in favor of what? I don't know why we no longer bother to enforce our border laws and so many others. Do you?" questioned Nick, stalking the stage as usual.

He continued through his usual litany of illegal immigration, lax enforcement of laws leading to rampant crime, the economic malaise gripping the country. Out-of-control inflation, falling wages, rising prices, high unemployment and a host of other problems all unchecked by the administration. The crowd was reaching a boiling point. Nick knew he had to tone it down or he *would* start a riot.

Shifting his tone, he stated how when he stands up and makes these points; he is considered subversive. How, he is accused of preaching insurrection and rebellion by pointing out the administration is not upholding the oaths they swore. He is the problem for merely pointing out this inconvenient truth. The crowd yelled 'Turner' and 'U.S.A.' in reply.

"I am also being accused of fear mongering. Of doing nothing but telling you how bad it is. How evil the Party is and the administration. How we are all headed to the death camps if they win. That I never offer solutions." Nick turned solemn as he paced the stage.

"I am a realist. I have to paint a picture of what the world *could* look like so you understand what your choices are. I never tell you what to do. Or how to think. Instead, I spend my time educating. Convincing you to think. To research. To make your own informed decision. This is what they are really afraid of. You. Thinking for yourself. Especially if you make an informed decision. Not one based only on what they want you to see and hear."

"Now we have the biggest banks in the country deciding to not do business with me. All three. At the same time. Coincidence? Hardly. This should concern all of you. Remember, cancel culture retaliates against all who dare to speak publicly against *their* accepted stance. Question them and now we can add their ability to prevent you from banking to their arsenal. How do you feel knowing this could happen to you?"

The crowd boo'd loudly at this revelation. It was clear not all of them knew what had happened to Nick.

"With no warning and no appeal, they can shut you off from spending *your* money. Doesn't seem very *American*, does it? Think long and hard about this and make choices to protect yourself and your freedom, so they can't do this to you, too. More to come on how we are fighting this. I can assure you, my campaign has plenty of money and we will continue to pay our staff and vendors, despite their attempts to cancel me. They are relentless in their attacks."

"I ask you, how does Greg Simmons or Kevin Moss feel about their efforts now? These people were my friends. They paid the ultimate price. Why in the world did they use my people to attack me?" he said in a pleading tone to the audience. "Why did they have to die? They died because these people are afraid. The Vice President and her elitist supporters are afraid. Of *me* and of *you*. They are afraid I will talk some sense into your brain. They are afraid I will inspire people to realize free is not free. Free is dependency and free is being paid for by someone. That someone is each of you." He had the crowd hanging on every word.

"Greg and Kevin knew this. They died to give me the chance to keep trying to educate and convince you. This is a burden I will bear forever. No one said this would be easy. I don't give up easily, either. I ask you to remember their sacrifice. It will not be the last I fear before all this is said and done, but remember, they died for *you*, too."

Nick paused to let this statement sink in.

"They sacrificed so you can still live under a Bill of Rights. Please don't squander that. We are rounding third and headed to home. I only have one more state fair in Arizona. I am running out of chances to talk to these big crowds. You must do your part. Please tell your friends and neighbors. Show them the *Turner Doctrine* pamphlet you were handed tonight. Read it, understand it, and spread the word. Before it is too late."

"Again, I thank you for letting me talk so long between bands. I have opened for your last group of the night before, so they are probably tired of hearing me say this to state fair crowds, but I need to say I did all I could. That I have given that 'last full measure of devotion', Lincoln spoke of in the Gettysburg Address. To ensure our continued freedom. Wake Up, Think for Yourself and VOTE. Thank you, Arkansas." said Nick with emotion as he turned to walk offstage.

The crowd stood and cheered. Nick left the stage, and the band came out. The crowd kept cheering and shouting for Nick. The singer turned and waved. Nick came back out and took the mic.

"Guys, you have to let them get started so they can do what you paid them to do. Play all those wonderful hits we love to sing along to. I will ask for one favor. Can you join me in a prayer for Greg and Kevin and grab the hand of the person to your left and right? Preferably people you do not know."

Nick grabbed the hands of the band, including the drummer and backup singers, who all came to the front of the stage. Even Nick's bodyguards joined in. The crowd started looking at each other and grabbing the hands of strangers on either side. Twenty-five thousand attendees in an outdoor fairground, raucous only a minute prior, were now suddenly quiet as a church.

"Father, we seek guidance. You have blessed us with so much. A bountiful land, safety far from our enemies. Boundless intelligence and freewill, allowing us to choose our direction and fate. We ask for your continued guidance and the strength to carry on. Ensuring we do not squander or take for granted the glorious bounty and opportunity you have provided us. You have sorely tested me this last week. I know not why Greg and Kevin are gone. I have to trust in your judgment. Please give us guidance, strength, knowledge, and wisdom to see evil and enable us to stand up to Satan wherever he rears his ugly head. Give us strength and resolve to continue to strive to earn your favor. To serve as good and just human beings. Doing right by our deeds and looking out for all our brothers and sisters. In your name, I ask for forgiveness for those who will not, or cannot. Amen," finished Nick.

The crowd shouted their amen. Many were crying as they started cheering again. Nick held up his hands, linked with the band.

"Alright, that's enough, I want to hear those songs too," announced Nick, laughing, and handing the microphone back and walking off the stage.

"God bless Nick Turner and may you protect him from evil. All right, let's have some fun," the singer said, breaking into one of her number one hits as the crowd started cheering and singing along.

Nick watched her and the band for a minute before heading to his Suburban with his security detail in tow. The secret service had tried to take over his protection, and he had flatly declined.

Having refused to protect him after the assassination attempt, Nick did not want or trust them. With the increasing violence from outside agitators at his rallies, Nick only trusted his own people now.

When they insisted, Nick secretly figured this was an additional way for Lexi to monitor his campaign. He'd asked a federal judge to rule. The judge said as a *candidate* he could refuse their help with security if he so chose.

Now he went with his imposing ex-Special Forces security, all vetted by Earl himself. They drove him to the private executive airport outside Little Rock. His chartered Gulfstream was fueled and waiting to fly him to Chicago. He got on the plane, buckled in and dialed Earl. They spoke for almost the entire ninety-minute flight.

Chapter 5

"Talk to me. Where are we?" asked Nick.

"The solution to the debanking is working. Your conversation with Martha and Everett to use their credit unions until Jeremy can charter a new one, is brilliant," announced Margie with a smile.

"Congrats, you're no longer broke," announced Denise. "Theodore is shifting enough campaign funds temporarily to their credit unions. They say the newly formed credit union should be chartered and up on Jeremy's servers no later than tomorrow. As soon as it is, Martha and Everett are going to announce they are merging theirs with it."

Nick's giant face was smiling on the monitor in the conference room in Denver.

"We didn't have to use your accounts or your money. The good news is almost all of your vendors would have allowed you to defer payments as long as you needed. Heck Nick, even the staff were willing to give up a paycheck if they had to. It was amazing," explained Denise, a little choked up at the show of solidarity with their boss.

"That's wonderful Denise. I'm just glad I don't have to work with the Bank of China."

"That *would* have been a bad look boss," laughed Margie, looking up from the conference table on the small video screen on Nick's laptop in his hotel room in Chicago.

"You all set for the day?" asked Denise.

"I think so. Earl and I talked last night. They are getting ready for the live press conference tonight. Did we get all the networks?"

"Yes," answered Margie. "We didn't offer it to ANC or FLCN as requested. But you have all the majors, NWN, RBS, EXN broadcast,

EXN cable, LN1, TeleEspana, and a few others. Plus, Hibi and the 2J's will both live stream and our website. You'll have your audience."

"Good. We can put this one to bed."

"So, David Copperfield, how exactly are you going to explain being on video with a packet of heroin in your hand??" asked Denise, still pissed at not knowing what or how Nick planned to fix this.

"Denise, you just have to trust me."

"Do I have a choice?"

"No. What's next?"

"We have you on with Billy and Autumn on EXN in thirty-seven minutes. You'll announce you have solved the banking issues. What else?" asked Margie.

"I'll plug tonight's broadcast, reiterate the Blue Morpho silliness and touch on the ballot's briefly as well. It's a different audience than Tommy, so it will be good to give them a little math lesson on just what it would take to win as a write-in candidate."

"Keep it brief Nick. I know you like to explain things. People watching over their morning oatmeal don't need either a history lesson or heavy math," cautioned Margie.

"They need it. Now whether they'll pay attention to it, I agree with you. I'll keep it clear." Nick watched as Denise and Margie grinned and nodded at Nick, agreeing to follow their advice for a change.

"OK. So, you're in Chicago today for the broadcast. Then back to DC for the Censure debate and vote tomorrow."

"I'll mention the colossal waste of time this Censure vote is on EXN in a minute, too. Anything else? They hate when I join at the last minute. Makes them nervous," smiled Nick.

"I'm glad others get to live our life, if only for a minute," remarked Denise snidely.

"With that, ladies, I will talk to you later today, I am sure," finished Nick, ending the call.

Earl Greene, Nick's head of security, laughed from his guest chair in the hotel room.

"I noticed you didn't laugh until *after* Denise couldn't hear you,"

"Unlike you, I don't seek out confrontation and conflict," replied Earl, his white teeth contrasting against his mahogany face and now almost full head of gray hair. It was coal black only eight months previously.

"We ready?"

"We are Nick. Do your call with EXN and then we can drive around a bit. Take a look at North Lawndale, maybe stop in on Nana, before we head to Ray's community center for the broadcast."

Nick nodded in agreement as he took a sip of his fast cooling coffee. He started the process of dialing into the virtual green room at EXN. He was becoming quite the networking technician, given his daily dial ins to innumerable news and radio shows.

#

Earl drove the suburban into North Lawndale, Chicago. Emblematic of nearly every large urban city in the US, these close-in urban suburbs were now in various stages of decline. Increasingly, they contained enclaves like North Lawndale, looking more like bombed out hellscape similar to cities in places like Gaza, Lebanon, and Ukraine.

Neighborhoods devastated by riots, ARL protests, and increasingly more military style gang warfare. In this neighborhood, much of the damage remained from the protests in 1968, following the assassination of Martin Luther King.

It had never been rebuilt. Left to rot and decay. A constant reminder of the protests, mainly driven by outside agitators, destroying buildings and locally owned black businesses. Afterwards, the protesters went home.

Those left behind, who could, left for better neighborhoods. Those who couldn't, remained to raise generations with fewer and fewer prospects for success. Or an ability to leave.

As they drove deeper into North Lawndale, the landscape suddenly changed. The streets became cleaner, the houses well kept. Litter, trash, and graffiti disappeared. Lawns and flower boxes on the fronts of houses appeared. Several blocks of houses showed fresh paint and whitewashed brick, looking more like the affluent suburbs you would find as you got further from the city.

"What happened?" asked Nick. Turning to look at a smiling Earl.

"You'll hear about it when we visit Ray at the community center. I know we have to scoot right after the broadcast to get you back to DC, but Ray and Kayla told me Nana wanted to see you. Her health has worsened since we saw her in April," explained Earl as they stopped the suburban in front of Nana's well-kept house.

Nick and Earl approached the door as his bodyguards stayed in on the porch. They were not happy, but Nick didn't give them a choice.

The door was opened by Roberta, who lived at the end of the street. They had heard her story during their visit in April as well.

"Bert, how are you?" asked Nick with a smile as she wrapped him in a big hug.

"Nick, it is good to see you. You too Earl," smiled Roberta in greeting. "Come on in. Josie is eager to see you. I watch her when Kayla is busy."

Nick nodded as he and Earl followed Roberta into the small house, to the kitchen, where Josie sat in a wheelchair. Almost a hundred, Josie's body had shrunken down to the size of a small child. Only her bright eyes betrayed the fire and drive, enabling her to earn a PhD in her sixties.

"Josie, it is good to see you," said Nick gently.

"Nick, I can't see you well, but my hearing is fine," she smiled her single toothed grin.

"Earl, you need to do a better job protecting him. No more shooting. Nick, you take too many risks. You keep talking like you do and they will do to you what they did to King. Don't underestimate the FBI," she said in an entirely serious and lucid tone.

"Josie, I have to do what is needed. Without risk, we can't wake people up to their danger."

"Nick, be careful. Don't trust anyone. I only have a little time left. I'm fine with that. You have driven around?"

"Yes, Earl showed me. It is amazing."

"Ha. It is not amazing. It's what we should have done years ago. It took you, a white guy, to finally kick enough people in the rear to motivate them to do what they were too lazy to do before. But thank you for providing the boot." She held up a slip of paper.

"What is that?" asked Nick.

"I made it Nick. I hoped to live long enough to vote for you. I did. It won't matter in our corrupt state. People are too dependent on handouts from Springfield to vote against keeping the checks flowing. But I cast mine with a clear conscience. I did my part."

"Thank you Josie. Every vote counts."

"Oh Nick, you are still so naïve. Try not to lose that attitude. What they are doing to you is only the beginning. They cannot let you succeed. Remember that. It will never stop, and you cannot let your guard down. Any of you," she ended, turning her rheumy eyes in Earl's direction.

"Roberta, could you be a dear and get the package?"

"Of course, Josie."

Roberta returned to the room with a shoe box. Nick recognized it as the box Josie had showed them in April. Full of campaign memorabilia from as far back as the campaigns of FDR in 1932.

"Her you go, Josie."

"Give it to Nick, please."

Nick took the box from Roberta but did not open it.

"Nick, I want you to have this. We both know Kayla can't appreciate the contents like you can. Have you seen her yet?" she asked with her nearly toothless grin.

Earl broke in. "He hasn't. We are headed to the community center next."

Josie laughed. Then started coughing. Roberta gave her some water. "Sorry Nick, I'm not supposed to strain. I am glad you'll get to see Kayla. Your talk had an impact, as you will see," she said slyly.

Nick didn't know how to respond to that statement.

"Thank you for the box. You know I'll cherish it. Along with the stories you told about them, I accept the stewardship of your box of memories."

She stared up at him, her eyes unfocused, but Nick still felt her boring into his soul. Then she smiled.

"Thank you. I have done my job. I pass on the torch. We cannot forget our past mistakes. If we do, we will continue to repeat them. I know you must go. Good luck Nick. I am glad you took the time to stop by an old lady's house in April. Like that first drop of snowmelt, it joins with so many others and is a mighty roar when the river empties into the sea. So are you. I wish you luck on your journey. Godspeed."

Roberta was dabbing at tears, and even Earl turned away as Nick merely held her gaze and smiled.

"Josie, I should thank you. That couple of hours and the wisdom you imparted, having lived through these moments in our history, are priceless." He held her hand and leaned over to kiss her cheek. He whispered in her ear, and her eyes brightened.

Nick and Earl thanked Roberta and walked out to the car, Nick carrying his shoe box of history.

#

"Ready?" asked Nick, thinking about Josie as they drove through revitalized streets to Earl's cousin Ray's community center.

"We are. I got everything you asked for. We are set up at Ray's. We did a dry run yesterday, and another with EXN this morning to make sure all the network feeds are good from our makeshift studio."

"Good. Everybody OK with this?" asked Nick.

Earl grinned. "You have no idea."

"What does *that* mean?" asked Nick carefully.

"You're not gonna believe it."

"Try me. I need some good news."

"First, Kayla is the leader of the Women for Turner chapter for Illinois. She is also on the board of the local Blue Morpho chapter working in North Lawndale and the South Side of Chicago," revealed Earl.

"That's great news. I guess we made an impression. Now I know why Josie was smiling. Glad to hear she kicked that ARL shit to the curb," said Nick with a smile.

"It gets better," said Earl as Nick listened. "Ray is the head of the Greater Chicago Blue Morpho effort. He has two Redemption Cities going and manages three properties donated by Howard Patterson. The effort is really paying off. He is combining this with his efforts to get the gangs off the street. And the kids in schools. The city and state are fighting him tooth and nail, but he is making progress despite this. A bunch of pissed off cops have joined his Blue Morpho and are providing security for the whole endeavor. The cartels and gangs are moving to other neighborhoods because of this."

"How's Kayla handling being around Ray so much?"

Earl laughed. "She'll be there. You can ask her yourself," replied Earl. "There is another surprise."

"Good or bad?"

"Definitely good. Care to guess who runs the local chapter of the Turner Rabble with over 1000 members?" asked Earl.

"Not a clue."

"EZee," said Earl, smiling big again.

"No shit?" said Nick, turning to look at Earl in surprise.

"You won't even recognize him. He lost 50 pounds, got his teeth capped. He looks like an investment banker," laughed Earl.

"Are people going to recognize him from the video?" asked Nick in a worried tone.

"No worries, he can't get rid of his tats," laughed Earl. "That one on the side of his cheek gives him away as a former gang banger."

"Good, you had me worried."

They pulled into the Community center. It, too, had changed. The brick was painted, the parking lot freshly paved and overhead lamps illuminating the entire parking lot. Nick noticed several portable buildings were now in the parking lot as well.

They walked into the gymnasium. Instead of a gym, there was a sea of temporary cubicles on one side and Nick could see the makings of a studio over in one corner, with black drapery backgrounds, stools, and a podium. Ray saw Nick and waved.

"Welcome Senator," said Ray as he gave Nick a hug. "Geez Ray, not you too. Nick turned and yelled out. My name is Nick, not Senator. Got it?" Nick heard a few laughs and giggles.

"How you talk," said Kayla from behind Nick.

He turned and stopped. A pregnant Kayla was standing in front of him with a big smile on her face. She smiled and gave him a big hug.

"Who's the lucky guy?" asked Nick with a snicker as Ray put up his fists mockingly. "I'm so happy for you two," continued Nick as Ray came over, putting an arm around his wife.

"Not as happy as Nana. Did you have time to see her yet? She made me promise to get you over there. She's not well," said Kayla, the regret clear in her voice.

"Yeah. Earl took me by already. I got to see her again. She is a treasure." Kayla turned away, overcome with emotion.

Ray turned to Nick as Kayla walked away to compose herself.

"Nick, we can't thank you enough. It's like you walked through and washed away all our sins. Or at least opened our eyes to our inattention. You should see the neighborhood. It is cleaned up, businesses are back. Gangs are gone and kids no longer have to wind their way through alleys and backyards. Mind you, it is only a few blocks of a really shitty part of Chicago. Look around. It is a huge turnaround."

"Earl drove me through. I had nothing to do with it. Just like I told all of you. Only *you* could decide to change things and then be able to make it happen. It was all of you working together who did this."

Ray smiled at Nick. "Of course, no one in the mayor's office or national news is interested in doing a story on how we did it and how to emulate it. The violence just migrated elsewhere. But our little patch is a safe zone. Nana could sit on her porch every night and the kids in the neighborhood came by to hear her stories. She's only recently declined. I'm glad you got to see her before she leaves."

"Me too. It was an honor to spend time with her. I feel privileged. How did you make so much progress so fast?"

Ray laughed. "Nick, you may poo poo your effect, but it is real. You talked to Eli as well on your trip. After, he came to me with an idea. We were able to pay the outstanding tax liens on many of the burned and crumbling buildings destroyed in the 1968 riots. No one wanted the properties, so we were able to get them for basically nothing."

"Local contractors donated time and equipment. We bulldozed them to the ground and others donated material and their time to help teach out young folk the trades. We put them to work, just like you suggested. We rebuilt the buildings. Pooling our resources, we opened up a convenience store, a grocery store and our own barbershop, hair salon, and even a medical clinic. Nick, we even get delivery services in the neighborhood again."

Nick put an arm around Ray's shoulder. Ray was one of the few people taller than Nick's six foot four. He'd played linebacker in college and with the Raiders professionally before a knee injury ended his career and steered him to the ministry. "Glad to help."

"Nick, just as you said, once we started cleaning up, others would come back. Several chain stores are now even in discussion about coming back. The funds from your Blue Morpho and TRDF have been incredibly helpful. We're even talking to Martha Summers about opening one of her stores in North Lawndale. That would be huge and could provide hundreds of great jobs. Our kids have hope again. Roberta is even sending Laila to school now that she and her grandson no longer have to dodge bullets on the way to school."

"Ray, have you told your story to anyone? We need to spread the word," suggested Nick.

"Nick, there is a lot of resistance. We acquire the buildings and then put them into a co-op owned by the residents. The city hates that because it gives us some tax exemptions. There are obviously other outside influences. Remember when I told you the cops got pissed and joined our efforts? It's because of what happened."

"What?" asked Nick.

"Once we finished building the grocery store and the little clinic, we had a group of Antifa thugs come by one night and try to burn them down with Molotov cocktails. Thankfully, the buildings are in the neighborhood with houses nearby. The folks were able to put out the flames and keep the buildings from burning down. Of course, the fire department still wouldn't come into North Lawndale without a police escort," Ray sighed, his frustration clear.

"When they got here, and the cops saw what happened and why and they saw how the entire community was united in their efforts to save our progress, I could see the light bulbs going off in their heads. We differed from what they usually saw down here."

"What did they do?"

"At first, nothing. We rebuilt the damaged part. Again, as we approached the opening, the thugs showed up again. This time, we were ready. We had some donated cameras set up. Once we saw them approaching, a bunch of us showed up to protect the buildings. Thankfully, these are thugs and not gang bangers with weapons. We could scare them off."

"Good. Antifa are just bullies. You stand up to them and they crumble," agreed Nick.

Ray smiled. "Yep. Unfortunately, whoever was paying them changed tactics. The next time, they paid the gangs to show up. We can't get into a gun battle. I told our guys to stand back as the gangs torched the clinic while we watched. They told us they'd be back if we built it again."

"I saw the clinic. How'd you get it built?"

"Someone sent me this little book by some dead Chinese dude," laughed Ray.

"I see you got the copy I sent?"

"Yes, I did. Read it from cover to cover several times. Especially the part about picking the time and place of battle. Doing the unexpected."

"I can't wait to hear this."

"So again, a couple of weeks later, we were once again rebuilt and finished this time. They were waiting until we were literally a day from opening with the equipment installed and ready to serve patients," described Ray.

"Sure enough, they showed up again. This time, though, it was not the biggest and the toughest of our guys. It was a row of moms. Sitting on all sides of the building. They tried to threaten them and tell them to move. Several of the gang member's moms were in our group. They started cursing them all out. One of them still tried to throw a cocktail and one of his compadres whose mother was there tackled the guy and beat him until he was unconscious. When he got up, he ripped off his gang colors and walked to his mom and stood there behind her. Several of the others did the same.

"The gang leader didn't know what to do. They were obviously being paid to do this. When they turned to go, they found themselves surrounded. We were behind them in case they went after the moms after all. There were also a dozen off-duty cops who had joined us as well."

"How did it end?"

"They tried to leave, but we had them hemmed in. We made them tell us who paid them and what they were told to do. They tried to say they weren't paid, but eventually we got some names. I was able to use my contacts, and we discovered a web of NGOs who were funding both ARL and Antifa efforts."

"Let me guess. World Harmony Society," said Nick.

"Good guess. We finally found a national reporter and did a minor story on our success and pointed out who was funding the agitators trying to burn it down. They gave up trying to stop us. At least for now. We're pretty established and the cops now patrol and respond when we dial 911. We also have a volunteer fire department with donated equipment and our own neighborhood watch. More like the old Guardian's Angels from New York back in the 70s and 80s. Citizens protecting each other. It's working," finished Ray.

"That's the right way, Ray. We can't fight violence with violence."

"I agree Nick. We've had some folks come from Baltimore, Detroit, Atlanta, Birmingham, and even Austin and LA to see how we have succeeded. We are hoping to start these 'urban oases' in other cities."

"Excellent. It doesn't surprise me Pavlovich's groups are involved. He is behind a lot of the VP's efforts. Anything that creates anarchy and chaos is a plus for him. Having you and your effort succeed and inspiring others to do the same in their cities is not good for his plans and goals. You showing people their own hard work can fix their problems without the city, state or fed is problematic. They want everyone to be beholden to the benevolent global state he envisions.

Keep an eye out regarding mayhem. I guarantee you he has not given up," remarked Nick.

Ray just glanced at Nick as he delivered this last advice in an ominous tone. They were slowly walking to the corner where they had the makeshift studio set up.

"I promise," he told Nick. "Let me show you what we have."

Kayla and Earl rejoined Ray as they walked Nick over to the studio corner. A couple of technicians were fiddling with the equipment, running sound and microphone checks, looking at monitors, verifying everything worked.

"Looks good. I assume EZee is ready for his 15 minutes of fame?" asked Nick, looking at Earl, Ray, and Kayla.

"He certainly is," came a voice from one technician, who straightened up from the monitor. Nick recognized the tattoo on his left cheek and his neck.

"EZee?" said Nick in shock.

He smiled. The gold teeth were gone, replaced by nice regular white caps. He had on a polo shirt, jeans, and sneakers. About as far from gang attire as one could go. "In the flesh. I go by Craig now, but I'll answer to EZee from the right folks," he said, holding out a hand. Nick pulled him into an embrace, and they both choked up a bit. "You look good."

"Thanks. I saw them take a shot at you. You're one tough SOB. Man, trouble follows you like that Charlie Brown guy with the dust cloud."

"It sure does," said Earl dryly.

Nick gave him a look. "Maybe it's really you Earl?"

"Ya right."

"Every time the bullets fly, you're there too," offered Nick.

"I don't think the sniper was trying to hit me off stage behind a wall," noted Earl.

"Maybe he really was that bad. He didn't get me either."

"OK boys, stop upsetting my baby with all this talk of shooting. We are past that here. Thanks to Nick," said Kayla.

"You did it. All of you."

"I am not sure exactly sure how or why, but it worked," replied Ray.

"Regardless, I'm glad. You should be proud. I just pointed out the obvious. You always had it in you. Hey how is Big D doing?" asked Nick, looking at Craig.

"Ask him yourself," said Craig, tapping the big guy working on the sound on the shoulder. He turned as Nick looked at Big D. He pulled down his headphones, smiled and gave Nick a big hug. "I never got to thank you for saving my life and then my soul."

"Glad I could help," said Nick. "I'm assuming you are no longer Big D either?"

"Darrell, nice to meet you Nick," he said, holding out a hand this time, smiling.

"You guys actually know what you are doing, or is this all for show?" mocked Nick playfully.

"You ain't no comedian. Stick with saving people," responded Craig. "Yes, this is what we do for a living. Sound technicians for TV and radio stations. When Earl contacted Ray, we killed two birds with one stone. We knew the guy who drove up was a narc or something. He was too confident for a newbie," explained Craig.

"Was I right? You had someone in the house filming?"

"You were. My girlfriend. She always used my phone so I could prove what deals I was doing when the boss man came by and thought I was skimming him."

"Great," declared Nick.

"This should put an end to that Bergamo bitch. Man, she been after your ass ever since you showed up in Washington," said Craig, shaking his head.

"What did you do to piss her off? Is she in love with you or something? And you turned her down?" asked Kayla with a laugh. "Hell hath no fury and all that."

Nick laughed nervously. "No, nothing like that. I think I embarrassed her one-to-many times in my early interviews and she has been after me ever since." Kayla just stared at Nick after his non answer as Earl came back to the group.

"Nick, Craig and Darrell worked up a little device they think could be useful to us." Darrell held out an I-phone looking device. He turned it on and waved it around.

"It picks up wireless transmission signals. It's a poor man's way of telling if someone is wearing a wire or transmitting a signal or tracking you with a tracker, that kind of stuff. Hold up your phone."

Nick held up his phone and the screen on the device Darrell was holding turned red whenever it crossed over Nick's phone. "Your security using earphones?" he asked. Earl nodded. He waved it toward them. It went to red as he crossed across each of their bodies.

"That could be their phones, though. Have one of them give you his phone."

Earl walked over to one of his guys and took his phone. Darrell waved it at the guard from his shoes to his head. When it got to his head, it turned from green to red. "See" said Darrell.

"What kind of range?" asked Nick.

"50-75 feet, maybe a little more," said Darrell, holding the device at his side, facing out.

Ray noticed it was red. "What is it detecting now?"

"What?" asked Darrell, lifting it up and watching it turn Green.

"It was red down at your side. It would have been facing Nick's bags," observed Ray.

"Nick probably just has his computer on or his phone is in there," said Darrell

"Actually, my computer is off and my phone is right here," said Nick, showing his phone.

"Do you have anything else that transmits a signal in your bag?" asked Darrell as they all approached the bags.

"Hold on," worried Earl.

He separated the bags. The overnight bag was green. That left the computer bag. It only contained the computer and Nick's infamous purple bound notebook.

Earl carefully removed the laptop and held it away from the bag. Darrell aimed at it. It was green.

"What the?" said Nick as he pulled out the notebook. The device stayed red, pointed at the notebook. He handed it to Earl. He examined it, pulling the notebook out of the purple sleeve. In the binder's spine, he found a small electronic tracker. It was about an inch long with a slim 1/2 inch long antenna attached.

"It's just a tracker. No sound transmission or recording. That lets the battery last a long time. It's the kind used by wives to track their wayward husbands. Private investigators use them a lot. Stick a magnet to them and put them on cars to keep tabs on who is going where," said Earl.

"What range?" asked Nick.

"A long way. It uses GPS to transmit back to an app. Like an Apple I-tag. This looks like a private job," said Earl.

"Any chance you guys can trace it back to who is tracking?" asked Nick.

"Ya, we might find out the IP it is broadcasting to," said Darrell, taking it from Earl. He took it over to a laptop and started typing.

"Well, somebody wanted to know where you were," said Earl. "Any chance it is Denise or Chuck wanting to keep track of you."

"Doubt it, this is almost never out of my hands or where anyone can get to it," thought Nick, pausing.

"Remembering something?" prodded Earl.

"Maybe. We'll see what the guys come up with," said Nick.

Chapter 6

"Let's do this," said Nick as he stood in the makeshift studio.

"We are a go," nodded Darrell.

Someone did a countdown from five and the light turned from green to red, signifying quiet on the set.

"Good evening. First, don't worry, I won't mess up *Monday Night Football.* I understand people's priorities," said Nick, breaking the ice with a wry smile.

"In case there is someone out there who does not know me. I am Senator Nick Turner, an independent candidate for President. I have taken the unusual step of buying time on any network and cable station which would accept my money. I have done this in order to tell my side of the stories being fabricated and reported upon by the various media outlets. I figure this is the only way to get the truth out. To bribe news networks who should want to get the facts out but won't."

"By now, you are probably aware FLCN has already been complicit in the death of two of my staffers, with inaccurate reporting and frankly outright lies, funded by some as yet unnamed source. Since that story has been thoroughly debunked and FLCN's role in these tragic deaths exposed, I have not sought to have this segment aired on their network."

"I see no reason to put money in their coffers when this is the result. If there is any justice left in our society. Any who value truth and the consequences of lying, FLCN and whomever is behind these lies will be held accountable and pay for their crimes," said Nick with passion, staring into the camera intensely. His anger was obvious in his tone and his body language.

"Next, it was implied I had been taking advantage of homeless people in my campaign offices and the non-profit organization I helped found along with a series of former Party mega donors. Many claim this is a scam, simply a tax shelter for these billionaires. This story originated on LN1, once upon a time the gold standard of news. Sadly, we have seen how far they have fallen. They claimed to have, again, anonymous whistleblower eyewitness accounts of my using and underpaying homeless in my offices."

"This has been disproven as well in a series of stories, interviews and the transparent review of the Blue Morpho Redemption Project books. Because of the generosity of these billionaires endowing Blue Morpho, it has given Venice Beach, California, and many other urban centers in major cities back to the residents and tourists."

"They have told their story of why they endorsed Blue Morpho to help solve the homeless problems the state and federal government have failed to address. As for the so-called whistleblowers, we have yet to have any of them identified. Where they worked or for them to produce any proof, they actually work, or worked, in any of our state offices."

"This was nothing less than a fabricated hit job designed to besmirch me, my campaign, and worst, the philanthropy of these wonderful Americans who have so unselfishly given their money to this effort."

"There is now pending litigation, as many of these anonymous accusations made against them would be serious crimes. I ask you to follow their lawsuits as they play out. It will expose the playbook the progressives will use against all of you."

Nick spoke to them as their neighbor or co-worker, not as a politician asking for a vote. Rather as a concerned friend asking for others to listen. And to think. For themselves and to use their common sense.

Off stage, Darrell held up a sign telling Nick his remaining time.

"I'm not even going to address the idea that I am printing ballots and putting my name on them in the Write In category. The sheer stupidity of this accusation and the idea we would do anything like this is so comical it would embarrass even the Marx brothers. The idea this is even possible through fraud is sheer lunacy."

"I can only hope this was not some pipe dream of either of my opponents to imply I would cheat. To be honest and forthright, I would suggest to anyone out there who is thinking of voting for me, please vote on election day. Please show up and show an ID to prove you are qualified to vote. I want my votes to be honest and legal. I don't want there to be any doubt about the legitimacy of *my* votes."

"My main reason for this time on the networks is to rebut the claim that I was filmed in the middle of a drug deal in Chicago, in April, by an undercover team of ANC reporter Lauren Bergamo and her cameraman. It is unfortunate that Miss Bergamo could not cover my entire visit to Chicago and my witnessing that drug deal specifically. I was indeed there, as her video shows. However, as is always the case with our American *Pravda* media, what they lack is the whole truth and context. They did not bother to ask me for the entire story before airing what they had. Today, I would like to tell you and *show* you the rest of the story."

"Yes, I was in Chicago. I went there with just my security chief, Earl Greene. We met with his cousin, Reverend Ray Coleman, who runs a shelter in North Lawndale, a suburb of Chicago."

"Much like 1968, today ARL led riots are burning down predominantly black neighborhoods and driving away critical businesses and chain stores from communities never to return. North Lawndale is hell on earth. Children pick their way through broken and dilapidated buildings and hope they have not crossed an invisible line somewhere which would get them shot for crossing into enemy territory. All of this I heard from Reverend Ray, whose shelter offered kids a chance to get an education they could not get in public schools. Where 83% of graduates are illiterate."

"Next Ray introduced me to some other residents, including an ARL activist who has since recanted and now understands their Marxist ideology is even *more* destructive. This person took Earl and me to see a drug deal in action. It was our request. We ended up on the doorstep of a dealer and gang member known as EZee."

"As you will shortly see, the drugs I have in my hand were dropped by one of EZee's crew and my natural tendency is to pick up what is dropped. Luckily for you and for me, EZee is not a trusting sort. His girlfriend filmed every drug deal going down for his own protection. Now we will play the entire video of what happened before Miss Bergamo's investigative report and, more importantly, what happens after. Roll it," said Nick.

The video played. It showed Nick, Earl, and Kayla talking to EZee. His crew dropping the drugs and Nick picking it up. Lauren and her photographer driving up. Everyone diving for cover as the shooters in the other car drove by and EZee and his crew taking shelter or running inside. Big D laying on the stoop in a pool of blood. It showed Nick working on him, telling Kayla to go get help and EZee asking why he cared and why he was trying to help. Finally, the video showed Nick and Earl carrying Big D into the car for the drive to the Hospital.

"As you can see, I was not buying or dealing drugs. I was observing and trying to understand what life was like in North Lawndale. We drove the young man to the hospital. The doctors were able to save his life. Unlike my accusers, none of my information is anonymous. Let me introduce you to Big D. Because of this experience, he is no longer a drug dealer or gang member. He has reformed and is a contributing member of society. I'd like you to meet EZee as well. He too has learned from this event and is no longer dealing drugs or leading a gang, either," Nick had turned toward Darrell and Craig as the camera panned to show them.

"In full disclosure, both guys began volunteering for my campaign, unbeknownst to me until I showed up yesterday to prepare for this filming. I fully expected to hear they were long dead in a bad drug deal. I was thrilled to hear this incident changed their lives. I would like to bring in the doctor, who operated on Darrell to prove we are not staging any of this."

A man wearing a doctor coat walked into the frame and introduced himself.

"I was the doctor on call at Community North that night. There is no doubt, if the triage Senator Turner did on site was not done, the patient would never have survived to even get to our hospital. He owes his life to the Senator."

Reverend Ray asked off camera. "Is it safe to say had the Senator not decided to get a firsthand look, without cameras, without entourage, without security, to see what life in North Lawndale is like, Darrell would be dead?"

"Absolutely," said the doctor. "We had 12 other gunshot wounds that night and 6 fatalities. He would have made it seven."

Nick looked back into the camera. "Thanks to all of you. Their stories and they themselves are available for anyone who wants to interview them or give them a lie detector test. I am not worried, because we tell the truth. We only have to defend against poorly sourced stories, outright lies, unscrupulous producers, and network presidents promoting this shit and calling it journalism. I am picked on relentlessly for referring to most of our news organizations as American *Pravda*. Now you know why," accused Nick, his frustration on obvious display.

"America, ask yourself. Why are they so afraid of me they need to drop four October surprises on a single day? Six in the last week total? What could I possibly be doing to warrant this kind of attention? I am behind the Opposition and a mile behind the Vice President. I'll tell you why. Because I speak the truth and I make people think. I say to you as I say to every group I talk to. Wake Up, Think for Yourself and Vote. In person. God Bless everyone."

The red light turned to green, and they were off the air. Nick took a deep breath and looked at the folks on the stage. Everyone clapped as Nick was surrounded by people hugging him.

"That was incredible," said Kayla. "If people don't think about what you said and why they were targeting you, they are hopeless. You don't want their vote anyway."

"Watching that and hearing you tell the story gave me the shivers," said Craig, he turned to Darrell. "I owe you an apology. I honestly didn't care if you lived or died," he said, shaking his head.

"Craig, I didn't care if I lived or died either, until I got the second chance. Then Dion came in and I saw how worried he was. It was then I knew I needed to change."

"Dion?" asked Nick.

"Little D," said Craig.

"Ah. Where is he?" asked Nick a bit cautiously.

"Don't worry, he got accepted at a military prep school this fall, thanks to Ray. Doing great and looking forward to going into the Army when he graduates."

"An admirable career, for sure."

"So how many stuck with us for the whole time and who is refunding me money?" laughed Nick.

"EXN, TeleEspana, Local Chicago affiliates and streaming on the web stayed on the whole time. LN1 dumped you after you trashed their story and NWN dropped you about halfway in. Same for RBS. Of course, ANC and FLCN were not even approached to air it live. I can only imagine how ANC is scrambling," laughed Earl.

"Nick," said Darrell. We reversed engineer the device. We found an IP address and tracked it down to an app downloaded on a phone with this number. Darrell handed it to Nick.

Nick looked at the number. "Son of a bitch."

"You know the number?" asked Earl.

"I do. I'll handle this one myself. It isn't anyone on the campaign," replied Nick, turning to Darrell. "Can you do me a favor? Can you go stick this on a train car or a Greyhound bus?"

Darrell smiled. "Can do. Good idea. You want it to go east or west?" he said with a smile.

"How about Canada or the North Pole?" said Nick with a laugh of his own.

"You got it Nick."

"Thanks guys, this was fabulous. Darrell, you say hi to Dion for me. Thanks to everyone for all you are doing for my campaign and for Blue Morpho. You guys do matter, and you are making a difference. Don't forget to vote.

Nick finished hugging Ray, Kayla, Craig, and Darrell and headed out to the Suburban with Earl as they headed to the chartered plane at Midway. On to DC and his next headache. While he was successfully dealing with each, they were preventing him from spreading his message to the people that mattered, the voters. He was doing exactly what they wanted him to do, not what he needed to do. Nick was allowing them to dictate the time and place of the battles.

Chapter 7

Mel knocked on Lexi's door. The "enter" he heard from behind the door seemed different.

Mel walked into the office. Lexi was standing with a drink in hand.

"Why am I surrounded by idiots? Don't we pay these guys well? Don't we feed them info and make sure they get first dibs on key items? We do everything to help their ratings and they screw up over and Over and OVER," said Lexi, her voice progressively rising. Mel shut the door behind him. Thankfully, it was late and few were still in the campaign office.

Mel walked over and tried to take the drink from her. She turned away and took another sip.

"How many of those have you had?" prodded Mel.

"Not enough," she answered. "I want them replaced."

"Who?" Mel looked around the room, half expecting Roland.

"Sherman, at ANC, that idiot at FLCN, all of them. They are fucking useless. Can't I just have them shot? What the hell good is it to be president if I can't order people to be shot?" she asked as Mel tried to get her to sit.

"Sit Lexi, put your feet up," cajoled Mel, getting her on the couch, putting her feet up on a coffee table on a pillow while taking off her heels. He went to the coffee machine and brewed a coffee. He set it to the strongest setting.

"Relax. What is bothering you?" he said, doctoring up her coffee with cream and Splenda. Lexi hated sugar. "Here, drink this."

"Ah, this is good. Thanks. Did you see Turner tonight? He was fucking brilliant," praised Lexi. "How did we screw that one up?

Everything we throw at him, he deflects or turns to a positive. Why are people paying any attention to him? Why isn't he on *my* ticket?"

"He was good," agreed Mel, trying to turn the conversation away from Turner. "But remember, Lexi, his organization is small. He has almost no support in the urban areas. He has focused on middle and working-class voters in the heartland. That's who is paying attention to him," continued Mel, getting his own coffee.

"Those are not our voters. They are ignorant and simple. Easy to persuade. All you have to do is tell them you are going to take away their guns, and he has their vote. Simple as that." Mel watched as Lexi drank more coffee, perking up.

"Our polling shows very little support for him in the cities, especially among black and Hispanic voters. Without the cities, he cannot hurt you. He isn't on the ballot in the upper Midwest. He has no chance in California. All you need to win is Minnesota and Nevada, or Iowa, Virginia, Georgia, or Arizona. You have a million paths to victory. He has none."

"He has to win two of the three states he is not even on the ballot. Then he has to take back Georgia and Arizona and we both know our operations there are too good to overcome. Blackbird is weak. He isn't going to get close to you and Turner isn't going to pick up enough of his voters to win. They'll split the moderates not voting for you and Turner won't get any conservatives with his pro-abortion stance. You're the one who is fucking brilliant," persuaded Mel in an encouraging tone.

She just looked up at him and then smiled. "Thanks. I still want those fuckers fired. What kind of shoddy journalism are they practicing? I mean, the LN1 reporter was green, but that Blue Morpho stuff should have been a slam dunk. Those guys are hiding their money and we should be able to make them pay for not putting their money behind us," railed Lexi.

"I want IRS and DOJ investigations opened on each one of them. The day after inauguration. Even if we find nothing, we can make their life miserable for a few years in payback. And Spalding. He especially has to pay. I warned him."

Mel just nodded. He had seen Lexi like this and he was better off not trying to debate her at this point.

"Bergamo is the one I am disappointed in. She seemed to have such a slam dunk with the video and all. How did he wiggle out of that one?"

"Clearly she wasn't there for the whole thing. She was literally dodging bullets at the end. She did have pictures of Turner with drugs in his hand. I wouldn't be too hard on her."

"I knew the ballot trick wouldn't work. Too obviously a setup. Shouldn't even have tried it. Now what?"

"We beat him up in the debate."

"He's definitely in?" asked Lexi, disappointed.

Mel just nodded, not wanting to give her news Turner was going up slightly in the polls, even after all the October surprises. They'd done too good a job taking out Blackbird.

"We start turning some of our ad budget toward him. Hit him on his climate denial and his ARL hate. Wanting to close the border. Even with his so-called assimilation plan, he is hating pretty hard on the immigrants who are here. Calling them terrorists and criminals tied to the cartels. He is way to the right of us on the key social justice issues," explained Mel as Lexi nodded.

"He's right about ARL and Antifa."

"Agree. We don't want them to be your problem. They have certainly caused enough issues for the current president," remarked Mel.

"I *am* the current president," quipped Lexi with a raised eyebrow.

"Well, when you put it that way, it was a problem for the last elected president whose biggest decision now is what flavor of ice cream to have after dinner," retorted Mel with a smile.

"What happens tomorrow?" asked Lexi, irritated.

"About what?" deflected Mel.

"Don't play coy with me. I'm not that drunk. Is Fitzpatrick going through with the Censure vote?"

"Fontana has been working him to get him to withdraw it, but he won't. They have limited the speeches to three from each side and Turner. So at least it won't go on for hours."

Lexi laughed. "Who are you kidding, Mel? If Turner wants to, he can stand there for hours, maybe even days, without a break. And he gets someone like Garcia or Crawford to spell him. We didn't get rid of the individual filibuster. He could keep going until the election if he wanted to. I want Fitzpatrick's head."

Mel contemplated before answering. They'd been through this already.

"Lexi, more than anything, Turner wants to be on the campaign trail. He isn't going to do an extended filibuster because he knows the vote isn't going to happen. Even if he lost, he doesn't care. He's out of the Senate in two months anyway. And we need Fitzpatrick's vote to pass our first hundred days of legislature. We'll deal with him when the time is right."

Lexi stared. She switched gears.

"Set up a meeting with Harriet. I want to go over the get out the vote and all the 'day of election' operations," ordered Lexi.

"Some of that is better for you not to know."

"Seriously? You don't think I don't know what is going on? Hell, don't you remember who put that putz in the office? I orchestrated most of it myself last time. I didn't get to be the first female Senate Majority Leader by relying on the Party National Committee plans. Just carve out some time."

"We can do it Saturday. We need to focus on the debate now. It's coming up on Friday. We have most of tomorrow, Wednesday and Thursday laid out for prep. George Mason is a short drive, so we will just stay here. I'll let Harriet know to be ready for a deep dive on Saturday morning."

#

"Well, that one hurt," said *America's News Channel* president, Sherman Hallberg, from his office suite as he watched Nick's presentation on EXN. "Any lawsuits?"

"Doubt it, our reporting was solid given what we had to work with. We couldn't have known or researched what happened prior to or after Lauren and Paul drove away," offered Sidney Blumfeld, corporate counsel for ANC.

"At least without asking, like he said. It was a worthy effort. I hope the Vice President appreciates it. I suspect she is going to blame us for helping Turner yet again turn a scandal into a triumph," sighed Sherman.

"He does appear to be bulletproof."

"Literally," said Sherman in an ironic tone. "Did we ever get anywhere with that investigation? Who the hell shot him and why haven't they tried again?"

"There is nothing. No one claims to have done it. No evidence pointing to anyone or any organization. If he hadn't had that sniper explain exactly what happens when a bullet hits and how hard it is to hit a target at that range, I would still claim he did it himself," mused Sidney.

"Me too, but nobody takes that kind of risk. Too bad he didn't ask to broadcast on our network. We could have used the revenue and the viewer bump."

"You're right on that. What are you going to do with Bergamo? You've pushed her pretty hard. She could bring you down if she went public with all you've made her do," worried Sidney.

"I don't think our little Miss Bergamo is going to do anything, trust me," said Sherman with a knowing smile.

"What about the Vice President?"

"I'll handle her. She's a lot more bark than bite."

"Really? Seems the other way around to me, but you have to take the call," shrugged Sidney.

"Lucky me," agreed Sherman, knowing the vindictive nature of the Vice President.

#

Lauren Bergamo sat in her condo in Atlanta, watching Nick's broadcast. She listened intently, seeing the aftermath once she and her cameraman Paul had sped away. She had a feeling something must have happened after. Her time with Nick in San Francisco confirmed there was no way he was doing anything with drugs.

She'd buried the footage, not thinking her cameraman would have a chance conversation and bring it up with her producer. She watched as

Nick worked to save the life of the gang member who was shot, bleeding out on the steps, picking him up and placing him in the car. Lauren was especially moved by his answers to the uncaring drug dealer, asking why he cared while trying to save the young man's life.

She started to cry once the people on the broadcast started coming through one by one to thank Nick for what he had done to change their lives, saving one, altering the course of others. A hero in every aspect.

"And that bitch Lauren Bergamo continues to try to bring him down," she said aloud to no one. She turned off the TV, poured more wine and sat in the darkness dreaming of what might have been, and what she would do, all while knowing Nick must truly hate her now.

Chapter 8

The Senate chambers held ninety-nine senators, most of whom would have preferred to be anywhere else. The lone absentee was an elderly Party Senator from Vermont, who'd slipped and broken his hip while boarding the plane to fly back to Washington. He'd had some choice words for Senator Fitzpatrick from his hospital bed when asked by a reporter how he felt about missing the vote.

Fontana had passed a motion by voice vote to allow only three speakers from both sides of the aisle, plus Senator Turner. He also limited the combined speeches to thirty minutes for each party combined and ten for Turner as an independent.

Party Senator's Williams of Washington, Harrington of Colorado and finally Senator Fitzpatrick spent their time citing examples of Nick's speeches inciting violence, preaching hate and support for racism, homophobia and encouraging people to rise up against the government.

Their speeches were greeted by raucous cheers from half the gallery and even louder boos from the other half. Fontana slammed his gavel so long and hard it broke while trying to restore order. He picked up the mallet head and smacked it on the tabletop until order was restored.

Senator Freddie Garcia spoke for the Opposition focusing primarily on the egregious breach of Senate rules. Using the serious process of Censure for political vendettas and petty differences of opinion. He gave a brief history lesson of the prior times Censure had been used. All primarily in cases that eventually led to indictments for mostly improper use of campaign funds.

"I will close with my remaining time and point out the unprecedented attacks we are now witnessing on Senator Turner and his campaign. Politics is a dirty business and Presidential politics is the filthiest of them all. But we are not a European court or an Asian empire where poison and assassination were commonplace and expected. We are a constitutional republic."

"Where every citizen has a voice and a say in how we are ruled through their elected officials. We have peacefully transferred power between parties who vehemently disagree. Yet in this campaign, we are seeing the rhetoric and vile words lead to violence and death. The death of Senator Turner's staffer and now that of his accuser, is both unfortunate and wrong on so many levels."

"This attack, from his senate colleagues on such frivolous grounds, and many of the others we are now seeing pop up, threatens our way of government. We must get back to healthy debate and use words, not violence, to convince our voters of our abilities to lead this country and its entire populace. Majority Leader, I yield the remainder of my time."

Fontana stood. "Thank you, Senator Garcia. The Chair recognizes Senator McKay. You have ten minutes."

Senator Allen McKay rose. "My fellow senators, while we do not agree with Senator Turner on all his stances, we do believe in the sanctity of our Senate rules. This vote is an egregious breach of these, and Senator Langston and I yield our twenty minutes to Senator Turner to enable him to offer a complete defense of his actions against these accusations hurled at him by our colleague."

This move was met with shouts from many Party Senators and cheers from the gallery. Fontana's face was white as a sheet as he rose to object to this move.

"This is not permitted, Senator. Nowhere did we make provisions for senators yielding their time to each other for this debate."

Senator McKay replied in a calm voice. "Majority Leader, I have consulted the Senate Parliamentarian. She has confirmed in the absence of a specific prohibition against yielding our time to colleagues, we are able to do so. I would also request that the time spent explaining this, not be removed from my yielded time. Thank you."

Fontana, knowing he'd been outfoxed, glanced at the Senate Parliamentarian, who briefly nodded in agreement.

"The Chair recognizes the junior Senator from Colorado. Senator Turner, you have thirty minutes. Proceed."

As he sat back in the leader's chair, Fontana felt sorry for Colin Fitzpatrick and immediately started reviewing in his mind potential female politicians in Massachusetts he could support in the primary to replace him. Lexi would indeed have Fitzpatrick's balls on her shelf.

Fitzpatrick had gifted Turner exactly what she had tried to deny. Free and easy access to a national audience of millions tuned in for this unusual spectacle of Congressional debate. Now he had thirty minutes of free air time before his largest audience to date.

Nick stood tall at the rostrum beneath the leader's dais. He thanked Freddie for his words and Senator's McKay and Langston for giving him their time.

"I find it ironic it is almost a year to the date when last I stood here preparing to cast my vote to preserve the filibuster. I doubt I will need all of this time, as these charges are so frivolous. Merely a difference in view and opinion. We have listened to three separate Senators stand and insult a large swath of our electorate who *support* law and order, sovereign borders, election integrity and sensible energy policies. Anyone with common sense also supports these policies. They are the bedrock of what has made America great. The fact my Party colleagues somehow think support for these is wrong or unpatriotic has me concerned about the future of our great republic."

"I and my followers also recognize the desire by women to make their own choices about their body with minimal coercion and sensible restriction. If espousing these views and exhorting people to make these choices, themselves, is all it takes to Censure a United States Senator, then we should adjourn permanently and save the electorate millions, if not trillions, of dollars."

There were some boos and some cheers from the assembled gallery. Fontana banged the head of his broken gavel, yelling for order.

Nick turned and stared at Fitzpatrick, who met his gaze defiantly.

"This is a personal accusation. There are no facts to support any of the spurious statements. Only rhetoric and vitriol. It is designed to do two things. First to sully my reputation, hoping to diminish my popularity, such that it is. Second, and more insidiously, the timing is suspicious, being so close to a national election. It pulled me, and sadly, thirty-three other senators, off the campaign trail, mere weeks before the election. These accusations, since they are not fact based, could have been levied against me at anytime since I announced my candidacy. Instead, you waited until now. If this is not election interference, I do not know what is." Nick paused.

"It is unfortunate we are not in the olden days. We could have easily solved this. You see, a personal insult of this nature would have certainly ended up in an old-fashioned duel. Let's call it the Andrew Jackson way. He was supposedly involved in 100 duels. I'd have been duty bound to meet Senator Fitzpatrick to defend my impugned honor."

"Perhaps we should re-institute this old tradition? Maybe we would cut down on some of this grandstanding and hyperbolic rhetoric. Folks might think twice before insulting colleagues." Nick finished and stared at the surprised and reddening face of Senator Fitzpatrick.

He continued, taking each of the Senator's specific claims and quickly debunking all of them. It was almost too easy for Nick to reference specific facts to rebut the claims and to cite the fact he never asked anyone to do anything other than make their own decisions. Based on *their* own research.

Claims he was leading a revolution, or asking for the toppling of the government, were easily disproved by specific video evidence he cited as available on his website or in Hibi posts.

Nick shifted gears, quickly highlighting worse statements made by senators, many of whom were still in the chamber today. He offered quotes into the record, as instances of much more egregious behavior, by primarily, Party Senators. Each calling for direct violence against groups of Opposition members, conservative voters, and supporters, and even Supreme Court justices and nominees.

In each case, the called-out senator rose to object and asked to be recognized. Nick denied their requests to yield in all cases. He simply stated he was quoting from the published record. If they cared to renounce or deny their own words, they could do so on American *Pravda* at their convenience, using *their* own time.

Fontana sat and fumed through the speech. This was the Filibuster debacle part two. He now feared for his own hide, thinking of Lexi's last words about everyone being replaceable. He quickly scribbled a note and handed it to a clerk with instructions.

"As Senator Garcia rightly pointed out, we can no longer have a civil discourse about issues. To present differing opinions to our electorate and to make our cases for them to review. Free to reach their own conclusions. This is apparently no longer permitted for a simple reason. They are afraid. Afraid the populace may choose to elect the 'wrong' candidate."

"Rather than recognize this and change their policies to win over the voters, they refuse. Now we get nonstop attacks against those of us preaching common sense. Whether through frivolous charges such as we see today, or 'lawfare' weaponizing the courts to tie up candidate's time and money defending against charges with little or no merit. This is the politics of personal destruction, used so effectively by my former party on so many occasions. Facts matter little. It is all about perception and deception."

"Trusting in the values and instincts of the voters in our great country to freely choose the path they sense is best, is too risky. As has been said before, the best way to win is to come up with a slate of stances to which a majority agree."

Nick continued and watched Fitzpatrick as he spoke about the tools the parties were using to manipulate the voters. He saw two clerks approach him, handing him notes. Nick watched as he opened one and shook his head. As he opened the second one, the color left his face. He closed his eyes for a second, then opened them and reread the note. Senator Fitzpatrick rose, asking him if he would yield for a question. Nick replied he would, for a question only.

Fitzpatrick was pale and nervous, a sheen of sweat covering his balding head.

"Senator Turner, first, I would like to offer an apology for my statements and accusation if you would accept it?" This caused gasps among the Party senators and cheers from one side of the gallery and groans from the other. Most astonished were his Party colleagues. The unwritten rule of Washington politics was never apologize.

"Second," continued Fitzpatrick, "upon further reflection of my action and of the words spoken here today. I would offer to withdraw the motion for Censure without a vote, again if you would allow it, as the accused. Also, while not a question, I apologize to all my fellow senators for making them return to Washington. Finally, I would like to announce, I will not seek reelection when my term is up in two years."

At this last, cheers broke out amongst Nick's supporters in the gallery and many senators from both parties were standing, yelling and speaking at this unusual speech. Nick stood waiting for order to be restored. He could only wonder what was in the notes.

Fontana was beating the mallet head on the table and yelling for order. Threatening to have the gallery emptied if he did not get it. He struck so hard the mallet head split, puncturing his ham fist and spraying blood on the dais. He calmly wrapped a towel he was handed around his wounded hand, waiting for folks to sit.

As they finally returned to their seats, Fontana looked toward Nick. "Senator, you may continue. Are you willing to accept the withdrawal of the Censure resolution? I cannot dismiss it without your approval, since you are the accused."

"I have a question for Senator Fitzpatrick. I want it to be clear, because I now have experienced some of the dirty tricks Washington can throw at a candidate these last few weeks. I did not threaten you in any way to make you withdraw your resolution. Nor did I force you to apologize or decide not to run in two years. Please acknowledge this, if true."

Senator Fitzpatrick stood. He was practically shaking. In a voice made unsteady by the moment, "I confirm Senator Turner has had nothing to do with any of my apologies or desire to withdraw the resolution and my decision to forsake re-election in two years."

Nick nodded. "In that case, while I would much prefer to spend my remaining fifteen minutes of national airtime, time I might add I have been unable to get from our media," there were jeers and cheers from the gallery at Nick's statement.

"Order!" banged Fontana.

"I will not waste more of the Senate's time on this. I trust my followers all know where I stand. For those who do not know me, but who may have tuned in for just this spectacle, I hope I have given you enough to know I value honor and truth more than power. I accept the apology of the Senator for bringing the resolution and for pulling all of us off the campaign trail. I also accept the removal of the Censure resolution. I cede my fifteen minutes of airtime back to the Vice President, who is no doubt very pleased with my decision to forego fifteen minutes of national airtime. Good day to all. I yield the remainder of my time."

Fontana jumped to his feet. "This matter is closed. The Senate is hereby adjourned."

#

Nick and Chuck walked from the Senate chamber where they were accosted by a gaggle of press reporters. Nick spied Lauren in the crowd. She was wearing a slim cut, form fitting red knee length dress with short sleeves and high neckline. A silver belt around her waist highlighted her figure. This was finished with a pair of matching red high heels. Her wavy dark auburn hair cascaded over one shoulder. He felt a pang in his gut. It took all his effort to fix her with an appropriate stare at her betrayal. She looked away from his piercing gaze.

"Senator, do you have any idea why Senator Fitzpatrick would withdraw the Censure resolution without a vote?" asked Ned Wheeler from EXN.

Nick stood for a second, biting off his smart comment. "Perhaps he was persuaded by the rebuttals from myself and Senator Garcia and realized many of his own Party colleagues would be forced to vote against the measure. My assumption is he decided to limit any further damage to his party and his colleagues up for re-election."

"We noticed Senator Fitzpatrick received several notes during your speech. Any idea what was in them?" shouted Meg from RBS.

"That is a question for Senator Fitzpatrick. As he answered when I asked, they weren't from me. You'll have to find some other culprit for that one." Nick scanned the press, settling on Lauren's face. "Ms. Bergamo?" asked Nick in a formal tone.

Lauren maintained a straight face and fought the flip-flops in her stomach as she asked a question. The other reporters all stared at one or the other, waiting for the inevitable conflict.

"Senator, while the Censure vote was rescinded, do you care to address the fact, your rallies appear to be inspiring more violent elements of those who claim to support you? Against minorities and LGBTQ followers. Even if you don't acknowledge them, they still support you."

Nick stood looking into her face, then he smiled. "No one gets to choose their followers. Jesus had Judas, after all." Lauren reddened at this statement as he continued.

"Nor can I be responsible for the actions of others. I am consistent in my message and I am confident you can go back and check the record. Just as we saw in there today, many of those senators were not upset about the words of hate they spoke previously. They were upset that I was *highlighting* the fact they had made them before. It is the same here. All I can do is tell these Gabriel's Angels I do not support them. I do not want their support. I cannot stop them from making their own decisions. A fully functioning justice system would prosecute *all* who commit crimes regardless of who the victims or the perpetrators are."

"I never tell my followers what to do, how to think, or especially how to vote. I tell them to use their brains. To think before they act. And, to take ownership of the consequences of those actions, right or wrong, good or bad."

Chuck pulled Nick away as other questions were shouted at him.

Lauren called out. "Senator."

He stopped and looked back.

"I *am* glad you were able to save that boy's life after the shooting."

Nick met her gaze and nodded, turning away and walking out of the Capitol.

#

"Your hand, OK?" asked Mel as he entered Fontana's office in the Capitol.

Sal Fontana held up his meaty right hand. It had a gauze bandage wrapped around it. "This is a scratch. I finished a shift on the dock once with a shark fish hook through my palm." He held up his fingers to show Mel it was about 4 or 5 inches long.

"You win the pissing contest," smiled Mel.

"Drink?" he asked as Mel nodded.

He returned with a couple of scotches. They took seats in front of one of the few working fireplaces in the Capitol.

Mel leaned over and tapped Sal's glass. "Good job, ending that before it got any worse. Or Turner did a weeklong filibuster."

"Ha. I was about to congratulate you for the same. It wasn't me."

"I saw on TV he got a couple of notes. He turned pale at the second one. That's when I figured you delivered some of Lexi's messages in dockyard threats," explained Mel.

"I assumed the same, except it was coming from you. My note just warned him Lexi would be out for bear and to prepare. The other note is the one that did it. I can only imagine the different ways Lexi threatened to fry up his balls and serve them to him. Must have been from her directly if you didn't send it."

"Hmm," mused Mel, thinking.

"Guess it doesn't matter. Though I am surprised he apologized so profusely. We *never* do that. Especially on our side. In fact, we have a procedure when we join Congress. They suck the remorse gene out of our DNA," laughed Sal.

"And then also announcing he is not going to run for a seat his family has held for fifty years?" added Mel.

"I know. Even more reason to think it was you and Lexi."

Mel didn't say what he was thinking. He just finished his scotch and strategized who they would run in two years for the seat.

Chapter 9

Roland Gill walked from the Capitol to the White House. He enjoyed having credentials that got him into most buildings in Washington, DC. What he would have done or who he would have killed for this access in prior times. Now, with the wave of his benefactor's hand, plural, he was inside. No vetting, no background checks, fingerprints or retinal scans. All of which would have told a different story.

He chuckled inside as he entered the West Wing of the White House. Now a familiar member of Lexi's detail, he smiled at the greetings he got from various staffers. How important all these people thought they were. The decisions they were making impacted so many without them knowing or even caring about the details. Details called people.

Roland suppressed a hidden desire to just kill all of them, knowing it would not matter one iota. The vacuum would be quickly filled with a new set of exactly the same parasites. Feeding off the host and providing no useful function. He had to admit, even he agreed with some of Turner's words occasionally.

He stopped in front of a small non-descript office. It was used by the Chairmen of the Joint Chiefs when he came to the White House for briefings. Roland knocked and entered, hearing an offer from inside.

#

Admiral Jason Kensington sat at the tiny desk in the office. He was sure it used to be a closet in the West Wing. Given the expansion of white house staff through the years, he knew he was lucky to even have access to this much privacy.

His rise in the Navy was meteoric by all standards. Only in his early fifties when he received his third star and then his fourth courtesy of his appointment to the Chairmanship. He was the youngest Chairman of the Joint Chiefs, taking the diaper distinction from Colin Powell, the previous wunderkind.

This role was the culmination of his lifetime of effort. Now he would have to choose between higher office in politics, the lucrative speaking circuit, or perhaps the chairmanship of a defense contracting firm when his term ended in October of next year.

Kensington excelled at pushing paper. Besides being the youngest, he was also the least decorated Joint Chief, having seen very little actual combat. Even serving in joint duty intelligence assignments during Iraq and Afghanistan, his roles were all rear echelon, planning and strategy.

His efficiency reports throughout his career highlighted his ability to meet his superior's every wish, often before they even knew what they were looking for. He had an uncanny knack for being in the right place at the right time. Always able to take credit for the hard work of others and use their effort and skills to advance his own career.

He'd left piles of officers in his wake during his rise to the upper echelons. No one would attend his retirement party. Unless they were paid or ordered too.

Despite this, he had a reputation for good staff work. In the modern Department of Defense, you couldn't rise without some skill. He was the best at the one skill most valued by the modern military of the United States. Securing funding for projects through politics. At this, no one was better than Kensington.

Always knowing who to compliment, or what side to take in an argument. How to wine and dine, cajole, and back slap the appropriate congress person or defense contractor at just the right time to do what was necessary for first the Navy and now the entire military.

Which programs to sacrifice and when, to get more funding for others. He handled much of the funding for the new wiz bangs as his first admiral had called all the cyber, drone, space, and hypersonic weapons programs. The modern military would soon replace pilots with drones and soldiers with AI and computer automation.

At this moment, he was in the midst of defunding once and for all the last remaining A-10 squadrons in favor of the F-35 for close air support. The Senators from Arizona and Missouri, representing the final air force bases with active squadrons, were making one last plea to keep some of them for active duty.

Kensington and the other service branches, including the Air Force, saw no reason to keep the A-10 *and* the F-35. Kensington also took great pleasure knowing it would piss off Senator Nick Turner. Anything he could do to piss off Turner made him happy.

He looked up at the knock on his door.

"Enter."

Roland Gill entered the room. Kensington had met him a couple of times since he had taken over security for the Vice President's campaign. He waved him to the lone guest chair.

"Sir, if I could have a moment?"

"Sure Gill, what's on your mind?" Kensington had a habit of referring to people by their last names. Another annoying trait his civilian colleagues disliked.

"I am sure you are aware the last debate is in a few days."

"Really? I pay little attention to this stuff," he lied.

"Oh? Lucky you. As you know, the Vice President and Senator Turner are sure to spar during the event."

"Get to the point Gill," said Kensington, not looking up, missing the deadly glare his rudeness produced.

"Ah direct. I like it," Roland's tone changed to one of dangerous forcefulness, causing Kensington to now look up, not used to being addressed this way.

"Task Force Echo," said Roland.

"Excuse me," replied the Admiral, sweat appearing on his forehead.

"You will go meet with the Vice President and provide her enough information to use against Turner in the debate. Something she can imply or bring up to discredit him and raise doubts about his truthfulness.

"How dare you come in here making threats?" Kensington stood up, anger and concern showing on his face.

Roland stayed seated. "Sit down Admiral. There is no need to get upset."

"I don't know who the fuck you think you are. Coming in here trying to blackmail me into divulging national security issues for a political campaign." He picked up the phone.

"Make that call and a file detailing all the dirty tricks you and your various commanding Admirals have done the last thirty-five years will land on the desk of several editors of both major US and international papers, besides US cable channels. You will be forced to resign in disgrace before tomorrow, if not arrested, for the death and destruction some of these decisions have caused. Criminal decisions, it seems in some cases," Roland delivered his threat in clinical terms.

Just as his note to Colin Fitzpatrick earlier in the day had detailed what would happen to him and his family if he did not stop the Censure vote immediately. Just enough info on past crimes to ensure compliance.

American politicians were amateurs when it came to the world of espionage. And hiding their malfeasance and indiscretions sufficiently from those with the resources to discover them.

"You're bluffing."

"Maskanah Syria, Shorabak and Moshtarak Afghanistan, al Quim Iraq, your role in the al-Sadr resurgence and the retaliatory strikes in Sadr City. How long you knew Bin Laden was in the compound in Pakistan and how many times *your* intelligence prevented missions? I could go on. But I don't need to, do I? I am not asking for much. Just give the Vice President something she can use against Turner. No one needs to be any wiser. You're already planning for your future outside the military anyway, correct?"

"How do you know all of this? Who do you work for?"

"I work for the Vice President. That is all you need to know. As for my sources, there are many. I do not make idle threats. Mention this conversation and it will be your last indiscretion." This last delivered with a steely gaze. Kensington blinked and looked down.

"Very well. I will do what I can, but I will not give her anything that would compromise our national security. If all you care to do is make Turner look bad, I can do that. With pleasure, actually."

"Excellent. Thank you for your time, Admiral."

Roland left the office and closed the door. Another loose end created he would no doubt have to clean up at some point. He was used to more precise missions. Being in Lexi's orbit was a constant bombardment of corruption, incompetence, and skullduggery. Roland smiled as he walked back to her office for their next 'strategy meeting'. He was enjoying the assignment. And it did have its perks.

Chapter 10

"We stand here mourning the loss of a young man, just starting off on his journey of life," said Nick, standing behind a podium at a memorial for Kevin Moss. He was at a funeral home in Salt Lake City.

"This is the second one of these I have spoken at today. I should be speaking at neither. Both fine men should be alive and thriving, and yet they are not," continued Nick, looking at Kevin's two sets of grandparents. His mother could not leave rehab to attend the memorial. His estranged father had not been invited to the service.

"Life is not without risk. We all understand this, having mourned the millions around the world who were struck down by the lab leak of the Chinese virus from Wuhan. We know every day we could be killed by a natural cause, hit by a car, or even struck by lightning. This is fate and out of our control."

"None of that happened to Kevin. What happened was entirely the fault of someone and that someone is not him," spoke Nick with conviction, looking directly into the cameras filming the event.

"Kevin loved what he was doing in our office. He was making a difference. Learning and even teaching the next set of interns after he became a full-time staffer. Training volunteers in our grassroots organizations. Kevin was liked by everyone who met him. He was funny, smart, and eager. He would have matured into a fine man and had a wonderful career, no matter the field he pursued. To be standing here is a crime."

"I will make you the same promise I made to Greg Simmon's relatives this morning." Nick was talking directly to the grandparents. "I will find out who was behind using this fine young man as a tool in their dirty political game. Someone is behind this. Either a campaign or someone working for or in concert with one. We all know the crime. We know the criminal. Now we need to find the evidence and I assure you, I will not rest until that person or group is unmasked. The ultimate decision maker punished for the lives cut short by their callous political tactics," finished Nick, sending a chill down the spine of all in attendance.

One grandfather leaped to his feet. "Senator, you find who murdered my grandson and you make them pay. Promise me you will do this," he said, tears streaming down his face as his wife pulled him back down into his seat.

"Sir, you have my word. I will find who did this, and I will avenge their deaths. Count on it," promised Nick fiercely.

"I will keep them in my prayers forever. They made the ultimate sacrifice for me. I cannot let that go to waste. You have my heartfelt apology, as I feel responsible. If I had not run, they would not have been in the line of fire. They signed up for a political campaign, not the Marines."

"Your grandson and my friends are not mere pawns to be used and discarded in their relentless pursuit of power," continued Nick, no longer talking to the audience in attendance. There was only one target for his anger now. The dangerous look in his eye and the tone of his voice made everyone glad they were not that target.

"God bless Kevin, for he is in a better place. Those who did this will not be so lucky." finished Nick walking from the podium and being surrounded by his four very large bodyguards as he walked to the waiting Suburban.

"Holy shit, did you see that look?" asked Paul, the ANC cameraman assigned from the press pool to cover this story.

"I would not want to be the guy who did this," agreed the pool reporter from AP.

Chapter 11

Nick was tired. He'd flown from DC after the Censure vote to Southern California for Greg's funeral on Wednesday morning. Then to Salt Lake City for Kevin's midday. Rather than waste the rest of the day flying back to DC, where the debate would be on Friday at George Mason University, they picked Phoenix as the place to prepare him.

They spent Wednesday evening and all-day Thursday at the Marriott Desert Ridge Resort in Phoenix. Denise played Lexi and tore into Nick personally, insulting him, implying he was unworthy of the Presidency, accusing him of treason and preaching outright revolution.

She attacked Nick's stance on climate change, his support for keeping guns in the hands of criminals and white supremacists. How he wanted to preserve the white patriarchy and keep black and brown minorities along with LGBTQ segregated as second-class citizens.

She mocked his support for restoring faith in God as a gimmick. To merely try to convince the religious to choose him versus having faith in government. She lambasted his constitutional approach as short sided and clearly revisionist. How it had been shown time and time again the Constitution was wrong, codifying slavery being an unpardonable original sin.

Session after session, each with a clear theme. The border and his stance to ignore the humanitarian needs of the weak and poor. How his constant attacks against education prevented teaching children key social justice themes to make them well-rounded citizens. His confused stances on abortion, scaring young women at a perilous time in their lives with threats of eternal damnation. Gender dysphoria, abolishing federal agencies, including the IRS and a host of other controversial stances.

Denise was wiped out at the end of each session. As they did more and more, she became concerned there was no way to adequately prepare Nick for the myriad of attack surfaces he was providing a good debater like Lexi.

Chuck played Blackbird and did much the same. Criticizing Nick's stances from the right side. His support for abortion as out of touch with conservative values and his economic policies as sure to get the United States involved in trade wars. His immigration policies likely to cause all manner of tension, both internal to the US with so many illegals already in the country, and concerns with the rest of the world about US inhumane treatment of true asylum seekers.

Nick stayed calm. Refusing to get flustered regardless of the attack style. Yelling, shouting, innuendo, statements question his personal morality, ethics, intelligence. Even questioning his own bravery. The only time he even flinched was a statement by Denise/Lexi regarding Nick allowing others to take the risks and pay the price for his deeds and stances. The rest rolled off his back as he answered each of the questions, ignoring all the other barbs and personal attacks.

Afterwards, Denise and Chuck both looked at each other, exhausted by their effort to break Nick. "You sure you've never done this before?"

"What?"

"Debate. High school, college?"

"Guys, every interaction with every person you meet in your life is a mini debate. You may not always be trying to win them over to your side, but you are learning the back and forth. I have been doing this my entire life. As long as you don't take things personally and remember the other person is entitled to and equally impassioned about their view, you can keep a clear head and civil response. Try convincing generals and admirals their pet operation is going to end up killing lots of soldiers versus the glory and acclamation they expect to receive."

"And then the guilt you feel when you could not stop the operations that resulted in exactly what you predicted. Lexi and Blackbird will bait me, they will attack me, they will accuse me of either doing or wanting to do horrible things to the country. But none of what they say would be worse than not finding a way to keep those soldiers from dying needlessly. I will stick to the facts of the moderator's question and refrain from rising to their bait."

"They'll be interrupting you every chance they get during the open debate. How will you handle that?" pushed Denise.

"We have six questions, right?"

They both nodded.

"I get two and a half minutes for each. I figure I'll get fifteen minutes to get my point across. They each get their fifteen, so that is half of the ninety minutes. Add in our two and a half minute closing statements, so that is another seven and a half. Fifty minutes of mostly uninterrupted talking. Forty minutes of *Animal House*. I'll let them scream at me and accuse me of all kinds of heinous crimes. If I don't get to talk at all during that, I am fine with it. It will just make them look that much less presidential."

"I guess that's one way to handle it. Getting in a shouting match with any of them would be a useless exercise," agreed Denise.

"Questions?" broke in Chuck.

"Guys, I've been in combat. I've been shot down behind enemy lines and have done things to survive my opponents cannot even imagine. I spent hours with a knife in my chest and a dead terrorist laying on top of me with an activated bomb vest. This debate may be life altering in the world of politicians, but I can't get too worked up over a couple of people for whom I have very little respect. Each pelting me with name calling and insults. I will survive. I always do," said Nick with a shrug.

"I guess that puts it a bit into perspective," added Chuck, laughing.

"Ya think," laughed Denise as well, picking up a copy of Nick's book they were using as a prop. She made a show of opening it, flipping through a few pages.

"Hmm, I see nothing in this biography chapter on being shot down behind enemy lines. Nor do I see any heroic details regarding things you did to survive. Or any other details about earning a bunch of medals you have in your hope chest? Actions, I might add, that would be of incredible value and interest to a bunch of people called 'potential voters'," finished Denise, with a frown on her face. "Nick, are you being serious and if so, why did you not cover any of this? This is what people want to know."

"Denise, it is not about me and what I did during the wars. It is about what I can do for my fellow citizens going forward. It will always be about that. Having everyone know about New York is bad enough. I am ready for this debate. Just trust that I have already been through other trials by fire."

#

Nick was asleep in the back row of the jet as they flew late Thursday night back to DC.

Denise and Chuck huddled in the front and spoke in low voices so they wouldn't wake him.

"Well?" asked Denise.

"He makes good points. We couldn't rattle him with anything. His strategy is sound, but once they start screaming at him and accusing him of things that offend his honor. No doubt partisans in the crowd will yell as well. How is he going to resist fighting back?" asked Chuck.

Denise just looked at him and the frown on his face.

"He hates bullies, Denise. Lexi is the ultimate schoolyard bully. I just hope he can keep it inside and not let her have it with both barrels."

"I'm more worried that he doesn't. Let's say he just stands there and lets them accuse him of all manner of untruth. If he says nothing, responds to nothing, is he going to come across as not having an answer? Of potentially freezing up under pressure? That would be disastrous," warned Denise.

Chuck shook his head. "Remember who you are talking about. There is no way *he* freezes under pressure. If it warrants a response, I think he will break his silence and make the point. I just hate to see him get pelted with shit all night.

"You guys ever hear of the parabolic effect?" asked Nick from the back of the plane. "Don't worry, shit washes off. Now get some sleep. You two are the ones who wore yourselves out trying to skewer me these last two days. Shut up and sleep. That's an order."

Chuck and Denise both smiled and reclined their seats to get comfortable as the plane flew eastward through the night.

#

As Nick got in the Suburban for the drive to George Mason University outside DC in southern Virginia late on Friday, Denise started going over the logistics of the debate one last time.

"You're on the right, as the viewer sees. This means you are last to answer on every question. Lexi is in the middle and Blackbird is on the left. He leads off with each answer. This also means you get to close off the debate with your final two and a half minutes. Make them count."

"Got it."

"Two and a half minutes, Nick. Only two and a half minutes. Make your points and move on," added Chuck, reinforcing the point. Nick simply nodded.

"Topic order is climate, then racism and social justice, crime, economy, foreign policy and finally healthcare. Remember, keep it concise: the audience is looking for something they can take away from each topic. Use powerful statements. Especially if you are not going to get into the shouting match in the open time after each question," pushed Denise, still worried and frustrated.

"Guys, this is not kindergarten. I'm not going to get into a 'look at me' contest."

"I get it. I don't agree, but I get it," groaned Denise.

"Any surprises? What can they try to do to throw me off my game?"

Denise just looked at Chuck sitting in the back with her. Earl was driving and Nick was in the front seat. They now had Suburbans full of bodyguards in front and behind theirs.

"I've been wracking my brain. You don't have a record to attack. All they can do is throw your words from the rallies in your face. You aren't going to run from any of those. Your October surprises have all been dealt with. Lexi is sure to bring up Blackbird's just to keep it front and center and force him to deny he did anything wrong, one more time for a big audience," explained Chuck.

"She won't touch yours with a ten-foot pole because she doesn't want to give you a chance to get more sympathy from these attacks. The ballot issue is probably a bad idea as well because it gives you a chance to respond with your thoughts on how they are the ones who are going to cheat to win, keeping you off the ballot. I can't think of anything else, can you?" she commented, looking at Chuck.

"I know there is something we're missing. Nick, anything you can think of?" asked Chuck.

"Nope," said Nick, half paying attention.

"Nick, take this seriously," carped Denise.

"Denise, I never take anything for granted. I've been talking about my thoughts on all six of these topics for almost a year. I know my talking points. I've handled her October surprises. I'm not afraid of their accusations, lies, or slurs. The thing I must resist is ripping her throat out in retaliation for Greg and Kevin," said Nick menacingly.

"Not trying to overstep my boundaries here," said Earl from the driver's seat. "But I think that might be a bad frame of mind going into a debate."

"Earl's right Nick. You can't hate your debate opponent. Be clear headed and nimble. You need to make sure your mind is clear and uncluttered with thoughts of payback or ripping out someone's throat. That is not a calming state of mind, just so you know," answered Denise, in a tone bordering on panic.

Nick smiled. "OK, no more revenge thoughts. Her time will come."

"That's not much better. Nick, sometimes you scare me," admitted Denise.

Nick sat, smiling.

Chapter 12

"Good evening and welcome to the third and final presidential debate. I'm Adam Mullen of EXN. I'll be your moderator tonight," opened Adam, sitting behind a desk facing the three candidates.

"Each candidate has two and a half minutes to answer each question with their thoughts and solutions. After that, we will have five minutes of open debate where I will ask follow-up questions each of you can answer and rebut each other's answers, time permitting. I would ask that we try to keep it civil. I would also like to warn the audience to withhold your applause and to refrain from commenting during the open debate sections for each question."

"Finally, each candidate will be given two and a half minutes for closing arguments. Straws were drawn prior to the debate. Governor Blackbird will go first on each question and final statement, followed by Vice President Smythe-Thomas and finally Senator Turner. Once the closing statements are complete, the debate is over. Thank you and without further delay, let's begin," announced Adam, arranging papers on his desk.

"Our first question is about preserving our planet and combatting climate change. Governor, you are first," started Adam.

Blackbird immediately launched into a litany of existing legislation and statistics about climate change and carbon emissions. About the need to speed up production of electric vehicles, but not at the expense of all gas vehicles. About reducing reliance on coal for power generation and a switch to natural gas power. He also stated there was a need for more investment in wind and solar and other clean resources to continue to reduce emissions.

He claimed his skills as a negotiator would allow him to work with other countries, and organizations to find compromise solutions. Without negotiating concessions from China, India, and Brazil, the world's emerging industrial economies whose footprints were growing, there would be no progress. He stated he was the man to bring them into the fold for the greater good of the planet.

Adam called on the Vice President next.

The benefit of being in the office gave Lexi the ability to read off a host of legislation, regulation, and international treaties the US had joined during their administration. As Lexi told it, as the administration's lead in climate change initiatives, every bit of US carbon emission reductions, every uptick in the use of wind and solar power to generate clean energy, was because of *her* leadership.

The advancements in clean energy technology or global cooperation were also a direct result of her efforts. Without her drive and commitment, without her ability to persuade, cajole, and threaten when necessary, nothing would have gotten done. Under *her* administration, all of this would just accelerate.

"Senator, your turn," announced Adam.

Nick stood tall, looking out over the crowd. "The climate is changing. For those of you who forgot or were never taught this in school, this spot we are standing in was once covered in ice over a mile thick. Think about that. And it all melted not once, but as many as four times. How did this ever occur without us? Man was around for at least the last one. Think all their campfires caused the ice to melt?" This got a chuckle from the crowd, earning a warning cough from Adam.

"I also don't think the dinosaurs farting cause them to go extinct, either." More laughter. "As you can see, if you spend even five minutes researching, there *are* actual 'facts'," said Nick, holding up his hands in air quotes. "Facts supporting the earth warming *and* cooling, all in only the last forty years. Yet they claim that science is settled despite these conflicting 'facts'. Anyone who disagrees is a denier."

"If that is the case, can we all agree that every scientist should resign tomorrow? Why do we need to pay them any longer?" More laughs.

"Science is never settled," said Nick, stabbing his finger into the podium to make his point. "Thank goodness. Because I really would not like leeches on my arm instead of a good antibiotic in it."

"Banning fossil fuels weakens our economy when those polluting much more than us are not slowing down their expansion. Or their efforts to overtake our country, economically, and in some cases, militarily. Making us less competitive while enabling countries like China, Russia, India, and Brazil to continue to operate and pollute at much higher rates. This isn't good for the planet or our own wellbeing. We are already reducing our emissions significantly, voluntarily."

"This administration is allowing our jobs to go overseas to countries who do not limit their emissions. Our economy suffers as we implement increasingly draconian measures. If *we* cut back as drastically as the Paris Accords suggests, even our scientists are united in claiming we'll have, at best, minimal effect on the temperature in a hundred years. We limit our economy without having a climate impact as others grow both their economy and emissions at our expense. Why would we willingly do this? It defies common sense."

"I am all for electric cars. I am all for wind and solar and nuclear power. But I am all for fossil fuel-based technology until we have perfected viable alternatives *that make sense economically for our country*," Nick finished, emphasizing this statement.

The red light on Nick's podium was flashing, signaling the end of his time was fast approaching.

"It will not get better through treaties, or limiting our economy by mandating x or y. Do not fall for the rhetoric of the climate change con artists and their propaganda. Filling your children's heads full of junk science. Our planet is trying to kill us constantly. Earthquakes, hurricanes, volcanos, and the universe is as well, with meteors and sunspots. Just ask those dinosaurs."

"Climate change is real, but it is *not* solely man made, so it can't be controlled by man either. Any more than the weather. I guess the scientists can keep their jobs. I would just like a little more honesty.

There is too much money involved now. *You* should become a science skeptic. Trust but verify," suggested Nick to the audience.

"All research is funded by someone. Like anyone else who has their job paid for by others, they have to make their customer happy. If that customer wants the temperature to climb, the facts can certainly support that. Or they can be reported to show them going down. Both statistics exist. Bottom line, unfortunately, as I have said, there are too many conflicting 'facts'. They are all up for interpretation."

"Thank you, Senator," said Adam. "As a follow up, Madame Vice President, you said you were in favor of economic sanctions for countries like China, India, or Brazil if they fail to live up to the obligations in the Paris Accords. As you know, China is the second largest economy in the world and will pass us next year. Yet in the Accords they are classified as a new industrial state, which allows them to continue to grow their emissions while we and Europe have to reduce ours. How do you reconcile this?"

"Adam, unlike the Senator whose policy is to simply deny the science, as evidenced by his long-winded denial of a problem, I live in reality. The reality is we need to take on China and we need to be smart about it. We need to work with the other members of the Paris Accords to alter the status of China and hold them accountable to reduce their reliance on coal for energy," replied Lexi.

Governor Blackbird interrupted. "Madame Vice President, you and your administration were the ones who allowed China to annex large swaths of Africa where coal is abundant and where their Belt and Road initiative is used to force these countries to provide concessions to the Chinese or face the withdrawal of their support for this infrastructure."

"Governor, I don't think you are in a position to lecture me about coal considering the amount of oil and fracking being done in the Dakota's supporting those fossil fuels you claim to be against," she responded sarcastically.

And so it went, back-and-forth trading barbs. In every retort, they took a swipe at Nick. He did not try to join the conversation. Nor did he respond as they baited him, insulted him, and claimed he was a climate denier. After three of the five minutes of open debate, Nick had still not said a word. He merely stood tall, a bemused look on his face, looking from speaker to speaker, observing as they attacked him and each other.

"Senator, you seem awfully quiet. Do you not have a comment regarding China's continuing rise in emissions?" asked Adam.

"Of course, I do Adam. I have made my position clear in my book and time and time again in my rallies. China emits more than the US and Europe combined. We have reduced our carbon emissions voluntarily each year before joining Paris Accords. By joining, this administration gave away our sovereign authority for no gain. Since joining, we have reduced our economic output and put limits on all of our heavy industries, costing jobs and GDP," replied Nick calmly with confidence.

"During that same time, China has expanded their own industrial capabilities tenfold. Under *this* administration, while their emissions have risen 66% from 27% to almost 40% of global carbon emissions. Opening a coal fired power plant every week for 10 years will do that. They will not willingly stop. We need to hit them where it hurts to get them to stop. We need to stop buying stuff from them," finished Nick.

Lexi laughed and Governor Blackbird said, "you want a trade war with China?" They attacked Nick again for his out of touch ideas and proposals for the remaining time. Nick continued watching, again choosing not to respond.

"Time is up for that topic candidates," noted Adam. "On to the next question."

The debate continued through questions about racism, immigration, crime, the economy and foreign policy. Governor Blackbird took the middle ground in each argument, always leaning toward policies of compromise and negotiated settlements.

Lexi doubled down on the progressive platform, supporting the efforts to push CRT and ARL into the schools. Continuing to keep the borders open to the massive immigration of asylum seekers. Defunding police until reform was clear and exploring alternate incarceration models in spite of the rising crime.

Her economic policies were aimed at raising taxes on wealthy individuals and investing heavily in green energy and services jobs. Forcing corporations, the government agencies, and military to continue their DEI initiatives to ensure diversity of hires.

Finally, her foreign policy positions were globalist in nature, diminishing America's role as the sole superpower and relying more on the UN and other world-based organizations to create collaborative, global policies.

Nick, in contrast, was succinct and to the point, offering common sense solutions. Stop treating blacks and other minorities like they are victims, incapable of doing anything for themselves, without massive government interference and assistance.

Close the border and focus on the assimilation of existing illegals, becoming citizens over time, starting at the back of the line. No mass amnesty. Fund the police, enforce the laws, jail and deport the criminals. Reestablish law and order.

Get America back to work. Lower or eliminate corporate tax, repatriate corporate wealth, and move jobs, especially manufacturing jobs back to the US. Continue to lead and innovate in areas like automation and AI.

In foreign policy, look after America first, while *supporting* allies but expecting them to help protect themselves. Remove America from organizations who would have a say in limiting any American government action they deemed inappropriate.

At the end of each of Nick's answers, the crowd cheered. Adam reminded them to control themselves, to little avail. It quickly became a free-for-all with raucous cheering from the gallery for each of their candidates and boos for their opponents. It was more akin to a UFC bout than a debate.

In the open debate portion of each question, Governor Blackbird and Lexi each tried to insult and label Nick's policies as racist, anti-immigrant, pro-racist cop, profiteering at the expense of the working man and war mongering with America first type policies.

Nick remained calm and only entered the conversations to directly answer follow-up questions from Adam or questions from his opponents. He let them act in a petty and hysterical manner, using all kinds of insults in the hope he would lose his cool.

They tried to paint Nick as both anti-American and dangerous to democracy. Accusations of returning to segregation or a nostalgic America of the past, where white patriarchy thrived at the expense of other races or genders. Nick just ignored their slights, causing them to flail even more in their attempts to get him to get angry and retaliate. He never took the bait.

Nick responded to one question from Adam regarding media coverage, citing his own rallies and the selective use of the violent attacks without the context of showing the responses were in self-defense.

"Adam, it gives me no pleasure to reply to your question, but I will try to make my point. The American *Pravda* media are a cancer in our body. It is slowly eating away at our souls. I want everyone to stop and think for a second. Imagine you turned it all off for a month? The cares of the world would fall off your shoulders. You would be free."

"Free to focus on what matters: your family, your friends, your world around you as you see it, not as others tell you to see it. Forced to have face-to-face conversations. This is how life should be lived. Think about it. Your feelings of anxiety and fear, of worry and concern, unrest and depression, anger and disgust. They are all because you are listening to American *Pravda*."

"If you want to solve the problems of the world, turn off your TV and trade in your smart phone for a flip phone. You are the solution, not the problem. Wake up. Only you can solve this problem. Stop waiting for others to do it for you. If you wait, you will not like the outcome."

Nick's other highlight came from an unexpected source. As Lexi finished answering a question from Adam about experience necessary to handle foreign policy, citing her years of committee assignments, treaty negotiations, and representing the country overseas as the VP, Lexi asked Nick a rhetorical question.

"Speaking of experience, Senator, we all acknowledge your heroic deeds, but is it not strange to move from active duty in the Navy after twelve years, leaving as a lieutenant commander and taking a lesser rank of captain in the Air National Guard? Did this have anything to do with a particular operation, Task Force Echo, for which you were cited for insubordination to your superiors, as well as striking a superior officer?"

Lexi beamed as she continued, the audience leaning forward in anticipation at this unexpected accusation.

"Did you not, in fact, retire from active duty in the Navy because you were given a choice to leave or face court martial and a dishonorable discharge?" asked Lexi, smiling devilishly as the crowd gasped in surprise at the revelation.

Nick paused for a second, pondering. "Madame Vice President, many of my military records have unique security classifications because of my Naval Intelligence work just before and after 9/11. To have gotten that service record unsealed requires an act of Congress and perhaps even approval from several agencies of the three-letter type." Nick fixed Lexi with a stare as he continued. The smile on her face became strained.

"I know for a fact you *don't* have these required clearances. Nor the SAP or SCI clearances for these timeframes, either. I can only assume one of two people has committed a serious felony, violating our national security. Either you, Madame Vice President, or the person who punched me. In fact, this level of classification was placed on these records, not because of me, but because of who hit me, to protect *his* career." The smile was completely gone from Lexi's face now as she made a show of looking down as if she was writing a note.

"Now I could file a complaint with the Department of Justice, but we both know it would not be acted on, as the DOJ in your administration is famous for not actually investigating actual crimes. Especially by members of this administration or their family," said Nick in a sarcastic tone as a look of anger crossed Lexi's face.

"Instead, your DOJ is focused on stripping away the Constitutional rights of our fellow citizens. Using surveillance and data selectively to ruin the lives of anyone questioning your administration and for pure political gain. Since you brought it up. I *was* involved in a fight with a superior officer," the audience murmured at this admission.

"*After* he hit me first, I retaliated. We exchanged punches. I was given a choice at my court martial. Yes, I did choose to leave active duty in the Navy and transfer to the Air National Guard to continue to serve my country." Nick's voice rose as he made his points. Getting angry for the first time in the evening.

"Would you like to know what happened to the other officer? He too should have faced a court martial and demotion for striking a *junior* officer under his command. But he knew a better admiral than I did. He is now the Chairman of the Joint Chiefs, Admiral Jason Kensington."

The audience was buzzing in conversation at this unexpected tidbit. Lexi stared back at Nick impassively.

"Care to know what we fought about, Madame Vice President? Since you have already committed the *felony* bringing up this highly classified topic? You should ask *him* about Task Force Echo. That is what we fought about. You will find out what kind of Admiral you have as the leader of the Joint Chiefs." said Nick, looking into the camera while Lexi tried to remain composed at her podium.

"I might also add that from the time I joined the Air National Guard, I volunteered to be deployed the entire eight years I was in the Guard without rotating home. *Not once.* I passed up opportunities to attend other non-combat assignments deemed politically important to rising to the rank of admiral or general in our current military."

"Instead, I did what our military is supposed to be concerned with. I chose to fight. To protect my fellow servicemen and women. I had no desire to punch my ticket and kiss the political ass necessary to rise. You might ask the Admiral how much time he spent in actual combat, on the line. Not back in HQ."

"I did this so others in the Guard with families would not have to risk their life being deployed to a war zone for months or even years while members of our regular army, who are paid to defend us full time, were instead being deployed to Korea, Germany, Okinawa, and other non-combat deployments." The red light on Nick's podium was solid red, time having expired for this rebuttal. Nick ignored it, figuring he was owed time he did not use in the other rebuttals. Adam did not stop him.

"If you bothered to check records that are *not* sealed, you will find I was one of the longest serving active duty servicemen in the war zone from any branch in the 20 years of the Iraq and Afghanistan wars. In fact, perhaps you should use your muscle to get all my military records unsealed. *I* have nothing to hide," smiled Nick.

"Nice try. Your attempts to defame me fall short and show once again the true nature of your character and that of your administration and its leaders. I look forward to testifying at the DOJ or congressional investigation of this felony disclosure," finished Nick smugly.

Nick's supporters cheered loudly as Lexi started to speak. Adam cut her off, asking for quiet. "That is all the time for the foreign policy question. We must move on to the last question."

#

"Son of a bitch. Did you know that?" asked Denise, looking at the monitor from a conference room down a hallway from the stage, turning to Chuck and Earl.

"Nope," admitted Chuck. "You know, Earl?"

"Not a clue."

"I wonder what he did to earn all those medals in his safe? Now it becomes clearer. I still think we should have been shouting from the rooftops if he has all these accolades," growled Denise in frustration again.

"Denise, you know that is not his style. He said it was classified so much even the VP can't see it. Maybe *he* can't talk about it either?" wondered Earl.

"I think there may be a lot we don't know about our boss," said Chuck in a questioning tone.

#

"Shit, she is getting killed." cried Harriet, watching on monitors in a different conference room nearby. Her head in her hands.

"Not good. Where did that come from? It sure wasn't in prep. If she accessed compartmented classified files without the proper approvals, Turner is right. It is a steaming pile of shit," added Mel, thinking aloud.

"She's the Vice President. How can there be stuff she can't access?"

"Trust me Harriet, presidents come and go, but the CIA, FBI, Homeland, NSA, and military span many administrations and they have secrets they don't share with anyone, unless they absolutely have to. I've been trying to get to this redacted data on Turner and I haven't had any luck at all. And I'm *not* going through normal channels. Obviously, Lexi found someone who could or else Kensington gave her this tidbit. If he did, he is an idiot, and he committed the felony,"

"Any idea what a Task Force Echo is?" prompted Harriet.

"Nope, and frankly, I don't want to know. I'm sure it is a cluster fuck and Saint Turner must have either tried to stop it or provided intel to tell them not to execute it. I know enough about Turner to know his sense of honor. I would not want to be the Chairman after this. Crap, just something else we have to deal with." Mel shook his head. "It may be time to ask him to resign his position to take one for the team. I just wish these people would stick with the plan and stop ad-libbing. It is killing us. Turner is just too fucking nimble."

#

"It is now time for closing statements candidates. Governor, you are first followed by the Vice President and then the Senator. I would ask that you respect each other's time. Please refrain from interruption or comment. There will be no rebuttal to any of these comments. At the end of the Senator's statement, the debate will officially end. Thank you. Governor, you are first," announced Adam.

Governor Blackbird touched on his experience in leading a state and his time as a congressman. His goal was to reduce taxes and tighten immigration, stabilize healthcare, and work collaboratively with corporation and the UN on climate change initiatives to help save the planet.

He vowed to work with law enforcement to ensure laws were equally applied and any racist tendencies or profiling would be eradicated. He touched on his abilities as a negotiator to reach a middle ground on key issues at home and abroad, with both allies and enemies.

Finally, he acknowledged he had made mistakes, but he had also done what he could to ensure their financial stability and saw to it that his 'other' family had not suffered. He closed with an exhortation to the voters to pick moderation rather than the radical ideas of Lexi or Nick and to 'heal our wounds' and bring people together in compromise. This was his goal.

"Thank you, Governor. Madame Vice President," said Adam.

She stood tall in her expertly tailored skirt and suit jacket, tapered to highlight her still attractive former model figure. Lexi was beautiful, confident, and exuded competence.

"We are at a crossroads in America," she said. "We face a crisis in our society where our past injustices can now be rectified. For our entire history, we have suppressed black Americans, preventing them from having equal opportunity, equal status, and equal success. Today we can break this cycle, to ensure equity of outcome and position."

"The free market has been allowed to pick winners and losers without regard for roadblocks we removed for whites and put in place for brown, black, and female Americans. This is slowly changing in the schools and in the corporations. We must continue this push. Raising generations of children taught without bias and without privilege. Understanding our priorities must be equity, climate change, real integration, and making sure the haves do not continue to amass obscene wealth on the backs of the poor and misfortunate any longer."

"This goes beyond just paying their fair share. It goes to equal participation in the cost of fixing these problems and ensuring all have equal access to school, healthcare, jobs, higher education, and safe neighborhoods."

"We must get our own house in order before we can hope to show or tell others how to change their own. Our participation in global affairs should no longer be as the arbiter of who can and cannot do this or that. It needs to be as a collaborative partner in global organizations ensuring cooperation and compliance with policies and practices benefiting all citizens of the entire planet."

"No longer should we be the sole beneficiary of our innovation and geographic location at the expense of those in Africa, Asia, or South America. There can be equal prosperity if we are willing to share the burden of lifting the downtrodden peoples of this planet. It is our penance for taking advantage of situations for our own wellbeing, while disregarding the harm we have caused."

"It is time for America to once again be a shining beacon on a hill, but to put our money and our resources to not only improving our own standing but to share that wealth in helping everyone."

"Finally, it is time to end the hateful rhetoric of the right. Those who fight against this progress, those who continue to hang onto the Constitution as if Moses brought it down from heaven. The time of the capitalist putting profit over people is now officially over. The fallacy of equality of opportunity, of pulling one up by the bootstrap, is a fairy tale for almost all but the luckiest among us."

"When one race starts with such a head start, it is no surprise they end up with the wealth and the power, leaving the others trying to jump and grab the first rung of the ladder. Well, this stops now. America will be a free and fair society, ensuring equality of outcome wherever possible going forward. No one will be left behind simply because they are black or brown, gay or straight, born rich or poor," finished Lexi. Her supporters in the crowd cheered, causing Adam to admonish them for this outburst.

"Thank you, Madame Vice President. Senator Turner, your closing statement," prompted Adam.

Nick looked into the camera with a firm look. "The Party has failed. It could not convince a majority of Americans its views, policies and overall ideology are better than Constitutional safeguards. You don't need to be told this; all you have to do is look at what they do when they are in power. It starts with attempts to silence all who dissent. Then they implement economic sanctions, as draconian mandates and regulations against corporations and citizens who do not agree with their policies."

"This is the opposite of a free market where ideas and supply and demand are the norm. The Party forces organizations to do its bidding with regulations that are not voted on or accepted through popular acclaim. Rather, they rule through executive order or the bully pulpit of social media and news organizations."

"The best way I can describe this is the Party is a Home Owners Association. People who inevitably end up in charge of HOAs have one goal. To make you live the way they want to live. This is why HOAs exist. They wouldn't be needed if the minority didn't need to force the majority to obey. They can't convince you their ideas are best, so they instead force you to comply, or you are fined. Eventually, you leave the HOA to get your freedom to choose for yourself back. Does this not sound like our government when the Party is in control?" The audience laughed, clearly getting the analogy. Adam asked for quiet.

"The Party has one goal. Use the Government HOA to make the rules for every aspect of your life. All under the guise of making things better for you. The more they control the levers of everyday services, the more they control the message, its distribution, and, most importantly, its enforcement. We already see this in the migration of people from blue state HOAs to free red states. Unfortunately, there is no other neighborhood in the US we can move to in order to escape their federal HOA."

"Our government is one of promise one thing and deliver the polar opposite. The word for this is hypocrisy. It is our fault, because we keep sending the same type of people to Washington and it just keeps doing the same thing. Regardless of who they are or even which party they are in."

"We need candidates who pledge to leave their 'plows in the field', serve for a short time, then return to those fields. Dramatically reduce the taxes and the expenditures of the government. Reduce our reliability on foreign countries for products and loans, especially China but others as well. We need to be an example and to lead by example. Encourage others to be like us because they want to, not because we want them to." Nick smacked a hand on the podium to emphasize his point.

"We are members of the global community, but we can no longer be the world's policeman. Our livelihood and our ability to continue to stay free must be preserved. Our system of government is better, with freedom of thought, freedom of action, freedom of speech."

"These are all ingredients in a recipe that has provided the world with innovation and served as a catalyst to make the world a better place. Yes, we make mistakes. But one hallmark of our democracy is the ability to pick ourselves back up and try again. Getting better until we succeed."

"This is the America we deserve and the America we all own. If we do not preserve this, we have no one to blame but ourselves. Your vote matters. Please do not squander it by believing the bullshit you are served daily by candidates, ads, and talking heads who are all being paid to convince you to vote for them."

"They do not care a wit about you, only your taxes, your vote and their power. Rely on yourself, not government. Reliance on government is just another form of slavery. Do not choose slavery over freedom. Use your vote, while it still matters and while you still can," finished Nick.

Both Lexi and Blackbird tried to break in after to rebut parts of Nick's closing statement, as Nick's supporters stood and shouted and cheered. The moderator killed all the candidate's mic's.

"Thank you, Governor Blackbird, Vice President Smythe-Thomas and Senator Turner. This concludes this presidential debate. Thank you to our studio audience and everyone watching. Please remember to go out and vote. Thank you and have a good evening," finished Adam as the cameras stopped and the lights came up.

Lexi was staring icily at Nick, who stared back, with no emotion on his face. Governor Blackbird simply left with his people, neither acknowledging his opponents or the moderator. Nick moved over to the moderator's table and shook Adam's hand.

"Thank you for trying to keep it civil."

"I did a pretty shitty job of it. Now I know what a kindergarten teacher feels like. Geez, you'd think they'd know how petty all those antics made them look," answered Adam, shaking his hand. "That's why

I used the mic spike to shut them down after your statement. I didn't want anymore of this crap."

"Well, I think you did a good job, considering what you were up against. You know you are going to catch it from all sides, for letting them talk, for stopping them, for letting the crowd boo them, and cheer me. You are going to be swimming in hate mail," laughed Nick.

"I'm an EXN Anchor, I am used to it," laughed Adam, gathering up papers. He looked up. "I see the Vice President and Governor are expressing their displeasure by not even bothering to shake my hand."

"Nor mine," shrugged Nick.

Adam handed off his microphone to a technician and looked around to make sure no other recording devices or mics were on, then he turned to Nick in a low voice.

"Nick, you mopped the floor with them. By not taking their bait, by not responding when they attacked. Sticking to your talking points, and not playing their game. They must have realized how bad they looked by the end of the debate. That's really why they didn't come up to thank me. They are pissed you were even in the debate. I just hope it is not too little too late for you. You should have been in all of them. Your polls were as high as Perot or Anderson. They both got into debates as third-party candidates."

"Well, at least we got in one. As always, we take what we can get. Thanks again," said Nick, shaking his hand one more time and walking off stage with Earl, Chuck, and Denise.

#

"All right, let me have it," said Nick, turning to look at Denise and Chuck in the back seats, as Earl drove them back to the DC campaign office from George Mason.

Denise was on the phone.

"Nick, I think you did fabulously, considering this was your first ever debate. Talk about going straight to the majors," smiled Chuck.

Denise ended her call.

"That was Margie. She gave me a rundown on what is going on. The liberal networks are trying to trash you, but really, they don't have any petulant moments from you to show. Your statements were succinct, and your message came through loud and clear. They are spending their time on your 'radical' policies," laughed Denise, as she recited Margie's points.

"The usual then," laughed Nick. "If that's the best they can do, I'd say we are OK."

"EXN is showing all the hysterical moments from Blackbird and Lexi attacking each other and you. They're also showing how well you handled it all, staying above the fray. Some of the talking heads are commenting on Lexi bringing up your service record and what kind of clearance or confidential status your record must have to require an act of Congress to view. Everyone wants to know what a Task Force Echo is," asked Denise in a questioning tone.

"First, it is *the* Task Force Echo. Good luck getting that info. No one wants that revealed. Trust me. Least of all the Chairman of the Joint Chiefs. I would really like to know where she got the info. There just aren't that many people with access, and quite a few of them have died in the last 15 years," said Nick.

"So why is your record so hard to access?" asked Earl innocently from his driver's seat.

"Nice try. There have already been enough felonies committed tonight. I'm not adding to the pile," replied Nick with a laugh.

"Actually, Margie said that is probably the biggest story coming out of the debate, how you handed Lexi her head when she implied you were less than honest about your military service," commented Denise.

"I welcome them looking through my records or at least the ones they can get too. Hell, even the compartmented ones protect others more than me. That one I'm not worried about. Besides, they'll ignore all the Freedom of Information Act requests. How is social media doing?" asked Nick.

"That clip is trending the most. There are a few others but most of them are memes about the VP and Blackbird being righteously indignant about your positions. The EXN ratings are higher for this debate than any of the other ones. All good there. I don't know how many voters we converted, but a lot of Lexi and Blackbird supporters got to see you in action for the first time. They had to come away feeling like you looked way more in control than either of the others," said Denise.

"Too bad so many have already voted. Having debates after mail in balloting is underway makes no sense at all," lamented Chuck.

"True. If I were a socialist, I thought her closing comments were pretty powerful. I could see a lot of young people and minorities agreeing with her," acknowledged Nick.

"Definitely the best part of her night and at the end, so that is good for her. She made implementing socialism sound like birthday cake, free college, and unlimited free phone plans for all. It is always a compelling argument and one tough to counter when your solution requires hard work instead," agreed Denise.

"I don't know how many undecided voters watch these debates, anyway. The best we can hope for is a few of Blackbird's supporters see Nick as a better choice and come to our side," declared Chuck.

"So, what is the plan now? It's ten days until election day. Tell me what I'm doing."

"Press conference in the morning. Maybe get you on Tommy again tomorrow night. We need to be prepared for Lexi to try something in the next week to suppress voter turnout," said Chuck.

"Nick, please, can we get an official video out to the grassroots orgs to start telling the truth to the pollsters? When people see how much you 'gain' in the polls, they may be inclined to jump from Blackbird onto the potential winning ticket," pleaded Denise.

"Yes, I can film it in the morning. It is time to release the hounds. I can mention it at the Arizona state fair. Even I am curious to see where I am in the polls. Maybe we can force Lexi into another miscalculation," wished Nick.

"Let's hope she is past any shenanigans," said Denise.

"You mean before they start stuffing ballot boxes?" added Chuck.

"That has already started, I can assure you," stated Nick.

Chapter 13

Nick and team were in their caravan of Suburbans, heading out of Phoenix. He'd spent Sunday evening speaking at his last state fair appearance and he'd just finished up a quick call into the Monday morning news program on EXN.

"I'm gonna miss those state fairs. I enjoyed the crowds of hardworking, everyday people. And the bands," responded Nick wistfully as Earl drove them.

"I'll miss the big crowds," lamented Denise, looking down at her tablet.

"That too," admitted Nick.

"Nick, tone down some of the rhetoric. I know you're mad, but it is really easy to get your followers spun up. You keep preaching violence is not the answer and then you get up there and are just so angry," cautioned Denise.

"I try, but talking about it just makes my blood boil. Luckily, Earl came out and told me to cool it last night. Thanks, buddy."

Earl just nodded from the driver's seat in response.

"Just watch it as we hit the home stretch. Keep it positive and issues based. Mistakes this late in the game are fatal."

Nick turned to give Denise a quick look.

"To the campaign, I mean," responded Denise, reddening and now flustered.

"Hey, I lifted the moratorium on telling the truth to pollsters. And mentioned the new credit union. I should get credit for those," responded Nick in a hurt tone.

"About time on the polling. Let's hope it is not too late to make a difference. And lighten up on the reporters. You didn't have to be so mean to Billy and Autumn for just asking about Task Force Echo. You know they have to."

Nick turned to look at Denise in the row of seats behind him. "I would prefer if they spent their time inquiring about my October surprises."

"Old news Nick. Old News," finished Denise shrugging.

#

Heading out of Phoenix, they began a trek across the swing state of Arizona, rallying voters to get out to the polls in a week. Arizona was incredibly important for all the candidates, along with Georgia and, to a lesser extent, Nevada. These were the states where it truly was a tossup. All had been won by mere thousands in the past few elections.

They stopped in Martha Summer's discount store parking lots in Prescott, Flagstaff, and Clarkdale, which was as close as they could find one to Sedona. The villagers having voted several times to not allow the construction of one of Martha's stores.

In Sedona, Nick drank coffee, talking to veterans at a VFW and wait staff and patrons at local restaurants. Nick joked at one, in response to a comment about not having Martha's stores in town, about how Sedona was like Boulder.

"Fifty square miles surrounded by reality."

He got the requisite laughs at the dichotomy between the uber elite enclaves and the necessity of all the service workers who worked in them having to live and shop miles away because of the lack of affordable housing or shopping for *them* in Sedona.

At each, Margie implored Nick to stay on schedule. He smiled at her as he refilled his coffee at stop after stop. Sitting on picnic tables and in folding chairs surrounded by everyday people at each one.

He laughed and told jokes and listened to stories of inflation, disastrous VA visits and the difficulty of surviving on fixed incomes. Nick connected with each group. Remembering names and sharing his own stories from other folks just like them.

Hundreds at a time at the VFW, American Legion, Elks, various restaurants and thousands in Martha's parking lots. Each time they left, there was no doubt those they spoke to would both vote and for whom. Denise fretted as she realized it was not enough.

Lexi had unleashed millions of dollars in attack ads against Nick in all the swing states. Targeting women, seniors, minorities, and young voters. Relentlessly making the point Nick intended to make their lives harder. Offering them no help.

No student loan forgiveness, no higher minimum wages, fewer social services or smaller safety nets. Lexi promised them more of everything. She knew how to play the game and what motivated people to vote.

Driving between Flagstaff and Las Vegas in the evening, Denise went over the next day's schedule with Nick.

"We'll either have to stop somewhere with good internet or stay in the hotel room long enough for you to dial into Brad Hudson's radio show. I don't want you dropping the signal if we are on the road."

"He's on from noon to three, eastern, right? Took over Limbaugh's spot?" asked Nick.

Denise made a sour face at Nick's reference.

"Yes, he did. Kept most of his audience as well," answered Denise in a tone making Nick turn to look at her. He smiled at her.

"Didn't like Limbaugh much?" he asked.

"Hardly. He was a pain in my and my candidate's ass for too many years."

"Did you ever bother to listen to any of his shows?"

"Are you kidding? I didn't have to," retorted Denise.

"Denise, you know me enough by now to know what I think about folks who make judgements without actually listening to or reading original sources." Nick raised a hand as Denise made to respond.

"If you had listened, you would have been treated to often the *only* conversations about the consequences of decisions being made by *all* administrations. Beyond the bluster and the humor, he did more to educate a swath of Americans than any other media or universities."

"I think you mean brainwash. Skulls full of mush. Dittoheads. Femi-nazis. That sounds like open minded conversations to me," responded Denise, her tone dripping in satire.

Nick smiled and shrugged. "That was his appeal. It was a wink, wink, nod, nod, kind of humor. Deflecting those who didn't listen to the words. They simply rose to the bait. Meanwhile, he educated voters on the important facts of the day and the unintended consequences of so many decisions, and why they happened. Say what you will, dismiss him, and now Hudson. These guys are doing their part to make people think. Limbaugh and his Operation Chaos idea are the reason I told people to lie to pollsters."

"Great, another reason to hate him," stated Denise, looking down at her tablet. "Back to his successor. He was really tough on you about your support for Dusty. Then, like everyone else, he came back stronger than ever after. You need to use this time to rouse his base to come out and vote for you. They are mostly conservatives, so stay away from your abortion stance. And your plans for amnesty for the illegals. Probably best to stay away from your universal catastrophic care tax too," counseled Denise, frowning as she added more topics likely to get Nick crossways with Hudson's conservative listeners.

"Denise, you aren't giving them enough credit. Despite the Party rhetoric, I find the conservatives are *not* one issue voters. By the way, my plan is not amnesty. It is *assimilation* over a period of time. We'll see where the conversation takes us. Conservative does not automatically equal religious right. Hell, if JFK were alive today, *he'd* be a conservative and maybe even Opposition."

"Don't offer that tidbit either, please," counseled Denise with a growl.

Nick smiled back. "We can make the call from our hotel and then hit the road. It won't set us back too far if we don't leave until mid-morning Pacific time. I can make some other calls in the morning or visit a breakfast place or two if you like."

"OK, I had hoped to get in a few more visits around Vegas before you talk at UNLV. Or rather Martha's store down the road since the University canceled our talk there. We have paid for buses to drive them from the University to the parking lot. I think a local eatery is even donating lunch. We'll turn it into a plus. Another black eye for the 'unbiased' university systems," proclaimed Denise, making notes on the tablet and looking up at Margie. She nodded and started drafting emails.

Margie's day now comprised rearranging Nick's visits to VFWs and other parking lots as he demolished the day's schedule with each first visit of the day. Just like every day on the road with Nick.

The various Turner Rabble and other grassroots orgs spread the word and gathered the folks to turn out at the various stops. Coordinating all this was turning out to be a full-time job. Margie would coordinate with Steve back in Denver. He'd spread the word to the various teams who communicated primarily through chat groups on Hibi.

While they liked to broadcast the schedule for major events so they could film them, these spontaneous ones, they kept as secret as possible. Trying to keep the protesters from showing up and seeking headlines. Everyone on the team and most of the supporters got a charge out of the clandestine nature of their operations.

Often protesters would show up, sometimes even buses loaded with them, only to find the talk over and Nick long gone. This added to the excitement amongst his supporters. Like they were getting away with something.

#

Nick sat alone in his hotel room, speaking into his phone as he dialed into the final hour of Brad Hudson's radio show.

"Welcome Senator. Sorry it has taken so long to get you on the program."

"In all fairness to your listeners, Brad, some of that was me. I didn't want to come on and talk about the trial or my support before it completed. Maybe that was a mistake in retrospect. And call me Nick, please."

Brad laughed. "Wow, that's a lot to unpack in only the first sentence. In any case, you are here now. Let's start."

They talked about Nick's various stances, and he listened to Brad explaining the concerns conservatives around America had. Rising crime, an open border, fentanyl in the schools, and progressive controlled curriculum in the schools. Weak foreign policy, emboldened enemies, out-of-control spending, interest rates, and inflation.

After the opening segment, responding to all the things Brad and his audience hated, Nick finally had enough.

"Brad, glad to hear everything you guys are pissed about. What are you doing about it?" challenged Nick.

"Excuse me?"

"I meant what I said. What are you and your listeners going to do about it? Guess what, electing me president isn't going to change any of this. I'm not a miracle worker. All of us got us here. Me, you, and *all* of your listeners. Why did this happen? We only have to look in the mirror to see who is responsible."

Brad laughed nervously, not sure if Nick was joking. "We did our part and voted against the President and his party."

Nick interrupted. "Your part? Voting is only the start. The Opposition has shown time and time again they are incapable of coming together to stop any of this. They are good at coming on your show and complaining about how bad it sucks. Including congressmen. Well, guess what? Get off your ass and change it. If voting isn't enough, figure out what else you can do."

"That worked really well on January 6th," remarked Brad.

"Exactly. That is clearly not what you need to do when you lose. Why did you lose? It wasn't just the presidency. It was your congressman and senators. Now it's your state congress and your sheriffs and district attorneys and judges. What's worse, when you do somehow achieve a slim majority, you squander it with internal bickering and petty squabbles. I'll give my former Party credit. They work in concert. When they are in power, there is no doubt about the agenda and doing what it takes to change the way things work. They aren't the problem. *You* are."

"Wow Senator, this is *not* what I was expecting. Frankly, I'm surprised. I expected you to convince us to vote for you. Not to blame us," responded Brad, somewhat miffed.

Nick laughed. "Brad, that's the problem. You get all mad when someone tells you the truth. You know, that's good. I want you mad.

I want you mad, not because I tell you how feckless your efforts have been, but because you can't come together until you *are* mad. It is time to come out of the shadows, wake up, stand up, and act. Quit calling into shows like this and complaining about how bad the Party is."

There was a pause of dead air as Brad processed Nick's statement.

"Did you hang up?" asked Nick, laughing.

"No, I'm here. I'm just thinking about what you said."

"Brad, obviously, I would like conservatives to vote for me. They sure aren't going to vote for Lexi. If it is between me or Blackbird or staying home, this is exactly what I am talking about. If you want to sit around complaining about how bad everything is, then please stay at home. Eventually, you'll realize you should have stood up for something. Before it was too late. Maybe they take your guns, or your house, or your ability to earn a wage. One day Tommy goes to school and comes home as Tammy. Maybe that's fine, but maybe you as the parent might want to know this is happening before it does. It will be something unless you swear fealty to their progressive policies. If you don't want to live that life. Now is your chance."

"We've had Senator Garcia on often and he agrees you are the only hope. Yet, you never tell us how you'll reverse all the harm the administration has done," pointed out Brad.

"That's because I can't Brad."

"That's not what we want to hear."

"Which goes back to my original statement. You are the problem. Because you don't realize there is no easy fix. You have to be as committed as they've been for the last hundred years. We didn't get here overnight. They took over the schools, slowly changing what was taught. Removing the parent and the family from the equation. Religion was marginalized and along with it the concepts of right and wrong. Ethics and morals learned by example and reinforced by two-parent households, church and schools. All slowly eliminated or neutered."

"They removed the power from the congress and handed it to the lobbyists and we did nothing. The deep state of federal departments are filled with career bureaucrats who *know* what the result is *they* want to achieve. They just slow down when the Opposition is in power, but they are never stopped. They decide the regulations and they are in charge of enforcement. By the way, that is called totalitarianism. We sure aren't voting on these regulations. Nor do they have to answer to voters. They decide how things change. Not the politicians. Not your elected officials, and certainly not your president."

"Geez, Senator, that is not a very hopeful message. If your goal is to get us to stay home and start drinking, you are doing a great job," commented Brad.

"Brad, I'm serious. You want the blueprint? Here it is. Elect me president. I'll start chipping away at the wall. But it is a gigantic wall. In two years you have to elect congressmen and women who pledge to abide by the Constitution. To reduce the size of the federal government. To return much of the work to the states. To significantly reduce the cost of government by eliminating the federal departments. And you have to do this at all levels of government. City, state and fed."

Nick paused. Brad did not interrupt, so he continued.

"The only way you do this is a united congress of moderates who can pass this legislation. It requires convincing a majority of citizens in the states to ratify the necessary amendments at *the state level* to make these changes not easily reversible. If it is just an executive order, it can be overturned by the next administration. You need a coalition of like-minded everyday citizens, *using the Constitution*, putting differences like abortion aside and uniting because of the eighty or ninety percent of things we *can* agree on. Short of this, the alternative is rule by the progressives. Totalitarianism," finished Nick.

"Senator, that sounds like a lot of work, with no guarantee of success."

Nick laughed. "Brad, when you started, did you ever in your wildest dream think you would be sitting here talking to fifteen million listeners daily?"

He could now hear Brad laughing.

"Exactly. You had a goal. Get ten more listeners. Get another affiliate. Add another hour or another advertiser. The goal was never to achieve fifteen million listeners. The goal was incremental progress. Do more, get more listeners. How did you do that? You created content they wanted to hear. You spread your message to your followers, who spread your message to their friends and family. You made provocative statements to get coverage from media. Even negative coverage made people curious. A percentage of them liked what they heard and stayed. This is how you made change happen. It is the same thing we need to do now."

"Nick, I need you to write the opening of my biography. In a minute, you summarized my journey. I never thought of applying it to our current political situation," admitted Brad.

"Brad, we have to start somewhere. Every journey starts with a first step. You push back and eventually, if you have the stamina, strength, and *resolve*, you stop their forward progress. Then you start pushing back from the far left toward the center. Where most sane people and common sense live. Where policies can achieve consensus without a bully pulpit, cancel culture to stifle dissent, or the megaphone of American *Pravda* making it *seem* like you have majority support. The challenge is to stop it there at the center."

"Nick, how I wish we could have had you on sooner. Especially before people started filling out mail in ballots. Especially any who have already voted for Blackbird."

"Brad, the far left is very good at mobilizing and making everyone else feel like they have no voice. We have a voice. We just need to use it like they do. No one will stop this if we don't. Stop worrying about being canceled. Stop shopping at online vendors whose principles you don't agree with. Stop giving your money to billionaires who turn around and use it to fund progressive causes or Ivy league schools where antisemitism is enshrined and celebrated. Sacrifice your latte or you next-day shipping. Freedom is *not* convenient. Go read a book about what your ancestors did to survive Valley Forge. Keeping the spark of freedom alive while their British enemies sat warm and toasty in *their* houses they'd confiscated in Philadelphia. How they endured, sacrificed, and died to enable us to have the freest and most principled government the planet has seen. If we don't squander it."

"I can agree with you there, Nick. We have forgotten how we got where we are and the sacrifice it took. No one is left who lived through the Depression. Our kids *and* most adults don't know what it means to do without. Even our poor live like kings compared to half the world."

"Brad, there is so much good information on the sacrifices some of our parents and all our grand and great grandparents made. They and the soldiers of the Civil War, Guadalcanal, Normandy and even Vietnam and Afghanistan all gave the last full measure not just for us, but for the ideal our country represents. We cannot do a disservice to their memories. To their *sacrifice*, by not standing up now when we are called to risk our livelihood to continue to preserve this for our children. Our D-day moment is approaching."

Nick was talking with his hands, as if exhorting a crowd, even though he was speaking through a phone.

"If not this election, then soon. We have to stand up or die trying, just as they did. Our ancestors had to fight and die to give us the privilege of making these changes with a *vote*. We don't have to do the same thing they did to stop this. We can do it with a simple vote. Let us understand this and use it while we still can. We still have a choice. If we don't use it, we may not have it in the future. Then we'll face more dire choices."

"I hope my audience realizes what you are saying and not just the words. No one but us can fix our problems."

"That's right Brad."

"We're running close to time, Nick. I wanted to ask you a question about the debanking. Have you found a bank?"

"We have Brad, and thanks for asking. As I said last week, one has to consider who you bank with, knowing these companies have this level of control over your ability to cash a check or pay a bill. Banks who can kick you out of the entire banking system without warning or appeal. Literally, they decide whether or not you can spend your money. This was an eye opener."

"Nick, that is truly troubling. The power they have. To debank anyone, anytime, with no excuse or an ability to defend yourself against the reason. It seems to go very much against our democratic principles," noted Brad in a concerned tone.

"I agree. Luckily, we were banking temporarily at Everett Spalding's and Martha Summer's employee owned credit unions. They worked with Jeremy Kwan, the owner of Hibi and the 2J's forming a new credit union where all are welcome. Freedom to Choose for Yourself or F2CFY. I believe it is now chartered and our funds will shift to them. I didn't want any of Martha or Everett's employees who disagree with my stances to be mad about my using their banks. I encourage everyone to decide for themselves if this kind of action is fair or just. F2CFY is open to anyone," finished Nick.

"I'm just glad you could overcome this obvious attempt to cripple your campaign. When private enterprise resorts to open warfare against a candidate, that crosses the line. I don't care what you say. When the three biggest banks in the US decide to debank you on the same day with no notice. You can't tell me that was not coordinated. You also can't tell me someone in the administration didn't have them do this. I've been the victim of so many attempts to cancel our advertisers. It is about time we start making our choices known and spend our dollars to support those choices, just like you said," ended Brad.

"Brad, everyone is free to do as they choose. I am not telling anyone what to do or whom to vote for or bank with. Thank you for having me."

"Nick, thank you. If you get a chance, tune in tomorrow, and hear what kind of responses we get from the call in guests."

"I suspect every minute of my time is going to be spent in a car or a parking lot talking to anyone willing to stand still long enough to listen."

"Good luck and God Bless senator. You really are our only hope for a stable and safe future."

"Thanks."

Chapter 14

"Nick, even before you hung up, we were seeing posts claiming you were calling for an armed revolution after you lose," said Margie as they pulled out of the hotel parking lot.

"Predictable. Take this down exactly as I say it, Margie."

'*To all members of American* Pravda. *Please get a copy of the complete transcript. Please report on exactly what was said. Any stories from this point forward, misreporting, or suggesting I "called for a revolution or armed resistance," will result in an immediate defamation lawsuit and a referral to the Department of Homeland Security, Disinformation Governance Board for review. See you in court.*'

The team just smiled as Nick narrated the exact phrases he wanted in the press release.

"You implied other things might be necessary," countered Denise.

"Dire choices are not the same as calling for open rebellion or an armed revolution. That is merely their opinion and interpretation. Both of which are seditious statements *they* are making, attributing to me, and trying to gaslight folks into believing I said them. They have used this playbook in the past against other candidates. I'm sure Penrose or Duane would love to take these cases on."

Margie laughed. "I'm sure you're right on that one."

"Especially Duane. I think he is having flashbacks to his protest days," laughed Denise.

"Thanks for choosing your words so carefully on Hudson's show," smiled Margie too.

"I'm well trained," replied Nick as Denise guffawed.

"Right. Trained my ass."

They flew from Vegas to Reno late Tuesday afternoon after his rally to six thousand in Vegas. He spoke to another five thousand in a parking lot at one of Martha's stores in Reno. Since it was private property, they'd gotten smarter and hired groups of security to prevent both the ARL and Antifa protesters from interfering.

This prohibition now also included not allowing any Gabriel's Angel's agitators. This usually led to some skirmishes, but it was on the perimeter of the events, nowhere near where Nick was typically setup on a makeshift stage of stacked pallets from the stores.

With Reno, they used their underground networks and chat groups to change the venue at the last minute to the other side of town and a different store than the one listed. They kept a couple of cameras on the old site to catch the befuddled protestors as they walked into the parking lot, only to find nothing more than a few parked RVs.

Neill and Ellie were barnstorming the rust belt states of Pennsylvania, West Virginia, Ohio, Michigan, finishing in Wisconsin and Minnesota. Their security detail drove all night between cities. Traveling on a tour bus rented to the campaign from one of the music acts Nick spoke in front of at many state fairs.

They'd offered it for free, but Denise quickly pointed out they needed to pay something for it to avoid controversy. Senator Garcia was speaking for Nick in the Carolinas. Trying to rally the religious conservatives of both states to his cause. It was all hands on deck a week before the election.

Even as they played 'hide the rally site' with the protesters, Lexi was rallying folks in the Northeast. She was drawing crowds of twenty thousand at stadiums and arenas. Her message was increasingly aimed at Nick after the disastrous debate performance. She doubled down on Nick's lack of experience and his propensity to say what he thought.

She painted a bleak picture of a Nick Turner administration. One where abortions would return to the back alleys, immigrants would be turned away or allowed to drown tangled in the barbed wire they would string in the Rio Grande. How immigrant children would be separated from their parents as they were being rounded up for deportation en masse back to their origin countries regardless of the asylum status.

As the world increasingly turned toward conflict, experienced leadership, like she showed defusing the latest Israeli-Hamas situation, was needed to restore order to the world. Turner would immediately pull the US out of the UN and any other world organizations, delegitimizing the foreign policy of the country, endangering both the safety and economic wellbeing of the entire nation, if not the world.

The crowds cheered loudly at Lexi's pronouncements and the airwaves were filled with pundits and stories about her crowd sizes, her superior leadership, the adulation of her followers, and the commanding lead in the polls. Task Force Echo, or the breach of national security by Lexi or Admiral Kensington, was never mentioned by anyone in American *Pravda*. Their curiosity was non-existent.

Media ad buys were saturating the airwaves with pro-Lexi and anti-Blackbird and Turner ads in all the swing states, specifically in the swing counties. The Party coffers were overflowing with funds. Money was not an issue.

Awareness and get out the vote were the key to victory. Nobody's ground game was as good as the Party's. Thousands of motivated young college-aged women were going door to door harvesting votes from nursing homes, urban neighborhoods and everywhere they were needed.

Thousands more were mobilized to drive those who wanted to vote in person, with transportation lined up to the polls on election day. Lexi and her team were ready.

Chapter 15

Nick and his team were finishing a barbecue picnic with his Texas ground teams in the town of Georgetown, north of Austin. Nick spent Thursday rallying voters in Allen, Fort Worth, San Antonio and then north Austin. At each he had overflow crowds of greater than 25,000, in high school football stadiums.

Just proving everything was bigger in Texas. Nick joked he wasn't quite as popular as high school football, since he couldn't fill the stadiums. One emcee who introduced him responded to his comment, saying they did only give people two hours' notice he was even coming, and there was a traffic jam ten miles long of folks still arriving.

As he was wrapping up, thanking his teams, and encouraging them to kick up the ground game in preparation for next week, he looked up and smiled.

"Fancy meeting you here," he said, shaking the outstretched hand of Jeremy Kwan.

"I had to come see the phenomena of Nick Turner live. I have to say the live show is much better than anything we show on Hibi."

"That's good to know. You moved your company down here, right?" asked Nick.

"Yep, just down the road, here in Georgetown. I live out south and west in a town called Dripping Springs, west of the airport."

"Geez, what a dolt. How is Kim? Has she had the baby yet?"

"Nope. I have her staying in town with her mother, right across from the medical center. Any day now. The due date is election day."

"I remember. Congrats man. You have to be excited."

"You have no idea," beamed Jeremy, his eyes disappearing again with a big smile.

"How are you doing against the man?" asked Nick, referring to the homeland investigations and accusations Jeremy and his company had counterattacked a Serbian cyber terror outfit and shut down half a city in Serbia.

"Good. We have all the info and have cooperated with Homeland. It wasn't us. My guys *could* have done what they say we did. It's easy enough. But we are careful and don't do things like that for exactly the reasons we are accused of. It was a rival cyber gang in Serbia whose attack cascaded across systems. They couldn't stop it and it wiped out half the power stations before the utilities pulled the plug to stop it from spreading. If they hadn't, it probably would have taken out half the Balkan countries' grids."

"That's not good. Is it really that easy?"

"Sadly, yes," Jeremy looked around. "Where you off to next?"

"Airport, I think. Heading back to DC. We have a weekend full of outreach to all the grassroots orgs. Then I hit the road Monday and Tuesday for last-minute rallies before we end up in Florida for election night. Why?"

"I have some other info on some of the questions you asked. Can I borrow you for an hour? I need a more secure venue," stated Jeremy, looking around.

"Let me tell them we'll meet them at the airport."

#

Thirty minutes later, Nick was walking with Jeremy into his office, flanked by two of his bodyguards. Jeremy looked like a child next to Nick and the two of them. As they entered Jeremy's private office, he let Nick's guys explore the office and the attached bathroom.

"Be right outside, boss."

Nick nodded. "I trust Jeremy." He received a grunt in reply.

"Remind me not to make any quick moves around them," he laughed nervously.

"As I'm being reminded constantly, I can't be too careful. When you piss off the most powerful woman in the world, it does not bode well for your long-term prospects," replied Nick with a sigh.

"I know we don't have a lot of time," expressed Jeremy, pressing some keys on his keyboard as the shades darkened. Nick could hear the familiar hum of white noise anti-surveillance curtain technology blanketing the room.

"First, the stuff you gave me from Baker's drive. All I can say is, wow. If you are top of her shit list, you only got there *after* they bumped off Vincent. In my mind, there is no doubt he was silenced. He should have spent some time in spy school. He was way too obvious."

"How?"

"I found some emails sent to a publisher asking a price and telling them what he was shopping. He obviously didn't go to spy movies either. Your average twelve-year-old could have been more stealthy."

"Unfortunately, if she ever finds out I have this, I'm right behind you on the list now. Right now, my major crime is giving you a voice and making it possible for you to get the word out. If she knew, I knew what they did to get the president elected. Yikes. I'm not built like you. I need a diaper."

"Don't worry, I'll make sure no one knows. We aren't going public with any of it anyway. Nothing we can prove. I won't stoop to their level of the politics of personal destruction, no matter how true it is. The bigger question is, did you learn anything? And can you stop it?" asked Nick.

"We have a pretty good idea how they manipulate the voting machines now. Of course, that was the way they did it last time. Some things have changed. The systems are much more locked down. But, as I have told you before, anything programmed by humans can be hacked by them. We know what to look for, and I think we have a way to prevent what they are planning from working."

"Will it work? Your plan?"

Jeremy shrugged. "Nick, we can't try it until election night. There is no beta. Only live. I've got smart guys. We have a good idea what to look for. What we can do is try to gather and record as much info as we can. I won't bore you with the details, but we think we can communicate with the machines. Not to change anything, they are preventing any changes from being made from the outside. By anyone, thankfully. But they do have to leave them open for monitoring. We can use this and I think we can make copies of the data as it is collected. Then we can analyze the before and after and see if there are discrepancies. It won't stop cheating, but it may help prove it later."

"That's good news," agreed Nick, not understanding half of what Jeremy explained.

Sensing this, Jeremy smiled. "Nick, good and bad. Whatever they are planning is already in the code inside. All we can do is maybe gather the proof they changed the voter's intent. The problem is, it is astronomical amounts of data. Even using Artificial Intelligence and Machine Learning, it will take months, maybe even years, to analyze all of it to give you the definitive proof you'd need to stand up in court."

"I get it. At least we would have the data this time. What else?"

"The bigger problem you have is the ballots themselves. Good old-fashioned harvesting and feet on the street collecting legal votes is going to kill you. She just has such a lead in organization. It is a well-oiled machine. I have to say I was impressed as I went through Vincent's info. They mix in votes from folks who are eligible but who have never voted, or older voters who haven't voted lately and just pump up the count."

"Not surprising."

"Remember, this was the last time. There are four years they have had to improve. Again, technology is making this easier and easier. Culling through lists. Using statistics. There are going to be a lot of votes cast by people who did not vote or who had no idea they voted twice. Sadly, many of these are not even going to get caught or thrown out. Same with illegals. It is going to be a mess and the time between November 7th and January 6th doesn't leave enough time for any kind of real forensic analysis. Especially with three of those eight weeks, essentially holiday weeks."

"You're just full of great news. Any suggestions?"

"Get your speeches ready to demand in person or, even better, biometric voting. Without one or both, there will be zero confidence in our elections going forward. We are on our way to banana republic outcomes."

Nick looked at his watch. "Jeremy, I gotta go. Anything else?"

"Nick, there was some disturbing info in there about what they've done to the President."

"Such as?"

"They've been pumping him full of experimental drugs. From even before the first election. A lot of these were being administered by a foreign doctor. Specifically, after one visit, Vincent noted the President's mental state improved significantly. This was early in the first term."

"After that period, he really declined. Vincent never got a name. He noted this doctor was introduced to the President by the Vice President. At one point, he also mentioned the White House physician was pissed and demanded to know what the treatment was. He was forced into early retirement. He died in a car wreck shortly after. No surprise, given what we know now. Someone ran him off the road. Never caught. I looked this up myself. Not in Vincent's notes. He either knew, wasn't curious, or was part of the order."

"There seem to be a lot of people dying needlessly in this orbit around Lexi, her campaign, and this administration," agreed Nick, carefully.

"Vincent did point out it was also during this period of clarity the President and VP were at loggerheads most often. He ok'd a couple of gas pipelines over the strenuous complaint of environmental groups and allowed selective drilling. He also canceled several earlier executive orders regarding funding for Planned Parenthood and other social justice activities after several high-profile incidents of corruption."

"This was also when the short-lived mandate to improve testing scores and tying this to school funding was proposed. That was the one the teacher's union was screaming bloody murder about, if you recall."

"I do. It was one of his few moments of success in my eyes when I was still in the Party. He showed his moderate streak. It didn't last. Now I know why. He slid again, and they made him rescind it?" asked Nick.

"Exactly. As he declined again, it got more aggressive. Whether they even bothered to try to restore his clarity again or not isn't clear in

Vincent's notes. All what is clear is the VP orchestrated the re-election. Vincent took over for the original chief of staff for the second term and here we are," finished Jeremy.

"Too bad it is all just hearsay. We'd have to find someone else to corroborate all of this for it to matter," mused Nick. "He didn't describe this 'doctor,' did he?"

"I don't think so, but I can check again. Why?"

"Just trying to get a sense of who it might be. Maybe we could track him down to validate some of this?"

"Good idea. I will review the notes again," agreed Jeremy.

Nick nodded.

"It shows something, Nick. They may be talking about you implying a revolution is coming. She is actually planning on leading it. You don't do all of this if you intend to play by the rules. Watch yourself. What happens after the election, assuming you don't win?"

"That's a good question. Thanks for the help with this. Keep me in the loop on the election shenanigans. We will have you on a direct feed on election night?"

"Yes, we have it all set up. We'll let you know what we see and what we find out *and* if we can stop anything."

"Thanks Jeremy."

"Nick, are you aware of what is happening with the three banks who debanked you?" asked Jeremy, in a way he assumed Nick knew.

Nick's blank stare told Jeremy he was not.

"You really don't know?"

"That's sounds less than ideal. What have I done now?"

"Nick, they're going down."

"Their stock prices? Good, serves them right. About time people started doing something to register their displeasure," commented Nick.

"No Nick, I mean they are on the verge of going under. All three of them."

"What?" asked Nick in such a worried tone, Jeremy's smile faded.

"I'm providing the servers and systems to run the F2CFY credit union applications. We are receiving millions of requests for new accounts and transfers from the three big banks. Tens if not hundreds of billions of dollars by now. Way more than they're able to handle with their reserves. Frankly, I'm surprised we haven't heard from the government yet. So far, it is just the individuals, your voters. Not the big institutional guys, but you know how the herd mentality works."

"Shit. This was not my intent. I just wanted them to feel some pain. Jeremy, this is not good. These guys employ hundreds of thousands. We don't want to compromise the banking system. Can we do a Hibi post from your office?"

"Now? Don't you want to run this by Margie and Denise first?"

"Nope. I need to get out in front of the official response. I walked into Lexi's trap. I didn't realize what I did and gave her an opening. I guarantee you right now, she is getting ready to tell the world I am not only trying to start a shooting revolution, but I have already started it by ruining the financial systems."

"Shit, I never looked at it that way. I can set the camera up here and we can record it."

"Ready."

Jeremy gave him a thumbs up.

"Everyone. Please listen carefully. I am just now finding out the extent to which folks are deciding to move their money and accounts from the banks who debanked me to the new Freedom to Choose for Yourself credit union. While I applaud your decisions, I ask you to slow down. I had no idea there'd be so many of you reacting the way you are."

"Our banking systems are not set up to support massive transfers of money from one bank to another on the scale I am hearing is happening. *There is no crisis.* Your money is safe in these banks. They are not going to debank you like they did me. I would ask that if you have not decided, please hold off and if you choose to still do this, open joint accounts and move your money between the two in a phased approach. Or even hold off for a few weeks."

"If too many of you make this move, it will have unintended consequences. Banks may need propping up to support all the movement of money. That comes with a cost. A cost you and I have to pay in taxes and higher interest rates."

"Remember, when you give your money to the bank, it does not sit there. It is loaned out as mortgages, to fund buildings, and roads as bonds. It is used to enable you to get a car loan or to charge that vacation on the credit card you are paying off for the next year. All I can do is ask you to consider the repercussions. I didn't ask you and I certainly did not tell you to move your banking. I just pointed out what happened to me."

"Now I am sure the administration or one of their minions is about to come on TV and blame me. Saying I started a bank run to somehow sway public opinion or to bring down our government. *This is patently false,*" emphasized Nick, using his hands.

"Let's remember who decided to debank my accounts. Actions have consequences. This is the unintended consequence of people deciding they did not think that was right or fair. Again, I am asking you to stop and reconsider. I don't want more chaos. We have enough already. Remember, this had nothing to do with the soundness of these banks."

"A quick analogy. You bake two dozen cookies and give some to your neighbors. They love them and they tell their neighbors. Suddenly there are forty people at your door who want cookies. You don't have all the ingredients because you were not planning on baking 40 cookies. It doesn't mean you can't, it just means you have to go get the ingredients."

"If all of you try to move your money at the same time, the bank doesn't have enough ingredients on hand to give all of you cookies. They can get it, just not instantaneously. All I am saying is to ask for your cookies next week instead of tomorrow. Remember, there is no shortage of ingredients. We can make all the cookies we need. It just takes time to bake them. There is no banking problem. Unless we create one. I don't want that to happen."

"Don't believe anyone who tells you I did this, or that it was intentional. Remember who debanked whom, and how this started. Thank you and God bless."

Jeremy gave Nick a thumbs up. They had stopped recording.

"Cookies, huh?" laughed Jeremy as he loaded the post.

"I was trying to think about something folks could relate to. Think it will work?"

"Maybe. Like you said, it is not really a run, just a 'I want to shop at x instead of y', but everyone wants to do it at once. Hopefully, some folks will decide to wait until after the election. Part of me wants it to burn down, but all that means is they will have to sell assets at a loss, probably to people who already have too much control."

"Exactly. Post it. I'll let Margie know so she can get EXN to also reference it before Lexi gets her message out there. I gotta go Jeremy. I'm surprised Denise hasn't tracked me down yet."

"Nick, one more quick thing. Remember when I told you they were advertising for hackers on the dark web?"

"Yes."

"The most notorious hacker of them all, Sebastian Kolsten, was found murdered in a $1000 a night suite in a Washington, DC, hotel a few weeks ago. Double tap to the head," explained Jeremy.

"And that means what?"

"Hackers are cowards. They would spill their guts if you threatened to pierce their ears, let alone anything more sensitive. He could be someone they used to set up the hack of the voting machines. Weak links are easy to squeeze for confessions."

"You think someone is cleaning up loose ends?"

"I do."

"Want some advice?" offered Nick.

"Sure."

"Call Earl. Have him give you the name of some of his special forces buddies. Computer code will not stop a bullet. Right or wrong, you have a target almost as big as me on you now. Especially now with the banking added to Hibi and the 2J's. Nixon's enemies list is a three-year-olds letter to Santa compared to what Lexi will do. When she can."

Jeremy's smile faded, sweat instantly appearing on his forehead.

"Talk to you on election night and thanks for all you have done," replied Nick as he got up to go.

Chapter 16

"Thank God you did that post last night," remarked Margie, as they watched the early morning press conference.

"How many hits so far?" asked Denise.

"About twenty million," responded Jer from a corner of the conference room.

"Is that enough?" asked Nick.

"Better than zero, for sure. You have over eighty million followers, so that means many haven't looked yet. It will help us when we rebut what Lexi is saying. Just as you said in the post, she is claiming this is you vindicating exactly why these banks debanked you. How you have tried to respond by forcing a run on them," noted Denise.

"American *Pravda* is going to eat this up. It also gives the cable business channels something to chew on as well," groused Margie.

"Do you think my post will slow folks down?"

"Honestly, I don't know Nick. If I were watching this hatchet job, I would say screw them and move my money anyway. You did what you could. Nowhere is anyone reminding folks you did not fire the first shot. Nor that you did not tell anyone to move their accounts. Just to contemplate the scenario if they faced the same situation. People used common sense and responded," offered Chuck from his place at the table.

The entire staff was in the DC office, including Colonel Bob, Nick's military advisor, Jenny his legal advisor, and Izzy, his medical issues director. This was the final push to the end.

"Bob, thoughts. Tactics?"

The colonel, an older gentleman still wearing a crew cut, thought for a second, looking at Nick. "I think you recovered nicely. You walked into the trap. And found a way out. Like Margie said, the fact your post was up last night steals some of their thunder and makes it easy to counter some of their more explosive accusations."

Nick turned to Margie, looking at his watch.

"Margie, can you see if Billy on EXN is willing to have me dial in to respond to the press conference?"

"Sure Nick, let me check," replied Margie, leaving the room and dialing her phone.

"Not too hard Nick. Calm and collected, OK? This could hurt us in North Carolina. One of those banks is Charlotte based. If they have to start laying folks off…" noted Denise.

"I just want to reiterate the banks started this with the debanking. All I did was respond and tell people what I did and why. That's it. I'm not going tit for tat with their accusations. They are playing to their base, anyway."

"And trying to keep those banks from having to sell a bunch of assets at fire-sale prices to come up with cash. I bet the Secretary of the Treasury was calling every big institutional investor last night to make sure none of them tried to pull out their money. A couple of them are the same as twenty million of your supporters. If it's just a million folks pulling out a thousand dollars each, it's much easier to handle than someone pulling out twenty billion," explained Chuck.

"Anyone have a count of the number of accounts F2CFY has opened? Just curious," asked Nick.

"Let me check," said Chuck, looking at his phone and texting.

Margie came back into the room.

"They're ready for you, Nick. Want to do it from your office?"

"Sounds good," said Nick, getting up to go.

"Nick." He turned to look at Chuck.

"I take back what I said. Twenty-one million requests for accounts so far. Total assets requested for movement, are you ready?"

"Hit me."

"Over three hundred billion."

"Holy shit. No wonder they're having a cow," blurted Denise.

"Nick, that puts them in the top one hundred largest banks in the world less than a week after opening, hell maybe even top fifty," noted Chuck, looking at his phone.

Nick just smiled as he left the office to talk to Billy McCall on the morning EXN news show.

#

Lexi stood alone in her campaign office. She'd returned from the Capitol where she had delivered her press conference, assuring the nation the three banks in question were both stable and able to handle the outflow of individual accounts. The institutional investors were not moving the money. What she didn't tell them was the lengths she had to go to in order to make this happen.

Lexi assured the world these banks had the backing of the United States and should they need any temporary loans to cover any immediate cash needs, beyond their copious reserves, the government would provide these at minimal cost. No one in the press even questioned why it was Lexi and not the president delivering this news.

She'd then railed against Turner's nefarious plans. Trying to destabilize the world's financial markets on the eve of an election was on par with his recent antics, implying insurrection was in the future when he lost. If his stances were popular and helped the average American, he would not need to resort to such evil deeds to sway the opinion of the public.

Rosemary Hurst, the Secretary of the Treasury and Willa Kreutz, the Secretary of Commerce, had taken the podium to explain the specifics. They both made it clear this was really lots of very small and insignificant accounts being closed in one bank and merely opened in another. There was nothing wrong systemically. No one was saying they were anything but rock solid. It was just retaliation by Turner for them reacting responsibly to his charges of spewing hate and inspiring violence against activists by his supporters.

"Madame Secretary, Senator Turner posted a statement last night, apparently upon hearing of the size and scope of the efforts of individual account holders to move their money. He specifically pointed out the banks in question debanked him first and he is on record as *not* telling people to move their money but just to consider the consequences of debanking without notice or appeal. The account holders ultimately make this choice," stated Ned Wheeler from EXN.

"I'll take this one Willa," said Lexi.

"First, of course he put that post up. He knew what was coming. We are onto his schemes. He is going to claim he didn't tell anyone to do anything directly. We've heard this before from him. 'Don't blame me. I didn't tell anyone to do something. They decided all on their own.' Right after he pushed them in the direction he wanted them to go. Over 700,000 people work for these three banks. He is putting their livelihood at risk with his antics. And they vote. Once the election is over, there will be investigations into what exactly was said, implied and the consequences of his actions," finished Lexi in a commanding tone.

"A quick follow up Madame Vice President. The banks did debank his campaign accounts, with no notice and no appeal. That much is true, is it not?" pushed Ned, earning a glare from Lexi.

"I am sure the banks had their reasons. As we can see by the retaliatory nature of Turner's attacks on them, perhaps these results show exactly why they were right in doing what they did."

#

"Shit Nick, can we get through one day without poking the angry Lexi bear?" grimaced Denise as they watched the recording.

Nick just smiled and shrugged.

"You did great with Billy, Nick. Very clear and concise. It is their fault for starting it. You didn't tell anyone to move their accounts. We have the recordings. They are free to bank wherever they want. Finally, going over the cookie analogy again tells folks there is nothing wrong with the system. Just folks exercising free choice to not bank with folks who would debank you for political reasons. That came through loud and clear," responded Margie with a big smile.

"More time spent chasing our tails and not talking to voters."

"We'll see how folks react. At least the stock market seems to have stabilized with your statement and the government guaranteeing people's money is safe in these banks," added Nick.

"There is that. Just something else for us to worry about," frowned Denise.

Chapter 17

"In our last segment tonight, we are pleased to be joined by Senator Nick Turner. What a couple of weeks, Senator. There is no doubt this has been both the most tragic and action-packed election cycle in our history."

"Thanks Tommy, good to be here. I certainly would have appreciated a less crazy one for sure. It just goes to show how much change is needed and how difficult it's going to be to make it happen. I guess I'll be seeing more of you in the next few days?" commented Nick.

"Indeed, you will Senator. I'll be joining the Senator as he does a whirlwind tour of the country on Monday and Tuesday until EXN's coverage starts on Tuesday night at 6pm eastern. What do you have in store for us, Senator?"

"I think the plan is to hit about ten states in two days. Lots of rallies. Put on your best walking shoes and comfortable travel clothes. We have a lot of flying and talking ahead of us."

"Senator, you have to be extremely proud of your campaign. No third-party candidate in the modern era has done this well. It is a real shame the debate committee kept changing the rules to keep you out of the debate. I even heard the Vice President's campaign tried at the last minute to change the rules again to keep you out of the last one," accused Tommy.

"I wouldn't know anything about that, Tommy. I'm just glad I got one chance to talk to a national audience. I heard the ratings were good."

"Good? Senator, your debate had the highest ratings by viewers and percentage, even topping the Nixon/Kennedy debate by percentage of total viewers. EXN thanks you. You chose a good time to hit one out of the park. It is a testament to the American people's desire to see what you had to say. You put that in contrast to the previous three debates. All snooze fests, with the lowest viewership ever for all of them. I can only surmise your message was the difference."

"Thanks Tommy. I just hope they heard the words and statements and think about what I said. I tried to stay out of the schoolyard bickering the other two were determined to get me in and just focus on the facts. As they say, sticks and stones and they were only armed with twigs. Running for president is serious business. It is not a pro wrestling match where you get points for style and flair. This is all about substance. I focused on the take downs and left the chair tosses and scissor kicks to my opponents," said Nick with a smile.

Tommy laughed. "Senator, I believe that is the first time I have heard a presidential candidate work pro-wrestling into a statement and then make an appropriate analogy. You are correct. Your opponents were there for show, but at the end you are the reigning champ."

"Let's hope it comes out that way on Tuesday," said Nick, smiling.

"Any comments on the debanking situation? It appears things have stabilized."

"Tommy, despite the false allegations of the Vice President and the cabinet, I didn't tell anyone to move their money. I simply told them to think. Something I have been consistent in doing since the beginning of my campaign. It appears over twenty million of those people did indeed think and decided they did not approve of the actions of their former banking establishments," finished Nick, a fire in his eye.

"Well put Senator," agreed Tommy.

"That's all we can do, Tommy. I guess I'll see you on Monday morning."

"I'll bring the coffee and Danish," said Tommy, smiling. "Good night and good luck," Nick smiled, not knowing if Tommy even knew he had just uttered Edward R. Murrow's famous catch phrase ending for his show.

"Thanks."

Chapter 18

Nick parked Chuck's Prius on a street in Chevy Chase, a block from Senator Bank's Georgian-style mansion. Nick walked up to the wrought-iron gate to the servant's quarters and buzzed the intercom. Hobson's voice answered. The gate clicked open. Nick glanced around, not seeing anything out of the ordinary. Previous times, he had felt he was being watched. With the revelation of the tracking device in his notebook, he started to be more careful.

He had a knock down drag out with Earl and Denise when he told them he needed to go out alone. Earl flatly refused until Nick told him he didn't want to embarrass his security detail by evading them. Finally, he just pulled rank and told them to deal with it.

Hobson let him in with a brief hello and a smile. He led Nick to the familiar library of the Senator. Senator Banks was comfortably seated in his well-worn leather wing-back chair. It appeared molded to his form. He had a large cognac in his hand.

"Nick, please come in. Can I offer you a drink, or more specifically, can Hobson pour you one?" offered Banks, holding his up in salute.

"What are you having?"

"An Armagnac. Specifically, a Laberdolive Bas Armagnac Vintage 1947 Domaine Du Jaurrey. It was given to me by Charles de Gaulle."

"I am not sure I am worthy," laughed Nick.

"Nonsense. De Gaulle was a sanctimonious SOB. Always the smartest man in the room. Not an ounce of humility. It was his way, always. It has been opened now. We have to drink it relatively quickly. Something this old when exposed to air has a relatively short lifespan," explained Banks.

"So why now?"

"It is not the only thing with a relatively brief life span in this room," he answered prophetically.

"Hmm," grunted Nick, choosing not to respond as he took the wing-back chair opposite Banks, thanking Hobson for his drink. He left and closed the library doors behind him.

"I aspire to have a room like this one day. I have a good start on the books. I just have nowhere this nice to put them."

"You must put down roots to build a room like this. This home is nearly 300 years old. It started out as a mere cottage. I have owned it for 70 years. My wife and I remodeled and rebuilt much of it, modernizing and stuff. We raised our daughter in this house." He took a quick sip, hiding his emotional response.

"They are both gone, Nick. I have no progeny. No grandkids, as my daughter was unable to bear children. She went first, lung cancer. I always told her not to smoke. But you know feminism was all the rage in the 60s and 70s and when it became unfashionable, she could never kick it." He shook his head sadly.

"A parent should never have to bury a child, and it is even tougher when you are both alive. My dear wife passed ten years ago. We were married for sixty-five years. She was truly my better half. My balance. You need a yin to your yang. You need something to fight for and protect Nick. Find a good woman. It makes all the difference, especially in this business. I think you are sensing this," he took another sip. Nick noticed a single tear streaked down a cheek in remembrance.

"Don't fight it. Ask Neill, he knows. If not for Ellie, he would long since have died, by his own hand, or someone else's. She saved him. He's a good man. Talk to him. Trust him and his judgement. In fact, trust both of them. They have experience and wisdom, something you are sorely lacking if you want to survive in this town."

Nick sat silent, listening. Sipping his Armagnac. "I don't even know how to describe this. I believe it is the most amazing alcohol I have ever tasted. Expensive, I assume?"

Banks shrugged. "It is only money. I frankly haven't priced anything like this, but my guess is a couple thousand a bottle. This one, of course, is priceless because of the provenance. Doesn't make it taste any better, but it makes for a good story."

Nick sat waiting patiently. He knew he had been summoned for a reason. "Senator, why am I here? Not that I don't love the stories, especially the history, but it is four days before the election."

"Indeed, it is Nick. There is plenty of money in the world. Old money handed down generation after generation. Rothschild, Morgan, Bettencourt, Otto, Lazard and Speyer. Other names you are probably more familiar with, Rockefeller, Vanderbilt, and Astor."

"These people, especially the bankers, have had an outsized influence on society. Go research the Federal Reserve some time. I have seen you rail against Wilson for the amendments to the Constitution to make income tax a reality and to make senators elected instead of appointed. While both were egregious, they pail before the masterstroke of progressivism in the Federal Reserve System."

"I am aware of the issue. It is a little hard to explain to people in a rally, though," admitted Nick.

Banks laughed. "Can't come up with a cookie analogy for that one?"

"Not yet," smiled Nick back, as Banks continued.

"Then you are aware, despite the rhetoric, China owns a relatively small portion of our national debt. What they did own, they sold most of at a large profit. The money we keep printing, and the corresponding debt, is held in the hands of bankers and sovereign wealth funds. There does not need to be a conspiracy theory or some mythical group drinking the blood of virgins to stay young. They are in plain sight," explained Banks.

"And your point is?" asked Nick, not understanding the purpose of the conversation.

"Nick, you scare the crap out of them because they have no leverage over you. You are not a creature of their system. Others have always been weak and easily controlled or replaced. You, on the other hand, are like hardened titanium. You are battle tested, literally. You do not panic. You do not take their bait and you do not have skeletons, at least none they can find," laughed Banks.

"I wouldn't know what you are talking about, Senator," replied Nick.

"We already discussed this on your last visit. I love how you handed Lexi her head when that idiot Kensington wanted to get his petty revenge on you. He is supposedly tendering his resignation first thing after the election. Congrats. You just made another powerful enemy."

"Kensington has been an enemy for decades," replied Nick, contemplating Bank's words. "You claim to know everything about my past. Does Dan Jacob's name ring a bell?"

Banks stiffened slightly. "Of course."

"You know he was murdered recently?"

"Yes." Banks adjusted in his seat a bit.

"Know anything about it?"

Now it was his turn to be evasive. "Why would I?"

"He sent me a note," revealed Nick.

"How did *you* know him?" asked Banks, confused, and then a look of concern crossing his face.

"I ran into him a couple of times early in my career in Navy Intel when we were doing our initial planning on both the invasion of Afghanistan and then Iraq. He showed up a couple of times, in joint briefings. I met him two other times, but I can't say where or when."

"I know where and when. I didn't realize you two met there, though," replied Banks. "What I can't fathom is why he was communicating with you directly."

"We could ask him, but unfortunately he's dead," replied Nick sarcastically.

"Don't be rude Nick, you don't wear it well. What did the note say?"

"Since we're throwing national security out the window."

"I am both dying and have higher clearances than even you. What did he say?" repeated Banks, now impatient.

"He admitted he committed treason."

Banks' face whitened. "What did he tell you?"

"He apologized and said *they* gave him no choice. Then he told me he copied some information from my file and gave them to someone looking for dirt on me."

"What! There is no way even *he* could access your history. I buried it deep for a reason. When Agent Henderson died, that should have been it. No one could get to those for at least fifty years. How did he do it?" This last was delivered by Banks to the air as he finished his cognac. He held his glass out to Nick, who moved to the bar to refill it.

"He didn't tell me any of that. He just said I was in danger and explained how he didn't give them what they were looking for. He also mentioned he would pay a horrible price for it, but didn't elaborate. Mainly he wanted me to know what he gave them and for me to know it," finished Nick, returning with Bank's drink.

Banks took it and reached for his lighter. Nick noticed there was a wolf's head logo with the Latin phrase *Nec Arpera Terrent* on the old zippo. Banks lit it and waved the flame below his cognac glass a few times.

"Fear no difficulties? You served?" translated Nick, tilting his glass at the lighter.

"Korea, in 51. 27th Army Infantry, Wolfhound Raiders. To us it meant 'No Fear on Earth'."

Nick nodded. "Know Colonel Hackworth?"

"Oh, yeah. He was a new mustang lieutenant then. He formed the Raiders," smiled Banks. "You remind me of him. Devil may care. Always throwing caution to the wind. Charge first, then adapt to the chaos he would cause. The opposite of what we have today in our military leaders."

"One of my heroes. Loved his books."

Banks continued smiling, thinking back to his former commanding officer, then twenty-year-old Lt. David Hackworth. The smile faded as he asked. "What did Jacob's tell you he gave them? He did not seem to be the kind to turn traitor."

"He didn't. He sent me a copy of what he sent. It doesn't have anything I think is bad. A bunch of after-action reports from the CIA. I got a sense he felt like whoever it was would not be happy with what he gave them. Since he was dead by the time I got it, I'm guessing he was right."

"You still have them?"

"Why?"

"Speculation is bad. You are probably not the only person who knows what Dan did. They probably don't know what he took or copied. In fact, I am sure of it. He was the *only* one who could even find a way to access any of that info. Now that he's gone, the security is unbreachable, trust me. For forty-nine more years, anyway. My suggestion is you shred the info."

"It won't matter. No one who cares would believe me if I told them I shredded it or not. What I find more interesting is the content of what he did take. It's all about me. Who cares?"

"Nick, in the right hands, this info is powerful leverage. What else was there?"

"Nothing about any of the worst things. One thing that was in there was Echo and info about my court martial." Nick did not mention it also included info on his allergy to pistachios. "The second piece I found even crazier was how full of lies the reports were. If this is the definitive record, it was whitewashed to hell and back from the *actual truth*."

"Interesting. Even more reason for you to hope they don't think you have a copy. Now you are a genuine threat to the CIA as well. Someone who can contradict the narrative as a witness to the aftermath of many of their debacles. That's why it was archived so deep in the first place."

"It is the past. Everyone already assumes all that shit happened. Even without the facts. Who is going to blackmail Jacobs and why? Whatever they were looking for, they didn't find it."

"Don't be so sure, Nick. I need to tell you something. I had hoped to not do this, because you have enough on your mind, but if I die, then there is no one else to tell you."

Nick sat up straighter, suddenly paying attention.

"Nick, I have weeks, maybe a couple months to live. Cancer is everywhere," he said, holding up a hand. "No sympathy required. It is long since time for me to rejoin my family. Perhaps I have been given the gift of sight because of this. Nick, you're going to lose. But in losing, you are the only hope the Constitutional loving citizens of this nation have.

When you lose, you'll be hunted like a dog. You are their Kryptonite and you must not take unnecessary risks. You will do what is right. I know this. The spark of righteousness is in you, along with both honor and passion. You'll know what to do at the right time. I know it sounds crazy, but it *is* your destiny."

"Obi-Wan, really?" Nick smiled at the Obi-Wan Kenobi reference.

"I talked to Sir Alec Guinness once about Obi-Wan. He hated that role," grinned Banks, before turning serious again. "Do you remember that night before Dolly showed up, and I told you *we* had our eye on you?"

"Pretty hard to forget."

"Do you remember a test you took as a sophomore in high school? The one with all the questions about specific situations, full of thought problems, and the difference between moral and ethical results. Lots of abstract, critical, and strategic thinking?"

Nick laughed. "I do. It was a weird test. No obvious yes or no answers. I liked it and thought it was easy. I remember my classmates didn't agree. But we also knew it wasn't being used to help us get into college, so nobody cared. In fact, I think they said it was a theoretical test they were assessing using going forward."

"That's right. We gave that test for two years to sophomores in the US. Before the teacher's union shut us down."

"What was the big deal?"

"Nick, over seven million students took that test in those two years. One of them got a perfect score. The next closest was 47%. High School wasn't challenging, was it?"

"I assume I am the one who scored perfect?"

Banks nodded.

"No, I didn't find high school challenging. I didn't apply myself beyond what was needed. I still graduated high in the class, but I wasn't motivated to get a perfect score. I played sports and dated girls. The 4.0 crowd did neither. I didn't want that.

"Precisely. And yet you scored perfect on a test most 4.0 students scored less than 15%. I was part of the task force that designed and implemented the test. We were looking for abstract thinkers who we could 'groom' for public service.

"That sounds ominous. Clearly you failed since I spent 20 years in the military. I would never have willingly run for dogcatcher, let alone the Senate. I only took this job out of a sense of duty when it was offered.

"I know. When your parents were killed, we lost any chance we had to control your future. You changed. Why?"

"You knew about the accident?"

"Nick, remember what I just told you. There are bigger forces. If we were watching you, others were watching what we were doing. Move, counter move."

Nick stiffened in his chair. "You said, 'when my parents were killed'. They died in a ten car pileup."

"Yes, they did," answered Banks.

"Son of a bitch," exploded Nick, standing to pace the library. "Who the fuck are you people? Six other people died in that pile up. Do you have *any* respect for life, or is everyone a pawn available to be sacrificed for whatever scheme you're running?"

Banks sat impassively, watching Nick process this information.

"Are you saying you picked me out and someone else killed my parents as a result? For what purpose? All it did was make me dive headlong into studying. To *find* a purpose which was to serve my country. To do all I could, knowing I could be snuffed out in any random activity at any time. To not waste time."

"Precisely."

"I don't understand."

"Nick, your parents died, so we would not have a chance to guide you on *our* chosen path. They bet you would do any of a number of things, but in all their scenarios, none of them would allow us to control your choices. They probably assumed getting a windfall of insurance money would enable you to do what other eighteen-year-olds would have done. Party. Head for the beach. Buy a Porsche. How surprised they were when you invested it and never touched it. They were wrong, but so were we."

"I now realize I *am* the Manchurian Candidate."

"Hardly. We push where we can, remove obstacles where possible, and enable you to be in the right place at the right time. You are the antithesis of someone being controlled or led," retorted Banks, with a snort.

"New York?"

Banks shrugged, sipping his Armagnac. "We merely ensured the two cars arrived at the intersection at the same time. What happened after was purely out of our hands. We knew you, and only you, would recognize a terrorist if he showed up, as our intel said was going to happen. We had no idea what he looked like. You were our only shot to stop it."

"You keep saying 'we'. Who are these others? Other Senators?"

Banks let out a deep belly laugh and immediately began coughing. He reached for his inhaler, taking a big puff.

Nick paced the room, running his hands through his hair.

"No, not other Senators Nick. Just as there is a group of globalists determined to rule the world as their giant fiefdom, there is a group of like-minded people who believe in the United States as the soul bulwark against their relentless efforts. We work in the background, striving to undue and thwart their various schemes. We have had marginal success. The globalists are relentless and have been at their plans much longer than we who have tried to stop them."

"Pavlovich?"

Banks nodded. "We think he is the leader, though it is very secretive. I belong to another group he chartered many decades ago. I have been in it for over forty years. I was *their* mole, deep in the Party. Working from the inside, feeding them information on various plans. Helping further their cause. Once I was closer to the inner workings. Now they suspect I am no longer a 'true' believer and hold me at arm's length."

"Senator, are you sure you are not hallucinating the plot for a movie? This is like so many of those new world order conspiracy movies. Is your group called QAnon?"

"Nick, you scoff, but what better way to deflect any curiosity than to create a fictional group, associate it with tin foil conspiracy, and then refer to anyone who comes close to the mark as a member of this idiotic conspiracy order. It is brilliant. Most of what people say is conspiracy and associate with QAnon, is in fact *happening*. Though, I can say, I have seen no virgin's being sacrificed to keep people young. Still just conventional plastic surgery," smiled Banks, trying to lessen the tension. It didn't work.

Nick stared at a wall of the library. He was having trouble believing what he was hearing. "So, you are in *both* groups?"

"Nick, trust me. Similar to you pulling people out of the Party fold to build your Blue Morpho organization. There is a group who would do evil in the name of globalization. Our group fights this evil, hoping to preserve America and her constitution as the beacon of freedom. Look for help in the most unlikely places."

Banks sat up in his chair, working himself up as he divulged these secrets to Nick. "You must never doubt yourself and you must promise me, as long as you breathe, you will not capitulate, no matter how bleak it appears. Promise me!" said Banks, leaning forward, his face flushed.

Nick, afraid Banks would have a stroke, quickly answered. "I promise. I will not give up this burden. I cannot. If the Constitution is not the guidepost for the society, then I have no desire to live in a society not following its tenets."

"Thank you, Nick," said Banks. He had now sunk back into his chair, seeming to shrink, the outburst appearing to have deflated his very essence.

"Senator, as you can imagine, I have a big couple of days ahead and I am afraid I must go."

"Wait a minute," said Banks, struggling to get out of his chair. Nick helped him stand. "Should I call Hobson?"

"Not yet. Come with me," said Banks as he led Nick into a second smaller office, also containing floor to ceiling bookshelves, a desk and chair were the only furniture. Banks led him to a section of this library on an interior wall. He looked through the books on the shelf, selecting one. He handed it to Nick.

It was an old book, with a dust jacket, *Thoughts and Adventures* by Winston S. Churchill.

"Very nice," said Nick.

"Open it."

Inside, Nick looked at the inscription written in a strong hand. '*Congressman Banks, I believe you will do great things in the American Congress. Never lose sight of America's greatest strength…Freedom,*'. It was signed Winston S. Churchill.

"Wow," said Nick.

"I sat with Winston after he had once again been kicked out of the Prime Minister job. I had dinner with him at Chartwell. He pulled this book out of his personal library. He signed it and gave it to me. I have cherished it my entire life. Whenever I am lost, I sit and read from it. To provide clarity. I hope it will do the same for you. Look in one more page, please."

Nick flipped the page. '*Senator Turner, may you find inspiration in Churchill's writings, as I have. As he saved Britain, you shall save American ideals. Good luck and God will bless you for your efforts, Baxter William Banks, Senator.*'

"I will cherish this. As you have made it your centerpiece, I will make it mine," said Nick, holding out his hand.

Banks took his hand, and then he drew Nick into an embrace and stood sobbing quietly. Nick wasn't sure what to do, so he just held the older man until he could compose himself.

"Sorry Nick, you will find as you approach the end, you get maudlin. Much as you have suggested, people look to faith and assume a day of reckoning will occur. I am living proof of this fear. Fear that I have not done enough to atone for my sins."

"I am sure you are fine, Senator," offered Nick.

"Only I will know. I needed to have this conversation and make sure you know you are not alone. Find a soulmate. It is important. Having something to lose will keep you from needlessly sacrificing yourself. You need something you do not want to lose, something you want to live for. Find her," said Banks once again in an almost otherworldly voice.

"I will Senator."

Hobson showed him the door. As he turned to look back, Banks was watching him, his head illuminated by the light of the reading lamp next to his chair. Nick shivered, as it looked almost like a halo. He was sad the Senator would shortly leave this world. He enjoyed the conversation and would have loved to have sat down and picked his brain for the stories he no doubt had.

Nick thanked Hobson as he cleared his head and checked his surroundings before walking to his car. He did not notice the car parked well down the street in the opposite direction. Nor the person shooting pictures of him leaving Bank's house from the back seat.

Part Two

Honest and Fair?

"Pay no attention to that man behind the curtain."

The Great and Powerful Oz, *The Wizard of Oz, (1939)*

Chapter 19

Nick came into the DC campaign office on Saturday morning bearing a couple boxes of donuts and a large container of coffee. As he struggled with the door, a couple of his staffers came to his rescue, taking the donuts and coffee to the conference room. He could see Denise and Margie had already been there a while. His donuts were added to a makeshift buffet in the back of the room already stacked with danishes, bagels, and lots of coffee.

"Are we ready to rumble?" asked Nick to the group, causing them to look up and laugh.

"What's with the wrestling lingo? First, last night and then today. Did you catch WWE or something?" asked Denise, checking the camera angles around the conference room table.

"Just seemed appropriate. I am in a good mood this morning."

"Relax, Nebraska isn't until this afternoon."

"Denise, you're such a buzzkill."

"That's why you pay me the big bucks. Stay focused."

"Don't worry, I am focused. Anything you want me to say?"

"Just be upbeat and positive, always. We won't have time for questions, but make sure you thank everyone for all their help and enthusiasm and give them the 'rah rah' to do their part to put you over the top Tuesday," explained Denise.

"Aye, Aye Captain."

"The group you're talking to will be on the white board over there," said Margie, pointing toward a wall. "It will also be in the upper corner of the screen, so don't pull a Gerald Ford and forget where you are or who you're talking to," she said pointing to the corner of the big screen at the head of the conference table.

"How do you even know who Gerald Ford was?" remarked Nick.

"Denise told me," she quipped back as Denise glanced at her middle finger extended.

Margie continued. "We'll be talking to campaign offices in every state. A couple more in specific cities or counties, like Laura in Orange County. Then we'll have some grass roots team calls. Lots of 'Women for Turner' groups, and a couple of 'Vets for Turner' and then a bunch of Turner Rabble groups. Especially in the plains and western states. Some of them are coming together on a single call. Unfortunately, we can't get to all of them, but we are trying to get to most. There are even a couple of 'Bikers for Turner' groups," laughed Margie.

"Really? Didn't know I appealed to the bicyclist set. Figured they would be Party for sure."

"Smart ass. You *are* in a good mood this morning," commented Denise, as the rest of the gathered staff laughed loudly.

"Sounds great. I sure would like to talk to any that have asked for it," frowned Nick at the idea he couldn't encourage all his groups.

"You do realize you have over a thousand grass-roots organizations we have chartered and sent money to?" commented Steve Gaines, Nick's head of grassroot organizing.

"I do?" responded Nick, flabbergasted.

"And that doesn't even include all your white supremacist militias. I guess you don't read *all* of your email," said Denise, giving Nick a side-eye as she adjusted one more camera angle.

"I try to hit the important ones," he said defensively.

"Yes, after every state fair, we usually get 20 requests to charter more 'Woman for Turner' or 'Vets for Turner' or 'Students for Turner' organizations. We even have a 'Quilters for Turner'. You should see the victory quilt they did. We have 'Dog walkers for Turner', from California of course, and 'Cajuns for Turner' from Louisiana," laughed Steve.

"Beekeepers, candle makers, carpenters, brewers, linemen, telephone that is, not football players, and a bunch of other groups," said Margie, chuckling as she read some off the list to Nick.

"We also have about 400 Turner Rabble organizations alone. If you spent any time on social media, Hibi especially, you'll see these motorcycle, boat, and pickup truck rallies of the Turner Rabble. I'm surprised Lexi's DOJ hasn't labeled them a domestic terror group yet."

"Give'em time. Especially if we lose," added Chuck drolly.

"Okay, let's get this party started," ordered Denise, looking at her phone. "First up is a Women for Turner group in Augusta Maine." Jer was off to the side, managing the dial in and getting everyone online.

Nick was greeted with an overflow crowd of hundreds of women wearing all kinds of Turner paraphernalia. He was overwhelmed when he saw it. Thanking them for their support, asking about the weather, he said some good things about having so many strong women supporting him. At one point, two women held up their hands to speak. They both appeared to be in their late seventies.

"Senator, I'm Margaret, Peg actually, and this is my twin Miriam. We just want to thank you. If it were not for you, we would still not be speaking to each other."

"Glad I could help. How long had you not been speaking?" laughed Nick, assuming they were Party and Opposition.

"We had not spoken to each other since January 22nd, 1973," answered Miriam.

"What? January 22nd, 1973?" repeated Nick, then he smiled, nodding. "Ah, opposite sides of *Roe*, I assume?"

"That's correct Senator. Ever since that was made law, we have been at odds. It got worse after it was repealed. Only your pragmatic approach allowed us to reconcile our differences and see it the way you described. As a matter between each of us and God. Thank you for that," said Peg, breaking down in tears as her sister hugged her.

There wasn't a dry eye in the building. As Nick looked around, the women were grabbing tissues in their conference room as well. "You both represent an unfortunate fracture in American society. One that has kept us from fully realizing our potential as a nation. While preventing our women from contributing *and* collaborating. From becoming the force you can be to solve so many of the issues every parent and family faces from the encroaching hand of bigger government. I hope this ends now and we can all move on to greater things with this divisive issue behind us. Thank you for those kind words. They warm my heart and confirm exactly why I'm running."

The room erupted into cheers of Turner, Turner, Turner, as Steve got on to thank them and encourage them to do all they can to help get out the vote. Getting any friends and neighbors to the polls.

"They'd better not all be like this. There isn't enough makeup in the room if this is the trend," growled Denise, to hide her feelings.

"Jer, please tell me you are recording?" sniffled Margie.

"I am. I learned from Greg to record everything Nick says," he smiled, as Denise and Margie broke into tears again at the mention of their lost colleague. Jer hugged Margie as Nick walked to Denise to do the same.

"OK team. Let's pull it together. If nothing else, we owe it to Greg to get through this and rally the troops," finished Nick.

Everyone nodded through their sniffles.

"Jer, get that first one posted. It's a great way to folks involved," suggested Denise, as they all got serious again.

This is how each call went. It seemed on each there was a cop or a fireman, healthcare worker, welder, vet or everyday person who had been affected by some position Nick supported. His explanation having converted them to his way of thinking. In each case, the person told a heartfelt story of how he or she changed because of Nick and his pragmatic views. These calls super charged Nick with confidence and gave him energy.

After the first few, Jer set up an automatic post to their Hibi social channel. As each recording finished, it posted. As the afternoon progressed, each of them would hit hundreds of thousands of views and a million or more by the end of the day as their supporters followed Nick's journey. Inspiring his grassroots followers just as if he'd been able to talk to each of them directly.

Around two in the afternoon, after munching on pizza, Nick joined a 'Women for Turner' call, suddenly greeted by Natalie's smiling face.

Denise watched out of the corner of her eye to see how he reacted. He played it cool, but his stomach was flip flopping like a first date in high school.

"Hello Women for Turner of Omaha and thank you for all your hard work and support," said Nick as the crowd of 400 in a high school gym cheered back at him. Natalie was seated at a table in front of the camera and the rest of the women and quite a few men were seated behind her in the bleachers.

"Thank you, Senator. We also have a bunch of our local Turner Rabble folks. We want you to know you have our full support. We know you'll carry the state of Nebraska on Tuesday night, with our help, of course," she said with a grin as the people behind broke into cheers of Turner. Nick only stared into Natalie's green eyes and she back, the cheering fading in the background.

"First, it's Nick. You know that Natalie," admonished Nick, causing Natalie's cheeks to turn a bright shade of red, accenting her freckles across her nose that much more.

Nick was glad he made her blush. "For those who may not know, one of my first stops after I announced was in Omaha. We went down to Stella's for lunch," cheers from some in the crowd. "Then to Natalie's B&B for dinner and a room for the night. The whole point of that road trip and the ones that followed was to get in touch with people like you. Like Natalie and her cousin Jamie. Hi Jamie," waved Nick as Jamie waved from the bleachers.

"Earl says hi too," said Nick, turning his head to look at Earl, who was watching and smiling off camera. Jamie laughed and yelled 'hello' back, standing and waving from the front of the bleachers.

"So anyway, I wanted to meet people like Bob and Jerry," who also raised their hands, waving at Nick.

"Everyone we met at Natalie's restaurant that night and all the conversations we had at Stella's and countless places like that were so I could get in touch with real people. To understand what *you* face every day. How inflation, jobs, and crime affect your life, no matter what the administration claims. How it is harder and harder to keep your children safe from the cesspool of social media. The prevalence of drugs in schools, and your concerns with the hypocrisy of CRT and defunding police. These are the things you need help with. This is what our government should be concerned with, how to enable you to succeed on your own, not to give you a handout or a leg up over your neighbor."

"That is not what America is about. America is about self- reliance. It is about leaving us alone to lead our lives and succeed or fail on the merits of our own two hands." The crowd cheered loudly, finally standing to cheer Nick's words.

"This is what I found out, and this is what I pledged my campaign to do. To get government out of your pocket, out of your school, and out of your community. You and your neighbors know what is best for you. Not some group of faceless bureaucrats making up regulations in Washington. With no idea of how they are affecting your life in Omaha. For this I thank you Natalie, your friends, and neighbors. Each of you contributed in your own way to my philosophy and my campaign. You are why I am the way I am. And for that, I am eternally grateful." More cheering followed Nick's confession.

"I hope I'm able to continue helping you and giving us all back the country our Constitution once enabled," announced Nick as the people behind Natalie cheered and Nat wiped her eyes with a tissue.

"Thank you to Natalie, Jamie, and Bob and Jerry and all of you for organizing these groups and driving so much support for our campaign not just in Omaha, but in surrounding states as well. Now get out there and help get everyone to the polls," smiled Nick as they closed down the call. He stared into Natalie's face until Denise told Jer to end the call.

As Jer prepared the next call, Nick's phone buzzed. It was a single smiley emoji blowing a kiss with a heart. He replied with the same. Denise noticed his smile.

"Important business?" she asked slyly.

"The most," said Nick, thinking about what Banks had told him last night.

The next call was ready, breaking Nick's reverie. This went on until they finished their last call at 9pm. They'd made one hundred and forty calls and were all exhausted. Nick told everyone to go home, get some rest, and be ready to hit it again on Sunday.

Sunday's calls wouldn't start until noon, to give folks a chance to get to church before assembling to take Nick's calls. After they finished, he went to his office and sat behind the desk in the sparsely furnished room. Chuck and Earl knocked at the door, carrying a couple of beers.

"Where's Denise?"

"Home. She was here at 5 this morning," responded Chuck.

Chuck and Earl took a seat in the two uncomfortable chairs in Nick's office.

"I thought those went well," admitted Chuck.

"I think Earl enjoyed seeing Jamie," said Nick with a grin.

Earl smiled. He had enjoyed seeing Jamie and, unlike Nick with his ladies, Earl was constantly texting and talking to her on the phone. They were both trying to convince Natalie to make more of an effort to talk to Nick.

"One hundred and forty calls, wow. That is a lot of support out there," commented Chuck.

"It sure is. I guess I really had no idea how extensive the grassroots support is," remarked Nick.

"It is what makes campaigns successful. You can only afford so many paid staffers. It is the volunteers and the grassroots people who make all the difference. They spread the word and get others enthused to join the crusade. You owe a lot to Steve. He really supercharged the effort and organized them from a mob into a force to be reckoned with. Still, you have more than most, and certainly yours are very enthusiastic," observed Chuck.

"And yet, I am sensing a purpose to your visit. Denise sent you, didn't she?" asked Nick, looking at Chuck.

"She did. Nick, we have done great things, but we need to face the possibility we may not win."

"Possibility? I think you got your adverb wrong. You mean probability," said Nick with a laugh.

"What will you do?" asked Chuck.

"I don't know. I am not sure if CSU will take me back as a history professor. I guess I could write a book. Everyone else does."

"Nick, you need to get serious," grumbled Earl.

"What do you mean?"

"Seriously?" they both said at the same time.

"Yes?"

"Nick, you have accused the future President of the United States of committing a felony. Of leading a group of global elitists hell bent on making us a totalitarian hellscape. You can't say things like that and not expect to have a target on your back," said Earl, belaboring the obvious.

Nick laughed. "So, you're saying they're going to be out to get me? More than they have already tried?"

"Big time. You need a plan, and probably a very visible one, so they can't just shoot you again," counseled Chuck.

"I'm not sure they shot me."

"What the hell does that mean?" asked Earl.

"As you say, I am not only a threat to Lexi, but to a lot of corporate interests as well. It could very well have been one of them."

"My point exactly. Chuck wants you in something visible. I want you underground and hidden. Let's say you lose. What are you going to do if all your followers are looking for direction? You *could* start a revolution and they know it," noted Earl.

"Not my style. And it certainly goes against the Constitution. When you lose fair and square or even unfair and square, you have to regroup, fix what went wrong, and try again. Complaining about it doesn't fix it," replied Nick.

Chuck shook his head. "Nick, rational thought and the Party does not go hand in hand. That's why we're at this point. That's your plan? Continue to oppose the administration?"

"I don't know what else I can do. I have to walk the path I have chosen. To use our elective society to change it within the system as it was laid out."

"And if she changes that system radically, even more than the filibuster? Say adding states, packing the courts, doing away with any voter ID, allowing illegals to vote. What then? How does the system allow you to have a fair fight when she can change the rules in her favor?"

"Chuck, if she does all this, she will lose the plurality she thinks she'll gain. Folk's livelihood will be impacted and when that happens, they will look for someone to blame. The obvious choice is Lexi. When that happens, we'll achieve a majority, not just in the Presidency, but in the House and Senate as well. Short of totalitarian rule and shredding the bill of rights, we will win in time."

"So, Pollyanna, what if she is successful in shredding the bill of rights? Then what?" asked Earl.

Nick looked at him, not wanting to verbalize the obvious answer.

"You know if it comes to that or even is leading to that, it would not be a stretch for her to arrest you for treason on any charge she wants. She'll own the entire justice process," said Earl.

"We'll deal with that if it comes to it. Let's go see if we can win an election first. I'm tired. I'm heading back to the office and my good ole Murphy bed. I'm gonna miss that bed."

Chuck laughed, shaking his head.

"Good night, Nick," they said as Nick left, followed by his bodyguards.

"You know they'll have to kill him whether he wins or loses," sighed Earl.

"I do. It is our job to not let them," said Chuck.

"Amen," replied Earl, without a clue how to stop them.

Chapter 20

Senator Banks was in his study as usual, having just finished a mid-morning breakfast of oatmeal and fruit with his coffee. He had the old-fashioned newspapers from the US and England on the desk. As he started in on one, Hobson knocked.

"Come in."

"Sir, this package came Express Delivery."

"On Sunday? Did you scan it?"

"I did, sir. It is metallic, but doesn't trigger any of the usual bomb characteristics."

"All right Hobson, I doubt anyone wants to waste their bomb on me."

Hobson left and closed the inner office doors. Senator Banks held the package up. It weighed about five pounds. He opened the box and unwrapped the contents. It was shaped like a brick. Made of stainless steel with what appeared to be a camera, pointing straight upwards. There was a card. It instructed him to press on a corner and wait for it to activate. Then they would talk. It was unsigned, but it was addressed to Senator Banks. He placed it in the middle of his desk and looked at it with a bit of trepidation.

He held a finger against a corner as the box lit up and a green light started blinking. A holographic projector in the top projected a stylized view of a Chinese zodiac wheel in the air directly above it, moving through images of the zodiac until it rested on an image of the Rat.

Senator Banks gasped audibly. He'd long suspected the existence of the Zodiac Council. Rumor persisted this secret council comprised twelve global elites, each represented by a Chinese Zodiac symbol. After forty years in the KSG, Banks had never been able to confirm it existed.

He knew enough about the Chinese Zodiac hierarchy to know the Rat was at the top. If this was to be believed, he was about to speak to the leader of this secret society.

A mechanical voice emanated from the 'brick'.

"Senator, for years, you have been a useful and loyal servant. Your inclusion in our various organizations, like the CFR, and your rise into the upper ranks of the 'inner circle' of Konigschloss, revealed our approval of your actions and the commitment of your spirit to the cause of globalization," said the voice.

Banks paused, digesting this. The Council on Foreign Relations was a more visible organization. Founded over a hundred years ago, it comprised the rich and powerful in all industries. As far as Banks could tell, the CFR was light on substance and heavy on ego. There always seemed to be a lot of drinking, pontificating, philandering, but not much global power mongering.

He'd attended these meetings since becoming a congressman and receiving an invitation over sixty years previously. And while yes, he had consistently been included in meetings with foreign heads of states and dignitaries, there was no master plan being discussed. He always smiled when anyone in Congress or the media would try to reference some global cabal running the world.

Banks knew the CFR was as far from this as possible. It really was one of the many vanity groups who surrounded themselves with sycophants, all claiming how important they were to each other. CFR, Bilderberg, Aspen Institute and Davos were all just excuses to bloviate. Nothing ever changed. And no one was ruling anything from them.

Konigschloss had always been different. More focused and serious in its efforts to 'direct' policy toward stated goals of globalization. With a much more exclusive membership made up of members who could affect this change. In their governments and industries. Secretive and exclusive, with no publicity. Focused beyond sovereign borders.

"And I suppose it would do no good to ask you to reveal yourself, though I have a pretty good idea who you are," asked Banks.

"Indeed, you are correct. As you know, our efforts have been global, putting the safety of the planet and its 8 billion inhabitants first. It is our goal, through the CFR, WTO, WHO, WEF, UN, IMF and other organizations, to move the disunited countries of the world into a true collaborative society. The inability of the United States to wholeheartedly support the global community efforts has prevented us from uniting the peoples and the resources they have, to prevent Armageddon and global planetary destruction," the mechanical voice paused.

"This you know. You fully understand our hopes and dreams, our tireless efforts to affect public policy in all civilized countries toward what is right, just, and good for all, not just the successful." The voice continued with the fervor of a genuine believer.

"No offense, Mr. Rodent, but I am long past my sell by date and your rhetoric won't work on me any longer. I admit to being ambitious and ideologic in the past. As I gained perspective and wisdom, I saw the errors of my ways and, frankly, my choices. What is the point of your *visit*?"

Rat ignored the slight on his name and continued. "You've been meeting with Turner. Why?"

"Turner is merely a colleague in the Senate. We confer from time to time to compare perspectives on pending legislature," deflected Banks conversationally.

The mechanical voice laughed. It was terrifying, like metal nails on steel. "If that were the case, I don't believe we would be having this conversation," replied Rat.

"Maksim, what do you want?" said Banks, pushing for a response.

"Nice try Baxter. You have long suspected the council or something like it existed. After all, you have been coming to the KSG retreats for decades. Now I can confirm it. You are probably wondering why you were never advanced?"

"No, actually I am not. I knew my inclusion was simply as a convenient mole in the US government's intelligence agencies. My wealth and influence pales before most of the other members of the group. Just as the inclusion of the President and those before him and now the current Vice President is merely you playing to their egos."

"Perceptive as always, Baxter."

"Surely by now, you know I betrayed no secrets likely to compromise the safety of my nation. I played along with your game, with one of my own."

"And now you have answered *my* question. You do indeed know why you were never invited to this council. As for your patriotism, have no fear, your weaker counterparts in the Presidency were more than happy to compromise your intelligence secrets in return for favors and activities beneficial to their own personal well beings, and of course, personal wealth."

Banks laughed, hoping his own was as disconcerting to his counterpart.

"Our presidents are generally weak and compromised individuals. If you knew anything about America, you would know they are not to be trusted with true secrets. Our intelligence agencies ensure they know as little as possible and are led to the conclusions we wish them to reach. This is our own safeguard against the people electing presidents of low character. The Vice President showed this during the debate with her felony disclosure. Exactly why we don't trust them with anything substantial."

"Perhaps. Yet they were useful idiots, as the saying goes."

"There must be a purpose to this revelation?" pushed Banks.

"I wanted to let you know you are not as clever as you think. We know about your efforts to counter our influence. We are really seeking the same outcome. Concerned with the poor decision of our world leaders and the inability by the population to do what is in their best interest versus what feels good," said Rat.

Banks laughed again. "You're delusional. You were the ones pushing the whole 'if it feels good, just do it and damn the consequences,' cultural rot. Encouraging anarchy. Neutering authority and introducing the religion of Climate Change. This is why the US is failing to lead. You continue to hollow out our willingness to stand for what we should believe. For right vs. wrong. This is your doing. I have seen it firsthand in the policies we have advocated and supported in KSG. How the 'philanthropy' of the world's richest elites and their foundations are directed to undercut the well-being of institutions and entire countries.

At least those that could stand in the way of your global goals. You forget you invited me to KSG and let me witness your efforts to drive this all this time."

"A progressive movement, of which until recently, you were one of our major proponents in the US Senate, I might add," replied Rat. "Look no further than the mirror to take credit for much of the cultural slide of your fellow citizens."

"Much as I would like to continue this conversation, it is past my nap time. What is the purpose?"

"Stop helping him. Consider this a warning. Turner cannot win. We will make sure he does not. You cannot change this outcome. Do not throw away your influence on a whim. You may have suddenly developed a conscience, but believe me, I know you and what you have done. There is not enough time left on your calendar to atone for the blood on your hands."

Banks looked at the ceiling and closed his eyes as the voice continued.

"Stop now and we will overlook this sudden lapse in judgment. You hold a position of prominence in the inner circle. Your words carry weight. You have consequence. You make a difference and you've contributed to the overall goals. Do not squander this lifetime of achievement on this whim of rebellious outrage."

"Democracy has had its cycle. Progressive Socialism is the next logical step. Only as a collective can the world once again thrive. America, as a lone super power for decades, did nothing to use its position to force change. Or to stop the damage that has occurred on her watch. It is time for the next batter to step up to the plate, as you Americans are so fond of saying."

"So, you aren't American?" asked Banks, continuing to seek the speaker's identity.

"Ah, nice try, Senator, but I will answer this one question. No, I'm not an American," said Rat.

"I will take your advice under advisement. What do I do with this device? Very clever."

"Remember Senator, do not interfere more. Let Turner have his moment and fade to oblivion. We are the future, remember that," ended Rat as the holographic image disappeared.

Banks summoned Hobson. He asked him to dispose of the 'brick' by putting it in a metal container and sealing it. He would tell him where to send it later. Hobson took the device and left for the garage.

The Senator sat contemplating the conversation in his study just off the library. He stood slowly, closing the door to his inner office. Shuffling to the bookcase opposite, he stuck his hand into the space where he had taken out the book he gave to Nick. Pushing a catch inside, a secret panel opened. He entered yet another smaller, more private den with only a small desk, chair and large screen TV. The bookcase door silently shut behind him.

He sat, turned on some equipment, made a few clicks with the mouse once the app loaded on the screen, and waited. In a minute, the Great Seal of the United States, with the unfinished pyramid, came up on the screen. A mechanical voice answered in the headset Banks had put awkwardly on his head.

"It is real. I got a call from the head of the Council. It is a Chinese zodiac, as we suspected. So, there are likely twelve. King Rat himself reached out. We were right to assume there was a coordinated effort. And he is not an American either. I am almost sure it is Pavlovich, just as we have suspected all along, with his Konigschloss ties. Also, as we suspected, he is driving all the global agencies to work on their agendas beyond what we discuss in the broader meetings," explained Banks to his counterpart.

Banks hated the headset. It always gave him a headache. He took it off and hit the speaker function. "…always knew those agencies were certainly working against American interests. None of this is a big surprise, other than confirmation there is a group directing efforts. It is good to know, but really it changes nothing. The Constitution is under attack and all we know now is it is confirmed. What did they want?"

"They want me to stop helping Turner."

"A little late in the game to ask you to stop helping. The election is in three days. That means it must be working and they are now worried.

Why else risk reaching out or confirming their existence?" asked Bank's companion on the call, their voice masked as well for security.

"True. I am trying to figure out how they know I was helping Turner. I have only met with him a few times and never in a way to draw unusual attention."

"You didn't hide it either."

"It was worth it. You know what this means," said Banks, ominously.

"I do."

"I'm dying, anyway. Two months max, most likely less. I wanted to make it through the election. My state has an Opposition governor so they can appoint a replacement for a year to help stop Lexi when she wins."

"We have done all we can do. This time around, though, we will not sit idly by as they stop all the audits and reviews. We will fight, because if we lose, we lose it all."

"Agree." mused Banks. "Let me send the device to you. It is clever and projects a holographic image. It must have used a satellite link once I activated it."

"Send it to Kwan. We have used him in the past."

"When I am gone, he would make a great replacement for the Framers."

"Excellent recommendation. I will propose it."

"Madison, you'll need to follow up with him on what he finds," said Banks, addressing his fellow member of the Framers by their own code name.

"Did you tell Turner about us?" asked Madison.

"No. There is no need for him to know anything about what we are doing. In time, he will find out. I alluded to help he may have from the most unlikely sources," answered Banks.

"What will you do, Hamilton?" asked Madison.

"What I have been doing. Help Turner any way I can with the time I have left."

"Farewell Hamilton. We will not forget all you have done for us and the cause of liberty. The risks and the sacrifices."

"Farewell Madison. It is your burden to carry now," ended Banks with a sigh.

Chapter 21

"This morning, the FBI executed a series of raids seizing fraudulent mail in ballots in eleven counties totaling roughly 500,000 write in ballots for Nick Turner. These were in official election boxes being transported to the central counting locations in these counties. It appears from the evidence collected so far, someone is trying to alter the election in Michigan in favor of Turner," explained Karen Coleman, acting director of the FBI at the hastily called early Sunday morning press conference.

"Director, how did you learn of this activity?" asked Lauren Bergamo.

"We received a tip regarding the transport of the doctored ballots," replied Karen, calling on another reporter, as Lauren shouted out a follow up.

"Were you able to determine from the drivers where the ballots were printed? To raid the actual warehouses and determine who did this?" asked Lauren, clearly annoying Karen with the question.

"We are interviewing the drivers to determine where they picked up the ballots. One of them had a video showing Turner campaign manager Denise Rojas inspecting these bins in one warehouse as they were loaded. We have not verified the authenticity of the video," she replied, as they played the video on a big screen behind her. ANC went to full screen on their broadcast, having been provided a copy.

"Did the driver say he saw Ms. Rojas? How was the FBI tipped off to know where to go in eleven different counties?" asked Lauren, continuing to dig for more details.

"At this time, we are not at liberty to reveal our sources or to comment further on the evidence," said Karen, clearly uncomfortable by this line of questioning.

"Don't you think it is coincidental you got tips to find eleven different trucks in eleven counties spread around the big state of Michigan? Have you run the registration for the trucks yet? Who rented them? Who hired the drivers, who paid them?" pushed Lauren, not giving up.

"Perhaps you would like to run the investigation, Miss Bergamo? We are doing all those things and more and we intend to get to the bottom of this attempt at election fraud as quickly as possible."

"Excuse me, director," responded Lauren, shaking her head. "Why would one of the drivers have a video of Denise Rojas looking at bins? That makes no sense. They are just drivers, as you said earlier. They didn't even know what they were transporting. By your own words, they weren't even present when the trucks were loaded. With the Deep Fake technology available now, it would not be hard to fake a video of her looking at the bins, of planting it on the phone of a driver and then 'tipping' the FBI off to show up in eleven different counties with specific descriptions of exactly what trucks to look for. This seems just a little too convenient. Especially given the number of bombshell attacks against the Senator in the last two weeks," finished Lauren, her tone clearly skeptical.

Karen stared at Lauren for a second before responding.

"Miss Bergamo, I believe your own part in those bombshells and attempts at deceptive reporting is well documented. We are the FBI and deal with facts. I think we are done here. Thank you for your speculation, but we will investigate the *facts* of the case. What is key here is we have stopped fraud on a massive scale from occurring in Michigan, apparently favoring Senator Turner," finished Director Coleman.

#

"What the hell?" asked Lexi, turning to look at Mel while Bergamo began poking holes in the FBI's case instead of just reporting the facts of the ballot seizure. She picked up the phone and dialed Sherman.

They'd been looking at the TV in her office, which showed a split screen with the FBI Director's news conference and ANC footage of the FBI stopping and arresting several drivers in different locations in the other. Examining the contents of the trucks, opening officially marked boxes of ballots with several agents holding up filled out ballots. 'Nick Turner' was clearly written out on the write in line on each ballot.

"Get that little bitch under control Sherman, what is she doing?" She listened as Sherman talked in her ear. "You had better fix this now. You didn't get exclusive coverage to film the seizures so you could fuck it up. I don't want to see *any* replays of her questions," finished Lexi as she hung up.

"Why would she be defending him?" asked Mel, raising an eyebrow at Lexi's reference to ANC being tipped for exclusive coverage.

"Beats me. She has pretty much made her career this last year reporting on and sparring with Turner," shrugged Lexi.

"She was embarrassed by Turner showing everything in Chicago. This is a pretty obvious setup, though. She is right. It won't hold up too much scrutiny. I wonder who tipped them off?" mused Mel, staring at Lexi.

"It doesn't have to stand up to any scrutiny. You know that. It is the same impression as being a convicted felon or accused of raping a teenager. Even *when* it gets overturned on appeal or turns out to be false, people still remember that initial accusation or verdict. Same thing here. People will hear this and won't hear anything else. They'll assume Turner is cheating to win," said Lexi, ignoring Mel's implied question.

"I thought you were friends with Denise? You just threw her under a semi."

"She understands this is the way the game is played," shrugged Lexi, getting up to pace the office. "She's been part of these on our side in the past. Her mistake was signing up to play on the enemy team. There is no allegiance in politics. You taught me that many years ago. She brought this on herself."

"Regardless, this will hang around her neck even when they find out it is a fake," noted Mel.

"Politics is a dirty and dangerous business. There are always casualties," answered Lexi, with no remorse in her voice.

#

"Get me on TV, now," ordered Nick, furious at the latest revelation.

He and the team were assembled on Sunday morning, going through the plans for the day when their phones started going crazy with breaking news.

Flipping through the various stations, all showing the footage of the raid and references to Denise being involved. None of the other stations showed any of the Q&A from the press conference.

All the pundits were laying into the obvious need for Nick to cheat to be relevant in Michigan. The guests were unanimous in their calls for Nick to admit to being caught cheating and to withdraw from the race.

"Nick, I didn't do it," wailed Denise, defensively.

"Of course you didn't. If people used their brain, they know this. Even Bergamo had to point out the obvious," added Nick with a bit of venom, causing Denise to glance at him.

"At least EXN is showing her questions. We need to send her a thank-you card for that one," commented Chuck. "Maybe she remembered some of her J-school training."

"She never finished journalism school," replied Nick automatically, before catching himself.

"How do you know that?" asked Chuck as Denise stared at Nick knowingly.

"I googled her when she started attacking me," deflected Nick, staring back at Denise, while the others looked at him, surprised at his knowledge of Lauren's schooling. "She was a beauty queen and got on TV that way." Nick's tone was one of sarcasm rather than admiration. "Can Margie get me on anywhere or do we need to do a press conference?"

Denise covered the phone mic. "She's working on it. Most likely a press conference. We should head to the capital and do it from the rotunda where the press is already set up. We'll get better coverage."

"It's the Sunday morning before the election. We'll be lucky to get any coverage," said Chuck.

Denise removed her hand and continued talking to Margie on the phone.

"Chuck, how many legit mail in votes do you think we would have in Michigan?" asked Nick

"Maybe 50,000 max, probably less. Our polling shows most of your support is going to be day of voting at the polls. The mail-in ballots are predominantly Lexi's base," replied Chuck.

"Earl?"

"Ya boss," said Earl from a corner of the conference room.

"Can you call your investigator buddy? See if he can do what Bergamo suggested. See if he can get a look at the truck license plates and reverse track those to their origins, who paid for them, and where they picked up the ballots. Review the ANC footage. Let's go through and see if there is anything."

"On it already," nodded Earl.

"Let's face it. They are all in Party counties. In fact, if memory serves, these are the *only* 11 counties the Party carried out of 83. This also means they have printing capabilities. And they have ballots. It means they are also printing ballots for Lexi. We might use this to turn the tables on her. She has all eyes on me for ballot fraud, but she is the one we need to catch cheating," remarked Nick.

"I still have friends in the bureau. Let me see if we can dig up any further details," agreed Earl.

"I wish we could get our hands on the video of fake Denise. If we could quickly confirm it was a fake, we could debunk the whole thing," said Nick.

"Fat chance of that. No way the FBI releases that to us," replied Earl.

"Wait a minute, can we play back the press conference, or even better, stream it on a laptop? Where is Jer?" asked Nick, looking around.

"I'll get him," responded Earl, talking on the phone while walking out of the conference room. 30 seconds later Margie and Jer walked into the conference room, Jer carrying his ever-present laptop.

"Jer, can you bring up the footage from ANC they just showed?"

"Sure, what am I looking for?"

"Stop it when the footage of Denise is on the screen. Can you take that bit and enhance it and look around the edges to see if there are any time codes of anything that could tell us when it was filmed?" asked Nick.

"Let me see what I can do," said Jer, staring intently into his screen, then getting up and hooking up to the big screen in the room so he could zoom in and explore every corner of the recording.

"Nick, we can do a press conference in 90 minutes. The networks need that much time to get folks to the rotunda to prepare," informed Margie, hanging up her phone.

"Good. We'll nip this in the bud." Nick glanced over at Denise, who sat looking dejected.

"We'll figure it out. Don't worry."

"I know, but it seems like she is using all of us to get to you."

"They're beginning to panic. I can't wait for the first polls to come in now that we have told our guys to tell the truth and they have enough time to answer truthfully for the first time," smiled Nick.

"The pollsters still have to call the right people for that to matter, Nick," said Jer, staring at each corner of the video, trying to find anything he could use to date it.

"Well, the final polls will come out tomorrow and the pollsters are always more accurate with the last poll so they can claim they got it right even though all their other polls are worthless," explained Nick.

"Nick, there isn't anything. No clock on the wall, no newspaper, no watches, no time codes. I'm not having any luck," said a dejected Jer.

Everyone stood and looked at the blown-up picture on the big screen as Jer played it in slow motion, frame by frame. Nick noticed one worker took a sip of coffee and set the cup down on a table.

#

Nick stood in front of a bank of cameras and microphones. He let out an audible sigh. Then he smiled and shook his head. Not the start everyone was thinking would happen. Then he laughed, further compounding their confusion.

"You know, I have seen some pretty comical things in my life. Including inept attempts to infiltrate bases in Afghanistan and Iraq. Even the worst of the attempts by the Taliban and ISIS to deceive us were better than this, the lamest of lame attempts. I don't know who is coming up with this bull excrement," challenged Nick, looking into the camera, "but Lexi, you should fire them." Several cameramen off camera were heard laughing.

"As most of you already heard with Miss Bergamo's obvious questions at the press conference," started Nick, looking through the assembled newscasters, where Lauren was not present.

"Why in the world would I be flooding only Party counties with write-in ballots? Wouldn't it be better to focus on the 73 Opposition counties? It would be much more believable, especially since so many of the current Administration's policies benefit the minority voters in the urban areas of Detroit, Ann Arbor, Lansing and Saginaw, where these ballots came from?" Nick paused, looking over the ten to twelve reporters they could round up on short notice.

"Who gets an anonymous tip to show up and track and stop eleven trucks? With detailed descriptions of the trucks and in eleven counties separated sometimes by hundreds of miles? I'll tell you who. This only happens when the person who organized the con provides the tip. At least ANC didn't get to film commandos coming out of the river to arrest sixty-eight-year-old pundits this time." More laughter from the crews filming in the background.

"Again, props to Miss Bergamo, but this is easy to debunk. Track the trucks. Who rented them, the shell companies behind it. Track them back to the pickup point? It will probably lead back to the warehouses, or at least the shell corporations involved. I can only assume our crack FBI is doing this right now and launching similar raids. If they are not, you have part of your answer regarding who is behind this."

"Something else to consider. Anyone who can print off and fill in ballots with my name to *frame* me probably has the equipment and ability to print ballots for someone else. Hmm, who is suspected of printing ballots and preventing observers from looking into the counting activities in Detroit's Wayne county in the past few elections?"

"We all know who. I bet if our FBI took Miss Bergamo's advice and hurried, they might still get to those printing operations before the real cheaters send their ballots to these same eleven deep blue counties. I will tell you this: if they stop counting ballots in Detroit or suddenly start pulling bins of ballots from under tables, there should be an audit of every vote in Michigan. Contact every voter and ask if they voted and for whom," suggested Nick, getting worked up.

"This is desperation and panic by at least one of my opponents. I think you know which one. Anyway, the icing on the cake is trying to include a video of my campaign manager supposedly coordinating all of this. And it was conveniently found on the phone of a driver who had no idea what he was carrying? How stupid do they think we are?"

"Why the F does he have a video like that on his phone? I would also like to admonish the FBI for once again, showing up in the last week of an election to throw out disinformation and attempt to swing voter sentiment. Obviously, the video is a fake. The FBI used to be a world class organization full of dedicated and serious investigators."

"For years we've been saying it is only the management, but you know what? Nothing has changed. One can only assume it goes deeper than the leadership. It is sad when the good people in the FBI won't or cannot stand up to the nefarious and potentially illegal activities of their superiors. It seems cancel culture exists within our intelligence agencies as well." Nick stopped again to allow his accusations to sink in. Then sighing continued.

"Once again, I categorically deny these allegations."

The reporters immediately started shouting questions. Nick called on Meg from RBS. "Senator, how can you possibly know the video is fake? The FBI only got it this morning. Do you have a copy?"

"Thank you for asking that question. We examined the video, as it is obviously a Deep Fake. You know those videos they make that are so realistic. Where they take your child's videos and images from KooKoo and create fake ones using them to demand money for being kidnapped. The things the FBI really should be trying to stop," noted Nick again sarcastically.

Meg interrupted. "Senator, you don't expect us to believe you figured out it was a fake looking at an image from a broadcast feed. I am fairly certain the FBI did not provide you with the original," she said somewhat defiantly.

"Meg, you are exactly right. Clearly, this was another sign of amateur hour. Here is what we discovered. The image over my shoulder shows the broadcast footage. We could isolate a curious object being set down on a table. As we zoom in and enhance, you can see it is the ubiquitous to go coffee cup. As you enhance the image, you can just make out Rafael ordered a caramel macchiato with an extra shot of espresso, but more curious, you can see he ordered it on Friday morning at 8:15. Unless Denise has a teleporter I am not aware of, she was with me and scores of others all day on Thursday in Texas and then all day in DC starting at 5:30 am with dozens who can verify these facts."

"Questions?" continued Nick.

"Senator," said Al from FLCN, "No offence, but you could just as easily have faked this view of the video."

"That is true Al. I am happy to take a feed from your laptop and do exactly what we just did with you or anyone else present to see we did not alter any aspect of what we showed you. As is always the case, we are happy to take lie detector tests or any other activity to prove our innocence. All I ask is for my opponents to be asked the same questions. Under the same conditions. I would be happy to sit side by side with my opponents to answer that question. I am confident of the outcome of *my* test. Schedule it. Any time, any place, and I will sit there right next to the Vice President," challenged Nick.

"Why do you keep accusing the Vice President? There is not a single shred of evidence pointing toward her involvement. You constantly try to deflect your scandals back on her. Frankly, Senator, it seems like you are the one trying to impact the election process with mis-information and wild accusations without proof," accused Al in rebuttal.

Nick paused before answering, staring at Al until he looked away. "Al, there is a phrase from Shakespeare, 'truth will out'. Eventually, the truth always surfaces. I want you and the public to remember exactly what you just claimed. I know what I have done and *not* done and take full responsibility for all my actions. I would also challenge both the Governor and the Vice President to pledge to join my call for full audits with random samplings of five hundred voters in each Michigan county. With observers from both parties asking these voters *if* they did indeed mail in a ballot for the election."

"Senator, why would we need to do that?" asked Meg.

Nick stared in disbelief for a second. "Well, Meg, I have been accused of fraud and cheating. I have just proved this is a frame job. Someone did this. I want to clear both my name and to ensure for the public, their vote is indeed being counted and not disenfranchised by a bunch of fraudulent votes being counted to change their will and choice. More importantly, I want to prove those who did not cast a vote are not having votes cast for them."

Meg shook her head, a frown on her face. "Why does it always come back to mail in ballot fraud? Senator, you are a broken record. There is no proof of any of this in significant amounts to impact *any election*."

"Meg, maybe that is true, but much of the electorate feels something is happening. They no longer believe the outcomes are fair or transparent. We need to restore confidence. The only way to do that is for ALL of us as candidates to pledge to do some sort of forensic audit of a random sampling of voters. Once we do this, we can put to bed any theories that people are having votes cast for them when they do not cast a vote. Why is this so controversial?"

"Senator, it sets a terrible precedent."

"So did lawfare and weaponizing the justice system. At least we can fix this one with a simple and transparent effort," challenged Nick back.

"It just makes it more likely every loser candidate demands this costly audit."

"Even more reason to do it on this biggest stage. Debunk the conspiracy theories. Only losers have to worry if the outcome is correct. In fact, my campaign will even pledge to pay the cost for this audit in Michigan after the election. What say you, opponents?" asked Nick, looking into the camera with a smile.

"Senator, you are so far behind in the polls, all this does is give more fuel to your white supremacist militia supporters to get violent when you lose," interjected Al.

"Nice deflection Al. The offer stands. Those without fear will accept my offer. Those who decline need to explain their reason for being afraid of a simple audit. I think we have sufficiently debunked this ballot hoax. Hopefully, the FBI will show some integrity and conclude this investigation immediately before they again affect an election outcome," commented Nick.

Margie broke in. "Ok, I think that about does it. Thank you for assembling on such short notice. Enjoy the rest of your Sunday. Senator, if you please," she said, leading Nick away.

#

Lexi sat in the oval office. Signing documents with the President's seal. She watched the interview on her phone. Smiling and shaking her head as Nick once again deflected an attack. He really was bulletproof. Just the right tone of humor and anger to shrug it off. His finding the coffee cup on the table made her lean back in the chair, thinking once again what might have been had they convinced him to join her side.

Her secure phone rang. "Yes, Mel, I have been watching," said Lexi, answering.

"Unbelievable. Now we need to come up with a response to his request for an audit," groaned Mel.

"We'll just stick with our usual stance of we have full confidence in the voters of America and our thousands of paid and volunteer poll workers. We have the safest and most secure elections in the world. Only losers complain about the integrity of elections. We will not dignify Senator Turner's conspiracy theories nor set dangerous precedents, allowing sore losers a podium to stir up sedition against their fellow citizens. Did you get all that?"

"I did. Brilliant as always. I'll get it on the wire."

"We need to figure out what we can do with him after the election. I still like the idea of recalling him to active duty. Can we send him to clear landmines on those beaches in the Falkland Islands?" chuckled Lexi. "I saw a documentary on that once. You know, the penguins can walk on the beach because they don't weigh enough, but if a human does, kablooey," observed Lexi.

Mel laughed. "I'll look into it. I think they cleared all those landmines already. Maybe Alaska or even better Guam. He is getting some traction on his continuous accusations that you are behind all this. All it takes is one person to cave in...," trailed off Mel.

"I know. I assume all our operations are complete and shipments have already been made?" asked Lexi.

"Yes, but with all this extra scrutiny, we need to be careful, especially in Michigan. We shouldn't need them anyway, since he really is a write-in candidate."

"No chances Mel. Hear me? No chances. We cannot afford to screw this up. And no loose ends. I don't want folks showing up on ANC talking about what they saw or did," ordered Lexi.

"Agreed. Just so I can be prepared. Do you have any more of these little surprises?" asked Mel, somewhat concerned.

"No. I give up. We'll have to rely on all our organizations to get out the vote," answered Lexi, revealing her part in this latest attempted frame of Turner.

"We have done all we can. Let it play out and we'll deal with any fallout."

"We can't take any chances. Use Roland if you have to. No loose ends."

"Lexi, we have it under control. We've been lucky so far. Even someone as good as Roland can screw up. If he does, he'll take us down."

"You sure we shouldn't just go all in from the beginning?" she asked, ignoring Mel's warning.

"No, you know my feeling. Turner is right, and he knows it. Only our ability to stop real audits and our stranglehold on the media stop this from collapsing. There is way too much talk about harvesting and ballot fraud. The lower we can keep the turnout and still win, the better. The votes are legal, so that will stand up to the first level of scrutiny. Any beyond that and people will start invalidating votes if they are curious and look for themselves out of curiosity. Only to realize someone voted in their name. We'll keep it in our back pocket as planned," he said.

"OK, but we can't wait too long. Our exit polling has sucked these last few elections, so we need to make sure our data is good."

"We will. We have operatives in every precinct and in every counting crew in all the swing counties in the swing states. Most of the team leads are already ours. Compromised thanks to all those WHS NGOs. They know what happens if they don't do as they are told. Just like the last time, so they know what to do as well if things start going south," offered Mel.

"You mean like water leaks?" scoffed Lexi. "We need to do better. How about a bomb scare, anthrax, or something like that? At least knock out the cameras first this time."

"We have better contingencies this go round."

"And the machines?"

"Lexi, we got this. Trust me," said Mel.

"I do."

Mel hung up. Lexi sat in the Oval, looking around. She was already thinking about how she would redecorate. The First Lady had horrible taste.

#

In as secure facility in Offutt airbase outside Omaha, millions of calls were monitored for keywords twenty-four hours a day. Most conversations were everyday phone calls. These were immediately erased, not having any of the keywords in them.

This program was designed to breakthrough secure communications. In theory any call being scrambled, encrypted, or masked was more likely to be one where these keywords would show up.

These calls were kept and other sophisticated programs tried to decode them to determine the subjects of the call and the locations of both the caller and the receiver. Once identified, whatever information was captured and decrypted would be tagged for review by an analyst with a high enough security clearance to determine next steps.

Calls from both allied and enemy countries were monitored without exception. It was at the discretion of the technician and their command structure which calls were tagged for additional review and which were simply deleted for containing indelicate, but not illegal information.

The sheer volume of information captured, analyzed, decrypted, and tagged for review ensured much of this information did not receive the level of follow up it needed. having the data was only step one.

Recognizing the value of the data and then responding quickly to the information were steps two and three. The American intelligence agencies, who still did not share information well between civilian and military intelligence were making little progress, despite spectacular failures, exemplified in both September 11th and October 7th. Progress was slow. Too slow.

Chapter 22

Mel and Harriet sat in the conference room in Lexi's DC HQ, late on Sunday, having just finished several hours with Lexi rallying their grassroots teams in the offices across the country. Getting out the vote and not assuming Lexi would win were the key messages. They'd sent Lexi out to get some rest and dinner while they continued.

"She's worried Harry. She thinks Turner is peaking at exactly the wrong time and that we didn't do enough to squash him when we had the chance. All our efforts to hang something around his neck haven't worked. If anything, they strengthened him. She is worried and when she is worried, she makes mistakes. Like the bit with the ballots this morning. Did you know about that?" asked Mel.

"Yes, she asked me to set it up and not tell you," admitted Harriet sheepishly.

"Geez Harry. Dirty tricks are not your strong suit. You should have told me. She knew I would have told her not to do it. Another set of ballots filled out with Turner's name? We already did that. And in Michigan, again?" Mel shook his head.

"It was the only place Josh still had printing capabilities he could use," shrugged Harriet.

"At some point, it becomes unbelievable. It brings unwanted attention to our own ballot efforts, when that is exactly what we are planning to ensure victory. Then tipping off the FBI? And ANC to be there filming the takedown of the drivers?"

"I gave ANC the truck descriptions and routes so they knew where the FBI would intercept," said Harriet.

"Shit. Let's get the pollsters on the phone and get this over with," said Mel.

"You worried too?" asked Harriet.

"Look at me. I am a skinny, balding Jewish political operative on a presidential campaign. It is my job to be worried," said Mel.

"Plus, she seems to have a new favorite. Where is the dark shadow?" asked Harriet.

"Lord only knows. I sure hope she doesn't have any other plans I'm not aware of. This is getting out of control when we need the most discipline. She's under a lot of pressure to deliver a big win this time."

#

Bert Minter, lead pollster for the Prescott Group and Wendall Krupa, the head of GrandSlam, were both on the video call on the big screen in the conference room. They were surprised and relieved Lexi was not in the conference room.

"Ok, how bad is it?" asked Mel.

"We have the Vice President at 41, Turner at 34, 17 for Blackbird and 8% undecided," answered Wendall. "Turner has picked up 16 and Lexi dropped 13. The margin for error is 5%."

"Jesus," blurted Mel, rubbing a hand over his balding head. "That bad. The debate performance was poor, but this is a big drop. I'm not surprised Blackbird dropped and Turner picked up some of those, but Lexi's drop is terrible, too. Bert, yours telling you the same?"

"We're showing the same thing. We have Lexi at 43, Turner 34, and 16 for Blackbird with 7% undecided. Our margin of error is +/-4."

"Explanation?" asked Mel pointedly.

"Honestly?"

"Please."

"We've been had. I think a bunch of Turner's supporters *did* successfully lie to all of us for the last six or seven months. That's the only way we can account for the big drop in her support, Turner picking up those fleeing Blackbird and her drop. It has to be the explanation. Even the debate would not cause 29 point swings in a week."

Mel sat digesting the information. "Electoral College?"

"We still show Lexi with around 330 electoral votes and she is still projected to flip Florida, hold Pennsylvania, Michigan and Wisconsin. Turner will probably win Ohio over Blackbird and probably Texas as well. Currently, we think Lexi will take both Georgia and Arizona, plus

Nevada. All the swing states. It is tightening, but it still looks good. Turner around 126 and Blackbird around 79," fudged Wendall, giving the most optimistic model.

"We see a similar split on the electoral college." Added Bert, supporting their positive outlook.

"Anything else?" asked Harriet.

Both Bert and Wendall looked away from the camera.

"God dammit, spill it guys. Lexi is not in the room," blurted Mel, getting frustrated.

"The races have tightened in all the states. Many of them are now within the margin of error, Florida, Pennsylvania, Michigan, Wisconsin, Georgia, Arizona, Virginia, Nevada, Iowa, between Turner and the VP. He is also within the margin of error in North Carolina, all the great plains states, the inter-mountain west, Ohio, and Indiana with Blackbird. We think he has a lock on Texas," said Bert.

"So let me get this straight. You're saying he would have polled how much higher back in the spring, five points?" asked Mel.

"No, probably closer to ten, which would have put him at fifteen when he started and then throughout the summer he was probably ahead of Blackbird the whole time, and Lexi was probably closer to where she is now. We think his supporters were lying and saying they were with her the entire summer. They fucked us," said Bert.

"OK, anything else we need to worry about?" asked Harriet, thinking.

"Turnout. Our models are showing an ungodly election day of turnout for Turner. He has preached from day one to vote the day of the election at the polls. The weather is going to be fabulous all across the country except for Hawaii, which is having a late season hurricane. So far, it looks like Lexi has a ton of mail in and absentee votes already in. Turner has very few. His voters are not using their mail in ballot," explained Wendall.

"OK, that may help us if there are long lines they may get discouraged," said Harriet.

"I don't think so. Our surveys show the more likely voter to be discouraged is the Lexi voter, who thinks she has it in the bag because of the polling and who would rather go start celebrating than stand in line to cast a vote for her. On the other hand, our surveys and conversations show Turner's voters would wait in a blizzard for 3 hours to cast their vote for him," confided Bert.

"Hmm," said Mel, contemplating their info. "OK gents. Please keep this minimized as much as possible."

"Sorry Mel. Our profession has such a black eye from the last few elections. We have to publish this stuff, if only to be honest. Hell, we are already going to get killed when these come out. They are going to say we did all this on purpose to help Lexi by showing her up by 30, only to be honest about this final poll. It is a sad day for our profession. We may not survive," groaned Bert.

"You gotta hand it to Turner. He single-handedly made a laughingstock out of all of us, and we walked right into the buzz-saw, proving his point," lamented Wendall, already thinking how to push his business more toward predicting sports analytics and online sports betting.

"Thanks for the info. Mel, anything else?" asked Harriet, wrapping up.

Mel sat contemplating the news and shook his head. They signed off the video call and sat in silence for a moment.

"You know, she was right. I should have trusted her instincts," said Mel.

"What?"

"She said we should be attacking Turner from the beginning. I always said he was so low in the polls if we started attacking him, it would just give his campaign oxygen. I figured why give him free press when he had little money? She was right. We should have hit him hard and stopped him. It didn't help that it took so long to win the nomination. It gave him time to get out there with his message and build a grassroots following," concluded Mel, shaking his head.

"What are you going to tell her?" probed Harriet carefully.

"The truth. Turner had his people lying to pollsters. We have dropped in the polls, but we still have a commanding lead and we are projecting around 330 electoral votes," said Mel.

"And when she sees the polls?" asked Harriet.

"I will point out we are still up."

"We don't win by eight million votes this time. What matters is we win the electoral votes. That's what I'll tell her," finished Mel, trying to convince himself.

"Works for me," agreed Harriet, picking up her phone and the list of numbers to get to work driving more turnout.

"I hope it works for her," said Mel.

#

Denise and Chuck were in Nick's office. Their faces betrayed how tired they were after wrapping up their day and another hundred calls to the grass roots. Finishing the last with their teams in Hawaii and American Samoa.

"Nick, you did great these last couple of days. Your enthusiasm and genuine joy at speaking to these grassroots teams was super authentic," said Chuck with a smile.

"Thanks, I really enjoy these. Frankly, they are the only part of campaigning I do like."

"The audience gets it. Nick, I have to tell you, every other campaign I have been on, what we just did the last two days is the part those candidates *hate* the most."

"I'm not surprised. That is our problem. Candidates forget they are auditioning for a job representing these people. Instead, they pander to them for a day, a few weeks or months to get a vote, and then promptly forget about them until it is time to pander again for the next vote."

Denise and Chuck laughed, shaking their heads looking at each other. Nick was truly the unpolitician.

Before anyone could respond, all three of their phones lit up with a news alert.

"Shit," blurted Denise.

"That is certainly convenient," agreed Chuck.

'Governor Blackbird's estranged daughter Lois Conrad was killed in a single vehicle accident in North Dakota earlier this evening. Apparently, she lost control of her car after hitting a patch of black ice on the highway after an unexpected freeze,' read the alert.

Nick sat back, ruminating on the rising body count from this election. He did not believe in coincidence.

Chapter 23

For crisscrossing the country, Nick's campaign had leased a 787 airliner from United to fly them and the staff. There were too many moving parts now for Nick to not have the entire staff with him. Handling innumerable logistics issues while staying in touch with all the happenings on the ground. They would leave Reagan National at 6 am for Pittsburgh and his first rally of the day scheduled for eight.

They were all on board by six, including Tommy, who would be allowed to sit in on strategy meetings but not to film them. As they got airborne, Nick sat in the first-class area with his team around him.

"OK, where are we Jer?

"Well, Blackbird is toast. Especially now with the news of his daughter's death. Dying in a car accident on early black ice? Even if it was an accident, many assume he arranged it."

Nick shook his head. "This is a political campaign, not Fallujah. The body count is getting way too high."

"What's that mean for us?" asked Chuck.

"Thankfully, you made my job easier by telling our supporters to stop lying. The problem now is my models are so screwed up from trying to account for hidden support that when I get actual support, I don't believe the numbers," he responded, laughing.

"The question is whether your message is getting through to the Opposition moderates. If it is, they will defect to you. If not, they will stay home. This is what Lexi is counting on."

"What do you think?"

"I think about half come over. Your abortion stance is likely to keep some of them home. Your debate performance may convince more to come over. No one likes to waste their vote and right now a vote for Blackbird is a throw away vote," said Jer.

#

They landed in Pittsburgh and headed to the stadium for a rally and an overflow crowd of 50,000. Nick spoke for thirty minutes, telling the crowd even though he was a write-in candidate, it was still worth their effort to go out and vote.

They left Pittsburgh, boarded the plane and made the short flight to Cleveland, where he spoke to 15,000 gathered at the airport. He used Ohio as an example of a state that had been in decline while the Party ruled the state. How they had slowly worked back to where they are now. A growing formerly rust belt state with some of the lowest unemployment in the region. A thriving tech and service economy, with companies relocating to the heartland for the lower cost of living and the educated and motivated workforce. Cleveland cheered him on and sent him on his way to Michigan.

He was in the air when the satellite phone rang. Denise answered it. She turned on the TV they had set up at the front of the first-class section. On the TV was the Attorney General of Michigan.

"Considering the allegations of mail in voter fraud against Senator Turner, we are going to err on the side of caution and not allow *any* of the collected mail in ballots showing a vote for Senator Turner to be counted and tallied. We understand this is an extreme case. We have asked our state Supreme Court for a ruling. Until then, given the extent of the alleged fraud, we feel it is in the best interests of the state of Michigan to sequester and not count these potentially fraudulent votes. Only day of voting will be counted for Senator Turner," finished the Attorney General.

"Don't worry, I already contacted Jenny to sue the AG and get an injunction against this order. This has no legal merit whatsoever, and it's designed to suppress your vote," observed Chuck. "We'll fast track it to the Federal Supreme Court if we have to. There is little doubt how the state Supreme Court will vote. They are all elected or appointed by Party majorities and they already voted once to keep you off the ballot."

"I know," said Nick. "Any chance they do this in Pennsylvania and Wisconsin?"

"I don't think so. They have no reason to suspect any issues. Plus, you really aren't losing that many votes there or frankly, in Michigan either. It is all about optics. It says you are cheating and calls into question any other mail in ballots," fumed Denise.

"Look at the bright side. There can't be too many more of these. They're running out of hours in the day before the polls open."

"Can we do a quick live shot from the plane? I want to get my thoughts out there?"

Margie nodded, heading back to a corner on her phone.

They landed in Detroit and headed for the baseball stadium. He took the stage in front of 40,000 Michiganders. 25,000 more waited outside the stadium, watching him on the outdoor screens having been denied entry by the Michigan State Police. Nick laid into Lexi in his speech. He all but accused her campaign and the Party Governor of orchestrating the mail in ballot fraud.

Nick stood tall at home plate on a temporary stage.

"I would ask that this time, the ballot observers in Wayne County actually be allowed to view the ballots rather than having to look at cardboard taped up by the workers to prevent anyone from seeing the ballot counting. What in the world could they possibly be hiding? This is another in a long string of obvious coverups and attempts to ensure the progressive agenda is implemented against the will of the people."

The crowd cheered loudly in agreement at this obvious lack of transparency.

Nick warned everyone who had cast a mail in vote to not vote twice, even on a provisional ballot, as this would mean both votes would be disallowed. He'd heard rumors someone was encouraging any who had sent in mail in ballots for Nick to do this.

This was just another ploy by whoever was trying to frame him to cancel his voters. The crowd booed loudly at this dishonesty. He implored his friends and neighbors in Michigan to help those who could not get to the polls.

It was always an uphill battle to win in a write in election, but he wanted to assure everyone who voted for him their vote would matter. It would be a vote against the corruption of Michigan, Pennsylvania, and Wisconsin officials who kept him off the ballot while allowing 40 others on it.

"12 people in three states have disenfranchised you. By 4-3 majorities, these courts have made partisan decisions rather than letting the will of the people choose their candidate. They don't want you voting for me. Why is that?" smiled Nick as he finished.

"This is what our fight is about, to take control and move it back locally. To take it away from faceless bureaucrats. Now is the time to stand up and fix the system. Do not let them keep you down." The people were on their feet and cheering Turner while booing every mention of the Governor, AG, judges and Lexi.

Nick had them whipped into a fervor as he left with one last request to be peaceful.

"Violence is never the answer. Don't give them a reason to persecute you. They will make it up, but never give them a legitimate reason to arrest you. Remember this always." Nick left the stage to thunderous applause as a band replaced him to play a free concert for his followers.

At the airport, Margie grabbed Nick's arm.

"Nick, Kyle Combs from NWN will put you on live to discuss the Michigan decision. He's the only one I can get willing to do this live. Even EXN turned us down," she finished with a frown.

"Let's do it. Now?"

"Board the plane and do it from the front section. I'll keep everyone else in the back and we can take off for Milwaukee when you're done. Keep it short, please. We are already behind schedule," she pleaded.

#

"We have Senator Nick Turner on for comment following the decision to disallow the Senator's mail in ballots from counting in Michigan. Senator," said Kyle Combs in a satisfied voice.

"Not disallow, Kyle, but sequester until the FBI concludes their investigation."

"It's pretty damning evidence against you, Senator. As everyone saw on TV yesterday morning. Multiple trucks stopped with more ballots, with your name filled in."

"Let me get this straight," interrupted Nick, getting upset. "They're going to sequester *my* mail in votes and only allow day of voting in Michigan. From my voters who prove their eligibility at the polls. For me? The only candidate demanding all voters be forced to show an ID to vote. But all the millions of other mail in ballots in Michigan, without ID verification for my opponents, are going to count? Did I get that right, Kyle?"

"No one else has been caught trying to cheat except you, Senator."

"What proof is there, Kyle, that I am the one trying to cheat?"

A look of disbelief showed on Kyle's face. "There are hundreds of thousands of mail in ballots with your name filled in on them. And a video of your campaign manager directing the loading of these ballots. How is that not proof?"

Nick laughed on camera. "Kyle, we already debunked the video as a deep fake. Denise Rojas could not have been where the drivers say she was at the time they say she was supervising the loading. And we have dozens of witnesses to prove that. That alone should be enough for the FBI to realize the false nature of this entire operation."

"The FBI has not come out and agreed with you, Senator. And apparently the Michigan Attorney General doesn't either."

"I see. No one in the media or public is questioning how multiple trucks were intercepted in multiple locations, all with ANC conveniently riding along with the FBI to film the take downs?"

"Senator, while you consistently accuse the FBI of partisanship, they continue to uncover these kinds of activities and stop outright election fraud designed to help *your* campaign," responded Kyle. "Are you not the one who tells his followers 'those who shout the loudest against things are usually the one perpetrating that which they complain about?'," questioned Kyle, holding up his palm against his chest. "Sir, perhaps you need to use your Mirror tactic on your own campaign."

Nick smiled and shook his head. "Kyle, if that were true, why would I be advocating for IDs for every vote? It is a clever twist to confuse the viewers, but I am the only one demanding we do forensic audits and ensure only registered voters and legal votes be counted. Instead, the Michigan Attorney General and the same four Michigan Supreme Court justices who kept me off the ballot in the first place will also disenfranchise a large group of voters who *did* send in mail in ballots. We won't even know how many of these votes there are."

"What else can you claim? The AG and court are clearly looking out for all the voters in Michigan and ensuring they do indeed have a fair and secure election," finished Kyle.

"Here's hoping our FBI can quickly finish this investigation and uncover both the hoax and those who perpetrated it, so my voter's votes are not disenfranchised by this administration."

"Senator, we *will* have the most fair and secure election in our time. It will be because of brave members of our FBI and courts standing up to your rhetoric and disinformation designed to undermine the faith of our citizens in these election processes. I wish you luck."

The screen went blank as NWN ended the transmission.

"That went well," said Tommy sarcastically from a corner where he'd been listening.

Nick let out a big sigh, turning toward him. "Unfortunately, what he says is believable to a large swath of people who ignore or don't see me exhorting at every rally that my supporters show up on election day, show an ID, and vote."

"Nick, you are too nice for this. You care about right and wrong and the truth. None of that matters in a presidential election. It is about one thing. Whatever it takes to win."

Nick looked up at the crew cut ex-Marine. He didn't answer him as Margie and the rest of his staff filtered into the front cabin. Nick knew Tommy was right. It didn't make it any easier.

#

The plane landed in Milwaukee. Nick gave the same speech to 35,000 at the ballpark there. They, too, were upset at the treatment of a presidential candidate and the arbitrariness of the decision at this late time. Nick made an exaggerated effort to spell out his name so folks would know what to write.

Once again, he made his joke about being lucky he didn't have a complicated Greek, German, or Polish last name. The crowd laughed, as they always did. Nick wrapped up his speech in Wisconsin and headed back to the plane. Shortly after takeoff on their way to California, once again Margie came in to the first-class area and turned on the TV.

"Now what?" asked Nick.

"Honestly, I don't know," said Margie. "Senator Banks called a press conference."

"Hmm," said Nick, getting a look from Margie, Denise and Chuck.

Chapter 24

Senator Banks sat behind a low table with a microphone in front of him. He did not look well. The skin of his face sagging off his cheeks.

"Thank you for coming on such short notice. I will be mercifully brief," he said in his southern drawl.

"Considering the unlawful actions of the Michigan Attorney General to so blatantly try to affect our national election tomorrow, my information may be even more timely," commented Banks in his wonderful orator's voice.

"I have come into possession of a recording between the Vice President, Alexis Smythe-Thomas and her chief of staff, Mel Arenson, where they are discussing the timing of the release of information concerning Governor Blackbird's family history. This recording has been compared and authenticated by third party experts who have confirmed it is indeed the Vice President and her chief of staff. I will play this for you shortly. However, before I do this, I would like to comment on the state of our election processes," he said, pausing to drink water and clear his throat.

"I've been in the Congress for almost 70 years. When I was first elected, Jack Kennedy was still a senator. I've seen the extent to which the Party will go to win elections. To achieve and maintain power."

"We in the Party have held at least one branch of power for almost the entire time since World War II. Until the 1990s. Ever since, we have seen a seesaw of flipping house, senate and presidential allegiance. Leading to more and more division. More rhetoric of the other side being evil or wanting to do the country harm."

"Most of this has come from my party. During those 40 years of our control, while we had Opposition Presidents, Eisenhower, Nixon, Ford,

Reagan, even Bush the elder. We still compromised with our brethren and put together legislation that both sides approved."

"For the last few decades, there has been no such civility. The bureaucracy has grown so large we in Congress can no longer control it. It has achieved a self-sustaining livelihood, controlling most of the true levers of power in our society. Because of this, legislation is no longer the role of the Congress, instead our role is to parade around on cable TV and support whatever blood feud of the moment we are executing."

"The same goes for the Presidency. It is now a contest in who can sling the best and dodge the return fire. If the President is Opposition, then it is the sole mission of the Party to oppose anything they do or propose. Regardless of whether we believe it is useful, necessary or in fact best for the country. We are not allowed by our orthodoxy to show support. This is wrong and dangerous for our well being."

"It is now all about winning. It matters not if human beings are discarded on the way to that victory. Whether they are left on the battlefield of ill-conceived foreign entanglements or simply the victims of vicious and baseless attacks of the politics of personal destruction. Practiced with such skill by we in the Party and perfected by our current candidate."

"I have played along with these games, because once upon a time, I really believed what we stood for. Helping the downtrodden and underprivileged. Undoing the remaining prejudice and affording minorities an equal shot at the promise of the American Dream. Yet in the last decades, I have watched as all that hard fought territory was ceded back. With ignorance, forgetting our own history, we have created pampered and privileged youth with no idea of how their privileged life came about."

"Betrayed by our education system into believing the BS they have been taught instead of learning the skills to think for themselves. I have looked on in horror, passively, these last few years as we regress as a society. The return of anti-Semitism and demands by minorities for segregated dorms and separate graduations based on race or sexual preference. Praise for terrorists. Allowing crime to become prevalent once more. Enabling our higher education to be turned into Maoist re-education camps without pushback. Our citizens are afraid to exercise their first amendment rights or to have an opinion for fear of being retaliated against, and now canceled."

"Most of you are too young to remember, but these are the policies of the East German Stasi, the Soviet KGB, the SS of Hitler and the black shirts of Mussolini. Where you are hunted down and jailed or killed for daring to challenge their totalitarian authority."

"Sadly, today we are in the same environment, where if you dare to speak against ARL, climate change, Party leadership, gender dysphoria, CRT, DEI, COVID lockdowns, vaccines, show support for Israel, or advocate for the Constitution, you are deemed an enemy of the state. A subversive. An insurrectionist. The only difference between those totalitarian regimes killing or imprisoning you, is our progressives simply make you an unperson. The result is the same." He paused again to drink.

"Their willing apparatchiks in social media and, as Senator Turner calls them, American *Pravda* media will do the dirty work for you. No free society can stay free if the exchange of ideas, thoughts, and vigorous debate are all stifled."

"I do this now, knowing my time in the Senate is drawing to a close. I am not a well man. I want to leave you with one final thought before we play the clip. Money begets power. Power begets control. There is no reason to acquire money or power except to use it to exercise control. In our global community, there are those who are of no country, who do not respect or feel we need sovereign borders or individual cultures. They feel national pride and culture are impediments to efficient rule. Not rule of countries mind you, but rule of individuals. Rule as they see fit. Rule of all of you. Beware these people, these Globalists, for they see you as nothing more than a number on a spreadsheet. Their decisions are not rooted in the reality of humanity. Rather, in the reality of their own making. Where their vision of the future is realizable only through great suffering. Not of them, but of you. You will pay for their utopian schemes and their attempt to remake our world in some form of universal corporation with them as the board of directors. It all comes down to money."

"As Eisenhower famously said in his last state of the union, which I was at, beware the Military Industrial Complex, it is far beyond that now. At the last minute, he was counseled to change his speech. He'd originally called it the Congressional Military Industrial Complex, correctly identifying the insidious partnership between government, private corporations and their devilish go-between, the lobbyist. It is clear today he was over the target and should never have removed Congress from the name. They are equal partners in this manipulation. Feeding the beast with the fruit of your labor. Taxes."

"I admonish everyone who cares about seeing their children and grandchildren grow up free to choose their own destinies. To beware the international banking system. They own and control everything. They control the Vice President and the President. They also influence the heads of state everywhere. Because they own access to the money. This means they have the power and the control. Most importantly, they can direct so-called free leaders to do what they want done. They have the *leverage*. All we have to counter them is a vote, a democratic society, and a Bill of Rights."

Banks coughed and finally, with another sip of water, he spoke once more, his voice getting weaker.

"Some will say these are the musings of a delusional old man. I can tell you with certainty that impending death brings with it a clarity to see what has been obscured in the past. I have sins to atone for. Not the least of which is my docile acquiescence to policies supposedly designed to help our people. Instead, our unintended consequences brought more misery or prevented them from escaping their poverty, poor schools, or horrible neighborhoods. I will pay for my sins on my day of reckoning, as Turner has reminded so many of us, is a possibility. To this I am resigned. But I will cower in fear no more. I am not afraid of death, but I am afraid for all of you, who are being led down a path to oblivion. No different from those who boarded trains to Auschwitz, or those being transported to the re-education camps of Western China today."

"As then, we know this is wrong. Yet we turn a blind eye. I beg you, for your own souls, do not follow any longer. Choose the path of knowledge and freedom. This is now a battle of good versus evil and, believe me, the side of evil is well prepared. Stacked with unseen allies and weapons to destroy any who get in their path."

"The greatest impediment to this global catastrophe was and is the Constitution. Our enemies fully realize this. There is a candidate who embodies what America used to be about. Standing up for ideals. Standing up for what is right. Looking to and following the guidelines our founders left in the Constitution. Using the freedoms guaranteed within. Debating and asking questions. Having civil conversation to reach common goals. Allowing our citizens to vote, in person, once, for candidates who they actually got to know and understand. I won't live to see it, but either we are going to continue to decline like Rome, or we are going to recognize our troubles and work to fix this. Only Nick Turner can lead us to safety. Leading us out of globalist bondage and into a new land and a new reborn American civilization."

Banks started a coughing fit. "Let's play the recording," he said, puffing on his inhaler.

As they listened, they could hear Lexi and Mel discussing the information they had dug up on Blackbird and how best to get it out. Deciding Beverly at NWN would be the best, then discussing how and when.

They talked about the package and how to get it anonymously to Beverly so she could follow up on the material, get it verified through county records. Lexi said she would make a call to make sure there would be no issues with accessing the proper files to validate the truth of the information.

Both could be heard laughing about what it would do to Blackbird's campaign. One can be heard saying, "well he is a big boy, and he did the deed that put him in this place. This really is a public service we're providing the country."

At the close, Senator Banks once more commented "As you can see, they found the information, had it leaked, greased the skids so the

NWN reporter could find and validate the contents and then sat back as their opponent was destroyed by American *Pravda*. While no laws were broken, at least not that I am aware. It is my final atonement to make sure everyone who is voting for or contemplating voting for the Vice President, understands the kind of person to whom you would give immense power."

Banks leaned forward. "She is a puppet of these globalists. Put in place to lead the diminishment of the United States. From our role as the beacon of freedom to one where we are just another member of a global community subject to their rules and whims. Remember, she will have the ability to turn the full force of the United States government against you if she wishes. Keep that in mind as you head to the polls tomorrow."

"I thank you for your time," finished Senator Banks. Several reporters started shouting questions. Banks looked up, recognizing Lauren Bergamo. He smiled at the resourceful reporter.

"Miss Bergamo, I believe I have the strength for one or two questions only."

"Senator, where or how did you get this info?" asked Lauren.

"It was provided by a reliable source. It will stand up to an examination of the voices, as I have said," replied Banks.

"But why? You have spent nearly seventy years in Congress. Why now? Why this way, just before an election? You have to know this will create a mess and tarnish your sterling reputation," asked Lauren in an almost pleading tone.

"Miss Bergamo, I am dying. Days, weeks, a month, at the most. That changes one's perspective. Call it an epiphany. I look back over my time in the Senate. I see the faces of the young men I served with in Korea, others I helped send to their deaths in Vietnam, Iraq, Afghanistan, and Syria. How we failed America on 9/11 by ignoring the problem and even analysis by our own people. I see the failure of our political system because of money and bureaucracy. I see good people chewed up and spit out by the vicious nature of our progressive slide toward socialism and ultimately totalitarianism."

"We are destroying our own citizens for expressing an opinion. We would not be where we are if we did not question authority, question the status quo, and challenge ourselves to do better. Instead, we are destroying ourselves from the inside out. This did it for me, when I realized we are the last barrier to world domination by the monied globalists. With America and her rugged individualism crushed, the peoples of the planet will not differ from the serfs of the medieval barons. Weak, subservient, and dependent on the ruling class for food and protection. We evolved from this to our current civilization. Why in the hell would we want to go backwards?"

"When I heard Lexi planning the leak of the info about Blackbird, I decided it was not right. I think Lexi will win anyway, but I couldn't sit by and let this continue. After what she has tried to do to Turner, with all the lies, the debanking, and finally the death of those poor young men, this is what I mean. Life is irrelevant to people like Lexi and those who pull her strings. You of all people know this, having been used by them as well to bring Turner down," Lauren blushed in embarrassment at his callout of her part in the effort to ruin Nick's campaign.

"As for my reputation. When I am dead, I will not care what others think of me. Others can think whatever they would like, then and now. Now if you don't mind, I need to excuse myself," remarked Senator Banks, being helped to his feet by Hobson and exiting the Rotunda press area to the nearby private Senate lounge.

#

"That was interesting," observed Tommy, watching the TV on the plane with Nick and his staff.

"I would say Senator Banks sleeps with a clean conscious tonight," suggested Nick.

"That's some endorsement," smirked Denise. Nick gave her a look.

"At least he didn't call you the second coming or say you came from Krypton to save the planet," scoffed Denise. "I don't think this will mean much in the scheme of things. Like he said, Lexi is a bitch. I could have told everyone that. Knowing she was the one behind a leak we all suspected was her, changes nothing. Blackbird is still an SOB. I'm almost with Lexi on this one. It was a PSA to expose Blackbird for the shit he is," she finished.

"Really?" responded Nick. "Come on, it is important for folks to understand what kind of vindictive harridan they may send to the White House."

"I have to agree with Nick on this one," added Margie. "You may know her, Denise, but a lot of voters may now think twice tomorrow knowing how gleefully she torpedoed her opponent's campaign. At least he also mentioned or implied her attempts at us have mostly failed."

"I hope it was worth it for the old coot," retorted Denise. "He just threw away a reputation as one of the absolute lions of the senate."

"What is up with you? You're a bear today," asked Nick, concerned.

"Just a tough day. We have so many moving parts and now Michigan and this on top of that. I need a drink and I can't have one, so that makes it even worse," she said.

"We're all tired. At least this one's not aimed at us," added Margie.

"Did you know this was coming? You alluded to something earlier?" asked Denise.

Nick shrugged "Lucky guess".

"Lucky guess my ass," commented Tommy.

"Sort of like you had nothing to do with my nomination at the Opposition convention."

It was Tommy's turn to shrug while smiling.

Their plane continued to fly to California as a couple of pundits lionized Bank's epiphany, while ten times more were excoriating him. Including many of his fellow Party senators. Branding him as a card-carrying member of QAnon. There was no doubt on which side American *Pravda* landed.

Chapter 25

About 500 miles ahead of Nick's plane, Air Force Two also sped toward California.

Lexi sat in her private office on the plane, watching Banks committing Hari-Kari on national TV. She sat impassively as Banks said his piece. She grimaced at first at the revelation of the recording, and then she smiled.

"Why are you smiling?" asked Mel, concerned they had just been exposed and his name with hers. He liked to keep a low profile.

"Banks said it himself. This was a PSA. If I am forced to answer, I'll say as much. I felt duty bound to get this information out so voters could make informed decisions about their candidates. Yes, it makes me look petty and vindictive, but what if I had not passed this information on and Blackbird were elected? Then this information ends up in the hands of Russia or China and they threaten to disclose it if he does not let them take Taiwan or Lithuania. I had no choice but to pass it on. I took no pleasure in doing it other than making sure it came out before the election and not after," proposed Lexi.

"You know, that might work."

"Of course it will. If Turner can do it, so can I," responded Lexi triumphantly.

"What about the rest, about the bankers ruling the world?" added Mel.

"QAnon conspiracy theories. Banks just needed a tin foil hat," replied Lexi, smiling.

"And the part implying you're a marionette, beholden to these bankers?"

Lexi turned her head slightly, contemplating the statement. "Am I a marionette if the way they want me to move is the way I want to move? A marionette implies an unwillingness, I prefer a dog on a leash, taking her master for a walk," said Lexi, laughing at her analogy. Mel merely nodded, having heard stories about Lexi's proclivities in her younger, wilder days.

"They ultimately go where I lead them and as long as it is mutually beneficial, everything works out well. I don't have to bite anyone for trying to make me do or go somewhere I don't want to go." Mel just wanted to change the subject.

"What's going to happen to Banks? That could be a problem if he dies. His state has an Opposition Governor and they won't have a special election for a year. Carson will get to appoint someone," worried Mel.

"Looks to me like we had lost his vote anyway. With Colorado back in the fold and we will pick up a seat in Ohio and another in Pennsylvania. That idiot in North Carolina may lose as well, so that could be another. We should be fine," observed Lexi.

Mel nodded. "Was the Michigan AG your doing?"

"Nope, that has Pavlovich written all over it. He is the one funding all these progressive AGs and Secretaries of State. He is doing more to remake our justice system than we ever imagined. In fact, we may have to deal with him at some point when we want to reverse all this crime. I can't have his people working against us when we deploy federalized police forces," commented Lexi.

"I agree. Pavlovich should fix his own country first. Belarus is a disaster," said Mel.

"He likes it that way. He has his own private army there and in Switzerland, where he spends most of his time. His army is better than the state army of either country," laughed Lexi.

"I'd like my own private army," chuckled Mel.

"Soon I will," said Lexi with a Cheshire Cat smile.

Chapter 26

Nick stopped running, bending over to tie his shoe. It was 4:05am, according to his watch, and the sun was nowhere near being ready to rise in San Diego. He'd started running twenty minutes ago and was making good time. Running from the Hotel Del Coronado, taking the Coronado Bay trail around the island.

He straightened up, looked at his four very large bodyguards. They were running in place as he took off to complete the last two miles of the loop back to the hotel. Twelve minutes and 46 seconds later, Nick walked into the lobby of the hotel.

Glancing at his watch, he was still within twenty seconds per mile from his best times when he was running every day. Despite all the travel, crappy road and hotel food, and irregular workout schedules. He was happy he was still running sub six minute miles at his age.

His private entourage was not even winded and probably thought Nick's pace was 'leisurely'. Two of them accompanied him up to his suite and stood outside after doing a quick review of the interior. Nick jumped into the shower. They were wheels up in an hour on the way to Colorado so he could cast his vote.

#

Lexi thought how strange it was to sleep in her own bed in her own brownstone next to her husband. This so seldomly happened since becoming Vice President. She still slept in the same bed with her husband in DC, more often than not, but that was all. They had served their purpose for the other. Except for the occasional alcohol induced revels, they each led their own lives.

Even today, election day, Pete would fly cross-country later to be with her when she took the stage for her victory speech in DC. Rather than tag along on her journey across the country.

She met her personal assistant, Anastasia, in the foyer who handed her the details of the day and a large, medium roast coffee with one sweetener and cream. Her secret service detail surrounded her, holding the door of the house and leading her down to the waiting Suburban's on the street.

The entire street had been cordoned off since she had arrived last night. She loved being Vice President and would enjoy being President even more. Harriet and Mel were already in the SUV as she climbed in. Ana got into one of the trailing vehicles. Lexi said hello to Mel and Harriet, but both knew not to engage her this early in the morning until she started it.

Rich, her lead Secret Service agent, was driving this morning. After voting, she would board Air Force Two at Moffett Federal Airfield and head to Arizona for a rally. "Let's go," she said. Rich nodded as they proceeded to the voting location.

#

Josh Stone, the 'Ballot Whisperer', had set up their monitoring HQ in a non-descript warehouse in Alexandria. They had torn down all the printing facilities in all the swing states long ago. The ballots were printed, delivered and in the hands of the official counting centers, delivered as any other mail in ballots from remote ballot boxes.

Except, of course, the ones in Michigan they'd printed at the last minute and filled out with Turner's name to be conveniently found by the FBI.

It had been such a rush job, the rest of the races on the ballot weren't even filled out and they were not in mail in envelopes. Just official cartons full of ballots to be tabulated by the counting machines.

Only Turner's name on the Write In line for President. These wouldn't have stood up to any scrutiny. But then again, they were never meant to be counted, only discovered.

He'd monitor the vote tallies directly from paid operatives embedded in each of the key counties counting staff. These operatives were the leaders of the counting in each county and where not, they were key operations and logistics personnel who could easily get the ballots in surreptitiously.

These additional ballots were pre-loaded in county vehicles, in officially labeled county ballot boxes and bins. Everything *was* on the up and up. The ballots were legitimate and from eligible voters after all. Many even included the correct driver's license numbers on the mail in ballot envelopes where a state required it. These voters just weren't aware they were voting, or for whom. Or more likely, were not aware they might be voting more than once.

Josh expected a low-key evening, unlike some elections in the past. His new system was near foolproof.

#

The President of the United States came out of his voting booth. He was carrying a book on the issues in his home state of Pennsylvania. As he came out of the booth, the First Lady grabbed him by the arm, steering him to the door. She whispered in his ear. He looked up, smiled, and waved before shuffling out, surrounded by the Secret Service.

"Oh my god, did you see him? I don't think he knew where he was," said a news reporter from the local NWN affiliate covering the Presidential vote.

"At least we know he is still alive. He has hardly been seen in the last six months," said the local RBS reporter.

"I can tell you one thing. He was not voting while he was in that booth. I don't think he would have recognized his name if we yelled it at him," said NWN.

The RBS reporter laughed. "Scary. He probably voted for Turner. This election can't end fast enough."

The footage of the President voting was the two second clip of him looking up and smiling and waving. Nothing else was shown.

#

Lexi left the voting booth with a big smile. She stood in front of the reporters. "Our election, by our citizens. All our citizens, not just those allowed to vote by the Opposition, is the most precious right we have as Americans. Today we change history. Today, we elect our first female president. We are ushering in a new era of progress. We'll make a country that is equal for all. Assure equitable distribution of wealth, jobs, opportunity, healthcare and prosperity."

"No one should be disadvantaged any longer by the white, male, bigoted dominance we have endured since our founding. Today America speaks and we will be better for it. Thank you," she finished and exited the polling place with her Secret Service entourage. Soon she was on the road, driving down the peninsula toward Moffett Field.

"Very nice," commented Harriet.

"I am just glad the day is here. Did you see the clip of the President? Couldn't we have said he voted with a mail in ballot?"

"It was important for people to see he was still alive. He hasn't appeared in months other than far away shots. People were questioning if he was still alive," stated Mel.

"I guess it was necessary. Thank God he didn't say anything. Lord only knows what would have come out," blurted Lexi.

"Moving on. We're off to Phoenix for a quick rally. Then to Atlanta before we get back to DC," read Harriet from her tablet.

"Did we dump Virginia?"

"Timing, and we are comfortable with Virginia, so let's get you to the suite," advised Mel.

"How many did he draw in California yesterday?" asked Lexi.

Mel and Harriet both paused. "He had some sizeable crowds, but these are the same people that signed petitions for recalls and then lost twice. I wouldn't read too much into crowd sizes," deflected Mel.

"130,000 in San Fran, 140,000 in LA and 75,000 in San Diego with less than a day's notice? I can read news articles."

"Those are not official counts," said Harriet defensively.

"It doesn't matter. This guy is catching on. We need to get this done. Fast," ordered Lexi.

"We have the systems in place. Everything is ready to go. The swing states are ours. He can't win. Without Pennsylvania, Michigan and Wisconsin, the math just doesn't work. And remember, Blackbird is going to win some states too."

"Good point," agreed Lexi. "I have crowd size envy."

"He is new and shiny. The fad will fade," noted Mel.

"I hope you're right," sighed Lexi as the caravan of Suburbans pulled into Moffett Field.

#

Nick was reviewing emails and comments coming in from well-wishers as they flew toward Colorado when Chuck nudged him. He looked up questioningly. Chuck motioned at the TV on the wall.

"We are sad to report today that Senator Baxter Banks was found dead of an apparent heart attack in his study this morning by his valet. Foul play is not suspected. As you know, Senator Banks gave a press conference yesterday presenting evidence that Vice President Smythe-Thomas had been responsible for the leak of information to NWN regarding Governor Blackbird's unknown family. Senator Banks, dead at 95. Rest in Peace," said the EXN news commentator in a solemn tone.

"Where's Jenny?" asked Nick.

Denise looked up. "I think she is in back. I can get her."

"Please."

He sat contemplating the death of his friend. Knowing what Banks told him, Nick knew there was nothing natural about this.

"Nick?" asked Jenny, coming up from the back of the plane.

"Jenny, I want an autopsy performed on Banks. Is there any way we can make this happen? You can tell them I spoke to him on Friday night, and he was fine. Tell them I suspect foul play, make something up. I don't know who his next of kin is, since his wife and daughter are both dead. Try to do something. I don't want this covered up like everything else."

"Could be difficult. Some of it is going to depend on who has power of attorney or if he had a will with explicit instructions on what to do upon his death. Let me do some checking," she said.

"Thanks Jenny. Try to reach his valet, Hobson. I know you'll do what you can," remarked Nick.

"Is Hobson a first or last name?" asked Jenny.

Nick laughed, "You know what? I have no idea. I guess that makes it harder, huh?"

"I'll do what I can," smiled Jenny, heading back to the middle of the plane.

"Lexi isn't going to like this. Carson will get to nominate an Opposition member to replace Banks for a year, so that flips another seat," noted Chuck.

"It is too coincidental for him to die the evening after he breaks his story," observed Nick.

"He didn't look well. And he said he had little time left," countered Denise. "It had to take a toll, throwing away 70 years of reputation. Could have been too much for a cancer ravaged body."

Nick shrugged and went back to his emails. Five minutes later, Jenny came up to the front.

"Nick?"

He looked up.

"According to Hobson, he left specific instructions that an autopsy be performed when he passed."

"Good. He must have suspected there might be foul play."

"Why would a 95-year-old senator dying from stage 4 pancreatic cancer suspect he might need an autopsy?" asked Chuck.

"Senator Banks knew a lot of secrets. Some of which he alluded to in his press conference. It could be some people about whom he knew stuff were thinking he might be inclined to spill more with his mortality looming. A 'what have I got to lose moment'. The name Jeffrey Epstein ring any bells?" noted Nick.

"Ok, but all they're going to find is cancer everywhere, right?" questioned Denise.

"Perhaps someone helped him along. That's all I want to find out. I owe him that much."

"Hobson also said Banks requested you speak at his service," added Jenny.

"Why?"

"He didn't say."

"OK, just schedule me in Washington then. Thanks Jenny."

#

Nick voted at his precinct in Fort Collins, Colorado. He stopped to make a statement.

"I walked in, I showed my ID, they confirmed I was a registered voter, I got my ballot and voted on paper, not electronically. I want to make sure there is a paper trail of my vote. As there should be for every vote so we can ensure, only eligible voters vote for our leaders. This is the fundamental right of every American citizen. To know how and who governs them is decided by eligible citizens of this great Republic. This is the right *legal* immigrants coming to our country dream of achieving. The ability to have a say in their government, to take part in self-rule."

"For the tens of millions who have chosen the illegal path to enter America, you have no claim to this privilege. You came here on false pretenses. Yet the progressives in the Party want to reward you with the right to vote. To vote for them in return for this bribe. This is a slap in the face to everyone who is an American by birth or by legal immigration."

"America is not a place or a destination. It is an ideal. It is not for the faint of heart and it is not free. Merely coming to America for economic reasons does not qualify. Democracy failed in Iraq and Afghanistan because we tried to force it on people who were disinterested in the work it required. Democracy needs tending. You must plow and seed, water, fertilize, weed and harvest, and improve *all the time*."

"We need to preserve this experiment in democracy. It starts right here," said Nick, waving at the people voting around him. "In the local voting booth where you are voting for national, state and local leaders. *You* are making this decision. It also starts with this," said Nick, holding up his ID. "It starts with proving you have the right to be part of this process."

"This is what the progressive fears most. An end to their ability to swing elections with tricks like ballot harvesting and mail in voting without validation. In the arena of ideas, they have failed. They have to resort to gaming the system. Well, it is really hard to game a fingerprint or an iris scan on a large enough scale to affect an outcome. It also makes it really hard for dead people to vote."

"We'll get there. Because to protect our democracy, we need to eliminate the noxious weeds in our garden. We need to keep them from overrunning our fields. Please go out and vote. Thank you," finished Nick, who turned to leave with Denise, Margie and Earl, along with his phalanx of bodyguards.

"Geez, Nick, you were supposed to say a few words and go off to the stadium. Not pontificate for 10 minutes," groaned Margie. "We are on a *very* tight schedule. You need to keep it to 15 minutes at the stadium."

"Alright, but things need to be said and I need to say them in case I disappear from the stage."

"I assume you mean if you lose and not if you physically disappear," replied Margie, looking at Nick.

He shrugged and smiled back.

"You also might want to not refer to illegal aliens as 'noxious weeds'," suggested Denise.

"I meant Lexi and her minions."

"Nick, you'll never learn," sighed Denise, shaking her head.

They made the short drive to the Colorado State University stadium. Nick spoke for 35 minutes, thanking the 25,000 in attendance. He joked about whether he could return to being a history professor.

Any perspective students would have to endure endless speeches. The crowd laughed dutifully. A group of protesters started heckling him at one point, but his supporters simply surrounded them and drowned them out with shouts of Turner, Turner, Turner, slowly isolating them in a corner of the stadium where they could no longer be heard.

He finished by once again exhorting the crowd to go vote if they hadn't already. Take part in defining their future. Don't leave these critical choices to others.

Margie was frantically trying to get Nick back on schedule. She was on the phone trying to get the Colorado Highway Patrol to give them a police escort. They declined. As they headed down I-25 in traffic, they were suddenly overtaken by several sheriff cars from the surrounding counties who turned on their lights and escorted Nick and company at high speed to the airport.

Earl smiled. "I still have a few friends here."

They boarded the plane and thankfully, because they were presidential candidates, the FAA treated them the same as the President and Vice President. Giving them preferred treatment to take off from Denver International. They were off to Tempe for a rally in Arizona. As they landed at Sky Harbor airport in Phoenix, they could see Air Force Two parked on the tarmac.

"Lexi is here too?" asked Nick.

"She spoke to 20,000 at Chase Field. You have over 100,000 waiting for you at the Fiesta Bowl," said Margie, smiling.

Nick arrived at the arena. There was an estimate of 40,000 people waiting outside the stadium and over 70,000 inside. Nick hated to just give them 15 minutes for all their trouble and spoke for almost 45 minutes. By the time he was done, Margie was already on her second dose of Xanax for the day. They rushed back to the airport, boarded the plane, and were airborne in 15 minutes. Air Force Two was long gone.

"Nick, I appreciate your desire to give them their monies worth, but this is not a rock concert, and you are not Taylor Swift. We need to hit as many places as we can as fast as we can before polls close. We are already at a disadvantage, moving west to east.

"This happens when you have western based candidates who want to be seen voting in their home states," noted Chuck, as Margie worked the phone adjusting their logistics on the fly.

"Chuck, I gotta do what I can. If we miss something, so be it. If we don't get to our suite before 9pm, does it really matter?"

Chuck shrugged. "Only if you have lost by then," he said, smiling.

"I have a gut feeling we are going to be up late tonight," said Denise from a nearby seat.

"I sure hope so," agreed Chuck.

"How's Tommy doing? asked Nick.

"He's loving it. He is doing man on the street interviews at all the rallies and he loved how your supporters handled the hecklers in Fort Collins.

Margie came back in, her face showing the stress. "OK, we put the kibosh on the stop in Miami, even at the airport. There just isn't enough time." Tommy hung back at the entrance to first class, observing.

"Whatever you say Margie, you are in charge of this run," offered Nick.

Margie laughed, "Hardly. I am in charge of fixing the schedules you destroy." She said it in a pleasant tone, resigned to the fact trying to keep Nick on schedule was hopeless.

"We're skipping Houston too. We're sending Neill there since he was in Dallas already. Neill is going to do Miami after he does Raleigh. Then he and Ellie we'll meet us in Orlando. You're headed to Atlanta now. You have the Arena downtown and Lexi has the ball park up in Cobb county," explained Margie.

"Then where?" asked Nick.

"Jacksonville and then Orlando. It's all we have time for. Next time live in an East Coast city and have your watch party in the west somewhere. Time zones are killing us," moaned Margie.

"Lexi is doing the same thing," observed Nick.

"Yes, but she is the VP and has a brand. The election is hers to lose. You have to fight for relevancy," added Denise.

"If I can interject some good news," spoke up Tommy.

"Ah, the intrepid roving reporter. Fire away," nodded Nick.

"Waterloo just released their last poll. Turner 44%, Smythe-Thomas 43%, and Blackbird 10% with 3% undecided."

"Are you fucking kidding? If you are kidding, the castration I promised will be with a butter knife," Denise growled.

Tommy held up his hand. "Scouts honor. Just got it from my producer. EXN is showing it on the screen right now if you don't believe me."

They looked at the TV as Billy McCall was talking about the poll.

"Waterloo is the only polling outfit that has come close to being accurate in the last five elections. This does not portend well for the Vice President. Both the VP and Turner are within the 3pt margin of error and there are 3% undecided. What is unprecedented is the precipitous fall of Blackbird losing as much as 30 pts in some polls and the rise of Turner gaining as much as 35 in the last week alone. I think we have an actual race now in what has seemed for the last two years to be a slow walk to a coronation for the Vice President," explained Billy on the TV monitor.

"Congrats Nick, you made it a race," said Tommy on the plane.

"Thanks Tommy. You and everyone else here had a lot to do with it. Now we just need the voters to show up."

"Don't we always. And hope too many of them didn't already mail in votes for the competition," noted Denise in a pained voice.

#

"It's one poll, Lexi," calmed Mel.

"Right, but that idiot on EXN said it best. Those guys at Waterloo are the most accurate. What if they're right? How can it be this close?" she asked, looking skyward.

"I'm not sure it is. It could be the popular vote will be tighter than usual, but electoral college wise, there just isn't a path for him. He would have to win two of the three states where he's not even on the ballot. That won't happen, no matter how popular he is. Most of these voters don't even know how to do a write-in vote," he said.

Lexi laughed. "You have a point there. Especially *his* voters."

"Knowing the electronic signature pads on these voting machines, we could probably challenge many of his write-in votes anyway," Mel pointed out in a hopeful tone, trying to calm Lexi.

"Let's hope we don't have to go that far. If I have to resort to those kinds of tactics, people are going to get upset."

"Relax, the electoral college is our friend like it always is, but more so this go round," commented Mel.

"Good thing that bill never got through, to eliminate it," remarked Lexi.

"Yes, that is true. We might have gotten lucky we lost on that one."

#

Nick and Lexi held dueling rallies in Atlanta. The baseball stadium, home of the former Atlanta Braves, now unnamed and awaiting a new politically correct moniker, held 45,000. Lexi barely had 25,000 and most of them had been bused in from the inner city and southern parts of the city.

In the middle of Atlanta, Nick spoke to a capacity crowd in the football stadium. 71,000 officially but more likely 80,000 with another 20-25,000 milling around outside watching him speak on an outdoor screen. Nick spoke for almost an hour, enthusing the crowd and getting them cheered on about their prospects if they could put Nick into office.

Atlanta, and Georgia in general, were ground central for the dueling factions of progressivism and constitutionality. Voter ID laws implemented by the Opposition governor and legislature were continuously challenged in state and federal courts to the point no one knew what was legal and what was not.

In the meantime, the aggressive state activists had ensured all eligible voters in Georgia had received mail in ballots and they were aggressive in quasi harvesting, even though it was still illegal. Unfortunately, in Georgia more than anywhere else, the issue was more and more often portrayed as black versus white.

Atlanta was majority black and had Party leadership, as it had for the last 50 years. Defund the police movements were successful in whittling the police force down to a hollow shell.

Buckhead leaving Atlanta, taking 40% of the tax revenue with it, had the expected effect of turning downtown Atlanta into a dangerous crime ridden area most evenings. Every tracked crime statistic had risen by greater than 100% since the split.

Meanwhile, Buckhead was targeted by activists and ARL protests nearly every weekend. Buckhead now had a police force and budget, which both exceeded Atlanta's for a fifth of the population. Many protesters were arrested for various crimes.

Buckhead was safe, but it felt like Berlin in the cold war. A pocket of freedom and constitutionality surrounded by the City of Atlanta where progressivism ruled and the rule of law was greatly diminished.

Nick touched on this during his speech, lamenting the fact this was happening in Atlanta. The most successful majority black city in the US. It was the Queen of the South and could do so much to show other urban areas how to grow and prosper versus fester and decline as Baltimore, New York, Detroit, Philly, Newark and Minneapolis had all done under progressive Party leaders for decades.

The people cheered and agreed as over half of Nick's attendees were black and Hispanic residents of Atlanta. They agreed wholeheartedly and cheered the loudest. "All I ask is a fair election, with open and transparent ballot tallies and the ability for folks to look at all the ballots. To make sure only legal citizens are voting. Is that unreasonable?" asked Nick, as the crowd cheered and yelled, 'transparency' over and over.

Tommy watched Nick work the crowd and shook his head as he taped a segment for the show tonight. "It is amazing how candidate Turner knows exactly what points to make in each location. His knowledge and empathy for the concerns of each crowd is amazing. I have now accompanied him on I think ten of these and in each location, it is like talking to your neighbor over the fence."

"He knows what they are worried about. Offering real world solutions, not promises. Standing side by side with them to fix things together. He is the unpolitician. The guy everyone wants on their softball team, teaching their kids math, leading the boy scout troop, or teaching Sunday school."

"He is the man's man and the woman's man as well. No matter how this election turns out, we have not seen the last of Nick Turner. He is a leader, and he has those willing to follow him wherever he leads," said Tommy, wrapping the segment.

"That was great," confided Chuck.

"I meant every word, Chuck. I would follow him, wouldn't you?"

"Absolutely. I was convert number one. I guess that makes me John, right? The first apostle?"

Tommy laughed. "I'd have to brush up on my New Testament. I think it was Andrew or Peter if I remember my Sunday School. Then John and James? I'll tell you one thing, regardless. Let's find Judas now and kill him before he can betray the cause," said Tommy in all seriousness.

Chuck nodded in response. They both turned, watching Nick wrap up.

#

"We're stuck in a ground hold," said Chuck, coming back from the cockpit to Nick and company

"Why? Weather is perfect," Nick said, while leaning down, looking out a window.

"Air Force Two. All traffic is stopped whenever the President or Vice President is in route or leaving. Lexi is due to depart shortly, so we are all stuck," grumbled Chuck.

"She probably knows we are here and is delaying our takeoff. Hoping to put us more off schedule," said Margie with a groan.

"Marjorie Wilson, I have never heard you criticize anyone. What has happened to you?" responded Nick in mock outrage.

"It's the company I keep. I haven't been called Marjorie since the last time I disappointed my parents," answered Margie, smiling.

"When was that? Elementary school?" asked Nick.

"No, when I decided to work for a politician instead of finishing my law degree."

"Ouch. Thank you for that. Chuck, please send Margie's parents a gift certificate to a very nice restaurant."

"Will do, boss," answered Chuck, laughing.

"Unnecessary," said Margie. "They hated you when I started. Man, has that changed. Mom is involved in a 'Women for Turner' group and dad is in a Turner Rabble chapter. They are both out driving elderly folks to the polls as we speak. As a matter of fact, they would be pissed if they even knew I told you they *ever* doubted you."

"Even more reason then. Chuck, make sure the card says I apologize for leading their daughter astray into the swamp of Washington," ordered Nick.

"You do that, and I will go work for Lexi," threatened Margie.

"Empty threat. Jer would never leave my campaign." Nick turned to look at Jer in the corner with his head down, trying to appear like he was not listening. "Right Jer?" asked Nick.

"Please don't make me choose," he replied, not looking up as Margie and Nick both smiled.

"All right, nix the gift card, Chuck," said Nick in defeat.

The plane started moving as the Captain came on, saying Air Force Two had just departed. They were next to go, so everyone needed to buckle up for takeoff.

"He got that one right," said Nick to no one in particular as he fastened his seat belt.

Chapter 27

Terry Mathis sat at a desk in Lexi's campaign war room in Washington, DC. In front of him were six monitors. Each showed a scrolling series of numbers as data was updated real-time. He clicked on one and it brought up a state-by-state count of ballots tabulated.

What he was doing was technically hacking, but since he was only interested in the data, not changing it, he didn't feel any guilt. He'd hacked the tabulation software nearly all the states were using to collate and upload information to the Secretaries of State offices.

Finding a particular vulnerability in the software code he could exploit, he saw everything. He would know the status of each state, county, and precinct long before the polls closed. This would enable Lexi's campaign to understand the situation in key counties before the polls closed. While they could still affect the outcome.

As he was toggling through the states in the Eastern time zone, his phone rang.

"Ya," he answered into his headset without taking his eyes off his screens.

"How's it look so far?" asked a voice with a lot of noise in the background.

It was Mel Arenson. He didn't acknowledge him and just started his update.

"Looking pretty good. You calling from a plane? It's very loud."

"Air Force Two."

"Got it. Hopefully, you can hear me. Turnout is very high. Some states are counting mail in first. Others already have them done. In both cases, the VP is building a good lead to start. Millions of mail in ballots already counted in the core northeast and mid-Atlantic states. She is way up. Blackbird has a small amount and almost none for Turner in any of these states.

"Good. Nothing crazy?"

"Actually, I think the VP is doing even better than projected in the mail in. Blackbird is the one underperforming. It is hard to compare as so many states have mailed ballots to *every* voter this time around. Before we could see how many were requested and returned and gauge the efficacy of the mail in votes."

"Meaning what? My head already hurts, net it out please," asked Mel impatiently.

"Meaning the VP already has more mail in votes than the President got in Michigan, Vermont, Massachusetts, Connecticut, New York, Florida, and Rhode Island. The same for Oregon, Washington and Montana who have already counted all the mail in ballots received."

"That's good news, right?"

"Depends, remember Florida had sixteen million registered voters last time, and they mailed in seven million. The President got about four million of those and still lost. Four out of seven is 57% of the eligible mail in ballots. Lexi is close to four and a half million now. But that is less than thirty percent of the total mailed out, because they went to over seventeen million with the population explosion. We're comparing different numbers. Anyway, you look at it, having that many in the can is still a great start for her."

"I will take that as good news and let her know we are off to a great start."

"Also, Virginia has really high turnout so far too. Both mail in and at the polls."

"That's what our poll watchers are telling us to. Long lines everywhere. All day. Not sure if that is good," remarked Mel.

"How about Michigan and Pennsylvania?" asked Terry, being curious. He hadn't looked up from his monitors to check on the news.

"Long lines. Couple hours to vote at most polling places. Weather is great and folks are staying civil unfortunately," lamented Mel, knowing the day of turnout would favor Blackbird and Turner. Their Party voting blocks were not interested in standing in lines to exercise their right to vote. They could only post so many KooKoo videos of standing in line before it got boring.

Terry could be heard laughing at the sad pronouncement of the Party voting base.

"How's Georgia look?"

"I already told you. Georgia is using different software. I can't get any info. You're as blind as everyone else for that one."

"Right, sorry. Florida?"

"So far OK as well. VP and Turner are both ahead of Blackbird. He is really tanking. He may not even keep either of the Carolinas."

"Call me if you see anything really crazy. You know what we're looking for," noted Mel.

"Yes, I do. I know the signal. We're still hours from the polls closing. As you know, most voting happens in the early morning before work and then four to seven in the evening in each time zone. We are just approaching four in the east," he cautioned.

"I know. Had a few minutes and thought I would check in. Monitor Pennsylvania and let me know if you hear of anything out of the ordinary happening."

"Out of the ordinary? Whose idea of ordinary?" laughed Terry.

"Good point. How about anything you think is noteworthy? Better?" laughed Mel.

"Much."

#

In a bunker in Omaha, Major Jenkins sat at a console listening to what he'd just heard. He had volunteered for the shift to allow his team to get out and vote. As he closed the file on the call, he made a secure copy, bypassing security protocols, and sent the copy wirelessly to the flash drive he carried in his pocket.

He was committing espionage at a minimum and treason if the prosecutor was so inclined, but he held a smoking gun in his pocket. The recording was then archived along with thousands of others they routinely recorded daily.

Many would never be touched. The technology was considered a prototype and information being collected was being put in deep archive for later mining to determine the efficacy of the tech.

Had the brass known the technology could listen in on a conversation on Air Force Two, they would have had a collective conniption fit. Jenkins scrubbed as much as he could to hide his tracks, knowing it was not complete, but the Army did not have the best and the brightest working in their information technology section. Those kids were all working in Silicon Valley, making in a year what it would take Jenkins four or five to match on his major's salary. He didn't care. He was a patriot.

Jenkins did not like what was happening to his country, to its military leadership, its capability to protect the land from foreign and domestic threats and most of all he did not like the ideology of the progressive movement which seemed hell bent on shredding his precious bill of rights.

#

Nick finished his rally in Jacksonville shortly after 5pm. He spoke for 30 minutes to give folks time to still get to the polls if they hadn't yet been. He headed to the plane with his team. All they could do now was sit back and wait. For someone like Nick, this was worse than being shot. Sitting around waiting for results was not in his nature.

Chapter 28

Nick and his entourage walked into the conference room. It was down the hall from the suite they reserved at the Hyatt Regency. The hotel was across the street from the Orange County Florida Convention Center, where his followers were gathered.

As they entered the conference room, those in the room stood up and started clapping. Nick acknowledged their acclaim and waved them back to their seats.

"Thanks, thanks. We made it. When I had my temper tantrum in Congress, I never imagined I'd be standing here awaiting the results of a presidential election. I couldn't have done this without the help of all of you. I want you to know. I appreciate all the crappy sandwiches, lousy hotels, late night flights, and the gallons of awful coffee." Everyone in the conference room laughed at his statement.

"Sit back and enjoy the night and remember it is all because of you we even made it this far. No matter the result, we will pick up tomorrow and keep moving forward. This is not the end, only the beginning. Come tomorrow, we will see where the path leads. Now for the hardest part, waiting," whined Nick, making a face as the group laughed.

Chuck turned to him, putting a hand on Nick's shoulder.

"Nick, I think I speak for everyone here and in all our offices and grassroots organizations around the country. We believe, and we believe in you. We know you have opened the eyes of millions of voters in this country. As you have said time and time again, all you can do is lay out the facts and hope the people are smart enough to understand their future is in their own hands. You have started a movement, regardless of what happens tonight. Let's hear it for the boss," said Chuck as the crowd cheered and shouted Turner, over and over.

Nick smiled and bowed, trying to keep his emotions in check.

Denise and Chuck led Nick through a door into a smaller adjacent conference room where they had phones, computers, and TVs set up to monitor the elections.

"Do you want to hang out here or in the suite in privacy?" asked Denise.

"Here is fine with the team. We win or lose together, no sense hiding."

"OK. We have ANC on this one, EXN in the middle, 2J's over here and then we will flick through FLCN, LN1, RBS and NWN on the one in the corner if something interesting happens on any of them."

"All right, now what?" said Nick, sitting with a sigh.

"Want a drink, something to calm the nerves?" asked Chuck.

"Nah, Pellegrino's fine. I'm not nervous, I just hate not having anything to do. I'll get over it. First polls close in what, twenty minutes at seven eastern?"

"Yes."

"Let's have some volume on EXN then. I don't want to listen to any of the other ones unless someone interesting comes on."

"Got it."

"What's the sequence?" asked Nick, knowing the answer but wanting to talk about something.

"Georgia, Indiana, Kentucky, South Carolina, Virginia, and Vermont are all first at seven eastern. Obviously, Georgia is the one to watch, but they won't know anything definitive until late is my guess," explained Chuck.

"Lexi is pushing real hard to win it. She doesn't need it, but we do. We'll know in a hurry the status of Blackbird. If our intel is right, we'll win Indiana and Kentucky and if we do, he is officially only going to hurt us with any states he wins. It is unfortunate, but he will still win some and that just makes it really hard for us," grimaced Denise.

"We needed Michigan, Wisconsin or Pennsylvania. The courts really screwed us over there. Even just Pennsylvania and we might have had a chance. We'll lose Vermont, of course, and Virginia is still purple trending blue, so no luck there either. South Carolina will go Blackbird because of Carson is still our current guess," recited Chuck.

"What does out exit polling say about Georgia and Pennsylvania?" asked Nick.

"Georgia is strong. The laggards in reporting are always the blue counties around Atlanta. Lexi had a huge lead in mail in ballots. Pennsylvania is a conundrum. I am not sure what to make of the data Nick, but our exit polling is 7 out of 10 are for you. The lines are long and have been all day all over the state, except in Philadelphia," answered Chuck.

"They're pissed in Pennsylvania. Pissed at their governor, at their supreme court, the President, and mostly they are pissed at the Vice President candidate. JJ hasn't lived in Pennsylvania for 40 years. The President going back to vote there as if he were a favorite son was also ridiculous." Denise's tone expressed her thoughts on these attempts to make hay of native sons.

"The Party is extremely tone deaf on their gauge of people and they are counting on you not being on the ballot. Is it enough? Probably. You would need three million write-in votes. Your mail in votes in Pennsylvania were miniscule compared to either Blackbird or Lexi. If Blackbird had just dropped out, I think you would have won here, and the election hands down," said Denise, shaking her head.

"Seven more minutes and we test our first theories," agreed Chuck.

#

Lexi settled into her chair in her suite in the Marriott Marquis next door to the Walter E. Washington Convention Center in DC. 10,000 of her campaign workers and donors were gathered to celebrate her eventual victory there. She'd decided to wait in the suite with just Harriet and Mel. Even her assistant Ana and her boyfriend were holed up in another suite with JJ and his wife to watch the results there.

She looked over at Mel and Harriet. Both heads down, looking at their phones. There were a row of screens in front of her, the center one showing NWN news with LN1 on the left and ANC on the right. A fourth smaller screen was in the corner with FLCN on at the moment.

NWN's volume was up but only slightly as the talking head blathered on about statistics and historic nature of yet again the potential for the nation's first female president.

"You mean first *elected* female president. Like I haven't already been doing the job this last year," commented Lexi at the TV." Harriet and Mel looked up but didn't comment.

"Five to seven," said Harriet. "First polls close. They should call Vermont first."

"Good. Anything else to report?" asked Lexi.

"Turnout is high across the nation. Weather has been great, so no one was forced to stay home. Blackbird is showing even worse than the polls, according to *our* exit poll surveys. My guess is a lot of his supporters just stayed home rather than stand in line to cast a vote for a big loser," remarked Mel.

"Or they voted for Turner," speculated Lexi.

"Some, no doubt, but not enough. We went to 90% turnout in Arizona, Georgia and Nevada with the ballots, just in case," noted Mel.

Lexi looked at him, not sure whether to approve or disapprove of not being consulted. "Why just those three and not the others?"

"Exit polling still has you winning them handily. No reason to risk the exposure, especially for those states where scrutiny is high, like Michigan."

"Makes sense," said Lexi. "Can you get me a glass of water, Harriet? Please."

Harriet was surprised at the cordial nature of her boss. She returned with the water. Lexi took a sip and then threw the rest in Mel's face.

"Never make that kind of decision without consulting me. Even if it turned out to be the correct one. This is too important for any of you to take into your own hands. I am the one whose ass is on the line here and I need to be consulted. Are we clear?" said Lexi, furious.

Mel dabbed his face with his handkerchief. He wasn't all that surprised. He'd seen Lexi in action before. He was just glad she didn't follow it with the glass. "Of course, Madame Vice President. How could I have been so short-sided after all these years to take the initiative to preserve your *ass* and increase your chances of victory without first consulting you in every decision? It won't happen again," said Mel, staring Lexi in the eyes.

Harriet's eyes were as big as saucers as Lexi turned to her with a smile. "Now, Harriet, can you get me a bourbon with two cubes of ice? Thanks," asked Lexi, holding out the empty crystal glass.

Mel looked at Harriet and laughed, easing the tension.

"Don't worry. She won't waste the bourbon or the Waterford throwing it at me. One was a gift from the Prince of Monaco and the other, I believe, came from the Irish President."

"You are correct, Mel. You know me so well," she said, smiling. "Make one for Mel too, as a peace offering."

"Here we go," observed Lexi as the NWN screen flashed a sign saying 7 o'clock on the east coast and the polls have closed in…

Chapter 29

"Welcome, it is seven o'clock on the east coast and the polls have closed in a handful of states," announced EXN's Billy McCall. "First up is Georgia and its sixteen electoral votes. No surprise to anyone, we cannot announce a winner with zero percent of the vote in."

"EXN is projecting our first surprise of the evening. Independent Candidate Nick Turner puts the first points on the board. We are declaring him the winner in Indiana, with its eleven electoral votes. Also, in Kentucky, we are projecting Nick Turner will edge out Governor Blackbird to take Kentucky's eight electoral votes. Over to you Adam," said Billy.

"Thank you, Billy. South Carolina, the state of the Vice-Presidential candidate Governor Carson, is still too close to call at the moment. EXN projects the state of Vermont with its three electoral votes goes for Vice President Smythe-Thomas putting her first electoral votes on the map."

"Finally, the state of Virginia and its thirteen electoral votes are also too close to call at this point. We are showing the Vice President with a comfortable lead, but with only 11% of the vote tallied so far," said Adam Mullen, the gray-haired veteran of many election night calls.

#

In Nick's conference room, it was all smiles as people hugged and high fived each other. Margie and Jer were hanging onto each other and jumping up and down as Nick looked on, smiling. Chuck shook his hand.

"Who'd have ever believed this when we started a year ago? Not only have you overcome the Opposition, but you are putting the fear of God into Lexi. I can guarantee it," teased Chuck.

Even Denise was smiling while she talked to Neill and Ellie, who had joined the group in the conference room from their last rally in Miami. Nick walked over and shook Neill's hand, hugging Ellie.

"Well, what do you think?" grinned Nick.

"I think you have a hell of a chance of pulling off the biggest upset in history. Nick, even pinch hitting, I can't explain enough the energy level and the enthusiasm I saw on the road. It is electric. People have been beaten down so much in the last 20 years and even more so in the last 10. They were without hope. You have given them back their hope and purpose. They can actually see a better tomorrow instead of the doom and gloom the progressives and frankly the opposition too, are always preaching is imminent. It is exciting and fun. I am generally not known for being either," laughed Neill as Ellie gave him a punch.

"You got that right," she said with a smile.

"I know we haven't had much time together since you joined the campaign. I want you to know how much it meant to me to have someone like you on the ticket with me. It was a comfort knowing you were out there fighting the fight on my behalf," thanked Nick.

Ellie jumped in. "Nick, it was our privilege to be included. No matter what happens. We've done our little part in this historic effort. We should thank you for the honor." She finished, giving him another long hug until Neill 'ha hummed' behind her. He put his arm around her. "I already told you to get your own woman," he said, looking down at his beaming wife.

Nick laughed and headed around the room, thanking folks as they listened to Billy, Adam and several other guests discussing the enormity of what they were witnessing.

"Rory," asked Billy on EXN, "What do you make of Turner taking Indiana and Kentucky right off the bat?"

"I'd say Blackbird is in for a humiliating end to one of the most poorly run opposition candidacies in modern history. We're talking McGovern and Mondale bad," answered Rory Kane. He was a middle-aged, rotund academic type with rimless wire glasses. His appearance evoked images of the old-time accountants wearing green shaded visors, reviewing the ledgers in the bank by candlelight. Rory was a geek with a PhD in statistical analysis and a penchant for getting things right. He was also equally famous for the chalkboards he used to show his math.

"Turner, on the other hand, is executing the most remarkable campaign presidential politics has probably ever seen. Starting less than a year ago with no national organization, very little money, no endorsements, and essentially no track record in Congress other than his historic vote against the filibuster."

Off camera, Adam could be heard laughing as the camera switched to him.

"Breaking with the Party and voting against the filibuster is more of a track record than many have for themselves after decades," quipped Adam. Rory looked a bit flustered at Adam's interruption.

"Sorry, Rory. Please continue," smiled Adam back at him.

"By skipping the primaries to run as an independent, he violated every one of the check boxes of a conventional candidate," finished Rory, his excitement returning to Nick's results.

"Perhaps that's what makes him so appealing," posited Adam.

"I agree. I think America has been crying out for a third-party candidate as the Opposition has been fragmenting more and more each election. What I think is different this time is the Party is fragmenting too. For decades they voted in lockstep, keeping their coalition intact. As the progressives have taken more control, the more moderate liberal has found themselves without a home. I think Turner is giving them a new one. They are wholeheartedly embracing his centrist and common sense platform," declared Rory.

"You think a lot of moderate Party voters are abandoning the Vice President to vote for Turner?" asked Billy.

"Three weeks ago I would have said less than 5% were inclined. But I think the combination of the Blackbird implosion, the five or six at last count, attempts to pin a scandal on Turner and the sensational failure of each, have not only helped Turner, but lionized him as the righteous and heroic figure so many believed him to be after the New York subway incident."

"I think the last straw and the one that really caused the massive shift, especially of female moderate Party voters, were Senator Banks' revelations yesterday. Wow, was it only yesterday?" commented Rory.

"It was just yesterday," responded Adam in a somber tone. "And today he is dead. If that is a coincidence, I will happily retire."

"I agree," said Rory. "That was the tipping point. When Senator Banks revealed the Vice President was behind the leaking of the info to NWN. Coupled with his press conference and then his convenient death, especially before he could reveal additional information? Very suspicious."

"He was in Congress for 70 years. He must have had a treasure trove of inside information. He made it clear he was clearing his conscience on Monday. He could have done a press conference every day for a month. Offering embarrassing tidbits without compromising national security," commented Adam.

"I couldn't agree more, Adam. All of this adds up to Party soccer moms jumping ship. Factor in the treatment they received when they tried to complain at school board meetings. I think it started a wave, just like taxes started the Tea Party movement. This time, it is more like a tsunami than a wave. I don't know if it is enough to give Turner the win, but it should make the Vice President sweat tonight," noted Rory.

"Excellent insight as always, Rory," said Billy. "The question on everyone's mind. Does Turner have a path to victory?"

"Honestly, Billy, no. If, and that is a huge IF, all the dominos fell just right, here is what he has to do. What really kills him is Blackbird. Every state Blackbird wins is one he needed. Not being on the ballot in Michigan, Wisconsin and Pennsylvania is just crippling. If he could have won two out of three of those, he might have had a chance. So here is one of my boards on this," said Rory, pulling up a black chalkboard with colored numbers on it.

"Ah, our first board of the night," said Billy with a laugh.

"The first of many, no doubt," opined Adam.

"Turner has to win all the traditional red states. This is where he is in trouble already. Blackbird is going to win the Dakotas. Not that many electoral votes, but if he wins the Carolinas too, that really hurts. That's 31 electoral votes. So that means Turner *has* to win Pennsylvania and either Michigan or Wisconsin and that is if he also wins Georgia, Arizona, Texas, Florida, and Ohio. Ohio is the only one I can say I think he takes. As you can see, he has to over perform beyond belief to even have a prayer. Strange as it may sound, Blackbird doing well is helping the Vice President most."

"Thank you, Rory. Insightful analysis, as always. We'll return to you again after the next set of polls close," closed Billy.

Chapter 30

"How come they haven't called Virginia yet?" asked Lexi. "We had a twelve-point lead there this morning."

"It's still early. They have to have enough votes in before they make the call. You remember how badly they got burned back in the Bush/Kerry election when the exit polls were all pro Kerry and they announced he was president before any of the polls closed? They don't want to repeat that," admitted Mel.

"If they don't call it soon, I want Whitestone from NWN on the phone," growled Lexi, pissed at the delay.

"Relax Lexi, nothing to worry about in Virginia. Georgia will turn once we get metro Atlanta in. I'm surprised by the vote counts for Turner. He's running second in Virginia. Even after threatening all those federal agency jobs. It looks like he is ahead of you in South Carolina, too. Second in Vermont. No surprise there since he is popular on college campuses."

"Get Whitestone on the phone anyway and tell them to call these things. Quit being such pussies," she said, finishing her drink.

"We'll get a bunch in the 8 o'clock calls. Let me refill your drink. How's the speech coming?"

Lexi glared at Mel but took the drink. "I want this to be a mandate, no more of these close majorities. We need it to get things changed. How is congress shaping up?"

"I think we're good. We should keep a majority in the house, probably 12 or 14 seats. Senate is going to be close, could be 50 or 51 since we lost Bank's seat for a year until the special election."

"Shit. I was hoping Hopkins could pull out Texas."

"Doesn't look like it. I think the administration's policies on letting the illegals flood in across the Rio Grande have killed any chances of turning Texas blue for another generation now. Our Party chairman in Texas went to work for Turner when we fired him after the primary. That's how bad it is down there now."

"Really? We'll see about that. There's a new sheriff in town and Texas is public enemy number one. And Florida." added Lexi with a vindictive glint in her eye.

#

"It's 7:30 on the east coast and the polls have closed in three more states," Billy McCall could be heard to say on the big screen in Nick's conference room.

"The state of North Carolina is too close to call, with Senator Turner and Governor Blackbird neck and neck with 40% of the vote in. The Vice President is running a distant third," recited Billy. "Adam, what about Ohio?"

"Billy, it's too soon to make a call in Ohio, too. Turner is doing well there with a double-digit lead with 35% of the vote in. However, it's still too early to make any predictions. EXN is calling the state of West Virginia for Senator Nick Turner. With 70% of the vote in, Turner is winning with a whopping 68% of the vote so far. This is an amazing stat, considering Senator Turner made only one visit to West Virginia early in his candidacy. His Vice Presidential running mate, the venerable Neill Rogers, held a rally in Charleston last week. I believe his wife is also a native, so maybe that helped. That's four more electoral votes for Turner," commented Adam.

"Our tote board has Turner in the lead with 23 electoral votes, Governor Blackbird has 9, with South Carolina being called for him and the Vice President with only 3," said Billy.

#

Ellie let out a whoop with a big smile as they announced Nick carrying her state of West Virginia. The room erupted into laughter at Ellie's attempt to cut the tension.

"No joke Nick, I think this is the first time a third-party candidate has had the lead since Teddy Roosevelt against Wilson and Taft, or maybe ever," offered Chuck.

"Let's call Guinness and find out," said Earl, who'd arrived from the convention center, where he was overseeing the security measures.

"Hey look who the cat dragged in," said Nick with a smile.

"I have spent the last hour arguing with the Secret Service. They feel compelled to take over the security at the convention center in case you win. They would not take no for an answer. They're co-mingled with our own security. Don't freak out if you see a bunch of guys in bad suits, earpieces, and sunglasses," growled Earl.

"Great, now I don't know who to trust. Just another log on the fire."

"Sorry I tried, but they do have a point. If this gets close, expect them to show up here as well. It is *their* job, after all."

"Oh joy," added Chuck with a frown.

#

"I still don't understand Virginia? They called Indiana and Kentucky immediately for Turner and they have like 15% in. Did you talk to Whitestone?" asked Lexi, pacing.

"I talked to someone on the desk at NWN. They are saying the exit polls are not clear and the strong showing of Turner in Virginia is preventing them from calling the state just yet," replied Mel, carefully.

"That's not what I want to hear. Where are these votes coming from?"

"The rural counties are coming in first. They are smaller and the counting is faster. Turner is winning these with 75% or more. The major metros are not in. The counties around DC and Richmond, where your votes are. Just be patient. I know it is hard, but if you make a stink, they'll think you're worried, and the pundits will focus on that instead of our obvious advantages," counseled Mel.

"Patient? I can always get another set of Waterford, you know. I don't enjoy sitting around and waiting."

Mel looked down at texts on his phone. "Good news. Looks like we are doing really well in Michigan and Pennsylvania. Wisconsin and Minnesota also look good. Looks like extraordinary measures won't be necessary. We've been monitoring the ballots as they are counted and so far it's looking good."

"Don't wait too long if we need to decide. I don't want any more videos of suitcases of ballots being pulled out from under tables. Speaking of that, how is Georgia looking?" she asked.

"We are still behind, not Blackbird, but Turner. None of the metro counties are in. Same as Virginia. Once they come in, we should take the lead easily. 8pm polls should close any minute. We'll get a bunch of calls then."

#

"Billy, we need to go to Jimmy King from our local EXN affiliate in Las Vegas, Jimmy?" called out Adam, a hand to his ear.

"Thank you, Adam. We have had a massive power spike of some kind around the city, it seems. Every one of the TrustedVoter machines has locked up and can no longer accept any new votes. The officials can still access the votes cast and tabulate the prior votes, so nothing was lost. It appears the power surge caused all the touch screens to malfunction. No new votes can be cast using the machines."

"The polling precincts are reverting to paper ballots. I hear there is an emergency ruling coming from the Nevada supreme court to keep the polls open at least another hour and as long as it takes for everyone who is in line at the time the polls close to cast their paper ballot. We have no idea if there are enough paper ballots available at the polling places. This is clearly a major issue and it will be a long night for the Nevada poll workers," he finished.

"Thank you Jimmy. Please keep us informed of any additional information," asked Billy.

"Billy," said Adam. "Looks to me like we have the same issue in Arizona. Let's go to April Sung in Maricopa county. April, welcome."

"Thanks Adam. Yes, we have had the same power spike throughout Arizona. I was talking to one voter who was in the middle of voting, before the machine locked up. He said the screen got really bright, almost like having a flashlight shined in your eyes and then it returned to normal, but none of the buttons on the screen functioned any longer."

"He was forced to enter his vote on a manual ballot and drop it in the drop box. Like Jimmy said in Nevada, they can still access the machines to tabulate votes already cast and tabulate them, so no votes appear to have been lost. In Arizona, the local county officials have already said they will keep the polls open at least another hour. Anyone in line when the polls close will get to vote no matter how long it takes tonight," finished April.

"April, thank you for that update," noted Adam. "We'd like to bring in one of our tech experts to talk about how the TrustedVoter machines work and what could have happened in this case. Robert Whitlock is the founder of a forensic accounting firm specializing in cyber fraud. Robert, welcome. What can you tell us about this situation and why is it machines in Nevada and Arizona only?"

"Thank you, Adam. Good to be with you. First, as with any electronic machine, they are all integrated circuit boards. Circuit boards have many ways to fail, power surges, shorts, physical damage, loosened connections causing an arc, etc. However, for a widespread outage effecting all systems of a specific kind, this has all the earmarks of a cyber attack," confided Robert.

"Wouldn't they need to be connected to the internet for that to happen?" questioned Billy.

"Yes, and no Billy. As you recall, there was a big stink several elections ago with the voting machines and the prospect they could have been manipulated because they were connected to the internet. Especially when it was shown, the data was leaving the machine and even the country before coming back to the machine to be counted."

"This included read/write access, meaning data could be sent and received and changes made from outside the system, leading to speculation of fraud or perhaps altering of vote totals of individual votes."

"Since then, laws have been passed to only allow monitoring of these systems during the election, meaning read only access."

"They are still connected to the internet?" asked Billy.

"Yes, but with this kind of access, outside systems can log in and monitor the systems, but they can't make any changes. Nor can they alter any information. This kind of connection would not allow anyone to load any kind of virus or malware into the system remotely. Think of it as a window to look through, but you can't reach through it into the house."

"What do you think caused the issue and why only these two states?" asked Adam, not understanding any of what Robert had described.

"I can only speculate at this time without doing a deep forensic audit of the logs and running diagnostics on the machines. For such a widespread result, something in the code on all of these machines malfunctioned. From what April said, it appears there was an overheating or possibly something known as overclocking of the GPU or CPU in the systems caused by a widespread power spike," answered Robert.

Adam laughed. "Robert, I don't understand anything you said, other than you sound skeptical of your own answer."

"I am. We've not heard of any slot machines or other machines in the casinos being affected the same way. They are essentially the same type of machine. A widespread power spike would have brought those machines down too. Seems a bit too convenient."

Adam laughed again. "I can barely operate my smart phone. Can you please lay this out in better terms for our audience, something we can relate to?"

Robert smiled. "Sorry Adam, of course. Have you ever used a device in your house for too long, or run too many on the same circuit, causing the breaker to pop?"

"You mean like your wife and three daughters all turning on their hair dryers at the same time?" smiled Adam in reply.

Robert laughed. "Exactly. This happens because you are trying to draw more power than the wiring can safely handle. The same thing happens in computers. It runs too hot, and it shuts itself down to prevent permanent damage."

Adam smiled, nodding as he could understand this analogy.

"Here it appears some piece of code executed something that drew or allowed too much power to the processors in the machines. Modern machines run most of the calculations using a Graphics Processing Unit, or many of them working in series inside the machines. They have taken over the role of the CPU of old. The CPU crunches numbers, the GPU makes all the fancy graphics and apps you use on your phone work. GPUs run really hot and need internal fans to cool them. If something turned off the fans, for instance, this would quickly cause an overheating situation."

"How could this malfunction happen in all the machines at the same time?" asked Billy skeptically.

"We have rolling blackouts in the west all the time now. The power company turns the power off and on to different parts of the grid. Places like polling buildings switch to generators until the power is back on. I suspect this happened. There was a power surge. It caused a piece of code to direct too much power to something because of the back and forth of the power surges and the constant change in current amperage. It caused the graphic interface to shut down to protect the system."

"This is not something you can fix on the fly without direct access to every machine. Because it happened to every machine, this has to be because of code in each one of them reacting the same way. I think if you check with the power company, you will find there were unplanned rolling black outs in Nevada and Arizona happening during this time. If not, then we have a mystery on our hands and we need to look deeper for an answer." concluded Robert.

"Wow," reacted Billy. "Seems awfully convenient for this to happen now. And in two swing states."

"Suspicious is more like it. The timing is too convenient, or inconvenient, depending on which candidate you are," ended Adam ominously.

#

"What the hell just happened?" yelled Mel into his phone, watching EXN for the explanation of the machine issues in Nevada and Arizona.

"We are trying to figure it out. I don't buy the surge theory, because it would more likely have shut the machines down than just causing the interface to lock up," replied Terry.

"Was it natural? A rolling blackout?" asked Mel, worried.

"It has all the hallmarks of a cyber attack, but I don't know how they did it with read only access. We'll keep looking."

"Keep digging. See if you can find out if they did have rolling blackouts. And see if there is any way to fix this," said Mel.

"Fix it?" laughed Terry. "Mel, I'm good, but there is no way you are going to do anything with these machines at this point. Whatever it was, cyber attack or natural cause, those machines are toast. These guys are back to the seventies, with paper and number 2 pencils filling in circles."

Mel hung up the phone, closing his eyes. The only person who would have an idea what happened was killed shortly after meeting with him. Without Kolsten, there was both no one who knew what he did and unfortunately, no one to fix anything.

"Well," asked Lexi.

"No idea what happened. The machines aren't going to be used going forward. I think we should bring in the extra ballots, at least to 95% in Maricopa and Clark. This is the perfect excuse while they are bringing in additional blank ballots to the precincts. There will be more bins going in. A few more and no one will suspect. That will add close to 250,000 more votes. We can have the last batch, to 100% ready as well, just in case."

Lexi nodded. "Make it happen. The die is cast."

Mel got on the phone to Josh to execute the 95% order for those two counties. This would consist of every polling place in these two counties getting additional bins of legal mail in ballots to open and tabulate and then report to the central counting center. They had to win now. There would be no way to hide this.

#

"What do you make of that?" asked Nick.

"No idea, but I suspect we may have help we don't know about. Anything affecting machines makes it hard to use them to cheat. This should be a good thing for us. The fact it is in the two western swing states tells me it is intentional," guessed Chuck.

"I agree. Let's keep an eye on things as they switch to paper. This probably gives them a chance to bring in more mail in ballots in the confusion," cautioned Nick.

"We'll have our watchers pay more attention," nodded Chuck, pulling out his phone.

#

"So much is happening," observed Billy. "It's 8pm on the east coast and we have a lot of calls to make. Let's get right to it." A picture of Alabama flew across the screen.

"EXN can now project Alabama and its nine electoral votes will go for Senator Nick Turner," he said.

"Billy, we are now projecting Connecticut will go for Vice President Smythe-Thomas with its seven electoral votes. We are projecting Delaware, and its three electoral votes also going for the Vice President," added Adam.

"At this point it is too early to call Florida, but we show Senator Turner with a slight lead with a little under 50% of the precincts reporting," said Billy. He continued, "We are projecting the Vice President will win Illinois and its nineteen electoral votes, the biggest prize of the night so far."

"Our election desk is projecting Maine's three electoral votes will go to the Vice President and the fourth open electoral vote is also being projected to belong to her," said Adam.

"The news keeps getting better and better for the Vice President. We are calling Maryland with ten electoral votes and Massachusetts with its eleven," said Billy.

"EXN is projecting Mississippi will go for Senator Turner. That's six more electoral votes for the Senator," said Adam. "We are not projecting a winner in Missouri at this time, but Senator Turner is leading with 40% of the vote in so far."

"In what can only be considered an upset, EXN can now project Senator Nick Turner will win the four electoral votes of New Hampshire.

It appears the message Senator Turner is delivering is resonating in the 'Live Free or Die' state. New Hampshire has a history of flopping back and forth in elections. It appears it is no different in this one," said Billy. "We are also projecting New Jersey and its fourteen electoral votes will go for the Vice President. Again, no surprise to anyone."

"We are projecting Oklahoma will go for Senator Turner. This is an upset, given Blackbird's Indian heritage. He had a 30 point lead as late as ten days ago. Turner overcame this deficit to not only win but to win with over 70% of the votes cast, with 83% of precincts reporting. This is a big deal," said Adam.

"It is, Adam. To make this kind of turnaround is exactly what I was talking about earlier. These shifts are only accomplished when lots of Opposition and Party voters are jumping onto Turner's bandwagon," said Rory, gesturing with different colored pieces of chalk in his smudged hands. "This could be interesting if the trend continues."

"In a bit of a surprise, we are not prepared to call Pennsylvania yet. So far, Senator Turner has tallied over one million election day write in ballots. He is still behind the Vice President by a million votes, but there are plenty of ballots left to count."

"Our sources on the ground tell us the turnout in Pennsylvania has been the highest both in terms of percentage and raw voters. We will keep a close eye on this as the night progresses. There are only about a third of the ballots counted, though. A long way to go in Pennsylvania," noted Billy.

"We are projecting Rhode Island for the Vice President and its three electoral votes. Our election desk has a winner in Tennessee. Again, it appears Governor Blackbird lost another large lead, as we are now projecting Tennessee will go for Senator Turner. This adds eleven more electoral votes to the Senator. Finally, Washington DC goes for the Vice President, but only with a plurality of 71%. That's twenty points lower than the last election," laughed Adam.

"That does it for the eight o'clock poll closings. At least the ones we can call," finished Billy, turning to Rory. "Thoughts, Rory?"

"So far not any genuine surprises, except maybe the no call in Pennsylvania and Turner's margin of victory in Tennessee and Oklahoma. I would point out that Turner is a strong second in every state he has not won, even in DC he got 28% of the vote. As you can see, even though the Vice President is now leading in the electoral college, Senator Turner is building an impressive popular vote lead. Look at Illinois."

Adam and Billy suppressed smiles as Rory lifted a small black chalkboard into view. Lots of wiped out numbers to be replaced by new quickly scribbled tallies.

"The VP has only 46% and Turner at 40 and Blackbird at 14. If that holds, only winning by 6% is a severe underperform for the VP. Same for Massachusetts, where she is only winning by 4 pts over Turner. You contrast that with Tennessee, where he is winning with 70% and the VP and Blackbird are both at 15%. That is an enormous difference. Turner is racking up popular votes even in losing efforts."

"Good points Rory," agreed Billy. "Let's look at the count so far. We have the Vice President with 78 electoral votes, followed by Senator Turner with 60 and Governor Blackbird with only 9 from South Carolina. Again, it takes 270 to win the Presidency.

"Folks, let's check in at the campaign watch parties and get a report on the mood there," said Billy. "First, Jennifer Tilson, on the floor of the Smythe-Thomas campaign at the Walter E. Washington Convention center just down the road from the Capitol."

"The camera showed a pretty blonde reporter surrounded by Lexi supporters shouting and cheering while music blared in the background. Jennifer shouted into the microphone to be heard.

"Billy, as you can see, the Vice President's followers are having a good time, especially with the results now showing her pulling away from the competition. It is one of jubilation and a sense of accomplishment as they continue to watch the electoral votes adding up." Back to you in the studio, Billy.

"Thanks Jen. Now we head down to our very own Tommy Charles reporting live from the floor of the Orange County Convention center in

Orlando Florida." Roughly 10,000 of Turner's supporters were laughing and cheering each update. Tommy, like Jennifer, was surrounded by mostly young people hooting and cheering about their candidate. As the camera turned to Tommy, he was smiling and laughing.

"Billy, this reminds me of my much younger days and the rock concerts I used to attend. The atmosphere on the floor is electric. Everyone here understands the historic nature of these results, and they already feel they have achieved a victory by winning *any* states. I have a sense this campaign and these people are here to stay regardless of outcomes tonight. What happens after is unknown, but unlike the Tea Party, I think this movement may have legs."

"Thanks Tommy," said a smiling Billy. "We'll check in again after the 9pm poll closing."

"Adam, it is 8:30 on the east coast and we can now call Arkansas for Senator Turner, bringing his total to 66 electoral votes. While we wait for the next poll closings, let's analyze some states we haven't called," said Billy, moving over to the big board where he could drill down into the specific counties in each state.

"Let's start with Virginia. In recent elections Virginia is becoming reliably Party. Driven mostly by the enormous growth of government workers during this administration. Most live in the Virginia counties surrounding the DC area and the counties around Richmond."

Billy tapped the touch screen and individual blue colored counties popped up amidst a sea of yellow counties in western Virginia.

"Drilling down, we can see the Vice President is winning the traditional blue counties, like Loudoun, Fairfax and Prince William, but not nearly by the margins of previous elections. The Loudoun County parents are still upset about CRT in their schools, apparently. This is why EXN has chosen not to call this state yet. There are still some rural counties to come in and they traditionally go solidly red. In this election, Turner is winning most of these traditional red counties with Blackbirds underperform. These are the yellow counties on the map," explained Billy.

"Let's look at North Carolina. As you can see, it is a sea of yellow, red, and a couple of blue counties. Here Governor Blackbird has a slight lead on Turner with more of the urban counties outstanding. Now, many of these will go for the Vice President, but that will hurt Blackbird more than Turner and we still have this as too close to call between the Governor and Turner."

"Florida is the same. Miami-Dade, Broward, Palm Beach are all in at less than 50% with Turner leading Blackbird and the Vice President by double digits. I think we are getting close to making a call in Florida, but for now, we are still waiting. The late endorsement of Turner by Governor Wilson helped him and hurt Blackbird for sure. Plus, the results of the panhandle will lag with the polls closing there an hour later."

"Finally, Pennsylvania. What is happening in Pennsylvania? Let's go to Rory for some more chalkboard work."

"Thanks Billy." Rory held up a chalkboard with numbers about Pennsylvania counties. "Pennsylvania really comes down to a couple of counties around Philly and two around Pittsburgh. This is where the Party typically makes up for the sea of red counties in Pennsylvania, or this year, the yellow counties of Turner on our maps. Turner is winning what are traditionally the red counties, and he is winning there with bigger margins than typical. In contrast, the Vice President is not winning the blue Party counties with as big a margin. Similar to the results we have seen elsewhere. What is keeping Turner from really capitalizing are the Blackbird votes. He is taking away 10-20% of votes that would have easily put Turner over the top. Blackbird is really the Ralph Nader/Ross Perot of this election. Drawing off just enough support from Turner, allowing the Vice President to stay ahead."

"Who could have predicted that? Until a month ago, the argument was how many voters Turner would 'steal' from the major party candidates and spoil *their* chances," interjected Adam.

"Not us or apparently the pollsters either," laughed Rory, continuing on his breakdown of the Pennsylvania vote. "The counties to watch, which are all still relatively low in reporting, are Montgomery, Chester,

Delaware and Philadelphia counties around Philly and Allegheny county in Pittsburgh. It is all about the conversion rate. Turner is pulling votes from both candidates, not just Blackbird. That is the important thing to note, the level of erosion of moderate Party voters. This makes this hard to predict and is why the networks, including EXN, are waiting. The Vice President needs to perform with traditional margins of victory there to overcome the lead Turner is amassing. What is amazing is the sheer volume of write in ballots Turner is getting and these are all day of voters. All these write-in ballots take longer to tabulate. It may be a while on Pennsylvania," finished Rory.

"How many write-in votes for Turner so far?" asked Adam.

"Over 2 million," responded Rory.

"Two million? Are you kidding me?" asked Adam in disbelief.

"I am not. It is amazing. It speaks to both the ability of Turner to get his supporters out and the nature of just how mad the electorate in Pennsylvania is. Turnout was 80% last cycle, we could see even higher this time. Maybe 90%, or more," said Rory.

"There is also another reason. Turner is an easy name to write and spell. There will be no doubt about the intention of the voter for each write in ballot. We can't underscore the importance of this if it comes to a recount or audit. All I can say is this is an amazing election cycle," ended Rory.

Chapter 31

"Pennsylvania? What the hell is happening, Mel?" groaned Lexi, exasperated as she watched NWN talking about high turnout and the surprising showing with Turner having over two million write in ballots so far.

"Turnout is high in Pennsylvania, just like he said."

"Then we need to go higher. Go to 90% in the key counties. Hell, go to 100%. We need to do it now before it's too late," said Lexi.

"Ok, maybe we start with 90? That won't be too crazy then."

"95% at least. If it is a turnout game, as he says, we need to up my turnout ratio."

"True, but if it is a turnout ratio, we also need to be mindful of our additional 20% who didn't vote last time around, some percentage of them are voting this time. We run a higher risk of ballots being invalidated and more effort being made to audit the vote."

"Mel, we have been over this. There are going to be close to 8 million votes cast in Pennsylvania. There is no way anyone can audit all those votes, even if we gave them full access between November 3rd and January 6th. Which we will certainly not do. We have nothing to lose, except the state, if we don't act now. Do it."

"OK."

"And do the same for Michigan and Wisconsin, too. Enough fucking around. I don't want to have this conversation every time. Get those ballots moving into the counting centers," said Lexi.

Mel walked to a corner and called Josh.

"Bad Moon Rising" was all he said once Josh answered, and he disconnected.

#

Josh hung up the phone. He'd been watching the tallies and expected the call. He made two calls. One to activate the drivers and the second to implement all the mini diversions to allow the ballots to be delivered in the confusion in each polling place. This scenario had been planned for and rehearsed. As the ballots arrived at their destinations, toilets overflowed, lights went out, workers fainted, fights happened and several other creative activities. In all cases, the cameras showing the back doors of every polling site suddenly when to snow on their monitors for eleven minutes.

#

"Rory, sorry to break in on your analysis," interrupted Billy.

"Let's go to our reporter on the ground in Philadelphia."

"Larry, what do you have to report?"

"There was a fire alarm about 5 minutes ago and everyone but a couple of security folks and the head of the counting evacuated the building. There does not seem to be a fire, but the Fire Department is waiting to give the all clear. Maybe someone pulled a prank. If that is the case, it was in very poor taste and it will set back their ballot counting. They are busy verifying and counting all the mail in ballots. They get reviewed and counted here," he explained.

"Thanks Larry. This sounds like an organized effort as we are getting reports from Delaware, Bucks, Lancaster, Montgomery, Philadelphia, and Chester county of similar things happening. Not sure what the point is except to cause confusion and delay the counting. Please let us know if you have any other updates," nodded Billy.

"We just received information from Nevada and Arizona. The Supreme Court of both states has ordered the polls to remain open for two hours beyond their normal reporting time. We can expect results from these two states to be significantly delayed," added Adam.

"I think it could be a very late evening indeed," agreed Billy.

#

Mel got a call "The levee is dry," he heard spoken in his ear before the call ended. He smiled and nodded to Lexi, who was talking to Harriet.

#

"Adam, looks like we can now call Missouri, just before the 9pm polls close. EXN can now confirm Missouri is going for Senator Turner with an additional ten electoral votes. He now has 76 total electoral votes," announced Billy.

"As we approach the 9pm poll closures in 15 seconds," drew out Billy, stalling for time. "It is now 9pm on the east coast and we have another slew of states with polls closing and we can call many of them. Over to you, Adam."

"Let's get started. With the outage in Arizona's TrustedVoter machines, we won't report on Arizona until 11pm east coast time. So next up is Colorado. EXN can project Senator Turner's home state is going for the Vice President. It was closer than expected, but the Vice President appears to be edging the Senator, but only by a point and a half. A far cry from the thirteen-point margin the President had in the last election. This adds ten electoral votes to her tally."

"Continuing his trend of flipping red states, EXN is reporting Senator Turner has won Kansas with its six electoral votes," said Billy.

"EXN is also calling Louisiana for the Senator with its eight electoral votes," said Adam. Before each of these calls, the screen would show the state being referenced flying in with the smiling picture of the winning candidate next to it in a frame.

"Surprisingly, like Pennsylvania, we cannot call Michigan for any candidate. Even with the Michigan attorney general keeping any mail in ballots from being counted for Senator Turner, there appears to be a voter revolt underway. At this time, Senator Turner is only 8 percentage points behind the Vice President with about 60% of the vote in. Once again, he has received over a million write-in votes so far. This one is far from over. I think we are sensing a trend here. Voters feeling like the decision is being taken out of their hands by the heavy hand of government," remarked Adam.

"It would seem like that, Adam. At this time, we are also not prepared to call Minnesota. The Vice President has a good-sized lead, but many of the traditional red counties have yet to report their ballots and Turner is still within striking range. We can call Nebraska for Senator Turner receiving an amazing 84% of the vote with 95% of the precincts reporting. Nebraska adds five electoral votes as Senator Turner also won the fifth electoral vote, which is awarded separately. It appears the heartland is shifting from Opposition to Turner."

"EXN is projecting New Mexico will go for the Vice President with five electoral votes. And with no surprise to anyone, we are also calling New York and its twenty-eight electoral votes for the Vice President as well. Senator Turner is running a close second in both states, closer than anyone would have expected," admitted Adam.

"Finally, we've not had much to say about Governor Blackbird tonight, but we can now project both North and South Dakota will go for Governor Blackbird, adding three electoral votes from each of them to his total. We should note, it appears the Governor will only win these states by single digits over Senator Turner. In fact," said Billy, looking at papers in front of him, "It appears Senator Turner has finished first or second in every state we have called so far. He has a two million popular vote lead overall because of this. Even when he loses, he is racking up the votes," noted Billy.

"There is no doubt who the most popular candidate is. It looks like we could be in for another argument on the popular vote vs the electoral college as the method of determining our president," agreed Adam.

"The polls in Texas have closed. It is too early to call it as well with 25% of the votes counted. Turner has a substantial lead, which is to be expected, considering he got the endorsement of Senator Garcia and the Governor," said Billy.

"The polls have closed in Wisconsin. To the surprise of no one, this one is also much closer than anyone expected. Once again, Turner is outperforming expectations with his day of write-in vote totals. The Vice President has a big lead, but it is still too close to call with only 17% of the vote in."

"In our last call this go round, we can project Turner will win Wyoming and it's three electoral votes, again with a whopping 84% of the votes cast.

"There is a lot to unpack there," said Billy. "Let's start with the current electoral count. Totals are 121 for the Vice President, 98 for Senator Turner and 15 for Governor Blackbird."

"We still have not called Virginia, North Carolina, Florida, Ohio, Pennsylvania, Michigan, Wisconsin, Minnesota, Texas, and Georgia," finished Billy. "We have a ton of electoral votes we still cannot award yet."

"Thoughts, Rory?" asked Adam, looking at the nerdy analyst.

Rory laughed. "I have lots of thoughts. I am thinking Senator Turner is going to win the popular vote, however unlikely that appears. That in itself is a miracle. An unknown entering the race late, with very little TV exposure, who spent his entire campaign speaking to small groups of people. Who didn't seek endorsements or court any big money? I wouldn't believe it if I wasn't seeing it."

"That is nice, but as we all know, it is the electoral college that decides the election. Does he have *any* chance?" asked Billy.

Rory took off his nerdy glasses. "Barely. He has a path, but it is narrow. Blackbird is holding on to his lead in North Carolina. If he wins, that will put a real damper on the Senator's chances. You can't easily make up those lost 31 electoral votes. If he can't win there, he pretty much needs to sweep the states still outstanding. As one of you mentioned earlier, I am surprised at the Vice President's weakness in key states. Like New York, for instance. The Party usually wins with low 60% to mid 30s. This time around she won with only 50% to Turners 44 and Blackbird with less than 6. Turner picked up the 30 odd percent the Opposition normally gets and then another 14 from the Party side."

"That's amazing Rory. Who are those voters?" asked Billy.

"Working-class whites, many of whom already fled the Party and suburban moderate moms. He seems to be doing much better than the opposition has historically with both urban black and Hispanic voters. What is also interesting is this was not a turnout issue, as the turnout for the state is up, like it is in every state. It is going to be interesting to unpeel all the voting segments afterwards. We have never had a cross over candidate like Turner, pulling large pieces of the center of both parties together on his side."

"Rory, is this a sign the Progressive platform is not as widely accepted as it appears? Perhaps people publicly claim support but privately reject it?"

"Adam, it could be. Until we have the actual breakdowns, it is going to be hard to speculate with any certainty. My gut tells me, and my research somewhat confirms, Turner's entire success is based on his offering a centrist alternative to the Progressive's bigger government with more spending and regulation. These progressive policies are already being implemented by the current administration. With more advocated in the platform of the Vice President.

"What about the remaining swing states, Rory? When will we be able to call them?" asked Billy.

"Virginia is surprisingly tight. We still have some of the western counties there which will most likely go for Turner and a few votes from Richmond, which should go to the VP. It is going to be close, maybe a point spread max," said Rory.

"That is a surprise. Virginia was turning reliably blue. The President carried the state by seven last election."

"You know, Billy, it is not really blue versus red. Turner should really be purple instead of yellow because that is what he really is. He is appealing to the disaffected moderates of both sides. Now admittedly a majority of his support is coming from the Opposition side, but that is part his stance and the other part such a weak Opposition candidate. I would say at least 20% of his support is coming from the Party. Maybe as high as 30%."

"Which means it is coming *from* the Vice President, not just Governor Blackbird," pointed out Billy.

"Yes. That explains close races in Virginia, and Pennsylvania, Michigan, Wisconsin, and Minnesota. I suspect we will see this in Nevada as well. If he had been on the ballot in Pennsylvania, Michigan and Wisconsin, I believe he would be president. There is going to be a lot of scrutiny on the legality of the rulings by the state supreme courts."

"I couldn't agree more, Rory. To keep a candidate off the ballot who is earning millions of write-in votes in these states. Somehow, he is illegitimate? Someone needs to explain that one to me. The unwillingness of the Supreme Court to take this case is also subject to scrutiny," interrupted Adam in an angry tone.

"Especially if Turner ends up winning the popular vote and losing the electoral college because of these states. They have a lot to answer for from their unwillingness to get involved to adjudicate the laws being used to keep him off the ballot. Anyway you look at it, the Vice President, if she wins, is not getting her mandate," announced Rory.

Adam laughed mockingly. "Where do you appeal a court deciding not to take a case and issue a ruling? Just ignoring it without deciding? If I read the Constitution correctly, this is one of the *few* official jobs our Supreme Court has. To be the last word on the Constitutionality of disenfranchising voters in this case."

"I think America agrees with you, Adam. Turner is fighting the good fight in these three states. Following the rules and processes, but consider Michigan where a single attorney general invalidated every mail in ballot cast for Turner? What happens to those votes? Those who mailed in ballots for Turner could not go cast a provisional day of ballot or risk both being canceled. These needed answering before the election, especially considering where he is in Michigan right now."

"Don't worry Rory, his appeal in front of the Michigan Supreme Court is scheduled to be reviewed *after* the election," replied Adam sarcastically. "When it no longer matters."

"Texas and Florida?" asked Billy, changing the subject to keep his elder statesmen colleague from saying something else he might regret.

"I think Turner will get both. It is taking longer because of the Blackbird vote. The EXN decision desk wants to be sure. I don't think EXN is interested in a repeat of that early Arizona call," implied Rory.

"Got that right," said Adam, remembering. "I am perfectly fine with us being last this time."

"I do like the idea of using purple instead of yellow. Maybe we can get that changed," laughed Billy.

#

Nick sat in the conference room, watching the discussion on EXN. Chuck and Denise sat on either side of him. Around them, the rest of the staff were talking on the phone or had their heads buried in laptops tracking west coast exit polls and trying to squeeze every vote they could out of each of the last states.

"What are you thinking?" asked Chuck, looking at Nick.

"I'm thinking what an absolutely complex, expensive, and time-consuming process our elections have become. What should be the simplest thing in the world is just another business to make a lot of people a lot of money. Like politics in general."

"Gotta love capitalism," shrugged Chuck.

"That's the best you can do? I make a prophetic statement on the corruption of a simple process of picking a leader and you claim hooray for capitalism," said Nick with a grin.

"Well, it's a job. Not sure what else I would do," shrugged Chuck.

"You could charge your parents for house sitting? That is the capitalist way, right?"

"Touche`."

"What are you two babbling about?" interjected Denise.

"Nothing," replied Nick.

"Nothing?" asked Denise, an eyebrow raised.

"What else am I supposed to do? I get to sit here and listen to all these experts tell me what I already see. A lot of confusion. My only solace is this is probably driving Lexi up the freaking wall," gloated Nick with a big grin.

"That part you have right. I would not want to be Mel Arenson right now. She is a bear at the best of time. Put her in a situation where she thinks she is being screwed out of something? Let's just say it is not a pleasant sight," confided Denise.

"Sounds like experience?" said Chuck, frowning at her.

"Oh, believe me, it is. I have seen all sides of Miss Smythe before she was a Thomas," confirmed Denise.

"Care to share? We have nothing else to do but wait," noted Nick.

"Someday maybe. Actually, what you should do is go up to the suite and see if you can get a few hours of sleep. This is not going to end until the wee hours if it isn't tomorrow morning. The way things are looking, there is going to be gridlock and maybe even some recounts from us and from them. If Virginia is as tight as Chalkboard said on EXN, you can bet Nevada will be closer. And Arizona and Georgia," suggested Denise.

"You're kidding right? And miss all this excitement," laughed Nick, pointing as Billy McCall was once again at his big board drilling down into counties and vote counts and 'what if this or that' happened? Basically, killing time until they had something substantial to report.

"Some of these guys live for election days. Billy is one of them," laughed Denise.

"What do you think?" asked Nick.

"I think we are being teased. We're being led to believe we have a chance. If there were any fairness in the world, we would have a chance. But Nick, I am so sorry you are up against Lexi. She is ruthless, she will do whatever it takes to win. You need to remember this. If she could sell her soul to the devil to make it happen, she would do it," said Denise, she was almost shaking. "She probably already has, in fact."

"Denise, it's alright. I knew it was a longshot. I get it. They cheat. Everybody cheats and not just stuffing ballot boxes. When the election goes on for two years, everyone's vote is essentially bought through some promise made to win it. At some point, enough people are going to stand up to them and no matter how hard they cheat, the people will prevail. If not now, sometime. They just need to know this. They can't give up. They need to keep trying. This is part of that learning experience."

She shook her head, on the verge of tears.

"Nick," interrupted Chuck.

Chuck was pointing at EXN on the TV

"We can now project Senator Turner will win in Florida, awarding their thirty electoral votes to him."

"Billy, we can also report Texas is in the win column for Senator Turner as well, with its forty electoral votes. And ready for this? EXN is now also able to project Senator Turner will also take Ohio and its seventeen electoral votes. With these three prizes, Senator Turner now has 185 electoral votes, the vice president with 121, and Governor Blackbird with 15," announced Adam.

"That officially puts Governor Blackbird out of the race. There are not enough electoral votes left for him to reach 270. It is the inglorious end to a spectacularly poorly run campaign and may very well signal the demise of the Opposition as a viable party. Just as the increasingly weak Whig candidates and presidents led to the formation of the Opposition party under Lincoln," opined Rory, giddy with excitement at these electoral revelations.

"Of course, the same could be said for the Party of Jefferson and Jackson. Starting with Wilson and probably exemplified most by Vice President Smythe-Thomas. The traditional Party is dead too. It is replaced by this incarnation of the Progressive Party. It is now officially between Turner and the Vice President," ended Rory.

"I think it has been that way ever since the October surprise. Blackbird could never recover. Turner thrived on all the attempts to sully his name. It just made him stronger and more presidential as he handled each crisis with aplomb and turned the tables on his enemies every time. This is what people are looking for in a leader," suggested Adam.

"Aplomb? Good word Adam," laughed Rory. "I agree. Trial by fire, visible to all, made him look very Presidential, trustworthy and confident."

"Just what many people are looking for after the last few administrations. Let's also not forget his military service and New York. There is no doubt this candidate is cool under pressure," added Adam.

"True. I think it is a factor of many things adding up to a swing of monumental proportion, driving behavior and certainly unintended consequences regarding the Vice President's campaign," suggested Rory.

"How so?" asked Billy, wasting time as they waited for some of the western polls to close.

"This is a case where traditional October surprises backfired and probably ended up making him a viable candidate and introducing him to many who had discounted or ignored him before. It also helped these happened just as folks were doing the mail in votes. Lots of voters can be swayed by something as simple as a good visual. In Turner's case, that visual was responding to each of these in powerful and honest ways."

Adam laughed. "This is a first. A candidate gets pummeled from all sides with scandal and innuendo and it *helps* him win votes?"

"It would have been front and center in their minds. Especially since there were so many and some of them were more obviously setups than others. When you add in Bank's revelations about the VP's roles in these October surprises and you now also have day of voting turnout through the roof. Most who were uncertain or on the fence swung to Turner. In addition, I think all of this and the general disgust with the state of our electoral process…," Rory paused for a second. "I think many folks who normally don't vote were suddenly motivated to cast a protest vote for Turner. Now we see the massive turnout in all the states, not just the key ones," finished Rory, leaning back in his chair.

Adam and Billy were nodding at Rory's explanation. "Well Rory, you just delivered your analysis with such 'aplomb'," smiled Adam. "It is hard to argue against any of your opinions. I doubt anyone can come up with better reasons for what we are seeing. I would not want to be the folks who recommended these tactics if there were indeed orchestrated by the VP or her team."

#

In the conference room, folks were hugging and cheering and tears were flowing. Nick was being patted on the back by various staffers. He shook his head at the turn of events so far this evening. They were wildly exceeding their most optimistic hopes. Now Blackbird was out. He could only imagine what was going on in Lexi's camp.

#

Mel watched as Nick won the three big prizes of the Opposition. Texas, Florida, and Ohio to get to a 64-electoral vote lead. It looked bad, but it was not terrible if their plan worked. It was closer in all the states, and the votes were coming in slower because of the write-in votes being cast for Turner.

Mel was trying to maintain a positive outward demeanor. Virginia was a worry. So were Nevada and Arizona and the machines. It made him wonder if someone had done something to the machines to stop them from cheating. He needed some wins to give Lexi something good to focus on. Instead of Turner winning.

She was calling network presidents left and right with all kinds of outrageous threats. At least they thought they were threats. They all called him after receiving her call, wondering. What he knew, and they did not, was she did not issue idle threats.

Lexi *would* follow through and she had the memory of an elephant. Especially if she felt someone did her wrong. It was his job to convince her not to go through with them. Some of these network presidents were actually useful. Others, not so much.

"Mel, get in here."

Lexi was pacing the suite, watching all the coverage where all she heard was how she was underperforming and how wonderful and amazing Turner was. She was fuming.

"Why is nobody calling Virginia or Pennsylvania? Or even freaking Minnesota. And Michigan and Wisconsin? They'll call Texas and Florida and Ohio for Turner. Do they think my threats are empty?" she warned.

"Lexi, they are just the network presidents. They don't run their election desks. They need to back up their claims if they call a state. I can tell you why Pennsylvania, Michigan and Wisconsin are not called and probably won't be until 1am, at the earliest," said Mel, fixing her a cup of tea.

"It takes forever to count write in ballots. Turner has a lot of them. Not enough to beat us, but a lot of them. Many are protest votes for the way the judges cheated him out of being on the ballot. You had nothing to do with that," he said, walking to her with the tea.

"In retrospect, we would have been better off to have the Supreme Court take the case and let Chief Wishy-Washy rule to put him on the ballot. We misjudged the push back. Now people are voting for him out of principle," concluded Mel, near Lexi as she sat, sipping the hot tea.

"Once they finish those, they will then have to count all the extra mail-in ballots, which we delivered later. It will look bad before we eventually win. Don't worry. It just takes time. Minnesota and Virginia are going to go for you, but they are taking longer because the margins are smaller, so they have to get in more of the ballots. Count them and wait until it is clear there is no way the outstanding votes can pass you." Mel sat across from her, but not too close, just in case. Her four-inch heels were called stilettos for a reason.

"There is no plot against you. Give it time. You know how these things work. Hell, you remember the first election and the second. We didn't know that one for weeks until the Arizona, Pennsylvania, and Georgia recounts finished. They were just as nerve-wracking," Mel pointed out.

"True, but I was just the VP then. Not the President. Are we doing everything we can?" mused Lexi. "What have we forgotten?"

"Nothing. It is going to be a long night, but we will prevail in the end. We did too good a job with Blackbird. Who would have ever thought that? We took him out so completely, Turner picked it all up. Live and learn."

Lexi gave him a half smile. "We have underestimated Turner for the last time. Mark my word."

For the first time, Mel noticed his nemesis had not been around once they made their way to the suite to watch the results. A chill went down his spine at Lexi's last comment.

"Where is Roland?"

Lexi stared back at him, her icy blue eyes on fire. He fought every fiber in his body to maintain his stare.

"Why do you ask?" she asked sweetly, knowing exactly why he was asking.

"Lexi, listen to me. I know you are upset. I get it. But we are already dealing with people assuming we knocked off Banks. If a network president dies or, God forbid, a presidential candidate, it will be the end. Please tell me you are not planning anything," pleaded Mel.

She stared at him. He looked up as Roland entered the suite. He stopped as both turned to stare at him.

"Yes?"

"How is security at the convention center? Everything ready for my acceptance speech, whenever that is," finished Lexi, glaring at Mel.

Roland smiled. "Yes. The teams are in place. The Secret Service has secured the premises. Not much for me to do since we are off the campaign trail now."

"Good. Maybe you can go home now," blurted Mel.

Roland smiled.

"Enough. Why was New York so close? It is embarrassing?" asked Lexi, shaking her head and pacing.

"Think about it, Lexi. He is the hero of the subway bombing. A lot of New Yorkers love him because of it. He got that vote. That is why it was closer than we thought. He also got almost all the Opposition votes."

"I don't get it. Why more people are not embracing our policies?" lamented Lexi. "We're only trying to make their lives easier. Providing a bigger and bigger safety net."

"It is the right wingers who keep carping on about freedom and privacy, until we have another 9/11 and then it will be why didn't we know and do something," agreed Mel.

"Don't forget freedom. They love freedom until they can't make their mortgage because they lost their job because of COVID. Then they're screaming for help. Help to feed their family, help to keep their home, help so they can go to the doctor without having to pay an arm and a leg. They have very short memories. It is always us who come through to help them. Not the feckless opposition. All they do is give you the freedom to starve, the freedom to fail, and the freedom to buy a gun. So you can go shoot people when you get depressed because your freedom doesn't help you when you needed it." Finished a very frustrated Lexi.

"You know, Lexi, that was one of the best rejections of Opposition policies I have ever heard you say. It came from the heart and it makes sense. We are compassionate, trying to do the right thing and help people as much as possible. Turner and Blackbird and the rest of them are not offering any help. They are just telling you, if you work real hard and get lucky, maybe you can get ahead. Maybe you just end up working real hard for your entire life and have nothing to show for it? Because you had to spend it all on the basic stuff we want everyone to have equally. Food, healthcare, schooling, and housing," offered Mel.

"We just need to up our messaging. And deliver on it to prove it to them," stated Lexi.

"We will. In your first 100 days, they will see change like we have never seen before. You'll make it reality and then we'll let the people judge for themselves," agreed Mel.

Roland sat in a chair, not reacting to their conversation. He *knew* things would change. Regardless of the outcome of the election. Plans were already in motion.

Chapter 32

"What's the word Harry?" asked Lexi as they waited for a late night room service dinner.

Harriet hung up the phone. "Good, I think. Turnout in the west is high, more so as they see it is tight, so that is good. Lots of our lazier young supporters stay home in California if they see it is already in the bag. Not so this year. They need to pull their weight. Northwest is strong as usual. Clark in Nevada, and Maricopa and Pima counties in Arizona are good too."

Lexi nodded.

"Our volunteers have been working caravans of people to the polls all day and going door to door to drive out the vote. A couple of minor skirmishes with Turner supporters doing the same, but nothing newsworthy. I overheard Mel explain to you what is happening in the upper Midwest. We just have to give them time. Our contingency plans are already in place, so we should see a late-night surge in all three as the last batch of mail in ballots are counted," described Harriet.

"Are we going to see the late-night spike like before?" said Lexi worriedly.

"I'm afraid so. Even worse. There is no way to hide it when they come in so late. Especially in Michigan, where there are no mail-in ballots for Turner."

"Mel, call the networks. Start laying the groundwork for the coincidence of our ballots being counted at the end. The order they get counted is not necessarily when they arrive. You know the drill," ordered Lexi as Mel nodded, already dialing.

"What are your thoughts on Virginia?" she asked Harriet.

"I think Turner got incredible turnout numbers in western Virginia, and I think a lot of our liberal DC supporters started partying early, figuring it was in the bag. They got lazy and complacent and didn't vote," explained Harriet.

"I could see that. The polls were showing a pretty easy win, unless they bothered to look yesterday," murmured Lexi.

"Worse, if the last poll they looked at was a week ago, you were up by 20+ points. They may not have even bothered to see it had tightened," said Harriet.

"Minnesota?" asked Lexi.

"That's what I was just discussing. NWN is about to call it. It is close, probably one and a half to two points, but it is yours. The pandemic hit them hard. People are really fed up with ARL and Antifa being unchecked in Minneapolis all these years later. Minneapolis now looks like parts of Chicago which never recovered from the '68 riots. So that hurt us with some of the urban liberals we usually can count on. Minnesota is basically as close to a socialist state as we have today. They have really fucked up the policing there," explained Harriet.

"They tried to kill Turner. He could get some guilt vote. From folks embarrassed, it happened in their state," added Roland from his seat against the wall.

"That too," laughed Harriet, nervously. She never felt comfortable around Lexi's head of campaign security.

"We'll fix that in January. Antifa isn't going to be a pain in the ass anymore on my watch. They served their purpose, time to stick them back in Pandora's box. ARL is another thing. I applaud the movement, but they are executing Alinsky's strategies poorly. It might be fixable. If not, off with their heads too," announced Lexi, with a hand chop, as Harriet looked on in approval. Her boss was back. The pity party was over.

Mel walked in with salads and a bottle of Chardonnay from room service. "Don't worry, Secret Service checked it," when Lexi raised an eyebrow.

"Would hate to get poisoned on election night," said Lexi with a laugh.

#

"We are approaching 10 pm in the east, but before that, we have another call to make," said Billy McCall. "EXN can now call Minnesota for the Vice President. It appears she will hold a slight margin of about 1 to 1.5 percent over a late surging Turner. That puts ten more electoral votes in the Vice President's corner."

"It is now 10pm on the east coast and we have four more states whose polls have just closed. Iowa is too close to call with only 50% of the vote in and Turner with a comfortable lead so far. EXN projects Senator Turner will carry the state of Montana and its four electoral votes," announced Billy.

"Normally, we would report Nevada as closed, but the Nevada courts allowed the polls to remain open for one more hour. I believe previously we said they would stay open two hours longer, but that was only Arizona. Nevada is staying open for just one more hour."

"Now both Nevada and Arizona's polls will close at 11pm eastern. Anyone in line when the polls officially close will still be allowed to vote there. The voting machines are still not accepting new votes after the power surge earlier this afternoon, so both states have been using paper ballots for hours now. Again, just to clarify, they did not lose any previously cast votes, nor are the machines down. They simply will not allow any new votes to register. No doubt there will be some serious investigations into this matter after the election," explained Adam.

"We have one more state to award from the 10pm poll closings. We are projecting Utah will also go to Senator Turner with its six electoral votes. Turner and Smythe-Thomas both picked up ten additional electoral votes. Turner is now 195, Smythe-Thomas at 131 and Blackbird at 15," finished Adam.

"Rory, what are you hearing about Virginia? The polls have been closed for 3 hours now. What is still outstanding?" asked Billy.

"Not much frankly, Billy. If you look at the board, it says 95% of the vote is in and Lexi is leading by a razor thin 21,000. The question is all about turnout. There were about 4.5 million votes cast in the last election in Virginia. We are already over 5 million for this election, so that makes it hard to know if 95% is accurate or not. 95% of what?"

"Good point," agreed Adam.

"Last election, total votes received but not yet counted? You see, this is why it is taking so long there. If we were to assume 5 million votes, then 1% is 50,000 votes and if 5% are still outstanding, that means 250,000 votes. So, 21,000 votes are not very many to overcome if that is the case," continued Rory, explaining the difficulty with predicting outcomes before all the votes are counted.

"As you showed earlier, Billy, the outstanding votes are in Frederick, Rockingham, and Bedford, which should all go big for Turner. Also, Virginia Beach and a sizeable chunk of Fairfax, which will both be Smythe-Thomas territory, especially Fairfax. It may all come down to Fairfax, which is showing 60%. Last cycle they have 600,000 and 419,000 were Party, around 70%. Extrapolating out, if there are roughly 180,000 votes left to be counted in Fairfax, the Vice President could expect to get as many as 130,000 or so too 50,000 for Turner."

"But we all know the turnout is not the same this election with Turner taking from the Party side, too. In this little conversation, you see how hard it is to predict things. We may actually have to wait for all the votes to be counted in many of these states. Trust me, nobody wants to be wrong and have to take a state they call back," he finished.

"Rory, I am exhausted just listening to this brief description of the process. No wonder it is taking so long," complained Adam.

"Turnout models are all wrong so far. These are an enormous piece of their projection models. When the turnout is higher than even the highest projections, their models really turn to," Rory paused, having almost committed a broadcast sin in his excitement. "Crap," he said, smiling. "All their models are crap right now, and statisticians hate to guess."

Billy and Adam were laughing. "Thank you for catching yourself. We have enough issues already with this administration without adding the FCC to the mix."

"Let's check in with our reporters on the ground at the Vice President's watch party in DC. Jennifer. How are things in the Smythe-Thomas camp?"

"Billy, they are still cautiously optimistic things will turn big for the Vice President. They believe all the Midwest states will go their way and combined with the west coast which is a traditional liberal stranglehold, it is really more of a question of when the party starts, not if. I've spoken to a few campaign officials who express surprise at Turner's showing. As they point out, he really is just taking the traditional red states, and not even all of those. They are feeling pretty confident right now. The music is playing, the food is out, the drinks are flowing, and people are getting excited, but nothing crazy yet."

"Thanks Jennifer. That's Jennifer Tilson, our EXN reporter on the ground at the Vice President's watch party in Washington, DC. Let's head to the floor of the Orange County Convention center in Orlando, where you will no doubt recognize our roving reporter covering Senator Turner's celebration."

Tommy's face came into the picture amidst a much more celebratory atmosphere compared to the Vice President. "Thanks Billy. I must say you would think Turner has won from the way his supporters are celebrating on the floor here. It was pandemonium when you announced Florida, Texas, and Ohio. You'd have thought we just landed on Mars. But in a way, they do have a lot to celebrate. No third-party candidate has come further, faster, and had this kind of showing. I think people here have a sense this is not the end, but a beginning of either a true third party or a party to replace the Opposition."

"What are you hearing from the campaign, Tommy? The math is pretty tough going forward."

"Adam, they know it is an uphill battle, and they are prepared for the outcome to not end their way. They've always known this was the longest longshot of all. Yet, here we sit on election night at 10:30 pm and an un-elected Senator, announcing a run for President less than one year before the election is leading with 195 electoral votes," commented Tommy

"It is inspiring, even if this is the pinnacle. I can feel the electricity and excitement at what they have done, but also what they have started. I can tell you, there will be partying here tonight, regardless of the outcome. One thing you will not see is disappointment. They have come farther than any of them thought possible and certainly farther than any of us in the media thought they would go. I dare say, they are putting up much more of a fight than the Vice President and her team ever expected. There is some sweating going on there tonight," said

Tommy, holding one hand over an ear because of the noise of partying Turner supporters.

"Thanks Tommy, we will check in with you again shortly."

"You bet Billy."

"I've been doing the math," said Rory, holding up a chalkboard. On one side it showed North Carolina, Georgia, Arizona, Idaho, Alaska, and Iowa. "Our first assumption is he can win states that go Opposition more often than not. That only gets him to 251, 19 short. Then he needs Pennsylvania, or Wisconsin and Michigan. He is still behind Blackbird in North Carolina and he is running out of uncounted votes to make up the difference. If he loses North Carolina, well, he needs a miracle. That would drop him to 235, 35 short of 270. To make that up, he needs Michigan, Pennsylvania and either Nevada or Wisconsin. It's really the only path left at that point," observed Rory.

"Or Virginia."

"True Billy, but given where the votes are outstanding and even accounting for extraordinary turnout, I still think the Vice President ekes out a win in Virginia."

"We are not hearing much from Pennsylvania, Michigan and Wisconsin?" asked Adam.

"They have to hand count the write in ballots. They are coming in batches of 100 or 200 and have been for the last two hours. As you can see, Turner is closing the gap in all three states. It is an extraordinary effort by his supporters. I'm also hearing there are still bins of mail in ballots in counties that still need to be counted around Detroit, Philly, and Milwaukee. Turnout is through the roof this time," reported Rory.

As they continued going through turnout numbers and what if scenarios, Nick turned from watching the screen in his suite. "We're going to lose North Carolina, aren't we?"

Chuck looked at him. "I'm afraid so. We have been crunching the numbers, there just aren't enough left. Mail-in balloting started before Blackbird's scandals and a lot of Opposition voters cast ballots for him. North Carolina does not allow you to change the vote or cast a provisional one. We couldn't make up the difference with day of voting."

"Crap. We weren't going to win the write in states anyway," admitted Nick, trying to keep the disappointment out of his voice.

Chapter 33

"Nick," said Denise, "Come over here, please."

Nick hurried over to a table where Denise was bending over a laptop showing a face talking excitedly. "Nick, this is Spencer in Pennsylvania. He works in our state office. Tell him what you just heard."

Spencer was smiling a huge smile on his very young and eager face. "Senator, I have a buddy working in the main counting office in Philadelphia and he says you are now ahead, just barely but ahead, and they are about done counting all the write-in votes in all the counties. The votes just keep coming in. I have heard there are a couple hundred thousand mail in ballots left to be counted as well, but they can't all be for the Vice President. I wanted to let you know," he said, smiling.

"Thank you Spencer, please let me know if anything changes," said Nick, smiling at his excited supporter.

He backed away and turned back to the EXN monitor. Somebody turned up the monitor volume.

"This is unbelievable. Senator Turner is now ahead in Pennsylvania with 98% of the vote in. His write-in votes keep trickling in from all counties. He's amassed over 4 million votes, all write in. This is not only unprecedented, it is almost inconceivable," said an amazed Rory, clearly astounded at the results.

"To put it in perspective, when the Alaskan Senator lost her Opposition primary battle and ran as a write in, she ended up winning the general election for senate. She only needed a couple hundred thousand votes to accomplish the feat," said Adam.

"Indeed, Adam, and if you look at Wisconsin, he is about to go ahead there, too. Michigan may be harder because he lost the benefit of his mail in ballots, but he is close there as well. Now keep in mind,

I'm being told in all three states there were late arriving mail in ballots collected from the remote site ballot drop boxes and these will need to be counted before any calls can be made. But those will more than likely be mostly for the vice president and Governor Blackbird, so Senator Turner needs to build up a lead sufficient to stand up to those counts," said Rory.

"The Vice President's camp has to be sweating bullets right about now," mused Adam.

"Maybe we can provide some good news for them," said Billy. "As of now, at 10:57 eastern time, with 99% of the vote in, EXN is projecting the Vice President will carry the state of Virginia and it's thirteen electoral votes. This brings her total to 144 electoral votes. Rory, we have about 45 seconds before the next polls close. Thoughts?"

"11,500 votes. The Vice President won by a tiny margin in a solidly blue state. I think that speaks for itself," explained Rory.

"OK, it is now 11pm on the east coast and the polls have closed across the west. In an evening of surprises, we cannot make a call in California. This is because of very long lines at polling places throughout the state. Everyone who was in line before the polls officially closed is given the opportunity to vote. In fact, we are hearing the polling line in some locations wraps around the block. We will not make any call until we hear everyone who was in line at the polls has completed their vote without interference from networks. We certainly hope the other networks follow our lead for the integrity of our profession," hoped Billy.

"EXN can project Idaho will go for Senator Turner, picking up the four electoral votes," said Adam. "We can also confirm the state of Oregon and its eight electoral votes will go for the Vice President, as well as the state of Washington with its twelve electoral votes. If you remember earlier, we told you the polls in Arizona and Nevada would stay open until 11pm eastern time. We can confirm the polls in both states are now closed, but we are not expecting any definitive results for a while as they tally the paper ballots and add them to the previously tabulated electronic machine votes."

"We have a lot to unpack here. Let's start with California. Rory, your thoughts?"

"There were over 18 million votes cast in California last election. California has embraced mail in balloting more than any other state, with 80% plus of ballots being mail in during the last few elections. That meant only 3.6 million people actually went to the polls. Mail in balloting greatly favors the Party candidates. This is not political bias, it is statistics. Of the 14 million cast by mail, the current President received over 10 million of those votes. Almost double the day of voting," explained Rory, trying to make the jumble of numbers understandable to those watching.

"Billy, our deal desk says it will probably be two hours before all the lines at the polling places are completely done voting. This is not just in certain places or because of a power outage in a precinct. We are being told it is in every precinct in the state except for San Francisco and LA, where the lines are only 100 people deep," laughed Rory. "It seems like many people are suddenly motivated to vote. Now it could be a bunch of Party voters who thought this was in the bag and are getting out to make sure, or it could be the opposite and there are a bunch of voters who could have cared less, who are now inspired by Senator Turner," Rory once again took off his glasses, rubbing his eyes with his chalk smudged hand.

"One thing is for sure, we are not going to know for probably," looking at his watch. "Four, maybe Five hours. I would start brewing coffee and maybe put in an order for a boatload of breakfast tacos."

"I don't know about breakfast tacos, but I could sure agree on the coffee. I guess it is time to switch from decaf back to regular," laughed Billy. "No surprises from the rest of the outcomes?" asked Billy.

"The winners followed the pattern of the evening, with Turner picking up the red states and the Vice President the northwest states. Again, the margins are much smaller than expected. Look at Washington. It's usually a 20pt win for the Party. It looks to be somewhere in the 44 for Smythe-Thomas, 41 for Turner and 15 for Blackbird. Oregon is usually a 14-16 point win. Lexi is only going to win by maybe 3, 47 to 44 for Turner and 9 for Blackbird. Now let's look at Idaho. This is a very conservative state. Turner is not anti-abortion and is not a traditional conservative on all points, yet he is winning with 75%, Lexi with 19 and Blackbird with 6. 75% is better than any candidate has *ever* gotten in Idaho. Look at Utah, another ultra-conservative anti-abortion state. Turner got 74%. Put this in perspective, Mitt Romney, their favorite son, only got 72.8% during his run."

Rory swapped out chalkboards with lots of numbers wiped out and re-written over the course of the night.

"Look at the popular vote. Turner has an 8 million vote lead. He has already surpassed the most Opposition votes ever cast in an election. And remember, this is an election with *three* candidates. If he keeps this up, he'll pass up the most Party votes won in an election. And he may not even win. I hear more arguments for abolishing the electoral college coming and the Party being put in the position of defending something they tried earnestly to get rid of the last decade or so," said Rory, excited and enthused by the statistical showing of Turner.

"Those are some amazing stats, Rory." Billy smiled at him geeking out on the turnout numbers. "Adam, you have some breaking news?"

"I do. Bad news for the Turner camp, I am afraid. EXN is now calling the state of North Carolina for Governor Blackbird. With those 16 electoral votes, Governor Blackbird may have killed any chance Senator Turner had of completing the biggest upset in history. The electoral counts are now, Senator Turner still in the lead with 195, Vice President Smythe-Thomas with 164 and Governor Blackbird with 31," said Adam.

"Rory?" asked Billy.

"Well, it is not over, statistically. But there are not enough electoral votes out there. Assuming he gets Georgia, Arizona, and Nevada, he still has to take all three of the write in states. It is so hard to flip states from blue to red or, in his case, yellow," commented Rory.

"Oh yeah, that reminds me, hit it fellows do the switcheroo," said Billy with a smile. All the yellow states on the big board suddenly turned a deep purple to make them distinguishable from the lighter blue of the Vice President.

"Now the states Turner wins reflect the actual makeup of his followers, Party and Opposition."

"I love it," said Rory. "My idea," he laughed.

"Hey, I'll give you credit," said Billy.

#

Lexi sat back in her chair in her suite. It was looking increasingly like two convention centers full of followers were unlikely to be spoken to for quite a few more hours by either candidate.

"Tell me we have enough ballots in Pennsylvania, Wisconsin, and Michigan to overcome his leads," said Lexi.

"Michigan easily since we are still winning. Pennsylvania and Wisconsin should be fine. You made the right call to go to 95% turnout. There are going to be a ton of people crying foul because those dumps are going to stand out like a flashing red beacon, but as you say, we will have won by then," said Harriet.

"Good. What about Nevada and Arizona?"

"Same thing, we should be fine, losing the voting machines hurt, but we should still be fine," said Harriet, less confidently.

"Georgia?" asked Lexi.

"Mel is on the phone right now. I am not sure it is going to be enough in Georgia. Apparently, one of our drivers failed to get his ballots in during the confusion. Something about getting stuck by a train for 30 minutes," said Harriet.

"Which county?" asked Lexi.

"Not sure. Here comes Mel. Mel which county failed to get the Georgia ballots?" asked Harriet?

"Cobb," said Mel dejectedly.

"Bad?" asked Lexi.

"Probably, that was 75,000 votes," said Mel, dejectedly.

"Do we need to put into effect the worst-case scenario plan?" asked Lexi.

"Not if you win California, Nevada, Pennsylvania, Michigan and Wisconsin. I am assuming you will win Hawaii with no contingency. We don't need Arizona or Georgia. No need to panic. I have told them to be ready in case we need them. We have a gal on the inside. We have parked them in an official Cobb County van outside the county office where the counting is happening. If need be, we can have her send some folks out to make sure there are no more ballots that haven't been counted. The problem is no one is going to know how it got there and she is going to have to give them a snow job about it not mattering, 'If they are ballots in an official county van, they must be legit and they need to be counted ASAP' or something like that," answered Mel.

"OK," sighed Lexi. "If we run into issues, we will contact her. Anything else?"

"Not at this point. We're just waiting. Pretty soon the networks will report Turner with good leads in all three write in states and then our mail in ballots will drop and flip all three."

"Even Michigan? Without his mail in votes?" asked Lexi in disbelief.

Mel nodded. "I have spoken to all the networks getting assurances none of them will call any of the states until all the write-in ballots are tallied. I can't stop EXN, but they got burned before, so they'll be careful," said Mel.

"What's up with California?"

"What do you mean?" asked Mel, confused.

"Don't be coy with me. Are those our people or his? California has never seen these kinds of lines. Ever. Are some of those ours? Are the little lazy privileged students waking up to the fact that if I am not elected, their mountains of debt won't be canceled and they won't be able to sit at home on their asses smoking weed and playing video games? If they're not our people, they should have been, if they knew what was good for them," said Lexi, fuming.

"I honestly don't know what is happening there. Some of it could be our campus folks rousting the college kids out to vote for those reasons. We gave them orders to get the vote out. I sense some of it is his. His people are motivated. You can blame the last few Party governors for turning paradise into a hellhole," said Mel.

"We won't know until much later. The other networks are not even showing vote counts, just like EXN. No one wants to be the one blamed by the losing campaign for suppressing votes in a state where voting is still in progress," explained Mel.

"Make sure that idiot at NWN doesn't even think about going to sleep. If he wants a cabinet post, he had better get ready to earn it," said Lexi, grinding her perfect teeth.

#

Nick sat in a chair in the small room off from the larger conference room, where his team was still busy on the phones and reviewing spreadsheets of data. Chuck stuck his head in the room.

"Did you eat anything?" he asked, giving Nick a beer from a Fort Collins Brewery.

"It's hard to believe we only picked these up this morning. It seems like a week ago," laughed Nick, taking a long pull, holding up a beer from his local brewery.

"I know. That's the way campaigns work."

"I had a slice of pizza and some salad a while back to answer your question. Not really hungry."

Nick looked at Chuck and then they both burst out laughing.

"Did you ever…"

"…think we would be here," finished Chuck. "Not a fucking chance."

"I thought we would make it to the election and get some votes. I didn't even think we would win a state, but here we are. With what, 5 million more votes than the Vice President," laughed Nick.

"Try 8, almost 9, and we don't even have any of California in yet. If nothing else, you have enthused or pissed people off so well, they are voting in droves. This is going to be the highest turnout election in the country's history, by far," revealed Chuck.

"Too bad it will be for naught. Is there any path?"

"Barring a miracle, no. But I think you just started a party, and you are going to have a ton of people in it from the start. Your career isn't over after all."

"I'm not sure I can keep this up. I think I've left everything on the field this time, Chuck," Nick said, tilting his beer.

"You aren't a quitter, Nick. You have started something. Regardless of where it leads, you're destined to lead us there. That much I know," said Chuck prophetically.

"All the same, I'm tired."

"I could close the door, you could catch a few Z's."

"My soul is tired, not my body. I'll be fine. The least I can do is put on a brave face until the end for the troops. They have done so much more than I ever would have believed. I wish Greg had let us help him. He was a big part of this success," said Nick wistfully.

"Indeed, he was. But his sacrifice helped you more than anything any of us have done individually. Maybe he knew that," said Chuck with a shrug.

"Maybe, but I would gladly trade the votes to have him back and Kevin, too."

"Nick, I fear there will be more losses before we are done with this journey," foretold Chuck, getting up.

Nick got up as well and put his arm on Chuck's shoulder. "I'm afraid you may be right, Chuck. I've never shirked from a fight before. I can't start now, especially since I brought so many friends." He smiled as they walked out into the conference room as it struck midnight on the east coast. Election day had ended. The election, however, was far from being over.

Chapter 34

"It's midnight on the east coast and we have two more states to call. To the surprise of no one, Alaska is projected for Senator Turner with its three electoral votes and Hawaii, will deliver its four electoral votes for the Vice President," said Billy McCall in an anti-climactic voice. If there were ever two sure things in a presidential election, it was Alaska and Hawaii.

#

Maksim Pavlovich woke up in his ornate canopy bed in his mansion, some would say castle, in the countryside outside Geneva, Switzerland. He carefully stretched, having learned many years before, his old sinews and bones did not take kindly to anything vigorous or extreme. He sat up and turned to the side of the bed, sliding bony feet into ermine slippers. Slipping on his centuries old Chinese silk robe, he shuffled to the nearby bathroom, where he stood for minutes to slowly empty his bladder. As he did every morning, he cursed his aged body, in which his brilliant mind lay imprisoned.

He made his way from the bedroom to the antechamber, where his manservant Fredric had laid out his usual morning fair. Bitter coffee, no sugar or sweetener. A bowl of oatmeal with almond milk, the usual newspapers, and his small glass of 'juice'. He called it juice, but it was really a concoction of his and the Doctor. Comprising herbs, human growth hormone and other items of less savory description, sourced in morally questionable and unethical ways. All combined to keep his organs and mind at their highest functioning state. It had worked on everything but his skin and bones, all of which continued to deteriorate no matter how they changed the formula.

He continued to fund all manner of advanced scientific work, from brain transplant to cryogenics to cloning. In the hope one of these offered him a chance at longer or renewed life. The Doctor continued to live simply because he was continuing the now multi-decade research project to provide longer life for Maksim through a miracle breakthrough.

For a moment, he almost forgot the American election was the prior evening. He opened his early edition of the New York Times. The headline just said the election was underway, with no results reported. Paper was so 20th century, he thought, finding the remote and turning on the channel to EXN.

He paused, a spoonful of oatmeal poised in front of his lips. He looked on in disbelief. First, the election was not over. Second Senator Turner was in the lead. Third, there were many states still undecided, including traditional blue states and states where his long cultivated operatives in all levels of the US government and judicial roles had conspired to keep Senator Turner off the ballot.

Yet these states were toss-ups as well. At 12:30 at night in New York? He had spent 100s of millions of dollars through the years to undermine and disrupt the judicial and election systems of America.

Single-handedly putting and keeping the last administration in power, only to have it get squeamish at the execution of the progressive platform supporting his globalist agenda. He now had a perfect foil in Lexi Smythe-Thomas. Maneuvering and helping her achieve every major outcome in her political career. This was to be the culmination of a lifetime of work, of planning, of effort, and sacrifice. Why was it not yet complete? What had caused this to happen? As if on cue, a picture of Nick Turner exhorting massive crowds in California during the days prior to the election showed on the screen.

Pavlovich had broken many a man and woman in his life. Once upon a time, with his own powerful hands. Now he worked through the hands of others. He stared at the image of Nick Turner he had frozen on his screen. He sat and finished his breakfast in silence, with Nick Turner looking on. Once finished, he drank his juice with a shiver, chased it with the last of his Himalayan bitter root coffee and started making phone calls. The election may not have been lost, but it had not been won yet either.

#

Everyone talked about this scenario and that. They showed pictures of the crowds Nick drew during the final days leading up to the election. They had Tommy on extolling the virtues of Nick and the sheer energy his rallies exuded. The love of him expressed by his crowds.

Once again Tommy implied, Nick had that quality, the once in a lifetime quality of leadership where your men would follow you into hell if you asked them too. Like Chuck earlier, Tommy sensed the cause was hopeless. But he also talked up the future, the future or lack thereof, for both the traditional Party and Opposition parties.

He referred to Nick's party as the New party. The New party would occupy the center and encompass the 50 percent of the electorate, 25% on either side of center, so the center left and the center right. This would leave the Progressives in charge of the far left and the Neo Cons in charge of the far right. He conceded it might be center left 20% and center right 30% as the lunatic fringe on the left was certainly more powerful and robust than the talking heads of the Neo Con right.

1am came and went. There was talk of Georgia and Arizona stopping counting as they had in years past. Both Secretaries of State in charge of elections in each state said there would be no stopping. They would go until it was done.

At 1:30am Nick peaked in Pennsylvania, with a 212,000 vote lead. At 1:34, he was ahead by 142,000 in Wisconsin and at 1:40 he was ahead in Michigan by 187,500.

"What do you think, Rory?" asked a visibly tired Billy McCall.

"Honestly, Billy, I don't know what to think. No other networks have called it. I know there are more mail in ballots being counted. I was told it was 225,000 in Pennsylvania, 152,000 in Wisconsin and 225,000 in Michigan. Unless these break at incredible margins for the Vice President, I don't see how these states are not going to go to Senator

Turner," said Rory, his excitement obvious, not so much for Turner, but for the statistical problems being front and center to the world.

"Yet we and nobody else are calling them. I am a statistician by trade and I can tell you statistically this is over. The probabilities of these remaining votes breaking sufficiently to overturn the Senator's lead are astronomically impossible. Not to mention in all *three*. And yet we wait." he finished shaking his head.

"I am told it will not be long now," said Adam, coming back, having taken an hour off. He looked refreshed and ready to go another 6 hours if needed.

"And California? Surely they are done voting?" asked Billy.

"Hang on, Billy, I am getting info from our decision desk. Apparently, California is about to declare that all polling precincts have closed as soon as some final stragglers in Orange County cast their votes," said Adam.

"What is up with Nevada? We haven't had much in the way of update since that first batch after their extended polling hours closed," observed Billy.

"My sources are telling me that not only did they have to do paper, there were a tremendous number of same day registrations. Nevada has about 58% of its population registered to vote. They're telling me they may have gotten this up to close to 70% with same day voter registration. If that is the case. That brings another 200,000 votes into play. I suspect many of those are going to be later Turner conversions. Right now, we have been stuck on 25% of the vote in, for over an hour. It shows the Vice President with a comfortable lead," said Rory, looking down at his notes.

"Well, it is 2am on the east coast and California has officially declared the polls closed and all votes cast. And," paused Billy. "We have nothing to report." We do not have a call for California. What we do have is 40% of the vote reported and the Vice President with 4 million votes so far and Turner with only 1 million and even Blackbird with 1.2 million. Now given these were mail in votes, you can't read too much into it. Given the turnout we have seen, I would guess we are going to be north of 20 million turning out. We also know the number of registrations soared to almost 28 million, an increase of 6 million in the last year alone."

"There are a lot of uncounted votes in California. Also, I would not trust the 40% in number either as it probably does not account for all the votes cast by mail, let alone the in person votes in the last 4 hours," cautioned Rory. Like the NFL draft expert who lived for draft day, the presidential election was the super bowl for political junkies like Rory.

"You must be a magician. The percentage just dropped to 30% but the Vice president went up to 7.5 million with the others only slightly gaining. It would seem they are still trying to get a handle on the total vote count.

"What the?" said Adam in the background.

"Adam, what was that" asked Billy, turning.

"Pennsylvania just posted 220,000 votes for the Vice President and 5,000 for Blackbird and it is now showing 100% and in my ear I am now hearing the EXN decision desk is calling Pennsylvania for the Vice President along with its nineteen electoral votes. She has a lead of almost 8,000 over Senator Turner. Rory, you're our guest. I will leave it to you to comment," said Adam, his tone hardly disguising his concern.

"If I read this right, the 225,000 mail in ballots remaining to be counted, 98% of them went for the Vice President. Just 2% for Blackbird and not a single mail in vote for Turner? In the immortal words of William Shakespeare, there is something rotten in Pennsylvania," Rory commented, not trying to be neutral.

"Ah guys, look at Wisconsin," said Billy as the screen showed the Wisconsin totals. Lexi jumped 74,000 and Blackbird went up 2,200, then Lexi jumped another 74,000 and Blackbird went up 1800. And the count went to 100% in. Lexi now held a slim lead of 6,000 votes over Turner.

"Ah, I am being told the EXN decision desk has now called Wisconsin for the Vice President and its ten electoral votes. That puts the Vice President's count at 188 and Senator Turner's at 202 with Governor Blackbird at 31."

"The producers are telling me, I need to point out, these mail in ballots were *not* just found. They have been at the polling places since well before the polls closed and it is just coincidence they were not counted earlier. The focus was on counting all the day of write in ballots rather than processing the remaining mail in ballots," reported Adam dutifully and then he stopped. The look on his face was one of anger. And concern.

"You go Billy," fumed Adam.

"Ah, sure Adam. Ah, we're also being asked to tell you the viewers not to read into this more than there is. It is just the way things were counted. Had they counted them first and then the write in ballots, Senator Turner would have fallen just short rather than appearing to have been slightly beaten by these mail in ballots counted last," said Billy, parroting what was being dictated in his ear.

In the conference room at Nick's hotel, the last thirty minutes had been one of an emotional high, followed by a plunge to the bottom. First, they'd rejoiced at the leads they had amassed in the three write in states only to watch them evaporate in a landslide of Lexi mail in ballots. Some staffers were crying, others were yelling about fraud and cheating.

"Margie," said Nick, calling out to his communications director. "Over here Nick," replied Margie on the phone and waving at him from across the room. He walked to her, and she hung up the phone.

Nick told Margie what he wanted to do. Chuck and Denise had joined the huddle, and they both looked at him like he was crazy. "See if you can do it, OK?"

#

Lexi smiled in her suite. Mel had been right. It was just enough to get those two. Now she just needed California and Michigan to come in and she was home free. Mel ended a call and walked over with a fresh drink for Lexi and himself. They clinked the glasses.

"Boy, that was close," commented Mel.

"Too close. We need to get our guys started on slow walking any recounts and audits for sure," agreed Lexi.

"Already have," said Mel. He glanced at EXN and there was Turner's face.

"What the fuck?" he said, turning up the volume.

"Thank you, Adam. I didn't know any other way to do this and reach as many of my voters as possible. We are also broadcasting on Hibi as well. I know a lot of you are upset. I know you see results like this where a drop of 200,000 votes without a single vote for me swings a tally from win to loss. I know you suspect there is something going on. I need you to trust. I need you to trust our system of government. The people who are running these elections. Who are counting and verifying and checking to make sure each vote is a legal vote." Nick stressed 'legal.'

"I need you to have faith. To have faith that the truth will always prevail. Do not suspect the worst. We are better than that. You are better than that. Now I don't want to hear of any violence. I don't tolerate that in my supporters. Violence is the tool of the progressives and we will not stoop to their level." He paused, staring into the camera.

"Please understand, I am serious. Nothing can be solved by violence. You just play into their hands and then you become a tool for them to use against all of us. Regardless of the outcome tonight, we are not going anywhere. There will be more elections. We will continue to play by the rules. Rules we all voted to put in and to abide by."

"We will count on our excellent courts and honest and just judges, the few remaining noble journalists whose sole job is supposed to be reporting facts. To root out and expose propaganda. We need to have faith in our elected officials who swear an oath to their fellow citizens, our Constitution, and to God to be honorable and honest. To have the best interests of their constituents at heart."

"Fear not, we will not be silenced and if it is not our time now, it will be sometime. As long as our hearts are true. As long as we have faith in our fellow man and woman and in a higher power, we'll be rewarded. The truth will be known. Count on it and keep the faith. Thank you for all your support and know that we have not given up. Like John Paul Jones, on the lonely quarterdeck of his ship during the Revolutionary War, when asked by the superior British ship to surrender, he said, 'We have not yet begun to fight.' He did indeed go on to victory. God Bless all of you and the United States of America." said Nick, signing off, ending the broadcast.

Adam dabbed at his eyes before speaking.

"I have been doing this now for over 60 years. I have seen it all. Crooks and charlatans. Leaders and sycophants. Liars and even the occasional honest politician. I have seen no one do something like that."

"Faced with what appears to be almost certain highly questionable activity at a minimum, he comes on and asks his followers to trust the very people who are perpetuating the deeds likely to cost him any chance of winning? There is being magnanimous and having grace, but good lord, that is unbelievable. I know I would be fighting mad if I were in his shoes and he comes on and threatens his own supporters if *they* get violent? Unbelievable. We should be so lucky to be led by someone with his character," Adam continued in a clear tone of admiration and approval.

"Explaining to his followers that being mad or striking out in anger is exactly what his opponents want and expect. No wonder this guy handled his October surprises so well. He isn't thinking outside the box, he just refused to see there even is a *box*. He refuses to react as *any* other politician would. You can't get cornered if the room has no walls." Adam was on a roll. No one tried to interrupt him.

"Sorry guys, I am frankly at a loss for how to describe what I just saw. I can tell you one thing, the last thing this country needs is more violent demonstrations. The ARL, Antifa, pro-Palestinian and pro-Hamas sympathizers, and other progressive supported groups have given us plenty of that these last few years, with little done to stop them."

"I applaud the Senator for doing all he can to nip anything in the bud. I will add my one cent's worth. If it is even worth that much. He is right on this one. Violence just gives them and the other networks talking points to use to more easily frame a negative narrative. Or to gin up more show trials in congress. It is the right message," Adam leaned back as he finished.

"Rory, give me a sec before you comment," said Billy. "While Senator Turner was speaking, Michigan has flipped to the Vice President as well. She gained 218,000 votes and Blackbird got 7000. That gives the Vice President a lead of 30,500 in Michigan and our decision desk is awarding the fifteen electoral votes to her," recited Billy.

"We do not know the number of Turner mail in votes that were sequestered. Nor do know if they have been counted or how they have been handled in case of an overrule of the Michigan Attorney General ruling to disqualifying them. If he wins on appeal, these votes would be added to his total. Stay tuned on that front, but for now, the Vice President has Michigan in her tally. Iowa has just officially been called for Senator Turner, so six more in his count. This now puts her in the lead with 212 to Turner's 208. We still have Georgia, Arizona, Nevada and California outstanding. Rory?"

"Thanks Billy", answered Rory, rifling through his notes, a stack of Chalkboards on the dais in front of him.

"Like Adam, I am glad the Senator got on and calmed down his supporters. I hope it works. It is clear they have a right to be angry. I understand the coincidences that are lining up to make this potentially look more nefarious than maybe it actually is, but the optics are bad any way you slice it. Bad for Turner because it killed what slight chance he may have had and frankly bad optics for the Vice President, who has made no bones about the aggressive first 100 days of legislation she wants to accomplish. With a cloud once again hanging over a presidential election, it is no way to go into what sounds like a foundational shift in how America operates," offered Rory.

#

Lexi sat watching all of this play out in her suite. "Damn. We wanted his folks out rioting and burning cars to make our point. Well, what do you think I should do?" asked Lexi, looking at Mel, who was nursing his bourbon.

"Absolutely nothing. We have our own operatives dressed in Turner gear, and word is no doubt going out to *his* Gabriel's Angel supporters, who will do that anyway, for the convenient ANC cameras, so we can pin it on his supporters."

"True, but we can't exactly round up our *own* operatives this time and hold them indefinitely while we bludgeon him with trying to overturn an election. I think he made it perfectly clear he isn't going to fall into *our* trap like they did last time," uttered Lexi, concerned and still watching EXN.

"You play it cool and you stay calm and presidential. We knew they would come after us. We knew the optics were going to be horrible. We can weather the storm, but we need to resist the bait. He is good. Way better than he should be and way more savvy than guys who have been working the political angles for 50 years. He is the most naturally gifted politician I think I have ever seen," praised Mel.

Lexi laughed and Mel ducked, expecting to have a glass sailing his way. "You just insulted him in the worst way. Calling him the world's best politician is worse than insulting his mother."

"I said naturally gifted. I did not say the best. I am looking at her," smiled Mel.

"Nice save," responded Lexi with a look.

"I meant it. Think about it. You have been through it all, seen it all, paid the prices, made the sacrifices, built up the markers, and are on the verge of achieving the ultimate pinnacle. For all his gifts, he is falling short. You are not. Because you know how the game is played. All his schtick about fairness and honesty of politicians and judges and journalists. It made me want to barf," stated Mel. "He is Alice in Wonderland without an author to write him out of this nightmare."

Roland laughed, shaking his head in disbelief at their conversation. "You both missed his point. He isn't talking to you. It was brilliant, because he is backing all of *you* into a corner. You are either honest or you are not. He is forcing people to pick sides. My experience tells me politicians hate to pick sides. They always want one foot in and one foot out. Ready to go either way they need to at any time. He took that away. There will be no safe middle going forward. Only us and them."

"Must have been all that strategy he learned in the military," offered Lexi, looking at him with an icy stare.

Roland shrugged with a smile. "Perhaps."

"Either way, we're going to have to do something about him," said Mel. "And I don't mean just shooting him." This last aimed at Roland. "We'll need to discredit him and his movement. Killing him now will cause a revolution we don't need."

"I agree. He is going to be way too popular and we can't have that. We still have to have elections for a while and I don't want him mucking any of them up," she finished.

"Clearly, we can't count on them to do something stupid like the last time," commented Mel.

"Agree. Get Sherman on the phone. Let's end this. I want him to call California and Nevada. We can wait until tomorrow in Georgia and Arizona. Guess we won't need your van full of ballots after all. Leave it there though. I want to see how they react when they find they missed them, and forgot to count them. Then we can be magnanimous and have then not count," said Lexi with a laugh.

Roland sat in silence. He had already heard from Pavlovich, who was not pleased.

#

Nick went into the conference room after his broadcast. Everyone cheered and most came up and gave him a hug. The tears and anger were gone. There was resignation and something else. A glimmer of hope for the future and realization this was not the end, only the beginning.

"Guys, I know I've said it a hundred times. But I'll say it again. You have all done so much. I could not be prouder. I'm being told there is a possibility we will get more votes than any candidate in history. Now that is saying something. What it is saying to me is we are just getting started. We will regroup and we will live to fight, *politically*, for another day," he said to laughter.

The people cheered once more and then broke off into tired groups. Denise walked up with Chuck.

"What did you think?" asked Nick.

"I think you are a conundrum," pondered Denise. "Who in their right mind, when confronted with such total and absolute voter fraud, costing you an election, would go on national TV and urge calm, while also urging his supporters to trust the wolves who just raided the henhouse and killed all your chickens. I don't get you. You should be furious; you should be marching in the streets demanding justice and rightfully so. Instead, you threaten your own followers if they get violent? Then you claim we should have faith in the systems that have screwed you so royally, to work this out?" Denise shook her head in disbelief and anger.

"You know exactly what you did, don't you?" responded Chuck.

"You bet. I keep them off balance. I picked the battlefield of my choice and I force them to march into the sun to get to me on the high ground," responded Nick calmly.

"Enough with the fucking Sun Tzu. Pick up the goddamn pitchfork and go stick someone," said Denise, totally exasperated.

"Denise, you need to calm down. There is nothing I could have done differently to alter tonight's outcome. You said it yourself. She was going to win, no matter what. What I made sure of is if we lost this battle, it costs them dearly. We emerge from the fight stronger and in a better position to win the war," explained Nick.

"Nick, you're delusional. If she becomes President, there is no safe place on this planet for you. No guards strong enough, no fortress big enough, no country brave enough to keep you from getting eliminated. By not winning this battle, you have ensured she will turn the full force and vindictive might of Lexi Smythe-Thomas on you." Denise's face was reddening as she laid into Nick for not fighting.

"When you combine that with the most powerful country in the world and intelligence agencies who have no qualms using their skills on their own citizens. It is a recipe for a slow and painful death which she will enjoy watching. Trust me, I know this woman. Hell hath no fury like Lexi Smythe." said Denise, tearing up in her anger and fear.

"Denise, by making that speech, I made it about them and not just me. About a movement and deeds against all of them and not just me personally. It has to be personal for *everyone* for this to work. It can't be just about me, as you pointed out. It has to go on no matter what happens." Before Denise could respond, Nick interrupted.

"We have any idea how many mail in votes we had in Michigan?" asked Nick, trying to get Denise thinking about the election again.

"Enough to beat her. Well over thirty-thousand, is my guess."

"How's the appeal?"

"Slow. Will probably just get thrown out now. You would have to take it to the Supreme Court. You know how the Chief Justice is. Without Justice Moore, he can't hide. He will vote with Party justices to deadlock at 4 to 4. Anything to keep from being dis-invited to the best parties."

"Michigan is truly lost as well?" asked Nick.

"Yep."

"I guess we had best go address the troops. I assume they are still there?"

"Oh yeah," replied Chuck with a smile.

Nick and Chuck walked into the larger conference room to tell them to head to the convention center. They were all standing around the big TV, watching EXN and looking dejected.

"Let's look at the big board and drill into the counties. Right now we have 70% of the vote in. The key items to look at are LA and San Diego," said Billy McCall.

"Hang on. OK folks, we are getting reports the networks and other cable stations have given California and Nevada to Lexi Smythe-Thomas. That puts her at the required electoral votes needed, in fact more, with 272 now and they are declaring her the next President," Billy had a hand pressed to his ear, listening.

"However, we at the EXN decision desk do *not* agree with their analysis. We still believe there are too many votes outstanding to call the election with 100% certainty. We will get some push back for *not* agreeing with their decision, but again, EXN has not called California or Nevada for any candidate at this point in the evening," reiterated Billy.

Chuck and Nick looked at each other, listening intently to the EXN analysis. Nick's phone buzzed. He left the group to go to a corner to take the call.

"Hey Jeremy, what's up?" asked Nick.

"Do *not* concede. My sources are telling me Lexi put the screws to ANC and the others to call this for her. I am also hearing it is much tighter in California than anyone is admitting. Same for Nevada. They aren't even close to being done counting the paper ballots or in Arizona either, for that matter. I'm not saying you will win, but I am saying she has not either. Please, don't give in yet. That is what they want," said Jeremy, almost pleading with Nick. "Nick, there is all kinds of shit going on in this election. We are capturing and saving everything we can get our hands on."

"Easy Jeremy, I'm not going to concede until all the ballots are counted. Don't worry. Just keep gathering data so we can use it to prove what is happening. No conspiracy theories this time. Only statements with facts to back them up," responded Nick, heading back to the crowd watching EXN.

"Let's look at the big board," said Billy, wandering over to the electronic state board. "We still have the electoral count at 212 for Smythe-Thomas and 208 for Turner. Outstanding states right now include California with 54 votes, Nevada with 6, Georgia with 16 and Arizona with 11."

"Let's go to Rory for some scenarios," said Billy.

"Billy, it is really pretty simple. If the VP wins California, she wins. She doesn't need any of the others, assuming they are also right about Nevada. Senator Turner would need California and Georgia or California, Arizona and Nevada. Arizona and Nevada are both behind counting because of the machine failures and the switch to paper ballots. California is behind because of the massive turnout. I don't have a clue what is going on in Georgia. They have been sitting at 98% for hours but no call. Turner appears to have about an 80,000 vote lead. It would seem to be over."

"Ok, I am getting an explanation for why we have not called California. Actually, let's bring our decision desk on to explain it. Welcome Nathan Meiers, our lead on the decision desk," said Billy.

Nathan was a disheveled looking middle-aged balding man with wire-rim glasses who was pulling on a hastily donned tie for his time on camera.

"Thanks Billy. Wasn't planning on being on camera tonight or I guess this morning now," said Nathan with a smile, staring into a camera from the decision desk studio.

"No problem, Nathan. I suspect by now, we all look pretty worn out. Except Adam, of course," said Billy, laughing. "Anyway, help us understand why they called it and we aren't."

"Sure Billy. It's simple. Turnout. We think they are using traditional models with only a slight adjustment for turnout this time. California is our largest state, but it is not particularly known for turnout, having been a deep blue state since the days of Reagan. People just stay home. Now with mail in balloting, they still have only slightly altered their turnout ratio. Typically, there are about 22 million registered voters. That is only about 55% of the 39 million residents. About 75% of those registered voters are voting mostly by mail, around 17 million. Stay with me. I know there are a lot of numbers being thrown around."

"It's been one of those nights," laughed Adam off camera.

"We are tracking two major shifts this election. We think the number of registered voters has surged to around 27 million, up 5 million from 22. And we think of these 27 million about 87% are voting this time around. The total number of votes is closer to 23 million versus the 17. There are 6 million more votes being cast."

"Sorry Nathan, just to clarify, we believe there are an additional 6 million voters? That is an enormous difference," said Adam.

"Indeed, Adam. Currently, they are showing 10 million cast for the Vice President with 70% of the vote in. Senator Turner is sitting at 6 million. What the other networks are not accounting for is the increase in registered voters and the increase in turnout."

"These, we believe, based on what we have seen in other states, is a surge in registrations and day of turnout and a vast majority of those are going Turner. Can he make up a 4 million vote deficit? That remains to be seen, but that is why we are not calling it. We think there are enough outstanding votes. Billy our count, only about 70% of the votes are in, not the 95% the other networks are claiming. Their models are flawed and, frankly, incorrect," finished Nathan.

"Nathan, Rory here. Where are you getting your data on the turnout?"

"Precinct captains. We contacted them and they told us they were seeing about a third more turnout than usual," replied Nathan.

"Interesting," said Rory, clearly thinking through scenarios in his head.

"Adam, Billy, I am hearing from our analysts. We are going to call Georgia for Senator Turner. There are still a few ballots outstanding, but not enough to swing the vote back," said Nathan.

"Ah, finally," said Adam. "So the sixteen electoral votes from Georgia go for Turner and brings him up to 224 electoral votes. EXN shows the Vice President with 212, Turner with 224 and Blackbird with 31 with 71 votes still up for grabs from California, Arizona and Nevada."

"Nathan, before we let you go, how much longer before we're sure on California?" asked Billy.

"Shouldn't be too long. The precincts are counting and sending in final tallies. Again, remember, the votes thus far were the mail in ballots, typically around 80% of the total. This year with the increased turnout I would put that number closer to 60%. So 40% instead of the usual 20% is coming from the day of in person. That is what we are waiting on. My guess is they were short staffed not expecting exponentially larger turnout on election day. That plus the lines have delayed it. Remember, all that day of is typically the Opposition who are voting for the Independent Turner 9 to 1 this election."

"Ok, I guess we are not done yet after all," said Billy.

"Not even close," laughed Rory.

\#

"Are they right?" asked Lexi.

"Possibly," said Mel, cautiously. "If their facts are true and the turnout is that high and that many more registered voters exist, it could happen. But those are a lot of factors that need to come true."

"We should have told them to hold off on Georgia," said Lexi.

"It had been sitting there for hours. They couldn't hold off any longer. Our woman on the inside of Cobb county is still holding it open, but she is slowly losing the battle. We either need to go now or forget about it," said Mel.

"Find them," ordered Lexi.

"Are you sure? This is even more obvious than the Midwest?" said Mel.

"Yes, I have a feeling we'll need them," advised Lexi.

"Ok," said Mel, pulling out a phone and texting 'baker carter' to a number.

Lexi's phone buzzed. She held it up to her ear. "What? You listen here, you little piece of shit. I made you and I can break you. You do this and you can kiss your FCC chairmanship goodbye," shouted Lexi, listening. "I don't care about the reasoning," she said, hanging up.

"Sherman?" asked Mel.

"Getting cold feet. He's afraid either California or Nevada are going to flip and they will look bad if they don't at least turn them back to toss-up."

"He always struck me as a bully with no spine," confided Mel. "You should let his ass hang out to dry."

"Ya, but if he pulls those back, it is going to look bad for us and them. This is certainly not working at all. What is your gut? Can we lose either of those states?"

"I can't see it in California. He had to make up 4 million votes. Nevada maybe. The turnout is way more than we thought and it is his voters showing up on election day. He's really motivated them by scaring them about you being a doomsday queen. We always thought Nevada could be a loss even back in April," said Mel.

"I will be doomsday for him, for sure," promised Lexi. "We have not talked about Arizona much since the machines went down."

"We used the confusion to ship in our mail in ballots, just like in the Midwest. You should have enough there since we had more counties to work with than Nevada, which was only Clark," Mel answered while texting on his phone.

#

"Oh, good lord," said Adam, listening in his ear. "Get Nathan back in here to explain this. I am not reading it," he said, visibly upset.

"Uh Adam, while we wait for Nathan, I am hearing ANC called back Nevada to toss up status. That moves Lexi back to 266. They are citing turnout changes, exceeding their model projections, just as Nathan suggested for why EXN had not called it," said Billy. "That is certainly embarrassing."

"Billy, like I said, I have been doing this for six decades. This is like my 13th or 14th election. I have never been part of a mistake of this magnitude. It is frankly unacceptable. In our competition to be first, we are all making mistakes, collectively and ruining any trust we have left with our viewers. Perhaps we should all refrain from prognosticating until all the polls are officially closed and 100% of ballots counted.

"That might put me out of a job," laughed Rory, trying to lighten the mood.

"OK, we have Nathan. What the hell happened?" asked Billy, also frustrated.

"Billy, it is not an excuse, but we waited almost 8 hours to call Georgia and we were told by Georgia counting officials there were not enough votes outstanding for anyone to overcome Senator Turner's 79,000 vote lead. Then officials in Cobb County found an official van parked out back with bins of mail in ballots that had not been carried in to be counted."

"Surveillance video showed the van arriving in the early evening and the driver entering. He was interviewed, and he said when he came in he got distracted by helping other workers who had knocked over some bins in the counting area. He assumed someone else had emptied the van. Surveillance shows no one tampered with the truck. They unloaded and are counting the ballots now. They promise to have them counted in Cobb County, the last county, to officially notify the Secretary of State of completed status as soon as possible. For now, Georgia is back in the toss-up stage. To be clear, all the networks called Georgia for Turner and we have all put it back in toss-up, along with Nevada and Arizona. And of course, our no call on California," said Nathan.

"Nathan, this is unfortunate. I feel we may never get our credibility back with the public," Adam continued carping.

"I agree. It is unfortunate, but this one was not our fault. It was the State of Georgia providing incorrect or at least inaccurate data about the status of the vote counting."

"Do we know how many ballots there are to be counted? Is it enough to overturn Turner?" asked Billy.

"We do not. Like everywhere else, turnout is historic," said Nathan.

"Ok, thanks Nathan. We will contact you if anything else changes," said Billy.

"Well, Rory, it is now three AM. Where are we?" said Billy in a tired voice.

"Turner is within a million votes of Lexi in California. With turnout already exceeding the highest prior election. Lexi has 11 million and change, Turner has 10 million and Blackbird has about a million. In Nevada, he is within 100,000 and he is leading in Georgia, as we already discussed. In Arizona, the counting is still very slow, but Lexi has a 200,000 vote lead at this point."

#

This time it was Mel's phone that buzzed. He answered and heard the nasal voice of Sherman Hallberg.

"Mel, she is irrational. I can't lie and make her win just by calling a state. If the votes change, they change. We have to salvage our reputation. California is no longer a sure thing. We have to move it back to toss up."

"I see. And you want me to break the news?" answered Mel.

"Yes. I have talked to the other network presidents. We all agreed we would switch it back, claiming the extraordinary turnout messing with our models and the massive lines of the day of voters breaking things. It is an accurate statement." explained Sherman.

"I understand. There will be repercussions, of course," said Mel.

"I did as she asked, even though the data didn't support calling it. I have done everything I can do without changing votes. She just has to live with the consequences, as we will for blowing this call," responded Sherman.

"We'll see," threatened Mel.

#

"Ha, I knew it," said Rory, as he watched the maps on some of the other networks change. He was off camera, but still on a hot mic.

"What do you have, Rory?" asked Billy.

"NWN just moved California back to Toss up. Turner is now within 100,000 votes. Guys, he has a real shot at taking California," said Rory excitedly.

"Let's go to Jennifer Tilson on the floor of the Vice President's campaign."

"Thanks Billy," said Jennifer. "What was absolute pandemonium, moments ago, has now turned to disbelief. People are consoling each other. Others are angry, saying the election is being stolen. There is a lot of rage, disbelief, disappointment and concern now on the floor of the convention center as people are confused and unsure of what happens next."

"Thanks Jennifer. Next, let's go to the floor at Turner's watch party. Tommy?" asked Billy.

Tommy was trying to speak into the microphone, but the noise was so loud they couldn't hear what he was saying.

"Tommy, get somewhere so we can hear you," said Billy. "We will bring him back as soon as we can hear him. But you can see from the pictures Turner's people are going crazy."

"They sure are. Can you imagine the roller coaster ride? Hope, then despair, then resignation, then hope again. It is emotionally draining for us up here. I can only imagine what it is like for those at the parties and for the candidates themselves," said Adam.

"Rory, give us the latest from your seat," said Billy.

Rory obligingly showed another chalkboard. "Votes continue to be tallied and Turner is gaining on Smythe-Thomas in California, her lead is down to 100,000 votes with somewhere between 5 and 10% of the vote outstanding. In Nevada her lead is now only 5,000 with 9% of the vote still outstanding. Many of these are still from Clark county, basically Las Vegas, but there are still some coming in from traditional red counties as well." Rory drew arrows on his chalkboard as he talked.

"In California, many of the outstanding votes are from central valley counties and far northern California. The bay area and Los Angeles county are already in," finished Rory, pointing to numbers on his handheld chalkboard.

"Billy, this is far from over. If you look at the outstanding votes in California, Placer and Kern are only 10% in and they are traditional red counties. San Diego and Orange county are also still reporting at 80%. Are there enough to overcome the lead of Smythe-Thomas, I don't know, but it appears Turner is picking up many of Blackbird's disillusioned supporters. He must also be winning over many of the moderate in the Party and, even more importantly, inspiring voters who have not been voting to get involved. As Nathan said, the networks claimed they didn't account for the same day voter turnout in California and that led to the erroneous early call. There is plenty of egg to go round for faces this time," said Rory.

"You have that right, Rory," lamented Adam.

"Billy, I don't want to say I told you so, but clearly, I did. Look at California. Placer County just came in with a huge batch. Check the total."

"Oh my God Rory," paused Billy, knowing he was not supposed to say God on air.

"Sorry about that, folks. Look at that, with Placer county reporting 95% in, Turner has now cut the lead to less than 30,000 with still what, 6, to 700,000 votes still outstanding?" asked Billy.

"Maybe more than a million," said Rory. "We need to start thinking about the possibility Turner could win California."

"You got it and look, Orange County is at 80% in. San Diego is 85% in. The real kicker is Kern County. This is deep red territory, and it is only in with 50%," said Adam.

"Guys, the EXN Decision desk is calling Nevada for Senator Nick Turner with its 6 electoral votes. This is a reversal of what all the other networks called an hour ago. Remember, EXN alone of the networks did not call Nevada or California and now we have called it. This puts Senator Turner at 214, Vice President Smythe-Thomas at 212 and Blackbird at 31," said Adam.

"Wow, this is an amazing night," said Billy, laughing. "Rory, Nathan is telling me in my ear how the other networks are coming unglued that we have called Nevada for Turner. I sure hope our decision desk has this right."

"Billy, looking at the counties and the current count and outstanding ballots, many of which are an uncounted day of paper ballots, there are not enough outstanding to make up the difference. Barring any last-minute discovery of tubs of mail in ballots. Which unfortunately has not been out of the question in Clark County in past elections," expressed Rory.

"Oh lord, please don't even suggest it," said Adam in disgust and concern.

"Rory, they may complain, but I am hearing all the other networks have made the same point as you. They are all changing Nevada to Turner, except ANC, which is still claiming Nevada is a toss-up," said Billy.

"I guess they are panicking right about now."

"Rory, you had to jinx it, didn't you," said Adam. "In a reversal reminiscent of Pennsylvania, Michigan and Wisconsin, the last batch of ballots conveniently found in Cobb county," paused Adam listening.

"You know what? No, I won't keep my opinion to myself," said Adam, obviously responding to voices in his ear and taking his ear piece out in disgust.

"I will call this as I see it, and if I lose my job, I don't care. What I see is not on the up and up. Senator Turner had a 79,000 vote lead when Georgia said they were done counting. Then they found these ballots, 85,000 of them. 82,500 of them were for Lexi Smythe-Thomas giving her a 3500 vote lead and the state of Georgia and its 16 electoral votes," said Adam in total disgust. He sat back in his chair, fuming.

"Tommy, let's go back to you. What's happening? Can you hear us?" asked Billy, trying to get Adam off camera.

"Thanks Billy. I can tell you people here are proud of what they have done. No third-party campaign has ever had a showing like this one and to still be in the running and leading the popular vote, they are frankly ecstatic. I was talking to the campaign manager on the phone and she said the other networks having to take back Nevada is just another example of the corruption of our electoral process. Billy, the corrupt media outlets intend to crown the next President and ignore the will of the people," said Tommy. "That was even before the news on Georgia proved it even more. The hits keep coming."

"Do you think we will hear from Senator Turner tonight?" asked Billy.

"Turner is not one to duck out of a tough situation, so I would suspect we will hear from him, even if it is 5am when it happens."

"It may be 5am and we may not get a final decision. I am being told that both Arizona's Maricopa and Pima counties are having issues counting in Arizona. Turner has a 154,000 vote lead with less than 5% still outstanding in both counties," said Billy.

"Well, Billy. I am not a correspondent, but an opinion host. I now put down my correspondent role and will preview my nightly show for tomorrow right now. This stinks. How many times do we have to put up with vote counting stopping in blue counties in key swing states to enable more ballots to be found to swing a vote from the non-Party candidate to the Party? Mark my words, Billy. At the end of the count in Arizona, just like in Georgia, Michigan, Wisconsin and Pennsylvania, Lexi Smythe-Thomas will end up winning. I, along with every other concerned American citizen, should be up in arms over what has now become a corrupt and completely discredited election process in the United States," condemned Tommy.

"Holy shit," said Billy.

"Sorry, Billy, what did you just say?" asked Tommy, concerned.

"Sorry, sorry, my apologies for my profanity," said Billy "Tommy, I am hearing in my ear, are you ready for this, the EXN decision desk has called California for," Billy paused for effect as the infographic spun in on the screen. "For Senator Nick Turner."

On the floor of Turner's convention, people were screaming and cheering, jumping up and down and hugging. Someone came up to Tommy and picked up the little crew cut former Marine and set him back down.

"Well, Billy, I guess you can see the response here. People are losing their minds. This means and Rory can correct my math, but I don't think Lexi can win the electoral vote now and only Nick can win if he gets Arizona."

"That is right Tommy," said Rory. "Senator Turner is at 268 electoral votes and the Vice President is at 228 with Blackbird at 31.

Tommy was suddenly looking unhappy. "Billy, am I still on?" asked Tommy.

"You are."

"So again, this is now going to be even worse. We need someone to seize all the outstanding ballots in Arizona and make sure no one meddles with or adds to the outstanding ballots remaining to be counted. It needs to be transparent. If Turner loses his lead after they have stopped counting, this will go to the house and once again, the common people could be screwed."

#

"Tommy has that exactly right," said Denise, looking at the screen in the campaign suite in Orlando. Nick sipped his coffee and shook his head.

"Who would have ever thought we would win California? Laura Wood was right. She told us we had a chance when we last visited. I laughed at her then. I will have to apologize. Hell, who'd have ever thought we would have 268 electoral votes or over 82 million total votes? In 10 months? Come on. What we have done is nothing short of miraculous. Greg would be so happy that we overcame everything they threw at us, persevered, survived and thrived. California," said Nick, shaking his head with a smile.

"What do you want to do?" asked Denise, as Chuck and Neill stood nearby.

"What are the other networks saying? Are they giving me California as well? How close are we?" asked Nick.

"ANC is holding out still on Nevada and California, but the other networks have done the math and realize Lexi can't catch you in either. You are leading Lexi by about 850,000 votes in California now and there are less than 250,000 still outstanding, primarily in Orange County and San Diego, and mostly day of votes they have not yet counted. There are sure to be recounts," said Denise.

"What do you think about Arizona?"

"We should win them, but it is Lexi, so I would guess we will lose the first count. Then we have to sue for the recounts and transparency. She'll want to go to the House and count on her leverage there," said Denise.

"What about Blackbird? He can't throw his electoral votes to us, can he?" asked Neill from a corner of the suite.

"Unfortunately, all four states he won have rules against allowing their electors to switch their votes from the winner in each state. Even faithless electors would be overruled. I guess the good news is Lexi can't get them either," said Chuck.

"We have to hope the count is honest tomorrow in Arizona," said Nick.

"A forlorn hope," said Denise. "I am so sorry, Nick. I never thought we would get this far, but to get so close and then have it snatched from you by corruption is too much to bear." Denise sat and broke down in tears, finally breaking under the stress. Ellie got up and sat with her.

Chuck, Nick, and Neill gathered in the center of the room. "I need to talk to the folks," announced Nick.

"Agree," said Chuck as Neill nodded. "We'll go with you."

\#

"Any other thoughts, Rory?" asked Adam.

"This is the worst-case scenario," said Rory.

"Turner wins California but no others. No one reaches 270. In that case, things are going to get really ugly. Especially considering the machine failures in Arizona and Nevada, the late surges of found ballots in Pennsylvania, Michigan, Wisconsin, and Georgia. The intervention of the courts to keep Turner off the ballot in those states. The attorney general's decision to invalidate all of Turner's mail in ballots in Michigan and the list goes on. The only winners will be the high-priced lawyers. Let's hope this does not happen."

\#

"Is there any recourse in California?" asked Lexi, surprisingly calm for 4:37am

"We did not plan for any contingencies for President. We did the usual harvest focused on winning back the congressional seats we lost in Southern California in the last midterm. We did not feel we needed to do anything on the Presidential side. We won with a 6 million vote plurality last time, when seventeen million voted. Hell, you even got more votes than anyone previously, over 12 million."

"But Turner made up a 6 million vote gap and added another million on top?"

"Yes, he did," confirmed Mel.

"First thing we need to do is keep him from winning Arizona. How do we make that happen?" asked Lexi.

"We have ballots in Pima and Maricopa ready. They will be found later this morning and added to the count. We moved them in with the supplies of blank ballots when they moved those in after the machines froze. It will take the county counts to unbelievable totals, but we'll just have to deal with it. You need to get on the phone with the judges and others," said Mel.

"That is already taken care of," replied Lexi, remembering the call she had received from Pavlovich shortly before 1am. He was one of the few people who genuinely frightened her with his power and his reach.

"How so?" asked Mel.

"Just trust me. That one is ok. The court cases aren't going to get any traction. Now we need to work towards Jan 6 and a vote in the house. We may need to bury the hatchet with Blackbird," mused Lexi.

"Good luck with that."

"Mel, he likes power. We'll see. I have to admit I don't know a lot about how the house vote works. I think every legislature gets a single vote in the house. And the Senate does the same for VP. We need to make sure Blackbird's states go our way. Right now we need to be putting pressure on the Opposition to vote for a known quantity, not someone with no experience. We need to start threatening them. Some of them have to go the way they voted, most in fact. We need to focus on Blackbird's and make sure they do not vote for Turner. Let's put the screws to them. Start doing background on every member of congress from those four states. I want them all in our court. Make promises, threats, whatever it takes. Got it?" said Lexi, in full command of the next steps.

"I do. You'll need to appear in front of the troops."

"Right, let's do that now," said Lexi as they left the room and headed to the Convention Center. Her phalanx of secret service guards formed up around her as she left.

Chapter 35

Nick walked out onto the stage. Denise, Neill, Ellie, and Chuck followed and stood in the background.

Nick held up his arms as his people cheered in the convention center, shouting 'Turner, Turner, Turner'. After a few minutes, Nick finally raised his hands to quiet the crowd.

"What have you done?" said Nick with a smile to the cheers. "You made all of this possible and, more importantly, all of you made it happen." More cheers.

"It is not over, but what a ride. We have come far, and we have proved you will not stay silent any longer. 83 million or more of you have voted to stand up and voted to keep your freedom. To reject the policies and the plans the Party wants to implement. But we are not finished. We have not won, but neither have they. We'll strive to make sure the counts continue in a fair and transparent manner in Arizona and elsewhere. We'll make sure the expected recounts are also transparent," said Nick as the crowd cheered and chanted 'No more Fraud, no more Fraud'.

"This is only the beginning. We have shown this party, all of you, have a platform and a voice. Regardless of what happens in the next few days, we need to win at all levels. We need to run people from our party in every city council and school board. In every state congress and senate, and at the federal level. We need our own people in the house and senate and in the presidency!" shouted Nick as the people roared.

"This is not an anomaly. This is the birth of a movement, of a new political party in this country and we will not return to silence. We have found our voice and our purpose. It is freedom and the preservation of our rights as laid out in the Constitution," said Nick, emphasizing the last.

"Looking at the tentative results, it looks like the Party has the slimmest of margins. The Opposition is behind in the House by a small margin and the Party extended their majority in the Senate to 51 49. We have to count on the Opposition to hold together and moderate Party members, of whom there are a few, to stand up for freedom and the Constitution."

"I am hopeful we will prevail, if not tonight or tomorrow, at some point in the future. We will continue to point out hypocrisy and fraud, corruption and evil and we will fight all legislation that limits our freedom and those of our fellow citizens. Whether or not they appreciate it," said Nick with a smile, getting the expected laughs from his cheering fans.

"Don't give up. Even when the odds are against us, remember, you have each other. 83 million others in this country and their families who believe as you do. We must keep fighting. We are not going to know anything tonight. They have stopped counting in Arizona counties." There was a chorus of boos and shouts of 'cheaters' and 'fraud'.

"We'll see what the daylight brings. I wish I could say I am confident, but we have seen this playbook before. Let's hope our faith in our democratic system is rewarded with a fair and transparent process to conclude this election." People cheered and shouted 'fair vote, fair vote,' and 'fair count, fair count,' and finally 'Turner, Turner, Turner.'

Nick held up his hands.

"Thanks to all the staff everywhere. To all the people who knocked on doors, walked from house to house, carried the message and debated their family members, neighbors, and even strangers. Now everyone knows the Flip," said Nick, holding out his hand and flipping it. "The Mirror." Nick held his hand in front of his chest. "And the third leg of our platform, Faith," said Nick, holding up his hand with three fingers raised. Everyone in the convention center raised up their hand with three fingers.

"You all gave me faith. You gave me the faith to continue when it seemed we were pushing the rock up the hill; with our nose," those in the convention laughed.

"I still have faith. And I will continue to work to help everyone. This is not an end, regardless of the outcome. It is merely a bend in the road, a bump in our journey to protect our freedoms. To reestablish policies our founders gave us. That made us the greatest nation on the planet. Only we can stop the downward spiral. We cannot count on anyone else to help us. All I ask is you," he said, pointing to everyone in the audience. "Have faith. Faith in yourself, faith in me and faith that we will never give up and never stop until we have reclaimed our freedom, our country, and our Constitution," said Nick, as everyone cheered.

After about 30 seconds, Nick held up his hands again.

"Alright folks, keep celebrating what you have accomplished. Win, lose or draw, we have already won, because we have done more than anyone ever gave us credit for. We have won more states, more electoral votes, and more popular votes in this election than any independent in history. If I can, I would like to have a moment of silence if you would allow me." The convention, a raucous and crazy place, became instantly and eerily silent.

"I would like to give thanks. Thanks for having the faith and belief that each of us has control over our own destiny. Faith in our system of democratic government. Faith in the goodness of our fellow citizen. Faith that they we'll do what is right, honorable, and within the laws we have all agreed to abide by."

"I would like to thank all who had the strength and courage to stand up against the evildoers. Against those who would persecute you simply for having a different belief system. A belief in our Constitution and its laws and guidelines which have allowed us to build this civilization. Finally, I would ask that all of you say a silent prayer for all who have sacrificed to allow us to stand here. So many do not have this freedom. Those in China, and Russia and those in thrall to the Party's secular Progressive religion, which preaches, much like Islamic Sharia, cancellation to any who do not follow their progressive religion."

"I say this now. We will not allow our freedom to be taken away. We will not allow our Constitutional rights to be destroyed. We will not dishonor the memory of the ones who gave their lives for our cause.

Greg Simmons, Kevin Moss, and now Senator Baxter Banks are just three of these. Casualties of the progressive crusade. Who will stop at nothing, who will use anyone, and destroy anyone who gets in their way. I say this has to stop. 83 million of you said the same tonight. This is not the end, regardless of the outcome. This is only the beginning and we will take this journey together. We will fight. We will fight to preserve our freedom and we will fight to preserve our Republic. We will fight for each other. We will support each other. Because we have faith, in each other, in our Constitution and in our higher power. Amen." finished Nick.

The crowd erupted as if they'd just won the Super Bowl, whooping and hollering. Many were wiping away tears and others were hugging their neighbors standing on the convention hall floor.

"Go home, get some sleep and rest up and I say this to every one of my followers. Do not, under any circumstance, commit any violence or damage any property. I do not want to see any scenes on the news of Turner supporters in any riots or acts of violence or property damage. You will see it, but it is being done by them so they can say it is you. I know their playbook. If you see something, film it and send it to us. But for now, enjoy this. It is all because of you!"

Nick walked from the podium, shook hands with Chuck and Neill and hugged Ellie and Denise as they walked offstage to the cheers of 'Turner, Turner, Turner'.

"Tommy, are you still on the floor?" asked Billy.

"I am Billy."

"What an amazing scene."

"Billy, I have never heard a speech like it. Even I had to wipe a tear. He is entirely right, and he said exactly the right thing. Rory can correct me, but I think we witnessed two things here tonight. One is the death of the Opposition party as we know it and the birth of a new party to replace it." Rory nodded on camera.

"I agree Tommy. In fact, I would also say we witnessed the death of the Party tonight, itself replaced by the Progressive party. With the showing by Blackbird and Turner, it is clear, most of the Opposition party have shifted to Turner's banner. And I would say, the additional 10 million who voted for Blackbird will break 4 to 1 to Turner's party. In the next election, if Turner can hold them together, regardless of the outcome of this one, you are going to see a monumental shift in power in the House and Senate," predicted Rory.

Adam jumped back in, "That did not seem to be a very hopeful speech from someone who, as he said, won more electoral votes, more states, and more popular votes. He sounded like he expects to lose despite all that. Does he know something we don't? He is ahead in Arizona, right?"

"Adam, that was a speech designed to prepare his followers for a long fight. I think he is being a realist. He has no allies in congress, in the supreme court, in most of the media. He has the common man, or a majority of them, but they are powerless because the elites make the rules. When they don't work, they are the ones who change the rules to protect themselves." Tommy was speaking from a corner of the floor where he could be heard.

"I think he is being honest and is telling his people to not expect justice to prevail. To be honest, I am glad he did not come out and give a mushy, hopeful speech. He told the truth. He fully expects he will lose Arizona and it will go to the House, where his party has no representatives. He actually laid out what he is going to do, regardless of outcomes. Formally found and build his party and then start running people to win at all levels. What you are seeing is the birth of a new centrist party. I say good riddance to the Opposition." said Tommy.

"Sorry, Tommy, we are hearing Arizona is going to stop counting, lock up the ballots, have security on guard and resume in 4 hours to finish the counting," said Adam, sighing.

"And so it begins again. Any time they stop counting, you can count on the Party flipping the lead. If there is anything we learned from previous elections, it is, when you stop the count, the fraud speeds up. If I were Turner, I would be demanding they continue counting even if it is the national guard doing it," said Tommy.

"If what I hear is true, Lexi is not being nearly so magnanimous. Outright accusing Turner and his followers of voter fraud and stuffing ballot boxes, citing the findings in Michigan as an example of the widespread fraud of the Turner campaign. Soon all the other networks will parrot these positions. It is a sad state of affairs we find ourselves in," finished Tommy in a resigned tone.

"Well, I don't know about you guys, but I need a shower and a change of clothes and maybe a few hours of sleep before I am back for the morning show. If I go now, I can just make it before I go on again in a few hours to report on the eventual outcomes," said Billy.

"We already know the outcome, I am afraid," said Adam in a sad and mournful tone.

Part Three

Will Justice Prevail?

"This process of election affords a moral certainty that the office of President will seldom fall to the lot of any man who is not in an eminent degree endowed with the requisite qualifications."

Alexander Hamilton

Chapter 36

Nick walked into his campaign office in DC on Wednesday mid-morning. He and his staff flew up from Orlando only hours before. Everyone heading home for showers and a change of clothes before meeting back at the office. The staffers cheered and clapped as Nick entered.

He smiled, acknowledging their praise, and returned the favor. Thanking all of them for their hard work. Heading to his conference room with his team in tow.

"Hi Jenny," said Nick as he entered the room. Jenny was on the phone and waved a greeting.

"We need to set up a war room to manage all the activities," stated Denise. "We can start here, but it will probably need to be a bigger room somewhere."

Jenny walked out of the conference room to finish her call. Denise's eyes followed her, annoyed she hadn't ended it.

"War room?" asked Nick.

"You know what I mean, Mr. Sun Tzu. There are doubtless going to be lawsuits we need to file to make sure there are recounts in Wisconsin, Georgia, Pennsylvania and Arizona. We are also going to need to fight Michigan to count our mail in ballots and possibly recount, depending on the outcome. We need watchers we can trust to make sure the counts are transparent. Each is going to require a team. This requires central command and control," continued Denise.

"Makes sense. Aren't most of these close enough to automatically trigger the recounts?" asked Chuck.

"They are, but we need to force them to do this in the open. We also need to make sure the machines are locked down with no access from outside or technicians. A court order to seize the paper ballot audits for the machines would be good as well, at least in the close states. All the things the Opposition tries to do every election and is never allowed. We now get to try with no one on our side, including them. We should also shoot for a random audit of the paper ballots and the mail in ones," rattled off Denise.

"What we need is a war room," announced Nick with a smile. The others laughed, and Denise even cracked one as Jenny came back into the room.

"Jenny, you know what that means? We've got to file lawsuits in all these states to make sure these things are transparent. And quick," finished Denise, as Jenny nodded at the tail end of their conversation.

"Already on it, Denise. We have paperwork being filed this morning in all of them. I had folks start working on this last night as soon as I saw we had a chance."

"Great."

Nick watched the interaction and smiled. "I get it. We need a war room and you need to run it, obviously."

"Nope. We need a practicing lawyer. Preferably one who has argued cases in front of the Supreme Court," countered Denise.

"Argh, lawyers? Really?" whined Nick.

"Not any lawyer. A great one. If we can find any to work with us," added Denise skeptically.

"What do you mean?"

"Hello, did you not pay any attention to these last few elections when there was major push back on potential election fraud? Where were you?"

"During the last election? Backpacking in the Italian Alps. The one before that, I was still in Syria, Afghanistan, or somewhere," shrugged Nick. "I have to admit, I was not paying much attention."

Denise stared at him for a second. "The last few times, the Party sicced their attack dogs on any lawyers who tried to make a case for fraud or transparency. They labeled them all conspiracy nuts, threatened their firms and, sometimes, outed where their families lived and worked.

A couple of Party congresswomen in Michigan and Georgia encouraged their followers to picket their houses. It got ugly. I think some of those lawyers are even out of jail by now," she explained.

"And *I'm* the threat to democracy?" responded Nick sarcastically.

"It worked. No one was willing to stand up and fight in the last election, when the results were even more in question. You can be sure it will be even worse with cancel culture so entrenched and America *Pravda* doing the dirty work of the Party more than ever. With only you having a chance to win outright, American *Pravda* and the Party are going to scream bloody murder at any attempt to swing a state to you for the win. No lawyer is going to stick their neck out for you, Nick. They owe you no allegiance," informed Chuck.

"We need lawyers who have nothing to lose," agreed Denise.

"Right, but the problem with those lawyers is they have an axe to grind and little credibility. I will see what I can dig up. We'll start putting the word out, but I wouldn't hold out much hope. Time in front of the Supreme Court is an absolute requirement?" asked Jenny, looking at Denise.

"Jenny, without that experience, we don't stand a chance," informed Denise.

"We can't just give up. What else can we do?" asked Nick. "What about Penrose?"

Jenny cocked her head. "Maybe, let me check. I doubt he had to take any cases to the Supreme Court from small town South Dakota," she laughed.

"How about Duane Cooper? He did such a great job on Dusty's trial?" suggested Chuck.

This time, Nick laughed. "Duane? The way he dresses? It would be the court scene from *My Cousin Vinny*. You can ask, but I'd be really surprised on that one."

"Our Arizona campaign manager is already filing official requests to have impartial observers from each party there for the remaining ballot counts," said Steve Gaines, who had joined them in the conference room.

"Steve, who is that again?" asked Nick.

"Joseph White. You met him on Tuesday morning," said Chuck before Steve could answer.

"Right, the guy who looked like a college professor, balding, with the glasses and about 40lbs too many," said Nick. "He seemed competent and committed."

"He *is* a college professor at the University of Arizona in Tucson. It is probably closer to 60lbs too many," laughed Steve.

"How can we help him?"

Jenny got a call and walked out again to talk, while Denise glared. Nick noticed.

"Must be important," commented Nick, as Denise turned to Margie.

"We need to get you on TV this morning demanding transparency," said Denise, looking at Margie, who was already on the phone herself.

"What else?" asked Nick.

"So far what we are hearing is they aren't going to start counting again until noon local. From what I can tell, there are a few outstanding ballots in Yuma. Those are paper ballots because of the machine failures and will be mostly for you. Maricopa has supposedly about 175,000 mail in ballots and suddenly Pima county, which had already said they were 100% finished, found four more bins of mail in ballots," replied Chuck.

"How do we fight that? It is clearly fraud. When did they announce they found them?" asked Nick, as Denise groaned in the background.

"This morning." Chuck shook his head.

"Geez. They don't even care about appearances anymore," groused Denise.

"The networks are saying they were delivered days ago and stored in a closet for safekeeping until the counting started. They forgot they were there," pantomimed Chuck.

"If they hold true to form, those will break huge for Lexi, right?" suggested Nick.

"Yep, count on it," replied Denise with a grim laugh. "If you get one vote in those, I'll be surprised. That would prove they were fraudulent and done before you became a viable candidate. In the other batches, at least they threw in a couple for Blackbird to make them look legit."

"Will they have enough?" asked Nick.

"Does it matter? If they don't, they'll just find more until they do," answered Chuck cynically.

"Look who is the font of optimism this morning." Nick glanced at the scowl on Chuck's face. "I'm pissed Nick. You won, fair and square. No one thought you had a chance. Lexi sure didn't. You rallied the common man to get to the polls. *Exactly* the way the system is designed to work. And what are they going to see? No matter how many vote. No matter how many 'stand up', who did not vote before, it will never be enough. Because the Progressive machine will just print more. It fucking sucks," said Chuck, visibly upset.

"When did Maricopa get their ballots?" asked Nick.

"Supposedly in the afternoon. They were busy counting all the paper ballots after the machine glitch," answered Steve.

"Perfect time to sneak them in during the chaos of switching to paper ballots," confirmed Nick.

Jenny came back into the office. "Who was that?" asked Denise snippily.

Jenny ignored her tone. "It was a friend of mine in the DOJ. She said they are already getting orders from up high to ignore or slow walk any lawsuits or appeals we file for recounts, access, or anything else related to transparency. That's why I stayed on the line. They won't be able to talk again after Arizona is announced."

"Great, things keep getting better and better," He turned toward Margie.

"Get me on TV. I'll do Sesame Street if that's all I can get."

"Yeah, right? You remember you voted against more funding for PBS. It was in the infrastructure bill you nixed. Big Bird is probably burning you in effigy right now. I'll try EXN," laughed Margie.

#

It was not quite the trip back to DC she had expected. Lexi arrived in her office to staff who were neither triumphant nor despondent, more like walking on eggshells and confused. Lexi, Mel, Roland, and Harriet were in her office.

"When will Arizona come in?" she asked.

"Depends. Turner is filing all kinds of lawsuits for transparent counting and better access to the remaining ballots. They are also challenging the 20,000 Pima county ballots conveniently 'found' this morning. They want to see documented evidence they arrived before the polls closed and the chain of custody documents. They want to see the same for Maricopa and its remaining ballots," explained Harriet.

"Anything we need to worry about? Do we have enough without Pima County?" asked Lexi.

Mel contemplated the ceiling before answering while Lexi waited impatiently.

"Well," she asked again in a terse tone.

"Yes, we made sure. When we snuck them in during the pause last night. Most of these are not as 'legal' as the others and they will take Pima to about 95% turnout, same as Maricopa, so we need to count on you and DOJ to stall any hand recounts or verification of votes from happening. As long as they don't start contacting voters to confirm they sent in mail in ballots, we will stand up to scrutiny or review. Signatures match. Our forgers were that good. I saw them in action and the voters are registered. Keep the verifications to that level and our counts are on the up and up. Much better than previous ham- handed attempts in prior elections where ballots were never folded and mailed, etc," responded Mel.

"Good. This is the entire ball game," announced Lexi.

"Should we be fighting having people watch the rest of the counting or not?" said Harriet.

"Absolutely. Anything to delay the counting is in our favor. It delays the recount and then it delays any hand inspections and such. We are trying to run out the clock until Dec 14 when the states have to certify. File our own countersuits. We need to do that now. Then we need to have our appeals court judges ready to overturn and file injunctions. We appeal every negative ruling. File at the deadline. Draw out the process as much as we can. I expect Turner will do the same, but he'll counter file as soon as he can to save the days," remarked Mel.

"Who is running this for Turner? Denise?" asked Lexi.

"Doubt it. Maybe now, but she needs to find a lawyer."

"Good luck with that," laughed Harriet. "After the last time, only a washed out and broken-down lawyer would take on these cases. They know we are going to hit them with both barrels. Ask the one who spent time in prison after the last election."

"His conviction *was* eventually overturned," smiled Mel.

"I agree. Northrup won't do it because she has a family. They are probably combing AA meetings while we speak. Turner seems to like the broken alcoholics," mused Lexi.

"Shit," said Mel, looking at his phone. "I thought we had this under control."

"What?" asked Lexi.

"Turner is on TV right now." Mel grabbed the remote and turned on the big screen in the conference room.

#

"Hello Billy, Autumn, thanks for having me on this morning," said Nick, shaking their hands and sitting on the couch on the other side of Autumn from Billy.

"Welcome Senator. That was some night," replied Billy. They were doing their usual morning show from the DC studio, later this morning, because of the late nature of last night's coverage.

"I'm so proud of all our staff and volunteers, but I am even more impressed with the millions of Americans, 83 million of them so far, who woke up and realized the dangers of the Vice President's progressive platform. They listened to what I had to say and decided they needed to get involved and make their voices heard. It was a great day for our Constitution."

"But was it enough Senator," asked Autumn. Distracted, she grabbed her vibrating phone on the couch next to her, as the TV screen cut to a closeup of Nick from the wide shot.

"Well, Autumn, from my point of view, it is merely a beginning. If we lose, it will not be from lack of trying, it will be because our system of justice is broken. We need transparency. Our people have little to no faith in their systems of election checks and balances. There is only one reason I can think of why *any* candidate does not want transparency and inspection of ballots to ensure legality. That reason is fraud. Those who are honest welcome scrutiny," pronounced Nick.

"Senator, do you believe there is fraud in this election?" asked Billy.

Autumn dropped her phone. It bounced off the couch they were seated on, onto the floor, between Nick's feet, causing Billy to look over at her. "Sorry," she said quickly, blushing as Nick answered him.

"You know what, Billy? What I believe is we should attempt to ensure the ballots are legal and the voters eligible to vote. Is that too much to ask?" asked Nick.

"But Senator, without clear evidence, how can you justify the expense and time these additional measures would take?" asked Autumn.

"Let me ask you a question. If a county says it has completed counting, sent the counters home and sent the votes to the state chairman. Then the next morning, in a close election where your state is the only one which has not finished counting the statewide results, the county precinct manager suddenly announces they have found four more large bins of uncounted ballots. Would you not be just a bit skeptical?" asked Nick.

Autumn shrugged. "Not necessarily. They could have been missed." Even Billy turned and gave his co-host a look at this statement.

"Ok, so let's give them the benefit of the doubt. But would you think it is out of line to ask to see the surveillance tapes from say 2am to 6am for all the entrances and exits to the 'locked' up counting headquarters? To make sure no one showed up in the middle of the night with these bins. You know, to maybe assure some people who might think something nefarious could be happening. Like, say, 83 million people who stand to be disenfranchised, should these ballots turn out to be fraudulent?" asked Nick.

"Seems reasonable to me," agreed Billy.

"But that is hardly proof of a need to do that," retorted Autumn, gaining another look from Billy. He was clearly surprised at her sudden challenges.

"Seriously?" Nick held Autumn's eyes until she looked away. "Well, Autumn, you have a trusting soul. I suppose you see nothing unusual about having hundreds of thousands of votes being counted with exactly zero votes for me in Wisconsin and Pennsylvania and they are coincidentally barely enough to overcome my leads?"

"Senator, they already explained how they had to count all the write-in votes you received, and it was merely coincidence that these mail in ballots were counted at the end," responded Autumn.

"You don't feel there is any reason to question any aspect of our voting process and we should trust that everything is on the up and up everywhere despite all these 'coincidences'?"

"I'm sorry you don't trust the system, Senator. Yes, I do and I trust that people who are counting our ballots and running our polling places are decent and honest people. I don't see a need to indulge your concerns and frankly the concerns of so many wild and implausible theories about conspiracies and widespread voter fraud. We have already been through this craziness in prior elections. All the investigations showed no widespread fraud, certainly nothing that would result in any changes in outcome. It is unfortunate we have not been able to declare a winner in the traditional manner, but the House of Representatives is sure to do their duty," commented Autumn.

"Interesting," responded Nick.

"What is interesting?" asked Billy, confused.

"It seems your colleague may know something none of the rest of us know. You see, by my count, I have a 174,000 vote lead in Arizona at the moment. If the counts are right, there are about 12,000 ballots in Yuma, 165,000 in Maricopa and now 20,000 immaculate conception ballots in Pima. That is 197,000 votes. I'm told I can expect about 60-70% of the Yuma county votes."

"Let's say that gives me a 180,000 vote lead. The remaining votes are 185,000." Nick turned from Billy to look at Autumn as he continued.

"In order to overcome my lead, help me out Billy, the Vice President would need, what, 97.5, 98% of the votes, with zero for me and only a few for the Governor. The statistical probability is so small it is almost immeasurable. And yet it is going to happen four times in one election? Is Arizona going to become a fifth statistical anomaly of massive proportions? If that is not proof enough to at least do some investigating, I don't know what is." Nick paused, a smile coming to his face.

"Why the smile, Senator?" asked Billy.

"I just had a thought. I will track down 51 statistic's experts and professors and have them sign a letter explaining how this is just not possible. I'm sure that is all American *Pravda* will need to agree with my stance. It worked before for this administration. Why not now and for me? Apparently, many of your prior guests this morning feel as I do. Yet it seems your colleague knows my being the victim of a fifth statistically impossible anomaly is a foregone conclusion?" asked Nick with an arched eyebrow.

Autumn was bright red, even her neck was flushed. "Senator, of course, I know nothing. How could I? I simply misspoke about the vote needing to occur in the House. It looks like you have a commanding lead," she said in a not very convincing tone.

Autumn was glaring into the camera as Billy responded, "What will you do, Senator?"

"All that I can, Billy. We will not give up. I owe all these people I awakened from their slumber, at least that much for their effort. We will file injunctions and lawsuits for recounts and hand inspection of mail in ballots. We will then file appeals to the inevitable Party loyal judge trying to stop our efforts at merely asking for transparency and fairness. Then, if those appeals fail to uphold the rule of law, we will take them to the Supreme Court. Frankly, given their track record of deciding any American election system integrity question is not worthy of their intervention, I do not have high hopes. We will still try. It is the process our founders laid out in our Constitution. They were just counting on the people in these roles to have integrity and to put the country first. All we ask is transparency."

"I think that about does it," stated Autumn, trying to end the interview.

"Billy, if I may," said Nick, ignoring Autumn's attempts. "I have one final thought and then you can bring on the obligatory Party operative to complain about my statements and even my getting on this show before the counting is complete. Why in the world would anyone be afraid to have the votes counted in a manner to put any thought of fraud completely and finally to bed?"

"Now is the time to do this once and for all. Prove our systems are honest, *to the people.* It is a simple, but admittedly time-consuming process, but one worth doing to unite the country. I say here and now, I would gladly welcome such scrutiny and remember I have millions of write in ballots in those three states. I am willing to have each one examined. The voter contacted and sworn affidavits signed on penalty of perjury. Why would the Vice President not welcome the same level of scrutiny for her ballots?" Autumn, could hold back no longer and broke in.

"Senator, you are asking for months of effort and millions of dollars so you can be assured of what all the rest of us already know. You lost in Michigan, Pennsylvania, Wisconsin and Georgia. This would set a horrible precedent. Every loser from now forward would request or demand this same effort. Frankly, this sounds like sour grapes," said Autumn in a serious tone, showing the interview was over.

Nick laughed. "Money should not be the issue. I have plenty in my campaign coffers. I can set up a 'GoFundMe' page and I guarantee it will have $100 million in an hour. But of course, they will seize the money or refuse to disperse it, saying we are violent, subversive, or corrupt because we dare to ask for transparency and a forensic audit. In the end, we will see who the country believes, me or the American *Pravda* media and the Vice President."

"Thank you for your time, Senator, and good luck," said Billy in an earnest tone, as they went to the commercial.

Nick bent over, picking up Autumn's phone, which she quickly yanked from his hand. He got up with a smile and left the set. Billy thanked him for coming and Autumn ignored him, looking down at her phone.

#

"Well, that sucked. Don't we have anything on EXN we can use to stop these Turner 'drive-bys'? He rarely goes on the hard news programs, only *Tommy*," mused Lexi.

"If your threats to Sheila aren't sufficient, I'm not sure what else we can do," answered Mel. He noticed she glanced quickly at Roland.

"Thankfully, most people were at work. Are we that obvious? It was almost as if he was in our conference room. He read us like a book and laid out exactly what we are going to do," said Mel.

"Did you see Autumn? Her tone suddenly shifted mid interview when she dropped her phone. Did you text her something?" asked Lexi. Mel shook his head no.

"Something rattled her. She practically gave away the fact we had primed all the hosts with info we expect to win Arizona. He laid the trap, and she walked right into it. These so-called journalists are useless," she finished, shaking her head in disgust.

"I agree. They used to be useful idiots. Now they are just idiots. And dangerous as we just saw. She recovered a bit, but she gave him the perfect foil to work against. He made a very compelling argument. His followers are never going to be satisfied with anything less than hand recounts and verification of each voter's eligibility," suggested Mel.

"Too fucking bad," shrugged Lexi.

"Thankfully, there is neither the time nor the money in the appropriate places. Even though what he said was true, no amount of money can compress time. With the court system hopelessly bogged down, they can't do it. We'll get more scrutiny, but we can weather it. You have to hand it to Josh and his ballot guys. They made it almost foolproof. As long as the machines self-destruct, we are covered there, too. Let's just stick to the plan." said Mel

"Which is?" asked Harriet

"Keep being presidential. Be gracious. Congratulate your opponent on a well-fought fight and then start explaining to the public how experience is the key to leadership in our country. How your years in the Senate taught you about winning and losing. About making tough decisions and how mistakes you made there have made you a better leader now. Point out as President, you don't get any do overs."

Mel looked from Harriet to Lexi as he continued.

"This is no time for on-the-job training. With so many foreign issues facing our country in China, Russia, Israel, Iran, and North Korea. Your time as Vice President has given you insight into the leaders around the world. Now is the time for leadership, not starting Armageddon by violent rhetoric like Turner spouts daily. You may even throw out the zinger. 'Those who can, do. Those who can't teach,' in terms of handling the pressure and responsibility. He did give up his military career. Quit because he didn't enjoy following orders any longer," suggested Mel.

Lexi looked up at the ceiling, contemplating Mel's words.

"When he left the service, he never entered politics or high pressure work environments. Instead, choosing the cushy confines of the college classroom. Contrast that to negotiating Iranian nuclear limits and peace between India and the Chinese. Or building a coalition of economic partners to rebuild Lebanon and keep its people from starving. Highlight what you just did in Israel. You can mine a lifetime of accomplishments completed in the face of adversity. All he has done is get stabbed in a subway," sneered Mel.

"I think I will leave that last bit out," laughed Lexi. "I have already stuck my foot in that pile before. But you make good points. I will be the low key, serious person offering the public a choice. Seasoned veteran who has paid her dues, learned by experience vs the flash in the pan flyboy with soaring words but zero accomplishments. He did not attach his name to a single bill in Congress in his time there. Preferring instead to grandstand. Contributing to the death of a venerated senator who deserved better. He is no team player, but a maverick who cares only about himself and his own personal brand."

Harriet and Mel clapped. "Perfect," they both said, looking at each other. "Do that a few times and he is toast," said Harriet.

In a corner of the room, Roland laughed and stood. They all turned to look at him, Mel especially staring daggers.

"You are underestimating Turner at every turn. You let him run around gaining momentum and turning your citizens against your policies. Allowed him to get and then turn down the opportunity to take a party nomination he knew would load him with a century's worth of Opposition baggage. Someone tried to kill him and it only made him stronger. Your pathetic attempts at October surprises, designed to ruin him through scandal, only resulted in the martyrdom of several of his staffers. The debanking debacle is crippling your biggest banks. Your blatant attempts to win through the voting booth have resulted in cheating on a scale impossible to hide without obvious manipulation of your compromised judicial systems. You have to rely on your willing dupes in the media to cover up your deeds. And you clap at a few words in a speech?" finished Roland, summing up the ineptitude and results of Lexi's 'sure thing' campaign cycle.

"Well, your solution is to kill everyone. Tell me. Did you take care of Banks yourself or did you farm it out?" accused Mel.

"Mel," cautioned Lexi.

"It's alright Madame Vice President. I believe you know who has *your* best interests at heart. I do what I can to protect your flanks. Perhaps now is the time to review some of your chief of staff's attempts to do this. His efforts always seem to end in failure or the opposite from the goal."

Now it was Mel's turn to laugh loudly.

"Roland, the game of politics is less concrete than putting a bullet in someone's brain or strangling drunks in their garages. There are a thousand moving parts. You have to adapt to the changes in real time. Some decisions work and some don't. Even with all these mistakes and the abilities of Turner to dodge literal and hypothetical bullets, we are still on the edge of accomplishing the goal. When we do, and we will, we'll deal with Turner and you can crawl back into the cage your master keeps you in."

Harriet's eyes were enormous and even Lexi was surprised at Mel's backbone standing up to Roland. Lethal and deadly, contrasted against the diminutive Mel with his eyeglasses and nearly bald head. Mel stood his ground, holding Roland's stare with one of equal intensity.

"Enough. We all need to work together to accomplish our task. We have made mistakes in the past. Now we need to be better and move forward. Finish this election and start cleaning up the mess," ordered Lexi.

Mel and Roland each relaxed and nodded slightly at Lexi's command. Round one ended in a draw. It was going to be a heavyweight match.

#

Nick munched on his salad as the rest of the team dug into the pizzas spread around the conference room. He watched as they worked and ate, smiling at the dedication.

"So, my merry band of munchers, where are we?"

Jenny spoke first. "The Governor of Arizona came through. He has said the remaining counting does not start until poll watchers from all sides are present in all three places. Further, he has dispatched the National Guard to watch over the ballots 24x7. He also ordered the surveillance video for the Pima County and Maricopa counting centers to be seized and reviewed by joint teams and law enforcement. Earl left for Arizona right after our meeting this morning. He will work with Joseph to get access to as much info as he can."

"We're also trying to get the voting machines quarantined in Arizona and Nevada. Georgia is still deciding what it will do with the machines and the ballots. All we really care about is Cobb County, but they are fighting us tooth and nail for access to that last batch of mail in ballot envelopes," noted Chuck.

"Let's stay focused on Arizona. We need access to a machine so someone can take it apart and figure out what was going on. Who is our best ally in one of those six states?" asked Nick.

"Ally? None publicly. Let me talk to Earl. Maybe he can find a sheriff who is friendly with a precinct captain who can get us access to a machine," suggested Denise.

"That's fine, but we really need a local judge to allow a public digital forensic examination of the machines. It needs to be public, or our efforts will be discounted as sour grapes and a frame job," said Nick.

"You mean like Autumn on EXN this morning? It sounded like she had been handed a script from Lexi's team. The others I get. Apparently EXN still has a bunch of liberals on the payroll too," said Margie from across the table.

"Well, well, I believe you may have completed your journey to the dark side," remarked Denise, as the others smiled.

"Margie, can you or Jer see if you can find anything on Edward Casper?" asked Nick.

"Who is that?"

"No idea, but that name was on a text on Autumn's phone when I picked it up off the floor. The text said 'stop him or we release what we have'. Remember, she dropped it during our interview and that is about when she turned attack dog on me. Maybe that name has something to do with it."

"We'll see what we can find," nodded Margie.

"That's the way they work. Blackmail, extortion, etc," explained Denise, knowingly. "As for the other, we'll start working on it. Again, probably Arizona, Georgia and Nevada are our best bets. We can focus our Midwest efforts on trying to get the Michigan mail in ballots counted. Do we even know where they are?"

"Probably need to talk to Earl on that one, too. He is running the team looking into the ballot fraud," explained Chuck.

"OK, ask him when he lands," said Nick. "What do we do if Michigan doesn't count our ballots and Arizona comes through for Lexi?"

Everyone in the room sat silently. Finally, Chuck said, "Pray."

"I see. Any chance we can convince Blackbird to endorse us instead of the VP?"

"You would think so, especially after what Bank's revealed about Lexi being the source of the leak. This is a strange town, and all Lexi did was reveal the truth about his past. He admitted everything. All is fair in presidential elections. She has way more to offer him. I suspect you are not willing to offer him a cabinet post or an ambassadorship, right?" asked Chuck.

Nick smiled. "You know me too well. No. I wouldn't offer him a cabinet post, but I could appeal to his humanity of what would happen if she wins."

"You are refreshingly naïve sometimes, Nick," frowned Denise. "You really need to toughen up. People are not in Washington for the people, at least not for long. They are here for themselves."

"Therein lies the problem," agreed Nick. "So, no noble deed from the Governor as a conscience clearing deed?"

"We can try, but that would constitute a miracle, so Chuck could be right after all," said Denise with a laugh. "Besides, the Governor has no vote. If it goes to the House, it is the newly seated congress in each state who casts the votes. Since you have no party, you are screwed if it goes to the House."

"Sounds like a prayer *is* in order then," acknowledged Nick with a nod.

Chapter 37

Nick stood in his office in the Hart senate building. His work as a senator was already beginning to wind down. His senate office staff had no reason to burn the midnight oil, unlike his campaign staff in *their* office across the Potomac. Shortly, he would sign letters of recommendations for the few senators he counted among his friends trying to find his senate staffers jobs with other congressmen.

He sat down in his office chair and put his feet up on the desk. He looked around the room and smiled. It would take all of 10 minutes to pack up the belongings he had brought to Washington. It had turned out to be a temp job, after all. He was looking forward to returning to Colorado.

"Hello," said a voice outside in the corridor.

"In here," yelled Nick.

Nick looked up as Jeremy Kwan entered his office wearing a visitor badge. He held it up.

"This was waiting for me downstairs. The guard said I could show myself up," grinned Jeremy.

"Pretty easy to infiltrate the Senate office building," replied Nick with a laugh.

"Nah, he was a fan and recognized me. I told him I had an appointment with you. He pointed the way. Don't be too tough on him. Plus, Carla recognized me too and pointed to your office," responded Jeremy.

"Have a seat. And of course, the big question, are you a dad yet?" asked Nick, smiling.

Jeremy grinned back, showing pictures of the baby with Kim. "Baby girl, Monday. Jenny Ariel Kwan. Kim and Jenny are doing fine. Thanks for asking."

"Congrats Jeremy. Can I get you something to drink?

"What are you having?"

"I think I have a fairly fresh six-pack. Haven't been in the office much the last few weeks," said Nick, pulling out a couple of 90 Schilling Ale's from Odell's Brewery in his hometown, Fort Collins. He handed one to Jeremy. They tapped bottles. "Here's to transparency."

"I'll drink to that," agreed Jeremy.

"What prompted this visit request?"

"Nick, as you know, I'm a geek. I have been involved online with lots of other geeks. First, let me tell you, there are many people like me out there with skills. They've been using these 'skills' to help the righteous causes. Some of these people help me on Hibi, both on the payroll, and some out of their own dedication to keeping the cyber world safe."

"Good to know they all aren't out there for profit and mayhem," countered Nick.

"Indeed. I believe some of these folks are ex-military, if not ex spooks. Hell, for all I know, they could be current spooks. Bottom line, they have been monitoring a lot of activity by foreign entities trying to influence the vote. What they have also seen is an almost total lack of effort by our own government to stop some of this."

"How so?" asked Nick, intrigued.

"Nick, we could track cyber-attacks against our voting machines from China, North Korea, Iran, Serbia, and Russia, to name only the biggest. We monitored these to see if they succeeded or if anything was being done to stop it. When it appeared nothing was happening, some of our hackers shut them down and sent attacks back at them."

"Exactly what Homeland is claiming you did to shut down half a Serbian city a few weeks ago?" asked Nick, eyebrow raised in question.

Jeremy smiled. "Yes, but we proved without a doubt that was not us. We also showed them who it *was* and schooled them on how we could detect this and how it happened. Bottom line. We are woefully unprepared to handle these kinds of incursions."

"What did you do? Are you telling me this because you expect another Homeland investigation?"

"Hardly. What we should get is a medal. I am happy to say, unlike our government, we fight back. We sent worms and DDoS attacks and flooded the offending servers and networks with a myriad of disruptive attacks to shut down their servers and stop the attack. It is very similar to what we do with trolls who try to flood Hibi. They try to shut down our servers and our routers and flood our message streams with millions of posts. We've become pretty good at stopping all of this. Like I told you before in Texas, we give ten times what we get," laughed Jeremy.

"What happens when you do this?" asked Nick

"Let's just say they are not as good at defense as they are on offense. I think they're so used to not being held accountable by our government, they have spent no time building defenses. What we send back are very sophisticated denial of service attacks where we simply do to them what they try to do to us. In the simplest terms, lets saying you are pouring gas into a can using a funnel. You know you can only pour so much or the funnel backs up and the gas spills. What we do is take the gas nozzle, turn it on full and lock it open. It overwhelms the funnel and fills up your garage with gasoline."

"They don't know what to do and they don't know how to stop it. Once we reach a certain point, we send a match and watch it all burn down. We have done this in centers in China and North Korea where their power systems are left open to attack. We simply start over-clocking their processors and turn off the fans."

"The servers literally melt down or catch fire. The Eastern Europeans are a little more savvy and have some protections. Only after we fried them too, for trying to overload our Hibi streams," said Jeremy, getting into the nuts and bolts, clearly excited.

Nick smiled at his enthusiasm. "I get it, you guys are good, our government sucks and there are lots of cyber baddies out there. Forgive me for not getting as excited as you. How does this apply to us, and don't get me wrong, I am happy you stepped in to stop the meddling in the election from these countries. There is no doubt which candidate they want to see win," offered Nick.

"Our government is not bad at this, per se. They have lots of smart people too. We don't have the *will* to stop it. They are being told not to retaliate. That is my opinion, obviously. Of one thing, I am certain. Nick the voting machines were rigged. Something was happening in them. Especially in Nevada and Arizona," confided Jeremy.

"Do you have proof?" asked Nick, now paying attention.

"We know they did something," explained Jeremy. "We don't have proof of exactly what or how yet. But we have collected all the data. We have info on how the votes were cast by the voter. We have the files from which the paper ballots were printed. We also have what was reported up to the counting centers. Guess what, in Arizona and Nevada, the three do not match. Every fourth vote for Blackbird was changed to a vote for Lexi," explained Jeremy.

"Exactly how did you get this information?"

"We followed the monitoring commands into the system and then issued our own monitoring commands, enabling us to not change, but *copy* information from each machine. Logs, audit logs, databases, etc. It is a ton of data, petabytes, maybe even an exabyte."

"Is that a lot?"

Jeremy smiled in return. "Yes. We can forensically reconstruct the changing of these votes. But it would take weeks or months to do this and then more months to track down each voter and get them to sign an affidavit they voted for Blackbird and not the VP. But we have the data," admitted Jeremy.

"Did you do this anywhere else?" asked Nick.

"We did not see this happening anywhere else. We still have the data from every state that used a machine. We looked hard in Georgia. We saw nothing this blatant standing out. At least for the machines. We can't stop people bringing in bins of votes on dollies. Or finding vans full of ballots. That's old school ballot box stuffing."

"Were you behind the machines frying in Nevada and Arizona?

Jeremy smiled. "Not me, I'm smart, but some of these guys make me look like I am playing with a chemistry set in my garage. Let's say I am glad they are on our side."

"Dare I ask how you did it? asked Nick.

"I am not even sure, but they figured out there must have been hidden code embedded in every machine, so TrustedVoter is in on the scam. Or at least it is an inside job from within the company. The code to do the re-tallying had to be present in the systems and activated from *within* the machines. Since nothing from the outside could have triggered them."

"So that is how it started. How did you stop it?"

"Same way we fried the hacker's servers. The machines had no defenses against our attacks. We sent millions of packets down the same pipe and used the same window to enter it. We overloaded the system with requests to monitor and focused the requests on things we could push through the port they opened. Turning the brightness up to the highest setting and overloading the user interface code, causing it to shut down the touch screen on every machine. This didn't bring down the machines, but it meant they could not be used to enter any new votes. If they rebooted, the attacks would simply have resumed and brought down the interface again. The only solution is to bring the machine entirely offline and do a hard reset. Clear the buffers and cache of waiting commands."

"They would lose all the vote data if they did that. With hundreds, even thousands of machines, there was no way this was going to happen. Nick, whoever put this code in has to know there is the possibility they'll be reviewed. It has to either have a self-destruct time code or some other failsafe to erase its presence if they turn the machine off or try to audit it. Routine maintenance and normal audit procedures are going to destroy the data we need. We have to sequester the machines, at least in Arizona and Nevada."

"Thanks Jeremy. I may not have won Nevada if you hadn't stopped the vote swapping. We'll see if it was enough. We are trying to get the machines sequestered, but TrustedVoter is fighting to get access to them to figure out what happened and to cover their tracks, no doubt," shared Nick.

"Nick, they're cheating. We have the proof, now we just need the time. Hell, we have the money between all the Blue Morpho and TRDF people. We can fund this. We can expose it all." responded Jeremy passionately.

"Jeremy, I appreciate what you have done and the offer, but there is nothing we can do with computers or any proof that requires computers, because they will claim we made it all up. They'll provide their experts to argue with our experts and it will all be us versus them," said Nick, looking Jeremy in the eyes as he explained the reality American *Pravda* had created in the minds of its ignorant viewers.

"Nick, you believe this. Don't you think we can convince the public of this with proof? What about the screen shots of the images? It shows the vote going in, and two of them changing from Blackbird to Lexi. Isn't that enough?" said Jeremy with desperation in his voice.

"Jeremy, you could easily have altered the data to show what you want it to show. By then they will have wiped the machines themselves of this data. If we get a machine in our hands, then maybe we can conduct a public digital forensic audit and maybe then you can discover the code and activate it to show what it does, but we still have to prove it was activated. We won't have any proof. This is why we need biometrics and paper ballots. Anything less is subject to fraud."

"Nick, if you don't win, how are you going to stop this? It is not right, and it is not fair." This is America, dammit," yelled Jeremy, standing up and pacing around the room.

"Jeremy, I'll keep fighting. We got 83 million people to vote. Maybe we get 90 or a hundred million next time. Eventually, we'll get enough that they cannot cheat through. Besides, it is not over yet. We still have Arizona and the chance for Michigan mail in ballots being counted."

"Ha. You don't think they got this far without contingency plans," warned Jeremy.

"No, I do not. Speaking of which. Is there any chance you can tell if they scanned and tabulated my mail in ballots from Michigan? How many there are? And where they are being stored?" asked Nick.

"I don't know, but I can try to find out," nodded Jeremy.

"That could be helpful."

"This is so wrong." lamented Jeremy. "What do you need me to do besides Michigan?"

"Three things. Do the work to figure out whose votes were changed. Even if we take a year to track them down. It will come in handy to prove to *the voters* they were disenfranchised, even if we can't change the outcome. Second, can you track down a cell phone number and see who texted to it while I was on the air this morning on EXN? Last, I want you to invent a biometric scanning method we can use as a method of identifying every legal voter in the United States," finished Nick, smiling.

"Sure, no problem. I'll have it done by next Tuesday. Is that soon enough?" replied Jeremy sarcastically.

"Can you do it?" asked Nick

"Theoretically, it is already done. Fingerprint scanning is already in place. They have it at the airport for the fast path access. Eye scans are better. But we don't have everyone's eye scan, so I get why you are starting with fingerprints. The challenge is the massive invasion of privacy required to collect and access every person's birth records to scan in their fingerprints. Next, you have the operational logistics of putting these scanners in every polling place and providing enough bandwidth to each to quickly scan and verify. The next problem you have is this requires internet access, which means someone can in theory mess with it or spoof it. So, you have security issues. It is a colossal challenge," said Jeremy, laughing, thinking through all the difficulties.

"Which is precisely why I asked you to do this," smiled Nick as he shook Jeremy's hand.

"Why do I feel like I just got conned?"

"Jeremy, last week you started a bank and fought off an attack by a government agency. Conned? Nah, maybe played. This should be a piece of cake. Welcome to Washington and impossible requests. I guess I am starting to get the hang of this politician shit at the end of my run," laughed Nick as he walked Jeremy out.

Chapter 38

Earl and Joseph, Nick's Arizona Campaign manager, along with representatives from Blackbird, and the Smythe-Thomas campaign all stood in a semi-circle around a terminal where a technician was preparing to play the footage from Pima County on election night.

He started the footage of the locked ballots and ran in fast forward mode from 2am local time on election night. They all turned to watch the footage on a big screen monitor. They could see counters counting and then everyone starts closing down and ballots were put in a cage which is then locked by the Pima county election chairman. The footage shows 3:47 local time when the chairman leaves the building. The time code goes forward until 4:30 and then turns to snow.

Everyone asked what happened. The tech ran the recording back and forth, but the snow remained. He fast forwarded until the end of the recording. Nothing but snow.

"I guess there must have been a glitch in the system," responded an Arizona election official.

Earl laughed. "Glitch. Pretty convenient."

The official gave him a side eye look. "I'd appreciate you not jumping to conclusions and creating disinformation," he said.

"Uh, huh? I'll wait until we're no doubt about to see the same 'glitch' on the next surveillance and any others we look at. You must really think the American people are stupid," quipped Earl.

"What are you accusing us of?" asked the official in a defensive tone as the technician reached near the same point in time from the second camera, covering the back door. The video also turned to snow at 4:29 am.

Earl turned to look at him, noticing the smirk on Lexi's state representatives. The Blackbird representatives were looking at their watches. "You were saying?" asked Earl.

"I don't know how this happened. Check your equipment," he practically yelled at the technician.

The tech queued up the files from the Maricopa County video cameras. He opened each file and attempted to play them. Each was the same, snow at the same time for both the entrance and the locked-up ballot cages. The tech turned to look at the state official. "Sorry, but all these files are useless from the points it turns to snow. There is nothing to see," said the tech.

Earl started laughing as everyone looked at him. "How convenient. You guys crack me up," shaking his head and walking out of the building. Joseph soon followed. Earl was already on the phone talking to Jenny.

"Ya, they were all blank. Just snow. No excuses, just a shrug and a claim of equipment failure. Yes, Joseph will have people reviewing the ballots, but the problem is they're going to be counted. There is no way we can disallow them. Tell Nick I am sorry," said Earl, ending the conversation. He turned to Joseph, who looked shell-shocked. "We should have had somebody watching the door. Why didn't we assume they would cheat," moaned Joseph, despondent.

"Joseph, they also said they had turned in 100% of the vote. Why would you think they would lie about that?" consoled Earl.

Joseph nodded as the representatives from the other campaigns came out laughing, including the election official. As they walked by, one of Lexi's looked at Earl and said, "Tough luck, huh". Joseph made a move, but Earl held him. "Don't waste the effort. This guy is a bootlicker," taunted Earl.

The smile disappeared from the face of Lexi's man. He made a move like he was going to say something. Earl smiled, inviting further confrontation. The election official intervened. "All right gentlemen, let's keep it civil. This is an unfortunate equipment failure, nothing more," he said, pulling Lexi's guy forward.

Earl added. "I don't care about civil. All we expected was transparent and honest. We got neither."

"Hey you saw the same thing I did. The equipment failed. That is out of our control," said the official, turning back to Earl.

"So, as an official of the Arizona election committee, aren't you concerned about the failure of your security and integrity systems at such a key moment? Especially considering Pima county reported it was done counting and voila, they conveniently find four bins of ballots and the surveillance is conveniently glitchy at exactly the time between when you are done and four bins appear? The American public will think this is much more than an equipment failure," remarked Earl. "You should consider what everyone else is going to think of your excuses instead of earning your pay from whomever."

"Watch your ass after we win," threatened Lexi's guy.

Earl walked over to the guy who visibly shrunk as Earl towered over him. "I was wrong. You aren't even a bootlicker. I'll be waiting," replied Earl, who turned, leaving with Joseph without looking back.

#

Three things occurred because of the 'equipment' failure. Pundits supporting Nick were going crazy online and on those few outlets still broadcasting their opinion in his favor. EXN was hosting guest after guest, citing obvious anomalies.

However, even they were juxtaposing these with guests contradicting those in favor of Nick. They were all circling the wagons to protect their franchises in an expected Smythe-Thomas administration.

Because Nick had no friends in Congress, there was no talk of subpoenaing officials in any of the swing states to answer questions on any of the anomalies or the increasingly glaring coincidences, all favoring the Vice President. No one in the administration seemed concerned enough about these to acknowledge or even investigate.

Even with all their complaints and evidence, ten times the number of pundits appeared on American *Pravda* media, countering those favoring Nick. Decrying the obvious hate and disinformation being spewed by Turner supporters to cast doubt on the legal ballots remaining to be counted. How Turner was trying to disenfranchise legitimate voters because he didn't want to risk losing.

Last, with the footage revealing nothing conclusive, the Arizona Governor and Secretary of State had no choice but to allow the Pima county ballots to be counted with observers present to verify the signatures and the eligibility of the mail in ballots. Starting Friday morning, they would resume counting all three sets of ballots.

On Friday, Nick and team gathered in the conference room, but the mood was resigned. They were watching special coverage with Billy, Autumn, and Rory. All present in an EXN studio talking about the expected outcomes.

Rory held up his chalkboard. On it he showed Nick with a lead of 174,000 votes with 95% reporting for the state. "Given the turnout models and assuming it goes as high as 90%, we can expect there are somewhere in the neighborhood of 175,000 votes plus the 20,000 or so mail in ballots found in Pima. I am also told most of the 175,000 are also mail in ballots left uncounted in Maricopa county, besides a few more paper ballots cast at precincts in Yuma county. Those should come in first and then Maricopa and finally Pima," said Rory.

"You seem to be right Rory, we just had an update. Yuma is now reporting 100% in and Turner's lead is now 182,000, having picked up 8,000 more votes in Yuma in this update," said Billy. "Do you think there are enough votes left for the Vice President to make up the difference?" he asked.

"Statistically, I would say no, but with this election and the propensity for these late tallying mail in ballots to go high 90s for the VP, it's apparently *possible*," pondered Rory. "What I find interesting is the commentary on the other channels. They are all talking about an upcoming vote in the house, as if it is a foregone conclusion the Vice President is going to have a statistical anomaly of impossible proportion. Again."

"That is true, Rory," agreed Billy as Autumn looked down at her notes, having already tangled with Senator Turner over this attitude.

Rory was still shaking his head. "Billy, let me give you an analogy while we await the data. This is like predicting a hurricane in January to hit in August. Not only that, but the city, the strength, the date, the height of the storm surge, the exact amount of property damage down to the penny, the number of casualties and what their names are," finished Rory breathlessly.

"Rory, that is a ridiculous analogy. Straight from the conspiracists. I think we should stick to the facts. What you are implying is a bit farcical. Here come those facts," said Autumn, trying to diminish Rory's analogy of the impossibility of the votes breaking a fifth time for the VP.

"The producers are telling me they are loading Maricopa as we speak," said Billy.

"Here we go," said Rory, his tone expressing his confusion at Autumn's rebuke.

They watched as Nick's lead dwindled to 17,000 as Maricopa turned to 100% complete. Billy shook his head as well. "How many ballots did you say were 'discovered' in Pima county Rory?"

"Why are you shaking your head, Rory?" inquired Autumn.

Rory laughed. "Autumn, despite your rebuke, we have now seen almost all of my hurricane analogy come to fruition. Pima county may now bring us the rest. If it holds true to form, we are about to see 18,000 votes for the VP and 2,000 for Blackbird in Pima county."

"Senator Turner said it best in one of his speeches. There is no such thing as a coincidence. This is especially true in politics. Statistically, is this possible? Yes, but 5 times in 5 different states always with the same outcome? Statistics are a genuine science. The science of probability. And the probability of this occurring is like being struck by lightning." Rory paused for dramatic effect. "10 times in a minute on a clear day. Impossible, no, but common sense would say it is highly improbable."

"Rory, as I told the Senator on Wednesday when he tried to claim the same thing, it really doesn't matter if it is a statistical improbability, it is what happened. You can keep coming up with your crazy analogies. Speculating about it or implying it is anything but honest counting.

Regardless, it is disingenuous and leads our audience to believe we do not have faith in the election counts," said Autumn in a lecturing tone.

Before Rory, who sat in stunned silence, could respond, Billy broke in.

"You were close on your estimate, Rory," he said in a deadpan voice. "The EXN decision desk is now calling the state of Arizona for Vice President Smythe-Thomas taking the state by a razor thin margin of 2200 votes. For the first time since 1876, we do not have a winner in the electoral college. Please explain to our viewers what this means, Rory."

Rory stared at Autumn with a not friendly frown on his round face. "And now we have the number of hurricane victims, their addresses and names in my analogy. Unbelievable."

"Rory, please answer Billy's question," responded Autumn, not acknowledging his words.

"Assuming all the inevitable recounts do not alter any of the awarded states, no one wins in the electoral college. This means the House of Representatives will have a vote to pick the next president. Each state gets one vote. DC does not get a vote, as they are represented, but they are not a state. Technically, the states would typically follow the parties represented. In fact, many must vote for whomever won the state. There are 26 Opposition led legislatures and 24 Party led legislatures. But since Turner is neither, it is unclear how these states would vote. Turner won 24 states, the Vice President 23 including DC and Governor Blackbird won 4."

"It is possible the Governor could play kingmaker by recommending the states he won, throw their votes one way or another, though that is a non-binding suggestion. Finally, the Senate will do the same vote, only they will pick the Vice President," explained Rory.

"The fact Turner has no party and has called all of Congress corrupt and weak defenders of the Constitution, I don't think it bodes well for him," said Autumn with a slight smile and a shake of her head.

"A candidate who wins more electoral votes, more states and about 10 million more popular votes is now relying on a House of Congress whose members owe him no allegiance. This was certainly not something the founders foresaw," noted Rory.

"Indeed not," agreed Billy.

"One other thought and a slight correction, Billy. 1876, was not a vote in the house. That election was decided by a bi-partisan committee of the House, Senate and Supreme Court reviewing ballots in three states for authenticity. The House has only voted twice to decide an election. Jefferson in 1800 and John Quincy Adams in 1824. My final thought is this," added Rory.

"Right now, there are 83 million Turner supporters, a clear plurality, who feel they have been robbed. I would dare say, a good portion of Blackbird's supporters would probably side more with Turner than the VP. Well more than half of the voting public, and we had historic turnout. Or at least it seems we did, favoring the positions and platform of Senator Turner. The House has to get re-elected every two years and of the 34 Senate seats up in two years, 21 of them are Party, including five in red states. If the Opposition vote to put the VP in office to keep the status quo, there will be a political bloodbath in Congress in two years," forecast Rory.

"Or maybe they need to vote according to what they feel is in the best interest of the country. Not the rhetoric and threats of violence the Senator has spawned with his divisive campaign," countered Autumn.

Rory gave her a strange look. "Most Americans are fair-minded and honest. They feel winners and loser should accept outcomes gracefully. There are the usual hyper-partisans on both extremes of the parties who want to win at all costs, but they are not a majority in either party. This is a watershed moment in our history, perhaps second only to the election of Abraham Lincoln in 1860. That saw the formation of the Opposition party from the ashes of the old Whig party. These are momentous times," said Rory in a solemn tone, not in his usual playful banter.

"Lincoln's election also saw the beginning of the Civil War. Thank you for that insight, Rory," said Autumn, cutting him off from saying anything further. "It is official. It appears the Presidential election will come down to a vote in the House of Representatives on January 6th."

Chapter 39

Luc Gauthier waited in the confessional of a small Catholic church in Dijon, France. Arriving at the specified time, he sat, considering the weight of guilt he suddenly felt. He'd not been to a true confession since he was twelve.

Knowing there was much to ask forgiveness for did not make the waiting easier. Only the guilt heavier. His Catholic upbringing, like many of his generation in Europe, had been abandoned by his early teens.

This was the only secure way to meet without the possibility of surveillance. He heard scraping on the other side of the wall. Hoping it was not a priest, he slid the screen open.

"The Lord blesses Camille de Soyécourt," he spoke in a soft tone in English.

From the other side of the screen came a reply, also in accented English. "Blessed is Thérèse Camille de l'Enfant-Jésus."

Luc sighed. "Sister Therese, is all well?"

"Inspector, it is. Annie is doing well and we are still protected."

"Excellent Sister. Was Annie able to discover anything in the information I provided?" asked Luc anxiously. He could not linger. He sensed he had lost a tail several times in the last week. He had been in Dijon for too long.

The screen opened an inch. He glimpsed the old and wrinkled face of Sister Therese in her Carmelite habit. She handed him a USB drive.

"The code is '*Amelanchier_0valis*', with a capital A and underscore between the words and the 'o' is a zero," recited the seventy-seven-year-old Sister Therese as she had been instructed by Annie.

Luc smiled, making a note of the code. She probably had no idea what she was saying. Or why. It was a flower for a serviceberry tree. Snowy white and indigenous to southern France. One of Annie's favorites. Thank you, Sister. I will review this and contact you in the normal method if we need to meet again.

"Inspector, be safe. I can sense you are being hunted."

"Peace be with you, Sister."

"And with you."

#

Luc left the Church and headed back to the small apartment he had rented for the week. Once there, he packed his meager belongings into his backpack. He would find another room in another city before he looked at what Annie provided.

Taking a circuitous route heading east before doubling back toward central France. Stopping often, checking for any consistency in cars following. Once he was confident he was not being tracked, he headed toward Orleans, inching his way closer to Paris.

#

Weeks prior, Luc provided copies of the Doctor's written material to Sister Therese to give to Annie. He could not visit the convent in the old monastery directly. Approaching once, he soon realized the surveillance he'd asked Chaumont to put on Annie was still in place.

Not wanting Alain to know he visited or his current appearance, he instead used an old system of communication he put in place with Sister Theresa when he and Marie had first placed Annie with them, years previously.

After the incident with Caroline, Luc had asked Gabi to move Annie to their larger convent outside Dijon. For protection and isolation. He thought it a long shot anyone would bother Annie. Given her autistic savant condition, she was hardly a threat.

Now reviewing what she had pieced together from reviewing the Doctor's notes and case files, he knew this was no longer the case. She had knowledge. If this were ever found out, it would require her elimination. He needed Sister Therese to hide Annie and not tell anyone, including Luc, where. He'd contacted Gabi to let her know he was alive, but not where he was. Now, because she knew where Annie was, he'd put her at risk as well.

The Doctor had been involved in much more than merely trying to extend his benefactor's life, as he'd divulged to Turner in his notes. Given what Luc knew of his expertise and background, Luc should have put the pieces together sooner.

Viral biology, molecular cell mutations, nanotechnology and bio-engineering. Exactly what was supposedly happening in the lab in Wuhan, China. He'd heard rumors of similar experimentation in the Ukraine prior to the Russian invasion and the first pandemic.

In his hands, he held proof of these and other efforts. And their goals. COVID was merely a start. More potent viral strands were being developed. Fentanyl variants were flooding the urban streets of Europe. Turning many users into veritable zombies. The walking dead.

As he continued to read, it was clear there were several other projects, each potentially catastrophic, being researched or prepared. But for what purpose or goal? Luc sat back, closing his eyes. COVID had decimated markets and economies indiscriminately.

It had sped up the natural deaths of elderly citizens around the world. Three years' worth of death by natural causes, accelerated into a single year. While also scarring the citizens of the world and impairing a generation of children. How could this have been a goal? Of anyone. For what purpose?

Looking down at his laptop screen, he contemplated several of the plans Annie's autistic viewpoint had dissected and recombined from the Doctor's notes. He could only hope these were failed projects and not all planned. She also obliquely confirmed his suspicion regarding why his wife and daughter were killed.

The human trafficking he had been on the verge of exposing was indeed coordinated. The outcome was even more heinous than just the forced sale of humans. Usually, this was for the predilections of rich billionaires and others with immoral tastes. Here, it was also for experimentation in the realms of molecular biology, organ harvesting, and augmentation.

The potential outcomes were both gruesome and incredibly questionable. Experiments in brain transplant and organ growth with hybrid extra-cellular augmentation. Just reading through these, Luc assumed he was reading a science fiction horror movie script. That this was being attempted, on living beings whose outcome was in all cases horrible death, made him ill.

The idea of organic material mated to silicon was already becoming reality. Companies were 'growing' mini brains to power these hybrid computers. This was being touted as a 'green' alternative to the massive power requirements of AI. The scene from The Matrix with humans being used to power 'the machine' was moving quickly from science fiction to reality.

The question of where and how it would be used was just being explored. The Doctor and his projects were way beyond this and the results left no doubt as to both the illegality of the process and outcomes.

And the immoral nature of the entire endeavor regarding wanton disregard for life. This and the outcome and potential havoc of so many of these prospective programs would make COVID seem like a common cold by comparison.

More than ever, he needed to speak to Nick Turner. His connection to the Doctor and knowledge of the Doctor's benefactor, who remained hidden to Luc, were of incredible importance. They needed to be exposed before more of their plans could be put into action.

Dolly was trying, but Nick was in the midst of a contentious election in America. What little news was being reported in Europe clearly favored the Vice President. It further implied Armageddon had been narrowly avoided by preventing the white supremacist and nationalist Turner from starting World War Three.

Nearly every head of state in Europe supported the Vice President and were vocal with this support. According to them, Turner would begin deporting millions of asylum seekers if elected. He had already proven this by endangering the world's financial systems in retaliation for his plans being exposed and stopped in America. He also made no secret of his disdain for world organizations aimed at helping the disadvantaged and maintaining global peace.

These snippets of information were broadcast from various news outlets in Europe with sensational headlines. Luc knew from experience to discount this rhetoric. Painting Turner to be a caricature of everyone's worst nightmare. He was often compared to Hitler and alternatively to the right-wing leaders of several countries and parties in Europe.

All of them were saying similar things regarding immigration, their economies and social justice reforms while preaching their own new brands of nationalism. The EU was a pressure cooker approaching its limits. It would have to release or explode.

Luc hated the press. Not because he was political, but because of the results it had on the populace. As a law enforcement officer, he had seen the deleterious effect of loose drug policies on the youth. The lack of deterrence for breaking the laws and the breakdown of societal norms. Most of these horrible outcomes were not given the coverage they should have been. By amplifying public opinion to force governments to change to better policies.

Instead, they focused on the social issues and continued to encourage the very policies causing the problems as the only way for a free society to continue to nurture, grow, and progress. Over this was the spectre of any crackdown, being the return of totalitarian fascism.

Suddenly forcing the citizens to obey the rules, cracking down on crime, no longer allowing a wanton disregard for other's personal safety and espousing economically responsible policies were the return of Hitler, Mussolini at worst or draconian restrictions at best.

He understood where Turner was coming from. He seemed an honorable man. In a position to do right and necessary things. For the right reasons. Not someone who craved the power. As many like Chaumont did. Who worked and connived in the sewers of politics to achieve it. For this, Turner's reward was to be pilloried in the public square.

Luc had fought against this in his own little way. Refusing to accept any corruption. No bribes to look away. Or advancement in return for favors or bending the rules during investigations of prominent citizens. He was righteous. His wife and child were now dead. Paying the price for his arrogance. For his incorruptibility. Because he tried to do right and fight against the unwinnable. He saw Turner headed toward the same result.

Yet, he'd also realized, the choice was simple. Right vs. wrong. Good vs. evil. A simple choice. In his hands, he held the plans for great evil. He was obligated to do all he could to get this information to someone who might stop it, or at a minimum, expose what was being planned.

Dolly had responded to his burner smart phone with a brief and cryptic correspondence that she would talk to Turner as soon as some of the craziness of the post-election chaos stabilized. He had little choice. He must wait. He debated telling Alain what he now knew. He had access to a head of state of a major European country. One that would suffer immeasurably if these plans came to fruition.

Luc did not trust his brother-in-law. Perhaps his sister, Madeline, the First Lady of France? In the meantime, he would let Sister Therese know to move Annie again for her safety and instruct her to destroy all the copies he had given her. He would also not tell Gabi where they moved Annie, for both of their protection. Then he would plan how to return to Paris. De Monfort had issued a warrant to have him detained for questioning. Luc would not give him the satisfaction.

Chapter 40

Professor Bishop was escorted into Karen's office by one of her staff. She waved at them, directing the professor to a small table. As the staff member closed the office door, Karen came from around her desk with a smile on her face.

"John, we have to make it a brief visit. I'm supposed to meet with the Vice President shortly."

John North/Steve Gaines, in his Professor Bishop costume, shook his gray-haired head. "This won't take long." Before he could continue, Karen interrupted.

"Has Turner done anything we can charge him with yet? He's gotta be reaching his breaking point. I figure any day now he is going to slip up and call for armed resistance. Then we've got him," smiled Karen gleefully.

John stood watching the obvious joy on the face of his boss at the prospect of Turner leading an armed uprising. He'd come in, expecting to disclose to Karen some facts they'd discovered in their efforts to fight off the ballot fraud. To enlist her and the FBI's help in investigating some of the fraud occurring.

He felt many of these efforts were being driven from the White House. They had to be. Too many coincidences, too many obvious circumstances of ballots miraculously appearing out of the blue. These efforts to compromise the election process, to distract and prevent Nick's voters from actually having their voices heard, were exactly why he'd joined the FBI.

To right wrong and root out, uncover, and prosecute people breaking the law for their own personal gain. John had been in Nick's campaign long enough to understand that far from being the menace the media, and now his boss portrayed Nick to be, he was the opposite. He alone stood for truth.

Only Turner was willing to count the actual votes and live with the consequences. The Vice President was not and was in fact, either directly or through her various minions, trying everything she knew to prevent this from becoming a reality.

At that moment, John realized he was trapped. No longer agreeing with his leader, nor even his agency and their mission. They were not interested in the facts. Or the truth. This put him in a dangerous position. If she suspected his change of heart, he would be off the case. More than likely, given his knowledge of events, he would be assigned to Alaska. Permanently.

He had a chilling thought. He'd remembered what had happened to others with information deemed potentially damaging to those in power. For the first time, he considered his wife and how this put her in danger as well. This would be the undercover role of his life.

"Karen, the pressure is enormous. The hits keep coming. Every time they have a glimmer of hope, it is snuffed out," smiled John, hoping his initial hesitation was not noticed. "It's beginning to get to him and especially the staff. They are on the verge of cracking."

She smiled in reply. "Good. It appears the Vice President is going to pull this off with the election going to the House of Representatives. No way they hand it to Turner. Then we'll have to deal with him. Believe me, all these speeches and riots, and now the banks. He is going too far. Now he is messing with the stability of the country, even the world. He is forcing a response from the administration."

John sat listening, not sure how she could come to that conclusion, when it was these same *banks* who had cut Nick off from being able to withdraw a hundred bucks from an ATM or to even cash a check.

"You already provided some of the more questionable grassroots groups and members. Given what is happening, we can expect a lot more violence when it becomes clear he's lost. Can you get us access to all the lists of the member groups?" she asked, looking him in the eye.

John didn't hesitate. "Let me see what I can do. There are a lot of names."

"You know most of them, right? We may need you to identify and prioritize the ones to track down and 'detain' to nip any riots before they start. I'm afraid this January 6th will make the other one look like a picnic. We're way ahead of the game this time with you on the inside. Once we round up a few, it will drive the others back into their caves."

John nodded in response, thankful for the fake beard and mustache hiding the strained smile.

"Can you stay under a little longer? We need to know what else he has planned. Catch him in a mistake." asked Karen, glancing at her watch. "I know it is a lot to ask after you have already given so much."

John sighed loudly. Karen thought it was the prospect of having to stay in character. John was happy she seemed to have missed his epiphany and moment of clarity. He smiled for real after a second and nodded.

"Of course. Whatever it takes."

She put a hand on his shoulder. "Thank you, John. You are one of the best. We will make it up to you. Maybe a trip to Aruba for you and Stephanie when this is all over," she smiled. "I have to go. Was there anything specific?"

John shook his head no. They headed out of her office together.

Chapter 41

Nick stood in the well of the Senate. Exactly one week after the election. It was his time to speak on the topic of providing emergency funding for the three largest banks in America. This emergency session of the Senate resulted from the relentless movement of individuals closing their accounts with these banks.

"Actions have consequences. In their haste to penalize me personally, they showed their ability to ruin anyone's life through the debanking process. Without reason, trial, or appeal. All of which are guaranteed by our Constitution and Bill of Rights under normal circumstances. Apparently not for your bank account, though. At least not with these banks," Nick's tone showed his concern for this ultimate power wielded by these institutions.

"In case no one noticed. Not once during the entire debate in the House and now the Senate did any Party member identify the reason all of this is happening. It is not because of insolvency. Nor is there any weakness in the banking system. No poor investments or questionable loans given to citizens who cannot repay them," Nick made his points, his voice rising and falling at each callout.

"Not a single one of my former Party colleagues noted it is *entirely* because of a *choice* these top three banks made. Not once has anyone on the Party side questioned the ability of a bank to decide whether you and your hard-earned money can take part in society. Money, I might add, you give to these banks in good faith. Money which they loan out and make money from while paying you a pittance of their profits gained from using *your* money."

Nick's voice continued to rise in anger as he made his points. "No, to them, this is all *because* of me. Because of the power I supposedly wield.

Somehow it was my mission before and now after the election to bring down these stalwarts of American finance. Me. One person. Against the trillions in assets they own. Against all of American *Pravda*, many government agencies, and all the other levers of power they control."

"This, my friends, is a watershed moment in our history. Even more than the election results. The silent majority has awakened and is coming together as the sane center. Rejecting the radical policies of the extreme right and left. I ask you to watch my speech where I questioned my debanking. How pundit after pundit came on praising the motives and actions of the banks to prevent me from making payroll or paying for lunch with a credit card." The crowd in the gallery cheered wildly at this as Fontana banged his new gavel for order.

"They rejoiced at the heavy hand of their progressive policies coming to fruition to crush me with the authoritarian hand of their arbitrary justice. No remorse. No quarter asked or given. No appeal allowed. In fact, on my website, you can watch a fourteen minute video of clips from the American *Pravda* media extolling the virtues and *bravery* of these banks for daring to debank me for entirely political reasons. They were giddy with delight."

Nick made his last points, jamming his finger into the rostrum, emphasizing his statement.

"No. Today we are here, because the unintended consequences of these joyful decisions now threaten the very institutions our media lauded only two weeks ago. It has shown the frail nature of the ability to destroy any of us. Today, we are here to bail out these institutions who so recklessly used their power to *destroy*. Me. And in doing so, they tore away the curtain and exposed the man, or woman, 'behind the curtain', manipulating things and lying to all of you. They also showed they wield the power to use this tool against all of you anytime they wish as well."

"I did not do this. You did. Somewhere between thirty and forty million of you have decided, of your own free will, to make a statement. To stand and protest this injustice. This abuse of power. I say today, like last week, there is nothing wrong with our banking system. This is simply free people exercising their freedom to choose."

"Unlike in 2008 when we paid for the unintended consequences of prior Party legislation, which allowed folks without a job, income, or down payments to purchase houses they could never afford. Because, we were told by successive presidents and congresses of both parties, it was not fair to deny someone the ability to have a house, simply because they couldn't afford it."

"We bailed them out the last time. We, the taxpayers. We paid for those policies. We paid for those mistakes. The politicians who enabled all that paid no price. Nor did the banks, or even the corporations labeled 'too big to fail'. Meanwhile, an entire generation of home buyers' credit was ruined."

"Well, guess what? Not this time. I did not cause this. And I will not enable the unnecessary use of taxpayer dollars to bail out companies who unwisely tried to use their power to destroy me. Because next time it could be you. There needs to be deterrence, so this never, ever, happens again. You burned your hand on the hot stove. I hope you learn to never do it again." Nick stopped and looked around the room, perhaps for the last time as a senator.

"Now I cannot speak for all of my fellow senators, but now is the time to stand on the side of right and fairness. The people are watching your vote today. Either you are with the banks and their actions or you are with the people. It is your choice. We are watching. Actions have consequences. Intended *and* unintended."

"Majority Leader, I yield back the remainder of my time," concluded Nick to thunderous applause from the gallery.

#

"Lexi, we tried, but Turner's no vote prevented the passage. I think he shamed the Opposition into sticking together. We only got Acker's from the Opposition. With one bank headquartered in Charlotte, he voted for the bailout. Crawford obviously did not. Not having Banks killed us. We would have had a tie," lamented Rose, the Treasury secretary.

"The pundits and papers are reaming Turner a new one, but since most individuals are not feeling the pain, it is falling on deaf ears. The banks are going through the sale of assets to cover the shortfall. One of them is going to sell all their branch banking and close out any individual account services," she noted.

"Shit. They were the biggest US bank in terms of the number of individual depositors. What does that mean?" asked Lexi, with a disgusted sound.

"It means the F2CFY credit union is now in the top ten largest banks in the country and is now number one in terms of *total* number of depositors. And they are intending to keep it all online. No brick and mortar. All those branches from the bank are being sold individually to the other top banks. No telling how many of their remaining depositors go to them versus their new owners," answered Rose.

"And the other two, are they holding their own?" asked Lexi.

"Things seem to have stabilized for now. They both had to sell off quite a few assets and take out short-term loans against them to cover the outflow. The third bank was much more exposed as they *were* the largest, with about 29% of individual accounts in America banking with them. Charlotte is going to take a hit employment wise as they will have to layoff a bunch of staff at their headquarters. No telling how many of the branches will close as well with their new owners. The stock of all three, and banks in general, are taking a bath."

She shook her head. "Where did they sell their assets?" asked Lexi, expecting to hear Saudi, UAE, or Qatar sovereign wealth funds as the answer.

Rose hesitated, knowing the answer would piss Lexi off.

"Rose?" pushed Lexi in a dangerous tone.

"F2CFY. They bought the assets with the money transferred as they are some of the least risky and best investments being sold at less than par value. They made better offers than the Middle East funds. So at least they stayed stateside," replied Rose, trying to put a positive spin on it.

Lexi's eyes had a dangerous glint. "Let me get this straight. He starts a run, then starts a bank, and the money is transferred to *his* new bank on paper. Because they can't provide the actual cash to cover the transfers, they have to sell assets to his bank. Which they then pay in cash to the other bank so they can just send it back to THEM? Unfucking believable. How is this legal?" wailed Lexi.

"It is not *his* credit union. And the other banks started this. This is the mother of all unintended consequences, just as he said in his Senate speech. I agree with you. These bankers are not the sharpest tools. They think they *rule* the world. Somewhere JP Morgan is laughing. Or crying at their ineptness." Rose shifted in the uncomfortable chair in Lexi's tiny west wing office.

"They're so used to manipulating markets and making others do as they say. This is a sobering event to many. Even more than the SVB debacle. Clearly, they forgot some basic economics. And they forgot about who actually owns the money in those accounts. Little people. Millions of them. It would be interesting if anyone in their actuary departments bothered to even bring this response up as a possibility," mused Rose.

"Rose, I don't deal in hypothetical. I deal with reality. And the reality of the moment is Turner is showing he has a lot more power and is a lot more dangerous than we even knew. He may believe he didn't make this happen, but they moved because he suggested it. How big are they now?"

"Almost 500 billion and close to 40 million individual accounts. Over 30% of all individual deposit accounts in the US are now banking at F2CFY. It seems pretty much every household that voted for Turner has opened an account. Makes them the largest credit union in the country, with the most members as well by a huge margin."

Lexi closed her eyes for a long second, thinking.

"Do we need to do anything, or is this behind us?"

"It seems to have stabilized. There are sure to be repercussions, but solvency is no longer an issue."

"Thank you for the update. Keep me apprised of any changes. No need to discuss this further in public, as it seems to only help him."

"Agreed Madame Vice President," replied Rose, realizing she was dismissed.

Chapter 42

Lauren stood on the perimeter of the funeral service for Senator Banks. There were more than a thousand people in rows and rows of white folded chairs in Arlington National Cemetery where Senator Banks would be interred, having earned the honor as a veteran of the Korean war.

She'd done some research on the Senator. Long forgotten by others, he'd been awarded a Silver Star and a Purple Heart in Korea. His wife and daughter were already buried in this section of Arlington, long filled except for the few remaining qualifying veterans.

As she looked over the crowd, she saw many prominent politicians, lobbyists, military leaders, ambassadors, and even a few high-ranking ministers from European and Asian countries. With almost 70 years of service in Congress, Banks had been a worthy opponent and a faithful friend to many generations of constituents and colleagues.

His fingerprints were on every major piece of legislation since the days of Kennedy and LBJ. As Lauren made notes in her notebook about who was in attendance, her cameraman Paul shot footage of the proceedings.

For such a prominent politician, there were very few TV crews. EXN appeared to be the only ones covering live. There camera was set up in the center aisle, facing the pastor as he delivered the sermon. As he concluded, he invited someone from the crowd to speak. A man in a military uniform stood in the front row, walking to the podium. Lauren was too far away to hear who and moved closer.

\#

Earlier in the day, Nick had pondered what to wear to the funeral service. He'd been invited by Hobson at the request of Senator Banks himself. Nick's surprise was only surpassed by the second request the Senator had made. As a result, he now wore his dress blue Air Force uniform. Given an option, he would have preferred to wear the dress whites of the Navy and his rank of lieutenant commander, but protocol, and the military was all about protocol, was to wear the uniform of your highest rank.

Nick had mustered out of the Air National Guard with the rank of full regular Air Force colonel. Two ranks higher than his navy rank. Colonel was the equivalent of a captain in the Navy, the ranks just below general and admiral, in their respective services. As a result, he wore the dress uniform of the Air Force for the service.

He smiled at the reflection in the mirror. He looked like a glorified flight attendant. The Air Force really needed to update their uniform. It was a matter of fact in the service the Marines were hands down the best dressed.

He stared at the rack of medals he'd removed from the box in his senate office. The same medals Denise had accused him of hiding during the campaign. It was an impressive display. He always felt self-conscious wearing them. Especially where generals and admirals were in attendance whose commendations paled by comparison.

Wearing his ribbons would have been bad enough, but a 'state' funeral and his dress uniform required he wear his medals. Nick knew this was sure to set off a shit storm of commentary. Just as him hiding this part of his past had with Denise. He smiled, knowing this was exactly what Banks wanted. Still scheming, even after death.

He took his rack of 'fruit salad' as these medals were often referred to by fellow soldiers, carefully folded them and the boards they were aligned on, placing them in his uniform side pocket. There was no need to show off for this crowd. He didn't want to deal with the fallout of this revelation on top of everything else. Banks would just have to understand.

He closed the wooden box on his desk. There were still quite a few medals remaining as he walked back into the kitchen and the safe where he kept them. Walking through the Senate office building, deserted on a weekend, he automatically returned a snappy salute from a Marine guard as he headed to the garage.

Walking to Chuck's Prius, he smiled inside at how easily he had reverted to military training. Even his walk had stiffened as his training returned. Just from donning the uniform. He drove Chuck's car the short drive from his office in the Hart building to Arlington National Cemetery across the Potomac.

Walking toward the grave site memorial, he could see the large crowd filing into the seats. It was an unusually warm day in November, perfect for an outside service.

"Commander," barked a baritone voice. Nick stiffened to attention, turning out of habit. Walking into view was a large black man in Navy dress whites, with his own impressive display of medals, including a Navy Cross. The highest bravery award of the Navy. Second only to the Medal of Honor. He stood in front of Nick, looking him up and down.

"Late for your flight, Miss?" he said in all seriousness. Nick relaxed and held out his hand.

"Good to see you, Admiral, sir."

"Don't sir me, Senator. What is happening to you is a crime. If you need the Teams to do a HALO insertion somewhere, just make the call," said retired two-star Rear Admiral Clarence P. Jackson, former head of the Naval Special Warfare Command, the SEAL team leader.

"How are you holding up?"

"The only easy day was yesterday," said Nick with a smile, replying with the SEAL motto.

Charlie smiled back. "What the hell are you doing wearing your flight attendant outfit?" His tone of disgust unmistakable.

"I should wear my ice cream suit instead? I made full bird before I mustered out. Technically, I have to choose the uniform of highest rank," remarked Nick with a shrug.

"Shit, you should have stayed in the Navy. Maybe you'd be the Chairman of the Joint Chiefs instead of that buttsnorkler Kensington," growled Charlie.

Nick laughed.

"Scuttlebutt says he is on the way out after what the VP revealed in the debate. Folks are not too happy you had to 'retire', and he paid no price after hitting a junior officer, first. Now he's a joint chief? That about sums up our military leadership," said Charlie, shaking his head.

"If it really happens, it will be too little too late," replied Nick seriously.

"Where the hell is your chest candy?" asked Charlie, looking at Nick's naked uniform. Only the silver eagles on his uniform shoulder boards announced he was a colonel. His only other items were his name tag, and his Air Force commander's insignia below the name tag on the right side of his uniform jacket.

Above his left breast pocket were his silver Command Pilot Wings. These were given to aviators with fifteen years' experience. Nick's commanding general, besides recommending him for promotion to regular Air Force colonel, had also waived this requirement.

Given the extraordinary number of hours and sorties Nick had flown in his eight years while in command of several squadrons, air groups, and finally an entire air wing in Iraq and Afghanistan. Accruing far more than fifteen years' worth of flying hours. Congress had agreed, approving the circumstances of the promotion. This was long before Nick's antics in New York City.

"Charlie, it seemed inappropriate," explained Nick earnestly. "I haven't even worn the uniform since I left. But Banks requested I appear in it for his eulogy."

"Inappropriate my ass. Banks was right. Lots of those medals are for saving my and my team's asses. Do you have them? And your Navy Intel pin? No way you are walking in their just representing the fricking Air Force," he demanded sternly.

"In my pocket," replied Nick, almost sheepishly, as Charlie held out his hand.

Nick pulled out his gold Naval Intelligence insignia pin and the huge rack of medals, unfolding the stack carefully several times. His medal rack was long, with over 30 medals arranged in order of precedence. Four to a row and overlapping the rows below. Nick put his Naval Intel pin on below the Command Pilot Wings, both up near his shoulder boards, while handing Charlie the others.

Charlie attached the rack of medals and made sure it was straight and the proper distance from his insignias. "Shit, Nick, even I didn't know about some of these. You *are* a bad ass. Looks like you're missing a few, if my memory is right," snickered Charlie.

"If I had them all on, I wouldn't be able to stand up straight," retorted Nick, insulting his buddy, who merely smiled. "I left off all the 'I was there' ones. The Air Force requires me to wear all of theirs, and I'm not. I guess they can court martial me, like the Navy."

"And the Medal of Freedom?"

"Got that as a civilian. Besides, Presidents give them to cronies like candy now. Even this President has one. With distinction, I might add. Shows what it is worth now. Don't want to muddy the waters. Not even sure I know where it is. I left the foreign ones off, too."

"Especially since we weren't in a lot of those places," said Charlie with a knowing smile.

Nick nodded with a smile of his own. "And since some of those governments no longer exist."

"Good point," responded Charlie.

"I guess we'd better get up there."

He and Charlie walked between the rows of chairs, both with chests full of medals for individual bravery and achievement. True warrior heroes of the United States military. Increasingly a rarity in the upper ranks of today's armed forces. The other guests stared at Charlie and Nick in their uniforms, eventually recognizing him. The whispers went up in volume.

No one had ever seen him in uniform. He'd become famous after New York and after he'd left the military. An usher approached them, asking Nick to follow him to a place in the front rows. Nick shook Charlie's hand.

"Good to see you, Admiral," Nick raised his hand in salute.

"And you, Commander," responded Charlie, saluting while ignoring the incorrect uniform and rank as Nick smiled and returned the salute.

Nick took his seat in the empty front row. He noticed Dolly Monroe in the row behind him, looking elegant even in her black mourning dress. She offered a weak smile. Nick could see she'd been crying and was trying to keep it together.

He knew how much Senator Banks and his wife Penny had meant to Dolly. It was as bad as losing her last parent. Nick nodded to her and turned as the Pastor began his sermon. He sat in silence, considering his words on faith and perseverance, stamina and purpose, redemption and hope. It seemed more aimed at him than at Bank's life. As he finished, he asked Nick to come up.

#

As Lauren looked on, an Air Force officer with more medals than she had ever seen, stood and made his way to the podium. As he removed his cap to speak, she was shocked to see it was Nick. She had no idea he was such a decorated warrior. None of her research on his available records had showed any inkling of him doing anything worthy of that many medals. Now all the scars she'd felt in San Francisco made more sense.

"Ladies and gentlemen, Senator Banks asked me to speak. As a veteran, a senator, a friend, and finally as an everyday American. I do not feel I knew Senator Banks well," said Nick, surveying the audience. "But in the short time I did, I can tell you he had a profound effect on my life. And my outlook on our future. In the time I spent with him, I also saw a committed patriot. Senator Banks loved his country. More than anything except his family. How do I know this? He told me." Nick looked down. Not to read non-existent notes, but simply to ponder his words before continuing.

"After my vote in the Senate, when I was being vilified and even accused of murdering Senator Wilhelm for trying to preserve our Constitution, Senator Banks asked me to visit him. I did and what we discussed inspired me to run for President," he said, pausing once again to look over the crowd of senators, generals and admirals, current and former justices of the supreme court, and a variety of civilians. Many of whom Nick suspected had served on Senator Bank's staff throughout the years.

Strangely, he noticed there was no representation from the administration. Yet another not-so-subtle statement showing how almost 70 years of support was so easily dismissed based on a single press conference.

"He told me politics is a dirty business and the more money is involved, the worse it gets. He knew he had little time left. I believe this gave him clarity. He saw how we were losing our way. The increasing coarseness of our culture. Our inability to debate ideas and achieve compromise. Worst of all, he felt we were letting our experiment in democracy slip away. Just as Rome allowed hedonism and selfishness to weaken their civilization to the point of collapse."

"Senator Banks had an epiphany. He looked back over his decisions and his fights for racial equality and voting rights. For abortion and women's rights. To end poverty and take care of the sick. He carried the water on every major accomplishment of the Party for 70 years. He told me this was all for naught, because we had forgotten what made all of this possible," pausing for effect, Nick finished. "You," he said, pointing to the audience as he continued.

"You and me and everyone else fortunate enough to be citizens of this country. We have freedom, we have free will, and we have the right to fail. To get back up and try again until we succeed. There is only one reason we are able to do this. Because a Virginian named George Mason insisted he would not sign the Constitution of Madison and Hamilton. Because it provided too much power to the Federal government."

"It did not protect the individual enough. Not from each other, but from their *government*. Remember, we'd just spent eight years fighting the strongest empire the world had ever seen. To throw off the shackles of an overbearing British government. A government who told you what you could and could not say, along with a host of other restrictions on freedom."

"George Mason was the father of the Bill of Rights, not Madison. Mason also insisted the Constitution abolish slavery. He never signed it. But he inspired Madison to introduce Mason's Bill of Rights in the first Congress. Mason saw ten of the original twelve amendments proposed and ratified. Coincidentally, the eleventh of the original twelve is now our 27th amendment. It restricted Congress from raising their *own* pay. Seems like common sense, huh?" The crowd chuckled a bit. "Well, it took over two hundred years to finally pass that one. And not by Congress, obviously, but 38 of the fifty state assemblies."

Nick paused again, looking to see if he was losing the crowd. People were alert and listening carefully.

"In that first meeting, Senator Banks and I found common ground in our love of our country and of our Constitution as the foundation for American success. Our Constitution is the envy of the world, not because of the way our government is set up. It is the envy of the world because it guarantees each of us freedoms. Freedoms the government cannot take away."

"These freedoms allowed everything to happen. This is why people risk life and limb to come here. They do not have a Bill of Rights where they come from. This document has enabled us to do great good and to also make mistakes and bad decisions. But it also allowed us to learn from our mistakes, from our experiences."

"Those of us in Congress and in the military take an oath to defend these documents. Until recently, every citizen would grow up pledging allegiance to these as well. It was core to being an American. Once upon a time, every school-age child not only said the pledge, they were also taught *why* this country was worth pledging their allegiance to."

"This was the reason they could start every morning, free to do so. To sit in their classroom to learn, free from worry. To one day take their place in our society to uphold these same values, morals, and ethics. Why it was worth fighting for and even dying for, to preserve its ideals."

Nick noticed most of the people in uniform were nodding and the civilians who were not in government were also nodding in agreement. Those senators and congressmen, and the government bureaucrats in the audience, all sat stone faced.

"After the vote to overturn the filibuster, Senator Banks sat me down, explaining how he had become part of the problem. He said he saw me standing against the impending tsunami of government control. Willing to sacrifice myself, and my fledgling political career, to protect that document of George Mason."

"That set of amendments that makes our Constitution the second most important document ever written, after the Bible. He said he felt deflated and diminished and ashamed he did not stand up and object before or after that vote. How he and each of his colleagues had provided the last swing of the hammer to shatter the Bill of Rights. Just as Moses had thrown down the Ten Commandments when the Israelites violated their covenant with God," spoke Nick, pausing. The crowd was enthralled by his less than traditional eulogy.

Lauren had moved closer so she could hear Nick better. She, like the crowd, was entranced by the story Nick was weaving. A pain in her gut, as she watched Nick, the ever-present reminder of her own guilt and weakness.

Nick continued in a slightly lighter tone. "Senator Banks had seen more than most. He regaled me with tales of meeting Churchill and JFK. Of his chance meeting with Martin Luther King and Elvis. His visit to a field in New York where three days of rain and mud had turned a field full of concert goers into faceless muddy revelers. He joked the drug companies made a year's profit on that weekend alone from sales of penicillin," confided Nick as the crowd laughed at Senator Bank's description of Woodstock.

"He told a lot of stories, and I am sure there are many he did not. The bottom line is, he had a life well lived. He always felt he was on the side of right and this made his fight more personal, more righteous. It was this nobility that made him take me under his wing, if only for a short time."

"He wanted me to understand the sin of pride all members of Congress and the bureaucracy suffer from in Washington. You see, in politics, you can never admit you are wrong. Ever," remarked Nick, stabbing his finger into the podium for emphasis.

"He wanted me to understand the disdain with which Washington views the rest of America. To promise to him that no matter what I did or where I went. No matter how much abuse and hatred this establishment would throw at me. I would not succumb to this disease. I told him I had thrown away my career in politics. So that temptation was gone. I also reminded him college professors wield little power, at least in the real world," deadpanned Nick to a few more laughs from the crowd.

"Most importantly, he warned me of the power of government. He lamented how money became the root of all evil in our society and in the world. The pursuit of it, the lending, the spending, all of it revolving around money. How this concentrates the true power in the hands of very few. Not elected politicians or even kings, but in the hands of those who control the flow of this money. Whoever has it, has the power to control outcomes." Nick paused for a second, looking over the thousand folks gathered in the noon sunshine.

"Senator Banks saw we really no longer had our freedoms. It wasn't a matter of the Progressive agenda to destroy the Bill of Rights and impose a government by bureaucratic fiat. It was about money, power, and control. It was no longer about right and wrong. We had lost our moral compass. We no longer cared about others. We only cared about ourself. Everything was measured by how it affected us personally. All of that was a function of money. Who had it, who didn't. He realized what he thought was right, was in fact death by a thousand paper cuts. He was wielding a hammer and a chisel, chipping away at the wall the Constitution provided. Slowly weakening the protection it provided us," continued Nick.

"Senator Banks said one day, the wall will collapse and when it does, it will wash away everything and everyone, like a biblical flood. The question is what arises from this flood? Will we go back to living in caves or will we once again unite in our freedom? Innovate and continue our journey to the stars? Maybe these were the ravings of delusion, but I think not," offered Nick, shaking his head.

"His body may have failed him, but not his mind. He could tell me what Churchill's cigar smelled like. What color JFK's tie was when he last saw him. I think he was plenty lucid, and I think he delivered a message. He certainly did to me. My campaign was not about power or control or money. It is about morality, ethics, faith, and most of all, hope."

"All things we have lost in our culture and in our society. It was about education and integrity. About understanding what George Mason gave us and realizing if we lose it, we cannot get it back, any more than we can get back the filibuster. Once paradise is lost, all we have left are memories. And regret. Memories of what we had and regret of how we squandered it in our inattention."

"I will cherish the time I spent with this great man. I will strive to earn the high regard with which he said he held me and for which I feel unworthy. But as he said, '*Good fights are worth fighting. Regardless of setbacks or obstacles, a good fight is fought until good is accomplished*'. I will not stop until I have accomplished this good. I thank you for your indulgence. Rest in peace, my friend. We are diminished without your presence," finished Nick, turning to shake the pastor's outstretched hand.

Instead of returning to his seat, he sat in a vacant seat next to Dolly in the second row. She took his hand in hers, leaning her head in, murmuring, 'thank you'. He caught Charlie's eye and saw him nod. Nick sat holding Dolly's hand as the pastor finished the service.

He stood with Dolly once the service was complete. Noticing Lauren and her cameraman standing to the side, he looked into her eyes. She smiled hesitantly. Nick put on his cover, turned, and escorted Dolly up the aisle without a glance back. They caught up with Charlie, who stood waiting.

"Admiral Jackson, have you met Dolly Wells-Monroe?" asked Nick.

Charlie smiled. "I had the pleasure of attending a gala years ago when I was still commander of the Naval Special Warfare Command. A pleasure to see you again, ma'am," said Charlie, taking the proffered hand and kissing the back of it with a bow.

Dolly smiled, looking up at Nick. "It seems I have underestimated the breeding of our military leaders. I see Nick is not the only scoundrel in the bunch."

Charlie laughed. "If it was good, I taught him. Any bad habits are his own."

"Thanks for watching my six buddy," retorted Nick sarcastically.

"What was that all about? It sounded like a declaration of war," commented Charlie, looking Nick in the eyes.

"Charlie, as far as I am concerned, we are at war. They fired the first shots. First my staffers and now Banks. This is going to get ugly. What are you doing these days?" he asked, as Dolly stood by, listening intently.

"I'm not sure I want to answer," replied Charlie, half smiling.

"Still at the same number?" He nodded. "Good, I'll be calling."

Charlie stood and looked at Nick. He held out his hand and shook it firmly. "You know, when we made you an honorary SEAL, we meant it. You are part of the brotherhood. We have faced battle together and lost comrades. You call and we *will* be there. I speak for all of them, Nick."

"Thank you, Charlie. I appreciate the confidence and the support." answered Nick as they both escorted Dolly to her car in the parking lot.

As Charlie walked away, Nick turned to her.

"I am so sorry, Dolly. I fear Baxter sacrificed himself to help me. He didn't have much time left, but I believe his revelations only hastened the end."

"Nick, if that is true, then Baxter went out fighting, as he hoped he would. I don't know what I'll do without both of them. It is such an empty feeling," she said, tears coming to her eyes.

Nick embraced her as she fought the feelings of loss. Soon she pulled away and looked into his eyes.

"You fight. And keep fighting," she said with a fierce look in her eyes. "His sacrifice, everyone's sacrifice, cannot be in vain."

Nick nodded, choosing not to speak, not knowing how to respond. He pulled her into an embrace again. "I will never give up," he whispered in her ear. He felt her nod against his chest in understanding. He helped her into her car and shut the door as she looked up, smiling again.

#

"Jesus fucking Christ, who is this guy? Did you see all those goddamn medals? How is all this hidden from us? I'm the Vice President, for God's sake," yelled Lexi.

"Maybe they're fake," suggested Mel, carefully.

Lexi gave him a look. "My grandfather served in World War II. Trust me, there is no way you show up at a service for a fallen military member where there are dozens of retired admirals and generals in the audience with medals you did not earn. Why is all this redacted? He sure wasn't hiding them."

"He was making a statement," said Roland from his seat in Lexi's office.

"Like what, 'don't fuck with me, I'm a war hero'? Shit, we already knew he was a hero from New York. And why the hell if you have all these decorations do you not reveal this while you're running for president? It makes no sense. Come to think of it, I don't recall seeing his Presidential Medal of Freedom. That is like a freaking Medal of Honor. Why wasn't he wearing that one too?" asked Lexi.

"That's a civilian honor. Clearly, he doesn't need to wear it when he has so many others," shrugged Mel.

"Whatever, I want some stories in the papers about how he is dishonoring the memory of a great man by turning his eulogy into a political stump speech. Why was he even speaking? Did Banks really ask for him to do this?"

"Apparently," said Mel. "Why don't you ask Rhett? I suspect some of this is their doing regarding the redactions. This has CIA written all over it. You may be able to convince him to spill what he knows."

"Tread carefully," suggested Roland, causing both to look at him. "Remember, Turner does nothing randomly. As you said, he could certainly have disclosed his military honors during the campaign. He chose not to. Why? And why now? He suddenly looks a lot more experienced than just being in the right place in New York. He now has displayed a chest full of reminders of leadership and bravery. *In combat.* While you are trying to paint him as inexperienced. And after the debate revelations, perhaps you should let the media ask the probing questions and not draw attention to it from your perch?"

Lexi pondered Roland's advice. "I'll call Rhett. Sherman did share with me he had pictures of Turner going to Banks' house a couple of times, but it wasn't like they spent a ton of time together. Mel, you make sure the media asks the tough questions. Do you think Banks really told him to run for President? Why? All that stuff about George Mason, geez. Nobody knows or cares about George Mason," sneered Lexi.

"George who?" responded Mel with a sly smile. "And yes, I do. I don't think he would have run if Banks hadn't put the thought in his head. And I would not put it past Banks to have asked Turner to wear his medals at his service, either."

"Another reason to hate the bastard. Speaking of bastards, are you getting anywhere with Blackbird? We need his votes. What does he want?" asked Lexi.

"I'm working it. He is still pretty bitter about the whole thing. He may not play ball; in which case you need to pull out the checkbook for the opposition congressmen in those states. There is always pork to be eaten. Both are pretty moderate. Perhaps you can entice them with posts in your administration? As Roland has pointed out, we have you scheduled on more shows to keep giving your speech about experience, and this is no time to turn over the reins of the government to a neophyte once again. His medals don't change the fact he knows nothing about governing. We already know he is brave, but so are you," finished Mel.

"Do we need to be more persuasive with the Governor? There are ways to apply pressure without eliminating people, contrary to Mel's view of my skills," suggested Roland with a smile. "I am not without my own resources."

"We have enough scrutiny with all the ballot issues. The last thing we need is more cars sliding off roads with Blackbird relatives in them," countered Mel.

"You give me too much credit. What's next, Bin Laden? I knew where he was, but no one called to ask me," laughed Roland in response to Mel's animosity.

Lexi looked from one to the other before settling back on Mel.

"Let's go with a full court press on Blackbird and find out what he wants. We ready for the House hearings?" she asked.

"Yes, we're all set for the House testimony tomorrow about election irregularities. We have both Opposition and Party ready to hammer the witnesses. They won't get anywhere. Just a bunch of unfounded conspiracy theories and posturing. The usual sour grapes the losers use to muddy the waters, trying to damage trust in our election systems," smiled Mel.

"No way they agree to do any deeper investigations?"

"Not a chance. Everyone has reasons to keep this from getting traction. Both sides have plenty to hide. Turner has few allies in Congress and none willing to sacrifice their careers on his behalf."

"Good. This cannot end fast enough for me," responded Lexi.

Chapter 43

Rhett Chadwick walked into the Capitol, heading toward the Vice President's office, responding to her 'friendly' summons. He smiled at members of congress, staffers, and reporters he recognized. He was a fixture on Capitol Hill. Pulling open the door to the Vice President's suite, Ana was standing in the foyer talking to the receptionist. She noticed the CIA Director and smiled.

"Director, welcome. The Vice President is finishing a call. It will only be a few more seconds."

"Not a problem, Anastasia," smiled Rhett, replying in his orator's baritone. He'd charmed many a young lady out of their knickers with his movie star looks, charm, and smooth manner. Anastasia was no different, blushing deeply as the older receptionist hid a smile. She was a veteran of Washington and had seen the Director in action on many occasions.

"She is finished," she said to the two of them.

Ana led him to the door, opened it before he could, closing it once she heard Lexi greet him.

"Rhett, thanks for making time to come over," said Lexi cordially. "Coffee? Or something stronger?"

"A cup of coffee would be great. I'll get it. You need any?"

"No, I'm fine," said Lexi, taking a seat in one of her leather wing back chairs

"How are you holding up?"

"I'd be lying if I said I wasn't a little concerned. This was certainly not what I, or frankly anyone else, expected."

"That's for sure," agreed Rhett, taking a seat in the chair opposite Lexi. He glanced at her crossed legs. They'd always been her best asset, even when they'd met so many decades prior working for congressmen as junior staffers.

"Rhett, did you see any sign of tampering from other countries?" asked Lexi, ignoring his glance.

"To be perfectly honest, we saw the usual suspects trying. We were monitoring their efforts. Then, suddenly, somebody hit them hard. I mean shutting down server farms, tying up their networks and shutting down some of them completely on election night. Whoever did it, knew what they were doing, and they slammed them."

"Not us?"

"Hardly. We've gotten a lot of complaints through non-official channels on the harshness of our counterattack. As you know, it is our policy to not respond for fear it will escalate things into attacks on our infrastructure, banking, and transportation systems. All of which are woefully unprepared to survive any attacks as we have already seen," commented Rhett. "Believe me, we're worried some entity was taking the protection of our election integrity into their own hands."

"Any idea who would do it and why?"

"Why is easy. They wanted to stop any meddling, and they did. Who is harder to say. There are plenty of both black and white hat hackers with the ability to see what was happening."

"Kwan?"

"Possibly, but he already has the magnifying glass on him from the existing Homeland investigation. As lame as it appears to be, he still needs to tread lightly. There are others, but I am not sure how many can mount this kind of response. We're trying to find them and stop them before they end up escalating things into something bigger."

"I have enough headaches without a full-fledged cyber war," sighed Lexi.

Rhett nodded at Lexi's admission. "Most of the time, China, North Korea, Iran are all more interested in stealing information than gumming up the works. It's the eastern Europeans and Russians who are the ones trying to create mayhem. They're more interested in ransomware. To get hard currency or bitcoin," explained Rhett.

"Keep me in the loop," nodded Lexi.

"I'm guessing you didn't ask me over to chat about cyber meddling in the election," responded Rhett with a smile, leaning back in his chair. Lexi remembered what a dashing specimen the Director had been when they were working in Washington. She and Denise, fresh out of Berkeley, and Rhett from Harvard with his new MBA.

"No, I did not. I want you to tell me what you know about Turner. Not the public info, but the rest of the story. I saw pictures of him at Bank's service and he had a chest full of medals. I've seen little mention of these in any of the military records I have access to." Lexi leaned forward.

"When I inquire, I am politely denied access to any redacted information on classified missions. This may cost Admiral Kensington his Joint Chief's role for telling me about Turner being forced to retire from Navy active duty. He, of course, neglected to say he was the reason, or that he also started it. And that it was a compartmented part of both of their records. Frankly, it was embarrassing," fumed Lexi.

"He should have kept his mouth shut. He knew better. Kensington let his emotions get out of control. Again."

"Again? Turner does that to people. What can you tell me?" she asked in anticipation.

Rhett laughed. "You weren't the only one noticing. There are hundreds, maybe thousands by now, of Freedom of Information Act requests being made as we speak. Stories about 'stolen valor' and 'how dare he stand up there displaying honors he didn't earn', etc. I can't talk about most of the medals. He *is* entitled to everything he wore."

"He is also one of the most highly decorated officers in the history of the United States, especially among those who have not been awarded a Congressional Medal of Honor. He even left a few off, believe it or not. That being said, I still can't tell you much," confirmed Rhett. "He was right on that part. You don't have the proper clearances."

"And when I become president?" asked Lexi archly.

"It won't change. If you feel any better, the current president doesn't have access either. There really is nothing dangerous. If there were, we would have leaked it to discredit him a long time ago to keep him from gaining momentum. Actually, it is exactly the opposite. Let me put it this way." He sat up straighter.

"Turner spent twelve years in Naval Intelligence. Mostly on joint duty assignments, planning and running many of our most sensitive black ops missions. From just before 9/11 until the first surge. He was one of the best strategists I've ever seen. He also has a tremendous grasp of the tactical requirements of any mission. Both the strategic *and* the operational level. Very unusual to excel at both. Naturally gifted would be an understatement."

Lexi merely nodded, holding back her rude comment.

"I was a CIA case officer in Iraq, Afghanistan and elsewhere in the Middle East, and eventually a station chief in Afghanistan when he was there. He is one of those guys who gets along with everybody. He impresses his fellow warriors and his superiors. Makes the enlisted man and non-coms want to follow him into hell. He is a natural born leader, as I am sure you can see in his ability to get 83 million votes in 10 months of campaigning," noted Rhett, wryly.

"So why in the hell did we let him out of the military?" blurted Lexi, showing her exasperation by raising her hands.

"We didn't. He quit. In disgust at our handling of Afghanistan. Threw away his career *and* pension. He got tired of telling everyone who would listen about how we were not learning any lessons from our continued failures," admitted Rhett.

He stared at Lexi for a second before continuing. "In a vault, deep in our archives, is a memo he wrote on July 17th, 2001. Let's just say we should have paid attention. That one won't see the light of day for another 70 years."

"Of course he did," groaned Lexi, leaning back.

"Lexi, he'd been on the job for less than *two months*. Fresh out of college and Naval ROTC as a *twenty-year-old*. Billeted straight to intelligence immediately, which is damn near impossible. I am not sure who or how that happened. But thank God it did."

"Someone was looking out for him his entire career. He wrote that memo after looking at the same intel other career intel specialists had reviewed. They couldn't put the pieces together. He saw something different, and we ignored it. Most likely *because* he was a twenty-year-old ensign, two months on the job and not even a Naval Academy grad."

Lexi looked at the pained look on Rhett's face as he remembered the consequences of this deadly intelligence failure.

"This rubbed a lot of folks the wrong way. The military is like a sorority. The pretty girl who pisses off all the others by just being pretty. There is nothing like vindictive 'sorority' women. And they hold a grudge, forever," smiled Rhett, holding her gaze.

Lexi smiled right back, a glare of steel while digesting his sexist analogy.

"Because of this pettiness, many of his recommendations and suggestions through the years were ignored or marginalized by his jealous superiors. He kept seeing these same REMFs getting promoted. Despite getting men and women killed by their inept leadership. Usually by ignoring his recommendations."

"REMFs?" asked Lexi with a raised eyebrow.

"Rear Echelon Mother...," said Rhett with a smile as Lexi finished the rest with a small laugh.

"Sadly, we have a history of both ignoring the words of these warrior leaders and then watching as they leave the service to become our worst critics. In Turner's case, unlike Hackworth, he kept his mouth shut, at least until now. Believe me, no one was more surprised than me when he showed up nominated to be a senator. Frankly, I'm surprised he took the role."

"I'm assuming Fontana knew none of this when they were picking him?" questioned Lexi.

Rhett shook his head no. "What I also didn't say about why he quit is the political nature of our officers now. Everyone who gets stars in our military today isn't getting them because they are warriors or leaders. They're getting them because they excel at one thing, kissing ass. In the military, they call them buttsnorklers," said Rhett, getting a loud laugh and a clap from Lexi.

"I love it. I want to use that in the future. Buttsnorkler! That is great," she said, still laughing.

"Turner rose through the ranks on merit and results. He didn't leverage any of this into accelerated promotions. Those buttsnorklers hated him because he was everything they were not," noted Rhett, sipping his coffee. "Those same leaders were happy to see him quit."

"They didn't want him outshining them? Hell, I see it around me all day. I'm surrounded by buttsnorklers," said Lexi, chuckling. "How did he get all those medals? Many are for valor. You don't get those riding a desk."

"A lot of it was serendipity. He had a knack for being in the right place at the right time to save several Marine and SEAL units whose missions he planned. You are correct, Navy Intel is usually a desk job, rear echelon, Pentagon staff duty. Turner insisted on posting in theatre as soon as 9/11 happened. To be closer to the other operational field intel units. Planning missions from within the war zone. Again, very unusual to expose someone with what he eventually knew to potential injury. Or worse, capture. Somebody made it happen."

"Other intel units? CIA?"

Rhett glanced at her, not replying. Smiling as he continued. Lexi nodded. In Washington, one quickly learned the value of non-verbal communication. It helped you lie truthfully at congressional hearings.

"Once there, he started being more and more hands on, earning the respect of many of the SEAL teams he planned missions for. Eventually, he would go along with the supporting teams or on the exfil choppers on the perimeter to observe, report, and gather intel."

She nodded as he continued. This time, Rhett leaned back.

"Lexi, you have to understand the unusual nature of this. Without earning the respect of those SEALs and Marines, no way they would let a pencil neck intel geek go along and risk mission success. Once he got in country, he started hanging with these teams, most of whom are enlisted." Rhett got up to refill his coffee, looking at Lexi, who shook her head.

"This further earned the dislike of his superiors. Fraternizing between enlisted and officers is looked down upon, especially by the buttsnorkling crew. They are all about schmoozing the commanders and getting the next duty assignment to advance their career. In essence, he got in country SEAL and special ops training from the best warriors in the business. He didn't start out as one, but by the time he left, he was as good as many of them."

"Great," she said, leaning back in her chair with a sigh as Rhett returned to his.

"Being on these missions also ensured he would have hands on grasp of what was happening and be ready to support if things went wrong. He was the master of contingency planning and turned many disasters into successful missions. Often embarrassing and contradicting his superiors, I might add."

Lexi let out a snort rather than comment about the military brass being risk averse. No one wanted to risk their post military cable appearances with poor decisions.

"Lexi, he has the best memory of anyone I have ever seen. Instantly recalling scenarios he has studied and applying them to the current situation. On more than a few occasions, by his quick thinking and action, ignoring orders, he saved the mission and, more importantly, the men. His commanders always smoothed things over so he could keep doing what he did. They knew he cared about both success and the men."

Rhett continued, setting his coffee down and using his hands to emphasize his points.

"Turner harkened back to the warriors of old. Those same leaders made sure he was awarded accordingly for all his deeds. He could have cared less. He didn't do what he did for medals."

"How do you know so much about him?"

"As the case officer or station chief, I was involved in debriefings for many of these missions. Many of the commendations were from these classified missions. Hell, I even signed off on recommendations for some of them."

Lexi shook her head at this new information.

"He's what the men in the service call a 'stud'. One of those warriors people strive to serve with and to learn from. One ticket punching buttsnorklers absolutely hate. This is why he did what he did for that Marine. It was the war all over again. The REMFs sacrificing the soldiers without remorse."

Lexi sat, listening to the story with rapt attention. Pieces were now coming into focus.

"Like we saw in New York, he is a man of action. Whenever he saw things going sideways, instead of telling them to pull out, he led teams to ambush the ambushers. Attack, not retreat. Changing tactics on the fly, always directing the support teams to deploy in exactly the correct place. In case you didn't notice, he has distinguished marksmen rifle and pistol medals from both the Navy and the Air Force."

Lexi nodded.

"Those SEALs taught him well.," Rhett laughed as he continued. "He even captured a top ISIS commander himself on one rescue mission. He noticed him trying to slip away dressed as a female Afghan villager." Lexi looked down as she sipped her coffee. It was going from bad to worse. She didn't interrupt as Rhett continued.

"Even with this success, occasionally some REMF would insist he go do his sea duty. Several times, he was forced to leave to serve on ships or joint duty assignments outside the war zone in places like Aviano in Italy. Plus, two years at the Pentagon where he went to the National War College. As the most junior ranking attendee." Rhett laughed again, sipping his coffee as he shook his head.

"Why the laugh?"

"Lexi, imagine a lowly lieutenant commander attending the National War College lectures with Navy captains and Army, Air Force and Marine colonels. He was the youngest lieutenant commander in the service and because it was the *National* War College and not one of the service War Colleges, this meant he was also there with the DOD, and state department stars, even international attendees. Only future admirals, generals, Secretaries of State and guaranteed future leaders attend these courses. While doing this, he also took advantage of being posted in DC to get a master's in international relations from Georgetown. *At the same time.* Graduating at the top of both classes, I might add," said Rhett, now smiling as he sipped his coffee.

"What else is new? I bet that went over like a lead balloon. The most junior officer at the NWC graduating above all his more seasoned counterparts," observed Lexi.

"Care to guess who one of his Navy captain classmates was?" posed Rhett with a smirk.

"Shit. Kensington?" answered Lexi with a headshake.

"From what I hear, they often clashed, offering differing views on how to solve problems," shared Rhett. "Needless to say, the solutions offered by Turner were always better."

"Figures. Go on."

"Good for Turner. Bad for us. It was during these periods when he was at the Pentagon, Aviano, or on a ship where we had our most visible failed missions and mistakes. They always occurred when he was not involved in the planning. Several times, SEAL commanders and Marine generals demanded he be reposted back to the war zone early, to no avail. Just more fodder for the ticket punchers to hold against him. When he got back, things were always better. He had a hand in planning all the successful surges and the Bin Laden raid."

"I still don't see where all these medals came from. He was a good planner, good at damage control, and turning around bad situations. None of those earn you Navy and Air Force crosses or even silver stars," pushed Lexi.

"I see you studied his medals."

"I had to look most of them up. My grandfather earned a silver star in World War II, so I recognized that one. I still have it in a box somewhere. He told me that was the last war where medals were earned. It always bothered him that so many high-ranking officers in later wars wore medals for valor just by being in the country during battles. Is that what happened here?" she asked hopefully.

"Lexi, the one thing the military still does fairly well is covet exactly to whom it gives its *top* awards for valor. True, lots of our generals and admirals *do* get commendations for just being in country during a battle. But for warriors and enlisted, they really do earn theirs."

"I figured that would be your answer," sighed Lexi.

"Indeed. A lot of those medals were because of his efforts to salvage these operations. To be honest, I am surprised he wore them at the service, especially after *not* wearing them when it could have helped on the campaign trail. Many of those were awarded for special operations and therefore not publicly known." Lexi perked up at this possible mistake.

"He is entitled to them, don't get me wrong, but usually you don't display medals you can't talk about if an admiral or a curious general asks about where and how you got them. A little inconvenient when you have to tell them it is classified beyond their clearance. If they push and look at the awards, they see the same thing you do, lots of black bar redactions," laughed Rhett.

"I bet that is uncomfortable," agreed Lexi. "I know it was for me when he told the entire country he knows something I can't know. Come January 21st, that will change, trust me."

Rhett stared at Lexi for a second before continuing. "You're welcome to try, Madame Vice President, but don't say I didn't warn you. Some things are better left unknown. Plausible deniability is often an appropriate defense."

"What else? Keep going," said Lexi impatiently, not wanting to dwell on the secrets of Washington's bureaucratic CYA machine.

"I once got wind of a compliance officer questioning his awards. He went to a Marine commanding general's 'Hail and Farewell' party. The compliance officer complained Turner had showed him a bogus DD-214. That is the form that lists what commendations you're entitled to in case buttsnorkling protocol officers ask."

"By this time, Turner was in the Air National Guard and apparently used to having his Navy citations questioned. Believe me, no one shows up at a formal military party carrying *paperwork* defending their awards," chuckled Rhett, at the silliness of carrying a form to a party. "Turner had to because his are so unbelievable without knowledge of his antics."

"He shows up at the party. He is in his Air Force uniform with all his ribbons. Mixed in with his Air Force valor ribbons is his Navy Cross, and a Navy Distinguished Service ribbon, two very high individual honors for valor and bravery. Also very rare. The protocol prick comes up and asks how an Air National Guard Major could possibly have a Navy Cross? Nick handed him his DD-214."

"The fact he even had the paperwork with him pissed off the officer. Once he looked at it, he started dressing Turner down, making a scene. Eventually, the General walked over. The officer turned to him showing him the form which had multiple pages of awards and in each description where you would normally see the description of the action for which it was awarded, were nothing but black redaction bars except for a few words," laughed Rhett as he imagined the scene.

"Blacked out dates and locations. Lots of mentions of 'valor' and 'above and beyond', each officially stamped and signed by commanding officers. Page after page of them. The pissant was explaining to the General that he would have Turner removed. The General gave the officer, a colonel I believe, a look, held out his hand and said hello to Turner, asking him how he was."

"He knew Turner?" asked Lexi.

"He did. Turner apparently smiled in response, telling him he was doing fine, enjoying flying his A-10. He congratulated the General on his celebration. The General turned to the officer, took the form from his hands, refolding it carefully, and gave it back to Nick."

"He then tore the protocol officer a new asshole, as only a Marine can. Telling him to never ever question the awards of an actual warrior and to never try to embarrass an authentic hero of the American armed forces. Especially one who had saved this general's ass frequently by his bravery in *combat*. One who had personally recommended Turner for and awarded some of those medals." Rhett continued to chuckle at the end of the story.

"Turner is legit, and this kind of episode is exactly why he eventually left. But I think he wanted to make a point at Bank's service to everyone by wearing his commendations. Or Banks backed him into a corner, forcing him to wear them. Either way, it's out there now."

Lexi sipped her cold coffee, nodding at the story, with a growing knot in the pit of her stomach.

"To be honest with you," continued Rhett, "his Navy Cross should have been a Medal of Honor. His headquarters commanding officers were career buttsnorklers who he'd crossed in the past with his actions. I don't know, but I suspect several of these started as Medal of Honor's and got pushed down to crosses, distinguished or even silver stars, since he didn't die during the events. The Navy Cross, I definitely cannot talk about."

"I can tell you Kensington was the worst. As was brought up in the debate, Kensington advocated Task Force Echo. This was after the Bin Laden raid where Turner was involved. Turner fought him tooth and nail on Echo, and showed what could happen, and why it was a bad idea."

"He walked through all the scenarios which could have compromised the SEAL teams involved. Kensington and the brass ignored him and threatened to write him up for insubordination when he wouldn't let it go. Turner was ready to resign at that point."

"How the hell do you know *that*?"

"Lexi, I was in the briefing room during the planning. It was a joint op. We had provided some of the intel," responded Rhett.

"It becomes clearer," she replied, glaring at Rhett.

Rhett shrugged at her glare. "Needless to say, the mission was an abject failure. Every single thing Turner predicted occurred. The one concession they had made because of Turner's protest was to have two extraction teams ready, instead of one to cover an exfil if things went sideways. Because of the extra manpower and some timely air support, the SEALs were able to retreat, dragging their wounded with them. But only because Turner forced them to be ready for failure."

"He literally prevented another 'Blackhawk Down'. Stowing away on the second exfil chopper. He killed 15 insurgents when the gunner in the chopper was hit as they were landing. This effort also saved the SEAL team mission leader."

"Is that why Kensington slugged him? For being right?"

"Actually, it's worse. They were in the officer's club days later and that SEAL team commander, Charlie Jackson, was thanking Turner for forcing the contingency plans that resulted in he and his men being able to retreat in an orderly fashion, without anyone dying.

"Admiral Jackson? The former leader of the SEALs?" asked Lexi.

"The same. Do you know him?"

"A little from my time as a senator. Coronado being one of their bases in my state. I've met him a few times at official functions."

"Charlie is a stud. From what I hear, he took a shine to Turner when he arrived in Afghanistan and was instrumental in letting him hang out with the teams. Wouldn't surprise me if he had a hand in Turner learning about being a SEAL," nodded Rhett, continuing.

"Anyway, as things went sideways, Turner jumped out and picked Jackson up when he was wounded running to the chopper. He killed two more insurgents and was wounded twice himself as he got him back to the chopper."

"In the O club, Jackson offered a toast to Turner. Kensington took exception to it. The SEAL officers had been drinking, celebrating being alive. Jackson and Kensington started having words and Turner got in between them to break it up. Supposedly, Charlie implied Turner was the only one who cared about the lives of his men, and Kensington flipped."

"In the ensuing brawl, Kensington ended up slugging Turner. Sucker punching him when he wasn't expecting it. From the story I heard, from Charlie himself. Nick shook off the punch, turned to Kensington and hit him so hard it broke his nose, lifted him off his feet, loosened his front teeth, and knocked him out when he landed," said Rhett, laughing.

"Wow. So, he *was* just retaliating? I know enough about the chain of command to know Kensington should have faced more serious charges for instigating it and striking the junior officer. What the hell was he doing telling me one side of the story?" asked Lexi rhetorically, leaning back again. "How did he wiggle out of it?"

"Buttsnorkling. He was in tight with the Vice Admiral in charge. He had big things planned for his protégé, Captain Kensington, so he arranged for only a non-official rebuke. He saw to it that Turner was brought up on charges and court martialed for the brawl and the insubordination prior to the mission. Then disobeying direct orders from Kensington by stowing away."

"Of course, his heroics during the mission were irrelevant. He would have been dishonorably discharged," explained Rhett. "Even with only the medals he earned in the Navy, it would have been a disgrace to the service to cashier someone of Turner's background."

"What happened?"

"Admiral Jackson, then only a commander, stood up for him at his court martial. At one point, fifty-nine Navy SEALs, Marines and Army infantrymen, including two Medal of Honor winners, marched into the room. All swore out affidavits they would not be alive today if it were not for Lt. Commander Turner and his bravery, superior planning, and operations skills over the course of his career, especially during Task Force Echo. Jackson made it a point that these were only those available on the court date and he could provide hundreds of other affidavits if necessary."

"They then went through the plan and Nick's arguments against them that were consistently overruled by Kensington and the other planners. The Court-Martial board made up of two admirals and a captain realized they were in a tough spot. The military does not have non-disclosure agreements, like corporations. They could not discharge Turner and keep him from talking, especially if it was a dishonorable."

"Turner could have roasted them in the press, and rightfully so. He would have lost his Navy pension because of the dishonorable, so they had nothing else to threaten him with," said Rhett, stopping, getting up to fill his coffee again, offering to take Lexi's.

"Don't even think about not telling me the rest of the story," she said threateningly, handing him the cup, leaning forward in her chair, mesmerized by the tale the CIA Director was telling.

"Don't worry, I've already broken national security laws. I'll have to make a note of your knowledge of these events now. And the pre-9/11 memo. Commander Jackson knew Turner wanted to fly. The Navy had prevented him from doing it because he was more valuable in Intelligence. Knowing two members of the court-martial board were ticket punchers who didn't want to go against the wishes of a vice admiral of CENTCOM, Jackson suggested Turner 'retire' from active Navy duty and transfer to the Air National Guard."

"He would get his wish and fly. He also received a reduction in rank as a cost of his insubordination. Turner had to join as a captain instead of a major, which was the equivalent of his lieutenant commander rank. Turner was fine with that. In true warrior fashion, he just wanted to fly and fight. He didn't care about his career. That's how he ended up in the Air National Guard," finished Rhett, returning with the coffees.

"Turner is forced to leave the Navy and Kensington got his first star," noted Rhett, sitting and shaking his head, remembering.

"Interesting," responded Lexi, non-committedly, fully aware of the way Washington worked. The competent rarely advanced. They lacked the killer instinct and will to sacrifice and climb over their coworkers to advance. The most prevalent trait of the upper echelon leaders in Washington and the military was a willingness to trample any and all to rise. Integrity was sacrificed as a cost of success.

"He got a Defense Distinguished Service Medal, before leaving the Navy, something newly promoted Captain Jackson and the lone warrior Admiral from the presiding court martial pushed through once they heard the case and realized the injustice occurring. And their inability to stop it."

"Is that a big deal?" asked Lexi, taking a sip of the hot coffee. Rhett had even remembered she liked it with one sweetener and cream.

He laughed. "Lexi, that award is typically given to Joint Chiefs and Supreme NATO commanders for joint command assignments. To give it to a lowly lieutenant commander in Naval Intelligence shows what he did to support joint operations on the ground was unprecedented."

"More importantly, it sent a message to Kensington and his guardian angel Admiral. The message there were others in the Navy and elsewhere who were on to this little miscarriage of justice. They stood their ground and made sure it got awarded despite efforts to squash it. That is another reason Kensington hates Turner. He only got his Defense Distinguished ribbon because he was awarded his fourth star when he was nominated as Chairman of the Joint Chiefs. Not because he earned it."

"Plus, even as a joint chief, he has next to no combat medals, no purple heart. I think officially Turner has five or six and probably has twice that if the truth were known. Kensington certainly does not have a distinguished anything other than his 'I was there' ribbons. In fact, all of our top brass have more ribbons and medals for doing nothing but punching tickets with all the right assignments, than actually doing anything remotely valorous. Patton and MacArthur would turn over at what has happened to duty, honor, and country."

"I can see why none of this is public," said Lexi, amazed at what she was hearing. She was even more amazed Turner had used none of this on the campaign trail. "And Kensington kept rising, as if nothing had happened?"

"He had connections and used them. If anything, his ticket punching was sped up. He is both the youngest joint chief and chairman as a result."

"Turner hid out in the Air National Guard, then? Seems like a lot more medals than what you described since he was behind the scenes during his time in the Navy. Even with that make good medal," mused Lexi.

Rhett smiled broadly. Then he leaned forward in his chair, shaking *his* head this time, cradling his coffee mug.

"Turner got a Navy Cross for some other hijinks and a Navy Distinguished Service medal for saving those SEALs on Echo. Frankly, that distinguished should have been a Medal of Honor or his second Navy Cross. The fact Kensington got his admiral to intercede and push it down to Distinguished is a crime as well."

"He earned two silver stars and a few other valor medals. As a Naval Intelligence officer. Not as a SEAL, a Naval Aviator, or a Marine combat soldier. Think about what he must have done to deserve that. And it is entirely earned. He was even more of a hero in the Air National Guard. Like I said, the guy is a danger magnet."

Lexi raised her coffee for a drink rather than respond what she was thinking at this revelation.

"He was involved in so many battles, supporting infantry and Marines on the ground. His A-10 is a low and slow plane. The infantryman's best friend. But it takes a beating from the enemy being that close. The Taliban, ISIS, Al-Qaeda, IRGC, and the Syrians are all terrified by the sound of an A-10 letting loose with its cannon."

"Trust me, terrorists and rebels around the world cheered our announcement removing the A-10 from service in favor of the F-35 for close air support. From ten thousand feet. That in itself tells you the F-35 is not truly providing *close* air support. Turner's A-10 was hundreds of feet and sometimes *less* from the enemy."

"Stick to Turner. What did he do in the Air Guard to earn those medals?"

"He saved so many lives in the eight years he flew all over the Middle East. He volunteered for every risky mission. Even as he rose in the command ranks. He flew more missions and sorties than anyone in the theatre. He was awarded two Air Force Crosses, only a few have earned more than one and he was also awarded two Air Force Distinguished Service medals, again something only a handful of non-general officers have accomplished. More silver stars, legions of merits, Distinguished Flying crosses, several more purple hearts and over fifty Air Medals for the hundreds of missions he flew besides other acts of valor. He probably could have worn at least 10 more medals than he had on yesterday."

"Syrians?"

Rhett smiled.

"Syrians means Russians. Were we engaged with the Russians, directly, in Syria?" asked Lexi in disbelief. "Does the President know this stuff?"

"Not *this* President. Let's just say officially, there are only two known instances where an A-10 is credited with an air-to-air victory and only against helicopters. That number might be closer to ten now and he might have also proved the A-10 can hold its own against much more advanced supersonic Russian and old Soviet fighters."

"Jesus, Rhett," blurted Lexi.

"In the right situations, that is. In fact, he rewrote the tactics manual for the A-10 because of what he could do in that plane. It may not be fast, but it is very nimble. Turn radius and being armed to the teeth with more ordnance than anything else flying. And a gun shooting depleted uranium shells, each the size of a bowling pin, at 65 rounds a second traveling close to Mach 3. It is a pretty formidable danger to an enemy plane expecting a missile. Especially against pilots who do not train like we do. Or fly like him."

"Turns out 30mm shells don't show up on enemy radar. At least not until too late. You hit a plane with a shell designed to kill a tank and that is all she wrote. Underestimating an A-10 flown by Nick Turner was a mistake several Russian, Iranian, and Syrian pilots made. Unofficially, he would be the first US ace since Vietnam."

"Good God Rhett! Iranians too?" said Lexi, shaking her head in disbelief. "How is this not known?"

"Lexi, you know how we work. We are really good at compartmentalizing things. And in some of these places 'where we have never been', it is especially true. Same goes for the enemy. They can't very well complain about losing planes in places *they* aren't supposed to be either," explained Rhett, continuing.

"Half his Distinguished Flying crosses could have been Air Force Crosses and one of those should have been a Medal of Honor as well. He flew his plane into a convoy of ISIL fighters reinforcing troops who had our infantry and local rebels surrounded on the ground. He stayed until he was out of ordnance and his plane was shot up as he kept strafing the enemy. There was nothing he could do, yet he stayed and tried. Sometimes, just the sight of an A-10 is enough to make the enemy flee." Lexi now sat on the edge of her chair as Rhett's story unfolded.

"He ended up using his plane, intentionally crashing it into the convoy, destroying half of it by flying his plane into the fuel and ammo supply truck. He ejected at the last possible second and ended up being captured. They tortured and beat the shit out of him for a couple of days before *he* managed to escape, killing most of his captors. He then evaded damn near the entire Syrian, Russian, and Iranian armies for weeks before making his own way back to friendly lines."

"We all figured he was dead. No ransom demands. We prepared for the fallout of them eventually trotting out his dead body for propaganda." Rhett's words were coming faster and faster, clearly enjoying the story he was weaving.

"Instead, he just shows up at a base in Syria a few weeks later. The intelligence gathered from his torturers allowed him to lead a SEAL team back. We killed the top ISIL operative in the area after his escape. He got an Air Force Cross for that. Shit, if he'd been regular Air Force, he would have the Medal hands down. The buttsnorklers strike again," said Rhett, disgusted. "It is not a wonder he lit into Kensington in that hearing. In my opinion, Turner has shown amazing restraint. Kensington deserved it and more."

"How come none of this made the news? Pilot shot down, captured, tortured, escapes, and leads SEALs back to capture and kill the enemy. Sounds better than most movies today," commented Lexi, still trying to process all she was learning.

Rhett shrugged. "The nature of the missions. Some are Sensitive Compartmented Information and Special Access Program classification levels. Most occurred in places we weren't supposed to be. Against enemies we weren't 'fighting' and leave it at that."

"I would not like to be the Air Force and Navy information officers handling all the FOIA requests. First the debate and now this," Rhett paused, smiling, sipping his coffee. "For instance, he wore his prisoner of war medal. I was surprised because what I just told you was classified at the highest level and the award of that medal would have been the same."

"Is that something I can hit him on? Violating national security by wearing it and opening up a lot of questions about how he could have a prisoner of war medal," asked Lexi in a hopeful tone.

"Nope. First, he can display any *military* medal he's entitled to, he just can't talk about it. And I checked his record and found out he was captured *twice* and escaped *twice*, the first time being when he was shot down in a helo in Afghanistan when he was still in the Navy. He escaped that time from the Taliban camp where they held him. They hardly even had time to interrogate him. How and what he did on that one is classified as well. He can certainly take care of himself, and he is not afraid to die doing it."

"Technically, he qualifies for two POW medals. Those info officers are going to have to answer with a lot of, 'thank you for your request, yes he is entitled to the medal he is wearing and no we are not at liberty to discuss the details of the missions on which they were awarded'," smiled Rhett, sitting back again.

"Sounds like you like him?" offered Lexi, listening to Rhett tell his story in a voice full of admiration and amazement.

"Lexi, he is a man's man. No nonsense and honest to a fault, even when it costs him. If he had an ounce of ambition in the military, he could be a joint chief, if not chairman. We retire our warriors, if we even have them any longer, long before they reach the highest ranks."

"You saw what happens when you publicly question the military leaders with that Marine colonel. They were going to court martial him after the Afghanistan pullout debacle. For simply asking why no senior leader was being held accountable for thirteen deaths. He was right. But being right in our military is not permitted when it points out failed leadership," said Rhett.

"For someone like Turner, following leaders like this, leading men and women into battle to watch them die because of this leadership, ceased to be acceptable."

"Turner left before we announced the pullout, but he could see it was going to occur and he warned us what would happen. Once again he was correct. When he left, he chose not to make a public statement and just resigned. No one in the upper echelons made any attempt to stop him."

"In fact, his commanding officer, who understood why Nick was leaving, recommended him for full air force colonel with just under 20 years. The general was a warrior and hand walked the promotion through congress, with Bank's help. Then he did what he did in New York after. Turner being Turner."

Lexi listened intently. She had totally underestimated Turner. As had everyone. Armed with this information, she would have done things differently. She would have made him an ally, or at least not an enemy. She shivered at the prospect of having Turner as her enemy. She was no shrinking violet either. He would be a worthy opponent. Game on.

Rhett noticed the shiver.

Lexi looked at him. "He has enough ambition to run for President. So, you're wrong there. Why exactly does the CIA know so much about Turner?" asked Lexi.

Rhett smiled. "That I can neither confirm nor deny. Turner was right about you not having the proper clearances."

"How does he know that?"

"Well, he has the clearance because he was on the missions."

"Would I be right to assume many of these missions were CIA black ops and Turner was working for Langley on these?"

"More like 'with' than 'for'. Like I said, he is a planner without equal. Beyond that, I can neither confirm nor deny."

"But I will give you one more piece of confidential info. Remember what I said about medals he was not wearing? Just like the President saw fit to give Turner the Presidential Medal of Freedom with Distinction, the civilian equivalent of the military Medal of Honor. The CIA may also have bestowed on a certain person, the Distinguished Intelligence Cross, the CIA's equivalent of the Navy or Air Force cross, our highest honor, *for bravery*, which, of course, is not a public award. These he *can't* display. In fact, this person might have two of them."

"Holy crap. Unbelievable," said Lexi, leaning back in the chair, stunned.

"It is a sad state of affairs when two civilian agencies are the ones to award him the highest honor when the military leadership is the one who has conspired to keep him from being recognized for his deeds," revealed Rhett.

"I sure wish you had shared this with me a year ago. Or even before, when he was just a senator. Things could be very different," announced Lexi.

Rhett shrugged. "There is a need to know, and there was nothing anyone needed to know. Also, we don't interfere with domestic operations. Turner, as a senator or presidential candidate, is most assuredly a domestic issue. If you excuse me, I need to get over to Langley for some meetings."

"Did Banks know Turner before he was a senator?" asked Lexi.

Rhett thought for a second.

"He was the head of the intelligence committee on and off for the last 50 years and on it for over sixty. Nobody was more plugged in than Banks. So yes, I would say it is probable that he knew about most, if not all, of what I have told you. We have to brief on most clandestine intelligence operations, at least to the intelligence committee leaders."

"Banks has been cozy with all the CIA directors for sixty years. He definitely knew about Turner's capture and escape the second time. Maybe some of his other escapades as well. Knowing what we know now, I would guess Banks was helping Turner throughout his career. Including the Navy Intel assignment right out of school. Probably the transfer to the Air Guard as well. However, I don't think he knew him personally before he became a senator. Why do you ask?"

"Just curious," said Lexi, standing as well. As Rhett turned to go, Lexi asked.

"Talk to Denise lately?"

Rhett visibly stiffened at the mention of Denise.

"You know I have not," said Rhett coldly.

"Oh," said Lexi coyly. "We were discussing you not even a month ago. Oh well, Paris was a very long time ago,"

"A lifetime. Good day, Madame Vice President," said Rhett as he exited the office.

Lexi smiled as he left, thinking.

Chapter 44

Nick's Washington campaign office was a disturbed anthill. Everyone scurrying back and forth, consultants and constituents, friends and reporters, in and out hourly. They monitored the recount efforts in Georgia, Pennsylvania, Wisconsin, Arizona and Nevada. They continued to fight the Michigan election and court systems to get Nick's mail in ballots released and counted. Finally, they were watching closely the efforts of the Orange County California recount efforts.

The press continued to hammer Nick on his sour grapes and attempts to paint the election as anything but fair and secure. Opinion polls were reflecting a nation tired of hearing about conspiracy theories. Or so American *Pravda* continued to trumpet non-stop.

On EXN and the 2J's, the opposite was front and center. Streams of voters and poll workers were interviewed about things they saw or how their votes were canceled and notification received long after their ability to do anything about it. *Their* polls reflected the opposite of American *Pravda*. Clear majorities favored full audits and voter IDs. Clearly, they did not agree the election was conducted in either a fair or secure manner. It was a tale of two countries, never more divided.

"Talk to me, Jenny," asked Nick in the war room they'd created in a much larger conference room on an upper floor of Nick's DC headquarters. There was flip chart paper taped to walls showing charts with lists and checked off action items.

"Georgia has finished the recounts. Not much to report, you gained fourteen votes. Next, we are suing to have an audit of the mail in ballots in six counties to validate their authenticity. Even a random sampling of a hundred or a thousand votes is better than nothing. We are hopeful this will go through. We'll have to pay for it, but we have plenty of funds," she explained.

"When does Georgia certify?" asked Chuck.

"Early next week, right before Thanksgiving. This is why we're pushing so hard to get this started. What I find strange is the Secretary of State is fighting back against us, saying the recount they just completed is sufficient and each of the ballots and votes were validated by poll workers prior to being counted. He is claiming there is no need for the time or expense of re-validating. Every vote counted was from an eligible voter. This is complicating things. But we are hoping to get a ruling today," stated Jenny.

"Well, we can't assume all Opposition officials are on our side just because we got a lot of the votes. We represent a threat to them as well, same as the Progressives. We don't have many allies in statehouses or in the judicial system. Everybody knows Pavlovich has made no secret of supporting far left Attorney Generals, Secretaries of State, judges, and District Attorneys everywhere they are elected. His web of NGOs has taken over all these positions with nary a peep from our government," remarked Chuck.

"Assume everyone is against us and is fighting any attempt at transparency," commented Nick.

"Us against the world," murmured Chuck.

"'Fraid so."

"Michigan is a problem. With Thanksgiving next week, they certify the Tuesday after and if we don't get a resolution on the mail in ballot issue, we're going to lose the chance to have them included. Earl flew up to Michigan this morning to meet with his investigators to see if they're getting anywhere. Our inquiries into the investigation by the FBI are being stonewalled. They refuse to provide any updates," fumed Jenny, obviously frustrated.

"Can we get an injunction to delay the certification until the courts rule and until we have exhausted our appeals?" asked Nick.

"We can have it tee'd up. If we try to jump the process, they'll just throw it out. Saying we have not exhausted our options with the lower courts. We need the FBI to release their findings, then we need the Michigan Supreme court to throw out their case. Or keep it in place. They just need to do *something*, so we can then go to the federal Supreme Court. But first, we need to get the FBI to do their job. We are in a holding pattern until they release a statement," complained Jenny.

"Seems to me that being the 'acting director' logically means Director Coleman isn't going to go against the Vice President's wishes. Maybe she's delaying the results to slow us down intentionally," offered Steve, who normally sat quietly in these meetings.

Nick glanced at him and nodded.

"You're right Steve. Acting FBI Director Coleman is Lexi's creature, so she'll do whatever Lexi asks, especially if she offers her the role full time," mused Nick. "I wonder if we can put some pressure on them. Maybe go public asking why it is taking so long? What else?"

"Arizona and Nevada will go through recounts without our prodding, as the race was close enough. It may take some more time because of the combination of the partial electronic vote and the paper ballots."

"Unfortunately, what we are hearing is the machines are not cooperating when the technicians are trying to understand why they failed. They are claiming they aren't able to find anything. Every time they try to troubleshoot, it is wiping the systems clean. Some sort of glitch, they claim. Of course, I don't trust anything we are hearing from the voting machine people. We're being stopped in all our attempts to subpoena the machines for a digital forensic audit," reported Jenny.

"You are full of good news. Do you have any?" asked Nick, softening the statement with a smile.

Jenny smiled too. She'd been going 20 hours a day since the election, as had all the staff. They were reaching burnout. Nick understood this. "Actually, there is. I wouldn't want to be the Party chair for Orange County, California," laughed Jenny.

"Why, what happened?" asked Chuck. "Last time I checked, they swept all seven of the congressional seats in and around Orange County, kicking out the five incumbent Opposition congresspeople."

"Apparently, the Orange County election canvassers panicked when Lexi started losing. Both the Opposition, and Laura from our team, have filed lawsuits for ballot hand counts and verification for the county. It's so bad even the local sheriffs agreed and have the place locked down and guarded 24/7. I believe they may have even sworn out an arrest warrant for the county clerk."

"Too bad it isn't Michigan," added Denise, joining the conversation.

"I guess that is bad news for Lexi and therefore good news for me, indirectly," agreed Nick. "What will that mean?"

"Depending on how bad it is, it could cost them some of those seats," noted Jenny. "California is one of the last to certify."

"Good. At least that will show cheating is happening," pointed out Chuck.

"Nick, I was texting with Earl. He says he thinks they at least know where the mail in ballots are being stored. It is in a warehouse in Detroit. He is going to set up surveillance 24/7. He says as far as his contacts can tell, they were *not* counted. No one knows if there is enough to catch up or pass Lexi," explained Denise.

"At least we found them," nodded Nick.

Denise was still looking at her phone. "Earl also confirmed what you said earlier. His sources tell him the FBI has already finished their investigation and has totally discredited the entire episode to frame you as an election fraudster."

"Apparently, one driver cracked under pressure and led them back to where he picked up his ballots and there were remnants of printing apparatus. He is not sure, but he thinks they also found some folks admitted to printing the bogus ballots with only the write in sections of the ballot filled out. Totally bogus. They're stalling," confirmed Denise.

"Good for you Denise. Looks like you won't be going to prison after all for election fraud," laughed Nick.

"You can laugh all you want. I'll sleep better when I hear it from the FBI," replied Denise, with no humor.

"Margie, how are you doing getting me on the calendars of all the Opposition legislators of Blackbird's states?"

"Your calendar is full of calls, starting tomorrow through next week. We want to get them all in before Thanksgiving," confirmed Margie.

"Good, I guess no rest for me," said Nick with a laugh. "Keep the faith, people. This is only the beginning. Keep that in mind. Thanks for all the work and the updates."

"Boss, can we talk about the funeral?" asked Margie.

"What about it?" asked Nick, knowing what was coming.

"Ah, let's see. We have over a thousand requests for comment on your medals, strangely enough, specifically the prisoner of war medal you wore," said Margie, trailing off questioningly.

"Nobody cared about any of the others?" laughed Nick.

"Well, someone like you, standing up there with more medals than anyone since Audie Murphy, leads one to speculate. Sporting a medal any other candidate would have worn at every campaign appearance also makes folks a wee bit curious," uttered Denise in her usual not so happy tone regarding this subject.

"Denise, you know it is not my style. Hell, the Medal of Freedom the President gave me trumps anything else I was awarded, and I didn't wear it. I only wore my medals because Banks specifically asked me to deliver his eulogy in uniform with them. That is all there is to it. I was just complying with his last request."

"Nick, sometimes..." said Denise as Chuck cut in.

"Boss, I think what we would all like to know is how we should respond," deflected Chuck diplomatically.

"You can do a brief press release. 'I served for twenty years in combat zones around the world in the Navy and the Air National Guard. During this time, I was awarded various commendations on missions, both classified and non-classified. I wore some of these awarded medals during Senator Baxter Banks' funeral. I can assure you; I have earned all of those I displayed and questions regarding these can be handled by the communications offices for the Navy and the Air Force'," finished Nick. "There, problem solved."

"Some? Are there more? You know that won't stop the questions," replied Margie, challenging Nick.

"I cannot tell you how I got most of those medals. There are national security laws, that unlike the Chairman of the Joint Chiefs, I am choosing not to violate. That is the nature of a war zone. Take it on faith that I would never wear something to which I am not entitled," said Nick, trying to move on.

"And yet, we asked you to write a biography, and you claimed and I quote 'Guys, I have done nothing'. You didn't choose to use them during the campaign. Which I don't understand. But now they are out there. And people are asking. Perhaps it is a sign we should use them to show your leadership and bravery? Two things Lexi is saying you are lacking in." ended Denise, voice rising, obviously still upset at the missed opportunity to capitalize even more on Nick's past heroics.

"Denise, I am not, was not, and will not use any of my deeds to make me look like something other than what I am. I know you think this is ludicrous, but the reality is, I don't care. I didn't do any of these deeds to earn recognition. I'm not suddenly going to talk about things I did, or that happened to me. Including getting shot down, captured, and escaping. The powers that be know what happened. If they have chosen not to make it public. I worked for them. It is their prerogative to keep it secret. It is not mine to talk about them."

Nick finished and looked around the room. He knew they were all dying to know about how he'd gotten all his medals.

"Those who do heroic things, in any walk of life, need not boast. They know what they did, and that is enough. Only pretenders claim glory and seek adulation for their false triumphs."

"Who said that?" asked Margie scribbling.

"Nicholas James Turner,"

Margie stopped writing and looked up.

"Next subject," said Nick, putting an end to the speculation about his service.

"Ok Boss, I'll go with that message, but it is going to look like we are trying to hide something," said Margie.

Nick laughed before answering. "It didn't work out so well for Kensington. Anyone else who wants to accuse me of something will suffer the same fate. I did nothing nefarious. They'll look worse for trying to paint it as such. Of that, I am confident. My conscience is clear, and my actions justified, always. I am *not* the one trying to hide my service record. Trust me."

#

Just before five, Jer walked into the conference room carrying a portable projector. Margie, Denise, Chuck, Steve, and Nick all looked up as he set it up on the conference table.

"What's up, Jer?" asked Margie, with a confused look.

He smiled. "Ask the boss."

As she turned to Nick, several other staffers entered the conference room, their arms full of pizza boxes, beer, and sodas.

"I decided we need a break. I thought a pizza party and a movie would be in order," replied Nick with a smile.

"Nick, we have a ton to do," blurted Denise as Nick held up a hand.

"Jer, we ready?"

"Yep, boss, ready when you are."

Nick turned to the room. Almost two dozen staffers were gathered.

"Turn off your phones, grab some pizza and your beverage of choice. Then sit down and watch. I appreciate what all of you are doing to get us elected. However, we have to be smart. This is not a sprint, but a marathon. I chose this movie because it shows exactly what can happen if we don't realize this and pace ourselves. Rather than me, I'm going to let Gregory Peck show what maximum effort is and what happens when you go too far," explained Nick.

They rearranged the tables and chairs into an impromptu theatre. As everyone grabbed their pizza and drinks. They sat and looked at Nick as he nodded to Jer. It was already dark outside, so they only had to turn off the conference room lights as the movie, *Twelve O'Clock High*, projected on the screen at one end of the conference room. Jer had even brought external speakers to provide good sound.

Everyone sat munching on their pizza and watching the movie. Nick noticed Jer and Margie were even holding hands, sitting next to each other. He smiled at this.

At the end of the movie, someone turned the conference room lights back on and everyone blinked at the now bright lights.

"What did we learn?" asked Nick, as if lecturing to students.

"Gregory Peck is a wonderful actor?" offered Chuck.

"Hey," said Jer, looking from Nick to his laptop, which now showed the poster of Gregory Peck in his uniform from the movie. "Is it just me, or does the boss bear an uncanny resemblance to Gregory Peck?"

Margie and Denise both turned and looked from the poster on Jer's laptop and back to Nick.

Denise laughed. "I'll be damned. You know, I always thought you reminded me of someone. Seeing you in your uniform, now I know who."

It was Nick's turn to laugh. "I should be so lucky. You're dodging my question. You all understand the message of the movie, right?"

"Sure boss," offered Steve. "You hit maximum effort and then you push through to whatever comes after that," he finished, smiling as Nick made a rude gesture. "I give up. Pace yourselves, please."

"That goes for you too, Mr. Peck," replied Denise, smiling.

Nick's face reddened a bit at this, obviously embarrassed this was what they took from the movie. Heather had once told him the same thing, so many years ago, when they had finished watching a revival of *Roman Holiday* at the local art house theatre in San Francisco. Truth was, he did look a lot like Peck.

Chapter 45

Lexi poured her expensive 24yr old Scotch into a glass with a single ice cube. She walked back to a chair in her office. Roland watched as she crossed her legs provocatively, dangling a red soled high heel.

"Who exactly do you work for?"

"You, of course," he replied, smiling.

"Ah, I wish it was so. If I am to trust you fully, I must know."

Roland contemplated how to lie, when there was a knock at the door.

Lexi straightened from her provocative slouch, pulled her skirt down and pushed her shoe back on her foot as she cried out an 'enter'.

Mel and Harriet walked into the room.

Lexi waved them into seats. Mel glanced quickly at Roland as he sat. It bothered him the amount of private time he was spending with Lexi. He was no prude and assumed they were lovers. That bothered him less than the pillow talk scheming. Lexi had insatiable needs, especially where there was power to be gained. Scheming for her had been *his* purview these last twenty-five years.

"We still gumming up the works?" asked Lexi, lightly sipping her scotch.

Mel smiled. "At every turn. They file, we wait and delay the response as long as we can, then they rule in our favor and the process starts over on the next appeal. They are running out of time and appeals."

Lexi nodded as Roland shook his head.

"You have an issue with this?"

"No. I find the hypocrisy enlightening. How your politicians stand and lecture the rest of the world how much better your justice systems are. You are so quick to point out corruption everywhere else as if the most egregious examples are not in fact happening in your own government. No wonder there is so much skepticism about 'American Exceptionalism' around the world."

Lexi shrugged at this claim, knowing he was right. She turned to Harriet.

"I assume the Supreme Court is not going to grant any of their motions to do these audits?"

"Not likely. These state and Federal Appeals courts are making the logical and correct ruling, despite Roland's cynicism. Turner hasn't produced examples of massive voting by ineligible voters. The recounts verified the votes were indeed from registered or eligible voters. His claim *they* did not cast the vote is mere speculation without more evidence," noted Harriet as Mel interrupted.

"There is no time to do what he wants. Publicly or privately. The pundits are also right in declaring to allow this would set a precedent for all future elections. We always counted on this being our defense against these accusations. Granting the loser power to delay the seating of any election winner until these expensive and time-consuming audits occurred invites mayhem."

"What about all the folks EXN keeps trotting out who say they checked online and found out they had voted by mail when they hadn't?" asked Lexi.

Mel shrugged. "It's EXN. What else are they going to say? Even for those folks they have on, there is no proof of *who* they voted for. What do you do in the worst-case scenario of an election official agreeing they should not have counted the ballot? They'd have to remove a vote from all three of you. What would that accomplish? Plus, how does the election official know the person making the claim didn't vote and then decide to get their fifteen minutes of fame by claiming they didn't? It is just their word against what the county shows as a signed ballot."

Lexi nodded at the brilliance of the scheme. It really was difficult to prove any fraud with mail in ballots. And very easy to commit it.

"Even Turner's door-to-door audit wouldn't ultimately change anything. There is no way to know decisively who a mail in vote was cast for. No way the Supreme's bring this chaos to our elections. These are DOA," finished Mel in his lengthy explanation.

"Ingenious indeed," acknowledged Roland.

"Agree. What else is there to worry about?" asked Lexi.

"Michigan," replied Harriet.

Mel nodded. "That one is a bit more problematic. The request is simply to count the ballots. It is harder to argue against, at least counting them. However, if there were enough to overcome your lead, Turner would have a better case at the Supreme Court to allow the mail in ballots to count. Especially if the FBI has finished their investigation. I assume this is what the FBI found?"

Lexi nodded. "Karen is holding off as long as she can."

"Won't be much longer. I know Turner filed a brief demanding the FBI stop meddling in the election and reveal what they found. The press is not so eager to forgive the FBI for their obvious bias and interference. Better them taking the hit than us."

"Agree. Karen is taking the hits to prove she is worthy of the role."

"I am not sure she can hold off until after Thanksgiving. If that news drops, I would expect the Appeals court would have no reason to not overturn the Supreme Court of Michigan's decision to not at least see how many there are," speculated Mel.

"And are there enough?"

"We actually don't know. It will be close. Too close," he admitted.

"We lose Michigan and that's it. I don't want them counted. We shouldn't take the risk," worried Lexi.

"Do we know where they are?" asked Harriet.

"Not officially," smiled Mel.

"How do we make sure they're not counted?" asked Lexi.

"I'll take care of it, if the ruling goes against you," announced Roland.

"Thanks, but no thanks. We don't need a pile of bodies and more FBI investigations. I have this under control. Trust me, Lexi," implored Mel.

"This is your domain, Mel. Handle it. How bad will it be?"

"Bad. Another giant coincidence favoring you and hurting Turner. But plausible. The pundits will tell the story with credibility."

"OK. Enjoy your weekend. Only a couple more weeks," sighed Lexi, the stress weighing on her.

"Lexi, maybe you should take the weekend off and head back to San Francisco, or maybe Napa. Just relax," suggested Mel with a glance at his rival.

Lexi laughed. "Soon. Hell, I can't even retreat to Camp David officially. I'll be fine. We got this far. Just a bit further."

Chapter 46

As Monday rolled around, Nick prepared for the short week before Thanksgiving. He'd spent the weekend trying to track down the remaining congressmen and women from the four Blackbird states with varying degrees of success.

Congress was not in session during the week of Thanksgiving. Pennsylvania, Georgia and Nevada would all certify prior to the holiday. They had various lawsuits filed for each state. Michigan was scheduled for the Tuesday after Thanksgiving. Wisconsin and Arizona were in the first week in December and California, just before the deadline of December 14. Barring any injunctions by the courts, these deadlines would stand. Nick was running out of calendar.

With the short week, his staff worked hard, especially in Michigan, as many of the folks necessary to move court cases forward in these states did not want to work the week of Thanksgiving. As with Arizona and Georgia, the initial recounts gave Nick a few votes but not enough to make much of a difference, only double digits.

The case to do the mail in ballot audit against the counties with the higher than normal turnouts around Philadelphia were shot down in the all Party legislature in Pennsylvania. The Court of Appeals for the Tenth district, just as the Eleventh had done in Georgia, upheld the state Supreme Court decision. Nick's team filed an expedited appeal as they had in the other states.

In Nevada, the Opposition Governor put an injunction against the Trusted Voter personnel accessing the machines in Clark County and was in the process of issuing orders for a full digital forensic audit to figure out what went wrong when the Clark County Party chairmen went to the Nevada Supreme Court.

The Nevada Supreme Court justices, all elected by a majority Party state, overruled the Governor's injunction. Claiming he did not have the authority to prevent the owners of the voting machines from accessing their own equipment.

There was insufficient evidence that TrustedVoter had anything to do with the malfunction and they granted them access to the machines for troubleshooting. An army of TrustedVoter techs descended on the central warehouse where all the Clark County voting machines had been moved after the election.

#

"Really, nothing?" asked Chuck, who was on the phone with their observers in Nevada.

"You expect the same in Arizona?" he asked back into the phone.

"OK, thanks."

"Let me guess. The machines wiped themselves clean when they turned them on and there is nothing to compare to what they reported on election night?" prognosticated Nick with a smirk.

"Now, how the hell did you know that? You know something we don't," accused Chuck as Denise, Margie, Steve and Earl all stared.

Nick smiled. "Jeremy explained what he thought would happen if there had been any cheating. He said they wouldn't have allowed the machines to be reviewed or audited. This sounds like what he described."

"Funny thing is, the Party is the one having a conniption. They were hoping to prove *you* were cheating in Nevada," laughed Denise.

"Well, it isn't going to let us prove they cheated in Arizona either," pointed out Steve.

"True. But I think the machines were always a head fake. The mail in ballots are the key. Do you remember the magazine article a couple of elections ago? Where they pointed out exactly how they had harvested their way to victory, stuffing the ballot boxes by voting 'for' people. I think they perfected it in this election. But if we can't get the judges to give us the time we need, it doesn't matter. We won't get the chance to ask Eddie and Eva down at Green Acres if they voted. For the first time in twenty years? Even though the voter rolls say they did. Without that confirmation, we can't *prove* any fraud happened."

"Nick, this is so unfair. The fraud is right there for anyone to see. What if you went on Hibi and had a bunch of folks show up at City Hall saying they didn't vote and demand to see if they are listed as voting?" suggested Margie.

Nick shook his head as Steve answered.

"Problem is those voters, or non-voters, are not watching Hibi. Or probably TV at all. They're the homeless, in retirement homes, rural and unplugged or urban poor who couldn't care less about casting a vote," answered Steve with a sigh as he continued.

"Exactly the folks they are counting on to not make a stink if someone cast a ballot in their name. It is a great system if you have the manpower to make it work. It takes too much time to gather enough critical mass to prove fraud on a big enough scale to get the FBI to develop a PCI or a judge to approve the investigation."

As Steve finished, Nick stared at him and Earl asked, "What's a PCI?"

Steve smiled big. "Don't you guys watch TV? Potential Confidential Informant. Watch *Law and Order* or *FBI*, some time," he replied, shaking his head as the others laughed. Nick continued staring.

"What does this mean for our appeals?" asked Nick.

"We don't have any in Nevada since we won. So, all good there," replied Jenny, who had joined the group a while ago.

"For Arizona, like you said, we are focused on the audits of the ballots. Same problem as all the others. Like Pennsylvania and Georgia, we're waiting on the Supreme Court. Same with Michigan, but that appeal is two-fold, one on the mail in ballot audit around Detroit and the second to at least count our mail in ballots. They have accepted the one about counting of our ballots and we expect a ruling on that shortly. Michigan doesn't certify until next week, so it could conceivably come before or right after Thanksgiving.

Finally, we have the request at the Court of Appeals to force the FBI to hand down their ruling and turn over all the information they found in their investigation. We're hoping that can influence the Supreme Court decisions. No movement on that one yet, either.

"Thanks Jenny." Nick looked around the conference room. There were a few other staffers on laptops.

"What?" asked Denise.

"I hate standing around with nothing to do. I hate waiting."

The team laughed.

#

On Tuesday, the United States Supreme Court upheld the earlier rulings by the state supreme courts and the courts of appeals in the various districts regarding the Turner campaigns request to order audits of random samplings of ballots. They cited a lack of conclusive evidence to warrant the extra time and expense, as well as the imminent need to certify the votes to allow the election to be completed.

They watched the reporter on EXN read out the Supreme Court's one paragraph response.

"We knew it was a long shot," replied Nick, trying to stay upbeat. "Where does that leave us?"

"We still have pending appeals in Michigan to count your mail in ballots. Now that they have ruled against our audit requests in Pennsylvania, Michigan, and Georgia, we are going to need something more conclusive in Wisconsin and Arizona to appeal to them for those states. Barring any new information, it is all coming down to Michigan," finished Jenny.

#

The Federal Court of Appeals handling Michigan took the case their campaign filed regarding the FBI information. The Court requested the FBI simply cooperate rather than force them to issue a ruling.

On the Wednesday before Thanksgiving, the acting FBI Director Karen Coleman, gave a press conference where she explained they had indeed done an extensive investigation where they found witnesses who confirmed they had been hired to print the ballots and deliver them in the trucks not to destinations but to be on certain highways and particular points at a specific rendezvous time.

This confirmed what the FBI suspected. The ballots with Turner's name were never intended to be delivered to counting centers but to be found by the FBI to raise suspicions against Turner's campaign. They were continuing to investigate who was behind this fraudulent act, and would report when they had more information.

With this exoneration, Jenny immediately filed a request for the Michigan Supreme Court to rescind its ruling, preventing Turner's mail in ballots from being counted.

The Michigan Supreme court rescinded the moratorium on counting Nick's ballots near noon on the Wednesday before Thanksgiving. The Michigan board of elections issued a statement saying they would convene to retrieve and count the ballots on Monday after Thanksgiving, providing a final total before the Tuesday certification.

Chapter 47

Nick and his team celebrated in the early afternoon on Wednesday before he sent them home and to airports to enjoy the holiday weekend. He would call them in if necessary, if anything changed. Otherwise, he told them he'd see them on Monday. Earl went to Nebraska, having been invited by Jamie to join her family Thanksgiving celebration. She also extended the offer to Nick, who politely declined.

#

Nick was in his Senate office on Thanksgiving. He had the radio on playing one of the pro football games, but he was not paying much attention. He was staring through a magnifying glass, still reviewing the information Dan Jacobs had provided. Trying to decipher some of the blurry portions to discover what else about his past was now known.

He was startled at a knock on the open office door. The office was deserted, but he saw no reason to lock the main office door. Dolly stood in the doorway, a big smile on her face.

"Why am I not surprised? Chuck told me I could probably find you here."

"I'm gonna have to talk to the guard. Apparently, they'll let anyone in," commented Nick as he stood and walked toward her. She looked spectacular, wearing black leather pants, block heeled black ankle boots, and a cobalt blue turtleneck sweater, flattering her figure. Her brunette hair falling across her shoulders, revealing sapphire earrings matching her sweater. She had her arms crossed as she leaned against the door frame.

"I told the guard Chuck sent me to spring you from your exile. He gave me a pass and told me where to go. He also said you were the only person in the building other than him and a few other security guards."

They stood staring at each other, like two teenagers, awkward, not knowing what to do next.

"Have you eaten?" she asked.

"No. I figured I would microwave something," shrugged Nick in reply.

Dolly shook her head. She walked to Nick and took him by the arm. Starting to walk him out. Then she stopped. Looking him up and down in his jeans, dark dress shirt, and cowboy boots.

"Actually, you need at least a sport coat. You have one, right?" she asked with a twinkle, white teeth contrasting against her subtle pinkish-red lipstick.

"I could always wear my tux jacket," he offered back. "Where are we going? The rest of my outfit acceptable? Or do I need to primp up for our date?"

"Jeans and boots are the new chic. I bet you didn't know that, did you?"

"Crap. Then I should change to sweats and running shoes. I hate to be in style." He returned wearing a black sport coat, a replacement for the one the EMTs had cut off in Minneapolis. Linking his arm to hers, he started walking.

"You drive the GTO?" he asked hopefully.

"Sorry. Being chauffeured tonight. I want to have a glass of wine or a martini."

"Fair enough." Nick locked the office doors as they walked out of the Hart senate building. The guard smiled, clearly admiring Nick's companion as he told them to have a nice evening.

Dolly let out a laugh as they walked out of the building to the waiting car.

"What?"

"I wonder if he thinks I'm a high-priced call girl," she smirked, turning to Nick with a wicked look.

"Ha. If that's the case, you're way out of my price range. We can just add it to my growing list of scandals," grinned Nick back as they both laughed, getting into the car as the driver held the door.

#

"I guess I shouldn't be surprised you can get a private table for two in the most exclusive restaurant in DC on Thanksgiving," said Nick, smiling.

They'd arrived and walked through the crowded main dining room to a private table near the back of the only three star rated Michelin restaurant in DC. The entire room had followed them as they walked with the maitre'd. Many snapping photos with their phones.

Nick, as always, felt self-conscious at all the attention. He turned to Dolly. "You're enjoying this, aren't you?"

She turned and smiled. "You *are* the most interesting man in the world at the moment."

"God help us," replied Nick in all seriousness as they sat. He looked at the packed restaurant over the divider separating them from the main dining area, then back at Dolly, who was still smiling.

"Actually, I met Rene when I was at the Sorbonne, and he was at Le Cordon Bleu. We kept in touch and I helped him with his first restaurant." She leaned over with a conspirator's wink. "I'm a silent partner in all four of his restaurants."

"Ah, corruption. I love it. Beats the hell out of whatever microwaved processed food I would have heated."

"That is a very low bar."

"Speaking of bars..." winked Nick as first the waiter and then a man who appeared to be the chef approached. He was animated, speaking in French as they rose to greet him. He was about five foot four and kissed Dolly on both cheeks as she turned to introduce him to Nick.

"Rene Vachon, Senator Nick Turner," said Dolly in a lilting French accent that cause Nick to turn and look at her.

Rene had to crane his neck to look up at Nick, who stood a foot taller as he shook his hand.

"A pleasure to meet you, Senator. Welcome to my restaurant," he said in barely accented English.

"The pleasure is all mine and please call me Nick. I am sure I am about to have one of the best meals in my life," laughed Nick.

"One of? We'll have to see if it can be the best. What is the competition?"

"Well," said Nick in a dramatic voice, "I had some wonderful roasted goat in Afghanistan once."

"Nick!" blurted Dolly in a startled voice. The look on her face was one of anger and irritation.

Rene didn't bat an eye. "Chapli?"

Nick laughed and nodded. "I might also add, I had not eaten a proper meal in almost three weeks, so my standards were very low."

"Mutton, not goat, just so you know," continued Rene as Dolly looked at Nick, still clearly annoyed. Not finding the humor in his story.

"I see I have irritated my hostess. To answer your question deliberately. I had the chance to have a unique meal at French Laundry once. A friend of a friend knew Thomas Keller and invited us to a meal there. It took five and a half hours and twenty courses. I didn't know half of what I was eating, but I ate every bite. I am just glad it was not on my credit card. I was a lowly Navy officer back then."

Rene contemplated the info. Then he nodded. "Challenge accepted. You can let me know after who won."

As Rene left and the waiter returned with martinis, Nick raised his in a toast. "I apologize Dolly. I can't help but act like an ass around you. You make me nervous." He clinked her glass as she glared.

"Let me get this straight. You have a chest full of medals, including one that shows you were captured and escaped. You've been shot. I don't know how many times. Lord only knows what happened to your back. A sniper tried to kill you, someone poisoned you at my party, and I make you nervous?" She delivered this in a bewildered voice.

He shrugged.

"What can I say? It's the only explanation for the wise cracking teenager resurfacing. As the words leave my mouth, my brain says, WTF dickhead?"

Dolly nearly spit up her drink, she laughed so hard. Nick also laughed at her reaction, having successfully put them back at ease.

They bantered a bit more, as a series of courses of various exotic foods arrived. Tiny portions of sea urchin, quail eggs, little pieces of Wagyu beef, Osetra caviar, Langostino mac and cheese with grated white truffle, and exquisite lamb, among a host of other magnificent and exotic creations.

Presented in artistic elegance on each plate and delivered by four waiters. One to set down the plate, while another removed the cover simultaneously for each course for each of them.

After twelve courses of tiny appetizers and entrees and several splits of different wines to accompany the various samples, Nick again commented on this alien world.

"What I took away from that fancy meal in Napa and this one is the size of the dishwashers they must have. By my count, that is now over fifty pieces of porcelain crockery they have to wash. Multiply that by everyone in this restaurant, and they must have an army of dishwashers."

"Nick, you are a piece of work," laughed Dolly, shaking her head. "Anyone else would comment about the taste of the food, the presentation, the whole gastronomic experience, and you are worried about the amount of dishes needing washing?"

He smiled, taking a sip of a red they were now drinking. They went through a few more courses, including some wonderful desserts. As they brought the final Petit Fors, the waiter pointed out the various ingredients. One had pistachios. Nick made sure to give that one to Dolly without mentioning his allergy.

Rene wandered by as they were both drinking a final cognac to finish their meal.

"Well?"

"The other was a long time ago. I can now fully appreciate both the care and the effort put into each of those exquisite courses. I would have to say you are the winner," replied Nick to a beaming Rene. Dolly even gave a little clap.

"Excellent. I will tell Thomas the next time I see him," said Rene with a nod and a victorious smile.

As they sat swirling the remaining cognac, Dolly turned serious.

Nick, did Chuck mention my friend in France to you?

The surprised look on Nick's face told Dolly all she needed to know. "I am so sorry, Dolly. He mentioned it, and then the hits kept coming. I totally forgot about it. What do you need?" he asked, reaching out a hand to grab hers on the table.

"I don't actually know. He married my best friend from college. He was an Interpol detective."

"Was?"

She nodded. "His wife and daughter were gunned down in protective custody a few years ago, in broad daylight. I don't know why. I lost track of them and my relationship with Marie suffered when I had my bad times." Nick squeezed the hand he was still holding.

"I got a cryptic note by messenger from him. He said he needed to talk to you. That it could be a matter of life and death for potentially many." Nick looked skeptical.

Nick, you don't know Luc. He is not prone to dramatics at all. His sister is married to the President of France. If he can't take this to him, it must be important.

He was now intrigued. Someone with connections like that and a history that cost him his family reaching out to an old friend rather than his brother-in-law, the President of France?

"How do I contact him?"

Dolly handed him a note.

"The phone number is at the bottom. Nick, I know you have a lot on your mind, but I can't imagine Luc would reach out if it was not important."

"I will contact him tomorrow. Promise."

"Thank you."

"No, thank you for getting me out of the office. This was a wonderful surprise. Not in a million years would I have expected to be sitting here after such a wonderful meal with you on Thanksgiving. I am truly thankful."

She smiled back.

They left the restaurant, once again stared at and photographed by an entirely different set of patrons as all the tables had turned over at least once since their arrival three hours before.

They sat in the car during the ride from the restaurant. Holding hands with her head on his shoulder. Each thinking about why the other was not making any move. Two proud and stubborn people. Nick was sure he could offer Dolly nothing but uncertainty and, even possibly, peril. Dolly sure that she could offer Nick stability and something to live for. Yet her pride prevented her. She would not throw herself at him again.

As the car stopped in front of the Hart building. Nick turned to her beautiful face, eyes mischievously staring back. Her red lips turned up in a slightly lopsided smile. He leaned in to kiss her, lingering longer than he should have. Squeezing her hands with his, he turned to go.

"Nick, remember what I said. The clock is ticking," she told him with a hesitant smile.

"I do. Every word. Thank you again." He shut the car door and tapped on the roof as he walked toward the darkened Hart building and his uncomfortable Murphy bed. Alone, as always.

#

Nick woke with his phone buzzing. He looked at it. 3:39am. The text was from Chuck. `Turn on EXN`. Nick reached for the remote, turning on the TV. He was greeted with a scene of what appeared to be an enormous fire in an industrial part of a town.

He got out of bed and turned up the volume, standing and looking at the screen. There were lots of fire trucks pouring water from aerials onto the roof of a line of warehouses. Nick had a sinking feeling when his phone started ringing. It was Earl.

"I assume this is what I think it is?"

"It is," replied Earl groggily. "My watchers said the fire started in the paint supply warehouse next door. By the time the fire trucks arrived, it had already spread to the warehouse next door where both the voting machines and mail in ballots are being stored. The fire even spread to the warehouse on the other side, where giant rolls of paper were being stored."

"There's no way they can put this out. *All* the paper mail in ballots, including your uncounted ones, are being burned to a crisp," explained Earl. "I'm sorry Nick."

"Are we really surprised?"

"No, but it seemed we were right on the brink. Now we will never know."

"Earl, we know and so do 83 million others. That's all that matters. Remember that. Get your surveillance teams to review their footage and see if there is anything suspicious in or around the paint warehouse we have on film before the fire. At least we can see if we can find any proof of arson."

"Will do."

"How was Thanksgiving?"

In the background he heard a female voice groggily asking if everything was OK?

Nick laughed. "I guess that answers that. Say hello to Jamie for me. In the morning. Good night, Earl."

"I will," said Earl, chuckling.

#

Nick answered further texts from Chuck, Denise, and Jenny. He told them all to go back to sleep and they could catch up in the morning. There was nothing any of them could do to turn back time.

#

As Friday morning rolled around, the Secretary of State for Michigan, Alicia Carr, yet another Pavlovich funded progressive, held a press conference.

"As you have no doubt heard, early this morning, the warehouse next door to where we had stored the voting machines and paper ballots, both counted and the uncounted mail in ballots of Senator Turner, caught fire. Because of the volatility of the materials stored there, the fire grew quickly and spread to our warehouse. The fire was too much for all the fire companies and aerial pumpers to contain, even though they called out every piece of equipment available in a 5th alarm."

She looked down at her notes, continuing. "The fire even spread to the warehouse on the other side of our election storage warehouse. Sadly, all our machines and the ballots were destroyed in the fire. Because of this, we no longer have the ballots, nor any idea how many were uncounted for Senator Turner. While this is an unfortunate disaster beyond our control, we have no choice but to certify our vote on Tuesday, with the current totals."

"Why were Turner's ballots not counted before now?" asked Keith from the local NWN affiliate.

"We did not bother to count them for two reasons. First, the state Supreme Court had disallowed them from being tabulated. Second, we did not want to risk a leak of how many potential votes might have been cast, to be used as leverage or to incite potential violence against our poll workers by Senator Turner's radical followers."

"And yet, if you had, it would be merely a simple task to disclose the count. Now, we will never truly know who won the election in the state of Michigan," accused Ned Wheeler from EXN.

"We do know who won. Based on the legal ballots at the time of the election, the Vice President is the legitimate winner. The fact the fire consumed Turner's and everyone else's ballots is irrelevant in the scheme of things, since nothing can be done to undo this," she replied in a righteous tone.

"Do you not find this convenient?" pushed Ned.

"I'm sorry, is there a question there? I don't see how a fire doing tens of millions of dollars of damage, and injuring several brave firefighters, can be construed as convenient. I believe we are done here. Let's let everyone get back to enjoying their holiday weekend. We will certify Michigan's election results on Tuesday. Thank you."

#

Lexi typed out a text on her phone to Mel, `excellent`.

He typed back, `relax & enjoy your weekend` with a smiley face.

`I am`. She typed as she put her phone down and rolled over in the bed to look into the smiling face of Roland Gill.

Chapter 48

Luc stood in his tiny fifth-floor apartment room. He'd rented it for a month when he'd snuck back into Paris a few days prior. It was in a cramped part of Paris, with centuries old four and five-story buildings. Far from the tourists and mostly filled with immigrants, it was perfect for his needs.

He paced back and forth from the room to the small balcony, holding the phone up to get a better signal. The balcony was about half a meter deep and one wide. With a low stone balustrade, his first thought was how this had to violate the building codes. A small child could easily topple over to the street below. Then he smiled. He doubted these buildings saw many code enforcement inspectors.

Looking down, the street below was a mass of small cheap Italian and French cars parked nose first into the sidewalk on both sides of the street. Many were even parked up onto the narrow sidewalk. There was barely enough room for a single car to pass between on the street behind.

Increasingly, scooters seemed to be the primary mode of travel as they buzzed up and down the street with blaring nasal horns and occasional epithets spewed in many languages from drivers and passengers alike.

All this noise and the smells of too many people living too close together, overwhelming antiquated sewer systems, wafted into the room from his half-open balcony door.

He turned back inside, glancing down at the single bar of service as he reentered the apartment, closing the door against the late November cold.

#

Luc was becoming increasingly paranoid. Sure he was being followed and on the verge of discovery. He'd hidden the USB drive Annie had provided. Sending word via weekly food deliveries to the convent in Dijon, he'd notified Sister Therese to move Annie and not tell him or anyone else where this was. He also gave her something to give to Annie with a clue only she would understand about where he had hidden the drive and the Doctor's original notes and files.

The copies he kept in his backpack had more to do with plans rather than the past and none of the Doctor's notes about *Daboia* or Turner.

With this complete, he'd had no choice except to reach out to his sister Madeline. He could only assume Dolly had failed to get Turner's attention. Reluctantly, he decided he must use his brother-in-law. He'd explained the situation briefly to Madeline.

He also contacted Gabi. He was not entirely sure why he did this, but he needed to talk to someone he could trust. He knew she truly cared about what would happen to Annie if something happened to *him*.

Waiting for a call back from both women, he paced the room, staring at the phone signal bars. Madeline was arranging a meeting with Chaumont. Gabi was arranging a meet to discuss what she knew about de Monfort and the hunt for Luc.

As he contemplated what else he could do, his phone vibrated in his hand. He answered, but there was no one on the phone, the call having dropped. Quickly, he opened the balcony door, to be immediately assaulted by the road noise, smells, and a blast of cold air.

Pacing the tiny space, holding up the phone, staring at the bars to see where the service showed the strongest. He leaned out, holding the phone as four service bars appeared. Finally.

The phone vibrated once more. As he made to move the phone to his ear, he was hit between the shoulder blades. His center of gravity was beyond the balconies' stone railing. Dropping the phone, he windmilled his arm, trying to catch his balance, turning toward the door to the balcony.

Just as he regained his balance, another blow to his shoulder toppled him over the edge of the railing. He grasped at the railing in vain with one hand, finding no handhold. As he fell the five stories to the pavement below, he looked up into the eyes of the face staring back at him. His own widened in recognition as his world went black.

#

In the room, the gloved hands of Luc's assailant gathered up his backpack and quickly scanned the room, finding no other belongings. As they turned to leave, the phone lying on the stone floor of the balcony vibrated loudly.

Picking it up, the caller recognized an international country code and a US area code. They did not answer. Placing it in the backpack and quickly exiting the room as sirens wailed outside.

#

"It is done."

Maksim Pavlovich nodded while listening to the encrypted voice on the other side of the connection.

"How? Where?"

"Paris. Just a few minutes ago. He was careless and left a phone on after using it. We had tapped the phones of those we thought he might try to contact."

"Did they recover the Doctor's notes?"

"Yes. There was a backpack full of files and papers they retrieved. It will be on its way to you shortly."

"Good. We will see just what the good Doctor has been committing to paper against our direction. How is our candidate holding up?"

"Worried. There are too many loose ends and Turner is a formidable opponent. He refuses to react as any politician would. Or even as any *normal* person would to all the injustice he is experiencing."

"This is a very dangerous situation. Our plans are progressing regardless. How are you doing about eliminating the potential threats?"

"It is ongoing. I have to rely on others, just as in Paris. This worries me and is not the best use of my skills."

"Patience *Daboia*. Soon enough, you will be back on the pitch."

#

Nick ended the phone call again. He'd been trying for hours now to get through to the number Dolly had provided with no success. There was also no message set up for the phone, not that he would have risked leaving one.

He'd try again tomorrow, but if there was no luck, he'd have to tell Dolly he could not make contact. It would not be from lack of trying. He owed her that much for not doing it sooner. Perhaps her friend had gone to the President Chaumont with his concerns, after all.

Chapter 49

Michigan certified their vote as expected on Tuesday after Thanksgiving. The team sat around the conference room in Nick's campaign HQ, yet again going through all the options. There were few left. Jer came into the room and turned the TV on. Everyone looked up at him in confusion.

"Watch. This was an hour ago."

"I'm Evelyn Krakowski. I am a canvasser in Dane county, Wisconsin," said a woman standing at the podium. She moved aside and an older man, probably well into his 60s stepped up.

"I'm Myles Adams, I too am a Dane county election canvasser. Evelyn and I are the two voters chosen to certify the election, along with the county clerk. We have called this press conference today to tell the public, neither of us is comfortable certifying this election result."

"Both Evelyn and I have reviewed random samplings of the ballots. We have discovered in that sample, mail in ballots supposedly cast by residents of the county whom we know personally. We also know they did not send in a mail in ballot. Because of this, we are not confident in the integrity of the ballots cast and we would request a larger investigation be completed to ensure we are not unlawfully certifying fraudulent votes," finished Myles.

"Sir, how many of these votes did you see for yourself" asked the local reporter from News3, the local LN1 affiliate.

"Myself, I saw seven I could verify with residents of the county I know. Six of them did not vote, and the seventh voted in person. Evelyn?" said Myles.

"I found five in my cursory look and all five people I contacted did not send in mail in ballots. Two of them voted in person, the other three did not vote at all," reported Evelyn.

"Excuse me, but you are talking about twelve votes. How many ballots did you examine to find these twelve?" asked NWN15's reporter.

"For me, less than 100. A 7% discrepancy, and those were the only ones I knew personally, out of the hundred. I don't claim to know all of our half a million Dane county residents," said Myles.

He could see the skeptical looks on the faces of the reporters.

"I was an insurance actuary before I retired. A 7% deviation on a sampling of 100 is off the charts and would result in any series being thrown out and rerun for accuracy. This is like your airplane engine stalling 7 times out of 100 flights. Highly improbable if you want to stay in business."

"I only looked at 50 and found five people I knew who had not sent in votes. This raised the red flag for me," agreed Evelyn.

A man in a suit, balding with a paunch, stepped to the podium.

"I am the county clerk, Arthur Edmundson. I want to go on record stating I do not agree, nor support their findings. Nor their request for further review of the mail in ballots cast. We are exploring our legal options to relieve them of their duties for failing to complete this effort and potentially risking the certification of the State of Wisconsin outcome for the Presidential election. The local Party has already filed suit against Dane county to force us to certify our vote. We will contact you when we have further updates."

"Looks like trouble in river city," smiled Chuck.

"I'll say. How long do you give them?" asked Nick.

"Since they only need to intimidate one into changing. End of the day," guessed Jenny. "My money is on the gal since she is the Party representative on the committee."

"Anything we can do to help or support them? The Opposition isn't going to since it only helps me."

"We can issue a statement saying we applaud their bravery and every American should want to do everything possible to ensure the count and the ballots cast are all legal and correct," suggested Margie.

"Sounds good. Let's get it out there," remarked Nick.

#

"Oh, good lord, what is it now?" asked Lexi

"Nothing we can't handle. A couple of canvassers in Wisconsin refusing to certify their votes. We'll have them replaced in due time. Don't worry about it."

"Then why are you here?"

"California," answered Mel.

"What is wrong in California other than my not winning a state which has been reliably Party for the last 40 years? asked Lexi archly.

"Orange County is becoming problematic."

Lexi shrugged. "We already lost there. What is the issue?"

"They're going to invalidate a large batch of the mail in ballots the harvesters provided. Some enterprising local precinct manager saw things getting tight for you and tried to help by marking the harvested ballots for the congressional races with presidential votes."

Lexi laughed. "I applaud their initiative, but by then, it was too late."

"Sadly, they didn't think it through. The problem is they used different colored pens on the same ballots and then reran ballots they had previously counted. This bumped them out for review. By itself this would have been ok, but they adjudicated all the duplicate votes to you. Also, double counting the votes for the Party congressional candidates."

"There were too many Opposition poll watchers, and we failed to keep them far enough away. Apparently, someone saw the different colors in the ink and got an Opposition judge to impound the ballots and demand a hand recount. When they saw blue ink and black on the same ballots, let's just say we don't have a suitable answer for that one," finished Mel.

"Meaning what, we lose some more votes? Won't make a difference," shrugged Lexi.

"It is going to cost us six seats in the house," explained Mel.

"What?" blurted Lexi.

"All six of the seats we flipped are going back to the Opposition. If things hold, we'll only have a three-seat majority in the house and 51/49 in the Senate. Right now, it is 51/48 with Bank's vacancy. Governor Carson will get to appoint a Senator and she'll choose an Opposition replacement until they hold a special election. At least we will get back to a reliable 51 once we swear in Turner's replacement. If we hold together, we can still get your agenda passed," assured Mel.

"This is not turning out quite like we planned, is it?"

"No, but we are almost there. As soon as we can get these recounts complete and the states certified, things will once again start progressing on plan."

"The sooner the better. Make it happen Mel, or Roland will, whether we like it or not," she said, resigned, not threatening. Mel understood completely.

#

"I support Mrs. Krakowski's stance for honesty and transparency," said Nick as he stood giving a press conference. "What I do not support is what has happened to her. From the moment she announced she would not certify the Dane County vote because of irregularities. She's been relentlessly vilified in the press."

"Her house has been picketed non-stop, including loud music and other noise throughout the night. No one in her house or those of her neighbors could sleep. Her husband's place of employment also has demonstrators outside. It seems some enterprising young reporter contacted someone in the County courthouse who was all too willing to dox Mrs. Krakowski for daring to ask for validation of the integrity of Wisconsin voting systems," accused Nick, letting his words sink in.

"To make matters worse, the schools of her children were disclosed and the most disgusting of all was the diatribe one of her daughters, a mere 7th grader, had to endure from one of her teachers. Explaining how her mother was a traitor to the cause and many other horrible things no 7th grader should have to hear. Certainly not about their mother. And not in front of a classroom full of her classmates." Nick's tone showed his disgust with the entire episode.

"There appear to be some decent people in the Dane County school system because at least they have suspended the offending teacher. She is, of course, being rewarded with appearances on most of your networks, acting as if she is the one being persecuted. Her implication is only Opposition or my supporter's cheat. The Party would never stoop to any fraud, regardless of the facts we see before our eyes. The teacher's union is jumping to her defense. For verbally abusing a twelve-year-old? How is this *ever* defensible from a teacher?"

"Irregularities occurred. Instead of embracing this and opening an investigation to understand the ballots in question, the entire efforts of Dane County, of Wisconsin, and the state Attorney General have been focused on removing Mrs. Krakowski from her position as an election canvasser."

"What makes this worse is she is a lifelong Party member. She voted for the Vice President in this election. She has volunteered and worked tirelessly to get the Party elected in Wisconsin. For years. It is pretty clear, the Party is not concerned with the truth. They are not concerned with free and fair elections. Only winning. I spoke to Mrs. Krakowski. I told her while I appreciate her effort to force transparency, it was not worth the well-being of her family when her party, her county, her state, and frankly, her country were not willing to stand behind her."

"They have focused on Mrs. Krakowski because it only takes two to certify, one canvasser and the clerk. Putting pressure on her to change her vote and agree to certify or to resign. Then they can replace her with a reliable sycophant who cares little for transparency and truth and only rubber stamps what their Progressive Party leaders tell them too."

Nick spoke with passion, articulating his points clearly. Lexi and American *Pravda* were already ignoring the story, relegating it to the back pages. The full press conference would only be shown on EXN and the 2J's. The truth no longer mattered, if it ever had.

#

A day later, Nick was once again standing in front of a gaggle of reporters and news cameras.

"Well, I want to congratulate every one of you here today. Put another notch in your cameras and your microphones. You have canceled another honest American," he was barely controlling his anger.

"You should pat yourself on your back. You have destroyed her and her husband's lives. They have both lost their jobs now. Their oldest daughter is now in the hospital, recovering from an attempted suicide last night. The relentless cyber bullying because of your coverage and amplification on the social media sewer were too much for her fifteen-year-old mind to handle."

"Evelyn has finally capitulated. She resigned. Her conscience wouldn't let her vote to certify an election she *knows* is fraudulent. I want each of you to go home and look in the mirror. Especially those with teenage children. This could have been your child. In fact, one day it probably will. I want you to look at and ask that reflection. Is this journalism, or is this the action of a black shirt working for a Progressive totalitarian regime? You are doing their dirty work."

"Mrs. Krakowski is not the problem. You are. Remember this as you continue to turn in your stories and sit their under the lights and read their propaganda to the nation's soon to be subjects. Explaining to them how giving up a few freedoms will lead to a better and safer life. The life *they* want you to live, not the life *you* choose to live. I commend you for your ability to destroy one woman, one family, for standing up for the truth. Well done," finished Nick, his voice dripping disdain and sarcasm as he looked at the press corp. None of them seemed the slightest bit remorseful of their part in ruining her life.

"Senator, there is no proof of any election fraud. Despite all the statements you make alluding to it, there is in fact no proof," said Meg, the RBS news reporter. "We have to prevent others from standing up and making baseless accusations."

"Really? Are you that clueless? Even in the few ballots they saw, there is fraud," said Nick, getting worked up. "That was the entire purpose of the complaint by Mrs. Krakowski. If I had won Wisconsin and these were *my* ballots being questioned. The FBI would be onsite, seizing every ballot and broadcasting the review of each one as if this were Florida and the 2000 election again. There is not more proof, because the election officials refuse to review the ballots. It is hard to have more proof of fraud if the election officials refuse access to ballots, now isn't it?" asked Nick. "Where has common sense gone?"

"Senator, it is easy to make these statements, knowing they will not be corroborated because there is no fraud and therefore no reason to review the ballots. You are free to make all the accusations you want, casting doubt on the state of Wisconsin and all those who have worked to ensure a free and fair election," responded NWN's reporter. "You cost that woman her livelihood, not us. By encouraging her to come forth because of your endless assault on the integrity of our voting systems."

Margie, standing behind Nick, could see him gripping the podium. She wished Earl was with her. He might keep Nick from reacting. She could not.

Nick shook his head and laughed, bottling up his anger.

"Let me get this straight. According to your twisted logic, you think I am making these claims, only because I know the people who are cheating will allow no one to see the ballots? To disprove me. Is that right?" asked Nick.

"No, Senator, the election officials know their systems are honest and true. They are not going to start a precedent of allowing review of every ballot every time a losing candidate says there was cheating," sneered NWN.

"Lest we forget, let's not discount the over 5000 affidavits we have received from the six swing states of less than honest activity. Similar to what Mrs. Krakowski detailed. These are from other workers in precincts, counting locations, and poll watchers." Nick noticed several cameras were now off, as was typical of all his press conferences now.

"These have been discounted by you and by your election officials. And many of these are from the Party. Just honest folks not blinded by political allegiance. Let's not forget the apparent attempt to frame me in Michigan that resulted in my mail in ballots not being counted on election night and then conveniently being burned up in a fire that is now being classified, surprise, surprise, as an arson investigation."

"This is a *Party* canvasser who risked her life and livelihood to bring this potential election fraud to visibility. She didn't do it for me. She did it for you," pointed Nick at the camera angrily. "How can you continue to claim this is all partisan complaining? What are *you* afraid of? That I am right?"

"Senator, what do you have to say about taking advantage of homeless people to go out and harvest your ballots in California and elsewhere?" asked Meg, clearly getting orders to change the subject.

"Does anyone have a question about how Mrs. Krakowski was treated or what has happened to her family?" asked Nick. "Which, by the way, is the topic of this press conference. Or her oldest daughter's attempted suicide?"

The silence that greeted Nick was deafening. Then all the reporters started shouting other questions at him. He looked at them with a look of disgust, turned his back, and walked away.

The story blasted on social media and replayed non-stop on American *Pravda* would be Turner fleeing because of the tough questions regarding his use of Blue Morpho's homeless, and the rebuttal of his cheating accusations. Not the treatment of Mrs. Krakowski or her daughter.

#

As Margie and Chuck caught up to him, he was seething. As they got in a Suburban to drive back to the campaign HQ, Nick turned to Chuck.

"Get hold of Coach. Make sure the Krakowski's are taken care of. If they want, put them to work in Blue Morpho. We would welcome people with these principles. If they want to move, let's make sure we help. Use the TRDF if they'll accept it," ordered Nick.

"Will do. I am sure they will. Their life in Madison is over."

"What's up Margie?" asked Nick, looking at Margie, who sat dejected.

"Nick, they really didn't care at all that they destroyed that woman and her family. There was no remorse in that audience. Have we really gone that far as a country that we wish harm on any who don't think the way they do?"

Nick shook his head, not replying.

"I don't want to live here if this is where we are. Not a single one of those reporters considers anything they did to be other than what was right and necessary. If it meant the end of the livelihood of that family or the potential loss of their daughter to suicide, they felt it was justified. *'They should have known what would happen if they dared to question the fairness of the voting systems. They got what they deserved',*" said Margie, shaking her head. "How can anyone believe or write that? How can they say that is right? What has happened to these people?" she started to cry as she reached for her bag and a tissue.

Nick leaned over from his front seat and patted Margie on an arm as she cried.

"Margie, there is much to lose on their part. They've been brainwashed into believing the Progressive agenda is the only salvation for our hopelessly compromised country. They are true believers. If we win and they lose, their entire reason for being ceases. There is a faction in the Opposition who believe the same. They just don't control the media megaphone," explained Nick.

"It's the same mentality that allowed the German people to not bat an eye as the Nazis rounded up the Jews, who they claimed were persecuting *them*. These were their friends and neighbors. But the propaganda and lies overcame common sense then too. Many of the progressive followers of Lexi now believe they are the ones being persecuted and anything done to their 'enemies' or to enable them to 'win' is not only justified, but done in self-preservation. It really is more akin to a fundementalist religion than a political view or party now. Any with a different *belief* is a mortal enemy to the cause. Because it is religion, you also cannot rationalize with them. Facts do not trump fanaticism."

Margie was shaking her head as she blew her nose and wiped her tears away.

Chapter 50

Nick looked around his senate office. He had already packed up what was non-essential. His office was spartan before, but now it was bleak. He got up and went to his coffee machine.

He pushed the start button and heard the reassuring whir of the grind as it made him another coffee. This machine was dependable. How many thousands of cups of coffee had it made for him in his time in the Senate? Soon it would make coffee for a former senator, presidential candidate, and unemployed college professor.

There was a knock at the door. Carla stood in the door.

"Senator, you have a couple of visitors. They are not on the calendar," said Carla, cautiously.

Nick could see Hobson, Senator Bank's valet, standing behind his aide.

"Thanks Carla. Hobson, come on in. My calendar is not nearly as full as it once was," said Nick, getting up to offer Hobson a handshake.

Hobson came in, trailed by a middle-aged man with a briefcase.

"Hello Senator. This is Mr. Wilkes. He is Senator Bank's barrister," said Hobson, looking around at the non-descript office.

"I am a lawyer, Hobson. I have told you time and time again, I am not a barrister. There actually is a difference," sighed Wilkes.

"Nice to meet you, Mr. Wilkes," Nick shook his hand.

"Take a seat, please. What can I do for you gentlemen?"

"Mr. Turner, Senator Banks' Will has been probated and I am here to read it for you," explained Mr. Wilkes.

"Really? He already gave me a book. That was more than enough," laughed Nick. Wilkes raised an eyebrow. Hobson had a big smile on his face, his crooked teeth betraying his British pedigree.

Wilkes held out the paper to read and looked at Nick.

"Senator Banks had no family, having been preceded in death by his wife, Penelope, and their only daughter, Priscilla, who was also childless. As such, he has done several things. He set up a trust fund to take care of Mr. Hobson," said Wilkes, glancing at Hobson.

"I would have expected no less. How long were you with him, Hobson?" asked Nick, interrupting.

"Over 20 years, Senator," answered Hobson.

"What will you do now?"

"That depends."

"On what?" asked Nick.

"You. Please carry on, Mr. Wilkes," said Hobson in his clipped British accent.

"As I was saying, Senator, after taking care of Hobson, Senator Banks has left everything else he has to you."

Nick sat in disbelief.

"Excuse me?"

Nick looked at Hobson, who was smiling even more broadly, genuinely happy Nick was the sole beneficiary.

"Yes, Senator. I assume you were unaware of this arrangement?" asked Wilkes, seeing Nick's genuine expression.

"That would be an understatement. What exactly am I inheriting?"

"The house in Chevy Chase, a seaside villa in Florida, a family estate in South Carolina on Hilton Head Island and, of course, the paper mill and slightly more than one million acres of Carolina timber. Further, he has bequeathed all the antiques, automobiles, furniture, artwork and, of course, all of his possessions, including his prized library," read Wilkes, turning pages.

"He has donated 25% of his cash and securities to various charities. The value of the remaining 75% of securities, investments, and cash is bequeathed to you in a trust to minimize the tax implications. As of yesterday, the value of these cash and cash equivalents and all the investments, *not* including any of the real estate, the paper mill, or personal property, is approximately $87 million," finished Mr. Wilkes.

"What?" responded Nick disbelievingly.

"I have already started the process of having all the deeds reissued in your name and all the various funds transferred to your ownership. The taxes have already been paid, so the $87 million is a post estate tax cash amount," said Mr. Wilkes.

Nick sat in shock at these revelations as Wilkes continued.

"The mill and the corporation managing this are in a blind trust with you as the owner, but not the managing trustee. This is to prevent any conflict of interest while you are running for President. If you are not elected, you can, of course, take over as the active trustee as they serve at your pleasure. The value of this is several hundred million dollars. Do you have any questions?"

"I have so many questions. Unfortunately, the person I want to interrogate can no longer answer. Hobson, help me out here. What the hell is this?"

"Senator, it is Senator Bank's wish for you to continue to be the steward of his family business ventures, his property, and most importantly, his library," expressed Hobson.

"Will you stay on?" asked Nick, dumbfounded by the entire proceeding.

"It would be my pleasure Sir," replied Hobson, with a slight bow.

"Only one rule. Call me Nick."

"Not a problem Senator" said Hobson, making it clear it he would not be calling him Nick any time soon.

"This is unbelievable."

"Not if you knew him, Senator. This is totally within his character, trust me. Shall you be staying the night at the estate?" asked Hobson.

"Not yet. I will come by soon though, so you can give me the tour. Have you taken care of all his clothes and things like that?" asked Nick.

"Yes, his personal possessions that are not heirlooms or something he would pass to you, have been taken care of," replied Mr. Wilkes, in an official tone.

"This was certainly a surprise," said Nick, rising to shake both their hands.

"See you soon, Senator," smiled Hobson.

"Hobson, what is your first name? asked Nick.

"Henry."

"Would you mind if I call you Henry?"

"That would be fine, Senator."

\#

Nick sat in his office, contemplating his future. Banks had certainly given him much to think about.

Chuck knocked and entered. Nick waved him over.

"You OK? You look like you saw a ghost."

Nick laughed. "Well buddy, if your parents ever kick you out of the townhouse, let me know. I seem to now have a nice place in Chevy Chase."

"You bought a house here? Great. About time you stop sleeping on this stupid bookcase bed," said Chuck, glancing at the Murphy bed in the wall.

"Not exactly."

"What is that supposed to mean?" asked Chuck, confused.

"It seems Banks took more of a shine to me than even I knew. Must have been the son he never had or something like that."

"What? He left you his house in Chevy Chase? That has to be worth a fortune. Being in the original upper crust section," noted Chuck whistling.

"And a villa in Florida, an estate in Hilton Head and oh yeah, his family pulp and paper business with around a million acres of timber," said Nick in a deadpan voice.

"Are you shitting me?" said Chuck, slapping his legs and laughing. "Unbelievable. You are the luckiest SOB on the planet."

"It's not funny."

"You're right. Not only is it not funny, it is also amazing. What are you going to do?

"Nothing. I am going to keep doing what I am doing. Nothing is going to change. But at least I will now have a bed to sleep in when I'm in town."

"Well, it is sure exciting hanging around with you. I'll give you that," quipped Chuck.

"What's up?" asked Nick, remembering Chuck came in for a reason.

"Do you want good news or bad?"

"Bad of course."

"There is no way we can get enough evidence of fraud in either Arizona or Georgia to build a case the Supreme Court in either state could use to contest the certification of the votes for Lexi."

"Just as we thought. They cheated, but they did it so well it is going to be impossible to convince a court in the time we have. I'll give them credit. They knew this going in and played to run out the clock. Slowing us down with frivolous suits, but ones that took time to resolve," nodded Nick, fully understanding the implications.

"What will you do?"

"Live to fight another day. This is not the time or place to go to battle with her. She has the high ground and superiority of force with the courts on her side. We only have public opinion, powerful but raw, and I don't want to waste that advantage on a battlefield of her choosing," said Nick, shaking his head.

"More Sun Tzu?" asked Chuck, smiling

"Of course," smiled Nick. "You said you had good news."

"Other than you being rich, the Supreme Court of California can't avoid the obvious signs of fraud in Orange County and is taking the case to review the ballots there. It could cost the party up to six seats they flipped," said Chuck.

"That's good for the country if not for me directly,"

"Too little too late," agreed Chuck.

"You giving up?"

"Aren't you?"

"No. There is still the chance some of Blackbird's states will vote the way their constituents want. There is still a chance," responded Nick.

"Okay," said Chuck, drawing it out. "In case it doesn't go our way, what next?"

"We cross that bridge when we get to it, okay?"

"Fair enough. What are you going to do with all that money?" asked Chuck.

"Nothing. I am going to act like it never happened."

"Good luck with that," said Chuck, laughing. "By the way, that probably makes you one of the richest members of Congress. With money comes responsibility," smiled Chuck.

"That's why I always tried to not have any. And only for another few weeks, then I'm out," laughed Nick.

"Have you seen Denise? We had some meetings this afternoon. She didn't show. I thought maybe she was with you."

"No, I haven't seen her all day," answered Nick. "You try her phone?"

"I did. It keeps going to voice mail. I'm worried."

Nick pulled out his phone and dialed. He waited. Suddenly he heard, "Hello" but it sounded different.

"Denise, is that you? You OK? It's Nick."

"Nick, you have to believe I am sorry. I am sooo sorry," said Denise, slightly slurring her words. It was clear to Nick she'd been drinking.

"Denise. What's wrong? Have you been drinking?" At this last remark, Chuck looked up in concern.

"Denise, where are you? Chuck and I will come get you."

"You can't. There is something I have to do. You can't stop me," she said, hanging up the phone.

Nick looked at his phone, but Denise had ended the call.

Chapter 51

Lexi sat on a park bench at the small park where she'd met Denise every month. Her secret service detail was nearby, but not on top of her at her own request. They did not greet each other as Denise sat at the end of the bench. Lexi noticed her friend looked a little rough, almost as if she'd been crying. She also thought she detected the smell of alcohol.

"You, OK?" asked Lexi.

"You know I am not," replied Denise hoarsely.

"Geez, Denise, did you fall off the wagon?" said Lexi, turning slightly to face her.

"Yes, I did. You sicced that bitch Bergamo on me. She called me, telling me she was doing an exposé. You are the only person who knows the things she asked me about. How could you do this? How could you betray me after all I have done for you?" asked Denise, upset.

"I have no idea what you are talking about. You need to pull it together. I didn't ask you to do anything. You're the one who told me about Kevin and Greg. You're the one who provided me with the info on the campaign. You did this of your own free will. I didn't do any of this to you," replied Lexi calmly.

Denise laughed. "Lexi, you have always been a piece of work. Was any of it real? Ever? You told me you loved me once. Was that a lie as well?"

"Denise, we were young. Those were heady days, pulling all nighters, working on the campaign. The attraction was real then. We both enjoyed it, right? But that was all it was, a fling. We both moved on to bigger and better things."

"We sure did. You used me to introduce you to Governor Whitson, who you then slept with and blackmailed to get your entry into California politics. Starting your rise to the top from your back," she snarled. "Throwing people under the bus and driving over everyone else who got in the way."

"Denise, this is getting boring. Do you have something for me? And lest you forget, it was me who held your hand when you had your daughter. It sure as shit wasn't fucking Rhett Bentley Chadwick IV, now was it?" Denise glared as Lexi continued.

"Don't you forget I was there when you needed me. When you washed out and hit rock bottom. I was there to get you into rehab and get that DUI reduced. Don't accuse me of using people. I take care of my friends and I destroy my enemies. You became the enemy when you hooked up with Turner. You should have stayed in New Mexico. You made the choice when you came back. I didn't," said Lexi, coldly.

"Lexi, I know you gave Bergamo the info. Just like you gave the info on Blackbird to Beverly. You're the only one who knows about our relationship. Only you know about my affair with Rhett. You were there when I had my daughter and gave her up for adoption. It was you who used this to force me to give you information on Nick's campaign and his people," accused Denise.

"You forgot all the other things only I know. Let's see, heroin, cocaine, how many abortions and, of course, the many, many drunken benders where only your good ole buddy Lexi stood by you. And let's not forget the 'accident'. You remember, the one that should have been manslaughter? You know how hard I worked back in those days to get all those incidents expunged from your records? So you could continue to work and manage election campaigns?"

Denise stared at her as she continued.

"You're a great campaign manager during the fight of the election. But you are a fucking colossal train wreck any other time. You need to be put in cold storage between elections. In between, you were a menace, thankfully mostly to yourself," said Lexi, shaking her head. "Do you have anything for me or not?"

"What you did with my info and how you allowed your media cronies to bully Kevin into accusing Greg, that is unforgivable. You have convinced yourself you're on some sort of crusade. How you are the savior. You are not. You are evil personified, and I will not let you destroy Nick and this country. I was weak. Not anymore," she said, sticking her hand in her coat pocket. Denise wrapped her hand around the contents of her pocket.

"Whoa Denise, hang on a minute here. Think about what you're doing," said Lexi, looking at her bulging hand in the coat.

"You know I liked it better when you went by Alex. Lexi is so bitchy sounding," commented Denise. "You know, one question people always ask, if you could meet Hitler in 1932, and you had the chance to kill him. To stop the holocaust from happening, could you do it? This is my chance."

Lexi had been making a sign with her hand. Her secret service approached, guns drawn, telling Denise to put her hands up. Denise turned back to Lexi and smiled. The sound of a shot rang out. The rest of the Secret Service surrounded Lexi and literally picked her up and threw her into the back of the Suburban as they drove away.

Two secret service agents stood over the body of Denise Rojas. A single bullet hole in her temple revealed the destination of the shot. One agent reached into her pocket, expecting to find a gun. Instead, he pulled out a crumpled set of documents wrapped around some photos. The agent looked up at his companion.

"Shit. She was unarmed," said the agent. "What do we do?"

The Vice President made a sign that notified them Denise had a weapon. She had been wrong and now an innocent woman was dead.

The second agent reached into his ankle holster. He leaned down and put a revolver into Denise's pocket.

"What are you doing?" asked the first agent.

"Our job, protecting Pegasus," said the second agent.

"This is not right."

"Do your job? That's an order," said the second, more senior agent, as the sirens of an ambulance and police signaled law enforcement. "There is no serial number on the gun, so it will be fine."

"Shit," said the first agent again as he spied news crews arriving along with the police.

Chapter 52

Nick continued to dial Denise's phone, but it would immediately go to voice mail. Chuck was trying as well.

"Where is she living?" asked Nick.

"I think she has an apartment in Alexandria, but I am not sure where exactly. I'm sure we have it in the records," replied Chuck, walking to the door. "I'll look it up."

Chuck left the office to go find the address and Nick stood pacing, waiting for him to return.

After a bit, Margie stuck her head in.

"Boss, I think somebody went after the VP. It is all over the TV. We have it on in the conference room."

Nick walked to the conference room. The talking head on EXN was describing how a witness saw the secret service converge on a park bench where the Vice President was apparently talking to another dark-haired woman when the Secret Service shot the dark-haired woman in the head and threw the Vice President into a car and screeched off.

By then, it was just a couple of Secret Service agents standing over the woman until the police and ambulance arrived. We don't have video of this, but the White House is saying the Vice President is fine, and no weapon was discharged at her. The perpetrator was armed and failed to respond to commands from the Secret Service, so they had no choice but to neutralize the threat. The name of the attacker has not been released as yet. Stay tuned for more on this developing story.

Nick looked at Chuck

His phone buzzed. He looked down.

"I am so sorry about Denise," said the text from Lauren.

"What are you talking about?" texted Nick.

"?? Denise was meeting with VP. She was 1 shot by SS."

"WHAT?" Nick typed back, yelling aloud as well as others in the room, suddenly looked at him.

"You don't know??"

"NO."

"Nick. I am sorry. I contacted Denise about story to confirm details of info sent to me."

Nick was typing a reply when the second text came in.

"I asked but she refused to confirm. I AM sorry."

Nick typed a couple of responses, deleting each without sending as he reached a slow boil. He put his phone away.

"Guys," Nick turned to Chuck, Margie, Earl, Jer, Steve, and Jenny in the room. "I think it was Denise who was shot."

"WHAT" was the general response to his revelation. Jenny collapsed in a chair, sobbing.

"If it is, and I say if, we are about to get hit with a shit storm. I need to know everything any of you know about Denise. Earl, call your friends, dig in and see what you can find out. Chuck, if you know things, now is the time to spill the beans."

"Margie, get me on Tommy tonight, even if it is for only 5 minutes. This is going to break any time."

"Nick," responded Chuck. "All I know is they worked together on the Dukakis and Clinton campaigns and she was friendly with her. I know Denise had bad bouts with alcoholism and was in a car wreck where someone got hurt badly. I think Lexi helped get the charges reduced. That was when she dropped out of the political scene.

"She hadn't worked on a campaign until you hired her. She was very good, but kind of a loose cannon reputation. That is really all I know," explained Chuck.

Carla stuck her head in the office. "Boss, the secret service is here."

Nick walked out of the conference room. Four secret service agents were in the foyer.

"Senator, we have a subpoena to seize all materials from the office of Denise Rojas, including her laptop. We can assure you any campaign confidential material will be kept in strictest confidence and not allowed to be seen by the Vice President," stated the lead Secret Service Agent.

Nick laughed. "No offence Agent...?" asked Nick

"Vargas," answered the agent.

"Well, Agent Vargas, you will forgive me if I do not believe a word of your statement. But I respect the law if others do not. I'll take you to her office." Nick led them to it, where they bagged up her laptop and files. They even took her potted plants.

"Guys, please show the agents out when they have finished tossing the place," commented Nick. "And keep filming everything." This earned a dark look from Agent Vargas.

He headed toward his office.

"Nick, this just came by courier," said Margie, handing Nick an envelope.

"Tommy will give you as much time as you want. He will put you on after his monologue. Word was already leaking. The person shot was Denise, who was meeting with the VP. And of course the liberal networks are going wall to wall on this being a sanctioned hit by you to eliminate your rival."

Nick stood and listened to Margie. Without comment, he headed to his office and opened the envelope. Inside was an SD memory card. Nick looked at his laptop, which did not have an SD card reader. He picked up his phone in his office.

"Jer."

"Nick here, do you have something that will let me read an SD card?"

"Sure, I have a USB card reader. I'll bring it over." Jer appeared 30 seconds later and gave Nick the reader.

"Thanks Jer. Can you shut the door on your way out? Thanks."

Jer paused at the door, shutting it but staying in the room. He was obviously shaken.

"Nick, how do you do it?"

Nick stared back, waiting for him to finish.

"I mean, you take hit after hit. They are cheating to high heaven and no one in the media, in the government, in the justice system is giving you the time of day. Despite the obvious contrived nature of all of this. How do you keep from exploding?" asked Jer, more worked up than Nick had ever seen him.

"Jer, let me ask you a question. Would we be any better off if I went on TV and cursed out every one of them as the lying, cheating SOBs they really are? Would anything be any different?"

Jer stood looking at Nick at the rhetorical question.

"Certainly not better. So that is why I don't do it. Because it wastes time, money, energy, and my internal happiness to play their game. Or to allow hate to overtake my soul. I believe in fate. And I believe in karma Jer."

"Both tell me there will be a right time and a right place and this is neither. Until then, I must soldier on and to do that, I have to allow what happens around me, and to me, to be of no consequence in my *mission*. Does that make sense?"

Jer stood for a few seconds, staring at Nick, processing what he'd told him. "Not really, but I understand the logic in a strange sort of way. I still don't know how you do it," he finished, shaking his head, opening the door to leave.

"Jer, thank you."

Jer stopped and looked at Nick. He smiled, closing the door as he left.

Nick inserted the card and opened it. There were a few files on the card and a video file.

After a few seconds, Denise's face showed up. She had been crying. Nick watched the 5-minute testimonial. He leaned back in his chair and closed his eyes, thinking.

His reverie was broken by a tentative knock at the door. "Enter." Chuck walked in with the rest of the team.

"Boss, it is official. The Secret Service just released Denise Rojas confronted the VP after taking a meeting based on their past friendship.

The VP said she threatened her and did not respond to the commands of the Secret Service. Unfortunately, they had to engage and shoot her. They found an unfired .38 revolver in her right hand. They are speculating she was despondent at the prospect of you losing the election in the House because of the VP's vastly greater experience and qualifications for the Presidency," quoted Margie.

"Jenny, first file an immediate FOIA request to review the ME's report on the body. Also, we want access to forensic reports on the gun. They will stonewall us, but file them anyway."

"Margie, let's get a statement out. First, we are glad the VP is safe. While we acknowledge her experience, 83 million people prefer my platform over her track record and experience. As for what may or may not have been said between Denise and the VP, we are aware they have known each other since college. We can only assume the conversation was a personal one rather than a political one. Clearly, this is not the first time they have met in this manner and the VP obviously trusted Denise enough to not have the Secret Service in the immediate proximity." Nick looked up at the confused faces of his staff.

"It's a tragedy the Secret Service felt obligated to shoot Denise instead of attempting to defuse the situation. It is also strange that a woman who has been anti-gun for her entire life would choose to bring a gun to this meeting."

"She has no record of ever purchasing a gun in her life. We welcome the investigation and the transparent release of all the information regarding this incident. We have lost a colleague and a friend and like our other staffers who have been casualties of this campaign and the media disinformation, I fear there is more to this story than we yet know," said Nick. "You get all that?"

"I did. Not sure I understand it. I suspect you know more than you are letting on," commented Margie.

"Let's just say you should pay attention to Tommy tonight," said Nick, who was not smiling. He looked at his watch.

"I am going to do this from the studio. Earl, can you drive me over?"

Chapter 53

"Well Lauren, here we are again. Only the situation seems different, as the story you are reporting on seems to have sped up," said Marty on his *ANC Tonight* news show.

"That is true, Marty. I have to also say, I hope I did not have a hand in today's events," replied Lauren with some sadness.

"How so?" asked Marty, a concerned look on his face.

"Marty, a little while back, I received a packet of information." Lauren held up her hand as Marty was about to speak.

"Yes, I know. Sounds exactly like what happened before, with Governor Blackbird. I did some research on this. The information provided is legitimate and timely. I reached out to Ms. Rojas and told her I was going to do a story on her political career and her return to prominence from her prior adversities. She decline to confirm or comment on any of my reporting. I thanked her and told her I would go forward with the story with no on the record comments."

"And you feel some of what you are about to expose might have driven her to confront the VP?" asked Marty.

"I don't know, Marty. I can only assume my timing was unfortunate for her. I do still believe the information I discovered applies to the current situation. And I would add, what I have discovered leads me to believe this information was not leaked by the VP or her team. Unlike the speculation from Senator Banks on the Blackbird scandal," said Lauren.

"You mean the alleged leak from the VP regarding the Governor," corrected Marty.

Lauren gave him a look. "Senator Banks' information seemed credible," said Lauren sarcastically. "But, of course, alleged leak."

"What did you find out?" asked Marty in an annoyed tone.

"I was provided information about Ms. Rojas to build an arc of interaction between the Vice President and her. First, it is common knowledge that both the Vice President and Ms. Rojas volunteered on the Dukakis campaign when they were freshmen in college," said Lauren, reviewing her notes.

"They both attended Berkeley. During this time, they had an intimate relationship, as shown in these pictures you now see."

The monitor showed a couple of pictures of Lexi and Denise, much younger, hugging, holding hands, and kissing at what looked like a concert. Ms. Rojas did not confirm or deny this relationship when I asked her.

"Both young women worked in politics after graduation, first as paid staffers on the Clinton campaign and then with other politicians. The Vice President with a California governor and then the staff of a California senator and Ms. Rojas first on a congressional staff and then a senator's staff as well. Apparently, while working on the hill, Ms. Rojas was involved in a relationship with current CIA Director Chadwick when he worked in a senator's office as an aide. Long before his career with the CIA."

"Ms. Rojas became pregnant by Director Chadwick and had a daughter whom she subsequently put up for adoption. I put in a call into the Director's office but it was not returned," said Lauren as pictures of Denise and the much younger CIA Director flashed on the screen. They were out and about having a good time in at least Paris, with the Eiffel tower and other landmarks in the background.

The last picture was of a very pregnant Denise sitting on the bench in the hospital and then a blowup of the picture with the reflection of a younger Lexi with the camera taking the picture.

"I could confirm the Vice President was there to support her while she had the child and the CIA Director apparently was not. Later, as both of their careers continued, Ms. Rojas became a prominent campaign manager, leading successful senatorial elections, including the

Vice President's senate campaigns in California and being part of several winning presidential campaigns."

"At some point, her drinking became too much, causing her to lose her job as a campaign manager for Senator Smythe-Thomas. Subsequent DUIs, a car accident, and criminal charges were filed. The Senator stepped in and helped Ms. Rojas' charges get reduced as long as she entered rehab and attended AA. Ms. Rojas retired from politics after this," finished Lauren.

"I am assuming this has a point. We are not a long form documentary show," said Marty with resignation.

Lauren gave him a peeved look. "Of course, Marty, our viewers need to understand this background to better appreciate what is coming," Marty nodded as Lauren continued.

"Ms. Rojas stayed out of the public eye and politics until she was recruited by Turner's campaign. I don't know if the Senator was aware of their extensive history or not. I have pictures of Ms. Rojas meeting with the Vice President at the same park where the incident occurred today. Once a month for the last eight months. They appear to be smiling and cordial. And there is no Secret Service nearby in any of the photos."

"As I started working on timelines, it appears Ms. Rojas was passing on information pertinent to the Vice President about the strategies of the Turner campaign," said Lauren as the pictures of meetings and the changes in clothing attested to a gradual warming up of the weather.

"Finally, and here is where I believe my reporting may have contributed to today's events. It appears at their meeting in September, Ms. Rojas provided an envelope. My research and timeline show this appears to be when the information about the Turner staffer Kevin Moss allegedly having a relationship with Greg Simmons was passed to the Vice President."

"Do you have any proof, Lauren?"

"The pictures the media used to imply an intimate relationship between Simmons and Moss were in the envelope. I *got* Ms. Rojas to admit she provided the speculative information about the possibility of the relationship, but she did not provide any conclusive proof. She felt very guilty about how the media bullied Mr. Moss into fabricating a story to pay for his mother's drug rehab."

"It was at this point I could tell she was breaking down and she hung up on me. I think knowing all of this was going to come to light, she probably went to confront the VP," finished Lauren.

"Lauren, that is a sad and twisted tale of intrigue and deceit. I agree your conversation may have spurred her to meet with the VP. But it also appears this was a regular occurrence, so it may have had nothing to do with it. The genuine revelation is the depth of the relationship between Turner's campaign manager and the rival VP's campaign," said Marty, trying to soften Lauren's revelations about the Vice President.

"It also seems the VP is partially responsible for the unfortunate deaths of the other Turner staffers. Politics is a dirty business. Perhaps Ms. Rojas' time away did not prepare her for the current cutthroat nature of the arena?"

"Lauren, I don't think you should draw any conclusions regarding the Vice President's involvement. That is pure conjecture on your part," accused Marty.

"Marty, I'll have to live with the possibility my reporting may have contributed to this incident. It makes me question our efforts, as we are the ones who amplify these stories, for better or worse," she stated quietly.

"You didn't do the deeds, Lauren. You offered her a chance to confirm or deny the information. It is unfortunate what happened, but it was not your fault. It is our job to report the news, even if the revelations are painful," countered Marty.

"Even when they lead to loss of life, Marty? I think we cross a line when our words encourage mayhem and violence. If it goes from reporting to tacit approval or even instigation of events?" asked Lauren with determination.

"Thank you for these explosive revelations, Lauren. Please keep us informed if anything else comes to light," said Marty as they went to commercial.

He turned to look at her.

"What the fuck are you doing? Accusing us of being responsible for murders or encouraging it? Jesus, Lauren. You may want to commit career suicide. Please don't step on the IED with me nearby," vented Marty, all puffed up.

Lauren laughed. "Marty, you made a joke. I'm impressed. You do have a sense of humor."

"I *am* serious," retorted Marty, even more puffed up.

"My apologies Marty, I thought you were making a joke," nodded Lauren, walking off the set, concerned at her part in the unfolding tragedy. And how Nick must feel about it.

#

"Was this the reason for the question about Denise when I was in your office?" accused Rhett angrily, standing in Lexi's office in the Capitol, pointing at the TV showing Lauren and Marty finishing their conversation.

Rhett had come over after the shooting and the subsequent call from Lauren Bergamo regarding comments on what she was going to disclose.

"Why would you think that? We were just reminiscing during one of our visits."

"She told me she had an abortion," said Rhett.

"You didn't seem too interested by then. If I remember you had moved on with that actress. Or was she a model? Who can remember? *We* didn't feel you needed to know she decided to have the girl," responded Lexi, watching Rhett's discomfort. She could only imagine the reaction of the holier than thou Congresswoman Murphy, his current wife, when he got home.

"Where is the daughter?" asked Rhett.

"Your daughter? Beats me. She was adopted. Back then, they kept it anonymous and did not allow contact between the parent and the new family. Why do *you* care?"

Rhett laughed cynically. "How do I even know it was mine?"

Lexi broke her calm persona, anger flashing in her eyes.

"Unlike you, who jumped on anything with a pair of tits back then, Denise was devastated when you discarded her and moped around until she found out she was pregnant. *You* were the only one she slept with."

"You're one to talk. Seems this was about the time you were bedding the Governor. Starting your rise to the top from underneath each new conquest," snarled Rhett in retort.

"Aren't we a pair? And Denise is the one who is dead," replied Lexi, her emotions under control again. "Like I said, I have no idea where *your* daughter is."

"Right. I would prefer not to have you treat me as you did Governor Blackbird with your little blackmail schemes. Remember, Lexi, two can play that game."

"My, my Director. That sounded mildly like a threat. Keep in mind, *I* did not leak Blackbird's family laundry, despite the late Senator Banks' accusations. Nor would I have provided Bergamo with any of this info about my past, either."

"If it wasn't you, who was it?"

"Clearly, I was under surveillance. Karen assures me it was not FBI. Is the CIA operating domestically? My Secret Service detail was unaware I was being watched when I met with Denise each month."

"Right. I surveilled you and then fed Bergamo information that makes me look like a dick and gives my wife a reason to bust my balls?"

Lexi shrugged in response to Rhett's rationalization.

"Jesus Lexi. You are a cold bitch. I always knew you were ruthless. But Denise was your friend. You had your agents take her out."

Lexi's icy exterior melted again as her eyes flashed in anger. She leaped up.

"I thought she was going to kill me. I didn't order anyone to kill her."

"Doesn't matter how, you're responsible for it. I hope you can live with it. You are stepping on a lot of toes and there are a lot of folks who would love to see you fall. I'm obligated to protect this country, and you, when you finally deal with Turner. Doesn't mean I have to like it." He fixed her with his own steely gaze as he turned and left her office.

Roland entered the office from the anteroom he had stood in during the conversation. Lexi flipped off the TV while walking to the bar. Her hand shook slightly as she poured the scotch.

"Well?" she asked, taking a large first gulp of her drink.

"He has a lot to lose. I think he's bluffing. From what I have seen in Washington so far, everyone here is more concerned about maintaining their status than they are in meting out revenge. He has a ten-year term, correct?"

"No, that's the FBI. I can fire him any time I want. But it would cause a shitstorm. He's career CIA, not a political appointee," she replied, taking another long pull on her drink. "Besides, we both have compromising info on each other. That works both ways. I can keep him in line. He may still be useful."

"Who provided the reporter with the information?"

"I don't know. We were nobodies in college. Why would anyone have pictures of two twenty-old kids kissing at a concert? I had no idea those even existed. Someone has a very broad reach and access to data that is very specific and very private," speculated Lexi.

"Whoever it is, intended her to expose you. Your calling in the Secret Service prevented that from happening."

"You're saying having them kill her was the right thing?"

"Then or now. She signed her death warrant by threatening to expose you," he nodded. "What did she have?"

"I don't know," replied Lexi.

"What did she know?" he asked, staring into her icy blue eyes.

She stared back, setting down her drink, while walking toward him after locking the office door. "Nothing. I'm done talking about this. I need to relax, she said, pushing him down on the couch."

He smiled. He would get the answer to his question one way or another.

Chapter 54

Tommy was finishing his monologue while Nick waited in the green room, watching Lauren's segment on his phone. No wonder she knew it was Denise when she texted him. The pieces fell into place.

Nick looked up at the monitor, watching Tommy finish.

"I am not sure what could have driven Denise Rojas to confront the VP and allegedly threaten her with a firearm to the extent she instructed her Secret Service agents to shoot her. Unfortunately, as is usually the case with this administration, we will probably never know the truth. Coming up, Senator Turner himself, to fill us in on what he knows about this incident."

As they went to break, Nick came out to be mic'd up.

"Thanks Tommy, I appreciate the opportunity to talk."

"Anytime Nick. I am so sorry for your loss. Is it true?" asked Tommy.

"No, it is not Tommy. That's why I am here. Did you hear about Bergamo's segment? Were your producers watching earlier?" asked Nick.

"No" said Tommy, shaking his head.

"15 seconds guys," said the producer.

"Trust me, I have a story to tell."

Tommy nodded.

"I would like to welcome Senator Turner to the show. Obviously, there are a lot of unanswered questions about today's incident," introduced Tommy.

"Thanks Tommy. I appreciate the opportunity to set the record straight. I also have the benefit of having been able to watch Lauren Bergamo do her segment right before your show. She admitted she had contacted Denise to tell her she had material from yet another anonymous source. Ms. Bergamo did research on this information and established Denise and the VP have known each other for 40 years. In fact, had been very close at one time."

"It appears my campaign manager was leaking info and some of that was used by the Vice President to allow another media outlet to bully my staffer Kevin Moss into making false accusations about Greg Simmons. Which, as we know, cost both of them their lives. This is what Denise was going to the VP to tell her. To let her know that this information was about to be revealed by Ms. Bergamo. She did not go to the VP to kill her."

"How do you know this, Senator? Those are some pretty explosive accusations," asked Tommy.

"She sent me a video via courier. If you can indulge me, Tommy. Your production staff has it queued up. It's about 5 minutes long," requested Nick.

"Let's play it," ordered Tommy.

After a second, a grainy picture of Denise appeared on the screen. She'd been crying.

"Nick, I am so sorry. I should have been honest from the beginning. There was a reason I was not involved in political campaigns any longer. I have too much baggage. It appears it is coming back to haunt me. I do not want it to hurt your campaign any longer," she sniffed loudly on camera, fighting back more tears.

"Nick, Lexi and I have known each other since college. We have been friends and were even lovers once a long time ago. We know a lot about each other and that put me in a compromising position on your team. I should never have accepted the position. Lexi knows too much about me. She has too much leverage."

"When your campaign started getting traction, she threatened to expose me and hurt your image unless I spied for her. She forced me to give her information about your plans. But even then, what I gave her really didn't amount to much until September."

"She started getting desperate and worried after you turned down the Opposition nomination. She said if I didn't provide something scandal worthy, she would share my past and embarrass the campaign.

Nick, I told her Kevin and Greg spent a lot of time together. I had them followed and pictures taken of them together at coffee houses and having lunch. That was all, I swear." This time, tears streamed down her face as she continued.

"She took the info and passed it on to the media and they bullied Kevin into making up the story about them having an intimate relationship. Now that bitch Bergamo has info about this and more, and she is going to do a story," spewed Denise, the hatred of Bergamo visceral in the way she said her name.

"I'm going to confront Lexi about this and tell her she needs to come clean and admit her part in the scandal, or I would confirm it with Bergamo. I don't care what she can do to me. I will leave my meeting with her and call Bergamo, or I will get a promise from Lexi to admit to it and go public. Then I'll come to you and resign. I am even willing to go on *Tommy* and explain this if you think it will help you."

"I am taking documents and pictures with me to show Lexi, confirming I have the information to force her to admit to this. It is stuff about things she did in the past even she won't want shared. It won't bring Kevin and Greg back and it won't make up for everything else she has done to you, but it will be a start."

"I'm meeting her shortly, so I will put this in a courier envelope. Again, I am sorry this happened, Nick. I should never have left New Mexico. I'll head back there after all this," finished Denise in the recording.

"Tommy, does that sound like someone who is on their way to confront and kill the Vice President? Would she be alluding to all the things she'd be doing after the VP refused to come clean? I don't think so," explained Nick.

"I agree it doesn't, but according to the Secret Service, she had a gun in her pocket."

"Tommy. I don't buy it. Where would she get a gun in DC?" asked Nick.

"They found a sheriff in New Mexico who said he taught her how to shoot. That she shot a vagrant in the leg there, who was trying to break into her house. She does own a gun and has shot someone previously," admitted Tommy, almost apologetically.

"Tommy, it was a giant revolver. A .357. The sheriff gave it to her. She did not bring it back from New Mexico. I know because I was there when she locked it up."

"The Secret Service is covering this up then?"

"Accidents happen and it the VP felt threatened. What better way to remove a potential threat than to have your Secret Service team take her out and pin it on your opponent?" inferred Nick.

"Hmm, excellent strategy," admitted Tommy.

"Where are the docs, Tommy? According to the official report, she had nothing on her but the gun in her pocket. No phone, no purse, nothing but a phone and a gun? She told all of us she was going to show Lexi documents and photos. Where are they?" asked Nick.

"Regardless, American *Pravda* is running with the story your campaign manager attempted to kill the Vice President to remove her from the race and assure your win," pointed out Tommy.

"And I get to bury yet another team member. What is wrong with our system? We defund police, we release criminals, we encourage anarchy in the name of diversity. We refuse to apply laws equally. We ignore our federal border laws, create chaos, and suffering for the very people we encouraged to come here for a better life. Our policies are doing nothing to improve and everything to destroy. Tommy, why can't everyone see this as plainly as I do?"

"Honestly, Senator, I don't know. It is counter to everything they should be embracing."

"The tyrants of history have always understood they need to control the feed of information, so their propaganda is the only source of truth.

"I couldn't agree more, Senator. How do we fix it?"

"Tommy, we should have counted my ballots in Michigan. Disavowed the late ballots in Arizona and Georgia. Put me on the ballot in Pennsylvania, Michigan, and Wisconsin. Let the people truly judge the ideas of the candidates they deem best able to improve their life. That would be a start. For a Party who claims the Opposition is always looking to disenfranchise minority votes, the only disenfranchising of voters I see is being done by a handful of Party appointed judges and Secretaries of State."

"Well put, Senator. That is a good point about disenfranchising voters. Hopefully, those who are honorable and voted for the Vice President can see how these efforts are preventing people from truly having their say in how we are governed and by whom."

"Tommy, we desperately need to unmake our current system of politicians for life. We need a volunteer system of public service. And not a rotating door from administration to lobbying to head of public think tank or talking head on a network and then back in another administration."

"This is what I stand for. Transparency. Instead, they have adopted a win at all cost mantra. No poor staffer, celibate gay man, recovering alcoholic campaign manager, or ninety-five-year-old senator dare get in their way. This has to end. The people have to wake up and see this is the choice. Servitude to their wishes forever or freedom to choose."

"Senator, you know I agree. I could not have said it better. I do honestly hope we can get to the bottom of this incident with Denise."

"Thanks for giving me the time, Tommy. God Rest your soul Denise," said Nick as they went to commercial.

#

"Did she have a gun or not?" asked Lexi, pausing the recording of Nick's interview in her Capitol office.

"Yes, she did," said Caleb Parker, the director of the Secret Service. It was clear he was not being truthful.

"Good God man, don't get under oath," groaned Lexi. "So, she didn't have a gun?"

"She was found on the street with a gun in her hand in the pocket of her coat."

"I don't know who the fuck you think you are talking too, but you had better start telling the truth, right fucking now," yelled Lexi, furious at the half answers she was receiving.

Mel intervened. "Lexi, she did not have a gun in her pocket. Only some papers. When the agents discovered this, they planted an unregistered revolver. It is better this way. The public can think Turner's campaign staffer threatened to shoot at you, rather than the Secret Service overreacting and shooting an innocent and unarmed woman simply talking to you."

"You made the distress sign, showing someone was threatening you with a weapon, Madame Vice President," reminded Parker defensively.

"So now we have a coverup I have to deal with instead of explaining how the Secret Service was in their rights to protect me from a potential threat. This is a giant cluster fuck," claimed Lexi, pacing the room. "You should leave now, Parker."

Caleb bobbed his head at the Vice President. "Madame Vice President," and left the office, leaving Lexi and Mel alone.

"It would have been better had they not planted the gun," expressed Mel.

"You think? Saint Turner is already on TV claiming I am on a murdering rampage, knocking off his staffers one by one in my relentless pursuit of power. He's right about Denise. I should have remembered she hates guns. Her father killed himself when she was a kid. She's been terrified and hated guns ever since. I should have realized she wouldn't shoot me. What was in the papers they found?" asked Lexi.

"No one seems to know where they are at the moment. In the confusion, they seem to have disappeared while they were trying to get the gun in her pocket before the news and the paparazzi arrived," said Mel.

"Great. Lord only knows what was on them. Find them," said Lexi, tossing back the remainder of her drink.

"Probably the same stuff Bergamo went through. Who do you think leaked it to her? It wasn't Turner, and it wasn't you. Who else?" asked Mel, carefully.

Lexi thought for a moment while she poured another drink to settle her nerves. "Rhett is pissed at me, knowing that he has to explain all this to his congresswoman wife. Banks is my guess," she said with determination after contemplating for a few seconds.

"Really?"

"We know there was more to him than met the eye. He was here forever. He could have stashed the info for this type of occasion," stated Lexi.

"Possible, I guess, but Bergamo said she just got it. I suppose he could have sent it before his death," guessed Mel.

"What do we do? I really liked Denise. I don't want to destroy her reputation. She really only loved working on elections. The rest of the time, her life was shit. This is not fair to her," admitted Lexi.

Mel, surprised at her showing feelings, looked at her.

"She's dead, Lexi. I don't think she cares. How many of those did you have before I got here?" asked Mel eyeing the crystal glass in Lexi's hand. "You getting soft on me? She tried to kill you to help benefit Turner's campaign. She deserves every vilification we can throw her way. It is the only way we can play it because of the ineptitude of the Secret Service," said Mel.

"Of course you're right. Maybe I was weak there for a moment. Poor Denise. They tell me she wouldn't have felt a thing. At least there is that," she offered.

Mel walked over to her and took her drink. He led her to a chaise lounge in the office. Helping her sit down, he took off her shoes and covered her with a quilt.

"Why thank you Mel, I didn't know you had it in you to be nice or thoughtful," said Lexi, exhausted from the adrenalin high combined with the alcohol.

"Too much hanging around you had knocked most of it out of me. You need to get a few winks. I will man the door for a couple hours," confided Mel.

Lexi smiled as she closed her eyes.

"Any idea where Denise's daughter is?" he asked.

"No. I told Rhett the truth. Back then, the info was well guarded to keep them from finding each other later in life," she murmured, already falling asleep. "What do we do if someone comes up with footage of the Secret Service planting the gun?" mumbled Lexi.

Mel filed away the knowledge she'd already had a conversation with Rhett on this subject. "We throw the stooges under the bus. You thought you were being threatened, and they erred on the side of caution. You yourself said they asked her to remove her hand from her pocket, right?" confirmed Mel.

"Yes, they did."

"There you have it. The fact they covered it up is their problem, not yours. Now get some sleep. I'll look in on you in a bit. We still have work to do, or I would get you home."

"OK," said Lexi, relaxing already as Mel left the office and told the Secret Service outside to not let anyone bother her for the next couple of hours until he got back.

Chapter 55

The First Lady led the President down the hall to the Lincoln Bedroom. She led him into the room. With the help of the nurse, they got him changed into his pajamas, gave him a warm glass of milk and a mild sedative.

As the nurse left, the First Lady bent over and kissed him on the forehead. He was already falling asleep. He had no recognition of her or that he was in the White House. And none that he was still the legal President of the United States. As was always the case, the First Lady sighed as she left and closed the door before heading up the hall to her bedroom in the residence.

She looked up and down the hallway. All the surveillance had been disabled in the hall. She did not want any footage to leak showing her feeble husband. She owed him that much. His country, which he had honorably served for over 60 years, also deserved to remember him for what he did. Even if he did not.

#

Later in the wee hours of the evening, a black clad shadow hugged the walls and entered the President's bedroom. There were no guards. Another request of the First Lady to reduce the number of people around her husband.

The figure moved to the bed. The President was on his back, snoring mildly. The intruder picked up a pillow and gently covered the face of the President. At first, little changed, but eventually the President's instinct kicked in and he weakly raised his arms to remove the pillow from his face.

The narcotics in his system made it difficult to focus or apply any force to fight. After five minutes of constant pressure, the intruder removed the pillow, checked for any pulse, waiting another two minutes to make sure he had passed. The intruder went out the way they came in. Silently, with no record of the intrusion.

#

In the morning, the First Lady entered the Lincoln bedroom, somewhat surprised her husband was still in bed. The nurse followed her in and immediately pushed past the First Lady to the President's side. Rigor had already set in. There was no doubt the President was dead.

#

Lexi sat on a settee in her spacious bathroom in her slip, drinking coffee and glancing at the news as she did her hair and makeup. Pete was still asleep in the bed. There was a commotion and her Secret Service team leader, Russ, stepped into the bedroom with several other agents. They all had their weapons out. "Madame Vice President, please get dressed quickly. We need to take you to the White House immediately."

"What's happened?" asked Lexi, rising and grabbing her dress from the rack.

Russ and his agents had their backs turned as Lexi pulled the dress over her head. Her phone started ringing. As she went to answer it, Russ grabbed it. She gave him a look. "Ma'am, we need to go NOW," he commanded.

Pete was up as well, but an agent separated him from her.

"I'm off to the White House. I will call you later," as she made an air kiss. The agents on either side of her lifted her off her feet and practically flew with her out of the house and into the Suburban. Her entire street was cordoned off, even more than usual. None of her neighbors would have been able to leave their houses.

Suddenly she was thrown against Russ as the driver executed a U turn and with a 3-car phalanx in front and behind as they sped off at a high rate of speed. She looked out the window and could see helicopters covering their route. Every cross street was blocked by police all standing outside their cars with weapons drawn.

"What happened? Were we attacked?"

"I'm sorry Ma'am. My orders are to get you to the White House and to confiscate your phone until we get there," answered Russ.

In less than five minutes, they pulled into the White House. Lexi could see Secret Service in full gear surrounding the building and up on the roof as they drove up. Under the portico, the Secret Service agents helped her out of the car where she was met by the Attorney General and the Chief Justice of the Supreme Court. "Javier, what the hell is going on? Were we attacked?" asked Lexi.

Javier shook his head. "No Madame Vice President, the President passed in his sleep last night. We need to get you sworn in." Lexi was led into the central foyer. "Madame Vice President, do you care where we swear you in?" asked the Chief Justice.

"Yes, in the Treaty room, please," said Lexi, now getting her bearings.

They all traipsed off to the Treaty room, their entourage now growing as Mel arrived as well as Joint Chief Kensington, the Secretary of State and the Directors of the FBI, CIA, NSA and Homeland.

Lexi put her hand on a bible they'd found in her West Wing office. She recited the oath as administered by the Chief Justice. A photographer dutifully captured the events. The now former First Lady was nowhere to be seen.

There would be no tearful Jackie Kennedy moment for this swearing in. Once the oath was administered, Ana, and the former president's press secretary, Amy, both said she needed to issue a statement and get on TV shortly.

"Amy," said Lexi. "Can you please get out a statement saying the President passed peacefully in his sleep last night," said Lexi, looking around the room.

"Where is the White House physician? It was natural causes, correct?" she asked. Everyone looked around and the White House physician was found as they made their way to the Oval office. Lexi was no stranger to the office or the room, but now she was officially president. She sat down on a chair in the Oval as all of her intelligence leaders stood in the room.

"Any threat increase? Anything?" she asked the assembled secretaries and directors. No one answered with any threats. As she prepared to say more, the White House physician was marched in.

"Doc, was it natural?"

"From our preliminary examination, it appears he had heart failure in the middle of the night. In fact, he may not have woken up at all during the episode."

"Thank you, doctor. I would not be remiss in assuring the nation our President passed in his sleep last night of apparent heart failure?" asked Lexi.

"No, Mrs. President, that is the truth. He was quite frail."

"Thank you," said Lexi as the doctor left.

"That sounds horrible, 'Mrs. President'. It makes me sound like Robin Williams in drag," frowned Lexi as everyone laughed.

"I'll do a quick briefing from the office here. Anything or anyone I need to reassure or threaten?"

"I don't think so Madame President" said Roger Brody, the Secretary of Homeland Security

Lexi smiled at this. "Much better. Thank you, Roger."

Homeland continued. "Just be forceful and make sure our enemies know you are not to be trifled with."

"Send in the camera crew. Thanks all. We will convene a cabinet meeting in an hour."

As they shuffled out and the camera crew came in along with the staff to touch up Lexi's makeup and hair, Mel sidled over to the other side.

"Congratulations Madame President," he said with a big smile on his face.

"Thank you, Mel. It's been a strange journey this year to get here. Nothing has gone as planned," said the new President of the United States.

Lexi's speechwriter came in and discussed the brief speech with Mel and Lexi until they agreed with the words and the tone. The speechwriter left to have it loaded into the teleprompter.

\#

"That certainly complicates things," fretted Chuck as he and Nick watched Lexi being sworn in. Then they watched her deliver her initial speech from the oval office, announcing the President had passed in his sleep. She assured the public there was no foul play and announced the President would lie in state.

She was confident all the current policies were the correct policies and would be continued as if nothing had changed. She continued to caution our enemies to not consider any mischief or they would face the full might and authority of the United States in this time of mourning and transition.

"She seems pretty comfortable at that desk," noted Nick.

Chuck nodded. "There have been rumors she has already been acting as president for the last 6 months to a year. Ever since she did the State of the Union."

"This makes our efforts to convince some of those Opposition members to support us harder. She gets to be in the role for the next month before the vote, acting and looking Presidential. Lots of folks are going to look at this as a 'why upset the apple cart and put in a guy who has only been a senator for less than two years' decision.'"

"I am afraid you're right, Nick. This is an enormous boost for her," responded Chuck, trying not to let his dejection come through in his tone. "It puts her in position to officially put pressure on groups investigating voter fraud. This is super convenient for her."

"Well, at least we are stable. I don't want our enemies to think they can take advantage of a vacuum. She has provided that," said Nick.

\#

Maksim Pavlovich sat in his study, taking calls and delivering directions to his widespread empire. His valet came in with his afternoon tea and the British version of the New York Times. He left and closed the door. He reached into the drawer of his desk and pressed a button. A holographic screen appeared, showing the American Stock markets. All of them were talking about the implications of the President dying and the swearing in of the Vice President.

Pavlovich looked at one of his phones. It showed a text he had received 6 hours before with a simple 'It is done'. He smiled, picking up the phone.

#

Mel stood off to the side as Lexi delivered her assurances to the public that she had everything under control. The speech was very presidential. It showed her calm and in charge. Announcing the President would lie in state was guaranteed to earn some sympathies and show she was not heartless.

The late President's real accomplishments would fill a thimble. His missteps a bucket, and his lost opportunities a 55-gallon drum. In a hundred years, students would be hard pressed to remember his name. He would be included with the likes of Fillmore and Arthur, Garfield and Hayes, Harding and Carter. Presidents with no real accomplishments and only remembered in trivia questions as no nothing presidents.

#

Lexi walked into the cabinet room. Everyone stood up as she entered. Unlike when she had been playing president, now she was the President. They gave her the respect they had previously withheld. She didn't have to worry about any of them leaking. They were all complicit and knew it. They would all cover their own asses and hers with it. As she sat, she surveyed the room.

"For now, we will keep everything the same until after the election is resolved. Then we can discuss who wants to stay on and who prefers to leave. I know not all of you approve of the last year, but it worked. We avoided a major incident. We kept our enemies in check, and we preserved the reputation of the late president. I would say that is commendable and all of you here today made that possible. For that, I thank you and our country thanks you. Javier, if you please."

The Attorney General stood and approached the President, handing her the signed copy of the emergency powers document they had signed so many months ago to ensure she could launch nukes as the Vice President.

"This is the only copy?" asked Lexi.

"Of course, Madame President. Believe me, this is not a document anyone would want a copy of for any purpose, at least no one in this room," replied Javier with a small laugh.

"Excellent. Who still smokes? I need a lighter," asked Lexi.

Les, the former union boss Secretary of Labor, handed his lighter to Lexi across the table.

She picked up the lighter, noticing its heft and the Marine Corps emblem embossed on one side.

"I'm not going to drench us if I burn this?" she asked aloud, looking up at the sprinklers.

Mel laughed from the corner, having been invited by Lexi to sit in on *her* cabinet meeting. "No Madame President, fire away." Everyone laughed at his euphemism.

Lexi made a show of lighting the document and waiting for it to flame up before she dropped it on a silver platter in the center of the table, where it fizzled out into a pile of ash.

"Madame President," said the Secretary of State, Susanna Bangura. "What are you going to do about the vacant Vice Presidency?"

"Good question Susanna. If we do nothing, the next in line is the Speaker of the House, correct?" asked Lexi.

"And then the Senator Pro Tempore," replied Susanna.

"Well, since the election will be resolved in a month, I suggest we continue without a VP and let the succession go to the Speaker if something were to happen. No sense giving a Vice Presidential pension to someone for a month's work. We are being fiscally responsible," said Lexi, eliciting laughter from the room. "Let's get a statement out saying this, except the last, of course."

They went around the room, briefing Lexi on the latest efforts since the last meeting before the President's death. At the end, Lexi asked the intelligence heads to stay. She looked around the room at the leaders of the alphabet soup of intelligence agencies.

"Ok, gents, and lady," said Lexi, nodding at Karen Coleman. "Talk to me about the election."

"We are monitoring the usual fringe groups on all sides. No one seems to be planning anything overt as yet. The usual rioting in the urban areas of the most progressive cities. I suspect once we get closer to Jan 6th we will have more chatter. The anti-government types now look to Jan 6 as a call to arms against government tyranny," answered Karen.

"Ya, that didn't work out so well, did it?" laughed Rhett.

"You're laughing about insurrection Director?" asked Homeland Security's Roger Brody in a serious tone.

"Insurrection?" said Rhett, in a disbelieving tone of surprise, looking at Director Brody and his offended look at Rhett's quip.

"I forgot. You were nowhere to be seen during that time. Working for Goldman running their Asia Pacific branch, right?" asked Rhett sarcastically.

"Yes, I was," replied Brody in an indignant tone.

"Well, for those not in the know," said Rhett, looking at Brody, while the others smiled. "We knew the folks were coming. We infiltrated the groups, and Karen knows this better than most, since it was mostly an FBI operation. We organized the groups, we brought Antifa elements in, gave them the clothing and the tools and instructions to fire up the more militant factions of the mob."

"Did you ever wonder why we kept so much of the footage out of the public hands? Ever wonder why there were so many journalists with cameras on the inside? Or pushed the sham committee and kept up the mantra of Jan 6 being as bad as 9/11? It was easy with our willing media. Even EXN had to play their part and denounce it."

"What we did was the greatest counter insurgency operation ever implemented," he paused. "And it was against our own citizens. Who would have thought? We convinced all these 'patriots' sticking their head out of the crowd would only get it shot off in the future. How exactly did you get to be Homeland Director and not know any of this?" finished Rhett, looking at Brody.

He stiffened. "My organizational skills. And in case you haven't noticed, we have had no incidents on US soil since I took over.

They have all been international, your area of ownership, if I am not mistaken."

Lexi stepped in before Rhett could retort. "Alright gentlemen, save it for the playground." She gave both of them a look, speaking volumes. "Rhett is correct about all these anarchist groups," agreed Lexi.

"Once again, the opponents of our change seem to have found a leader and this time he is not someone who is easy to manipulate into missteps. This makes him exponentially more dangerous. We have to double down on his supporters and turn up the heat. We cannot allow him to take his popularity and use it to thwart our plans."

"The entire last administration was led by a President who turned out to be incapable of executing and holding the line on our decisions. Every time we tried to make progress, he would cave and pull back 80%. That will not be the case going forward. We will use all the levers of government to ensure our policies are enforced."

"When Turner and his rabble push back, we need to be prepared to push back twice as hard. Intelligence is more important than ever now people. Let's keep our eye on the ball," she said, getting up as they all rose. "Karen, please stay."

As everyone filed out, Lexi turned to Karen. "Thanks for your efforts in Michigan. It was enough to run out the clock up there."

She nodded.

"Karen, I cannot put forth your name for the Directorship until I am officially president after the inauguration. Once that is done, yours is the first I will put forth in nomination."

"Thank you, Madame President. I will not let you down," answered Karen Coleman with a beaming smile. She had done it.

Chapter 56

"Wisconsin and Arizona both certified their votes. Only California is left," said Chuck as they once again huddled around the conference table.

"Didn't take long, did it?" said Nick.

"Nope, they both caved. Wisconsin certified two minutes after they swore in the replacement for Krakowski and certified Dane County," reported Chuck.

"I'm a bit more surprised about Arizona. I thought we had a real chance to fight for a hand inspection of the Pima County late ballots, but the Governor and Secretary of State suddenly crumbled. I'm guessing either Lexi got to them and threatened funding for something or sweetened the pot to give them something to expedite things," guessed Chuck.

"We have an open lawsuit to inspect the ballots, but it was rejected by the Arizona Supreme Court citing lack of evidence, so we appealed to the Supreme Court. I'm not holding out much hope there. And it will be after the fact, so it will change nothing." replied Jenny.

"Duane arguing the cases for us at the Supreme Court?" asked Nick with a smile.

"Oh yeah, and he is champing at the bit. He can't wait to stick it to the man, or so he says," smiled Jenny.

"He realizes this isn't the sixties, right?" questioned Chuck.

"More like the late seventies, that was his time as a public defender in NYC. Think, Peter Finch in *Network*. He's definitely 'mad as hell and not going to take it anymore'. Frankly, I feel the same way," grimaced Jenny.

"Man, what a time. New York was almost as bad as it is now," offered Chuck.

"The fashions were worse, all that polyester. Yuck," Jenny made a face.

"All right, you guys. What's up in California? We're safe there, right?" asked Nick.

"Us? Sure, even Lexi can't make more than a million votes appear out of thin air. But the Party has some problems. The courts ordered a hand recount of the mail in ballots in Orange Country. Almost 5,000 of the ballots were invalidated because of dual markings," explained Chuck.

"The Party lawyers have appealed this to the California Supreme Court. This will be a genuine test of the law, as the election supervisor and the county clerk have both been arrested and charged with many counts of voter fraud. It will be really hard for the California Supreme Court to overturn the local judgement," finished Jenny.

"This time we have the proof we have been seeking in all these other cases? Too bad they are last in line, or we could use this example to get the Supreme's to allow some access to Arizona, Wisconsin, Pennsylvania, and Georgia," sighed Nick.

"Too little too late. They would say it was those two people and not an example of widespread fraud," said Chuck in a depressed voice, as he sensed they were running out of options.

"What will happen, Jenny?" asked Nick.

"You know boss, I think the court might actually uphold the judgement. The judges can't ignore this much evidence. They would have to defend the decision to the Supreme Court," she said.

"What's the result?" asked Nick.

"The six congressional seats the Dems won will go Opposition. This will mean they only have a 3 or 4 seat majority in congress," said Chuck. "Find a few Turner rebels, and any Party led legislation gets stalled."

"Good. That should give the President some heartburn," said Nick, grimacing as he had to refer to Lexi as the 'President'.

"When will the court rule?" asked Nick.

"Next day or so. That will give them enough time to appeal to the Supreme Court, if needed, before they have to certify on the 11th."

"What is your feeling on the states?" asked Chuck.

"I only had to convince one congressman in South and North Dakota. I think I got through to Guthrie in North Dakota. Johnson in South Dakota is a Blackbird supporter through and through, so no chance there. South Carolina is a toss-up. I think I have three for and three against. The last is not going to tell me. North Carolina is out. Too much animosity about Wilhelm, even though the Governor is on my side. It will come down to South Carolina. If it goes, Lexi, we are going to lose. Even if we get it, we are 25/25. I have no idea what will happen then," shrugged Nick.

"They keep voting," explained Jenny, answering his question. Chuck laughed, while Jenny looked confused.

"I think he knew that. I think he meant he had no idea how the tie would eventually change," smiled Chuck. Jenny nodded and blushed. "Sorry."

"Jenny, do I have any more recommendations to write or endorsements to give? I want to make sure all the people in the office land somewhere," remarked Nick.

"It's under control."

"Well, I guess there is not much more we can do. Where is Earl?"

"He's still in Michigan. He refuses to give up, even though they have already certified their votes," noted Chuck.

"It gives him something to do."

"Nick, why don't you go to your new house and have Hobson show you around? You can't avoid it forever," suggested Chuck.

"That might be a good idea. Give me something to do. Hard to believe we were so go, go, go, for so many months and now all I can do is sit around and wait."

"Ironic, isn't it? You won the election, she is now the President, and we still haven't certified the election results," remarked Chuck.

"Ironic? More like Bizarro World," laughed Nick.

#

Nick couldn't bring himself to go over to Bank's house, now his house. He wasn't ready.

His phone rang. He picked up, hearing an excited Earl.

"Nick, we got 'em. We got the bastards this time. I have three eyewitnesses to fraud. Printing ballots for Lexi, delivering them to six different states. They have pictures and videos. It is the smoking gun we have been looking for," said Earl.

"Calm down Earl. Are they credible?"

"Hell no, but they do have pictures and they can describe the operations and the people. Are you ready for this? One of them even claims to have seen Mel Arenson in the warehouse. We have no pictures of that, but it is something to keep in our pocket. What do you want to do?"

"We should call a press conference and go public with this and the pictures. Make sure you have them at a safe house. The FBI will probably want to take over as soon as we break the story. We need to immediately have Jenny file an injunction against the states to rescind the vote certification. This could be what we are looking for. Let's get Duane involved as well."

"Got it. We need to hurry, Nick. We're running out of time. With the holidays coming, everyone is going to disappear," said Earl.

"I know," replied Nick, walking out of his office and waving to Chuck and Jenny to join him in the conference room. "Hang on Earl, I have Jenny and Chuck. Tell them what you told me," said Nick, putting his phone down on the conference table on speaker.

Earl explained to them again what he'd found. Nick watched as Chuck and Jenny got more and more enthused, going through what they needed to do. They called in Margie as well so she could work on the press conference. They were back in business.

Chapter 57

"Mel, what the fuck is this?" asked Lexi, looking at the press conference Turner was having. He introduced several tattoo'd and pierced twenty somethings who swore they were part of an operation to print ballots for the former Vice President.

They talked about the operations in the warehouse to print the ballots. One said he was part of the group of people who helped load and drive grocery delivery trucks to the various counties in the six states where the ballots would be used. The second talked about how they had stations for each of the six swing states, with ballots printed, folded, and forgers to sign them.

The most credible witness was a young black woman, covered in tattoos. She spoke in great detail about how they used computer programs to review the list of eligible voters from data they'd received from the states, specifically the swing counties. Building their own lists of voters least likely to vote from this data. Using these, they could print up the mail in ballots to fill out and vote for them. They also showed some blurry footage of the operation in a warehouse.

"I thought you told me this was as secure an operation as possible and no phones were allowed in or out," accused Lexi.

Mel recognized the black woman from his trip to the operation. So far, she had not mentioned meeting him. He also studied the footage they provided. Two things were evident. There was some sort of operation going on with lots of people and desks. The second, thankfully, was the footage was obviously shot from a low-resolution device, like a webcam or laptop camera rather than a smart phone. You could make out one sign saying Wisconsin, but nothing else. Also, their footage was from a distance, so no faces could be made out.

"Looks pretty inconclusive to me. And look at these guys. Turner could have picked them up off the street and paid them to say anything," noted Mel, trying to sound confident.

"Doesn't matter. He is casting doubt once again. Can they reverse the certification in Michigan?" said Lexi nervously.

"No, only the Supreme Court could do that. Call up your good buddy, Chief Justice Wishy-washy, and tell him you need a 4 to 4 decision on any suit coming his way. We can count on the Michigan Supreme Court. They have done what you have asked from the beginning. The evidence while damning is pretty circumstantial. The entire operation was torn down months ago. If this is the best they can do after a month of investigating, we can handle it. I suggest the first thing you do is have the FBI take over. They can 'look' into the witnesses. I am sure they all have rap sheets a mile long."

"I'll talk to Karen," agreed Lexi.

#

"As expected, the FBI took over," said Earl, seated in Nick's office in the Hart building this time.

"They take the witnesses as well?"

"Yes, 'protective custody'. Said they could protect them better," worried Earl.

"My ass. I feel sorry for them. They stuck their neck out for us, and they're going to get chewed up by the media first and the FBI second," responded Nick.

"Is it enough?" asked Earl.

"I don't know. Jenny told me the Michigan court is going to say it is inconclusive and the witnesses are of questionable credibility. We'll have to take it to the Federal Court of Appeals who will uphold it and then to the Supreme Court. Then it will all come down to Duane," said Nick.

"We better put something in his cornflakes. He only seems to work well when he is hopped up on something. 'Organic' of course," laughed Earl, holding his hands in air quotes as Nick smiled.

"He's sneaky good, Earl. I have seen him in action. He is very good at manipulating opposing counsel into corners," stated Nick.

"The Supreme Court is different, right? They make their case to the judges. No back and forth between the counsels," asked Earl.

"You know, I'm not sure how that works. Maybe we can ask Jenny." He picked up his phone and dialed.

"Hey Jenny, sitting here with Earl and we had a question. At the Supreme Court, do the counsels for both sides present to the Supreme Court justices like a *Law and Order* episode?"

Jenny could be heard laughing on the speakerphone.

"Nick, nothing is like *Law and Order*. Total BS. If those guys tried half the stuff they show on TV, they would have long since been disbarred and working at Starbucks. No, for the Supreme Court, we file a legal brief making our case, laying out our evidence and any precedents we are citing to help them follow our argument. Then we get one hour alone with the Court where our counsel makes the verbal case and gives the justices a chance to ask questions. Opposing counsel gets the same. Sorry, no *Law and Order* antics or courtroom confessions of the guilty within the forty-four minutes of the show."

"Thanks Jenny. How is Duane doing?"

She laughed again. "He is a trip, I can tell you that. But his briefs are the best I have ever seen. Now I can see how he got Dusty off for those murder charges. If we had courts which ruled solely on the law, we would have won all these cases. But with political state Supreme Courts packed by the Progressives and that Pavlovich monster through the years, no honest arguments stand a chance. Plus, the court of public opinion taints the jury pool so there can be no impartiality, as we have seen."

"Having Justice Moore die when he did came at the most inopportune time. It changed everything. I hate coincidences," mused Nick aloud.

"And the President conveniently dying to make Lexi more presidential?" added Earl.

"What are you two drinking? Conspiracy juice?" laughed Jenny.

They just looked at each other, not smiling. "Regardless, it made the Chief Justice the swing vote again. That does not bode well for justice," answered Nick.

"He is a total embarrassment to the law. Terrified of having to make a consequential decision. I think it will be the same here. Maybe Duane can get one of the others to break ranks. Hell, Justice Feinberg is too old to be drinking anymore anyway, so what if she misses a few of those cocktail parties he's so worried about being dis-invited from?" laughed Jenny.

Nick and Earl also laughed dutifully as they hung up after thanking Jenny.

"Nick, how do you do it?" asked Earl in a strained tone.

"Do what Earl?"

"Put up with all this unfairness."

"Jer asked me the same question a while back. What is my other option, Earl?"

"I don't know. I want to stick my head out a window and scream," said Earl.

"Funny, we were just referencing Howard Beale."

"Who?"

"You know the guy from *Network*, who stuck his head out the window and said he wouldn't take it anymore.

"Nick, you saw where I grew up. We didn't even have a TV, let alone cable."

Nick laughed and pointed to his window.

"Feel free if it will make you feel better. But it won't change anything. I could rage. I could go on TV, and denounce the results day and night. Eventually, people will tune out. Complaining about injustice or cheating is irrelevant in the scheme of things."

"I think they already are," answered Earl ruefully.

"Exactly. Ask all the conservative pundits what all their complaining has done. Nothing. The only way to move forward is to play the game better than they do. Right now, they have the overwhelming force. I cannot afford to get in a pitched battle with them. I have to work on the flanks, find their weak spots. Use deception and intrigue. I have to keep chipping away. Most of all, my army and I have to live to fight another day. Make them feel like they are invincible and only then will I have an advantage. Right now, they are too dangerous. I can't afford to squander the only advantages I have until I know I can win."

"Sounds like George Washington's job in the Revolution."

"Indeed. Well done, Mr. Greene. All he had to do was to survive and keep his army on the field. He didn't win many battles. What he did was *not* lose. He knew public opinion in England would eventually sour about funding an expensive foreign war in a land the size of the colonies. They were already in debt from the Seven Years' War and other European escapades."

Earl nodded. "I should have paid more attention to those strategy lectures."

"There are more forces at work here than Party vs Opposition vs Me. We just have to survive. They have too many weapons right now. *Pravda*, the courts, the congress, and the entire bureaucratic state. They are all like a cancer in the body. We need to be the chemotherapy. They are going to fight us off like no tomorrow. Like the body when fighting cancer, we are going to have to take the country to the brink of death in order to survive, I fear."

"That is certainly reassuring," uttered Earl.

"At least we are diagnosing we have cancer and not ignoring our pain and symptoms. Now we have our diagnosis. My intent is to hit it with everything I can. We eventually kill it or die trying.," noted Nick.

Earl sat looking at his boss. He was worried how he could keep Nick alive long enough to accomplish a task the whole might of the US government, and maybe even the world, would be united in stopping. He also knew Nick was entirely correct in both his diagnosis and his treatment.

#

Mel dialed Josh Stone's phone number for the millionth time, getting voicemail again. With the revelations in Michigan and the staffers who were obviously in the warehouse when Mel visited, he was worried about any other potential revelations. Josh not responding had him conjuring up all kinds of scenarios. Everything from FBI interrogations to an EXN expose suddenly appearing.

He glanced up at the knock on his campaign office door. Roland was standing in the doorway.

"May I come in?"

"Do I have a choice?" responded Mel.

"No," replied Roland, shutting the door as he entered. He reached into his pocket. Mel immediately thought he was going to get shot. Instead, Roland pulled out a smartphone and threw it on the desk in front of Mel.

Looking down, Mel could see the lock screen showed a pop up showing his number had tried calling 32 times, the last one, five minutes ago. The background of the lock screen also showed Josh Stone with his arms around a wife or girlfriend.

"He will not answer, no matter how many times you call. His phone plan isn't *that* good," finished Roland with a smirk.

Mel stood up. Handing the phone back to Roland.

"Keep it. I got what I needed from him."

"Which was?" asked Mel, wondering.

"The names, addresses, phone numbers of every operative in your ballot printing operation. You were careless, thinking you could do all this and no one would talk."

Mel shrugged. He had been worried, but he also had a few hundred other things on his mind running the campaign. "Looks like you missed a few."

Roland smiled. "For now. We'll see what tomorrow brings." He turned to leave.

"She is president now, Roland. This means the entire world is out to take her down. Remember this as you start indiscriminately eliminating everyone. America differs from your usual Eastern European haunts. Even from Israel. Just remember. Even the best make a mistake. And it ultimately costs them."

Roland stared at Mel, who did not flinch or blink. He opened the office door and left.

They were playing a dangerous game.

Chapter 58

As expected, the Michigan Supreme Court refused to hear the lawsuit from Nick's campaign. The Sixth circuit federal court of appeals also declined to take the cases, since the Michigan court did not provide a ruling to appeal. Jenny filed the paperwork to appeal to the Supreme Court, to have the certification rescinded, and a full-blown audit, including verification of each mail in voter.

While awaiting the Court to accept or deny the case, one witness recanted their sworn affidavit under FBI interrogation, saying they were probably high at the time they signed it. This was the person who claimed to have the video evidence.

Because of this, his evidence was no longer accepted. The FBI returned the phone to him. He promptly reset it to the factory settings, wiping all the data as they watched. No copies having been made, of course.

The second witness was arrested during interrogation for outstanding warrants stemming from grand theft to sex with a minor. They were booked into county lockup awaiting arraignment and trial. The media had a field day destroying the character of this witness at the FBI press conference announcing this turn of events.

The media and even the FBI were calling on the Turner campaign to drop the charade of voter fraud and drop the lawsuits and accept the outcome of the upcoming vote in the house. It was clear they expected this to go the way of the President.

Finally, the third witness died while in an FBI safe house of an apparent heroin overdose. There was no autopsy. With no direct next of kin, the body was cremated before Nick and his team could find a judge to order a third-party examination and autopsy.

American *Pravda* summarized their allegations as last gasp antics from Nick's campaign subjecting the country to lies from convicted child molesters, drug addicts and criminals. All designed to undermine the faith of the common citizen in their fair and secure election systems.

According to snap polls issued by each of these outlets paired with their partner 'papers of record,' the results showed Nick's approval ratings diving, now significantly below Lexi. Especially in trust and the ability to lead categories.

Those few voices continuing to highlight the coincidences of the convenient deaths or canceling of anyone daring to come forward, challenging the government narrative, were drowned out.

Boycotts were organized, protesters circled corporate headquarters, and sponsors were threatened if they continued to contribute to amplifying Turner's conspiracy mongering. It worked as many knuckled under to these threats. Even EXN's reporting took a decidedly neutral view of the proceedings. The body politic was fighting back against the chemo.

#

"We are no longer investigating the alleged voter fraud in Michigan and elsewhere. The recanting, and credibility of the witness statements, all of whom had extensive criminal records, leads us to believe these witnesses were coerced or bribed into making these statements," said acting FBI Director Coleman.

"We are opening an investigation into where and how these statements were obtained. The massive amounts of money forced to be spent by localities to unnecessarily validate the integrity of our election processes we already know to be accurate. The unfortunate death of witness #3 from a heroin overdose was the last episode in this unfortunate tale. And we fully believe it was a tall tale concocted to sow doubt in our electoral system and the process by which we ensure our votes are legitimate. I will now take your questions."

"How did witness #3 get the heroin, if she was in a safe house surrounded by FBI agents?" asked an LN1 reporter.

"We are investigating this as we speak. We believe it may have been smuggled in during one of the food deliveries," said the Director.

"But why? That makes no sense? If she had no contact with the outside world, how in the world would she order heroin? Also, from our research, witness #3 had no prior history of drug use. And her 'extensive criminal record' you refer to were all arrests for peaceful protests. Hardly anything comparable to the other two's records of violent crime," noted Ned Wheeler from EXN.

"It is under investigation. That's all I can disclose at this point because of the ongoing investigation," replied Karen impatiently.

"Director, were you able to establish where these witnesses said the operation was taking place?" asked NWN.

"We did locate the warehouse. We investigated the premises and seized surveillance photos from the industrial park and the surrounding traffic footage. There was nothing on any of the surveillance to show any activity. The empty warehouse contained no evidence of an operation of the size suggested by the witnesses."

"In fact, the type of effort they stated would have required excessive electrical service and none of this was recorded or provided according to the local power authority. This led us to question the first witness specifically about this, leading to them recanting their testimony and admitting the video was fake," explained Karen.

"Will you disclose the name and location of the witness now that they have been released and the video evidence destroyed?" asked Lauren Bergamo.

"We cannot at this time, as we are reviewing charges against them for making false statements. In time, we will release this information when our investigation concludes."

"Can you disclose where this operation was said to have occurred?" asked the NWN reporter in a follow up.

"In the DC area is all I will say at this time," shared Karen.

"Director, do you not find it convenient that all three witnesses who described the operations and provided the video evidence of the operation in action are all now discredited by the FBI? The agency reporting to the person who stands to benefit the most. And is it not unusual for the witness who died to have been cremated without an autopsy?" asked Lauren.

The director looked at the usually reliable ANC reporter, who was now becoming increasingly critical of the FBI. She paused for a second before answering.

"Ms. Bergamo, first we are the FBI. It does not matter who the President is. We investigate and seek the truth. The *truth* is, these witnesses were clearly rehearsed. Coordinating their story and somehow creating the video evidence to support it. Right now we are trying to find out if they had help in this effort," she trailed off, clearly implying the Turner campaign had been involved.

"As for the unfortunate demise of witness #3. It is under investigation. The woman had no immediate family, is my guess," responded Karen quickly.

Lauren continued. "Guess, Director? Cremation is usually after 30 days for an unclaimed body, not 30 hours. This situation, on the heels of the obvious attempt at a frame up with the ballots before the election in Michigan. And your announcement of the FBI investigation a week before the election leading to the State wrongfully disenfranchising Michigan's mail in ballots for Turner. Then the convenient arson destroying these ballots on the eve of them being counted may have swung the election away from Senator Turner. How do you defend the FBI's actions in these cases?" accused Lauren.

"That is all for now. If you have any further questions, please direct them to our office. Thank you," she turned to go when a question was shouted from the back.

"Is this a cover up, Director?" She stopped and looked out over the crowd, trying to see who asked the question. As the reporters continued to shout questions, she turned and headed out.

#

"Who killed the goddamn witness?" asked Karen once they were back in her office. This directed at her lead investigator, Ron Luchesi.

"Honestly, we don't know. It happened overnight. When she went to her bedroom in the safe house, she was fine. The next morning, we knocked and when she didn't answer, we went in. There was a needle in her arm. There were signs of a struggle. The window was also no longer locked. Our agents stationed on the perimeter swear they saw and heard nothing. Clearly somebody got in, held her down and injected her with the heroin. She was not a user, so it would have ended quickly," replied Ron.

"Did we do an autopsy?"

"Of course we did. The heroin was almost pure fentanyl. It would have killed her in 30 seconds. She fought hard. Broken nails and a chipped tooth. It also looks like whoever held her hit her hard in the face at least once. She had a broken nose and a fractured cheekbone. The blow was delivered with precision and force. Probably knocked her out, or at least senseless. Long enough to inject the heroin."

"Shit, why did we leak she died of a drug overdose? And how the hell do we come up with a plausible story about how she got it? Shit, shit, shit," said Karen. "How could no one hear the struggle?"

"I don't know. Once the election is certified, we can just ignore it."

"If we can get that bitch Bergamo to stop asking questions. How do we explain the cremation?" asked Karen.

"Clerical error. The witness, Maya Flores, was cremated when someone mis-wrote the date on the form. It is true, she had no next of kin, so no one was going to claim the body anyway," recited Ron.

"And the other two witnesses?"

"Well, one is headed to lockup for his other crimes, so we can monitor him to make sure he isn't giving any press conferences. We'll watch the third one too. He'll screw up somewhere and we'll detain him. Then we can figure it out."

Karen breathed a sigh of relief. "Good. The last thing we need is any of them showing up on ANC being interviewed by Bergamo about our interrogation tactics. Stonewall any requests for information. We'll 'lose' this until after the election is finished."

#

"The Supreme Court of California in a 5 to 3 decision ruled in favor of the plaintiffs in the case of *Blackbird, Turner, et al.* vs *Orange County Board of Elections*. Citing the overwhelming physical evidence presented.

They immediately ordered the disqualification of every duplicate vote adjudicated incorrectly by the local election judge."

"They also ruled every mail in ballot which contained a vote for a congressional candidate in one ink and the presidential vote in another color ink be summarily discarded. Further, the Court suggested the State of California perform a full forensic audit of all mail in ballots counted in Orange County to determine the level of fraudulent votes cast," read the legal news reporter on EXN.

"This action and the change of vote tallies prompted each of the Party candidates for House seats to switch from winners of their contests to losers to their Opposition opponents," added the reporter.

"There is no precedent in the history of federal elections of such widespread fraud and subsequent disqualification of congressional seats. It is also important to point out, this ruling was handed down by the California Supreme Court which comprises eight judges appointed by Party governors. We can only speculate on the ramifications of this ruling on other pending cases."

#

"Even they couldn't duck this one," gloated Jenny to Nick, Earl, Margie, Steve, and Chuck, who were all present in his Senate office conference room watching as the EXN Reporter standing in front of the Supreme Court building in Sacramento read the majority opinion.

"Good luck getting California to conduct an audit on their mail in ballots. They would find a good deal of them are from homeless and mentally indigent 'voters'," promised Chuck, making air quotes.

"They won't do it. But it helps us because at least they ordered it. They did this because they knew the Party operatives of Orange County were guilty of widespread fraud in the harvesting activity," stated Nick.

"What time does Duane begin his argument?" asked Chuck.

"11am. The defendants go first at 10am," said Jenny.

"We'll head over around a quarter to noon to wait for him to finish," said Nick.

"There will be a gaggle of reporters out front. Do you want to say a few words?" asked Margie.

"We'll see. I'm not inclined to contribute to the circus. I've already made my points."

Chapter 59

Duane Cooper stood in front of the eight justices of the Supreme Court of the United States to argue the case of *Turner* vs *the State of Michigan*. The deceased Justice Moore's empty ninth seat emblematic of Nick's bad luck.

Duane began with the usual statements, going through the legal issues outlined in the brief. The State of Michigan had overstepped their boundary in withholding the ability of the state election boards to count the mail in ballots pending an open FBI investigation.

He continued to cite precedent and call into question the lack of foresight in not counting the ballots and then holding them in escrow until the investigation had been completed. This would have established if the number of votes would have changed the outcome of the State of Michigan's electoral award.

Secondarily, he argued the entire process of balloting in the state and the specific cases of *just* the six counties around Detroit having twenty percent higher turnout than historical precedent. The collection and counting of these ballots at the end of the voting process leads the entire country to question the integrity of the vote in Michigan. He fielded several questions from the Justice's during his initial review of the legal brief, some skeptical, some dismissive and some genuinely interested.

He cited precedent from the Supreme Court case *Marion County Election Board* vs *State of Indiana Democratic Party*, specifically the majority opinion written by the then increasingly liberal Justice John Paul Stevens where he stated:

'with the National Voter Registration Act of 1993, Congress established procedures that would both increase the number of registered voters and protect the integrity of the electoral process. The statute requires state motor

vehicle driver's license applications to serve as voter registration applications. While that requirement has increased the number of registered voters, the statute also contains a provision restricting States' ability to remove names from the lists of registered voters. These protections have been partly responsible for inflated lists of registered voters. For example, evidence credited by Judge Barker estimated that as of 2004 Indiana's voter rolls were inflated by as much as 41.4%, and data collected by the Election Assistance Committee in 2004 indicated that 19 of 92 Indiana counties had registration totals exceeding 100% of the 2004 voting-age population' end quote," said Duane.

"This was in 2004. We are decades later. This combined with the excuse of COVID has been used to remove all safeguards against voter fraud. With the added incentive to encourage fraud, these same poorly maintained lists of registered voters are used to mail ballots to every 'registered' voter. Add in years of automatic voter registration during driver's license issuing and renewal and you are essentially sending ballots to everyone. Regardless of a stated desire to vote, or even a historical record of prior voting in national elections. Another quote from Justice Steven's opinion in *Marion*:"

'but they do indicate that Congress believes that photo identification is one effective method of establishing a voter's qualification to vote and that the integrity of elections is enhanced through improved technology'. That conclusion is also supported by a report issued by the Commission on Federal Election Reform chaired by former President Jimmy Carter and former Secretary of State James A. Baker III, which is a part of the record in these cases. In the introduction to their discussion of voter identification, they made these pertinent comments:

'A good registration list will ensure that citizens are only registered in one place, but election officials still need to make sure that the person arriving at a polling site is the same one that is named on the registration list. In the old days and in small towns where everyone knows each other, voters did not need to identify themselves. But in the United States, where 40 million people move each year, and in urban areas where some people do not even know the people living in their own apartment building let alone

their precinct, some form of identification is needed. There is no evidence of extensive fraud in U. S. elections or of multiple voting, but both occur, and it could affect the outcome of a close election. The electoral system cannot inspire public confidence if no safeguards exist to deter or detect fraud or to confirm the identity of voters. Photo identification cards currently are needed to board a plane, enter federal buildings, and cash a check. Voting is equally important. Commission on Federal Election Reform, Report, Building Confidence in U. S. Elections (Sept. 2005), (Carter-Baker Report)'

Duane looked up from his notes at the stoic faces of the eight Supreme Court justices.

"Further, in his opinion, Justice Stevens included the following statement regarding fraud:" '*There is no question about the legitimacy or importance of the State's interest in counting only the votes of eligible voters. Moreover, the interest in orderly administration and accurate recordkeeping provides a sufficient justification for carefully identifying all voters participating in the election process. While the most effective method of preventing election fraud may well be debatable, the propriety of doing so is perfectly clear.*'

"Clearly, Justice Stevens was most concerned with confirming both the eligibility of the voter, and also the integrity ensuring only the eligible voter indeed cast their own ballot. This can logically be extrapolated to also extend these arguments to mail in ballots," argued Duane.

"But we are not arguing the efficacy of photo ID requirements in voting," responded Justice Rodriguez.

"Indeed, Madame Justice, but we are arguing the efficacy of voter eligibility and the concern of the legitimacy of the vote being cast by the aforementioned voter," countered Duane.

"Again, Counselor, this is not about verifying the eligibility of the voter, but the certification of the votes and whether the State of Michigan has exceeded their authority in disallowing ballots from being counted," retorted Justice Rodriguez.

"I disagree with my esteemed colleague," said Justice Benton. "This is all about voter integrity and the confidence of the public in our election processes. This is about ensuring the votes counted are the votes cast by the people who are listed on the ballots. Your citing Justice Steven's opinion from *Marion* is timely and pertinent because it gets to the root of the problem. Bloated registration rolls and no safeguard for verifying these rolls are in fact ensuring, beyond a mailing address, the voter sent the ballot is indeed the registered voter or perhaps even an eligible voter entirely. Also, the vote received from said voter is also required to have no verification beyond a signature, that as Carter and Baker stated in the report, is easy to forge," she finished.

"Madame Justice, are you trying the case for the Counselor?" asked Justice Rodriquez in a disdainful tone, as Duane tried to keep the smile off his face at the impending cat fight.

"No more than you, Justice Rodriguez," replied Justice Benton archly.

"Please continue Counselor," said the Chief Justice interceding.

"Of course, your Honors, in keeping with the arguments of both Justices' Rodriguez and Benton, I would site one last passage from Justice Steven's opinion in *Marion* as pertinent to our current case:"

'*Finally, the State contends that it has an interest in protecting public confidence 'in the integrity and legitimacy of representative government'. While that interest is closely related to the State's interest in preventing voter fraud, public confidence in the integrity of the electoral process has independent significance, because it encourages citizen participation in the democratic process. As the Carter-Baker Report observed, the "electoral system cannot inspire public confidence if no safeguards exist to deter or detect fraud or to confirm the identity of voters.'*

"I would submit, this case is not solely about the actions of the Supreme Court of the State of Michigan, but also about the entire process, including activity beyond mere coincidence. While we have no physical evidence of specific voter fraud, I would again submit, the only way to guarantee the integrity of elections where a majority of the ballots are delivered by mail is to build into the process some amount of time and effort to randomly sample a statistically valid number of the physical mail in ballots. So we have evidence and confirmation of the *legitimacy* of the votes and the voter. We contact the individual voters of these random samples to confirm they did indeed submit the vote in a mail in manner. Have them sign an affidavit confirming this, under penalty of perjury.

"Without this, we have no concrete way of confirming the integrity of these elections and, as Justice Stevens said in his opinion, citizen participation will diminish, but the number of votes may not correspondingly shrink. I would submit the statistical anomalies of six counties in Georgia with over 90% turnout. Six Counties in Michigan with over 92% turnout. Four counties in Arizona with over 93% turnout and I would also cite Pennsylvania, Wisconsin and Nevada as yet more examples of twenty percent increases in voter turnout. In only these counties where ballots were discovered at the end of counting!" Duane was on a roll, confidently disclosing his statistics.

"As you no doubt saw in Wisconsin, a single canvasser had the courage to question the votes. They saw physical evidence of potential fraud. As Carter and Baker cited, they actually knew the aforementioned voters did not submit mail in ballots, let alone vote in person. This is clear evidence of fraud. This in itself should raise a red flag and put into action upstanding and honorable election officials to validate and question whether they got it right," ended Duane.

"Once again Counselor, if you choose to spend your hour before us, regaling us with tales and your opinions on how elections should be run, that is your choice. We are here to review the law and whether the Supreme Court of Michigan has overstepped their authority in restricting the access to the mail in ballots of candidate Turner. Even if we were to find in your favor, what would the proposed remedy be?" asked Justice Rodriguez.

Duane made to answer when Justice Molinari interrupted. "I would remind Justice Rodriguez, this is indeed the Counselor's hour, and it is not only our job to judge on the ruling of the Michigan Supreme Court, but on the entire election process. How these votes were handled and if they were adjudicated properly. If you please Counselor, continue."

"Thank you, your Honor. Next, I would cite the Supreme Court's 6-3 judgement in favor of Arizona's HB 2023 dealing with both in precinct voting and banning ballot harvesting. While neither applies directly to our current argument, the opinion by the Majority explains precedent that is relevant to this case. For those who choose to vote early by mail, Arizona has long required that '*[o]nly the elector may be in possession of that elector's early ballot.' In 2016, the state legislature enacted House Bill 2023 (HB 2023), which makes it a crime for any person other than a postal worker, an elections official, or a voter's caregiver, family member, or household member to knowingly collect an early ballot—either before or after it has been completed.'*

"Further, the opinion went on: '*One strong and entirely legitimate state interest is the prevention of fraud. Fraud can affect the outcome of a close election, and fraudulent votes dilute the right of citizens to cast ballots that carry appropriate weight. Fraud can also undermine public confidence in the fairness of elections and the perceived legitimacy of the announced outcome. Ensuring that every vote is cast freely, without intimidation or undue influence is also a valid and important state interest. This interest helped to spur the adoption of what soon became standard practice in this country and other democratic nations the world round: the use of private voting booths*'.

"Your Honor's, with the time remaining, I will, in fact, ask you to consider your role in our country," stated Duane in a solemn but firm voice.

"We have lost confidence in our election processes. We have lost confidence in the one person, one vote mantra under which we have successfully operated for well over two hundred years. With the expanded usage of machines. Which require humans to program and are not easily understood. Machines, to which many reports presented to Congress have proven time and time again, are subject to manipulation and hacking. We have traded legitimacy for efficiency. What does it matter if we have made the possibility of fraud more prevalent? Now able to be done in the safety of a parent's basement or a server farm in Iran, China, or Russia," said Duane, raising his hands for emphasis.

"While COVID may have indeed required extraordinary circumstances, why did they not also trigger extraordinary measures to ensure the mail in balloting was indeed fair and true? We are now several elections removed from that election and yet, voter confidence is lower than ever. So how is it we have achieved such high turnouts with such disdain and disgust at this process?"

"Let us apply the rule of common sense. The states with incredible turnouts are well known to be the states that swing elections. These statistically unlikely turnouts are limited to only the well known, blue counties in the six states that swing elections."

"We have no access to the physical voting machines to have third parties review their logs and other files that may prove one way or another the election and results match the votes cast. And yet, in each of these states, five of them anyway, the machines have mysteriously had these logs erased and in the other case of course they burned up in a fire that also burned up uncounted ballots that may have changed the outcome of an entire election."

"When fraud has been alleged, pointing out physical evidence, collectively the person raising the red flag had her life ruined and her position replaced by someone who had seen not a *single* ballot of the election, yet could vote to confirm the ballots cast were authentic and legal."

"We had others offer tales of massive fraud on an industrial scale and yet all three witnesses have recanted or conveniently died. Causing their complaints to be dismissed from lack of evidence or the complainant being incapable of testifying."

"This is worse than the most notorious gangster movies." concluded Duane, pausing and looking across the Justices. Most were paying attention. Justice Rodriguez was reading something on her phone, not paying attention to his statement in the least. He paused, looking at her until several of the Justices looked to see what he was looking at. As he prepared to continue, he shook his head in disappointment.

"I ask you, I beg you, to consider the role you play. You are the last bastion. The final sea wall between the safe existence of our election system and our one vote, one person, in person voting democracy, or the impending flood that would wash away any and all election safeguards. Turning our elections from democratic to no better than Iraq, Zimbabwe, Venezuela, North Korea."

"It is in your hands. It is an immense burden, I know. But if you don't act to protect the integrity of our voting system, who else can? At a minimum, I ask you to draw a line in the sand. To demand better of our states. To insist on the safeguards to test the voter accuracy. I ask you to find against the order of the Michigan Supreme Court and as a remedy, since the votes no longer exist to count, that instead you order a forensic audit of the mail in ballots cast for President Smythe-Thomas."

"Validating each with the voter listed to confirm they did cast the mail in ballot. If you were to allow this effort, it would once and for all establish mail in balloting is safe, accurate, and set a precedent you and both parties can use to argue against any future suits claiming mail in voting is rife with fraud."

At this last statement, Justice Rodriguez lifted her head as if to protest this statement. Before she could interject, Duane finished his statement. "I thank you for your time and willingness to address the systemic problem of election fraud in this country. Thank you."

"Thank you, Mr. Cooper. The case is submitted."

"Wait, I want my comment on the record," said Justice Rodriguez.

"The case is closed," repeated the Chief Justice.

Duane smiled and picked up his notes, turning to leave the chamber. He may have earned the enmity of Justice Rodriguez for the remainder of his career, but it was worth it.

Chapter 60

"Well, how did it go?" asked Jenny, as Duane, Chuck, Nick, and she walked from the Supreme Court to Nick's Senate office.

"Let's just say Justice Rodriguez took me off her Christmas card list."

"Geez, what did you do?" asked Jenny, looking at Duane wearing his outdated corduroy jacket and bolo tie with his long ponytail swaying as he walked.

"I appealed to their sense of duty and integrity. Frankly, it was all I had left. They still can't magically produce mail in ballots that weren't counted. I cited *Marion* and Arizona HB 2023 heavily. That's what set off, Rodriguez."

Jenny laughed. "I bet it did."

"Care to enlighten us?" asked Chuck.

"Justice Rodriguez is the biggest proponent of the living constitution on the court. She fully believes it is the Supreme Court's job to 'fix' the laws Congress passes. She is also the biggest supporter of removing any need for voter IDs at the polls and was the most vocal supporter of going to all mail in ballots. Not just for registered voters, but for everyone. She is about as partisan a Justice as we have ever had on the court," answered Jenny.

"I think I may actually have made the Chief Justice care. I'm at least making him think hard about planting a stake in the ground around voter integrity. This is a perfect case for him, because there is not really much he can do to alter the outcome."

"I asked them to do a random sampling of mail in ballots and confirm those registered voters actually voted. I told them if they did this in a transparent and non-partisan manner, it would go a long way to providing confidence in the voting again and possibly set a precedent to stop any further cases like this," said Duane.

"You backed them into a corner," laughed Jenny.

"How so?" asked Nick.

"If they don't do something, then they are agreeing the current fraudulent voting practices are not fraudulent. The transcript will get out. After what Duane asked, which is a perfectly reasonable way to resolve this issue, especially in a state where Nick lost by 30,000 votes."

"They should support this random sampling to validate the count in Michigan and the election across all the swing states. If they fight it and don't do it, then the fix is in, and the Court will lose all credibility because they won't order this simple review. Rodriguez will fight this tooth and nail. And if she does, we will know there are over 30,000 fraudulent votes among the mail in votes for Lexi," said Jenny.

"Exactly," grinned Duane.

"I guess you are as good as advertised," admitted Nick with a smile.

"Hardly. It didn't help Dusty, did it?" frowned Duane.

"You did all you could then and now, too. I appreciate it," said Nick solemnly, his smile disappearing quickly.

"Now we wait until they give their judgement. I would still bet they deadlock four to four. The Chief is so against doing anything remarkable," noted Duane as they entered the Hart building walking to Nick's office.

#

Several days later, Jenny came into Nick's office. "Nick, they're about to release their opinion on the case."

"Be right there."

He walked into the conference room. It was filled with staff. An EXN blonde stood in front of the camera with the ruling in hand.

"Adam, it looks like they voted 5 to 3. I am reading the ruling as we speak. Summarizing, it appears they are agreeing there are too many coincidences and too many incidents of questionable voting practices and results to find for the defendant. Further, they are admonishing both the Attorney General and then the Supreme Court of Michigan for overstepping their power and materially affecting the national election with their irresponsible and reckless conduct regarding the decision to not count a presidential candidate's ballots."

"Wow, they wrote reckless and irresponsible in the ruling?" whistled Adam as she continued to read.

"Yes, they did. They're recommending the Attorney General and each of the Justices of the Supreme Court in Michigan who supported this decision resign, as they have tarnished their impartial role beyond redemption," said the reporter as she read.

"That is a strong condemnation for a legal ruling," said Jenny, looking at Duane, who was smiling.

The EXN reporter continued. "While there is no physical evidence of voter fraud, and since Michigan has already certified their vote, we do not feel it is in our power to turn back the clock to count votes that are unknown in quantity. We recommend they begin with a complete audit of their mail in votes, including forensic discovery and confirmation of each mail in voter with a signed affidavit. We will not order this, but we recommend the State of Michigan do this to restore credibility in the election process and in the election itself for their citizens and those of the country at large. Anything less will rightfully leave the public feeling the process was less than honest," read the reporter.

"Shit," said Jenny, in a very unladylike tone. "That was our last hope, getting him to decertify the vote, so we could do an audit and change the outcome."

The EXN reporter continued. "Hang on, Adam, there is more. The Chief Justice says, while they do not have the authority to decertify the vote, they have the power to disqualify the entire state because of the confused nature of the voting. The Constitution gives the states the right to run the election in the manner they choose, but it leaves the power to the Federal Government to determine the validity of the results delivered. Concluding there is not enough time to do a complete forensic audit of the mail in ballots to overcome the evidence of potential fraud. As a result, we feel it is in the best interests of all parties to disqualify Michigan's electoral votes from the results of this Presidential Election. It should also be noted that this does not disqualify Michigan from casting a vote in the House of Representatives," finished the EXN reporter.

"That was interesting. For a Chief Justice who does not like controversy, he just issued an opinion creating a massive one," pronounced Jenny.

"Yet it does not really change anything. Lexi didn't need the votes and Nick didn't gain any," said Chuck.

Nick and Duane looked at each other, smiling. Chuck and Jenny noticed. "Why are you too so happy?" asked Jenny, confused.

"Do you want to tell her or should I?" asked Nick.

"By all means, Senator," said Duane with a mini bow.

"Jenny, please prepare a brief and file it with the Supreme Court asking them to rule on the number of electoral votes needed to win the election now that Michigan has been disqualified. Since they are removed from the total, that takes the total number of electoral votes from 538 to 523. The number to get in order to win a simple majority is no longer 270, it is 262. Therefore, the Turner campaign should be declared the winner of the election without delay," explained Nick.

"Holy Shit," said Chuck. "Will that work?"

Duane shrugged. "Maybe. Depends on whether the Chief Justice has broken out of his shell or not. And if they once again want to have the Supreme Court accused of deciding a presidential election. On the surface, it makes sense. It will all come down to whether or not he wants to stick his neck out."

"But it is right based on his own logic. A disqualified state is no longer part of the calculus of the electoral college. There are now 49 states and DC," agreed Chuck.

"Let's get it filed and see if they will take the case and then if they will issue a ruling. They shouldn't need any argument. Either Michigan is disqualified, and the total changes, or Michigan is zero electoral votes but still counts in the total," said Nick.

"I will get it filed immediately," responded Jenny, almost running from the room.

"Where is Margie?" asked Nick, looking around.

Margie and Jer were standing in a corner watching the TV. She turned at her name. "Here Nick," she said, walking to him.

"Margie, get me on Tommy tonight. 2 minutes, 30 seconds, I don't care. I need to get this out there," said Nick.

Margie nodded and was already dialing.

\#

Lexi sat in the sitting room next to the presidential bedroom. Mel was there as well. They both had drinks in their hand as they watched the news discussing the Supreme Court ruling on Michigan.

"I trust Michigan isn't doing an audit of the ballots cast," assumed Lexi.

"No fucking way. At least not if any of them want to work in politics again. And the temerity of the Chief Justice to demand the Supreme Court of Michigan resign? After we fought so hard to get them their roles. I don't think so. Our friends in the media are already hammering the court for overstepping their boundaries," offered Mel.

"Good. Let's keep it up."

Both their phones buzzed. Mel grabbed the remote and turned to EXN. Senator Turner was on with Tommy.

"So let me get this straight," said Tommy. "You are asking the Supreme Court to rule on whether Michigan counts in the electoral college, having been disqualified. And if that's the case, your claim is there are no longer 538 electoral votes, but now 523 without Michigan?

"Yes. If true, we no longer need 270 electoral votes, only 262 to claim a majority," nodded Nick.

"With your current total of 268, you're asking them to declare you the winner?" replied Tommy, leaning forward in an excited voice.

"That's right Tommy," replied a smiling Nick Turner.

\#

Lexi dropped her drink on the carpet of the room. Her face drained of color as she turned to look at Mel in terror.

"He can't do that, right?" she wailed.

"I don't know. If the Supreme's rule this way we are screwed. There is nowhere to appeal. They are the Supreme Court. We could choose to not abide by a ruling if not in our favor. You are the President after all, but that would get ugly. My suggestion is you handle the Chief Justice carefully. Don't bully him."

"Right. First thing in the morning and I'll have a civil conversation," said Lexi, her face still drained of color. "Turner refuses to go away."

"It sure looks that way," said Mel.

#

"Hello Rob," said Lexi the next morning, speaking to the Chief Justice of the Supreme Court, Robert P. Harris Jr.

"Madame President," answered the Chief Justice warily.

"I am sure you know why I've called?"

"I do, and I thank you for not making me come to the White House. I think that would set the wrong tone."

"I agree. That's why I called. Listen, I understand your position. It is difficult. But I would ask that you consider things. You have already disqualified Michigan. A move many believe is beyond the power of the Court to execute."

"Yet we did not *order* them to do the mail in ballot audit. We left it to the state. Had we ordered it, we both know what we would have found. And you would have lost right there," noted Rob, interrupting.

"Perhaps, but you might have been overstepping your boundaries again. You made the correct decision to leave it to the states to unravel their mess. You need to consider the long-term effect of any further rulings. Do you want to be remembered as the guy who screwed Michigan voters to put Turner into office? This would be worse than *Bush vs Gore* in terms of the destruction of all credibility of our voting systems and of the Court itself as an impartial arbiter. If you vote to allow Turner to win, you are playing kingmaker," said Lexi.

"And if we don't, are we not doing the same for you?" he asked.

"I am already King. So, no, you are letting the process play out as intended."

"If he won, despite all the efforts otherwise? The lasting effects to our Republic are really the slow destruction of voter confidence and their overall desire to continue to take part in a rigged game. And if it comes out later, with definitive proof of fraud. Then what? At some point, the voters pick up their toys and go home. But this is bigger than that, I fear. Turner is tapping into something. What it is, I don't know. Win or lose, this election isn't going to pop the pressure relief valve," suggested Rob.

"Maybe so. Do you want to be the one to punch a hole in the boiler's side and let all that steam out catastrophically? I can diffuse it and let it dissipate in a manner that will not destroy the country. Can you say the same if you anoint him president? All I ask is you contemplate the consequences of your decision and the impact it will have on the country and its institutions if the ultimate reviewers of justice no longer interpret the laws made by Congress. Instead, start implementing by judicial fiat. That is a tremendous burden and one you will bear personally," forecast Lexi.

"As President, I am prepared to make those decisions and bear the consequences. As Chief Justice, that is not your role. Do you want it and the responsibility that goes with it? I thank you for taking my call this morning."

"Thank you, Madame President," answered the Chief Justice of the United States.

As he ended the call, he turned to look at his wife of less than a year standing at the kitchen counter sipping her coffee. This job had already cost him his first wife and family, a messy divorce, and half of the family fortune willed to him by his father.

As he looked at his very much younger wife, all he wanted was to live a quiet life of pleasure after so much angst, conflict, and drama. He contemplated the sacrifices he'd made to achieve his realized goal of leading the Supreme Court.

He did not want to be the center of the universe. Glancing again at his wife in her silk robe, he made eye contact. She smiled coyly, turned heading toward the bedroom, the swirling of her robe revealing her nakedness. He smiled and followed her back to the bedroom to forget his troubles. At least for a little while.

#

In a room in the Offutt Air Force Base in Omaha, Nebraska, a soulless machine dutifully recorded the highly encrypted conversation. Storing the information from the call in a file in an equally heavily encrypted portion of the supercomputer's flash storage array.

Chapter 61

Nick stood in the doorway of his Senate office. He looked back into the room. It was now empty of anything belonging to him. His few possessions had been boxed up and sent back to Colorado. The bulk of Congress was long gone for the holiday break, the last sessions having ended a week ago. Next week, a fresh set of legislators and those re-elected would return for the next congress.

Nick turned and walked out with no trace of remorse. Chuck stood in the hallway, with a small box of his last possessions. He handed Nick the bronze plaque which once hung outside the office in the hallway. Announcing this was the Senate office of The Honorable Nick Turner of Colorado. Nick took it from him with a smile.

"Well, it was interesting, for sure," responded Nick.

"That is an understatement of mammoth proportions."

They took the elevator to the bottom of the building and the parking garage, walking to Chuck's Prius. As they left the building, Nick looked at Chuck.

"What next?" asked Nick.

"When? I'm going to visit my parents in France for Christmas."

"They left the Villages in Florida? In December?" noted Nick sarcastically.

"They wanted to experience strike season in France," responded Chuck, laughing.

"I believe that is a year-round phenomenon now. Enjoy."

"You heading to Colorado?"

"I don't know. I may stay here, explore my new mansion and the library. That could take years."

"Once you get settled, you can give me the tour. Banks' library is legendary. Oxford and Cambridge are probably pissed."

"They both asked me about getting it. I politely declined," laughed Nick.

Chuck navigated Washington traffic, chauffeuring Nick out to his 'new' house in Chevy Chase. As they drove, neither spoke much.

"When do you think the Supreme's will rule on the motion?" asked Nick.

"No telling. They have gone home for the holidays. It could happen during the break or on the 3rd or possibly not at all. They could ignore the request as well." admitted Chuck, trying to shrug as he drove. "Too bad he didn't disqualify Michigan from voting in the house. That would have made all the difference. Who knows, maybe that is one option they *are* considering."

"Well, it makes it hard to have a relaxing holiday with this hanging over our head," remarked Nick.

"That's for sure. Here we are. Impressive. Welcome to the world of old money," grinned Chuck.

"How does it compare to your parent's brownstone?" asked Nick with a smile.

"Different. Theirs is in a block of connected houses, like those on the upper west side in New York City. You have," he paused, "a.... yard I think they call it," laughed Chuck before finishing in a shocked tone.

"Yes, I do. Maybe I'll get a dog."

"I would recommend against that. Me thinks you aren't going to be home much for the next few years," guessed Chuck.

"I think you're probably right. Enjoy your vacation. I will see you on the 2nd or 3rd at the campaign office, then we can end this thing," announced Nick, shaking Chuck's hand as he collected his last box of belongings.

#

Nick walked up to the front door. Before he could knock, the door opened, and Hobson stood there. "Ah Senator, welcome."

"Henry, I told you, please call me Nick," he said, entering the impressive foyer.

"Sir, I have been addressing the owner of this house as senator for decades. It is more natural to me than a name. Please allow me to continue," said Henry.

"OK, I guess you're not going to change. Soon, though, I won't be entitled to be called senator any longer."

"You'll always be a senator. May I take your bag?" asked Henry, accepting Nick's backpack with his laptop and a few remaining items from his office, ignoring his statement.

"Let's put them in the library. This way," said Henry, leading Nick from the foyer down a hallway, pointing out a sitting room, a formal living room, and a hall bath before approaching a door at the end of the hall leading to his extensive library.

Henry led them through the main library, through a doorway into the small secondary room, where it too was covered in floor to ceiling bookshelves as well. Nick had briefly entered the room on his last visit when presented the book by Churchill from Banks.

An ancient and ornate writing desk took one corner with a phone and lamp on the desk. The desk chair was another well-worn leather chair on wooden legs and old-fashioned casters. In contrast to the first room and its plush area rug carpets, this smaller annex had hand scraped bamboo floors with what looked like a small Persian rug under the legs of the desk. Henry set down Nick's bag in the corner.

"This is where the Senator spent most of his time. In here or in the main library. The true master suite is upstairs, but the Senator converted one of the main floor bedrooms. He stopped climbing stairs many years ago. The entire upstairs is basically unchanged since his wife died over 10 years ago."

"Where is the kitchen?" asked Nick.

Henry led him back down the hall, turning into another wing, through the large dining room with its massive table with a dozen extra chairs against the surrounding walls.

Antique china and buffet cabinets lined the rest of the wall space. The upper half of the walls were covered in original paintings. Nick recognized a few of the artists. This was where Banks, Dolly and Nick had dined during the summer.

They continued on through a large butler's pantry into a spacious and surprisingly modern kitchen. It gleamed with stainless steel appliances, double ovens, warming drawers and a massive gas stovetop with 10 burners and a wide flat top griddle.

There were also double sized fridges and freezers. Nick turned and gave Henry a look. He smiled.

"The Senator's tastes were limited to mostly sandwiches once his wife passed. When she was alive, this house was famous for decades as the hottest ticket in town for parties and holiday gatherings."

"This kitchen was her pride and joy. Mrs. Banks updated it several times through the years, always keeping it up to date with the most modern improvements. This last update was completed just before she passed. The Senator hated to come in here. It reminded him of so many happy times. It was the only time I ever saw him break down," said Henry sadly.

"Well, Henry, we'll make them proud. One day, the parties and the laughter will return. I promise," said Nick.

"That would make him happy. He always felt bad living in a house like this and using only the library, bathroom, and a bedroom. I think that is one reason he left it to you. He felt you would return it to its glory days," offered Henry.

"Why don't you make one of those famous sandwiches? I'll eat it in the office."

"You got it, Nick," said Henry with a mischievous smile.

#

Nick sat in the chair behind the desk. It felt surprisingly comfortable. He looked in the desk drawers. There were the usual pens, stapler, highlighters, and notecards. There were a couple of business cards. Nick took them out, looking at them, wondering why Banks had kept just these in the desk. Henry came in with the sandwich and a local dark beer.

"Thanks Henry. Did Senator Banks have many visitors?" asked Nick, as he took a bite of his sandwich.

"Hey this is great. What is it?"

Henry smiled. "Braunschweiger, Vidalia onions, lettuce, and Dijon mustard on local pumpernickel. It was one of the Senator's favorites. It can be strong. I would suggest you *not* invite Ms. Monroe over after eating this," he said with a big smile. Nick grunted back at his comment.

"As for visitors, the Senator rarely had visitors. In fact, in this last year, I believe you and Ms. Monroe were the only ones who came by the house. He did frequently have calls. I assumed they had to do with his Intelligence or Appropriations committees. Reach under the bottom drawer. There is a button. Push it," suggested Henry.

As Nick pushed the button, the door to the office closed, the windows blacked out, and other lights came on in the office. Senator Bank's office doubled as a SCIF.

"The Senator would lock down the office for many of his calls. I would always tell because there is a light in the main library which would tell me it would be impossible for me to enter the inner office," explained Henry.

"Good to know. Thanks Henry." Nick pushed the button again to disengage from SCIF mode.

"Anything else?"

"No, that's all for now," replied Nick, continuing to devour the sandwich.

He finished it and started perusing the volumes in the library.

#

Nick was in the massive dining room as Hobson served him Salmon picatta, asparagus spears in garlic butter, along with a small Caesar salad and a slice of warm Focaccia bread.

"Where is yours?" asked Nick as Hobson turned to go.

Hobson smiled. "Senator, I don't eat with you."

"Why not?"

"I think you should have this conversation with Ms. Monroe. She can explain it better. Also, I need to show you the garage after dinner," said Henry.

"What's in there, a Dusenberg?" asked Nick.

Henry smiled. "Hardly."

After a slice of cherry pie and coffee, Henry suggested they take a stroll to the garage.

It was brisk, late in the afternoon, with a bite in the wind, but not bad for December in DC. They walked out a side door off the kitchen mudroom, down a path of granite paving stones, through a garden to a large carriage house. There were four garage bays.

Henry stood at the door and entered a code, showing Nick the sequence to deactivate the alarm. Once inside, he entered a second code to deactivate a second silent alarm attached to a local security company with a three-minute response time.

He flipped on the switches. The lights burned brightly, revealing four automobiles. The first was a gleaming Mercedes S550 black sedan. Nick ran his fingers over the pristine finish.

"This was Mrs. Banks' car. The battery is removed, but I can put it in if this is a car you would expect to drive. Senator Banks couldn't bring himself to sell it," said Henry.

Nick shook his head. As he moved down the row, the next was a late model Range Rover in a medium blue color. Nick looked at Henry.

"Yes, this is my daily driver. A nice car for driving in Washington, high enough to see, but not so huge as the ever prevalent Suburban and Escalade. If you would like to drive this, I can certainly drive the Mercedes," offered Henry.

"Oh no Henry, carry on as usual. What is next?" Nick went around the Range Rover. In the final two bays were two examples of exquisite automobile craftsmanship. "E-type right?" asked Nick.

"Yes. A 1961 Jaguar E-Type, gunmetal gray with original red leather interior. He bought it from a collector in Dubai who bought it from the original owner. This was his pride and joy. I only saw him drive it once, but according to Mrs. Banks, in his younger days as a senator, he would commute to the Senate office building. He even convinced another senator to give him his parking spot where he could park it in a corner of the garage, away from traffic and other cars. It is a beautiful car. There is an older gentleman in Alexandria who takes care of it once a year to make sure nothing is failing."

"Is that an American car?" asked Nick, looking at the fourth car.

"Yes. It is a 1948 Buick Roadmaster convertible. It was his father's car. He used to drive it once a year as a tribute to him," said Henry.

"It is fabulous. I don't want to drive any of them, so just keep doing what you've been doing," said Nick, thinking. "On second thought, at some point, the Mercedes maybe, so prep it, please."

"Of course," said Henry.

#

Nick spent the beginning of the holiday getting familiar with his new house. He explored the rooms, sometimes with Henry in tow and others on his own. He looked in every nook and cranny. Examined every piece of antique furniture. The master suite was spectacular. He wished he had met Senator Bank's wife, Penny.

She had impeccable taste and understood how to acquire and remodel things to be timeless. The bed in the master bedroom was said to have come from Versailles itself. It was a huge four poster and required a step stool to mount. The first night Nick spent in it, he felt like a little kid getting to sleep in his parents' bed.

In a house of this age, he expected antiquated fixtures and issues, but it was clear, at some point, an extensive modernization project had occurred on the property. All the fixtures and electrical systems were modern, with touch and voice activation if you so chose.

The master bathroom was straight out of a luxury spa, with stacked stone on the walls, marble fixtures, a massive walk-in shower and a partially sunken soaking tub. There was even a steam shower/sauna in one part of the ensuite.

He shook his head, marveling at this sitting unused for over a decade. Nick also found in one corner of a room he called the study, an elevator.

Banks' decision to live on the main floor was more an issue of missing his wife than not wanting to take the stairs.

Nick invited Henry to join him for Christmas dinner.

"Henry, how does one become a man servant if you don't mind my asking?"

"In my case, it was Mrs. Banks. She was a marvelous woman, kindhearted, sharp as a whip, and, as Senator Banks said many times, his better half. She found me while volunteering at a clinic. I was recovering from an addiction to morphine. I hurt my hip in the British Army."

"After my service, I found work in construction around London. During my work, I was injured on the job and the National Health Service doctor told me I did not need surgery and prescribed a strong morphine-based narcotic."

"Soon I was addicted. Lost my job and was arrested for breaking into cars to steal anything I could pawn. A kindly judge sentenced me to rehab rather than prison. I came to the states to rebuild my life after I kicked my habit. I found work at a DC people's clinic, trying to get my life back in order. She volunteered there."

"I got to know her, and I confided I did not know what to do next. She offered to have me come by the house, a sort of handyman role. I had no idea who she or her husband were," explained Henry, thinking back to that time over 20 years ago while sipping the wine he had selected for the prime rib madeira they were enjoying for Christmas dinner.

"What did Banks think when his wife shows up with a new, much younger handyman?" laughed Nick.

"He was actually the one who told her to bring me to the house. He was getting up there in age. I think he was in his mid-seventies and she was in her early seventies. He wanted someone around to talk to her and help her out around the house. They had a cleaning lady and Senator Banks had a driver. That's how I started. As a handyman around the house and helper for Mrs. Banks. Eventually I moved into one bedroom, though I keep an apartment nearby officially. I became the caretaker of the estate and of them. I have enjoyed it, and they were, and have been, very good to me," he finished.

"If you don't mind my asking. Did you not have any desire to marry or start a family of your own?" asked Nick quietly.

"It would seem strange that a man my age would be content in the service of an older couple and then, upon achieving a financial windfall, continue to provide these services to you? Is that the question?" smiled Henry.

Nick smiled in reply.

"Nick, I am not gay, nor am I a serial killer, a predator, or a pervert of any type. I enjoyed my time with the ladies while in the Army. I have had a series of unfortunate events, most stemming from the morphine addiction, that have rendered me incapable of any intimacy. Even given this, I have, from time to time, had relationships with women I have met. Most of them have a hard time understanding both my chosen profession and my inability to satisfy them in the conventional manner. I am not sad, nor am I lonely. What I do is a noble profession. While not as prevalent in America, it is an established role in places where there is still titled nobility. You, sir, are as close to the English Duke as America has. Even more so with the inheritance and its trappings."

"Henry, my apologies for prying. Banks may have qualified as a Duke. I feel like the seventh son of a Count, nowhere near an Earl or a Duke," laughed Nick.

"Don't sell yourself short, Senator," commented Henry.

"You know you will have to call me Nick after January 3rd when my successor is sworn in. Might as well get used to it. I will just be Nick again."

"We'll see, sir," said Henry, getting up to clear the plates and prepare the dessert.

Nick's phone buzzed.

"What's up?" said Nick into the phone.

"Nick, people are protesting the vote in Michigan. Several of them were hurt in a fight with Antifa. No fatalities, but some are now in the hospital," said Margie.

"On Christmas?" asked Nick

"Fraid so," responded Margie.

"All right, I'll record a video you can post and get up on Hibi. We can't have our people getting violent. It gives Lexi what she wants."

"I'll look for it and get it posted immediately. Merry Christmas."

"You too Margie. Jer with you?" asked Nick slyly. He could imagine Margie blushing on the phone.

She paused for a second. "Yes. We're at my parents. He is right here. Do you need to speak with him?"

"Nope, you two enjoy your holiday," said Nick with a smile. At least two of his staffers were having a happy Christmas.

"Thanks Nick."

#

Nick turned on his camera from his inner office on Christmas evening. He spoke into the camera, highlighting all the reasons not to give Lexi and her crew the footage they craved.

He cautioned them to avoid anyone not showing their faces and record everything! To under no circumstances rise to the bait and fight back. Turn around and walk away. No matter what.

"Call the police. They are on our side, because we are on their side. Violence is the tool of the black and brown shirts of the communist, the fascist, the anarchist and now the Progressive. We are better than that. Be smart and stay safe. We will prevail and we will restore a true Constitutional based government. Merry Christmas and God Bless."

Nick stopped the recording, reviewed it, and sent it off to Margie.

"Not bad, but you know that is not enough," said Henry from the doorway where he had watched.

"I know, but I can't play into their hands. If we fight, we lose. They control the media and the spin. If we look like we are a rabble, it will be January 6th all over again. I have to do everything I can to prevent that from becoming a reality."

"Why not go on the offensive?" asked Henry.

"What is the objective?"

"Force them to count the votes. Force them to validate all the mail in votes," said Henry.

"The key word is force. It won't work. There are too many levers of power they control to derail any effort to get to the truth. Chuck asks the same thing. We have very few assets on our side of the ledger. I have to be very careful in how and when I use them, because we have zero margin for error," explained Nick.

"You have the patience of Job. I could not show the restraint you are," expressed Henry.

"I hope I am not destined to live the rest of Job's story before this ends," retorted Nick in an ironic tone.

#

Nick flew up to Detroit to visit the three people in the hospital from the protest. It was clear they were targeted by groups aligned with the Party. The media was highlighting the retaliation of Turner's folks after they were hit with rocks and frozen water bottles while the local police stood by with orders to not interfere. When Turner's people retaliated, the Antifa thugs fell to the ground, acting like they were being beaten as their allies took photos on their phones.

Before Nick left, he made sure the hospital knew to send all the bills to the Turner Rabble Defense Fund offices. This charity could pay the bills, something he could not with his campaign funds.

As Nick headed back to the airport, he called Margie and Chuck and reviewed what he'd heard.

"Boss," said Margie. "What do you want to do? These pop up protests are showing up all over the place."

"Not sure there is much I can do. All I *can* do is keep encouraging them to stay peaceful. The one thing we need to do is keep them from being in DC on the 6th."

"There is a really big one being organized in Texas and another in Georgia, Arizona and Ohio. I am hearing more and more about these planned protests," said Margie, concerned.

"Maybe we should make it a rally. Should we try to do it in an arena or maybe at the Texas Motor Speedway?" suggested Nick.

"That's a good idea. Let me see when we can do it."

"What about after the vote on the 6th? Maybe do a giant thank you rally in Texas and simulcast it to other places around the country, except Washington?" offered Chuck. "Channel all that energy into a giant countrywide rally?"

"I like it. What do you think Margie?" asked Nick.

"Well, it certainly gives us more time to plan and it would be warmer in Texas," she said with a smile. "It might give us a way to nip some of the other protests and turn them into peaceful rallies. Do we want to do it the afternoon of the 6th? What if you're elected?" asked Margie

"Then I fly to Texas as President and thank everyone," said Nick, laughing.

"See if you can get Tommy to broadcast live from Texas. Win or lose, he should jump at the chance," agreed Chuck.

"Will do," said Margie

"Let's get a video up on the site as well. To warn people not to march on Washington," voiced Chuck.

"Actually, let's spread that word through the local Turner Rabble and other grass roots. Talk to Steve. Keep it off the social channels. I have a feeling they are going to try Jan 6th part two, assuming we will show up. Let's try a head fake," mused Nick aloud.

"It's risky Nick, if some of your followers don't get the word," stated Margie.

"Yes it is, but it is also a test of our ability to communicate to the followers without using the internet or social media. I have a feeling this is going to be important in the future. Let's see if it can work," responded Nick.

"Got it. Jungle telegraph it is. Sons of Liberty, meet the Turner Rabble," laughed Chuck.

"That makes you Paul Revere, Margie. And you're Joseph Warren, Chuck."

She just laughed in reply. Chuck frowned. "It didn't end so well for Dr. Warren."

Nick shrugged. "Just stay away from Bunker Hill."

#

Nick stood on the roof of his house. Banks had built a solarium with both a glassed-in atrium and an outdoor deck. Nick stood on the deck, brandy in hand, as the clock struck midnight. He could see the Washington Monument and the Capitol in the distance as the fireworks announcing New Year's fired off over the Potomac.

He sat down in a chair in the cold crisp air of the now first night of January. Watching his breath in between sips.

"Mind some company?" asked Henry at the doorway carrying two cups of steaming coffee. "I thought you might want something warm."

"Thanks Henry, sure come on out," said Nick, putting his brandy down on a table and accepting the coffee from Henry.

They sat watching the last of the fireworks light up the Washington sky.

"Henry?"

"Yes."

"Banks told you to stay close, didn't he?"

"Yes."

"Would I be right in guessing your time in the 'British Army' might have been, say, SAS?" asked Nick, not looking at Henry.

"Possibly."

"Banks orchestrated all of this, didn't he?" asked Nick.

"That I cannot answer. He gave you this house for a reason. I suspect you will find your answers in his inner library. Think back to the conversations you had, the topics you discussed. I was not privy to the plans, but I was privy to some concerns. My service was not just as his manservant, but bodyguard as well."

Nick turned to look at Hobson, surprise clear on his face.

"I am not sure what he was doing, but there were several attempts on his life in the last two decades. It seems his public persona as a liberal scion did not mimic his private actions. I know from my conversations he became disillusioned with the progressive takeover of the Party years ago."

"He saw their endgame as anti-ethical to what America used to stand for. He felt we had lost our way. He was too old to stop it, but I believe in you, he saw someone who might have a chance. He told me to protect you and to help in any way I can."

"Thanks for the honesty. Not much of that going on in this town. I appreciate the effort. Exactly how do you plan to protect me? And from what?" asked Nick.

"There are many ways to do that. It happens constantly. You may not see it, and we are not perfect, but we will strive to do better."

"We?" asked Nick. Henry smiled in response.

"In case you missed it, someone tried to kill me in Minneapolis," replied Nick with a little laugh.

"Did they?" said Henry in a dry tone.

"You can't be serious. No one can make that shot."

Henry shrugged in reply, sipping his coffee.

"Henry is not your first name, is it?" asked Nick. "Perhaps I will call you Augustus?"

Henry stiffened slightly at the name. "Of course, it is your prerogative to call me as you see fit."

"Augustus Henry Benedict seems like a fitting moniker. What do you think? Perhaps I'll just call you Caesar Augustus."

"A noble moniker for certain, but undeserved," replied Henry.

"Did you know, rumor has it the King of Diamonds in the playing card deck represents Caesar Augustus?"

Henry laughed. "Ah, the sin of pride. You are quite resourceful, Colonel. How did you ever figure this out?"

"If it is any consolation, most of it was conjecture. But it just came together. Why did you leave your calling card? If I can find it out, so can others?"

"A slight risk. I needed you to know. The others would not follow the path you have followed. It would make no logical sense."

"Who made the gun?"

"*We* are not without resources or allies. Perhaps in time.

Nick nodded, realizing he would not get an answer.

"Thank you for hitting your target."

"I missed."

"Excuse me?"

"Nick, I was *not* supposed to hit you. It was supposed to be an assassination attempt to have you shot *at*. Not actually shot. You were so animated, and I was so far away. By the time the bullet got there, you moved into the path."

"I *was* right. No one would take that shot."

"You are correct. As was 'Bob'. I presume he gave you the last clue to point you to my history. What were the odds of you selecting an ex-pupil to explain the idiocy of having yourself shot?"

"Serendipity for sure. He passed me the info on who the King of Diamonds was. Then I connected the dots and yes, you are correct. No one would follow the path I did to you. Most would stop at your grave. You look surprisingly intact for someone 'blown to bits' in the Iraq War."

"Subterfuge was certainly the intent."

"Plus, your story at Christmas reinforced my theory. A little too implausible that you would just show up to be found by Mrs. Banks."

"Necessary to explain my sudden arrival in the Bank's household as his valet. Unfortunately, the morphine addiction and its aftermath are an authentic part of the story. I suffered the injury in the SAS. Once it became clear I could not continue my prior career, my 'accident' explained my disappearance. I was recruited to assist in these endeavors and placed here to protect the Senator. I have grown to love the job, my charges, and my adopted country," he concluded.

"In that case, I guess I should thank my guardian angel."

"Yes. The Senator and his friends nearly had a heart attack when they found out I actually shot you. As it turned out, it helped you more than anything else. It is so unbelievable, it became believable. It renewed my faith in God that I didn't end up killing you that night."

Nick laughed. "The Lord works in mysterious ways."

"Amen, Senator."

Chapter 62

"That takes care of that," said Mel as he and Lexi watched NWN news on the morning of the third of January. They were in her Capitol Office. With no Vice President, the Senator Pro Tempore would swear in the new senators. Normally, it would have been Lexi's last duty as Vice President had she not ascended to the role of president.

As they watched the TV, NWN's legal reporter went over the missive received from the Supreme Court. They declined to take the case of whether the Electoral College numbers were altered by the disqualification of Michigan from the vote. Since the election was conducted under the premise of 538 electoral votes being available and therefore a need to achieve 270 to achieve a majority. It is beyond the authority of the Supreme Court to render a ruling changing the rules of how the election was conducted or the requisite majorities needed to be declared the winner.

#

"It was a long shot," acknowledged Nick to his newly depressed staff gathered at their campaign HQ. They're campaign had been a series of incredible trials as they seemed to be on the cusp of victory time after time only to have judges or states change the rules or simply ignore them to prevent their team from gaining a victory.

"Doesn't make it any easier," responded Chuck.

"Got that right. Do you want to issue a statement?" asked Margie.

"And say what?" Nick eyed his senior staff.

"Good point."

"Everything ready for Denise's service?" asked Nick.

"Yes. It will be a small service. Her parents are dead and she has no living siblings. She has an aunt and uncle who'll be there," noted Chuck.

"We'll fly out in the morning and back right after," stated Nick.

"Chuck, join me in my office please," asked Nick, leaving the conference room and heading to his office.

"What's up?" asked Chuck worriedly as he entered and closed the door.

"Did you know Senator Banks?" asked Nick, turning to confront Chuck.

"Huh?" said Chuck confused.

"Did you know Senator Banks?"

"Sure, I met him a few times when I was working with Senator Richards. Why are you asking me?"

Nick stared at him. Did anyone tell you to stay on when the Governor picked me?

"I don't know. I guess I never thought about it. Why the third degree?"

"Think harder?" ordered Nick, his tone turning dangerous. "Who told you to stay? It is important. Was it the Governor?"

"No, I only shook his hand, never talked to him. I'm thinking, maybe I just stayed," said Chuck, shaking his head.

"And you say I'm a terrible liar?" said Nick sarcastically.

Chuck tried smiling back at him.

"You picked Denise as well," noted Nick, not backing down.

"Where are you going with all this?" asked Chuck carefully.

"This is all a farce. My appointment, being manipulated into voting against the filibuster, running for President. Hell, even getting shot. Someone is calling the shots, and I didn't agree to be a marionette," replied Nick angrily.

"What the hell are you talking about?"

"Chuck, time to come clean or you are out the door right now."

Chuck looked uncomfortable. "Nobody talked to me. They blackmailed me into staying."

"How so?"

"Dad, or more correctly, Mom and Dad. They told me I needed to stay on when you came on board or investigators would be tipped off to some 'creative financing' of my father's and he would be told of some dalliances of my mother, when he was working overseas setting up factories years ago. I didn't know if any of it was true, but staying on seemed the easier solution," admitted Chuck.

"Banks had nothing to do with that?"

"As far as I know. I got a letter in the mail, no conversations. After I stayed, I got a second letter. All it said was, 'Good choice'. Do everything you can to help Turner adapt and succeed. Help him navigate this pit of vipers," explained Chuck.

"Those exact words?"

"Yes. Why do you think you are being manipulated?"

"Somebody told me. Banks was in on it. Hell, he may have been the one leading it for all I know," confided Nick.

"But you have made all the decisions. You said the words, you made the speeches. I watched you struggle with the vote. No one made you vote against the filibuster. You did that on your own. No one roused 83 million people to vote for you. That was all you. If anything, if you were manipulated into this, it has turned out pretty well, wouldn't you agree?" asked Chuck, holding his hands up.

"Maybe, but I don't enjoy being played. And I am not somebody's pawn," said Nick, pissed. "What made you pick Denise?"

"Nick, you have to understand. I really didn't have a choice," said Chuck sheepishly.

"More notes?" said Nick.

"No, this time my father called me saying he had been getting threatening phone calls. They told him to call me and mention Caracas."

"What is Caracas?" asked Nick.

"It was a junket to Venezuela back when Chavez was calling our former president the Devil. Richard's was down there with Lexi when she was the Majority Leader as part of a Senate state visit to discuss more joint trade. The last night we had a get together at the hotel bar. Denise was there and got shit faced. It was the last time. Lexi fired her when they returned to the US. Then she had her accident shortly thereafter and went into rehab."

"So that word led you to Denise?"

"You had just announced your run. You remember me telling you no one who was any good was available to run your campaign? They were all running the primary campaigns of the other candidates."

"When my dad called, I knew it was the same people. They knew I was in Caracas with Denise. They also knew I would put two and two together. They wanted Denise on your campaign. I pointed you that way, but again, you decided, not anyone else," noted Chuck.

Nick shook his head.

"You picked Earl, right? You hired Jenny, Margie, Jer, and most of the other staff. Some of the policy people were holdovers, but their influence has been minor."

"I liked Banks, but clearly he was playing *Wizard of Oz*. Maybe he thought he was helping me," said Nick, thinking.

"More likely, he thought he was helping the country. Maybe he felt bad for spending 70 years supporting policies that got us to this point, like he said in his press conference," offered Chuck.

"Could be," admitted Nick. "Alright, sorry for the third degree, but I needed to know. I'm getting a little paranoid about all my staffers paying the price for this campaign."

"I deserved it. Sorry I wasn't honest from the get go."

"Water under the bridge. A lot of water," laughed Nick, relaxing.

"Indeed. More like rapids. And we have been a piece of wood," agreed Chuck.

Nick got up, held out his hand to Chuck, who took it. "Thanks for all you have done."

"Thank you for what *you* have done and what you are going to keep doing. Regardless of how you got to where you are, there are at least 83 million people who are happy you were pushed into this."

"Let's hope they are not disappointed. Let's go put Denise to rest and then we can find out how to get justice for her," said Nick as they walked out of the office.

Chapter 63

Nick looked over at the crowd assembled for Denise's service. It was a small group. Perhaps some were scared away by the circumstance of her demise. Or maybe she didn't have that many friends. Most of the assembled were people who had known her from her days on the family farm.

After the service, Nick and the team stood around chatting with these folks who knew Denise. Laughing at some stories people were telling of her childhood. Apparently, she was quite the hellion as a child as well. Nick walked over to the aunt and uncle.

They both smiled. "Denise was only ever happy when she was in the fight," said Rosie. "She would call when she could to check up on us. She was always so excited and proud of what you were doing. Senator, you gave her purpose. She made the most of her time out here, but it was clear she was not in touch with the earth. Her heart was in the political world."

"I take your words as comfort. I want you to know this. Washington is a cesspool. I can assure you, Denise did not have a weapon, and she did not threaten the President. I will get justice for her, no matter how long it takes," promised Nick, in a fierce tone.

"Senator, do not let it consume you. Everyone knows politics is corrupt. Even here in New Mexico where we vote year after year to send the same Party politicians to Washington. Where they then forget they are from New Mexico, the minute they arrive. We understand and are resigned to the fact what happens here is of little consequence in Washington. We do not differ from Kansas, Nebraska, Kentucky or any state without large urban cities."

"Money and power are not found anywhere around here," said Juan, spreading his hands and turning. "Look around. We have no oil. We have little farming. What we have are a lot of native Americans who are happy to take the Government's money, get drunk and die in their brand-new Ford Pickups on the road."

"Juan, give him the box," said Rosie.

"Oh yeah, hang on Senator," said Juan as he went to an older Ford pickup and came back with a file storage box.

"Here. We don't know what is in here, but maybe it will help. She had us keep this for her, so the FBI missed it when they searched her property," said Juan, handing the box to Nick. He peeked in and saw a pile of papers, letters, and pictures.

"Thank you. I'll let you know if I find anything personal and I will send it back."

"It's OK Senator, you are as close to family as she had," said Rosie. "Keep it."

"Please call me Nick. I am officially no longer a Senator."

"Nick, thank you," they both said and laughed.

#

He carried the box back to the rest of the crew. They crammed all seven of them into a rented Suburban and prepared to make the 2-hour drive back to Albuquerque, where the plane was waiting to take them back to Washington to watch the vote in the house. As Earl drove them to the airport. Nick's phone buzzed. He looked down. He deleted the text. Chuck looked at him.

"Anything important?"

Nick shook his head no and watched the landscape of New Mexico as they drove.

Chapter 64

Nick was in the main library in one of the comfortable leather wingback chairs. He was reading a first edition of *Advise and Consent*, the Pulitzer prize-winning novel by Allen Drury. Drury was a political reporter during the 1940s and 1950s. The glory days of Washington.

The book was all about the Senate, with senators arguing back and forth over a Secretary of State nominee. Nick chuckled frequently as he read the book. Those were the days of 'honor' in the Senate, or as close to honor as there had ever been.

He wondered aloud what Drury would think of today's Senate and, more importantly, the demise of the smart and savvy reporters digging for facts and reporting these to the public. Still letting them form their own opinions, rather than forming it for them.

Taking a sip of his beer, he looked once again at the inside of the cover. There was a dedication from Drury to then Congressman Banks. '*To Baxter Banks, you can go far. Follow the path of Bob Munson and let your conscience guide you. Allen*', Nick pondered the inscription.

Bob Munson was the Majority Leader of the Senate in the novel. Struggling to assist his party's President get the Secretary of State nominee through confirmation when he does not like or feel the nominee is worthy. Written at the height of the Cold War, the novel's focus was the infiltration of the government by communist sympathizers.

"Excuse me, Nick," said Henry, finally giving in to Nick about him not being called senator any longer. Nick looked up.

"You have a visitor."

Nick put the book on the table.

"Who?"

"A beautiful woman. She says she knows you. Ms. Lauren Bergamo," Henry read from the card she had given him.

Nick visibly stiffened.

"Sir, shall I say you are indisposed?" offered Henry.

"No Henry, I can't duck this one. Bring her in please," replied Nick with a sigh, standing.

Nick wandered to a corner of the room, looking at the books. He could hear her approaching heels on the hardwood of the hallway as she entered the library. Nick turned. Lauren stood in the doorway.

She was a vision in a form fitting long-sleeved dark green knee length jersey dress with a deep cowl and tall black leather high-heeled boots. A wide belt around her waist highlighted her perfect figure. Nick noticed her hair was a bit more auburn than in San Francisco. As stunning as ever. She smiled tentatively.

"Would you like something to drink?" asked Nick in a neutral tone. "Gin martini?"

Nick nodded at Henry, signaling two.

Lauren looked around the library, admiring the woodwork, and the thousands of volumes contained on the shelves. She walked toward the opposite corner from Nick, reaching out to touch the wooden ladder, moving it back and forth on the rail.

She looked down at the track in the hardwood, allowing the ladder to circle the room.

"Very nice," she said, turning to Nick. Her smile, against the light pink shade on her lips, dazzling as always. Nick did not respond. He stared at her until she broke eye contact.

"Nice place you have here. A far cry from sleeping in your Senate office," she said, trying to get a response out of him.

Henry came into the room carrying a tray with the two Martinis and a small plate of cheese and crackers. He placed them on the table between the leather wingback chairs. "Anything else, sir?"

"Nothing Henry, thank you. Please close the door on your way out," Henry made a simple bow, turned, shutting the door as he left. Nick went to the table and picked up the drinks, handing one to Lauren.

"What shall we toast?" he asked sarcastically.

"Your inability to use your phone to respond to a text?" retorted Lauren with an arched eyebrow as she gently tapped her glass on his.

"Clearly you did not understand the message implied in my not replying. It appears the subtle approach did not work."

"I always wanted to see this place," remarked Lauren, ignoring his retort, still admiring the room.

"Several of my older colleagues bragged about being invited to parties here decades ago, when ANC was still respectable."

"Visiting hours ended a long time ago. Why are you here, Lauren? Your conscience getting to you?"

"Actually, yes," she admitted.

"Well, that surprises me, given all the things you've done and all the pain and suffering your 'reporting' has caused. I guess getting the story is all that matters to you. No matter who is hurt," commented Nick, practically snarling.

Lauren took a long pull on her drink. "Henry makes a wicked martini," she said, stalling.

"Out with it. I have things to do," barked Nick.

"Back to asshole, Nick, I see," snapped Lauren with a fire in her eye.

"You have a brass pair. I'll give you that. You bugged me. You followed me around. Your stories hurt people and may have cost them their lives. And you have the guts to stand there and tell me *I'm* being rude," accused Nick, almost unable to contain his anger.

"Please believe me. I never meant for any of this to hurt anyone," she replied, shoulders slumping.

"Was San Francisco just another ploy to get a story? You said you were a lousy Mata Hari when we parted. I'm the naïve one. I believed you then. You were wrong. You have out Mata Hari'd even the real one. I hope you're proud and happy. Come tomorrow, you're going to be partially responsible for keeping Alexis Smythe-Thomas in power and enabling her to drive this country right over the fucking cliff."

"That's not fair. I told you there, I followed you. What we had was real," pleaded Lauren, her eyes misting.

"And now I know how you 'followed' me. In Chicago. To the meetings with the Governor and the Vice President. To my meetings here with Banks. You have a lot to answer for, Miss Bergamo," said Nick in a disgusted tone.

"I figured as much when it showed up in Canada. I admit I planted the tracker that day I came by your office. I was being an investigative journalist. You were the biggest story in town. You embarrassed and treated me like crap on camera. I wanted to get back at you," responded Lauren defensively.

"Boy, did you. Do you realize how many deaths you have been involved in because of this?" His eyes were piercing as they stared.

"What do you mean? I haven't done anything to anyone," responded Lauren, continuing to defend her actions.

"Really? Are you going to stand there and say you had nothing to do with getting involved in Chicago? Who knows what would have happened if you hadn't pulled up? I could have been killed. One of those young men almost was." Nick sat in his chair.

"You can't blame that one on me. You were the one at the drug deal. The one holding the drugs and standing on the stoop when the drive by happened. What I did had nothing to do with that," denied Lauren, taking the other chair facing Nick.

"Maybe, maybe not. Who knows what would or could have happened if you hadn't been so eager to broadcast my meetings with Lexi and the Governor. That was after San Fran. You could have told me what you did. You could have told me you had the footage. These all had an effect and impacted the election. They made Lexi do things she might not have done if they hadn't occurred. Maybe Greg and Kevin would still be alive if Lexi wasn't so desperate to frame Denise into providing the info. Did you consider that?"

"Nick, those could have helped you for all you know. This is not rational. You can hate me because I used the tracker to get the scoop, to print the stories. If it wasn't me, it would have been someone. I do feel bad," said Lauren, looking down at her boots.

"You still don't get it, do you? It is all about the story to you. By whatever means necessary. Damn the torpedoes and if anyone gets hurt, all is fair in love and presidential politics ratings coverage?"

Lauren crossed her legs. Nick noticed, peeking out of the top of one boot, was a boot sock he'd bought for her in San Francisco. Nick returned to staring into her eyes, trying to ignore anything else. She was tearing up a bit.

"You know what was worst. Is the ease with which you shared this information to be used against me. I'm sure you got some great kudos from your bosses for the Chicago tapes and for the scoops on my meeting with Blackbird and Lexi. But when you leaked my meetings with Banks, that led directly to his death. I think you should go now. I find your actions irredeemable," finished Nick, standing and turning his back to her.

"What do you mean about Banks? He died in his sleep," responded Lauren, confused.

"No, he did not. He was murdered. In that room right there," Nick pointed toward the inner office. "Someone told somebody I was meeting with him and whoever that was, felt Banks was a traitor to the cause. Your information from your little bug led directly to his being murdered. But Banks was old and dying. No, what was the final straw for me was Denise. You felt compelled to trash her in the press by baring all her life's foibles. For *ratings*. What kind of person are you?" accused Nick, his voice rising in anger again.

Lauren's hand was shaking. The empty glass slipped and fell to the area rug beneath the chair. She fell to her knees, sobbing. Not fake sobs, but full body sobs. Nick watched. The look on his face showed perhaps he had been too hard on her. He moved to help her up off the floor. She raised her head with streaking mascara and yelled at him. "No! Stay away. I *am* a monster."

Nick backed off, then moved in again. "Lauren, let me help you up. You are not a monster. I was being overly mean." As he helped her up, she shook loose from his grip, turned, and yelled at him again. "NO,

I am a monster, a murderer," sobbing again, covering her face with her hands as her body shook.

"Lauren, calm down. You're not a murderer. Banks had lots of enemies," consoled Nick, moving to her, feeling bad he had been so harsh.

"Nick, stay away. I am a *killer*. I killed your baby. I am a murderer. Stay away," she said, holding out her hands, tears streaking her mascara further.

Nick stood still. "What did you say?"

Lauren stood, her shoulders continuing to shake as the sobs racked her body.

"I got pregnant. I had an abortion. The same day you got shot. I'm so sorry Nick."

She collapsed again, but he rushed in and caught her before she could crumble. He held onto her as she sobbed into his chest until the shakes subsided. Then he led her to the loveseat in the room.

"Wait here."

Nick disappeared into the inner office and returned with a decanter of brandy. He poured a good amount into his empty martini glass and handed it to her.

"I know you hate it, but take a few sips. It will help." He picked her glass up from the floor and set it on the table.

She took a sip, making a face, but took a second sip, handing the glass back to Nick. Nick handed her his handkerchief. She wiped her eyes and her nose.

Lauren looked down at the handkerchief, now smeared with tears and mascara.

"Oh god, I must be a real sight to see," she sniffed. "Thank you for the brandy. It helped."

Nick continued to look at her. She noticed him staring and looked him in the eye.

"Please don't look at me like that. I don't deserve your sympathy, or your pity. I've done some horrible things. I failed to stand up and people were hurt by my actions. Or rather, inactions," she said, tears welling up again. She took the glass and downed another sip of the brandy.

"Please say something, anything," she pleaded.

"I wish you'd told me."

She looked at him. "I so wanted to. By then I was already taking advantage of knowing you were meeting with Blackbird and Lexi and doing those stories. When I figured out I didn't have the flu or COVID and was pregnant, things were falling apart."

"You were being attacked, and some of it was because of my reporting. I figured at that point you wouldn't want to talk to me, not trusting me to have a conversation. I didn't know what to do. There was no way I'd get past Margie. Or Denise, for that matter. Nick, I wanted to talk to you, but I also knew it wouldn't matter. My contract says I couldn't get pregnant. The last thing you needed was a one-night stand showing up pregnant with a child just as you headed to election day," said Lauren, looking down at her drink, unable to meet Nick's eyes. "Then you got shot..."

"I think you know me well enough to know I would have been there for you, to support you in any decision you made. You know my stance on abortion. You also know I fully respect your decision. I could have provided you emotional support," he finished, a strange feeling returning to his gut at almost being a father.

Lauren took another long pull of brandy, emptying the glass.

"I know. I was feeling sorry for myself. All I could see is my career ending, your candidacy taking a hit and my bosses at ANC using this information to harm you." She shook her head, sniffling. "They harmed you anyway."

"They found out?"

She nodded.

"How?" asked Nick, taking the glass out of her hand, pouring a little more.

"The admitting nurse where I had the procedure. The form asks for a father. I put 'unknown' at first. Then, I felt it was my right to list the father." She laughed bitterly. "As if I cared whether they thought I was a slut. So, I wrote your name. The nurse must have seen it. She made a copy and kept a picture of the form on her phone. I think she sold it to ANC. My cameraman innocently asked my producer about the drug deal footage we took and where the story went. You have to believe me when I say I was never going to do that story. Paul didn't know it was you. Hell, come to think of it, I almost got him killed, too," she said, slumping.

"Eventually it got to Hallberg, and he put two and two together. He came to me and threatened to end my career by going public that I'd aborted your baby, unless I did the story on Chicago. So again, I was weak and only concerned with myself. I gave it to him. Thank God you were able to stick it to them. You probably single-handedly killed that network. At least something good came out of it," she finished, taking a sip from her new glass.

"That's also when he found out about Banks. The photos of me watching you go in and out of this house a couple times. I don't know who he shared them with, but that had to be where it started. I am sorry Nick. I never meant for anyone to get hurt, I promise," she whimpered, her shoulders slumping again.

"Lauren, this business sucks. This town sucks. The people in power are mostly evil and irredeemable. I have no doubt I will not be president. The dominos are lining up and the deep state is circling the wagons to make sure I don't win."

"I am so sorry, Nick. I actually thought I was helping by implicating Lexi in Denise's troubles," revealed Lauren.

"I'm sorry too Lauren. I was being harsh because I felt betrayed by your actions. I was taking everything out on you. That was not fair."

Lauren laughed, shaking her head.

"You are an amazing person, Nick. Here I show up, after all the trouble I have caused, the deeds I have done, killing our baby, and you are apologizing to me for being mean? Unbelievable," she smiled and Nick felt a pang in his heart for what might have been. Even now he was incredibly attracted to her, with mascara streaks and puffy eyes.

He took her hand. She shivered.

"They think they've won. Lexi thinks she can enact whatever she wants and the people will live with it. They couldn't be more wrong. They did the one thing they couldn't afford to do. They woke up the silent majority. We will not go quietly into the night. It is my job going forward to make sure they don't give up."

"What will you do?" she asked, looking into his eyes and shivering again at the determination she saw.

"I intend to keep fighting. Nothing you did or had done to you is irredeemable in itself. We all make our decisions, and we live with the consequences of these actions. It is called personal responsibility. Something sorely missing from the progressive movement. So many in this town don't see it that way. They think they don't have to face the consequences of their actions. I am going to show them they are wrong. Like the biblical Michael, I am going to show them their actions *do* have consequences. They will have a day of reckoning," noted Nick prophetically.

"How?" asked Lauren in a meek but concerned voice

Nick laughed, defusing the tension. "Don't worry. I'm not going to change my spots now and suddenly advocate for armed resistance. I'll organize my followers, build a third party, and kick the party *and* opposition out of congress in the midterms. Hopefully, with her small majorities, we have one more election where Lexi will not have total control of the outcome. This is our last chance. I'm willing to sacrifice myself to make this happen."

"Congress was always supposed to be the most powerful branch of government. We punted on our stewardship and allowed the bureaucratic state to supplant that role. The only way to win it back is the majority rule of smart, honest, and patriotic men and women in the House and Senate. That is my revenge. Use the rules they so disdain to topple them before they remake the country," explained Nick.

Lauren smiled.

"What will you do?" asked Nick.

"Me? I don't know. Technically, I'm still under contract to ANC. If I leave, I still can't go report or work in the industry until the noncompete expires. This is what I do. I'll go back and fight to get the truth out there. Force them to silence me or let me out of my contract. Maybe I'll dye my hair blonde and work for EXN," teased Lauren, smiling.

"Don't do that, at least the hair color part," smiled Nick.

"That is certainly a sexist thing to say."

"That's the pain in the ass reporter I know. The one who gave better than she got. Who was relentless in the pursuit of the story. I think that's your calling. You'll be bored with anything else," suggested Nick.

"You're probably right, Senator," replied Lauren with a smile. "Besides, I need to atone for my past deeds. No better time to start."

"Just Nick now. They already swore in my replacement. I'd better get used to it. It would be nice to know I have a friend in enemy territory who is motivated by the truth," offered Nick.

Lauren stood, wondering if their relationship had been irreparably harmed by this conversation. Regardless, they could still be friends rather than enemies. She would work to rebuild his trust. She could live with that. It was a start, for now anyway.

She stood in front of Nick, holding his hands. "Just a friend?" She gave him a hug and kissed him on the cheek. He looked down, staring into her eyes. They both realized they had been a family, maybe never together, but in spirit, if only for a little while. He kissed her on the forehead.

"You should fix your face. I don't want Henry calling the cops thinking I've been beating you. Hallberg would love to run that story," laughed Nick as he retrieved her purse and coat from the chair by the door.

As she pulled her mirror from her purse, she gasped.

"Oh, my God Nick. I'm hideous." She immediately went to work with her tissue and makeup brush as he laughed. As she worked to fix her face, she asked.

"How did you end up with this place?"

"Banks had no relatives, so he left it to me. Don't ask me why."

"Wow, talk about a rich uncle."

"You got that right. I've never been more surprised in my life."

"You know what?" she said, looking up. "It suits you."

"I don't know about that, but I am enjoying the books. How did you get here? Uber?"

"No, I drove my rental and parked on the street. I didn't want to take the chance I would freeze on the sidewalk waiting half an hour for an Uber after you threw me out on my ass," she admitted.

"Let me walk you to your car. This is a sketchy neighborhood."

"If this neighborhood is sketchy, then our country really is in trouble," asserted Lauren, as Nick helped her into her coat. He walked her to the front door. Henry was nowhere to be seen. Nick walked her down the front walk to her SUV in front of the house.

As she opened the door, she turned and put her arms around his neck and found his lips. Nick did not resist. When they broke the embrace, the vapor clouds from their breath were very dense in the cold air. She turned and got in the car while Nick held the door. She looked at him and smiled as he shut the door.

He shook his head at his weakness. "What are you doing?" He said to no one in particular.

Neither noticed the car down the street, filming their entire embrace.

Chapter 65

With no Vice President, the Speaker of the House presided over calling the roll for the Electoral College vote. There was endless speculation in American *Pravda* of faithless electors going both ways in the weeks leading up to this vote. Or worse. The threat of a lawsuit by the states and the precedent of the Supreme Court disallowing any faithless electors from counting in prior elections quelled this threat.

The roll was called. As expected, the electoral count came out as 268 for Turner, 224 for Lexi without Michigan, and 31 for Blackbird. This was recorded and noted that no one was declared the winner in the Electoral College.

The electors left to be replaced by the legislature. The Speaker of the House was replaced by the Senate Pro Tempore, who would preside over the House vote for President, and the House Speaker would preside over the Senate vote for Vice President.

Outside the Capital, there were 3000 National Guard troops deployed and hundreds of Capitol Police. Fencing and barbed wire surrounded the Capitol as if it were preparing for a siege. It looked like a third world country where the people were being prevented from congregating by the fearful government.

The liberal media channels were predicting massive protests by Turner supporters and a repeat of the attempted overthrow of the government by the unhappy rabble whipped into a 'violent frenzy by Turner's rhetoric'. ANC was having a field day showing the massive police presence.

They all played endless loops of footage from the original January 6th riots.

The problem was there was not a *single* Turner supporter to be found. Even the black clad Antifa agitators had nothing to do but stand on the perimeter, stomping their feet to keep warm. Several groups of Gabriel's Angels also showed up, expecting to throw some punches.

With no crowd to incite *or* blame, they stood looking at each other. It was another in a long series of intelligence blunders by the current administration.

Inside the well secured Capitol, the assembled senior congressmen and women representing their states were ready to cast their single vote per state to determine who would be elected president.

For the first vote, they had already previously agreed to do it according to who won the states in the election, there being no precedent since 1820 and no winner possible from this first vote. 24 states voted for Turner, 22 for Lexi including Michigan and 4 for Blackbird.

DC did not get a vote since it was not a state, something the Mayor had been complaining bitterly about for the last month on cable news. Lexi had vowed one of her first tasks would be statehood for DC.

Nick's only comment was to suggest they read the charter of Washington, DC, intentionally carved out of *any* state to remove the idea of partisanship at the seat of the federal government. DC had become the most reliably blue electoral votes in the country, even surpassing Hawaii.

These revelations and suggestions were ignored by American *Pravda*. The exception being the 2J's. Even EXN seemed to approve of DC's constant mantra of 'no taxation without representation' rallying cry.

The next vote would be the telling one. The talking heads on the networks pontificated and debated who would go what way. They all assumed Lexi would win Blackbird's and end this nightmare. After all, she was clearly the most qualified and had already been in the role for the last month.

Nick and his senior staff watched from the conference room. "No surprises so far," commented Chuck.

"What do you think, Nick?" asked Earl.

"Guys, I honestly don't know," he responded.

As they called off state by state, there were no surprises. The first state to change was California, now switching its vote to Lexi, again not surprising with the massive majority of Party members in Congress from the state, even with the flip of the six seats in and around Orange County back to opposition winners.

It continued until they reached the first Blackbird state. North Carolina. It went for Lexi. They boo'd in the conference room except for Nick. Next was North Dakota. It went for Turner. Everyone cheered in the room. They hoped the others might follow. South Carolina came up next. It went for Turner.

They held their breath. If South Dakota could go his way, he would win. South Dakota, with a governor wronged so personally by Lexi herself, went for Lexi. Everyone in the conference room was deflated. They knew this was their best chance, and it had passed. The vote ended in a 25-25 tie. They would vote again after a 30 minute recess.

"Nick, do you want to call anyone?" asked Chuck, hopefully. "The South Dakota congresswoman was promised an ambassadorship. You could offer her the Secretary of Education role. She was a teacher, after all."

"Nope," said Nick

"You sure? All you have to do is offer Blackbird something or the Congresswoman and it is yours," said Chuck as Earl, Jenny, Jer and Margie all looked on.

"Chuck, we have been through this. This is a perfect example of all that is wrong with our system and Washington. I cannot betray 83 million people by sacrificing my integrity to win a rigged vote. By suddenly starting to make promises in return for favors."

"Either they have heard from their constituents and are going to vote the way they want them to vote, or they are going to go against their voters and ensure they are going to lose in the mid-terms. We have to get back to first principles. This is not my pride. This is a commitment to do this and do it in a way we can sustain. Selling out would compromise all we have worked for," informed Nick.

"I hate to see them win this way," said Chuck, frustrated.

"They are not winning Chuck. And 83 million and maybe half of Blackbirds fifteen million know it," retorted Nick as they started up the next vote. "When do we catch the plane for the rally?" asked Nick.

"Two hours, boss," replied a dejected Margie.

"Thanks." Nick walked to his office and sat in his chair. He closed his eyes and meditated.

It was done. Now he could look to the future.

#

As expected, Lexi made a deal with the lone North Dakota congressman, promising him a role in her administration. Neither he, nor the South Dakota congresswoman, heard from Nick or his campaign to make a better offer for them to vote for him. Determined to get something for their votes, they both voted for Lexi, who won the next vote 26 to 24.

The two 'bribed' Opposition Congress persons from the Dakotas would not have to face the wrath of their constituents in the next mid-term election, after all. They would both be out of Congress and into the administration.

"Well, that does it. The current interim President, Lexi Smythe-Thomas, is now the official winner of the election and will be sworn in on January 20th," reported Marty, the anchor of ANC's special coverage of the vote in the House, in a satisfied voice.

"Justice has finally been served," crowed Jamal Adebayo, an ANC contributor, former Anti-Racism League group leader and staunch supporter of the new President.

"Now President Smythe-Thomas needs to arrest Turner for the violence and fraud he has perpetrated on this country. This is the most racist, homophobic, and anti-American presidential race we have ever witnessed. His speeches are full of sedition and his followers are all ready to commit violence at his mere command. For the good of the country, she needs to lock him up and throw away the key."

"Those are pretty strong words, Jamal," interjected David Pierce, the now retired Party congressman from Ohio. "I believe we need to have honest debate in this country. If we don't allow it, we will never heal."

"Ha," laughed Jamal. "Congressman, that is why you retired, because you wanted to compromise, and your district in Cleveland wanted to fight injustice and white suppression."

"Now wait a minute," said the former congressman. "Just because you don't agree with Turner, 83 million people did, more than voted for the President. Those people are constituents too and they need to be heard."

"Baloney," retorted Jamal. "We know Turner cheated in Michigan, Pennsylvania, Wisconsin, and probably in California too. He may have a vote total, but in the end, justice prevailed, and the true president is now elected. If there are 83 million white supremacists and their Uncle Tom supporters from the suburbs, you had better watch out, because this will not continue," he finished with glee.

"Let's move on and talk about what happens in Congress. With only a three-seat majority in the House and one in the Senate, will the President be able to pass her aggressive agenda in the first 100 days?" asked Marty. "Congressman?"

"I would recommend she temper her expectations a bit. There are moderate Party members in the caucus who are hearing from their constituents regarding some of the more radical changes proposed. She should take care of what she proposes. It remains to be seen how many of her cabinet will cause vacant House and Senate seats needing to be filled from special elections. The Party lost one seat with Banks' death, so that makes their majority precarious."

"She needs to push on hard," disagreed Jamal. "The last administration betrayed the cause. They talked a good game and then retreated from every progressive promise they made. America is different. It is ready for change. Ready to push back on the oppression of white-run corporations, white-run schools, and frankly white-run congresses to make a more equal society. One where minorities and diversity are not just celebrated, but in charge. This country is getting browner by the day. It is time for a new day and President Alexis Smythe-Thomas is going to lead us into it."

#

"What do you think Turner is going to do?" asked Billy McCall to his panel on EXN. "Adam, let's start with you. You have seen more of these than all of us combined."

"Why thank you, Billy. Yes, I am old, if that is your point," he smiled, softening the statement. "I like to think I am wise as well. If I know Turner, he isn't going to disappear. Tommy may have better insight on this, but I would guess he is going to start a third party. It remains to be seen if he can keep together enough of a coalition to make a difference, but I bet he tries. Tommy?"

Tommy's face was red. "You know, guys, this is wrong. What is the matter with our country? What is the matter with our people? We sit idly by when we know fraud on a massive scale has been perpetrated. How do we let this charade move forward without stopping and saying this is wrong?" he cautioned.

"Tommy, there is no physical evidence of any fraud on a scale large enough to affect the election," noted Billy diplomatically.

"How do we know Billy? Have we subpoenaed the ballots? Have we demanded forensic audits of the machines? Or the mail in ballots? Are we going to ignore the coincidences of the fire in Michigan, all the voting machines in Arizona and Nevada being wiped clean, the lack of interest in matching mail in ballots to actual voters in Wisconsin as those two canvassers claimed?"

His colleagues sat silent.

"No, we are just going to do nothing. Demand nothing. And let them get away with it again. This sickens me to my core. You know what? We deserve everything the President is about to inflict on us. Remember this. This was our Normandy. This was our chance to unmask the enemy within and expose the massive fraud. Maybe our last chance if the President is successful in her plans. We failed to establish our beachhead and were forced to retreat from the beach. What happens going forward is as much our fault as hers," said Tommy, even redder.

Billy quickly segued to Rory.

"I don't disagree with a lot of what Tommy is saying and feeling. From a statistician's point of view, all I can say is there are too many anomalies of such statistical significance for any of this to be correct. One outlier maybe, but we have dozens of plots on the graph that are so off they are impossible, not improbable, but impossible," said Rory, holding up a graph of plotted points.

"For instance, these are the correlated counting of votes as they come in. As you can see, they follow a pretty standard pattern of up and down, not deviating from the norm by more than one standard deviation. And then wham, we have a couple of dumps, where the plot is out here," he said, holding up a pencil and stretching it to a point in the air 3 feet from his graph.

"This doesn't happen once, it happens *23 times in 7 states*. This is not possible. What is also not rational is how no one in the media or in government at the local, state or federal level is even the slightest interested in understanding how or why this happened. From *either* party. We have collectively stuck our head in the sand as the bulldozer approaches, agreeing en masse if we don't look, maybe it will not run us over," said Rory, shaking his head.

"Personally, I hope Turner does something. What I don't know, but somebody needs to keep advocating for truth and honesty and transparency. No one else is doing *anything* to make it happen."

"Thanks panel, we are about to switch to the Senate for the formality of the vote on the Vice President. Unlike the House, they will not hold a first vote in line with how the states were awarded and will instead vote for the candidate they want to be Vice President. I would expect Jefferson will be quickly confirmed at this point."

As the noise in the Senate chamber announced the starting of the vote, Billy turned to the panel to ask another question.

"Adam, with the slim majority in the House and Senate, do you think the President will tone down her first 100 day's agenda?" asked Billy.

"Ah, Billy, I think something is happening," said Adam as they turned their attention to the roll call.

Alabama, Alaska, and Arkansas had all voted for Turner for Vice President.

"Huh, can they do that?" asked Billy, looking at Rory.

"Beats me," he replied, with a confused look, looking down at his phone, typing.

The call went on with all of Turner's states voting for him and Lexi's voting for Jefferson. They came to North Carolina who voted for Turner. Then North Dakota, who also voted for Turner.

"Holy Crap, if he gets another Blackbird state, he's going to be elected Vice President," explained Billy to his confused panel and audience.

"Why would he want to be Vice President?" asked Tommy.

"I don't think he would," laughed Adam. "Especially to Lexi's President. I suspect he knows nothing about this, or he would have shut it down."

South Carolina voted for Turner and South Dakota as well. That would give Turner 28 if the rest of his states stayed true to form.

#

Chuck knocked on the door. "Ah boss, we have a problem," motioned Chuck, turning and heading back to the conference room. They had EXN on, covering the Vice President vote.

"What now?" remarked Nick, hurrying into the room.

"You've been elected Vice President," announced Margie disbelievingly.

"What?" groaned Nick in a startled voice.

#

"What?" screeched Lexi in the Oval Office, looking at Mel.

"Don't look at me," responded Mel, frantically picking up his phone to make a call.

"Is this allowed?" asked Lexi.

"Adams had Jefferson as his VP and they hated each other, at least during their presidencies," noted Mel.

"Can he decline?" asked Lexi. "How the hell did this happen?"

Mel started to answer when the person on the other side picked up. Mel began talking into the phone. After a couple of minutes, he ended the call.

"Folks are telling me the twelfth amendment prohibits this, but with him being third party and getting more votes than you, there is an argument being made it is at the discretion of the Senate to choose from the eligible candidates, not just the VPs. They are setting this up to force the Supreme Court to issue another controversial ruling to undercut you."

Lexi stood in the room, anxiety showing on her face.

"You'll need to give the Chief Justice another call," suggested Mel.

"What the fuck?" barked Lexi, running her hands through her blonde hair. "This nightmare won't end. Can we impeach him if he accepts?"

"Maybe, but on what grounds? Plus, remember if we lose a single senator, he is the tiebreaker as VP," reminded Mel.

"This is horrible. We can freeze him out of every meeting, every plan, almost make him a non-person. But at what cost?"

"Maybe having him close is better. We can keep an eye on him. The Vice President is ceremonial for the most part. The minute he goes against us, we can impeach him," said Mel.

"That would keep him from running for president again, right?" responded Lexi thinking out loud.

"Yes, if he is found guilty, then the Senate can pass a resolution to ensure he can never be president."

"Maybe this is not such a bad thing?" agreed Lexi.

#

"This is horrible," noted Nick. "I don't want to be Vice President to Lexi, or anyone else for that matter."

"But it could be good. You could gum up the works from the inside being VP," suggested Chuck, thinking outside the box.

"And get myself impeached and banned from running for president ever again? It gives Lexi way too much control over me."

"Think about the pros and cons. I think it could be good. As long as you don't do anything she can impeach you on and get a conviction, it could be helpful to the cause," countered Chuck.

"Chuck, I am breathing. To Lexi, that is an impeachable offense."

"But she has to get a two-thirds majority to convict. That will be difficult," stated Chuck, still thinking it through.

"What I want to do is going to piss off every member of congress. Starting tonight. There is no way they don't convict me and stop my goals."

"It may not happen, anyway. I hear they are already preparing to appeal to the Supreme Court. If they say you are eligible, please think about it," pleaded Chuck, looking at his watch. "We need to scoot to the airport."

Chapter 66

As the popular country band finished their set, Nick took the stage.
It was a mild January late afternoon. The crowd of close to 400,000
cheered him on from inside and around the grounds of the Texas Motor
Speedway north of Fort Worth.

The crowd had been arriving the entire day, just like a NASCAR
event. It was a festival atmosphere. To the uninformed observer,
you would never have guessed this was a rally for the *loser* of a
presidential election.

The idea of keeping it low key and spread via word of mouth and chat
groups had worked beautifully. Again, everyone involved felt like they
were a secret agent on the way to a clandestine meeting. By the time the
traffic snarls happened, law enforcement was none the wiser about what
was occurring.

Besides the four hundred thousand on hand, the event was being
simulcast to stadiums all over the country. Nick and his team had rented
every major stadium not being used for sporting events on this evening.

Hundreds of thousands were also gathered at venues from the
University of Hawaii stadium to the Rose Bowl. At almost every
pro baseball or football stadium in the country. Just like in Texas,
Nick's fans had been arriving all day and a giant tail gate celebration
occurred at each.

Later, it would be estimated over eight million people gathered in
these venues to watch Nick's speech live across the country. Many other
millions of his followers watched live on Hibi, EXN and the 2J's.

None of American *Pravda* paid any attention or even gave it coverage.
Instead, they tried to make hay of staged protests at the Capitol, where
not a single *real* Turner supporter stood. Only paid agitators, Antifa,

Gabriel's Angels, and no doubt FBI infiltrators waiting to incite more 'spontaneous' insurrections. Nick was too smart to fall into this trap. The nearest Turner rally to the Capitol was miles away at the football stadium in Baltimore.

Nick stood looking out over the capacity crowd in the stands and filling the infield. There were plenty of American flags being waved. Several award winning, mostly country music groups had provided impromptu concerts in the hours leading up. The crowd was in a lively and patriotic mood as Nick waved his arms to quiet them down.

"First off, I had no idea I could be chosen to be Vice President. Besides, I know how the Supreme Court will rule. Don't you?" the crowd laughed. "Why would I want to be Vice President?" finished Nick, shaking his head and smiling as the crowd roared.

"Thank you all for your support and your tireless efforts. This is not a concession speech. I am conceding nothing, other than a vote in the house of representatives following the rules in our Constitution. Lexi won that vote. I acknowledge she is the rightful elected President."

The crowd booed loudly at this admission.

"I don't want to hear anyone claiming I am an election denier. Looking backwards at what and how the vote happened changes nothing. We can only look forward. It does not change the fact that we," he opened his arms wide to encompass everyone, "got more votes than any candidate in history. As an *independent third-party* candidate. We won more electoral votes than our opponents and more states. This was all because of you."

The crowd roared in appreciation.

"This is not the end of our movement, either. This is a victory celebration. The victory belongs to each of you. You are now aware of the damage the policies of the Progressives have done to your children, your police forces, your schools, your local government, and your corporations."

"These policies target you through these institutions. They only do this to harm you. Not to help, despite their twisted explanations. When you are docile, and afraid to speak your mind. When you cower at home, afraid to make a joke or render an opinion on the subject of the day. At work, church, or in a restaurant, fearful the woke police will call you out, they win." Nick walked back and forth as he talked, dressed in jeans, cowboy boots, and a dark sweater.

"They want you lonely and afraid. Locked up in your home. Scared of people, scared of germs, scared of interaction with others. Certain that people are out to get you because of your skin color, who your parents were, your preferred gender, or what your job is. This is only a taste of what it means to live under a totalitarian regime. *1984* is no longer fiction. It is a handbook. The handbook of the Progressives. They think they have won with their candidate now in a position to execute the platform she described at the convention."

The crowd booed loudly at this statement and the prospect of a future where these policies were accelerated, not contained.

"Guess what? They aren't the majority. You are. We are. The rule of law and the Constitution survive in each of you. And each of you shows this every day. This was an election, not a coronation. I'm going to let you in on a little secret. Three and One."

"This is the razor-thin majority they have to implement their changes. Three in the house and one in the Senate. Many of these Party congressmen and women and senators live in your states. They work for *you*. Never, ever, let them forget that. Make your will and desires known. If they vote against your will, make sure they know you are not going to re-elect them if they keep doing this."

"The one thing I have learned from my short time in Washington is this. The politicians who get there want to stay. They will do or say whatever they need to in order to maintain their status. If you threaten them with losing, they have to change or lose their job."

"We have the power. We are the silent majority and guess what? We are not *woke*, we are *awakened*!" shouted Nick to huge and sustained cheers from his supporters.

"Here is what I think *you* should do. Some of these congressmen and women are going to be offered cabinet posts. When they vacate their seats, you, all of you who are now awake, need to make sure you nominate and elect folks who think like we do. Not rubber stamps for the Party or the Opposition. Make them pledge to stay for only a little while. To treat this as the temp job it is." Folks cheered Turner, Turner, Turner and term limits. Nick waited for them to quiet.

"When the founders laid out our system of government, they created the people's house. The House of Representatives. They gave it *all* the important tasks. The power of the purse and the ability to declare war and to sign off on *all* laws. Sadly, in the history of our country, the people's *representatives*, your congressmen and women, have allowed the Senate, the Presidency, the Supreme Court and, most disastrously, the bureaucratic fourth branch of the government to take more and more power. The unelected bureaucratic state has taken over the roles and responsibilities of the 'people's house'. Through lobbyists, their foot soldiers, they write the bills the congress votes on and then the bureaucratic state decides what is in them and how they are enforced on *you*." The crowd booed.

Nick stood and shook his head. "This is our fault. Yours and mine and our parents and neighbors and all who came before us. You know why?" asked Nick rhetorically.

"We let them get away with it. We did not stand and say no more. Or vote them out to be replaced by better representatives. To hold them accountable for their reprehensible punting of their responsibility. To *us*. No, we continued to elect them even after they gave away the power of the people to the unelected and the elites in these institutions. The remedy is simple." He had four hundred thousand revelers, listening to every word he was saying.

"Congress is made up of 435 elected congressmen and 100 elected senators. We elect them. We lost the Presidency, true. You know what? The President does not make a single law. They don't have a say in the budget. They don't get to declare war. Executive orders they issue are illegal and should not be allowed and frequently are overturned by the Supreme Court once they review them. The solution is again, *you*."

"Starting today, we have to recruit our next congressional candidates. Not from the professional political ranks. Look to your right and your left in every stadium where you are gathered. We need common sense folks who work for a living. Who agree to abide by the Constitution. To serve for defined amounts of time. To put each of you first and not the Party, the elites, or the establishment."

Folks were standing and cheering at this prospect.

"Did you know, in the ancient Greek democracy, public officials were subject to the idea of *accountability*. Their finances were audited before taking office and then after. If the wealth grew significantly, they could be sentenced to death for using their power to amass wealth. This might be a good rule to enforce on our own elected officials," suggested Nick with a shrug. The crowd laughed and cheered at this suggestion.

"We need debate. We need to make sure whomever we pick represents our moderate, middle of the road values. People who have morals and ethics. Believe in the importance of family. Agree parents should be involved in their children's rearing. Who are against schools and doctors filling our vulnerable children's heads full of life-changing advice. Without the knowledge or consent of the parents. We need candidates who will let children be children."

The cheers were deafening this time and Nick stood while the crowd cheered and chanted. He took a sip of his water as they continued.

"Candidates who are beholden to us. Who will fight the progressive policies and their damage to the majority. We cannot let minority mandated legislation become the law for the majority. This is the genuine gift of the founders. The ability to overturn bad choices. To repeal bad laws. To undo unlawful executive orders. Anything this President can mandate in the next two years can be undone in two more *if* we stand together. If we support each other."

Nick held his hands up.

"Make no mistake. *They* will fight you tooth and nail. They have already proved they will do whatever it takes to win. Just as they have in this election. As we have uncovered and laid bare and will continue to uncover in the coming weeks, months, and years for all to see the ends to which they will go to protect their elite entitlement. We need to work to take this bureaucratic state apart, brick by brick. Keep what makes sense, and we all agree is necessary, and remove those pieces which are useless."

"We need government by citizens and for citizens. For the benefit of all citizens, not just those few with their hands on the levers of power. I have nothing against the rank and file who work in our federal and state agencies throughout the country. But we must reduce the mechanisms of the centralized federal government. Returning many of these tasks to where they belong. At the state and local level, close to the people affected by these decisions. Where the decision makers can both see and be held accountable for the consequences of the actions."

"We need to remove as much extra regulation and red tape as possible and we need to move our economy back to one of freedom to choose. Unleashing the innovation this country was once famous for. We will once again reclaim our greatness. My fellow Americans, we are silent no more. We are awake and we will not be silent *ever* again."

More full-throated cries of support.

Earl, offstage, was cringing at each of his threatening actions. He would not be surprised to see the black helicopters landing to snatch Nick. He was throwing the gauntlet down in the most public view possible. There could be no denying the intent of Nick Turner or his followers.

Nick stopped pacing, smiling brightly.

"For over 250 years, America has been an example. It has been an alternative. We have drawn to our shores countless souls seeking individual freedom, not for political purpose, but to enjoy the freedom of liberty. Of choice. To make their own decisions and live with the consequences of their own choices. This is called personal responsibility."

"This is the most important trait of self-government and self-rule. Of freedom. The freedom to choose and the freedom to live with those consequences. To be responsible to oneself, to your community, and to your fellow citizens. This personal responsibility has disappeared in America. It has been replaced with no bail. With no fault this, and no fault that. With policies holding you blameless for your actions because you have been oppressed or you are some gender, race, or age. My friends, this is all bullshit," said Nick as the crowd roared its approval.

We have a choice. Our choice is simple. Do nothing and watch as the Government grows more and more powerful. As it spends money, it does not have. As it lowers your standard of living. Rewards those who choose not to work hard, enjoying the fruits of the labor of those who do. All in the name of equality of outcome. Equity. Get used to that word. It is an insidious word. It is one the tyrants of the world have used to overthrow governments. To persecute individuals and to establish themselves in power. They appeal to those less fortunate. The marginalized. Most of whom are that way because they have been accepting government help for generations. Assistance not designed to help them get out of poverty. Instead, keeping them in poverty permanently." Nick paused as he let his point sink in.

"They use the power of the state to lock people into poverty. Then they use the power of the state to destroy any who threaten their power."

"I say today, here now. As an American, you are owed *nothing*. By the state, by your parents, by your neighbors or your fellow taxpayers," the stadium was as quiet as a tennis match, as Nick delivered his challenge.

"You are provided with an opportunity in America. With a set of laws, designed to apply equally to all who have the right, as an *American* to have this freedom. The freedom to choose to do or not do. The freedom to *earn* your way to whatever you want. There is no rule or law that says you get to have what someone else has just because you are an American. That is socialism. That is Equity. That is the road to slavery." Nick was practically trotting back and forth on stage, full of passion.

"We fought a war over a hundred and fifty years ago to stop this. Then, for over the last one hundred, we have re-instituted economic slavery in the form of progressive politics and the bureaucratic state. No more. We are a merit-based society. We have equality of opportunity. My job is to slay equity wherever it rears its evil head. Equity is about rewarding those not willing to put in the work. You work, I take. And give it to folks who will continue to vote me into power. That is bullshit! No more!"

He stopped center stage as 400,000 shouted their agreement with his direction. They continued for two minutes while he smiled and sipped his water. Yelling Turner, and God Bless America. Finally, he raised a hand.

"We must stand and demand equality of opportunity and deny equity whenever and wherever it appears. In school, in our jobs, on our TV programs, in our churches and most especially in our elected officials. Remember, they all work for *us*. We are their bosses. And it is time to give them an honest appraisal and give them fair warning. Shape up and start abiding by the laws of the Constitution or expect to get fired in your next election."

As Nick finished, the crowd went bananas. Shouting and yelling, jumping up and down. Nick smiled at their antics, drinking more water and looking at Earl, who was looking down, shaking his head.

"Let me give you an example of exactly what I am talking about. Earlier, this bureaucratic state, through its cronies in the financial community, tried to remove my campaign from being able to cash a check or pay a bill." The crowd jeered at this action.

Nick laughed. "Ah, the unintended consequences of actions. I am sure when they did this, they did not expect we would recover. They hoped I would go away or my vendors and employees would quit since I could no longer make payroll or pay my bills. They tried to cancel me and failed."

The crowd again growled their displeasure at being reminded of this attempt to rig the election process by financially ruining a candidate.

"They certainly never expected this would cause innovative Americans to found the Free 2 Choose For Yourself credit union. They also never expected that forty million of you would move close to five hundred *billion* dollars out of the three *formerly* largest banks in our country. How many of you are now in F2CFY?" Most in the crowd raised their hands to show they had moved.

"F2CFY is now in the top ten largest banks in the *world*. And because it is a credit union and not a bank, guess what? It is not for profit. It is for you. Using your money to help you. Not to drive corporate profits. Congratulations. See what we can accomplish when we move as one?"

Nick smiled as the crowd went wild again, realizing what they could accomplish together.

"I like the name so much, I am thinking of calling our new political party Free to Choose For Yourself. F2CFY or just F2C. It rolls off the tongue," smiled Nick as folks in the crowd started shouting F2C. Nick smiled as he continued.

"Today we launch our party. I can tell you what we stand for. Common Sense. Voter IDs, term limits, and an end to lobbyists writing our laws for the bureaucratic state to enforce. We will fund police while holding them and citizens accountable for their actions by enforcing our laws equally. Crime will no longer pay." Nick marched back and forth reciting his platform that had garnered him 83 million votes.

"A powerful military, a secure border. An economy favoring America first. We will not reduce our economy at the direction of globalist or these world organizations claiming to speak for the benefit of all. A strong and growing American economy benefits the entire world. The rising tide lifts all boats. We will once again be that tide." Nick was greeted with raucous cheers at these statements.

"We can do this and still reduce emissions, slaying poverty and racism. Fair taxes, paid equally by all, to fund only what we need. A balanced budget. You have to manage your household budget. Well guess what, so does our country. It will not always be easy. It may mean doing without some things we have become accustomed to. But this is America. We do not back down from our challenges. We overcome obstacles. To do this, we will work *together*."

"Regardless of gender, race, age or party. Good is good. Right is right. Common sense needs to become common again." Nick paused as his fans cheered. He held out a hand to calm the crowd.

"I understand this will not be easy. There will be roadblocks. Those who benefit from the way things are today will not go quietly back to their mansions. They will fight us to preserve their hold on power. One thing I can promise you is we will no longer let American *Pravda* tell you what and how to think."

There was a mix of cheers and boos at this statement. It was pretty clear to everyone in attendance who the enemies of freedom were.

"I don't believe in censorship or trying to silence anyone's voice. What I do believe in is people thinking for themselves. If we *all* do this, they will have no one to talk to except their sycophants. The other dirty secret is they *need* you. They need you to keep paying your taxes and keep staying home, allowing them to keep amassing their power. We stop this at the ballot box. It is the *only* way that will work."

"With a new majority in the House and Senate of F2C candidates, we would immediately shrink the size of government. This means we will eliminate and shrink these organizations significantly. Many of these need to be eliminated or rebuilt from the bottom up. This includes all the intelligence agencies and our military leadership."

"They have forgotten they are accountable to the people, not the other way around. We should not fear our government, they should *fear* and *serve* all of us. If this is not the case, something is wrong."

"We have to defeat those in the Party and the Opposition who do not view America this way. They need to be replaced with those who believe in a government by the people, for the people, following the Constitution. From this day forward, we are putting them all on notice. We will use this greatest gift of the founders to remake our country. One vote at a time, using the mechanism they have provided. Elections. This is the *revolution* of the ballot box."

Nick stood as everyone cheered as one. Excited at the prospect.

"Think for Yourself. We have the freedom to choose our path and to reject the path of indolence and government dependency. Hard work is good for the soul. Let's roll up our sleeves and get to work. Thank you!" finished Nick to thunderous applause.

Nick stood soaking up the adulation of the crowd. As he was preparing to leave the stage, he turned back and waved at the crowd.

"One more thing, and this is very important. Especially to all of you gathered right now in large groups everywhere around the country. We are non-violent and we need to stay that way. They will do everything they can to provoke you. To goad you into responding. To get you angry. To get you to lash out and hit back. *Do Not Do It!*"

"I cannot reiterate it enough. Folks, you cannot play into their hands. No matter how angry you are, don't give in. Remember, we are working toward our goals. If you give in, you let down everyone standing around you. You make it harder for everyone else. Because they will take every incident of violence and use it to scare everyone else from standing up. This is now a tug of war. We can only win at the ballot box."

"We are trying to stand up for freedom and they are trying to intimidate you into cowering in fear once again and doing nothing. So here are some simple rules. Be paranoid. But never ever get violent. Debate, but respect other's opinions. Walk away from physical confrontation. Please. Take up boxing, hang your rugs on the clothesline and beat them. Find a board and hammer nails into it. Do anything else."

Everyone laughed at Nick's suggestions for venting frustrations.

"Save your anger for a time when we will use it to do good. At the ballot box. I ask you to do this for me, for everyone who has made the ultimate sacrifice for our crusade and for everyone else around you. If we stand together, against all they throw at us, we can prevail. But only together. Remember this."

Everyone cheered again. After a few minutes of the clapping, shouting, cheering and Turner chants. Nick raised his hand one more time.

"One last request and then the bands can come back and we can celebrate what we *have* accomplished. You note in my suggestions of what we stand for, I did not mention religion."

"You know by now, my view of faith. It is between me and my higher power. How any of you choose to define this relationship is yours to choose as well. It has to be. Too much damage has been done by advocating or favoring one view versus another. Tolerance and personal responsibility. Adherence to fair laws. Morals, ethics, right and wrong. These are all hallmarks of civilized society. To live as if someone or some entity is watching. Expecting to be called to stand in judgement of your deeds in this mortal life should be a part of everyone's being. If it is, oh how the world changes. None of us will ever know if it is true, but why take that risk? Where is the harm in living a life in this manner?"

"I would ask you to indulge me in one last prayer." Nick bowed his heads as did four hundred thousand in his stadium and countless millions around the country as he began.

"First, I must thank you for providing free will. The freedom to use this gift to craft a civilization where all exercising this free will can decide for themselves how they choose to live. Thank you for giving us willpower and perseverance. For *not* making this easy. Forcing us to strive to overcome adversity and, in doing so, learn from both failure and success. To understand the power of sacrifice and the satisfaction of doing right. Most of all, thank you for giving us the opportunity to shape our own destiny. To decide, one person at a time, how we can work together to be greater than we are alone. If we lead our lives, make our choices, build our society and the relationships within as if you are watching. To enable each of us to know this and, in doing so, to always strive to do good and achieve all you hoped we would when you enabled us to make these choices ourselves. Thank you for the opportunity to serve and to succeed. God bless America, Amen."

In Texas, and stadiums around the country, the shouted Amen would certainly have set the record for the loudest noise at a concert or event.

#

Nick joined Chuck, Earl, Steve, and Margie off stage. "Well, that is done."

"Done?" laughed Chuck. "Earl is on the phone trying to hire the 82nd airborne to protect you from Lexi. There is throwing down the gauntlet and then there is kicking burning sand in someone's face. Wow Nick, that was some throw down. It wouldn't surprise me if she doesn't already have the FBI on the way to arrest you."

"She doesn't have the balls to do that now. She works in the shadows. Her attacks will come from the perimeter. Lexi knows she can't win by making me a martyr. Instead, she'll go whole hog after anyone who stands up. The little people. Make an example of them and try to cow everyone else into submission. Destroy their lives and broadcast it so others will know what is in store for them. Just like Evelyn in Wisconsin. We need to be ready to help as many refugees as possible. The TRDF is not going anywhere soon."

"Of that you can be sure," agreed Chuck.

"I wish you were not so forthcoming with your plans. Doesn't that violate your mantra of picking the time and place of your battles?" asked Earl in a serious voice.

"Reality is best when the truth is told. It is not reality if it is constructed of lies spewed and propped up by officials and outlets telling and promoting the lies. Eventually, the truth will come out and those who have been lied to will be rightfully angry with those pushing the false narrative." Earl shook his head as Nick continued.

"I need to hit them between the eyes with this. So *they* know what to be on the lookout for and to recognize it for what it is. Besides, I didn't reveal *how* we are going to accomplish our goals," said Nick with a big smile. "There is strategy and then there are tactics. You can't win without both. I only revealed a part of one."

"Maybe the 82nd and the 101st Chuck," groaned Earl at the enormity of keeping Nick alive long enough to achieve his goals.

"Earl, there are many forces at work here. Many more than just Party and Opposition vs F2C. There are many who stand to gain and lose, depending on what happens next. Our enemies are many, our friends few and complacent. Soft because of our hegemonic umbrella of projected power."

"As this umbrella is pulled back, these soft allies are finding out how weak they are without us. How unprepared they are to confront the worldwide evils of religious fanaticism and plain old greed. This is not just our fight, it is the fight for the future of the world and perhaps the entire planet's future. Climate change is not the biggest issue. As always, it is the human's propensity to kill each other for power and control."

"We hold our fate in our hands. There are those who have maneuvered in the background. Perfectly happy to allow individuals to claim ownership and leadership positions in public roles while they pull the marionette strings in the background. These are the true foes we face. They are making their move. They have hollowed out America and they think they have succeeded by finally co-opting the Constitution out of relevancy."

"Where exactly is all of this coming from? You suddenly join QAnon?" asked Chuck, entirely serious.

"Hardly Chuck. I have had a brief peek behind the curtain. I have seen the wizard at work. This campaign is starting to tear the curtain down. Exposing the puppeteers out of concern, they may lose control. I think, actually I *hope*, they are moving too soon. They may think we are weaker than we are."

"I believe there is still a backbone in this country. It has laid dormant, simmering silently as the world changed in ways it did not agree with. I now realize I have to accept the mantle of Cincinnatus, like it or not. Banks made me understand this and revealed some of the bigger picture. They killed him for it, not able to let him live long enough to expose more. Earl, heat the forge. It's time to beat my spade into a sword."

"Please, please don't say that where any of Lexi's minions can hear you," winced Earl as they turned to walk to the waiting caravan of Suburbans.

Nick put his hand on Earl's shoulder. "You really aren't cut out to be a farmer, my friend."

"But I was willing to try," lamented Earl as Nick laughed.

Chapter 67

Nick sat at Bank's desk, feeling the edges, examining the drawers. The button for SCIF mode was on the underside. As he inspected the drawers, one seemed shallower than the desk opening it fit into. He pulled out the drawer and examined it, noticing a slit in the back about the size of the letter opener on the desk.

Pushing it into the slit, he met resistance. He pushed a little harder and heard a click. The bottom of the drawer liner was now raised up on the back side. Pushing the opener under the edge, he lifted the drawer bottom up. In the 1/2 deep void underneath was a key and an envelope addressed to him.

He looked at the key. It was a modern electronic key with some type of electronic code built in. He had no idea what kind of lock it would work in. He picked up the small manila envelope. The contents were two note cards. The first read.

"*Make sure you put Churchill back on the shelf where it belongs.*" Nick smiled and shook his head. The second contained several quotations, each apparently written at different times in pencil and ink pen.

The first and probably oldest being at the top was from Ben Franklin. '*Only a virtuous people are capable of freedom. As nations become corrupt and vicious, they have more need of masters.*'

Below this was a second quote, '*The issue today is the same as it has been throughout all history, whether man shall be allowed to govern himself or be ruled by a small elite.*' Thomas Jefferson.

The quote was in ink but under the words 'small elite' Banks had apparently written later, in pencil, the acronym 'KSG' and then again, in a different shade, 'Zodiac'. Neither of these meant anything to Nick.

While reading the final quote, a sudden chill ran up his spine.

'For the Son of Man is going to come in the glory of His Father with His angels, and will then repay every man according to his deeds. Matthew 16.27.'

That was all it said. More cryptic messages in Nick's ever more cryptic world. He turned the card in his hand, thinking. Leaning back in his chair, grabbing the crystal glass from the desk top coaster.

Taking a sip, savoring the taste of the 24yr old scotch and glancing at the two melting ice cubes in his glass. He stared out the window, looking at the top of the Washington Monument in the twilight. His phone started vibrating. Glancing down, recognizing the number, he felt a pang of guilt after Lauren's visit. After a couple of rings, he answered.

"Hello."

"I saw you lost," said a melodious and laughing voice.

Nick smiled. "Did I?"

"Well, if you don't think you lost, I guess you can ignore my call," said the voice.

"It's not over, sadly," remarked Nick in a disappointed voice.

"True, but denial is the first stage. If you need help with your grief, you know where to find me."

"I appreciate the offer," responded Nick in a more upbeat tone.

"Well, until then, good luck," replied the voice.

Nick hesitated. "Thank you for everything. For the support, for the call, for believing."

"It works both ways, fella. Stay safe."

Nick took another sip of his drink. It looked like his next trip home to Colorado would go through Omaha.

Chapter 68

Maksim Pavlovich sat in his expansive library. It was an ornate room, with mahogany bookcases lining the walls of the first floor, a spiral staircase leading to a second-floor catwalk circling the room, and another entire floor of nothing but bookcases filled with books of all ages.

The collection was considered the most complete in the world outside of Oxford and Cambridge. He sat back in his well-worn leather chair, behind a desk used by Catherine the Great.

His walls of bookcases were only broken up by three pieces of priceless art. Nestled in a niche between bookcases was Van Gogh's 1888 *Portrait on the Road to Tarascon*. One of Van Gogh's self-portraits, featuring bright yellows and greens with the artist carrying his art supplies. The painting was assumed to have been destroyed in World War II in a bombing in Dresden where the Nazis kept it as the war turned against them.

A second slightly larger niche in the bookcases on an opposite wall held the most famous lost painting of all. T*he Portrait of a Young Man* by Raphael. It showed the artist as a young man painted in 1513 or 1514. Yet another painting stolen by the Nazis, never to be recovered and returned to its rightful owners.

Finally, on the wall opposite the man's desk hung a massive painting, almost six meters square. *The Nativity with St. Francis and St. Lawrence*, by Caravaggio. Yet another of the world's most famous stolen paintings. It had previously hung above the altar of the Oratory of San Lorenzo in Palermo, Sicily, from which it was stolen in 1969.

His eyes wandered around the room, taking in the trappings of his massive wealth. He turned back to his desk, pressed a hidden button, and a holographic projection of a screen appeared in midair above and in front of his desk.

On the screen, he watched as Lexi Smythe-Thomas took the oath of office. Leaning back, he smiled. On one corner of his desk was an exquisite sculpture of a Chinese dragon made from bronze with rubies the size of quarters for eyes. At the feet of the dragon was a small jade rat. He preferred the look of the dragon over the simple rat, but the rat represented the top of the hierarchy.

The eyes of the dragon sculpture seemed to gleam in pleasure in the light from the hologram as it showed the completion of the United States Presidential inauguration ceremony. Phase one was done. Now to start phase two. The destruction of America, by America.

He continued to stare at the screen in the air in front of him. As a smiling Lexi took the Presidential oath of office, with her husband standing beside her, behind her stood her newly sworn in Vice President. The smile left Pavlovich's face as he stared. The unexpected spanner in the works. Nicholas James Turner, Vice President of the United States.

End of Book Four

America at the Brink

Connect with the Author

- Author website: www.ejriceauthor.com
- Facebook author site: https://www.facebook.com/ejriceauthor
- Substack Blog site: https://ejriceauthor.substack.com/
- Twitter account: https://twitter.com/EJRiceauthor
- Instagram: https://www.instagram.com/ericriceauthor.
- TikTok: https://www.tiktok.com/eric.rice.author